AND MIGHTY OAKS

❖

MURRAY CAMERON

To order additional copies of this book, contact:
Xlibris
1-800-455-039
www.Xlibris.com.au
Orders@Xlibris.com.au
773475

AND MIGHTY OAKS

A boy from the final year at St Ninian's Academy, Fearnas, carrying a small canvas travel bag, his school years successfully completed, was leaving, walking away from his schooldays, his adolescence, and his way of living. Whatever he had gained from the seventeen and a half years that he had lived until now would have to do; it was all he was ever going to get from youth. Even his last steps through the tall cast-iron double gates would be changed—changed to paces. These new paces would have a different rhythm, a different and consistent length, and be directed, from now on, to new directions not entirely under his control. Already he had lost control of his life. What he had to do next, he had not chosen to do. He was fit, he was healthy, and he was male. He had been commanded, in pain of legal punishment should he resist, to become a soldier in the armed forces of Great Britain.

That suited Roddy Mckenzie just fine; fate, through the National Service Act, had dealt him an ace. He had spent all of these five years at St Ninian's Academy not unhappily, but impatiently wanting to be elsewhere—Burma, India, the Middle East, Africa. Each half year gave birth to a new ambition to strike out in a different direction. Two years of soldiering would surely provide some of the life he sought. These two years would give him time to decide in which direction he would choose to go. He had no concerns.

He was not conscious that he was void of feeling. He was not conscious that he was feeling none of the sentiments associated with departure. He was suffering no pangs of severance, or loss, or fears of the new, or excitement of adventure ahead, of seeing the world, of making new friends; he was void of sensation beyond the purpose of his steps and just functionally aware of voices, shouts, and laughter behind him of adolescents at play. Were he to be asked what he was taking away with him, he would struggle to find a sensible answer. No one was going to ask the question. Somewhere, sometime out there, the answer would be exposed in response to a need.

Out there was Fort George, the Highland Brigade Training Depot. He was walking towards significant change without the faintest feeling of its significance. In less than two hours, he would no longer be addressed as 'boy' but as 'man'. The loose ease of his youthful walk would become more erect, more rigid. The steps would be a measured length and be called paces. The word 'step' would be changed to 'pace'—'step' being reserved for the rhythmic pattern of even paces.

St. Ninian's Academy, that building of finely cut sandstone on which his back was now turned, was the setting in which all the most important changes within his six years of successfully completed secondary education had been acted out. He had never given thought to what those changes had been. Now his physical steps were taking him away from secondary education through the tall cast-iron gates where the railed stone wall was the boundary of the school world. He would pass through these gates into change. No longer would his world be directed by the guidance of parents, headmaster, teachers, or of his own volition. That would be the first, the greatest change. Now an institution of harder edges and higher demands would dominate twenty-four hours of every day of his life. There was no group of boys at the gates to see him off; that would be too stupidly sentimental, and anyway everyone was blasé about people departing to serve in the forces or to go abroad to live forevermore or just to take up a job somewhere in the empire or a dominion. He turned left and passed through into his future.

Fewer than fifty yards along the footpath at McAuslan's wireless shop, where he used to take the acid-filled glass accumulator battery to be recharged, Alexander's Bluebird Bus would shortly pick him up and, within the hours of the stipulated time limit, take him to the place ordered by the army.

He had gone only a few paces when a military car pulled up slightly ahead of him. Its driver called through the open passenger window, 'Are ye for the Fort?'

'Aye,' said Roddy Mckenzie, 'I've got to join today.'

'Jump in!' said the young driver in khaki uniform.

'Ach, the Fort's no' that bad an' ye'll no be there that long. There's two things on at the meenit, Malaya an' Korea, so when ye're finished, ye'll go tae battle trainin' an' then off: that's where ye'll be goin'. I went to Malaya wi' the Seaforths an' no long back. There's nothing for me back in Strathnaver, so I signed on to make five years.' Thus was he driven to the Highland Brigade Training Depot, Fort George, to begin his two years of compulsory National Service. He didn't know, until the young Seaforth soldier alongside whom he sat told him, that he was the CO's (commanding officer's) driver. The fluttering pennant and the rank identification plate on the front had had no meaning for Roddy. It suddenly dawned on him that he was going to enter Fort George riding in the CO's car!

The soldier at the gate presented arms. It would not be too long before Roddy learned what the 'Present Arms' salute meant. With the members of his squad, on that piece of the world sacred to the RSM, the parade ground, he learned how to execute the required drill movement in perfect harmony and timing: Wah!-2, 3-, Wah!-2, 3-, Wah! His dignified and respected entry to the bosom of HM Forces ended quite abruptly, but in the case of Rod's intake, not with the harshness that happened to many at different depots scattered all around Britain. Nor was it, for Roddy, traumatic. He had been evolving, throughout his childhood, by some natural process, to become a soldier. When you were old enough (or not), you put on khaki and off did sail. Isn't that what boys who have become men ever and always do? How could it possibly be a Land of Hope and Glory with an empire 'on which the sun never sets' if these transformative human youngsters from Great Britain didn't turn into men and go forth to war?

His squad at the Highland Brigade Training Depot at Fort George was as mixed a group as could possibly be imagined: a Muslim from Newcastle called Kutakis; a Hindu tailor from

Birmingham; a representation from no fewer than three of
the major public schools—Eton, Harrow, and Rugby—and one
from the lesser Sherbourne. Universities were represented by
St Andrews, Edinburgh, and Glasgow. Engineering tradesmen
fielded two who had just finished their apprenticeships at
Inverurie Loco Works; motley others, schoolboys like himself
were drawn from all over Scotland, including the inevitable
'Shake' Mckenzie from Lewis, and from London's heartland,
a man from Lambeth. Verily was it a Tower of Babel as they
chattered, made introductions, and decided which iron bed
would be whose so that they could dump the two 'biscuits'
and the blankets they had just signed for at the Q Store. It
seems the army believed in its own law of perpetual motion.
Immediately the first installment of kit was put down, there was
another shouted command of 'Fall in outside!' They hastened
down the stone stairs each step, like an ancient whetstone,
worn to a curved tread from two centuries of the coming and
going of army boots. Talking of which, it was the issue of 'Boots
Ammunition, pairs one, and brogues highland pairs one' that
took place next. After that, self-flagellation being no longer
fashionable it seemed, they were issued with a hair shirt and
a battle dress uniform made of finely spun steel wool. Very
important items included a folded set of two aluminium mess
tins and a fork, knife, and spoon set that clipped together in a
little bundle; an enamel mug, 'mugs, Emmanuel'; a 'housewife'
which, when rolled up and secured with its tapes, its pocketed
linen would hold button cotton, darning wool, needles, and
your razor. Now like crabs or lizards, they shed their first shell,
or skin, and put on what would be their identifying dress for
the next two years, but unlike crabs and lizards, they had to be
taught the finer points of wearing it. This led inevitably to mean
that if they had been dressed as soldiers, they now had to move
about like soldiers. And so to 'square bashing'.

For all the negative writings on the subject of army drill,
nothing of that kind emerged from Roddy's squad whose
members seemed to see its merits and the need for it or that
it had to be put up with. They did their best to master it: even
the university graduates who were not unfit overcame their

bolshevist tendencies and their low regard for the young corporals who took over after Sgt. Shenton, who had done the hard part of initial moulding, put their backs into it, and said they felt it doing them good. Very shortly their rifles were issued to which they immediately became enslaved. However, this too was taken up with goodwill, and on frequent thorough inspections throughout the days, very few spiders' nests were found. It seemed the only time they didn't carry a rifle was when clutching their mess tins; knife, fork, and spoon sets; and their 'mugs, Emmanuel', at the end of a rigid left arm, they 'doubled' through the Ravelin gate up to the distant, massive mess hall to join the long queue for army grub. For the public school boys, it was a matter of delight to have better quality food than they were used to: it seems that quails eggs and roast pheasant was the stuff of vacation time menus. After a week or so into their ten-week basic training period, Roddy with some others including the Inverurie lads and all of the public school boys were drafted off to a leader training wing for potential officers and non-commissioned officers. From now on, they would wear a thin white band on the epaulettes of their uniforms including the denim working dress. Apart from that, nothing much changed except that they were pushed harder and marched to the mess hall in quick time like light infantrymen. These hard energy days seemed to pass very quickly. Having learned to merge with and disappear into the wet heather and crawl silently on their bellies amongst thorny whins and having met the required scores on the rifle range, it was time to erase the face blackening and get down to serious 'bullshit' to create a handsome soldierly sparkle to impress the senior officers, and any loving parents who could make the trip, when they mounted their passing out parade.

That was the end of a beginning. As national servicemen, they were not permanently part of the regiment at whose depot they had enlisted. Now they would be allocated to regiments engaging in battle against the enemies of freedom. It was at the end of basic training that Roddy happened to bump into a Fearnach called David Clark, badged Cameron Highlanders, from another squad. It was the end of ten hard weeks, why wasn't he looking happy? The members of his squad had just been apprised of their destiny, and when Roddy asked where he was going next, David's face and voice interpreted his feelings. He replied, '43Highland. Korea.' That was Roddy's regiment.

Roddy was just one of two and a half million young men called to do National Service between 1945 and 1963. He did not see this service as disruption to his life that so many young men did of theirs. National Service did disrupt lives; there was much senseless bullying by people, protected by rank from any reasonable retaliation, and intelligent young men were made to undertake absurdly, stupidly contrived tasks. Sensitive souls were destroyed, and some men were given the stimulus to become 'hard men', a mental condition from which they would never recover. They would be social anarchists, thugs, troublemakers, and criminals for the rest of their lives. As these tragedies were occurring, it is undeniable that for many others, it was an experience from which lifelong benefits were derived.

The big world war was over and we had won. The country was presumably at peace, emotionally and financially exhausted by war. Why then, after all that, should every fit young man of 18 years and over have to drop everything, good prospects or not, and be one of the six thousand who were called up every fortnight to serve in the armed forces?

The difficulty was that there were still more military tasks for British soldiers to do. All around, colonial empires, including their own, were sundering. Major problems were beginning to bite. The Dutch ally, of the now-finished continental war, was trying to regain its Indonesian colony from a new vigorous body of Indonesians who had a government of its own, ready to function the moment the Japanese should be defeated. They would never undergo the Dutch regime again. The British came to help the Dutch. A promise was also being given to helping the French in Indo-China. Nations that have kings and queens and empires are prone to support colonials whose nationals have the effrontery to want to be rid of them. Bloody ingrates! It was a lost cause for the Dutch. The Yugoslav communists wanted Trieste. But international law said it should remain Italian until otherwise decided. This list could go on and on, and only two more major problems need be mentioned here: Palestine and Cyprus. 'The Emergency' in Malaya was an economic drain of fighting forces, materiel, and money. There were morale and life-sapping conflicts that would remain long-time suppurating sores. The promise of independence for India had to be met with the ensuing horrors of the separation into different geographical areas for Hindus and Muslims and heartbreaking moves of populations. Outside of India, more of the empire's problem chickens would come home to roost. But Britain had not yet taken up its position at the first dot point on the graph illustrating its own demoralising, loss-of-empire learning curve. Then came the bipolar power division between Russia and the Western Allies; the American policy of containment, and the dread of universal communism.

No politician in Britain's Labour government found it easy to reach the inevitable conclusion that Britain had to go to Korea. And with hundreds of time-served men bound for release, who would be the soldiers of Britain's contingent?

Britain from a soul in torture had found itself agreeing to peacetime conscription. National Service began at first for a duration of eighteen months with a five-year period of Reserve Service, and on the outbreak of the Korean War, with an extension to two years.

Somewhere in the enormous moving, churning mix of mighty international powers, struggle with and conflicts between and amongst ideologies, and people wild to throw off the rule of foreign nations, tiny, minute bits of human material had to be found to fire the shots and take the risks. The youthful Roderick Fraser Mckenzie, now beginning his military life as a national serviceman of the Forty-third Royal Highland Regiment (on battle maps, look for 43 Highland), was to go into battle as a national serviceman, part of Britain's contribution.

It was May 1952 when 43 Highland was ordered to Korea. The battalion would be assembled at the old, hutted wartime camp at Pinefield near Elgin, the capital of Morayshire, twenty miles to the east of Fearnas. The battalion was spread around on the plain by companies and platoons in the timber or curved galvanised-iron Nissen huts where they would be quartered for the six weeks of their battle training when not out on Dava Moor. There was no training pamphlet yet for Korea, so a composite of the age old of jungle, desert, and European training was scrambled and rolled into the training for Korea. But the essentials were there so that you could fire fifteen rounds per minute from a Lee Enfield, keep a Bren Light Machine gun serviced and firing accurately, fire a two-inch mortar, hurl grenades, become an undetectable part of a landscape. You could get up and over hills all day and the next and the next with sixty pounds of kit, and if the gods were not on your side, do it carrying the platoon wireless, or a spare valise for the Bren, or a cartouche of two-inch mortar bombs or 'tools entrenching' (a spade) or any of the other luxuries of an infantryman's life. Apart from your own ground sheet, you would have an oblong sheet of heavy canvas—your half of a 'tents half shelter'—a little more than the length and breadth of a man lying down. On the edge of one long side, there were grommetted holes, and on the other, metal pins which could be passed through the holes and opened out to secure the piece of yours and another man's sheet, and lo, you had a two-man tent. During the occasional hour in bivouac, you would be glad to get in there and, with heath beneath your groundsheet, get a bit of kip. It was that glorious time in the Highlands just before the late summer turns to October's sharper bite. Perfect for what was going to happen in the next weeks.

'The Lines', which the rows of tents were called, were barely formed when the command came to fall in. There was a briefing for a night attack, enough time to go to the cookhouse and have a meal before moving out across a part of the miles and miles of the Dava Moor. A signal from a forward scout alerted the platoon, 'Contact front', and the platoon immediately spread into their classic positions with the gun on the high ground. And so it had begun and would go on over the weeks, mixed with returns to Pinefield for range firing of rifles, stens and brens, kit inspections, last medicals and jags, and to sweeten moments of dullness or slovenly effete dawn slumber, there was 'pokey drill' until the strain displaced your eyebrows and you finally could hold a rifle by the muzzle and extend it parallel to the ground

with your arm outstretched. In no time at all you would be off
on the ocean cruise that you had never got around to dreaming
about—but first, seventeen days' embarkation leave.

Before the 43 Highland's draft had mounted the long special
train at Elgin station, Roddy had been made a 'draft corporal'.
This did not mean promotion; it just meant that he would fill
the role of corporal—'acting, unpaid'—until the draft reached
its destination and was taken onto brigade strength in Korea.
When the draft reached Southampton, Roddy's berth ticket was
taken by Sergeant Ferguson who organized a switch of berth,
saying, 'I want you up by the bulkhead door.' Roddy was having
his first experience of differentiation by rank and 'the loneliness
of command'.

The troopship *Empire Fowey* ploughed its way across the Bay
of Biscay at a bit less than its possible, majestic eighteen knots.
The tossing and heaving was not confined to the vessel's hull.
Almost every soldier was seasick. Some were not being sick as a
result of the ship's cruel twisting and plunging but by being in
confined space with men who could not help but vomit where
they were, or on their way to the now putrid lavatories, or some
sheltered corner in a lee. Roddy had to organize parties to
try to minimize the foul swill. Later, in the Mediterranean,
there were big broad swells, but now they were as nothing to
the storm-hardened squaddies—the sun was shining—and on
rotation, they could get on the decks to enjoy almost four weeks
of this enviable luxury, at the expense of the British taxpayer.
While they were being so pampered, the same kindly folk were
enabling them to draw a quid and a half a week—with grub
and a suit thrown in! 'Cor, you couldn't get better than that,
could ya?'

Then, at Pusan in south of South Korea, there was an
embarkation on a troop train bound on a long tedious,
uncomfortable, noisy grind to Tokchon. From there, 43
Highland was taken by truck to within twelve miles or so of the
forward positions. There was a stumbling, cursing march of
twelve miles, in full kit, over rough, hilly ground. In just over
three hours, they had reached where they were to take over
from the American troops who were withdrawing and moving

to another area. It was the blind leading the blind, some of the platoon moved forward, to take up defensive positions in the scattered perimeter weapon pits. For those who had not been taken forward, a miserable, acutely cold night was spent, mostly sleepless, on a ground sheet with the meagre covering of a single blanket. Every two hours someone would be shaken awake to go up and take over the guard positions. They were in the front line. At sparrow fart, the company commander, Major Erik Barron, had taken a small patrol out to assess whether this was strategically the best place to be. It wasn't. So tactically, D Coy would move up onto a higher hill to their left, commanding a broad view of the enemy's front and the river below. In the process of the move, the barely new morning was made an official day at the front by the fall of mortar bombs all over their present position. When the enemy had delivered their morale-boosting (whose?) salvos, the move continued. They would have to get organized quickly; but there was no point in getting too elaborate too soon. There was a general feeling of happiness that they were going to create their own position from scratch.

It seems impossible that such a feeling could arise. But British troops have ever been cast into worlds totally foreign to them. Of such lands, Korea was maybe the most foreign. Yet these young national servicemen were now soldiers, they were in the army; they, with the remnants of regulars, had come to Korea to fight and quite possibly die, fighting what was described by a world external to them as an enemy. Armies inoculate troops against the external world. The army creates a kind of incunabulum within which an absorbing demand for self-maintenance and alertness to danger, patterns, and rules of behaviour dominate activity. All is congealed into dependency. The need for such dependency and trust is real and testable. Without trust, how could you ever possibly sleep? How could you move over ground without covering fire? How could you survive hunger without the idea that, somehow, today or tomorrow or maybe the next day HQ company would get something to you that you could eat and stay alive? All the orientation of training, sharing risk, making joint efforts to attain objectives, being together night and day, wet and dry, hot and freezing, shapes a social environment of shared dependency and leads to the minor delight of having your own home, even if it is just a bleak rocky hill in a very foreign land with a dangerous enemy at your front door.

The Commonwealth Division had a different way of looking at the war from the American view. The British believed that with the enemy, suffering the difficulties attendant to having a long supply line, and the allied forces forbidden to cross the parallel, the Commonwealth Division's strategy was now to occupy defensive positions at key strategic points that could provide each other with support, and the whole supported by their own three-inch mortars, an artillery regiment, and air cover.

43 Highland was fortunate, much more so than the Argylls who had come first, because in the beginning of this new world, there was not light. All was dark in the administrative pre-dawn of the British participation in the Korean War, the curtain of dawn was abruptly and raggedly raised; the Argyll and Sutherland Highlanders drawn from the far corner of the wings, the warm, balmy louche life of Hong Kong, and wearing the wrong costumes for the drama they were about to enact were thrust upon a bare stage—there were no props available for the stage manager to have arranged.

They went into action immediately, numerically under strength, without their own support weapons, and for the Korean climate, woefully underclad. In no time they were engaged by an attacking enemy. As they struggled with this formidable force, they were being scorched by napalm. In error and confusion, despite identification panels being in place, the napalm bombs fell and exploded in massive brilliant clouds and black stinking smoke, sending the flowing, flaming wave of gel over the Argylls. The napalm bombs had been dropped by low-flying American aircraft. As the troops were scrambling to escape the burning, clinging gel and to escape the closing enemy, the aircraft returned and strafed them. There were many casualties.

How would Hemingway have described the land over which these living men moved and had their being? Which of the young soldiers ever thought beyond another bloody hill? Here there were no magic woods with paths dim and silent where one might come across a glade in which a princess sat by a pool, praying for your arrival as she looked so dreamily into the still blue mirror. It sparkled from her reflected eyes as she combed her long black hair, smiling coyly, shyly, and blushing like a rose at the thoughts in her mind. Perhaps, looking at hill after hill into the distance, an artist could make a subject for a water colour where the fading washes told of the remoteness of the hidden horizon. Perhaps the Samichon River could have some attractive pastoral charm as it flowed flatly where there was depth above the rocky bed, rushing white and noisy when forced between the rocks or over a ridge, generally meandering across an ancient space washed flat and spread, till at its sides the high land, eroded over time, had descended to its flood line. Now it was a minor defence which the enemy would have to cross to reach you. The enemy was in static defensive positions scratched into the rocky ground. Somewhere over there, on the other side, there were mortars. Where exactly? They were ready, at a whim it seemed, to send bombs thudding and blasting in amongst your hoochies and into the stony earth above the tunnels that army engineers and Korean workmen had dug into the hills covering them with more earth and rocks to absorb the impact of high-explosive shells from enemy artillery firing from far behind the hills.

D Company, 43 Highland, with its officer commanding, Major Erik Barron, now had its own private hill with its own 'postal' address, Hill 353, and which, because of its rough shape on the spur, was called 'Sickle'.

Second Lieutenant McRae had led a reconnaissance patrol out of the position to report on the terrain, confirm significant features and the accuracy of the available maps, report enemy strength and movements, and pick out some likely approaches to the enemy lines. On their way back in tactical formation, they came across a wrecked village not far from their company's temporary forward standing patrol post. When they had gone through the village and reformed, declaring it clear and apparently long neglected, Roddy said *sotto voce* to Lieutenant McRae, 'Did you see what I saw back there, sir?'

'I don't know what you saw, Mckenzie, so tell me.'

'Timber, sir. Timber for hoochie building. Before the place is covered in wire and mines, I suggest we get down there pronto and rob it out.'

'Good thinking, Mckenzie. When I go up and report to the Boss'—everyone called Erik Barron 'the Boss'—'I'll talk to Sgt. Ferguson on the way through so when you get "dismiss", back you go.'

'Thank you, sir'—and with a good wee bit of cheek—'We'll see if we can get anything for you.'

McRae liked it and said, 'I can't frame a recommendation for a Mention in Dispatches based on your generosity, Mckenzie. Sorry.'

Like good soldiers, they didn't make a picnic of the asset acquisition, but went back to the village armed and in tactical formation with bits of rope, and one very good piece, they'd found lying on the platoon site near where they had decided was to be their new piece of real estate: 'Charmingly located rustic residence of unique design in a rural setting with attractive glimpses to the Samichon River.' The space was the floor of a small re-entrant with a hillock each side, and rising up steeply to the back, three defensive walls already built by nature! It was on the reverse side of a small hill on the platoon position half facing the enemy front, and just round it, a pace or two, or a crawl away, they had dug out their basic weapon pit. At the village, they posted sentries while the robbers went to work. 'Bags that door!' Woodie growled. Heard or not, they hastened to take possession. Whenever time allowed, they improved their weapon pit and really slogged at getting the hoochie site cleared. They didn't have a saw to cut the door to size, so it took additional digging, and creative architectural and engineering design, to install it in all its beauty. The result was that when it was opened, you had to take a big step up to get on to the interior floor level. There's inevitably a critic of another man's genius and here was one, deriding the door-opening design of the gun section's hoochie.

There was constant patrolling and sometimes the company would have to advance and take and hold ground until some larger objective had been met.

Then the necessary tactical decision to withdraw would be resorted to. Yes, it can be done, but at times it is far from easy to put into effect. The pretence of presence must be kept, as the thinning out and withdrawal is taking palace. Section by section, platoon by platoon, you've to try to keep everything operationally offensive while you're still trying to get the hell out of there. Each man knows that this is really bad. The nearest last known point of their lines may be a mile away over hills and stony, scrubby, broken-up hillsides. Korea is a world of hilltop after hilltop. In between are deadly spaces perfect for enfilade fire. And while on the move, every minute of time, someone will be watching and waiting to kill you. You may even be hit by friendly fire of the artillery supporting your withdrawal.

Previous attacks on 43 Highland, on D Coy, and 6 Platoon had been severe enough. On one occasion, the enemy reached to within a hundred yards of the wire, which their shelling had successfully torn open. But with the mutual support of the companies to left and right and the supporting artillery being called down by a young gunner officer in D Company's forward standing patrol pit, the attack broke up and the enemy withdrew. During all the activities of preparing the defensive position, patrolling actions, and during attacks, Major Barron and Lieutenant McRae had been observing Roddy. Once again he was wearing two stripes but this time was promoted substantive corporal. The help given in building Lieutenant McRae's hoochie being a factor of no influence on the promotion.

They were under attack again, but this attack was different. It looked as if the enemy had decided to make a determined all-out investment in troops and ammunition. They had seen the importance of Hill 353 in holding up their plan to advance southward. Thousands of shells had been exploded in 43 Highland's positions, and D Company's area was apparently where they were going to concentrate their force. The faces of the hills in front of them were covered in scrambling Chinese troops in such numbers that they could not be concealed; they were simply pouring down the face of the hills like ants on a dropped bun. They expended huge numbers of men, but a mass, spread out along the front, had got through the barrage and the wire and were scrambling onto the base of the hill. Each enemy soldier was recognizable.

Woodie was on the gun, firing aimed bursts at the rapidly oncoming horde that was stumbling, scrambling, falling, and picking themselves up and still advancing. One of the platoon's men, who broke from the line, had thrown down his rifle and was running back. Young Second Lieutenant McRae stood in front of him and drew his pistol. 'Return to your position or I will shoot you,' he voiced in a firm, clear command. The dazed man looked at the officer standing firmly there aiming to fire at his chest. He hesitated for seconds. He scurried back to join the other men in their firing positions. Those who had seen and heard the event admired the young commander's strength. They were all in this together. Any weakness would mean defeat, capture, or more likely, death.

'Aw, fuck!' shouted Woodie and rolled away from the gun. Freddie grabbed the gun and continued firing until the magazine ran out. 'Quick, Donnie see's a hand. Woodie's hit. Come tae the gun an' bring the mags closer tae it.' Freddie pulled out his groundsheet and rolled Woodie on to it. Seizing both hands full of Woodie's jerkin and the ground sheet, he pulled them and slid Woodie away over the top and down the reverse slope, calling out for casualty help. But everyone was on the line. The enemy had now opened up their defensive SOS task, and shrapnel shells were falling thickly into the platoon's position. Leaving Woodie to be rescued, Freddie turned to start back up to the line. His first pace directed him towards a bursting shell. His chest and his belly were torn and spread around in the air. His remains fell back nearly on top of Woodie. But Woodie was dead anyway.

It was desperate on the ridge. Major Barron had got hold of a two-inch mortar. It was one of those with a short firing lanyard on its base and he was loading and firing hell for leather; Roddy was right beside him giving him covering rifle fire, which he was doing without delay except for swift actions to change magazines. A Chinese soldier armed with a burp gun had dropped out of sight on a steep rise. Roddy stood up to see him (not the time to think about firing from cover), aimed, fired, and dropped him.

He was cocking his rifle to fire at another who had appeared alongside the dead man when a burning hot punch hit him just above his left hip. The round had torn through his waist belt and the bottom of his left ammunition pouch and carried on taking webbing and clothing with it. He was hurled backwards and fell to the ground dazed winded and hurting. A Coy had by now engaged the enemy's right flank, so 6 Platoon was getting strong support on its left. The Welch Regiment, off to the Forty-third's right, were now engaging the enemy. Suddenly the enemy bugles were sounding here and there along the front. The troops in front of 10 Platoon's position turned and ran, being shot down as they went. There were some prisoners. Major Barron helped to carry Roddy down, and as he was being taken over by some very efficient Indian ambulance men, he trotted beside them, looking down on the bloodless white face on the stretcher, and said, 'Well done, Corporal Mckenzie. You're in good hands'. Then he turned and set off quickly to reorganize the remains of his scattered, battered company.

Roddy was taken to a field hospital where the remarkable Indian surgeons somehow patched his torn flesh, severed nerves and muscles, and within three months of recuperation, care, and guided exercise—which he carried out conscientiously—he was back with the battalion from the big military hospital. He was posted to HQ Coy on 'light duties' working as a clerk for the adjutant. Here he learned a bit about the role of subalterns in a battalion, the battalion's administration, and generally hobnobbed with the powers of 43 Highland. It was a different world. The administrative non-commissioned officers and other ranks seemed to come from a different army. He found the men with whom he shared a tent a different breed, not of such a kind as Freddie and Woodie. Perhaps it was because he had time to let his senses surface: he couldn't understand how bereft he felt, or get his brain to find a way of accommodating the shattering sadness of his loss and the finality of death. 'Just as well this whole thing will soon be over. This is a different game: I'm not enjoying it anymore.'

His spirit recovered when he was back in the line. From that time, and for more arduous months, they survived and functioned as a fighting force. When it was their time to leave the line and depart for home, the battalion had completed its tour of duty, and when preparing to depart, there was a well-merited tune of glory in the air around them. As a man who had been wounded, Roddy was offered a flight home to UK which he declined—he wanted to go back to Blighty in the company of the men he had served with when they could all disband together.

However, political powers had another plan for 43 Highland. While they were at sea, it was announced that the ship would be changing course to head for the African port of Mombasa, Kenya, where they would be engaged to quell an uprising of the Kikuyu, the indigenous Africans who wanted to take their land back from their colonial rulers. It was hard to find anyone with positive feelings about this change. Everyone felt he had done his share and didn't include killing Africans in their ideas of a soldier's duty. The squadies could sense that some of the officers were equally unhappy.

Pre-history and history gives many examples of racial migrations and equally as many examples of the swamped original holders of the land rising in rebellion against the newcomers. These shifts of different ethnic groups encroaching upon lands held by peoples of different ethnicity had taken place as a result of increasing populations and the need for new food sources, climate change, rivers changing course, and often with the added demand for more extensive regional power to counter perceived threats to existing powers. The Bantu races' movement into southern and eastern Africa fits that ancient pattern. Their arrival into what has, since ancient time been known, and now commonly known as Kenya, is part of the wide spreading journey of the Bantu peoples. It is absurd in the extreme to hold the view, as some English people do, that the Bantu races now in Kenya are Johnny-come-lately land grabbers. This conclusion justified shifting Kikuyu off their tribal lands to allocate those lands to white settlers. Of course the Kikuyu had no 'legal titles' to the land. It is impossible to draw any sensible similarities between the Bantu migrations and the European 'Scramble for Africa' of the nineteenth century. The

Highlands of Scotland have tasted the same bitter cup. There is much more similarity between the Celtic migration to Britain and the Bantu migrations in Africa. The Roman and Norman invasions of Britain are of a completely different category. People of Britain had, by the end of the eighteenth century, transformed any native love of their land, remnant threads of which may still have remained, into a metaphor encapsulated in the mythology of a 'Land of Hope and Glory'. It is too late for all but a very few exceptional types, such as was Laurens van der Post, to understand the primordial meaning of our term 'land' to aboriginal peoples—the Bushmen of the Kalahari, the Scottish Highlanders of long ago, the Australian aboriginals, the American Indians, and many others now being derided into extinction by modern social engineering, misguided 'do-gooding', and a flood of conscience money eagerly soaked up by innumerable groups legitimately (or otherwise) enjoying the ride on the gravy train.

The task of 43 Highland was to help the Kenya police to round up Mau Mau insurgents. The Kenya police had armed white officers and armed African askaris. Mau Mau by no means represented all Kikuyu and certainly their strategy and cruelty was condemned by Kikuyu leaders, yet all the tribes of Kenya wished the colonial system gone. In their fight for Uhuru, the political battles were being fought against powers set up by British authority whose professionally staffed bureaucracy erected an insurmountable barrier to reason as seen by Africans. The Africans' weapons of hand wielded panga's and do-it-yourself rifles were more dangerous to the user than the enemy. Because the whites, one way or another, controlled almost all the land except the racial reserves into which had been driven the people whose land had been taken Mau Mau went off into the high, wooded, and difficult-to-traverse highlands. Practically all the employment was provided by whites, farmers and traders, making political funding very hard to come by. The pressure around the theme of African freedom, Uhuru, was building to the point where the only tool to effect a mind change by Europeans was terror. At least Sinn Fein had weapons, could make bombs, and had access to money. Here were people thought by whites, who appeared quite rational in many other regards, deciding that the Africans were childlike, incapable of ruling themselves, thus requiring the guidance of civilised gentlepeople who had designed systems and laws appropriate to primitives of such a low state of mental and cultural development. Sadly, that kind of thinking was endemic and deep rooted in the colonials from the first to the most recent arrivals, reinforced to the point of being the strengthening and sustaining mythology, almost a religious infection of values. Infection finds its vectors and these had, sadly, bitten not a few military personnel.

43 Highland, after a train ride from Mombasa to Nairobi, with a break on the way to listen to the pipes and drums, pitched up at the broad paddock of Gilgit where they set up a camp of tents and began a brief period of acclimatization to the high altitude. There was a lot of running, route marches, ambush drills, and to stiffen the spine, a lecture on the tactics of the very nasty Mau Mau. While this was going on, the officers jumped into vehicles and shot off to see where the battalion would have to operate and make a plan. The result of these endeavours was that three companies would set up Coy HQs in three areas— two in the Aberdares and one at Meru. It was to Meru that D Coy would go, an area much different from the lofty Aberdares where troops would be operating in the cold drizzling wet at twelve thousand feet.

The land around Meru is natural savannah grass land on red lateritic soil with a variety of acacia species and, here and there, Doum palm trees. Wildlife abounds, and troops who had never even heard of Kenya before that announcement on the *Fowey* were now stunned to see family groups of enormous African elephants, graceful tall-horned eland and zebra with stripes more brown than black, and now and again, a rhinoceros. Flocks of tiny seed-eating birds wheel swiftly around the scrub, settle for a while on a patch of ground, rise again en masse, another moving, swishing cloud. The major strategy was patrolling—to keep the enemy on the move, to find out where the enemy was, where they may have camps, to ambush and capture, to disrupt communications and their supplies of food. So the patrols moved from their tented base camp near a fine coffee plantation homestead up into the more heavily treed, and in some places beautifully forested, ground which rose up out of the plain. If encountered in these treed areas, the Mau Mau could speedily disperse to elude pursuit. If patrolling located a more established camp, an ambush could be planned. Food supply was a major problem for the camps, so night and day patrolling of paths and ambushing were normal practice. In the Aberdares, the Mau Mau used a clever ruse for resupply. Somewhere, a distance from their camp, they would light a smoky fire, the air force believing this to be in a camp, would plaster the area with bombs, killing just about everything living. The Mau Mau then moved in, picked up the remains of the slaughter, and lugged it back to camp.

There was much scenic beauty. Towering cliffs gave magnificent views down into lakes and lush forests; there were high, mighty waterfalls and panoramas of mountain ranges. One day, with the excuse of a personal orientation reconnaissance, Major Barron told Lieutenant McRae he wanted a corporal and eight men to accompany him for a day. The company cook provided sandwiches (delicate works of military culinary art as may be imagined), and with their water bottles full, wearing battle order, the major leading, the corporal behind him and the others in the patrol following, they marched off, rifles at the slope until through the front gates and a few hundred yards more until clear of the camp. The exercise began, rifle slings were slackened out, they took up tactical formation and at an easy climber's pace, worked through the forest glades and into the dappled shade of the higher growth. Shortly the major halted his small column, gave them 'stand easy', and asked them to gather round. He then briefed them for the day's exercise. They would be doing a tactical patrol exercise under jungle conditions searching for signs of enemy movement with another objective of meeting up with and joining another patrol. 'I'll bring up the rear but I'm not on patrol strength so bear that in mind. I'm not going to give my estimated time when you should reach the objective.' He looked at his watch, took a few steps away, and said, 'The patrol starts now.' Roddy made them 'harbour' and called a man over. He got his map and compass out, worked out where they were, pinpointed the RV, gave people their task briefing, and the patrol set off.

Roddy and his men arrived, spot on at the RV. 'Let your men stand easy, Corporal. Just find somewhere to sit and gather round. Right, let's hear about your patrol commander. Who's game to start?' Robby Ellis put his hand up and gave a very good description of Roddy's beginning to the exercise with the description making the patrol secure while he did his preparation and gave the briefing. 'Right, well done, Ellis,' said the major. 'What else did anyone notice, keeping on the subject of the commander?' And so it went till all the learning points were brought out and made his summary and confirmation of the points. 'Did you enjoy the exercise?' They all spoke at once and, with some enthusiasm, agreed that they had all felt the benefit and just the way the training had been handled. 'You were as military as was needed, sir, and I felt encouraged by that. The debriefing was a new experience... made me think about things I'd missed...I won't forget what happened.'

'Thank you, Henderson.' There were murmurs of agreement and free responses and cheery sounds and someone said, 'I was wondering what I'd first do if I came face-to-face with a rhino, sir, but I'm no' gaen' tae spoil oor lunch.' He told the corporal that if he'd finished with his men, he could dismiss them and break off for a half-hour lunch. 'Corporal Mckenzie, I'd like you to join me.' Roddy stood up smartly and, saluting, said firmly, 'Sir!' Then, from the men who had also risen to their feet now, he posted sentries. 'Take your webbing off but have it ready,' were his last words.

Major Barron and Corporal Mckenzie sat on a shelf with a cliff rising sheer behind them, providing a back rest. Before them the western view was majestic lit by the sun; under an artistically placed bunch of white cumulus clouds stood the majestic shape of Mt Kenya still looking large though miles distant. To its left, one could swear that the straight blue line they imagined they saw must have been Lake Naivasha. From here to the horizon further to the left was yellow grazing savannah fading as it disappeared west and southward. Ahead and to the right, there was what appeared to be some farmland following the earth shapes vast flowing green sheets of coffee bushes. Somewhere could be heard the muffled roar of a major waterfall. And right nearby, the equator passed on its circuit silent, invisible, imaginary.

'My god. . . what a view!' exclaimed the major.

'Without making a cliché of the word, it is spectacular! Unforgettable. I'm very lucky,' were Roddy's words.

'Then you're doubly lucky, because you're lucky to be alive! You're Fearnachan, aren't you?'

'Yes, born and bred. My old parents are still at the gate Lodge at Woodend and I was born and lived there till the call up.'

'I'm Fearnachan too, born in the Fishertown. My mother died giving me birth, and since my father was still fishing, I lived with a relative of my mother's, a Mrs. Duggie on Society Street. I went to the Links school first then to Millbank Primary and finally Gordonstoun before entering Sandhurst. Then there was the war, so I've been away from Fearnas for a long time. Talking of time, your service with the colours will be completed in ten weeks. Any plans?' asked the major.

'My plan is to give my brain time to settle to see how I'm thinking. I'll go up to Fearnas to see my parents of course, but I don't see myself staying there for long. I think I've earned the time, if not the money, to gad about a bit for a short time,' was Roddy's reply.

'You know I retire almost at exactly the same time as you finish? And if you were to ask me the question I asked you, I would give you the reply you gave me! Have you ever done any sailing?' was the major's next question.

'An hour and a half on the Fearnas Sea Scouts' gaff naval cutter,' was the most Roddy could offer.

'The reason I'm asking is I've got a yacht down at Cowes. No, I haven't, my brother has, but I'm the one who uses it most. I just fancy cruising around—but I'm dead set on doing a Fastnet—go round into the Med and pretend . . . soak myself in leisure. I have no female commitments at the moment. But after the Med, who knows? Do you fancy coming along for the ride?'

'When can we start?' Roddy asked enthusiastically.

'Okay, we've both got immediate duties which we want to do. After that, I don't think either of us wants to spend time lingering. Give me your Woodend comms details.' He pulled a message pad from his leg pocket and printed his London address and telephone number. On a similar sheet, Roddy wrote his Woodend details.

'If I can wangle it, I'll see if we can get on the same aircraft from here, then when we get to London, we can have a dioch an doruis before you get on the train.'

'Sounds super, sir. I'd better get back to the lads now.'

The half hour was nearly up, so Roddy asked them if they were ready to go. They were. 'I'll tell the Boss,' he said.

They fell into patrol formation and worked their way back—on the path.

The major had little difficulty in making the necessary flight arrangements; string-pulling skills proved not to be required. They were in fact listed to take the same flight; the listing later appeared on BROs.

After a big farewell for Major Barron in the officers' mess, there was a marching out parade for the draft, which included Major Barron, bound for the UK, and the end of their military service. Needless to say, they did not sit together on the aircraft. There was slightly better seating for'ard for the four officers. The flight hedgehopped its way: Nairobi–Entebbe–Khartoum–Wadi Halfa–El Adem–Malta–Blackbush Airfield whence by train to London. Roddy could not be the major's guest at the Naval and Military Club because they were in uniform and Roddy was an NCO. It was close to the train's departure time by the time they got to the city from the distant airport in the north-east corner of Hampshire, near Camberley. They were not the only men in khaki at the Euston station bar nearest Platform 13. But Erik Barron was the only officer.

For these two, active service and service in action had ended. They were sailing *Fear Naught*, he and Erik, around the coast of southern Spain and soon would sail through the Straits of Gibraltar on their way, eventually to Mallorca when Erik, in a combined statement-cum-question, said, 'Surely you're not going to go through five years in the reserves as an NCO? You can do better. Don't let stupid social status hold you back from taking a commission. Would you consider going to War Office Selection Board?'

'If you're suggesting I'm good enough, I'd go like a shot.'

'Mckenzie'—and this was his surname used in an intimacy of friendship—'I think I know you better than you know yourself. If I pulled strings to get you through WOSB and you found out, you might, might just forgive me, but you'd cancel your application for Officer Training College.

'When we get to a phone in Almeria, I'll ask a friend of mine who's a staff colonel in Southern Command Infantry Brigade when the next Wosby is. Depending on what he says, you may have to go back by land. If there's sailing time, it would be a great race back, eh? Now shall we go into Gib or on to Almeria?' They went on to Almeria then battered their way back to Isle of Wight, on courses calculated for fastest time, with all the sail the old girl could carry yet minimum beating for two on two off watches. What those two masochistic lunatics did could scarcely be thought fun by more normal people. The truth is, great days and grim days, those two revelled in it.

From Cowes—shaved, showered, sober, and properly dressed—the WOSB candidate got on trains to Barton Stacey and arrived with so much time to spare he had to lounge around for a full thirty-seven minutes before candidates were allowed to enter. With all his sensitivity switches on and his mental eyes wide open, the external Mckenzie 'played it cool'.

The report from Erik's staff colonel chum was that his candidate performed brilliantly and would be actively influenced by his command staff to sign on and go to Sandhurst. Erik knew and Roddy knew that that was not included in their objectives. In Britain, holding a service commission was a small step up the social ladder. This was the result of a historical stereotype grown from the hundreds of years to the present; when all commissioned officers had been drawn, at the very least, from the upper classes and could help explain why British officers stayed aloof from other ranks. Erik knew that whatever else Roddy should choose to do, having gone through the process and having earned an army commission that it would be a helpful inclusion in any curriculum vitae, in addition to the other social and leadership skills and lasting friendships he would inevitably acquire. For Roddy, the penny dropped when on an occasion he and Erik had to join some others in London, Erik was able to say, 'Let's meet at the Naval and Military Club.' The social ball had begun to roll when in yacht clubs, Erik would always include in Roddy's introduction: 'We were in Korea together.' Ipso facto, Roddy must be an officer.

One day an old Sandhurst friend of Erik's, Hugh Verney, with his wife, Miette, was invited to come for an afternoon's sail on *Fear Naught*. In the course of the afternoon's gentle summer cruise, the vivaciously French Miette was drawn to this very charming and attractive male animal who was Erik's companion. When it was announced that, on Ninian's invitation, *Fear Naught* was going to be Roddy's billet while he completed OCTU, Miette was aghast—outraged!

'That will never do. *Ma fois! Ce brave célibataire* cannot be imprisoned on a yacht! Who will he ever meet except boring old matelots? Hugh, what about our little cottage by the stables?'

That is how Roddy came to take up residence in that very ancient yet charming cottage of two and a bit rooms under an enormous chestnut tree by the stables and loose boxes at Ranelagh Estate, Hants. It is also how, quite coincidentally, while looking for employment, there happened to be a vacant position for a groom / stockman / farm worker on the Ranelagh home farm. It was how one Roddy Mckenzie happened to be the successful applicant. The fact that he lived near the job was possibly the convincing factor. Mind you, insouciant enquiries by Hugh had scratched up a vein of gold. Roddy had in his youth spent much time with workhorses and . . . and . . . ponies . . . and riding hacks! Hugh immediately envisioned a groom for his polo ponies and someone to have practice games with during the week. 'Know anything about polo?' Hugh had asked as if coincidentally. Well, Roddy explained in reply, only what he had seen as he watched the Indian soldiers (not one of whom didn't have Khan in his name) play in the Farmers' Field. He had ridden the change-over horses, walked them cool, and ridden them back to those horrible concrete-floored stables behind the long dyke of Woodend. He didn't mention that he had tried tent pegging, with success waiting sometime in the future. And these same beautiful, strong-muscled horses from New South Wales in Australia, that could spin on a sixpence, pulled guns and limbers and ammunition wagons? Shame! Nor did he mention that these Indian horsemen, far from their homes and families, almost put him on strength with the regiment, surely on ration strength—when he once had the flu, two tall lean men wearing pagris came to the Lodge bearing for him curry in a jug and chapattis in a rumal. On many evenings after primary school, he shared with the soldiers in their hut the evening meal drawn from the big cookhouse on the other side of the field.

Roddy could not have struck a sweeter situation than that at Ranelagh. Hugh was right behind his army reserve activities even the social events like mess dinners, two-week exercises, and courses. Roddy insisted that since he was getting army pay for these absences, he should not be entitled to draw wages from the farm. 'Fine,' said Hugh, 'if that's your wish.' Without mention to Roddy, he promptly had the estate factor's office open a special account in Roddy's name for the farm wages he would forego.

There was something of infectious enthusiasm in the air around Ranelagh where it concerned the young hero of a modern war. Apparently the ex-soldier had become somewhat embarrassed at using the Ranelagh home farm's Land Rover— offered by Hugh without request—to go to his army nights and weekends and refused ever to take it out to do simply personal things like going to the Barley Mow for a pint. That is, were he not summoned to accompany Hugh who was a frequent visitor. It was Hugh's gathering point for local intelligence and sharing in the usual rumours, sage pronouncements, fiery polemics, hyperbole, lies, belly-laugh humour, and cures for ring bone in the white hooves of chestnut horses. Hugh had thoughts too about how the world appeared to be shaping that gave him a feeling of uneasiness. Our fathers' thinking us so hopeless that there was no possibility of a socially civilized world continuing seemed appropriate now. Times really had changed. Philosophies of a new kind appeared to be lining up to take over the future. He made a studied but sincere purpose in making sure he spent time with the farm labourers and the young people who worked in Winchester and other larger towns not far away. After saying hello to a group of young men standing back from the bar each with a pint of ale in hand, he said to one, 'Oh, ho,' he sounded facetiously grim, 'Bit dodgy, eh, that third try of yours, Eddie Winstanley? Oh—mm, bit dodgy. Spectators who've played see more than umpires do. He thought there was a fumble for the ball, and maybe there was, but in my view, that ball was passed forward.' He clapped him on the shoulder and put his arm across it and with the solemnity of a wise old gaffer, 'Your conscience will give you so many sleepless nights that when we play you next time, you'll be so buggered you won't be able to run with the ball.' Then changing tone, he went on, 'I'm off to have a pint without shame in losing. It was a bloody good game.' And as he looked around the group, he said before leaving, 'Cheers, lads.'

'Ah, fumble or no Major Verney, we'll beat you next time as well,' called Eddie to the figure departing through the throng. On hearing, Hugh looked round, smiled, and waved. There was laughter from the listeners around as he made his way through to his group. The old locals had theirs at particular, special, sacred spaces. His group, like the others, was well established and territorial. It would form down by a window in the side wall of the room, a back wall behind them with strategic access to the tail end of the bar, and most important of all, easy access to a toilet. Near their window was a door that led out onto a lawn and terraced garden much used in the good weather. Even so, it was more used as an egress than entrance because the members liked the business of chatting here and there with the others in the bar on their way to their corner.

This was a group into which Roddy had become inducted. In every gathering, the gentry, as acknowledged by the structure of their society, was always represented and one member was absent only when the House of Lords was in session or he had been called to some higher duty not in the House. There may even have been as many as twenty at a time in that august body of cheery chaps. It was to this group that Hugh Verney, on an

occasion of Roddy's absence, raised the subject of transport
for Roddy. 'Roddy's getting very embarrassed about using the
farm's Land Rover every time he goes to his reserve parades
at Winchester. He jogs or comes in here on his bicycle, or with
someone who happens to be coming. It's hard to know what to
do to help him. Let's face it; I don't pay him too much.' There
was a silence in the group, and some were thinking of their
penurious pasts when, as perhaps the son of a vicar, even a
decent bike was luxurious. Out of the silence, Colonel Sir John
Davenport said 'When we bought the Grange from Norman
Wallbank's widow, there was an old car in one of the sheds. Joan
said it was his pride and joy. She said he'd had it from his flight
lieutenant days until he was a wing commander in Bomber
Command, in fact he was using it right up till the night in 1945
when his Lancaster was blown up by the latest Gerry ack-ack on
his way home from Dusseldorf. His son was going to use it, but
what attracted young females after the war wasn't a two-seater
Alvis beetle-back built in 1927, so it stayed in the shed. Joan
somehow didn't want to move it and so left it behind. It was
there, and we inherited it with the property. Our Christopher
talked about doing something with it but never did. He went off
to nuclear science, and any ideas he may have had about an old
car evaporated. It's still there. I wouldn't be surprised if it didn't
still work like a clock. What d'ye think, Hugh, might Roddy be
interested?'

'Dunno, but I'll try him out on it. I think it would be great
fun to own.'

'Don't get carried away, Hugh, old chum. If you want it,
you've got to buy it. If Roddy wants it, I'll give him a free ninety-
nine-year lease.' It was later agreed that money should change
hands to give symbolic significance to the transaction. And so it
was that at the Barley Mow, on a special occasion of pomp and
ceremony, the transfer took place, that of twenty-five pounds
sterling passed between hands, and a shake to follow. Roderick
Mckenzie was now the lease holder of a two-seater, drop-hood
1927 beetle-back Alvis Speed Twenty in British racing green,
complete with hens' nests and eggs and enough hay in the seats
and all over it to feed two teams of Suffolk Punches. Now, a

vehicle like that, suitably cleaned and polished, would attract the kind of females he would like to drive around with. What a shame, there would be no convenient room for their friends. The dickie seat would surely put friends off. Besides, with the neatly fitting lid closed, who was to know it wasn't a luggage boot? Cleaned up and 'restored', with as much enthusiasm by Hugh as Roddy, the lustrous tourer caught every eye and was soon a common sight on the roads between Ranelagh and Cowes, Winchester, various military establishments around the county, the Judo Club in Southampton, and—well of course—the Barley Mow. Though he was never spotted personally, it was concluded that he certainly followed his interests with dedicated zeal. For those all over Hampshire who didn't know the owner, it was thought variously that perhaps he was a keen angler, a butterfly collector, a student of forestry, or particularly keen on picnicking in secluded spots. The Alvis was part of a new life of halcyon days. It was about days getting hot and greasy fixing the cast-iron meshing of gears on a reaper, in driving to tiny timbered pubs to drink pints from pewter pots, or in the Alvis as apollonian aegis to feverish passionate groping and kissing that went on and on; it was driving under trees that arched across hedged lanes and hay meadows that were lakes of blooms in colours that would challenge Turner in his driven dream of trying to mix a colour to achieve the emotion in the scene that shape and colour had contrived. It was girls with dresses that flowed, made of floral patterned seersucker with short puffed sleeves which showed arms that had quickly browned in the few long days of summer sun. It was heavy showers that made you pull up the hood or scamper for cover under a hedge or tree where you looked at each other in the moist closeness and kissed again, kissed raindrops from eyelashes and cheeks and noses and ears. And he watched as hair was given a wild shake, ruffled to catch motionless air, perhaps to dry fluffy if that was your style, or schoolgirl straight, which had its own attractiveness if its colour and the face were right.

For Roddy there was no dark ignorance on which it was his duty to shine a light, but there was much that he needed to learn. Time, circumstance and experiences, new people, and the caring

people—Miette, Hugh, Erik, Ninian, and Nora, his own mother
Flora, and in a unique, quiet way, Mary Dugal—these many, and
more, were the rich soil and the climate where his learning would
flourish and his personality would be nurtured. Now, two years
of frontline soldiering were left behind; a world lay before him to
be discovered, he was being offered an overflowing cup, he was
drinking of it in this golden world.

In his little brick and flint stone cottage, he began to learn
the recuperative joys of cooking. From the abundant fresh
vegetables and fruit of the farm's gardens, he applied his
imagination to the creation of meals that he enjoyed to eat. He
scolded himself for his failures and had another glass of wine to
celebrate his successes, each meal undergoing, sometimes cruel,
objective analysis. He had a flagstone floor on which a large
patterned rug of eastern birth was serving out the last years of
long service, a cast-iron fire in fine work of the iron-moulders
art, complete with an oven that he grew to understand and
could load with a dish which, at some late hour on his return
from Winchester (or the Barley Mow), he could sit in his castle
and enjoy. He was never unaware of his good fortune. He had
within a loose tangle of ideas, strands thick and thin of beliefs,
values, aspirations, thoughts, and reflections. How often had
he felt, experienced, the consciousness of the role of class in
society? This role was sometimes a locked gate on a pathway to
some desired end. He needed a key to unlock this gate. Hadn't
one such gate just been unlocked? Here he was, on the strongly
defended perimeter of a territory, a small part of which he
wished to claim. With the help of Erik, Hugh, and Miette, and
the men of the Barley Mow, a defensible position had been
established and a path through some of the obstacles had been
indicated.

Erik had laid the ground for Roddy's future when he invited
him down to share their 'rehabilitation'. Now, by turning the
necessity of Roddy's reserve duties into the invention of seeking
a commission, he had indicated Roddy's first path. He must go
to War Office Selection Board, he must pass through Officer
Cadet Training Unit, he must achieve a commissioned rank.
Both this process and its outcome would put Roddy well on his

way. As someone may desire, beyond all else, a first in classics at Oxford, Roddy wanted to lead a platoon in the field. There was no imagining now how that may come about, but when it did, he would be ready.

If 'serious' is the word, Erik was serious about the rehabilitation lark and did not undervalue it. Without diminishing the effect of the tonic leave, a share of time in healthy pursuits could be nicely be devoted to thinking. In the meantime, in between time, some organizational feats were going to be necessary. How were they to include perhaps any or all of a Fastnet Race, a Round the Island Race, a Mediterranean cruise, a run up the west coast of Scotland, and social days with friends on the Solent? When would Roddy's first on-shore commitment begin? Projected sun-lazy bumming about the Med had been an early casualty with Roddy's need to dash back for Wosby. Now he turned his mind to neglected interests and ideas about ways in which he may be able to help young people to create free minds and healthy bodies. He would get himself involved in the Outward Bound movement by providing experiences of sailing and cooperation in teams for young people while he enjoyed a facilitator's role and lots of cruising.

For Roddy, the military programme was going to dictate life for the next six to eight months or so but would not consume it. Living and working with Hugh and his people on the expansive Ranelagh lands was sheer joy. Working with Hugh's magnificent Percheron horses, for which he had a quite prosperous stud, was for Roddy a labour of the heart. When not procreating, they were used on the farm for ploughing and hauling carts and implements principally for the delight of the crowds whose visits helped make the estate financially viable. Polo was fun and satisfying because it was helping Hugh as a friend. The estate spread over ten thousand acres of Hampshire and the Home Farm was only one of four. Miette, who had been a theatrical agent and producer, had latterly concentrated her enthusiasm and feeling for heritage by working with Hugh and applying her not inconsiderable promotional and marketing skills to saving the whole estate, house, home, and land from the auctioneer's gavel and the taxman's purse. Theirs was a happy, fulfilling, and commercially successful Endeavour. Roddy was very sensitive to the good feelings around Ranelagh. In everyday thoughts, he learned humbly to accept their special care for him. These joys of the present would not and could not go on forever. Once his commission was achieved, the future stages of his establishment and development must be speeded up. These stages would not be spent here.

Perhaps it was the animal fecundity everywhere around him, perhaps it was the invigorating way he lived his life—or was it the passing of the seasons? It was not spring, but a young man's fancy was turning to love, or at least the delightful prospect of falling into it—perhaps, should love not entrap him in its soft and seductive coils, he could at least do something about ending his continuing virginal life. Surely that could be achieved with basic goodwill and equal intention between a male and a female? And didn't he, on his part, he asked himself as he cruised down to Cowes, have both of those? He needed to fix a problem on the toilet valve before the weekend when Ninian, Erik et al. were planning perhaps the last comfortable cruise of the season. He was making his way out in the dinghy when he was hailed by some people from a French yacht. Making his way alongside, he was greeted amiably in French by two Frenchmen to whom he replied equally amiably in French (thank you, Miss Laing and Mollie Bonne) and carried on a short conversation during which he asked them what he could do to help. They said they wished to sail on but that they had given these two ladies, who were happy to go to Cowes, a passage across the channel. Could Roddy put them ashore? *Pas de probleme.* The two girls, with their limited soft baggage passed down after them, nimbly got themselves into the dinghy, waved arms and made cries of 'See you in Australia one day!' Roddy had scarcely time to clear away when a man was in the bow of the French yacht letting the mooring go. A few questions about the girls' intentions revealed that they had made no plans for accommodation on the island. He explained that he was going to be staying overnight on board *Fear Naught* and that they'd be welcome to kip there for the night if they wished. 'I've actually come out to fix a valve on the loo. When I've done that, we could go ashore and you could decide what you want to do about accommodation. We could perhaps have a meal and a drink and we'd come back aboard later on if that's how you decided.' They looked at each other not knowing what to do, so he said, 'Okay, I can imagine you want have a look shoreside first. If you don't mind waiting while I fix the valve, I'll take you in as soon as I've done it. How's that?'

One asked, 'How long do you think the job will take?'

'I think the best part of an hour. If it looks as if it's going to take longer, I'll run you in anyway.'

The one who had introduced herself as Jill turned to the one she had introduced as Emma saying, 'Let's go to the yacht now.' They really had no trouble with yachts: they and their kit were aboard in a trice.

He showed them around the yacht in which he took an almost proprietorial pride. 'I've crewed in a Fastnet in this yacht with its owner, Ninian Barron, and his brother Erik who was my company commander in Korea. Ninian, and Nora his wife, will be coming down. She does sail, but she'll be staying with my boss's wife on Ranelagh Estate where I live and work.' He was saying this as they looked around. 'You can tell this is a loved, respected working yacht. It's got that feel and look about it.'

'Yes, you're right. It's exactly that,' he said, very pleased by this observation. 'Can you amuse yourselves while I fix the valve?' He fixed the valve inside the hour he had suggested, and during that time, the girls had decided that they'd like to stay the night at Cowes rather than go to the mainland today. 'Good stuff,' said Roddy, 'let's go ashore and gaze at the dazzling glitter of Cowes on a Friday night. I'm going to take some shore shoes just in case we end up at the dance. What about you two, we can put them in one bag.' As they skimmed ashore in the rubber boat, Roddy suggested, 'Let's say we have a quick look around town for accommodation first then we can go and play?'

'Good idea,' said Jill. 'If we fail, we still have tomorrow.'

It was late on a perfect English late summer afternoon and a few cumulus clouds had risen as high as physics would permit into the pale blue sky; the surface breeze was warm, and if conditions held—as the barometer indicated they might— it would be a perfect day for cruising on the morrow. They puttered in to the Cowes Corinthian Sailing Club, got the bags ashore where Roddy, and two very fit Australian girls made easy work of hauling out the big dinghy and making it fast. 'Right!' said Roddy, 'lets fix up the accommodation!'.

'We're here, Jilly,' cried Emma with delight! 'We've done it! We're on English soil. Can you imagine getting here a better way than this?'

'No, no way. We couldn't have imagined or planned this. Thank you so much, Roddy.'

'Right! First, let's fix the accommodation!' said Roddy, looking at these two lively girls delighted to be on English soil. Their enthusiasm was reaching him, and he was happy to be with them. 'C'mon, let's go up to the club and stow our gear. Perhaps someone up there may have some tips on accommodation.'

This Club was not grandiose, but once past the 'working parts', very pleasantly sunny and comfortably furnished. A steward suggested an old hotel called the Duke of York—not pretentious, not expensive, and not too far away. Simply to express their appreciation for his wise counsel, they thought it meet to have a drink at the club before going up to claim their accommodation which, to compound their indebtedness to the steward, he had begun to arrange by getting 'The Duke' on the phone, which he handed to Jill to complete the transaction. 'Done,' said Jill as she gave the phone hand piece back to the steward. 'Thank you for your help. That was kind of you,' she said to the youngish man whose eyes had scarcely left her.

'My real pleasure, miss. I hope you'll like our town and the island. If you strike any snags, just drop in. If I'm here, I'll see if I can help you. Now, would you like something to drink?' he asked, looking at Roddy.

'I certainly would, Freddie; but let me ask my overseas guests. What would you like to drink to celebrate your arrival on British soil?' Two gins and tonics were part of the order, and Roddy had a beer. The Friday evening crowd had been gathering. Apart from active sailors and local members who lived on the island, the lounge was filling—a vacant table by a window remained.

Jilly said, 'Shall I pounce on that window table while you and Em get the drinks?'

'Well done. Move now,' said Rod like a terse command. And off she went. 'We can saunter gently over, Emma,' he said, 'because all drinks must be served by stewards.' Reaching the table, Roddy questioned Jilly, the holder of their drinking territory. 'I thought you'd have hoisted the Southern Cross by now to signal a re-occupation of the motherland?'

'Nah, didn't want to start a stoush'—in her best twist on Australian vernacular—'we may not want to stay.'

'Oh! So it's no-man's-land terra nullius.' And turning to Emma, he said, 'It seems this territory is not occupied by an established civilization. Let's squat, Emma. Are we botanists or anthropologists or explorers?' he asked Emma, putting on a serious face.

Jill said, 'By the time you've made up your minds, we'll all have done a Burke and Wills. His Majesty's ship supply is trying to put a hook down and get some rations ashore!'

A steward, tray in hand, was right behind the pair. Roddy put his arm on Emma's shoulder. 'Bear away, Emma. Vessel with right o'way!'

It was surely time to make better introductions. It was a pleasant ambienza in which to be doing such a thing. The sky outside still a very pale blue and a breeze was hinting at a rougher passage back aboard, at the same time pulling together clouds where their complex surfaces would allow the cunning lighting scheme of the setting sun play with lights and shadows to present a memorable sunset. Apart from a few quite remarkable oils and the mandatory model ships, there was nothing pseudo-nautical about the decor—it was a very cosy middle-class chintz sitting room. The sounds were low and comfortably sociable. The girls were looking around and quickly getting a sense of the place.

'Okay, you're the new arrivals: it's up to you to declare yourselves. Who's going to start?'

'Toss you, Em,' said Jill, whereupon Jill told her word-scant story. Her name was Jillian Lowing. She worked for the Bank of New South Wales at head office in Sydney and as a cadet, and as part of that cadetship was attending Sydney University where she would be returning to complete her final year as a master of commerce. She lived in a flat in Kirribilli with Emma

who was secretary to the manager for the Pacific of a shipping
agency company and another girl. Roddy's eyes had opened
wide when he had heard the name Lowing. 'What a coincidence
that would be!' he thought. Emma went on. She worked right
on the water front in the office of a shipping company in the
not-very-salubrious but busy and lively Five Dock. She was happy
in this salty very male environment of clerks some past seagoing
types. She came to and returned from work (as did Jill) by the
green-and-yellow steam ferry from the little jetty on the north
shore, at the bottom of their street. Roddy listened to their
stories with sincere interest and active imagination.

At last, he could ask, 'Jill do you have any brothers or sisters?'

'Yes, I have two brothers. One is on a farm not far from our
family farm at Deniliquin, the other is presently with a stock and
station agency—Goldsborough Mort—at Jerilderie.'

'The reason I was so keen to ask was that when our battalion
was on its way back from Korea, we were diverted to the Mau
Mau rebellion in Kenya. In the area where our company was
operating, I palled up with the local Kenya police officer whose
name was Michael Manning Lowing who came from Deniliquin.
Is it possible . . . could it be . . . he's some relation of yours?'

'That's my brother Mick,' she exclaimed, 'the one at
Jerilderie! He's not long back from Kenya.'

'Well, I'll be blowed! You must tell him about this and give
him my very best wishes. He told me a lot about Australia,
and taking it from Mick a bit more seriously, I added it to the
more colourful information I'd heard from the Australians
with 3Bn Royal Australia Regiment. The result is I heard many
stories about Sydney, its character and life, its artists, poets,
writers, cartoonists, dancers, musicians all living right there, in
or around Sydney; all unpretentious and accessible, habitués
of the special pubs and cafes, mixing in the daily living in the
unique cultures of each of the suburbs.'

Jilly talked about her Saturday sailing, crewing on a Jubilee
from Kirribilli Yacht Club, where she was a member. Both Jilly and
Em could talk about 'the bush' and their young lives in Deniliquin
and Wagga. He wanted to get up and go to Australia—now. There
were more drinks and thoughts about dinner, which somehow led

to his having to raise the issue of tomorrow. 'Girls, I hope you're early risers, we've got to be off *Fear Naught* at sparrows. I need to be on the first ferry because we're having the annual Gymkhana and Fete at Ranelagh. How could they run it without me? Now, you have your kit with you. You may want to change your plan and take the last ferry to the mainland or stay here and leave the island at your leisure. On the other hand, we could give our apologies to the pub for a cancellation and come out to *Fear Naught*. Then we all leave to get the first ferry in the morning up to Ranelagh where you may enjoy all the fun of the fair at Ranelagh, stay overnight at our local pub, and I'll get you to Winchester to catch a London train on Sunday morning. Sleeping aboard will save you the cost of one night's accommodation—then, with the lower prices at the Barley Mow, more cash for London, which, in your plan, is probably a higher priority than Cowes, lovely as it is. No need to move the kit,' said Roddy. 'Shall we go to the pub and undo the booking? Perhaps we can eat there, then find the local *palais de danse?*'

The pub made no fuss about the cancellation when Jill informed them of their change of plan. The dining room was delightfully old fashioned and had obviously been in continuous use for most of its existence. The menu was made to match— roast beef, roast lamb, roast pork, roast chicken, and grilled local bream, and my goodness, a nice little wine list. 'Shades of Deniliquin,' commented Jill, 'but a good bit more refined.'

'How are the prices, Roddy?' asked Emma.

'I'm not really any good on prices: I very rarely eat out. But they're within reach for a farm labourer on reserve officer's pay. You can't believe how delighted I am to take Mick Lowing's sister and her chum out to dinner.'

'What say Emmy and I buy the drinks?'

'Don't give him the choice!' chimed Emma.

So they wined and dined on roasts which were—surprise, surprise—not overdone. These were two pleasingly sophisticated young ladies who, after the menu choices were made, had no difficulty in nailing down two French wines ripe for drinking after the briefest parts of seconds during which they had been allowed to flex their muscles in the airy world outside a bottle.

A waiter told them where to find the nearby palais and how it had had its wartime heyday to brilliant bands of American servicemen. That venue for good bands had continued long after the troops had (or had not) returned home. Dancers, from all over, came for the bands that played here—great bands from the north and London. Tonight's band was to be Lew and June Smith's 'Swing High'. Roddy danced all night enjoying the vivacity which, so clearly without artifice, was their abounding healthy charm. Their healthy, firm, well-muscled bodies were a joy to have in his arms. Their lightly tanned skin seemed to bloom like ripe stone fruit. Then it was time to pick up their kit and drag the dinghy out. On the sea, lit by a bright moon, a convectional breeze was making splashy little waves. Once aboard, logic dictated that Rod should use the washing facilities first so leaving a clear field for the girls. But first kisses, cuddles, good nights, thanks, and chatter of enjoyment shared.

The night breeze was still blowing when they woke at dawn. As they whisked along the lanes—not as swiftly as it seemed and sounded—Jill and Emma had the opportunity to gaze around and appreciate England's green and pleasant land. They marvelled at the small patterned fields behind hedges of hawthorn, or tree boughs trained by clever pruning. All around there seemed to be trees—oaks and elms standing by ashes, limes beeches, and by the streams' edges, weeping willows all set in a world where it seemed you could stretch out your arm and reach the horizon. Soon they drove past a double set of very tall gates: the cast-iron castings were shaped as leaves and branches; at particular, aesthetically sited areas, there were lions, horses' heads, knights in armour, the towers of castles and oaks, their boughs spread. Set into the stonework on either side brickwork recesses had tasteful but very large clear signs reading 'Ranelagh Estate'. If they were more of an advertisement, that was intended. Many other estates had suffered and died from a combination of vitiating taxation, owner penury, sad neglect, and lack of imagination. This was not the case at Ranelagh. Here taxation bills had been met by a committed, hereditary, ancestral owner and his wife who, with him, applied her skill, taste, imagination, and marketing flair to its glory and long-term aesthetic, productive, and financial future. Their care had filled Ranelagh with life.

This weekend's Fete and Gymkhana was part of a disciplined, thoughtfully executed marketing plan. They drove along the wall and turned into a leaf arched lane of copper beeches from which the roof of the large old house was now visible some way off, above the wall. Ahead there was a cluster of tall trees and farm buildings, and before reaching them, the Alvis was pulled up on a grassy patch where yellowing grass, of the type that can grow almost anywhere, and here, despite the shade of that enormous tree, its thin stems had grown through the summer and had seeded to wait until they starved, broke down to pushed aside by the new growth of next spring. The walls of the little house, made of big flint pebbles, had soft orange-red bricks to form edges that held them in place.

'Here, dear ladies,' announced Roddy 'is my "wee bit hoosie". Come and have a look.'

The cottage under the spreading chestnut tree was a storybook fairy-tale illustration, emotive yet real—the women loved it. In the stark white interior of the main of the two rooms, a burnished black stove immediately caught the eye, the smooth scrubbed surface of an ash table supported, by stained oak legs, had the girls imagining a vision of pastry being rolled out to fit a pottery pie dish to put into the hot oven beside the glowing log fire in the grate, whose door would be swung open to receive its game-filled feast. This bright square room was kitchen and general living room with a cosy armchair and old Eastern rugs whose faded reds and blues were still alive and commanding. The big dresser with cupboards on the bottom must have held every cooking vessel ever needed for there was nothing on view in the uncluttered space of the little room. 'Hugh's wife, Miette, whom I hope you'll meet, was responsible for revitalizing what was a tumble down ruin. He pushed aside a heavy red-brown curtain in a back corner to reveal an old painted door with a brass knob. 'This is more of Miette's flair at work.' A little square room, not an obvious addition, had been tiled to the full height of the walls making a complete wet area for a shower, a toilet, and

a wash hand basin. An eye-level window along one wall let a
viewer see onto green pasture and yellow cropland through the
boughs of a copper beech. Showing them the contents of the
pinewood dresser, he was saying, 'Please I'd like you to make
this your base for the day while you enjoy the activities. Look,
tea, coffee, biscuits although you'll possibly opt for some of the
good eats on the stalls.' A glazed white lidded box declared
'Bread' in bold capitals. He lifted the heavy lid and pointed.
'Bread,' he announced, 'Home-made!' He paused and had
wanted to explain, 'I'm going to be a bit rude and leave you to
your own devices while I go and look after my animals.'

'Can we come with you? We're not "just another pretty face,"
you know?'

'By all means, do,' he said.

They had put on their hiking boots, more suitable for fixing
the loose boxes and lugging feed around. Roddy was preparing
tack for the afternoon's polo. They were in their element as
Roddy could see, as he admired their competence and approach
to their tasks. One of the girls had led out a horse, a tall sorrel
gelding, and was deftly brushing it when Hugh arrived. 'Hello,'
he greeted Emma. 'Good morning,' he said cheerily, 'Do we
have a new recruit? I'm Hugh.'

'And I'm Emma, Jill and I asked Roddy if we could help.'

This tall man with the cheery weathered face and sparkling
eyes would surely be the Hugh that Roddy so much admired.

'Excuse me, I'll call her.' Emma threw back her head and, in
a tone starting low and ending high, sounded, 'Co-oo-oo–ee!'

A tallish blonde girl holding a pitchfork appeared from a
loose box. 'Oh,' she said on seeing Hugh, 'Good morning. I'm
Jill Lowing, volunteer Gymkhana worker.'

Roddy appeared having interpreted the call as meaning
"Come!"

'Good morning, Hugh, you've met the Australian volunteers?
Sounds like something from the Boer War, doesn't it?—They
came across from France yesterday in a French yacht. I provided
a ferry in *Fear Naught's* dinghy.'

Hugh was captured by the natural charm of these young
women.

'When can you spare them from their labours? They must come and meet Miette. Nora's here. The Barron boys have just dropped her here and gone on down. Roddy, could you play Four for us this afternoon? Leigh Benson's got something aeronautical on at Odiham today—can't come. I'll take "Rupert". Do you mind taking "Trumpeter"? You know how to handle him.'

'Certainly,' Roddy said enthusiastically.

Hugh, speaking to the girls, enquired, 'I hope the Mckenzie hasn't been singing "The Mucking o' "Geordie's Byre" at you. Just threaten his beer supply: that'll silence him,' in a manner that the girls recognized as being a bit military. Addressing Roddy, he said, 'When you're ready, bring the Australian contingent up to meet Miette and Nora.' To Jill and Emma, he said cheerily, 'I'll look forward to seeing you later. In the meantime, enjoy all the fun of the fair.'

Hugh, in his enthusiasm about his encounter, found Miette and passed on his news. 'I had just been down to the stables. Roddy's got two charming young Australian women down there. Thought you might like to cast your eye on them. Sorry, can't wait, just going to put the boards down.' And he was gone.

It might have been thought, quite understandably, that with an enormous outdoor fete to organize, which she would officially open in two hours, that she would be dashing hither and yon, over the extensive area of the grounds and numerous stall venues, making last-minute decisions and arrangements. On the contrary, all the planning had been done—efficient, well-briefed staff each had his or part of the activities under control. She was cool, calm, and collectedly going around being gracious everywhere, welcoming stallholders and wishing them a successful day's trading, praising their displays, and generally engendering happiness. Hugh had just gone. Miette immediately got into her little Morris estate car and went to the stables. She found Roddy.

'Roddy?' she demanded. 'Where are these two Australian women that my husband is so excited about?'

Just then, from one of the doors, a tallish female with loose blond hair, a very neat figure, and a fluid walk, her back to them, walked along the stables, asking in a mature, modulated voice, 'Emma, are you using the broom?'

From a further door, a young woman with black hair pulled back from a face that was so much more than pretty, walked out, a yard broom in hand. She saw Roddy and Miette who immediately called out, *'Bon jour, cheres demoiselles!* My husband told me we had overseas visitors.' Roddy introduced the visitors, and Miette was *enchantee* to make their acquaintance. In the animated exchanges, Miette invited the girls to lunch. They explained that as they were travelling light, costume choice was somewhat constrained. Skirts would do, they were assured, and perhaps they had some shoes.

When Miette had gone, Roddy suggested that since the official opening would be at twelve o'clock, they may like to go and prepare themselves, then have a wander around the park and the stalls. He wouldn't be able to join them for lunch, he said, because he would have to take the horses up for the first chukka at two o'clock. 'Thank you so much for your help. You saved me a heap of time. I'm very pleased Miette asked you to lunch, I think you'll find her great fun to be with. Nora is Ninian Barron's wife. Ninian's the one who actually owns *Fear Naught.* When I get sorted out after the polo, we can get together and can go up to the Barley Mow and fix your digs. I'd to offer to have you to stay, but I'm afraid my wee hoosie is much too small for comfort.'

'Roddy, don't be too concerned about us. It's nice of you to ask us to come and we enjoyed what we've been doing this morning. We'll be watching you play. May the home team win! By the look of him, Trumpeter is a fine strong horse—hope he does well for you.'

'Thank you, both. Cowes would be nice for you, but I'll be looking forward to what you have to say about Ranelagh and its people when we have a beer tonight. I think you'll find anything you need. There should be plenty hot water. Oh, towels are in that big cupboard in my room. If there's something you can't readily find, - rummage!' He was thinking how much he had enjoyed them. 'God, what would I do if I had to choose between them?' he asked himself.

He was pleased that Hugh had asked him to play, although he faced the fact that it was not in a goal competition and that it was simply entertainment for the crowd, therefore, being an unofficial game, it would not go towards goal scoring count. He didn't know who the other players would be or how they would react to a newcomer being in the team. It would be his first-ever polo game. He just had to get in there, he was thinking, and play his best. Eventually it was time to saddle up the Ranelagh ponies and get them up to the ground.

The weather was holding up magnificently, the sun was bright, and there was just a very gentle breeze, which wouldn't please the sailors but would be just fine for the crowds of people who had come to this pleasant place to enjoy the diminishing days of warmth before winter arrived, which it quite suddenly would. Jill and Emma had changed and enjoyed being out among the crowd. They loved the children's Animal Farm. The pony rides which the estate ran as an income earner (the price included in the entry ticket) were totally occupied while aspiring riders impatiently awaited their turns. The girls thought how much it was like an Easter show in country Australia. A pair of brightly harnessed stud Percherons with plaited and beribboned manes and tails were pulling a long hay wagon on which benches had been fixed. It too was proving a favourite not only with younger people; there were some aboard who would have had to be lifted up. Jill was remarking, 'It's not hard to imagine the pleasure it must be giving these old people to gaze around, while those beautiful animals plodded through the roads and paths of the grounds; under the arching trees, looking into the gardens, seeing the animals, the well-cared-for old buildings, with fields and trees and pastures of this magnificent estate stretching all about.'

'They look so happy and in touch with what they're seeing. I wonder what histories of association are going on in their minds?' commented Emma.

As they wandered, they were seeing stalls where estate grown cut flowers and plants were for sale; fruit and vegetables from the gardens; honey and jams and preserves made in the big copper pots in the huge bright kitchen at the rear of the main house; rolls filled with hot, farm pork were attracting customers. There was a stall in the centre of some small tables selling cider from the estate's own brewery. All the seats were filled with merry drinkers and the foaming cider suds were wetting quite a few white-haired whiskers. There were girls in floral frocks and bare brown arms who were partaking equally heartily. As they were watching, a noisy old Fordson tractor passed by hauling a flat trailer with benches of laughing, shouting children aboard. It was a pleasure for so many to walk through the estate's gardens. The gardeners were in attendance and enthusiasts were assaulting them with questions on care, and growing and pests and every other kind of question which fills the minds of ardent gardeners.

There were decorative trees in a rising gradient of growth, gardens of shrubs, roses, and meticulously trimmed flowerbeds. From the kitchen doors, the cook could walk in to a high-walled garden, hers to command well, almost: Miette was an engaged enthusiast and the gardener was a dedicated expert. It called out 'abundance' from row upon row of vegetables brightly green that made reds look richer and were a perfect foil for rhubarb and Swiss chard and yellow pumpkins. Herbs there were too, which added flavour and piquancy to every dish the cook prepared—of course Miette ensured Provence was represented. Tall though the walls were, they did not encroach, so there was room for raspberries, gooseberries, and fruits. What could not thrive in the weather without, lived within the luxury of glass and hothouses.

After taking his horses up and tethering them, Roddy went to the tack room and put on the old boots the knee padding and a helmet that Hugh had given him to wear when they practised. When Hugh came down, he brought a Ranelagh shirt for Roddy, saying, 'It should fit, Roddy, it's an old Four that I found in a togs drawer up in the house.' They could have walked up to the ground, but you never knew when the Rover would be needed, so they drove up companionably, agreeing they were very lucky to have such brilliant weather. The last items of the Gymkhana part of the activities were being cleared from the ground, the jumps, and the lines of poles for the bending races, their holes filled in and packed smooth. Their saddles removed, the globular ponies were blowing, and girls and boys were happily together caring for their steeds in a warm atmosphere of chatter. The very sophisticated young adult male and female show jumpers, who seemed to turn britches and jodhpurs into items of elegant allure, were caring for their tall hunters, lively beasts with pricked ears and roving eyes in heads held high. Some of the riders, with the last bit tack off and put away, had decided there should be no further delay in opening the odd bottle of bubbles. So now the two polo teams, formed in files, walked onto the field, the number one of Ranelagh facing the one of the visitors.

The game had been going quite well; friendly competition was allowing sufficient challenge to make the game interesting. As they passed on the field, Hugh had given Roddy, on two occasions, a 'Well done!' for especially good plays; and the number two had done the same.

It happened in the last period of the last chukka when the play was running up to the rivals' end. Roddy was well up in the centre: a ball came from his left to cross his front. With a well-executed near-side hit, he had placed the ball forward where he could ride onto it and get a clear offside forehand shot. The opposing goal was wide open. His next stroke would be an almost certain goal. At a gallop, the number three of his own Ranelagh team aimed for a wipe-out of Roddy and thundered across at an angle of about ninety degrees, directly to unhorse Roddy by striking his pony at the withers and crashing him off the ball. After the heavy blow, of horse-on-horse contact, the hindquarters of his speeding pony bent the neck of Roddy's mount, twisting it away and down as it bore on at the gallop. Trumpeter was clawing with his front legs to get a grip on the ground while scrambling to spread his back legs for balance, his belly just touching the ground. It was with great skill that Roddy struck balance for himself and his horse to hold the staggering Trumpeter from rolling over. There was a loud groan from the spectators. The opposing number two shouted at the Ranelagh three, 'You should be shot for that!' The Ranelagh number three followed the ball at a gallop. Now it was very easy to hit before the other side could turn around. He swung his mallet, played completely offline, and shot the ball past the opposing team's left goal post. Hugh observed the action with anger and disgust. The bell rang to indicate time while the game continued, but it seemed, somehow, that the players were happy when the horn was blown.

'Aubrey Bardsley! Attempting to crash a teammate whose shot it clearly was, was the worst, most disgusting display of bad sportsmanship I've ever seen.' Hugh was keeping tight control of his seething, hot anger; his eyes had narrowed, as he signalled detestation to the fatuous face he addressed. His voice was cold, measured.

'Damn it, Hugh, he's only a farm labourer. He shouldn't have been on the field.'

'I'll decide who plays in the Ranelagh teams. You can decide not to play. A decision you will never be required to make in the future. Whoever, or whatever, once the team is formed, it must play as a team. Two very fine ponies and a player were put in serious danger by your unmanly action. It would be a bitterly sad day to see a man who survived wounding in the front line and two of the severest battles of the Korean War, killed by an oaf on a polo field. Leave Ranelagh now. I don't want you amongst sportsmen, and I daresay they don't want you.'

Bardsley said nothing, no apology, no contrition. If anything, he looked confused to hear Hugh saying such things. Then he realized that Hugh's body was taut with anger. He turned without a word. He left the pony he had ridden at the tethering line. He strode quickly to his nearby car and drove away. By some, wishing to evade the major issue, Roddy was being congratulated on the brilliant near-side shot that had put him in a prime position to score. Others were using the word 'appalling' about the crashing incident as they talked amongst themselves. 'Bardsley rather let you down, Hugh,' the visiting captain was saying. 'That was a very succinct dressing-down you gave the fool and a good decision to keep the young idiot off Ranelagh. I hope not too many of our new young men are going to turn out like that.'

Hugh turned to Roddy who had heard every word between Hugh and Bardsley. 'Roddy, I must apologise for that event. I've never experienced anything like it my life and I'm certain I never shall again. I imagine you heard what Bardsley said to me?'

'Yes, I did, but you really can't take responsibility for that. Thank you very much, Hugh. I feel privileged. You have done all that you could possibly do. Putting today's extreme event completely aside. May I say I'd be very unhappy if you put yourself in an invidious social position on my account? I don't ever feel that you have excluded me. You cannot imagine how much I appreciate what you and Miette are doing for me. I feel more about what might have happened to Trumpeter. And being on sick report would be the worst thing that could happen to me at the present time. Believe me, I'm relieved. Please, Hugh, go and see the ladies and Captain Robert. I'm happy looking after the horses: they did well today.' Hugh put his arm forward and placed a hand on Roddy's shoulder grasped it tightly, looked at Roddy squarely, and then without a word, went off to do what he had suggested.

Jill and Emma were finding Miette and Nora quite remarkable and very sweet women—mature, confident, and suave. They were conversationalists who were widely experienced—interested, empathetic, rational, emotional—all of these expressed with sometimes devilish humour and sincere joy. Every story was greeted with shared sympathy or delight. When the polo began, they turned their attention at the game and the people whose fortunes interested them. The expanse of the ground with spectators grouped and spread all around between the trees and circling boards, which kept the ball from running out of play and marked the boundary, painted a colourful, gay ambienza.

The spectators had been enjoying the game until the play of events towards the end changed everyone's mood. Those who didn't know it was against all etiquette and the rules shrank at the near disaster for the ponies and the rider who had been attacked. It was rather disappointing that such an event should have occurred. Miette was upset and was sad for Hugh. Bardsley knew the etiquette as well as anyone on the field; he knew the sanctity of team. She could see, if no one else could, that he had wilfully thrown aside these guidelines to express a baser feeling. Like a child in a tantrum, he vented his feeling of social supcriority and exclusion. Hugh rejoined the lunch table, the ladies, and Robert Morley, the old sea captain, widower from a neighbouring property, who had been a friend of the family since Hugh's father's time. Jill and Emma realized it was bad sportsmanship. 'Imagine that happening in rugby?' they said when they saw the flagrant action. Miette and Captain Morley were eager to show that what affected them both in that upsetting event was what had happened to Hugh. His captaincy of the team had been insulted, as host he had been insulted his chosen team member had been given a shocking slight, and two very valuable horses with a ruined shoulder each, or worse, could have been put out of action for the rest of their lives. To cap it all, of the two men at risk, the man in Roddy's position had been in the most danger. Yes, it was all bad. He told the group what he had said to Bardsley. *'Bien fait, mon cheri,'* called Miette and came around them to hug and kiss him. She squeezed him and remained by his side with her arm around him. 'Bravo!' said the captain. 'We can do without people like that.'

The spectators were leaving and some came to say thank you to their host and hostess, while on their way by, others who knew Hugh, men and women, stopped to say how they were feeling for him and what an absolute cad Barnsley had shown himself to be. Miette, still holding Hugh, said to the girls, 'Roddy will still have a lot to do, but we can go up to the house now.'

'I've been sitting on my backside all afternoon; I need a walk on deck. I'll go down and get in Roddy's way, be a bit of a nuisance then walk up with him,' said the Captain. There were things he wanted to say to Roddy. The girls, Nora, Miette and Hugh packed the baskets and cushions and set off for the house. Miette and Hugh were walking hand in hand, Hugh with one basket, the girls and Nora with the other baskets and cushions. She had attached herself to the Australian ladies: and they walked together a little apart and slightly behind Hugh and Miette.

When Roddy and the captain hove into sight of the small terrace on the side of the house, Hugh said, 'The Mckenzie will be needing a drink. I'll go and get some beer for him. Is there anything I can get for you ladies when I go in?' Jill and Emma noticed Hugh's nickname for Roddy and what it implied about the friendship underlying their relationship. What did it mean that Miette had a special meal, not leftovers from the lunch, prepared and kept especially for what she knew would be a very hungry young man?

Everyone wanted to say something to Roddy and each did almost all at once, so there was something of a babble for some seconds. Miette took Roddy's hand in both of hers and held it up to her breast. 'I'm so, so sorry, Roddy,' she softly said. Hugh arrived with the beer. Then there was joking and much lighter chat and talking about what next for Jilly and Em.

'We haven't got him signed up yet, but we want to recruit him for Australia,' Emma said.

'If you're successful, it will give another reason to visit Australia again. We didn't see enough on our first visit. We loved it, is that not true, *cheri*?' She later said to the girls as the little party was chattering, 'Roddy has to leave *demain au premier chant du coq*, so why should you go to the Barley Mow tonight? I have single rooms, very small which we have made for people who come here for conferences or training, why don't you stay there, Roddy can come up from his cottage and have breakfast here, which I shall make, then you may drive away in his automobile *sportif* together and I shall be able to say *au revoir*?' And so they did; and all happened the way Miette had in mind. Their French/English breakfast was served at the huge cooking table away from the enormous Aga cooker which was hot it perpetually was. Kitchen or not, there were white curtains with blue cornflowers echoing Provence pulled back from the tall windows.

'We see too little of our Mckenzie. On Thursday he will leave again for two weeks *pour devenir parachutiste*. Hugh and I always miss him when he goes away. But you can't possess a soldier.'

En route for Winchester, the capital of ancient England, the conversation, as they bowled along, was of Australia and his firming decision to go there. He left them at the station where they would take command of their travelling future. He stood there, a young lieutenant in denims, cuddling two delightful young Australian women. Their visit had been brief, but they

had adored everything, inevitably they had fallen in love with
Miette, and Hugh was close behind. They knew the pair would
come to Australia and they were already envisioning how they
would make the experience wonderful for them. Roddy had
been provisioned with names addresses and telephone numbers,
theirs and Mick Lowing's. Well, really, if you couldn't kiss and
cuddle these lovely women, then hopes for an amorous future
were bleak. He did and imagined there might have been some
mutual enjoyment.

Being ordinary infantrymen, and lieutenants to boot, except
for three NCOs on the course, and 'weekend warriors', the
Parachute Regiment instructors took them as fair game to be
given a hard time, which for the first few days they did. Like
WOSB, you knew at the end of the course whether you had
passed or failed. The selection was good, and the only man who
could not graduate was a bloke who broke his ankle on the first
jump. As happens on courses, there is someone you pal up with,
and Geoffrey Lancaster, who was actually a regular, palled up
with Roddy. Abingdon was fine, but Oxford nearby beckoned, it
being, one supposes, the economic law of supply and demand- it
had more pubs!

Hot on the ending of this course came the two-week platoon
commanders' Infantry Battle School at Brecon. That too was
worthwhile, effective training; suitably demanding; and for
someone, as Roddy was at that time, totally enjoyable. When
one can set the endurance clock to a fixed time plus a bit more
for 'stuff-ups', a fortnight of very demanding slog in the field,
short sleep, and forced quick decision making makes two weeks
shrink to bearability. Wot, no shelling? Sheer bloody luxury!
Anyway, the directing staff wanted to get away and bag the
remaining gun-shy game before it cleared out. Thus, to all
intents and purposes, the major weight of the infantry training
season calms down.

Roddy was not totally ashamed about his contribution to
Ranelagh's peak period. He had seen the grain crops off and
the abundant hay season's mow safely stacked. He had helped
Hugh develop shots, which meant that he too had to develop
shots to feed Hugh's practice. The ponies had taken to him,

as had all the people on the farms, in the gardens, and in the kitchen. He had dutifully served God and Mammon, lived in an incredibly *bequwemes Hauschen*. What others could there be for sheer care and gentility than Hugh and Miette? He would never be able to thank them for what they had done.

Geoffrey Lancaster's rank as lieutenant had just been made substantive, and his name had appeared in the *Gazette*. Added to the fact that there were some old-school chums who were going to be around at that time, but not for much longer, he would most likely be joining the battalion presently in BAOR 3 Germany. He knew of Roddy's plan to leave for Australia, and since his parents would be absent in the Caribbean, it seemed like the perfect time for a party. Geoffrey, Roddy, and Mark Phillips had been on the parachute course together, so it was a small celebration for them. His twenty-year-old sister had lots of friends who would be in party mood (as ever) and available to come. It was to be a casual dress affair. His sister had organized a very good band and the household staff liked parties—all was set for a good time.

Roddy didn't mind the odd party, so he was happy to be there. He had been chatting with Mark and some females and just excused himself to go and find a drink. He had turned round and was about to take his first pace when right in front of him and about to collide, was a gorgeous tall blonde woman. Each stopped, and he found himself looking into her radiant face. The radiant face lit up yet further.

'Gracious me!' she exclaimed. 'Are you Roddy Mckenzie from Fearnas?'

'Indeed I am,' he confirmed and, with a smile, continued, 'and I'm guessing that you may be Miss Jane Dugal?'

'Yes, I'm Jane Dugal. My gosh, it's a long time since last I saw you. You're looking very well.'

'Do you know anyone else here? Are you with a group?' she asked.

'No, I don't, really, except Geoffrey and one other army bloke. But I don't feel lost. I'll see what's going on and where the fun is.'

'Well, maybe the fun will turn up. Come and meet two friends of mine. One's another school marm and the other's a GP. C'mon!' With a free, girlish friendliness, she picked up his hand and, giving it a little squeeze, gently pulled him forward towards her friends. His physical fitness expressed itself in an emanation of energy which gave one the thought that should one touch him, one would feel a powerful electrical shock, and as she touched his hand, she felt a powerful vibration tingle in her arm and spread through her body. To keep her feelings at the level of girlish friendliness was going to be difficult.

Roddy responded to her inviting mood. 'Super! Let's go,' he said, returning a squeeze.

She had still not let go of his hand and was still holding it when she brought him to a group of males and females. Jane waited in the pause while the group sensed and responded to the arriving couple.

'I'd like you to meet Roddy Mackenzie. He's from my very own part of Scotland.'

She went on then to introduce Roddy to each of the five— three women, one of whom was Edwina, Geoffrey's sister, and two men. From their greeting, it seemed that they were very pleasant people.

Victor (one of the men), noting that Jane was still holding Roddy's hand, said to Roddy, 'And how did you capture the fair Jane?'

'Ah, secret mountain magic, but I'll let you in on the secret. I stirred the most beautiful puddings of soap suds in her castle in the Rhododendrons in the magic forest of where was it?' And he turned to Jane to hear her say the name.

'Himalayalanddesh!' she announced, loading the sound of the name with exotic mystery. 'The secret land beneath the jangli trees on the slopes of the Himalayas where you climb through a steep mountain pass to the Forever Land. We didn't have much to carry, just a white enamel jug with blue edges purloined from cook, soap we pinched from the gardener's lavatory which always had the dry mustiness of summer, and spiders, and a doll's tea set. So we twisted and slashed our way through the dense lianas and mossy boughs.' Changing her voice from struggling jungle explorer to lecturer, she explained, 'Actually it's absolutely bare under rhododendrons. Nothing will grow there. But we grimly struggled on, day after day, until we reached the Magic Future land, the lawn. It must have been all of twenty yards away, but we did bend and wriggle through the rhododendrons, just like going through the forested foothills, until you leave the tree line. And I haven't seen much of him since, and this evening, here he is.'

She had turned and was looking into Roddy's face as she was saying this, and as she returned her gaze to the group, they could not help but see the happiness shining from her eyes.

Herbert may have felt that the ace he was going to play had already been trumped.

The small band had begun to play 'I Get a Kick out of You'. Roddy smiled brightly at Jane and said with delight, 'Oh, boy. Old-fashioned dancing.

What do you think? Like to try?'

'Love to.'

Roddy, turning to include the entire little group, said, 'Excuse us please; must try this.' And off they went.

They slipped into the beat immediately like old troupers in a chorus line. Jane loved Roddy's fluid but controlled movements. His guiding arms were so easy to follow. No pulling on the snaffle, just a rein on the neck and the pressure of a knee. The little band was very good. Their tempo was spot on and their changes from trumpet lead to sax, then giving the trombone his chance were 'just nice'. Anyone with a sense of rhythm and an ear for music had to enjoy it. What Roddy and Jane had begun suited the mood of the other guests and soon everyone was on the floor. The ballroom had been designed for grander events, for ladies in crinolines, couples in long lines for contra-dancing, so Geoffrey's guests found themselves on a vast, calm ocean of parquetry, which Roddy took advantage of to lead his partner into gliding, swooping turns in the quicksteps.

As they were making their turns with elegant verve, with her face close to his, Jane said, 'You're something of a sophisticate, Roddy. Where did you learn to dance so well?'

'Ah, I'm betrayed by the signs of an ill-spent youth, but you won't believe me when I tell you. Perhaps I should make up some excitingly exotic yarn.'

'Which are you going to choose?'

'Perhaps the dull truth is best; inventing an exotic yarn may give you the wrong impression. Towards the end of each year at St Ninian's Academy, we would learn and practice country dances so that we could enjoy all the parties that were held over Christmas. Then on our final year, we learned waltzes, quicksteps, and foxtrots. In the closing weeks before the seniors' dance, the girls would join us for the dancing classes. It was great fun.'

When the music ended, they left the floor, and as they walked off, Roddy said, 'Thank you, Jane, I enjoyed dancing with you so much. Shall we try again before the night's out? That is if your program doesn't fill up immediately. Will you keep a spot for me?'

'Stop and I'll pencil you in now,' she said and looked down at her imaginary programme with her hand up holding an equally imaginary pencil. 'How about the gavotte?'—she looked up—'Or would you prefer the second minuet?' They laughed, and as they walked off, Roddy's arm was lightly around her waist. She kept close to him, their bodies touching, and she glanced at his face as they went. Their group had broken up and gone to remix with other friends. They were on their own, and as they stood on the edge of the dance floor, the others who had been dancing were now chattering. Jane said, 'Shall we go and have a drink? I love the lawn and old trees but perhaps not this evening.'

From the ballroom, doors opened into a large drawing room which looked rather like the portrait room in an art museum. There were sofas, armchairs, and low tables, and the returning dancers were choosing where to sit. As Jane had hinted, it was too cool to brave the terrace and a wood fire had been lit in an enormous grate below a long mantel piece on which a selection of silver and gold objects was on display.

When Roddy was returning with the wine, she stood up and watched him approach. She couldn't and didn't try to define her feeling as joy or excitement, and she loved seeing this male approaching her. 'Thank you, Roddy,' she said, taking the glass. 'I did enjoy dancing with you,' she said earnestly. 'I'm so glad you asked.' This was no trite politeness. She wanted him to know that his having asked her to dance had been something special. Then she smiled and her voice lightened. She looked at him roguishly and, narrowing her eyes to slits, declared in a threatening voice, 'Now I can begin my inquisition. Shall we sit?' They sat before tall windows across which the curtains had not been drawn and a gibbous moon was still pale in the darkening sky. She immediately engaged Roddy's eyes. She looked very beautiful, fresh, and vive, Roddy was thinking. 'Why is Jane Dugal looking at me in this way? Why is she so warm and vivaciously friendly?' went flitting through his mind.

When they'd settled, with a laughing smile, she moved from the jest to interest.

'You mentioned "another army bloke", are you still serving?'

'Yes, I'm in the Hamps' Reserve battalion. I'm living on Ranelagh Estate where I'm working for Major Hugh Verney. It's really great being with Hugh. I get to do everything around the place, from milking our home cows to ploughing, fixing fencing and machines that break down. Oh, and another thing, at least once a week I have to play two or three practice chukkas with Hugh. In between times, I look after the polo ponies.' Jane was listening with interest. She really wanted to know.

'When Geoffrey and I went on the parachute course, Hugh didn't just let me off, he wanted me to go. He's happy about all the army duty I do, even the social stuff. Say there's a dining-in night or something like that and I have to go off early to travel, he'd be unhappy and quite upset if I didn't go. I don't accept pay for army duty time off. I'd do anything for Hugh and Miette. They're just super people.'

'You sound very happy down there with Hugh.'

She appeared to think for a few moments. 'You must come over to Arlstorp and see the school and meet some of the others.'

She was about to go on but Roddy spoke. 'Talking about others,' he said, 'aren't we neglecting your friends? We should go and find them, c'mon, bring your glass, we'll get another drink on the way.' They found Meredith, a teacher, in conversation with a male teacher from a neighbouring boys' school. The doctor had joined others elsewhere. Roddy opened the conversation saying, 'I must apologise. I've been monopolizing Jane.'

'Don't apologise. You haven't seen each other for years: I see Jane every day,' said Meredith. 'You've met Herbert Asquith, a friend and collaborator of ours, he's science master at St Swithin's School.'

'Hello again, Roddy, Meredith and I have just been talking about a school concert which Jane and we two are involved in putting on. We're providing the male voices and I'm in the orchestra.'

'That sounds like good fun,' said Roddy, interested. 'What are you going to be producing?' he asked, looking at all three.

'We're going to do *Salad Days*,' said Jane, replying for the three. 'I think you'd enjoy it. The performers really are very good.'

'Oh, I surely would! The first thing I do when I think of *Salad Days* is break the rule; I don't remind myself that, "We Said We Wouldn't Look Back".' And without hesitation, he sang the little piece of melody, which was the main number of the show. 'It's such a lovely duet. The melody's jumped into my head now. I'll be humming it for days. I believe school shows are often underestimated, then, when people go to see them, they get an excitingly pleasant surprise. That's what we used to hear after our St Ninian's Academy shows.'

'I do believe you,' said Jane, 'When I was doing my Dip. Ed. after my degree, one of the other girls, who'd been at St Ninian's, was ecstatic about a certain young singer in one of their shows. I can't for the moment remember what the song was but I think it was either "Passing By" or "Where E'er You Walk". It was you she was talking about. It was just before school finished and you immediately went off to join up. She said she hadn't seen you since and wondered what had happened to you. I think she may have had a crush on you.' Another level of softness transformed her face. 'You'll sing that song for me one day perhaps,' she said wistfully, meaning what she said. He didn't respond, just wondered who it might have been. 'Getting back to our show, would you like to come?'

'Of course! I'd love to come to your concert! If you can give me the dates and times, I'll see if that fits into Hugh's plans. When is it going to happen? I'd enjoy that very much, you must have heaps to tell me about what you've been doing since I last saw you so long ago.'

'The details aren't really established, oh, I'm sure they are, and have been for months, but I don't know precisely. I'll have to make sure.'

'It looks like you'll have to telephone me when you find out. I don't have a telephone at my cottage. I can agree with Hugh about not wanting to put one in. He's perfectly happy to take calls for me. He jumps in the Land Rover and dashes down if anyone should ring, no matter when. He invites me to use the house phone whenever I wish, but he knows damn well I never would—unless the sky was falling, in which case a bit pointless. But I'd hate to intrude on a friendly household just to make a phone call.'

Jane later phoned to give Roddy dates and times for the show. A friendly male voice answered.

Jane: 'Hello. Is that Major Verney?'

Hugh: 'The same. Who's there?'

'I'm Jane Dugal. Good afternoon. I'd like to speak to Roddy Mackenzie if I may.'

'Of course you may, but I'll have to get him to phone you back. Will that be all right? Just give me the number.' She does and he writes it down.

'You say Jane Dugal. Are you by any chance Major Ronnie Dugal's daughter?'

'Yes, I am.'

'Then Roddy's father works for yours.'

'Yes, has for years. They were in the Forty-third Highlanders together. He and my father get along famously until they're working on a project together, then they argue like fury. It's not fair really Father has the trump card because he just walks away. This leaves Sandy fuming. Father really enjoys that. He chuckles all the way back to the house. Father is really naughty. Except for projects like putting up high-wire fences for raspberries, they understand each other very well. They were both in the same company on the Somme together, and when Father first came up, Sandy literally led him by the hand and took him round the complexities of their trench lines. Apparently the trenches are a bit like a Hampton court maze for the uninitiated. Yes, they understand each other very well.'

'I'm not going to ask you about your relationship with Roddy. He's a very fine young man. What shall I tell him?'

'The show is at 7 p.m. in Trent Hall Girls' School, Arlstorp. Meet there at 6.45 or earlier. I shall be at the auditorium. There will be signs everywhere.'

'Jane, I'll pass the message and I'll see if I can get Roddy to come up here and phone you to confirm. Anyway, listen, you must come down and see us. We've got plenty of room. Female voices and views always welcome. Miette would love to put a young female on strength.'

'Thank you, Hugh. That would be very nice, and thanks for getting the message to Roddy. Good-bye.'

'Yes, that would be nice.' And she pictured herself down there with Roddy. 'Yes, that would be very nice.'

A knock at the cottage door, a call—'Roddy, are you home?'—and Hugh the messenger was there. 'Roddy, message from Jane, she just rang about her school concert. I've written down the joining info. Here.' He handed him the slip of paper, saying, 'You'll go of course?'

'If we have nothing on here, I'd love to,' he replied.

Then Hugh said, 'Best not to keep her wondering. Do you want to come up and ring her back?'

'Yes, thanks, Hugh.' He left the cottage door wide open and got into the Land Rover alongside Hugh. 'I like the style of her, Roddy. She has a very natural charm in her voice. Must get her down here one day. She'd be a nice fresh face for Miette.' Perhaps that was not all that Hugh was thinking. He had already thought about his matchmaking role and the social complications. He satisfied himself with the thought that he was only giving them a better chance to see each other. How they got on was entirely up to them. He told himself that Jane and Roddy equally understood 'the signs on the wire in front of the social minefield'.

Jane answered the phone. 'Jane? Hello! Roddy here. Hugh has just brought me the info about the concert. I'm looking forward to coming down to see you, seeing the concert, and meeting your teacher friends. I love genteel white-haired old ladies with their spare knitting needles stuck in their buns. I bet they're all very wise and will give me sage advice to guide me through life.'

'I hope you won't be disappointed. I shall tell my teacher friends exactly what you said and all I can say is, "Look out!"'

'Oh gosh. I'll have to gird up my loins.'

'Suffer in fear and trepidation until then,' she said in a deep, ominous voice, then, 'Thanks for confirming so promptly, Roddy. So glad you can come. I'm looking forward to seeing you.' The sound in her voice told her truth.

'I'll try not to think about the hazards of hat pins and knitting needles and concentrate on the delight of seeing the concert . . . oh, and you too!'

'G'bye, Mr. Roderick Mackenzie. Let your agonies begin.'

'Be sure there will be much wailing and gnashing of teeth the shadow of fear will be upon my but-and-ben. *Beannachd leat, a bientot.*'

In the morning, before he set off for Arlstorp for some small reason, he had to go to the estate office that had grown to take up the larger part of a wing of the old manor. Miette and Hugh shared a lovely old room that belied the efficiency, acumen, and drive that underlay the business, the commercial success that was Ranelagh Estate. Where others struggled—or didn't— and had failed, the quiet, rustic, genteel, dreamy pair seemed somehow to survive. 'Well, they sell lots of cabbages, dear,' a lady who lived in a crumbling pile miles away would say to her husband as he stared into an empty grate. The trip to Arlstorp would take an hour, plus or minus, through lanes and narrow roadways, favourite subjects for calendars and magazines and even more pleasing in reality. There was no point in an early arrival because Jane would have much to do. Miette did not seem to think so. 'Roddy, *mon cher, il faut que tu ne sois pas en retard!* Jane will have the show to think about, she cannot wait for you, she will become anxious, she is so sweet, and you must care for her, *mon cher.*' Miette was in crisis mode. Miette? The world could be about to fall asunder and Miette would calmly be calculating choices, yet here she was getting into a tizz. Hugh came in. 'Aren't you off yet?' Maybe he was thinking about how long it might take to travel to Arlstorp when the family was first granted Ranelagh by Henry II. 'You mustn't let the girl down.' He looked at these concerned faces. 'Get going! Go and meet Jane!' they seemed to be saying. They were really serious! 'I'll be leaving within minutes,' was all he could say.

He had to exit Ranelagh quick-smart! Having oceans of time to get to Arlstorp, he chose a winding, western, roundabout route. Soon the England he was enjoying so much would become a memory. It was the England of postcards, calendars, and the inspired output of a legion of great painters in every medium. Rivers and brooks had to be crossed where willows crowded the bridges and oaks and elms were sentinels in the fields. Scattered copses, filling hollows, broke the tyranny of the straight lines that hawthorn hedges thought to establish, and little roads took bends on perfectly flat land for some reason lost in time, but now must stay because 'they were always there' and now a form of right of custom meant that they had become 'possessed'. His little car seemed to be enjoying the run, a chance to blow the coke from her valves, to thrust her tribal Alvis radiator into the wind her exciting speed was creating.

Trent Hall was an old public school for girls, and sitting comfortably on the bank of the Trent stream that flowed through the old British-Norman town of Arlstorp settled, for many a long year, amongst ancient well-grown trees now in the diminishing glory of autumn colour as their falling leaves filled the lane sides with deep bands of rosy-red colour as they shut down for the wintry months ahead.

The performance hall was on a wing of the school a short distance from where Roddy had been directed to park the Alvis by a girl on duty. An avenue of trees led towards the stream that he could see at its end. Jane was waiting but not idly or alone, though apparently not as a duty posting, but warmly greeting parents and guests as they arrived. He paused to watch and loved the radiant young woman he could see. She happened to look up and see him. She ran across to where he stood under the trees, clasped him in her arms, and kissed him. It was a magic kiss that had grown within her over the hours since she had seen him for he had been scarcely out of her thoughts. He held her close. They looked at each other through a long, warm, absorbing silence, each drawing in the delight of seeing the feelings their eyes were expressing that no words could.

They had respectfully left the best seats for parents and friends, but where they were, on a rising curve off to the left, there was very little of the action they would miss. The 'pit orchestra' struck up and he turned towards Jane and said, 'This is always exciting, don't you feel?'

'Oh yes, I love it,' she said, giving a little wriggle, seizing and squeezing his hand. He found it so moving to see these young people, really not so much younger than he, so enthusiastically and competently creating a world to be imagined by an audience. Their voices were clean, clear, and energetic; even the males, who frequently can't be made to relax and lose stiffness and reserve in stage situations, had captured the fantasy, the bubbling mood of the catchy music and the story. The excitement, the energy, the voices, the acting, and the 'pain' the principles projected— everything in the youthful energy and exuberance found its way to Roddy's emotional interior. Roddy was caught wiping tears from his eyes.

Leaving this evening of student theatricals, he saw himself a player with a role that he had been living for nearly a year. About to depart from England, he could feel himself leaving, in a way, a vibrant stage production, set in Hampshire. He would never forget the characters, the roles they played, and how he had been drawn in to participate. He had been given a role— the others were every one, an actor, a producer, a director. He required no mask. He was his character. He had but to be the person whose role the story had caused, and it was his story which had defined the role.

After the performance Jane, Meredith and Herbert had some duties to perform, but the bumping out was in the hands of some sports, Phys. Ed. people and senior 'stage management students'. There were public officials and 'sponsors' who had to be met, and Jane, rather than leave Roddy in mid-air, invited him to join her, Meredith, and Herbert in doing their duties in meeting these public demands of 'showbiz'. It turned out to be very pleasant and Roddy opened himself to the process feeling as, unconsciously, he always did, that he could learn from a new experience. There was a general dispersal of pupils and parents, and those parents who had come further afield went off to accommodations nearby. Next day was a sports day which involved Jane in girls' golf and Meredith in the swimming events. Herbert had a cross-country event, a kind of paper chase–tracking event. They went together to the house that Jane and Meredith shared to a supper snack and a glass of wine for which Roddy retrieved a bottle of Chardonnay from the dickie seat-cum-cellar of the Alvis. The supper was pleasant and the foursome related well to each other. Everyone wanted to know Roddy's plans. 'This trip to Australia will be principally reconnaissance,' he began. 'I heard a lot about Australia from soldiers from 3 RAR I met in Korea, and those blokes really impressed me.' He told about his battalion's diversion to Kenya and the emergency. 'I spent quite a bit of time with a chap, Mick Lowing, in the Kenya police who would soon be finishing his engagement and returning to Australia. I'm sure he didn't intentionally paint a rosy picture—it sounded really attractive.' He then related a bit about the amazing coincidence of meeting Jill and her being Mick's sister, he breezily related the story of Jill and Emma by starting with, 'I picked two lovely Australian girls from a French yacht in Cowes.' Jane visibly stiffened. She knew she had—and immediately reminded herself that she had—no proprietorial rights to the dashing young Mckenzie. 'This trip will be principally reconnaissance,' he went on, 'I have immediate army obligations here, which will take another two months. I will have continuing service obligations. If I put a bit of polish on my rural youth at Woodend and Fearnas and my period with Hugh as farming experience, perhaps the bank will come to the party. Mick said they particularly liked people with a good service record. Apart from military service, I really am very poorly qualified for civilian life and I know I'd go round the bend working indoors all day. I'm living in a very special small world at the moment and that has actually, to all intents and purposes, reached its end now.' Roddy could not fail to notice that Jane's bright mood was dimming. How could he comfort her? Had his response to her affection misled her to think of some relationship for the future? Perhaps the other two had felt Jane's despair. The conversation seemed to have reached an end. To explore the topic further would increase Jane's discomfort. 'You'd be just the bloke to come on our cross-country tomorrow,' Herbert said in an attempt at levity and change of tack. 'I'd love it, Herbert. Unfortunately I'm duty dairy man and livestock attendant all weekend. No complaints, I really live a pampered life. It most certainly is my turn.' Herbert stood up and said he ought to be pushing off. Roddy saw that it was his time too. Jane and Verity who shared Jane's house saw them to the door. Herbert drove off, and Meredith left Jane and Roddy on the step. 'Good night, Roddy. I enjoyed meeting you. Glad you could come to our show and that you enjoyed it so much. I hope I'll see you some more before you set sail on James Cook's trail.' The two were alone now, on the front steps, Jane was quite disconsolate. 'Oh, Roddy, every word of your story tonight made me feel as if it were a tall ship, or life itself, drawing away from me to some place away beyond the soul's horizon. Now, when we've only just met, and I feel already that there's much that is already binding us. Oh, we must make the most of it, Roddy.' She paused, anxiously, and asked, 'When shall we meet again?'

He knew then that their inevitable final parting would be aggravated by sharing more time together, yet he wanted to have more time with Jane, as much time as possible. 'Shall we try for next weekend? I've got Hamps on Friday night and Saturday until about half past four. If you'll be free on Sunday, maybe we can meet then, but Hugh must have first claim. May I phone you one evening?'

'Oh yes, please do. I do have school things to do some evenings, but if I'm not at home, Meredith or Joy will take a message.' She explained that she had school after-hours work, sometimes tutorials, sometimes clubs and societies.

It was arranged that Roddy would phone after eight o'clock one evening, as soon as he could find out what Hugh may need. He would go up and phone from the telephone box at the Barley Mow.

She clung to him in silence for long minutes feeling his breathing and his firm body, her head full of indefinable ideas of a sweetness that she could recognize—with no logical consideration, no flash of a thought process—as a symptom of being in love. Then raising her head from his neck and looking at him, she said, in an attempt at rationally sounding speech, 'Thank you so much for coming, Roddy. Good night. I shall look forward to hearing from you.'

He brought her back deep into his embrace and gently, slowly kissed her lips, held his face against her cheek before slowly disengaging as he was saying, 'Thank you, Jane, thank you so much for such an enjoyable evening. I'll call as soon as I know what Hugh's up to.' Before she went in, she waited until the quiet burble of the Alvis had become part of the silence of the night.

Miette did come to the stables occasionally, but only as a requirement of Ranelagh operational functions. What was she doing there early on a Saturday morning? She'd had her coffee with Hugh and dashed off. She had to restrain her little estate car. Like a romping pup, it wanted to dash ahead of her. She was working on a plot and needed up-to-date intelligence. Roddy was contentedly going about the care of 'his' horses and was really surprised when he heard Miette's beautiful alto call out in French, 'Roddy, mon cher est-ce que tu y es?'

'Oui, Madame Miette, j'y suis.' She began immediately in French, not particularly unusual, but most often used when she felt she needed to be specific—or if she was up to something! She asked about the concert, but the name 'Jane' was demanding to be uttered; she wanted to get to the 'nitty-gritty'. (Truth is, she was actually uncomfortable with the sound shape of 'Jane', so after encountering the discomfort, she had switched to 'Jeanne'.) 'Jeanne is such a lovely woman, *tres gracieuse*. Have you fallen in love with her yet?'

He was stunned by the direct question about such a personal, intimate matter. Roddy had already become accustomed to

Miette's direct approach, after all, he was the son she had never had and she adored him, and Hugh cared for him very much—yes, almost as a son. He was conscious of her care for him; he knew how much affairs of the heart drew her interest.

He couldn't believe he was hearing himself say the words when he said, 'Yes, I believe I have, and I think she has with me. Neither of us has said so. But that has not been needed.'

Miette moved quickly forward, seized him in her arms, and kissed his cheeks. 'Oh, I'm so happy,' she cried. Her excitement, he could see, was making her tremble. 'I must tell my Hugh! Now, what I have to say is that we are planning a very small dinner for two lovely friends of ours and another equally lovely couple the man of which you will know. I would love you to meet them. They are such interesting people. When we have established the day, I will ask you and Jeanne to come. Please give me her telephone number and her address. I think it will be next weekend.'

'That's very sweet of you, Miette, and I know Jane will be pleased to come if she can. I'll bring the information up to you later if I may.'

'Yes. Your ponies will not starve if you go and do it now. I'll be in the kitchen.'

Miette wanted to build the Roddy and Jane love relationship. She wanted to be involved in their being in love: she wanted them in her family, to snuggle with them. She wanted to arrange the dinner. She had chosen her very favourite people, Tearlath and Isabelle Cumming, whose careers led to their living such interesting lives. Meeting them would be an experience for her young lovers; perhaps they may become new friends to extend their lives? She had also chosen old Captain Robert Morley and his vivacious wife, Margaret. 'Believe me; these people are not too old for you and the young Jeanne to spend an evening with. Yes!' In her mind, of course she was addressing Roddy.

A small dairy herd was kept at Ranelagh to provide cross-bred calves for the market; milk for everyone on the property and for the young pigs on the home farm and rich manure for the house gardens and the commercial plots. The herd, the calves, and the pigs were attractive continuing exhibits on Open

Days. Roddy had not quite finished and he was just putting the cups of the Alfa-Laval milking machine on an udder when there was a call. It was Miette.

'Roddy, were you planning to go to the Barley Mow after work tonight?'

'Well, Madame Miette, the thought had crossed my mind, I was thinking a pint of Speckled Hen would go down very well, but I cast aside that self-indulgent whim. Then I was wondering whether the Barley Mow Society might be having a meeting and insufficient members present to form a quorum. But I cast aside even thoughts of social obligation and was simply going up in that direction to make a telephone call. Is there something I may do for you?'

'Ah, *que tu fais de la bêtise*! Please, even if you finally decide not to go to make a telephone call please'—and she feigned to beseech—'be so gentil as to go and take this very important letter to the post box—*pour l'amour de moi*.' She gave him a peck on the cheek, turned around, and was gone. He looked at the envelope in his hand. The letter was addressed to a 'Mlle. Jane Dugal'.

He'd actually got the milking finished; the washing down completed, and the cows had wandered off. He heard the Land Rover pull up. 'What ho, Roddy, have you finished?'

'Yes, Hugh,' he replied, 'all my ladies have turned their backs on me to seek greener pasture.'

'D'ye fancy a pint at the Barley Mow?'

'The question wasn't put to me quite that way first time, but this is the second time I've been asked a similar question in the last half hour. Your question has an easier answer. Yes, I do. Give me a few minutes to tidy up a bit.'

'Well, we're both farmers, let's not stand on ceremony, let's go as we are.'

'No, Hugh. You're done up like a pox-doctor's clerk and I'm in my dungers. It'll take me minutes, five at the most.'

Before they entered the pub, Roddy excused himself and took Miette's letter to the post box. Hugh was standing by the Land Rover watching.

'You, sir, are a witness to my having posted a letter. It is going by Royal mail—by royal command.' Thinks: bubble, bubble.

'Couldn't Hugh have posted it? Ah, there's something going on here, methinks.'

From the usual, there were pleasant greetings, and the rugby supporters were very buoyant. The team had won and that had required resounding encouragement which demanded lubrication throughout the match. So spirits were high amongst the rugby followers. Hugh had shifted his pint with inordinate swiftness even the thirsty Roddy appeared to be dragging.

Hugh turned off, on the way back, to follow one of the hedged lanes that led upward to one of his much-loved forests of broad-leaved trees; their foliage had passed that heart-stopping glory of russets and reds and yellows and oranges and were shedding the last of their autumn glory to build a future soil.

'That letter,' he was saying as the Land Rover climbed the winding road, 'you just posted was an official invitation to Jane Dugal to join us for dinner next Saturday evening. When you get home, I shouldn't be surprised if yours isn't there. I realize you've got Hamps on Friday and Saturday, but you should be finished the duty part by 16.30. Why I wanted a quiet moment with you was to tell you a bit about Tearlath Cumming, one of our guests, because I know he will not talk about himself at the meal. I imagine you've heard about the playwright of that name? That was a stupid question because to save foreigners the agonies of pronunciation, he writes as Charles Cumming.'

'No, I haven't. I haven't seen as much theatre as I would like to and I can't recall having read about him or his work.'

'We got to know him through Miette's work as Isabelle de Crespigny's theatrical agent and she was Tearlath's favourite performer. You'll learn best about the wonderful Isabelle from Miette. I'll do the best I can to paint a picture, but I won't do justice to the man.'

'He is a small dark man who sometimes, or often, looks serious but his deep brown eyes brighten in that pale face when he looks at anyone. He appears as if he were entirely made of muscle. We came to know, on the good authority of Isabelle, that he lived in a stone cottage somewhere between Rerrope Cottage and Aitnoch Hill, nearby Lochindorb, on Darnaway Estate, not very far from Fearnas. It is coincidental, and there is no connection with him, that Darnaway is the family home of the Cummings. He was known as a quiet chiel who kept very much to himself, but should anyone chap on his door—if, or whenever, it may have been shut—that person would be given the warmth of welcome to gratify the heart of any traveller weary and lost or simply intending a social call.

'He would go off from the cottage for months at a spell. On his return, he would scarcely have opened his door when he was out and off, a heavy-canvas bag with leather edgings across his broad back and a fishing rod on his shoulder. He always, without fail, had on an old stalker's tweed hat which, when he was at home, it was thought, he probably wore in bed.

'It was suspected that he worked for the government as a secret agent and spent much time in smoke-filled bars in deep dark souks in strange cities which explained the pallor of his skin.

'Of course there was a change of story when, just before summer turned to long warm evenings and the smell of hot pine resin hung on the air, a very smart touring car would arrive at his house. Out of it would step a tall, supple blonde woman that a breeze might blow over, so light and lissom did she appear.

'This gave rise to a new quite different surmise spiced with a piquancy that was beautifully romantic for she was known to spend the hours of darkness alone with him in his very wee hoosie. He was most certainly a writer of plays which were performed in London at the Theatre Royal in Drury Lane. His plays attracted the best West End, and overseas actors and actresses too to play major roles. And this sylph had partnered the lovely Norrie Carr in *The Major Amiss* which went on to full houses season after season.

'Of course! That's it; they were convinced: "He's a writer of plays like James Barrie and Jack Priestley!"

'Strange to relate, both the surmises of the estate workers, and farmers all around, were correct. Tearlath Cumming was involved in clandestine work when called upon, as he had been during the Second World War. He continues now, at the whim of MI 6, to get into the saddle, most likely a camel's, and ride off to talk with men who knew the small dark man. These men purposely spoke with him in their variety of Arab dialects, knowing full well he would work them out and understand. He would understand not just the dialect's subtleties but the deeper meaning behind what was being said.

'Before he left St Ninian's Academy, he had excelled in the studies of Latin and Greek, French and German. He knew where his path lay and he had had to think deeply about his choice of university. His reading was of the Arab world. The complexity of its subtle language, theology, cultural, and political systems held him in fascination. He needed, and sought, a school of Arabic studies where there was no exclusion of Arab thought, no distinctly Western sourced and developed programmes. Oxford seemed the best choice because he could major in anthropology, Arabic studies, and Arabic language. He wanted to study the Arab cultures from the inside to the outside, from its inner base to its intellectual apex. He abhorred the thought of academic studies of Arabs which seemed to be dominated by thinkers and writers who were quite divorced from, and had made exclusive to them, their studies of "the Orient".

'He imagined he would have a spare ten per cent of time to indulge his study and love of theatre from Shakespeare to Sheridan and Moliere to Milne. So now, when he was not on a journey to meet with Lawrence's sheiks, princes, and kings, and Arab or Persian families of the present day, he sat quietly and wrote plays of great vigour and charm which not even the most perspicacious critic could detect were often based on the effects of his Arab experience and how academe can create studies that are aloof from their subjects.

'No one has the command of intelligence studies of the Arab, Persian, and Western Indian sub-continental worlds than Tearlath Cumming. And when you meet him, you may wonder whether I have been telling you the truth.'

Roddy was silent for a while. 'Thank you, Hugh. That was a completely absorbing piece of description. I look forward very much to meeting this man. I must take care to conceal the awe that your story has made me feel.'

It was all very exciting. Her Roddy had found a charming woman. That's what Hugh had said, *n'est-ce pas?* And hadn't he gone to her to share the musical at her school? And were not

Isabelle and the intriguing 'Sherlah' coming for the weekend?
Hadn't she already invited Margaret and le Capitaine Robert for
dinner on Saturday? *Eh bien,* she must invite the young couple!
'That would make it perfect for Hugh,' was her considerate
thought. Now she must call upon Mlle. Dugal to prepare her
for the meeting of new people, *naturellement.* She had penned
her invitation on the demand of proper etiquette, *mais, bien sur,*
there was not much time. *Alors,* she must have to take the liberty
to speak with Mlle. Jane on the telephone so that she might
make an arrangement to make a visit at her house in Arlstorp
to tell her all about the other guests.

Miette was never too grand to drive her little estate car
everywhere. It had become widely known. *Tant bien,* the Wolseley
was too big, thus did she arrive at *chez* Jane.

The tall, elegant young woman with blond hair drawn back
from a very beautiful face came to the door. 'Madame Verney, je
suis Jane Dugal. Je suis enchantee de faire votre connaissance.'

Miette responded in French then elided into English. The
most important role for her to play was to be teller of a story,
a love story of such decorum, such sweetness, such movement
of the heart. Isabelle de Crespigny had been put forward as a
contestant for the leading role in one of Tearlath's productions
by Miette Verney, the theatrical agent. The playwright himself
was to be present at the auditions. The character whose role
the successful auditioning actress would play would make the
play a triumph or a disaster. Isabelle was the second person
to audition. His decision was made instantly. He knew, with
his whole being, that this woman had the depth in her own
character without which the role could never be interpreted.
And she was gracious and very beautiful with a voice tone whose
whisper would carry through a thunderstorm. Even the words
she had chosen to use in describing the piece she had chosen
for her audition was acting, and voice range it demanded was
of the most subtle kind. He didn't want to hear the others, but
he pleaded with this French willow wand to wait until he had
done his duty by the others. The role would become Sigrid de
Crespigny's, and forever would be. It established her fame. It
began a friendship which became love.

Their relationship was, to say the least, unusual. She was a professional actress of the first quality with a world of fame and fortune awaiting her; he was a man of the most unusual character leading two lives of diametrically opposite kinds. But their lives were meant to be one. There was rhythm, resonance, and accordance in the beating of their hearts. And they both were servants of discipline. Before they were married, Isabelle would visit Tearlath at Rerrope. After an exhausting season, she would take a sleeper on the overnight train to Forres. At his garage where her Riley tourer was kept, Willie McIntosh would have removed its dust cover and have one of his men make it ready. Willie himself would drive to the station to meet her. The station master would open her carriage door with special external key and greet her with almost palpable affection. A Highland Railway porter would push the iron-wheeled luggage barrow out of the station to her car. She never gave tips. She always brought a present for their wives and often a wee bottle of something, or pipe tobacco of a special mixture. Oh, how she loved the drive up to Darnaway, whatever the weather.

As she opened the little wooden gate at the end of the flowered path leading to the cottage where the dark green door would be standing wide open, she would call out a beautifully executed Australian, 'Coo-ee!' finishing with the abrupt rising note of a whip-bird.

The small dark man would come into the doorway, remove his hat at the end of a theatrically sweeping arm to signal 'salaam', and casually return it at once to the jaunty angle on his head where it belonged.

He looked into her eyes and asked with seriousness, 'Can the sun really go to rest tonight while you are here?'

'Let it cease its triumphant labour of this glorious day and allow the gentle evening its place in the circle of time. Tearlath Cumming, it's delightful to see you again: and to see you here where I'm so sure you really belong.' She stopped and had to lower her head, to pull him into her embrace, and to kiss him on the cheek.

'Come away ben into my wee hoose,' he said in an accent and turn of phrase that were now an imitation of that he had had around his ears as a child. 'Where would you like to sit, within or without?'

'I'd like to sit here where I can enjoy that lovely light from the back window. It's so gorgeously "cottagey".'

'It's so wonderful to see you here.' The expression was loaded with a quiet happiness as if serenity had just swept up the whole afternoon in a spiritual embrace. It might have been spoken by a male lead in one of his plays, however, in his intonation was that nuance which rendered reality as different from the best of artifice. 'I could offer you a cup of tea, but it doesn't seem appropriate to the occasion. I've got some very nice sherries—mm?' he intoned, in suggestion. 'However, when I got home, the highland fairies had visited. The fridge was running. And guess what? There's a bottle of Laurent Perrier in there, too cold to put my fingers on. I can see I've got some pears and some cheeses. What say we go out the back in the evening sun and start our holiday? You and Norrie and the rest of the cast must be falling to bits. Oh, but have your leisure,' he feigned to complain, 'even if your indolence will make a pauper of me.' He touched her lightly on her shoulder as he looked at her eyes, then pausing touched her cheek. He put his cheek against hers, slightly pressing the hand on her other cheek, then gently moved away to go to bring the champagne.

'You know, I walk in here as if I've always known it,' she said in the voice of dreams, 'I feel that if I ever had to run away from anything, this is where I'd want to come. It's all about you, Tearlath. It's your spirit that suffuses this house of peace.'

'And it was like that, and it was how they lived, and it was how they loved. They are married now and I have seen no difference. You would have had to wait so long for Isabelle to have told you her story of her love with Tearlath. I have told the story with respect for her, because I wish you to enjoy Isabelle and Tearlath when you come to dinner. I have become like you Scots people. If I did not know that you are sib, you would never have heard that story from me. Your whole being speaks to me, and I feel I have found another treasure to love. I'm looking forward so much for you and Roddy to come to us.'

'You have paid me a great compliment, *chere madame*. I feel an honour has been bestowed on me. I can't thank you enough for the way you have prepared me for our evening. I shall wait impatiently.' Showing the same ease and grace with which she came, Mme. Verney, now to be addressed as Miette, departed in her little car for Ranelagh.

Hugh made the introductions, the old captain and Margaret first. 'Tearlath [he pronounced it—and there really is no other way—Cherlae] and Isabelle de Crespigny [and there was still a direct bloodline to the Huguenot de Crespigny family lineage], Miette and I would like you to meet these lovely people, Lieutenant Roderick Fraser Mckenzie [and he pronounced the *z* in *Mackenzie* as if it were a *y* and with another change into the Gaelic that renders the sound nothing like *Mckenzie* at all], late Forty-third Royal Highland Regiment, wounded on active service in Korea, presently Royal Hampshire Regiment; and the erudite Miss Jane Dugal, master of science of St Andrews University, presently labouring on a doctoral thesis which will be of such mathematical abstruseness that she will end up, like Bertie Russell, struggling to find someone capable of marking it. We are so pleased that they have been able to join us tonight.'

Roddy said as he shook hands with Tearlath, 'I'm delighted to meet you, sir.'

'Please call me Tearlath and may I call you Roddy? You would have served with Ike Barron?'

'Indeed I've had the honour: he was my company commander and now, probably most unusually, we are firm friends. It's through Erik that I was introduced to Hugh and Miette.'

Miette jumped in. 'And it was I who got him to come and live here! *Ce cher bel homme*,' she said, clutching his arm, then at once Jane's, 'and you see, Roddy has brought the lovely Jane'—and changing her tone—'although my Hugh thinks it was his idea.'

The ladies were gowned and indisputably gorgeous, Margaret no less so than the younger women. The men were in dinner suits of various cuts and each had tied his own selected style of black tie.

Autumn is the perfect season for a meal in rustic France or Britain. There is game galore and mushrooms of many kinds. Miette would have loved to do the entire preparation herself, but the Ranelagh cook was a professional for whom cooking was never a chore and she loved pitting her skills against Miette—is that true? Or did she just enjoy cooking with another person who really cared about the choice of ingredients and working with someone of equal devotion, skill, and touch? Ranelagh Estate was bountiful in game and funghi from its woods and all the most desirable vegetables directly from the good, nurtured soil of Ranelagh's gardens.

To tantalize them by having to guess the menu would be unfair. Here it is: Tomato Consommé (Yes! And all three males gasped with delight), Salmis de Faisan with truffles (from an area of the estate not to be disclosed), venison (cooked to gloriously rare), mushrooms, potatoes (with skins on) on butter salt and pepper, capsicums (the greenhouse growing triumph of one of the gardeners—singed peeled brought to the table *au moment juste*), red cabbage, gooseberry full with home farm cream. There was a flor fino or Semillon for the soup, a Chateau Neuf du Pape, and huge dark Cahors red for the rest, with a St Emilion for those who would. Since there was also a selection of cheeses including a fine Stilton, Hugh had released a tawny Portuguese (port of course) acquired through the good offices of Ninian Barron. The conversation was catholicity itself, and to Roddy's great delight, there was much about the theatre and fascinating contributions on international relations from Jane, Miette, Robert, and Tearlath. Full stops were given a brief moment of glory, and except for exclamation marks, there seemed pause for no other punctuation. Oh, what a night it was. It was such a night.

Margaret would have stayed as long as anyone there, but she had a duty to get the captain to his cot before his next watch. At one point, Tearlath and Isabelle excused themselves on the grounds that it was the hour when normal people go to bed. Hugh said he had always admired Tearlath's perspicacity, and Miette? Well, she simply confirmed with Jane that her room had in it all that she may need at that she remembered how to get to it. She said to Roddy, 'Your house is too ascetic to invite Jane down to talk; you must stay here as long as you wish.' Her embrace of Jane was as of a mother welcoming home a child after a painfully long absence; for Roddy, its intensity was a release of joy.

The dinner had been a success from every aspect, perhaps the mood was the result of all the wonderful conversations; the non-stop demand on recollection and on 'mental togetherness' to frame arguments. Jane had been in similar situations with more than a few infantry officers and was surprised at Roddy's performance; he was bright beyond the norm. His skill in questioning was amazing, and 'Would that mean . . . ?' and similar were some of the skillfully used devices he employed to clarify questioner's situations before a required opinion could be proffered. He'd be a champion in uni tutorials. The other males respected his contributions to the pool of views and arguments, as did the women it would appear.

What was Jane feeling as she sat through those delightful hours of conviviality? She had found herself focusing and refocusing on Roddy—his skill and charm, his knack of phrasing his statements to show a balance in giving and taking and keeping himself just at the level of the others. Of course he never really could in such experienced, successful company. But he didn't have to struggle to get away from the sidelines.

Why was she so surprised at his *savoire faire*? What has she expected? What on earth had she been thinking—or not thinking? What had she been supposing? Were there some inferences she had secretly been making with herself about the boy from the lodge and the Girl from the House? She, with a master's degree and honours now working on a doctoral thesis, wasn't at all happy about what she had found lurking within her. Jane was feeling more and more attracted, more and more comfortable with him. Was that good or bad? Was there a deeper instinct that needed to be honestly dealt with? These fleeting thoughts were niggling and inducing uncertainty. Uncertainty about what? Surely to feel love for him was enough?

They were in one of the smaller sitting rooms at Ranelagh where it might be imagined Miette and Hugh spent time if they ever stopped running their business at great speed and energy. Hugh and Miette had gone. They were alone, standing together.

Despite all of the sociability engendered by the meal and the quality of the conviviality each was reserved, hesitant, Jane leapt the little gap before reserve had reached discomfort. She was close to him, and she took his hands lightly, holding them by their sides.

'Wasn't that the most delightful party in every way?' she asked.

'It most certainly was. It's the first experience of its kind I have ever had. My god, those lovely people know so much about the world from so many angles.' He was full of exclamatory enthusiasm. 'Just to hear opposing views traded . . . disagreements over subjects were simply clinical differences of points of view, of looking at the issue, and thinking about it. No one was pushed to agree with another's point of view, or to win the argument. Possibly all the discussions I've ever been involved in have had instances of that. I have learned so much from that group tonight!'

'I'm always disappointed when a person becomes annoyed if another person won't succumb to what he imagines is his superior argument. It was a learning night for me too. I hung on every word of the exchanges. I'm thinking now that I've Erik Barron to thank for all of this. He made an appreciation of me and my life situation, and obstacles I would likely face in the future. I can see that he decided he wanted to help. He showed me where a path began and left me to choose whether I wanted to follow it. Then he set up a situation in which I'd meet Hugh and Miette with results that he guessed would be as likely as inevitable. That put me in the mentoring care of two of the world's most wonderful people. Hugh knows he can't do all he'd like to do for me within his society, but tonight he has shown me that the social life of Britain's elite is not something that can be broadly generalized and that generalization be taken as applying to all cases. Maybe it also a fine demonstration that, amongst it all, we are at will to choose our particular friends.'

'Are you going to choose me, Roddy?'

He held her hands a little more firmly, his voice was soft, his eyes searching her face.

'I have, without your permission, already chosen you. But as there are for Hugh and Miette, there are limits, restrictions on me as to what form that friendship may take.

'I'd like to go beyond and above friendship,' and he became tense as he said, 'but that would be the most utterly selfish, careless, possibly even destructive choice I could make.' As he went on, Jane was listening very carefully as his voice changed again.

'Hugh and Miette had very carefully chosen the people to whom I could be introduced. I can't really know their motivation to invite me tonight. Say, they wished to invite you for an occasion, that would have been simple; and they would trust your knowledge of the rules to invite a person appropriate in the normality of your society. Tonight they wanted to put us together and I imagine they wanted to leave it to us to resolve for ourselves any difficulties that would arise were we to fall in love.'

'And can't we do that, Roddy? Fall in love?' The question she had just posed was laden and back grounded by those other questions which had been circling in her mind, but she was searching his eyes. He was looking into her eyes and he felt what they were saying with the question.

'Shall we sit?' he asked and took a hand gently in his; they went together to one of the small sofas covered in large floral prints spanning Vivaldi's seasons.

'I know there's an awful lot of humbug in our British society. Are you painting too dark a picture?' she asked

'I've had some experiences while I've been at Ranelagh that have influenced me to shape some views and I've added those to my existing stock. My conclusion is that I can cope with the rules; and indeed I think I have been doing that since I've been back in Britain. As you put up with the cold of winter, you do so in the certainty of the warmer seasons.'

'Does Hugh never take you out, say, to polo games?'

'No, he hasn't except to do my job. I stick closely to that and play my role as Hugh's employee all the time other people are around. I can sense the difficulty he has at times when he has to be the master, and I, the servant, as customary. He could in no way involve me in the social aspects of the events. I clearly understand that, without the slightest ill feeling or misunderstanding, I've got to know a bit about the polo set, and you probably know what it's like. It would be very difficult for Hugh. If I were to be to be around socially, Hugh would be letting the side down which could cause unpleasantness. I think he knows there would be people who would find it almost necessary to be rude and unpleasant to me and he would hate that. There seemed to be an opportunity for easing the rigidity at the Ranelagh Gymkhana when I was even asked to play. Hugh thought he had all the bases covered, yet there was an incident. It would possibly be worth hearing about it from Miette, but briefly this is what happened.' And he gave a brief description of the event.

Although he had tried to pare all possibility of drama from his description, the bare facts were enough. Jane was pale with shock. 'Oh my god, that was ghastly!' She gasped.

'It was something I was equipped to handle. My main concern was the hurt it caused Hugh. It was a shocking insult to him. I might just mention something more if I may, which will perhaps shine some light on the form of my beliefs.

'On the way back home from Korea, our trip was diverted to Kenya to go and help re-establish peace for the British planters. They had, not all that many years before, moved the tribal Kenyans off their land and simply taken it for themselves. They were English urban twerps with no knowledge or understanding of their own history; puffed up with the myth of white superiority, further bloated now by their ownership of land which they would never have successfully achieved in Britain. You know that land ownership has forever been the key to access the social system. Now they had it.

'I was only a corporal at the time. When they spoke to me, you would think they were red tabs, top brass, staff officers. I hated it and hated them for it. It was sickening to see them take officers as if they were somehow people at their level. I realized how horridly stultifying to human progress such behaviour was and how many more problems it would yet cause nationally and internationally. Now they were wondering why the Africans were upset. They couldn't understand why the atrocious killings of whites had taken place. I was so fascinated by this perversion and blind ignorance of reality that I undertook a historical study as soon as I got back. Korea was bad. Kenya was worse. I hated my duties. I had to scrape the shame off my memory. I'm not going to go into the study of the settlement of Kenya. Our social system took thousands of years evolving, and then developing over hundreds of years to be what it is now. It won't suddenly be changed by political parties of either kind or the Beatles and Carnaby Street or science, and certainly not the church.'

He was in great difficulty to know how best to say what needed to be said next. 'I fell in love with you the moment I saw you at Geoffrey's. I love you too much to have said those words which, if you felt as I felt, would cause so much pain . . . cause you the discomfort and real pain of trying to jump the horrid abyss of two conflicting social worlds. Jane, my darling, our stars are crossed.'

'Oh this blasted class system!' she vehemently almost cried out. 'I see you as different, as a freshly minted spirit of a new kind. This is only the third occasion we've met; each has been a joyful addition to the last.' He took her into his arms and held her quite tightly. 'Maybe one day our positions in relation to the stars will have changed. I feel sure it would be disastrous now to tempt the fates. Perhaps it's now too late in the hours to go on. Let's go to sleep now remembering the happiness of our dinner with those dear people we'll be seeing again tomorrow?'

To all that he had said, his voice shaped suggestions, questions. Jane, realizing the impossibility of resolving their problems in these early hours of the morning, held him again tightly and stood up holding his hand.

Her eyes searched every aspect of his face, and softly she said, 'Good night, good night! Parting is such sweet sorrow that I shall say good night till it be morrow.'

'Angels guard thee sweet love, till morn,' was all he could only think to say.

She walked with him to a side door over which a light had been kept on. They kissed again. He turned to leave, walked a

little, then as he turned from his path to look back, she raised
her arm and waved. He waved as he watched her close the door.
The light went out leaving and a starlit sky.

———∘∘∘—⚭—∘∘∘———

The Sunday breakfast was to be in the big kitchen at
Ranelagh. Miette was preparing coffee when Jane arrived. They
exchanged 'good morning' kisses, and Jane told Miette how
much they both had enjoyed the dinner; the impact it had made
on Roddy and how he had prized it as an important learning
event. The huge scrubbed wooden table before the enormous
Aga cooker was bare. Dressing the table could wait; she was
eager simply to put out her big French breakfast coffee cups
so that she might hear what Jane would tell her of her evening
with Roddy. *Naturellement*, Miette placed the cups at a corner
so that they would be very close together. This was going to be
a tete-a-tete *intime, n'est-ce pas?* First she took in Jane's face. She
was looking for signs.

'He is a very charming young man, our Roddy, *d'accord?*'

'Yes, he is a very charming young man and his charm is
of a very special kind. Hugh will have told you of how Roddy
and I have known each other since childhood and the social
relationship. I had not seen him for many years until I met him
at Geoffrey's party, *il etait un coup de foudre. Aussi pour lui.*' She
continued in French to tell how Roddy viewed the oil-and-water
situation of the classes and how she knew in her heart that what
he had said was undeniable.

'I can't stop my feelings, Miette, but I haven't any clear idea
about what I'm going to do. Roddy is so very practical; I know
what he says is true.'

'I am sad because I too know he is right.'

She said this with an expression of despondency. 'I know
that I have been naughty in encouraging you two, but I believe
we . . . you . . . should have these moments of transcendent
sweetness in our lives, whatever must happen after those
moments. My Hugh has so enjoyed having Roddy here. He too
can see Roddy's special qualities; they have a rare relationship,

those two. Perhaps because they have both been soldiers, they have found a way to cope with friendships that life will cause to be strained by parting. For them, sometimes the cruel fates made physical parting final by death. But this is not the case for you; you will both be alive to live and love again and you will always, always have these moments to remember.'

She took Miette's hands. 'Oh, Miette, you sweet, sweet person, my feelings are rebelling against your wise words, but I will come to my senses.' She seemed sad, distressed, and unresolved; her mind still full of the issues that beset their love and their lives together.

'To have to be thinking about me, when he needs to focus on establishing a way of life in the world, would be totally unfair. It could change his whole life direction, could spoil his chances of making the life he creates—his. I've thought about this in the lives of other people; we can only be our best for others, when we are the best of ourselves. The burden of knowing he was sacrificing himself for me . . . oh . . . I don't know how I could cope with that.' Then she became silent, as if not present, for what seemed a long time. Miette was still holding her hands. She was still holding Miette's hands.

This is how Tcarlath and Isabelle found them. Miette spoke in French to Isabelle. 'We were just sharing some moments of joy and sadness; were we not, *ma chere* Jeanne?' They kissed each other then and greeted the pair with kisses, brightening up for them, and rejoining in the gladness that each shared in being with the others. Jane joined in the French conversation which spoke of the weather, the coffee which would be coming how they had slept and how delightful the dinner had been, and Roddy was with his cows and Hugh had gone to discuss some work on a cottage with a builder who could only come today and what would they prefer for breakfast and . . .

When Roddy was not at the regiment or was needed for a yacht race or polo, he was always happy to do the weekends for the dairy man, or the lady who shared the dairy work. He could still do that and get down to Southampton for the Judo Club.

When they found him, he was again at the small home farm dairy. Two female figures had appeared against the light coming through the doorway of the clinically clean milk room and creamery; he looked up and greeted them.

'Ah, sweet ladies the weighty burden of my toil is lightened by your coming!' he called from the end of the room.

'These are beguiling words, mon brave monsieur, but are we not to be kissed?'

'For such a delicious pleasure, I must prepare my heart *pour faire de mon mieux.*' And he strode with dramatic swiftness from the back of the white room to the doorway.

For the dear Miette, there were decorous three kisses on the cheeks. So shameful in the company of a senior lady, and she the mother of neither, he drew Jane to him and held her in his arms—and kissed her on the lips. 'The angels did what they were asked to do,' he said. 'Bonjour, chere demoiselle.'

'We came to ask, if you were going to be free to join us all for lunch, bearing in mind that Jeanne must leave this afternoon to return to her *eleves,*' said Miette when the two had become disentangled.

'I would love to. Thank you. Do you happen to know what Hugh may have planned for the day concerning me?'

'Hugh also extended the lunch invitation, *tout va bien.*'

'There is little left for me to do here. So I am free.'

'Then you must make the most of your time with Jeanne and join us a *treize heures chez nous.* Jeanne may like to see the estate, *les terroires differents, notre domaine.*'

'Ah, good idea that would be very pleasant,' asking Jane, 'Shall we take the horses?'

'Oh, yes, that'd be super! Knowing this is a horsey place I put in a pair of old jhoddies and boots.'

'If you go up and change, I'll come up to the house and meet you.'

When they met, Roddy suggested that they should begin the safari at 'The Residence', his house among the chestnut trees, then go and saddle up. They strolled, hand in hand, down to the cottage.

'Roddy, it's marvelous!' she cried, as they approached the little knobbly-walled cottage under the huge, almost bare trees. 'Now that truly is, well, picturesque.'

'I'm a very lucky lad. I love living here. Come and see inside.'
He proudly showed her every neat, clean corner.' There were
a few books in a small bookcase among them an old copy
of Trevelyan's *History of England* and a well-worn J. M. Dent's
Everyman's Library Edition of the *Anglo Saxon Chronicle* discarded
by the Adult Education Board.

'My, you're serious about getting to know the foreign *desh* in
which you find yourself!'

'Yes, I'm curious about the ancient past that made the people
around today who and what they are. I spotted both in a second-
hand bookshop in Portsmouth. You can't imagine how chuffed
I was. I've enjoyed them; as I move around, I try to imagine
the scenes as they might have been many years ago. Just love it.
I look at a scene and I can't help saying to myself, Constable,
Cotman, Hilder. Before I go, perhaps you may know some little
shops and galleries that you could show me.'

'There are a few very nice ones I'd love to show you. It really
would be joy to do that.'

In the big tack room, Roddy selected a couple of hacking
saddles and two bridles with snaffles. 'But come and have a look
at my horses and see which one is the one you will choose.' Jane
looked at a tall flea-bitten grey.

'Can you see the Arab in her?' asked Roddy. 'She has a
pedigree that covers pages of the stud book. She raced as 'First
Minuet', but in civvy life, she's called 'Sally'. 'Say her name to her
and see what she does.' When Jane did, Sally shook her head a
little, breasted the door and stretched her neck out to Jane, and
stuck her head against her face.

'I think the choice has been taken, but not just by me.'

'It looks mutual. You'll like her.'

Jane saddled her mare as Roddy, alongside, saddled
Trumpeter.

It was the perfect day to be out and mounted, the sun was
shining through scattered cloud which caused shadows on the
stubble fields as they floated by. Where the boughs covered the
small internal roads and lanes, there was a patterned carpet of
lighter and darker tones. The land around was showing good
heart, in rich burnt umber where ploughing had begun. The

beautiful, bountiful Ranelagh was revealing itself now in broad
sweeps of hay meadows then of stubble fields, plough lands,
green rows of root crops followed slopes gently up and down,
here and there an ancient oak that would certainly have been
growing long before Trevelyan wrote his first word on a slate.

Roddy was speaking. 'It would be impossible to imagine
Bardlsey's foul arising from mere dislike. People may be disliked
for any number of reasons, often some kind of behaviour which
causes you displeasure. He didn't know more about me other
than that I worked for Hugh. The cause was the difference of
social level. It must have been a powerful influence. It caused
him to do something against a major rule of the game, a breach
of etiquette—my playing in the team being Hugh's choice, the
universal binding rule of team membership, sheer bad spirit to
benefit from an easy shot set up by another player, and as Hugh
very rightly said, putting two very good ponies in bone-breaking
danger.

'He broke all those rules, which seem to have more moral and
practical legitimacy, simply on the grounds of social superiority.

'To me that epitomizes the power of that force and its
persistence into the present. It says very clearly, that whatever
other rules there may be, the class rule overrules all of them.
It may well be that Bardsley believed sincerely, within his own
soul, that it was he who had upheld the highest order of rules
and that Hugh had sinned heretically against it. Bardsley didn't
apologise for any transgression. He closed the game with the
trump card: "He's only a farm servant." In his mind, he had no
requirement for apology to anyone or for anything. I must say,
that on the morning of the game, when Hugh asked me to play,
my first thought was: have you covered all your flanks? You're
playing me because someone has dropped out. Am I the person
to play? I felt I shouldn't question Hugh and that it would be
wrong to do that. Heaven knows what repercussions there may
now be amongst Bardsley, Hugh, and the people around.' There
was a small pause and then he said, 'A small rise in temperature
can cause an enormous cyclone.'

'Roddy, do you know what I'm feeling and thinking now?'
She meant it rhetorically and went on before he could say a

word. 'I wish human problems could be solved by mathematical methods, but they can't be. The laws of operation of non-human systems have their own vagaries yet remain more manageable than the systems humans create. Even this class question, or problem, only exists when the system is put to absurd extremes: extremes which, in terms of one system, causes damage to another human system which has been tried and through long application has given satisfactory results. Humans can make instant judgements about when the rule should be applied, even to what extent, in what circumstances or at what level within the levels of the system. All animal populations have class, hierarchical systems: certainly all mammals have pecking orders which ultimately help the group to establish coherence and, through that, on to survival. Sometimes it can be, and can certainly on observation, look very cruel look. Generally the family, or the major group will afford a way to a solution. Depending on the make-up of the errant subject, it could lead to death. Generally, even certain amounts of unhappiness are tolerated when it appears to lead somewhere more bearable or ultimately desirable. Would it be destructive to our system if we were to love each other and live together?'

'I can't answer that question with a simple yes or no. It is so sad that the system has given rise to this discussion, but we've got to have it. I can see any number of couples dodging the issue and plunging on. I think we two, both of us, know we have to look before we leap. Unless many other elements of our problem were to change to improve our possibilities, a wrong decision now could cause our love to exist under bitter pain. It may take time, but we may have to see which elements of the equations we can shift. I tell myself I'm being realistic, and simultaneously, I ask if I'm just being selfish. I'm living here in a demi-paradise, a fool's paradise. It can't continue. Miette and Hugh have supported me for a purpose, my purpose. That purpose has been met. I have to get out and build a future or I shall be useless, a handicap to anyone who chose to love me. I've now actively begun planning a move to Australia. I'm making a choice to go to Australia. I'll make a reconnaissance and then a decision. I've now got to move quickly. Financially

I can't afford to hang about. Hugh volunteered that he would
employ me until I wish to go up to Fearnas; he's said so. I know
in my bones I'll do well. I want to succeed if only to give Hugh
a form of reward for all that he and Miette have done for me.
And of course for Erik who set me on my way. I'll have to stay
in UK until Christmas, go to Fearnas, have Christmas with my
parents . . .'

At these words, Jane visibly quailed. He could not miss seeing
the look, almost of alarm, in her face.

'Something has happened Jane,' he said, seizing her hand.

'My god. A whole ghastly picture flashed into my brain. In
a fraction of a moment, the shocking reality of what you have
been saying exploded in a cascade of pictures . . . of me riding
past the Lodge, so aloof, so high, so dignified, so different. How
can you be at the Lodge for Christmas? With me, just up the
drive at Woodend . . . unable to invite you into my family home?
How will the days be?' She was trembling.

'I hadn't come to the point of thinking about that. I'm going
to be leaving my parents for an uncertain time; and their lives
are shortening. I must be with them before I go.'

'Of course, of course you must'— emphasizing the word—
'be with them for Christmas.' She paused to think beyond the
shock, then said, 'I'm beginning to see other ramifications . . .
even if my brother weren't to be home . . . if you came to the
house . . . as a guest . . . what would that mean to the future
of the relationship between your father and my father?' She
went on, speaking very rapidly emotionally, angrily. 'Hector
would create a fuss, and he and Dad would have an unholy row.
What would happen if Hector invited friends? Oh god. I can
see this all so horribly clearly now.' Tears were just in check.
She pulled herself together and said with what conviction she
could assemble. 'I can see my parents any time. I'm not going
anywhere. There will be other Christmases. You go, Roddy. I
can go up afterwards if I want to.'

This was the reality which Roddy had, unhappily, understood.
A problem of social status had now become theirs, to be faced
now. Jane had offered a solution, but she must have begun to
realize that this solution was a compromise called upon to solve,

not entirely satisfactorily, this one, just this one, immediate problem. In the alarm and dismay of this painful realization, he did not have time then to say that he had booked a passage to sail on the Stratheden from Tilbury on New Year's Day. 'Our love must wait.'

'I don't want you not to go home to your parents. At the risk of being very callous, may I suggest that we may have to say our farewells now or when I leave Ranelagh. We will be moving in different orbits in Fearnas; I'll only be there for seven days. This is one of those sacrifices our love would become bedevilled by and here you are making the sacrifice.'

She was about to throw herself upon him and squeeze him so very hard when voices could be heard and the sound of hooves. His face, she saw, had its own pain.

He stood up, holding her hand. 'Come,' he said, in attempted normality, 'we must not be late for Madame Miette's lunch.'

'No. That would never do.'

'Let's have a canter across the stubble. The paths are for the paying passengers.'

As they cantered at a diagonal across the field, it did, just a little, break the tension they were feeling.

He called to her. 'Let's go straight to the house. Please, you go in. I'll take the ponies back.'

Outside the door, he dismounted, and as they stood before that lovely old house, where the oaks and the elms stood by, each with a handful of reins, they threw their arms around each other and hugged and kissed.

From the front drawing room window, a French lady was watching. She smiled outwardly with pleasure in their love, but with an inward sadness, she was feeling about the uncertainty of their future.

Roddy mounted cavalry style without using a stirrup. 'C'mon, Sally,' he said and posted away at a gentle trot.

There was a glass sunroom at the same side of the house as the office which had been designed to accommodate small casual lunches as well as being a comfortable sitting room. And that was where they dined.

'If you are comfortable, ma chere, it is not necessary for you to change, come I'll show you the toilet.'

The others—Hugh, Isabelle, and Tearlath—were spread around in lounge chairs from the comfort of which the men had risen to greet her.

It could neither have been some coincidental, nor some tacit understanding: it must have been the result of discussion and agreement. Never for a moment before, during, throughout, or after the lunch was there the vaguest mention of or allusion to Roddy's known plan to leave Ranelagh. Nor was there any mention or question about what plans Jane and Roddy may have for the coming days or some distant future. Australia was left to lie, an enormous island in the distant Southern hemisphere, silent save for the people from its north who had settled in it and wandered its length and breadth for the last sixty thousand or more years. What an interesting discussion it may have evoked. But for the purposes of preventing social pain, its mention was a taboo.

It was impossible not to speak of Scotland and that ball was thrown into Tearlath's court. This gave him license to draw from his inexhaustible mine of facts of history or anecdotes of people; poachers and princes; stories, always a story, of lands and lochs and vast heather moors; of grand Cairngorms, the Black Isle, which wasn't an 'isle', the big Firth of Moray and the beautiful little firths of Beauly, home to Lord Lovat of Commando fame, and the Cromarty scene of a naval mutiny, with the two cobblers sharing their awl, throwing it from side to side of its mouth where they sat at their lasts and where the sea found its way in; and back, beyond, Ben Wyvis and the glorious sunsets or the merry dancers of the borealis. Of course theatre was talked about; the great success of the Paisley Repertory Company and their Gorbals Story production, the rising vigour of theatre and review in Edinburgh, the satires from the Cambridge Footlights Club; and from ex-servicemen a wholly new creation of English comedy and satire.

Hugh was ardently in the midst of it all energetically injecting his unique enthusiasm for the arts, theatre, music, and a favourite passion—watercolour painting—of which there was charming evidence in this very room. For a Hampshire country squire? Amazing. Not so amazing perhaps was the extensive general knowledge of Miette; about the political world, on every aspect of drama, its theatres, producers, and players; Isabelle, with an encyclopedic knowledge of Scottish history and European literature. To the sheer competency in their expositions, there was added an ability to make incisive, perspicacious comment increasing the enjoyment of their listeners each by her individual, unique, sparkle. Jane was a competent, thoughtful contributor perhaps, more subdued today, and with less evident emotion in her views and responses. Roddy had come from the arid years of military service but listened eagerly to, and was mindful of, every syllable from these brilliant people. He could not set a value on the richness of the treasure trove from which he had been invited to draw.

Roddy had to seize his moment to withdraw. 'I don't want to disturb this totally enjoyable conversation. But having made animals our slaves they have in turn made us theirs. A bevy of bovine beauties will be bellowing at me to relieve their discomfort. Please excuse me. Thank you, Miette, Hugh, for inviting me to share all this pleasure.'

Jane, surprised, stood up too. Sadness shaped her eyes. 'I'm afraid I too must look to my duties. I'll have some girls that I'll have to see back from exeats.' She had taken Roddy's hand and attempted a lightness. 'As Nancy Blackett might say,' addressing Roddy with this shared allusion, 'I'll have to lash up and stow, and when I have, I'll come down and say cheerio on my way home.' Both were on the point of kissing and their bodies could be seen to arrest a started movement. Instead they squeezed hands and exchanged rather wan smiles. 'That would be lovely, Jane,' he said, fearing it would sound as limp when spoken as he heard it in his head. Addressing Isabelle and Tearlath, he said, 'Tomorrow things will be fairly humming here, so I'll come back, if I may, when the cows are out and say proper farewells to you.' Not to leave a heart hurt and a kiss missed, Miette got up, gave Roddy a little hug in the confine of Jane's proximity, almost linking the pair, and kissed him on the cheek. And rising on a circulating tide of metaphor and citation, she drew herself up to declaim,

'Go quickly to your kine, young man, or there will be nor cream nor cheese, nor milk for my morning chicory. You will come anon when our needs be met and the maiden Jane has ridden off to succour her returning charges. Go at once!' Isabelle must have been quite envious, or even professionally threatened, by such an imperious performance. But she did applaud.

Normally, Roddy would have revelled in such exchanges; today they just managed to lighten a gloom within. He did not look about him as he walked to the milking stalls. The cows stood in the order of their coming, their own social system having decided how it would be. He was glad to give them his attention and addressed each by her name. He had all but finished when he heard Jane's car arrive, Hugh having given her guidance on how long the milking would take. Jane walked in at the end of the stalls where the second last of two cows had the gate before her stall swung open, a pat on her rump from Roddy, and she clopped away. Jane had not spoken. He caught her in the corner of his eye and straightened up. He too was silent. He saw the female figure that was so powerfully erotically seductive in her riding clothes; the shirt that moulded her breasts and the cut of the jodhpurs which shaped her hips. They moved quickly towards each other. They embraced. The blood was rushing in his body and he could feel the warmth burning Jane's cheeks, her body trembling. Warning lights were flashing in his brain. He had to break away. He had to stop the inevitable outcome of this urge. The sound of suction on the milking pump was saying 'no flow'.

There was a bellow of annoyance and impatience from Stella, the last cow. She wanted to get out! Jane had shared equally the intensity of what had been happening. She did not want the heat to cease. Something inside her was demanding, 'Now! Now!' For Roddy, it was a chance to gain control of his senses, to overcome the surging that was still going on in his body. It was a crisis. He had to take control. He knew, in cold, commanding clarity that if he failed in self-control, he would have done something in hot blood, in lust, albeit as the consequences of deep, emotional, passionate loving. He knew that the consequences would damn him forever in his own soul. Let his virtue, if that is what it was, be sneered at, were it known of by others. So let it be. Who would care for a cow's displeasure in the heat of passion with a beautiful, adoring woman who wanted you urgently with all her body? Roddy knew that it wasn't Stella's call that made him break away from Jane's embrace, it was something infinitely more important, and if Paris is worth a mass, self-control is worth a sneer. The need for that control was now; he had to make its effects the least hurtful he possibly could. This was no easily entered, easy quit, short, happy, but swift relationship. This was significant, important love between humans capable of caring deeply, of sharing a thousand thoughts and interests, a love that would never cease to grow. It was worth more than Paris—more than a crown—infinitely more than the rituals and pleas to invisible gods and the promise of a life ever after. It had to remain intact now to be recoverable when the trials were over. He did not have to think all these thoughts in the press of the present hectic moments of burning passion while here together; they were so much part of him that no consciousness was required.

What was required now was calmness. Standing there at the end of the dairy, he took her hands in his, and holding them to turn them up, he raised them and softly placed a kiss in each palm and formed them gently as if in prayer, and holding them, he enclosed the kisses.

'Keep them for me. They were my kisses for you. Please, may we keep our last days free from the compelling demands of our bodies? I know that may sound stupid and you may wish to judge me on that. Oh, my lovely Jane, I want us when I leave—as leave I am committed to do—to leave with all our love fresh, beautiful, forever clear, and able to be cherished in our dreams, an anchor to a firm ground of love that has infinite life.' He wanted to break from the ponderous sincerity of what he knew he had to express, however badly.

'Come, sweet, my love, you have the next generation of good British women to care about and I have germs in the dairy which are multiplying even now. May I'—now adopting the facetious theatrical—'call upon you at your residence? I shall whizz there wearing my helmet and goggles in my wind-speed Alvis!'

'Take your puncture kit. I may have tatting to finish and you'll have to help me with my threads.' She seized him and gasped and gulped in a gush of tears and sobbed and spoke somehow, 'Roddy, you are the most remarkable animal. I do love you, please do come—to the house—but not until seven tomorrow.' They kissed briefly, as a married couple might, when the husband leaves the house to go to work. She sat in the beautiful brown leather seat of her black Austin Ruby saloon car with the window down and said again, in a quiet affirmation of a fact, 'Oh, Roddy, I love you so much. Let's live every moment inside our love. We'll have to try to let the painful reality be something outside. Tomorrow will seem so long until you come. *A demain. Je t'aime.*' She drove the pretty rounded little car up to the drive, turned into the road for Arlstorp, and disappeared from view. Inside him there was a weight of sadness, almost physical, that asked him to sit somewhere and let the weight flow out, diminish. The real world had different ideas. He set to and sanitised the dairy and the milk room.

That done, he had to go up as promised, to the house to farewell Isabelle and Tearlath. The folk saw him as he came by the windows of the summer house and Hugh rose to let him in. 'Roddy, you are with us again *ceud mile failte*!' called Tearlath across the room. 'The lowing herd is winding slowly o'er the lea, I'm sure. You may not have ploughed, but plod homeward your weary way you surely have, for *an tocadh* [emotion] is a heavy load to walk with on your back,' said Tearlath. How did the ladies contain their curiosity to know *que'est que c'est passe entre ces deux*? They knew their men were equally anxious to know, and for people with such sophisticated social skills, their eagerness didn't seem to be able to help them phrase the appropriate questions. Tearlath asked a question. 'Hugh, dear friend, aren't you going to offer that poor work-worn man a drink?'

'For the Lord's sake, you *hielan teuchtar*, he's hardly in the door . . . and you giving him an elegiac soliloquy . . . my words of welcome and my offer of a dram were stopped in my throat by its torrent.' He relaxed his theatrical glare and turned to Roddy.

'Roddy, I'm not as neglectful a host as that gnome from under the tree roots of Darnaway's alders would claim. What would you like?' This was going to become, as the lunch had been, Tearlath's kind of gathering where a bit of gentle ribbing and literary and other allusions could be indulged in. He was very sad that Jane had gone, not only because he had lost a listener from the thralls of his yarn spinner's web. He had been affected by her charm and had found her a very bright participant in the small debates and discussions which had made sitting together at the dinner of the evening before and this day's convivial and pleasantly rewarding gathering much joy.

'Hugh, thank you. If there's a drop of that glorious Rhone red that has been spared heilan plundering, I'd be pleased to have a glass.'

'Indeed. It's just there.' He indicated a small table across the room on which all the wines and glasses and an ice bucket were arrayed. 'Do you mind if you help yourself?' And he indicated the table on which all the wines and glasses were arrayed. Though the room was a place for relaxed leisure, the glass he brought back was of Edinburgh crystal. He had barely settled at a low table when the absent Jane became the topic. She had won every heart and the ladies vowed to claim her continuing friendship when Roddy had gone to Australia, and Hugh volunteered that he might attempt to recruit her for polo if and when the demands of being a boarding-school house mistress would permit. Isabelle was first to introduce the topic of Australia when she mentioned that she had made three visits with Tearlath when J. C. Williamson, over a period of five years, produced three of his plays in the state capitals. John McCallum and Googie Withers had been there a number of times and had been rapturous about Australian audiences and the hospitality that enabled them to have short stays on sheep and cattle stations and vineyards. They were dined to death on crayfish, and other fish which they were invited to come and catch from private launches of very hospitable owners. They acknowledged that it could be very, very hot. The Cummings would be in England for Christmas so Roddy would not be able to visit them during his short stay in Fearnas. Isabelle insisted that he must check any time he visited Fearnas to see whether they were up at Rerrope. In his conversation of farewell, Tearlath made a point of saying that since he was a pal of Ike Barron, it was certain that he would be meeting Roddy again.

From then, the days sped by, and of those days, they could spend so few hours together. Whenever they were together, there was much laughter, not to paper over the deep-down pain, but because it was in the essential nature of each of them to be of a positive, happy disposition. Jane took continuing delight in the contrasting aspects of Roddy's theatricality and child-like love of new experiences and ideas. 'Oh, Jane,' he would say, 'I'm learning so much from you. Every hour we spend together seems to expand my life by years. I am the most fortunate man in the world. Your love for me fills my being to explosion point.'

She loved his innocence and naiveté, his natural grace, his sincerity and emotional depth. When she spoke to him about any subject whatsoever, his quick, flexible intelligence seemed to reach the core of the idea at once. 'Why? Why? Why? When I crave this man, when I love him so profoundly, can he not be mine? Oh, the stars in their unchangeable positions: damn stellar metaphors! Damn human systems seem as fix't as stars.'

Hours had to be wrenched from these fast flitting days. Each had work to do, and both were wholehearted in their work efforts. The heat of sexual desire had to be sublimated in a kind of cultural saturation, delightful diversions in concerts, plays, galleries, meeting with teachers in rustic pubs—once at the Barley Mow when the 'end-corner boys' had, coincidentally, gone. The group, activated by their usual Greenwich meantime angle of the sun's meridian, never a navigational minute out, their cleverly calculated course through rounds of drinks put them on the homeward tide, when even the tardy left before the full.

The truth is it was a magical time for these two. In their will to ignore the fear of an end, a spice, piquancy, was added to their pleasures. They were so headily, so rapturously in love that sadness could scarce compete. There were one or two more occasions with Hugh and Miette at Ranelagh when their lives too seemed to be affected by the sadness of the pending departure. They had a brief visit with Ike in London and drove to Aberdeen to be with Nora and Ninian. Life was just so packed full. 'If only, if only, if only.'

The fullness of life was getting to the point when singling off of berthing lines would have to begin. He'd have to see Sir John Davenport about returning the now-cherished Alvis. He talked with Hugh. 'The contract was made at the Barley Mow. It seems appropriate that negotiations for its termination should take place there.' And so they were. Trust Hugh to have got on the brigade net and talked with the knighted colonel and to the others, such as the captain, to ensure rigidity of process and that all negotiations were above board. It was verily a convocation which took place. For Roddy, it felt like going on an interview with the brigade commander. What a fine body of men! Decent blokes all! There was a complete muster—no one on sick parade, no one on leave, and no one in detention. Roddy was the cynosure of friendly eyes when up spake the worthy Knight. 'Freddy, you're a lawyer, say the words.'

And Freddy did. 'Roderick Fraser Mckenzie, you have leased a vehicle, to wit an Alvis roadster, British racing green in colour, from its legal owner and lessor Colonel Sir John Davenport. All intelligence indicates that it has been kept in exceptionally good nick and that it has been used solely for the purposes of pleasure. There is no requirement for details of such pleasure to be disclosed and the observation of beautiful blond-haired ladies in the passenger seat are not required to be explained. At other times, its use to facilitate services to HM Forces in defence of the realm is worthy of distinction. It is not my task to make laudatory remarks. But with Sir John's leave, I would venture to say that you have been an exemplary lessee with just one reservation which I shall put before the lessor and that is that the vehicle has followed a propensity to direct itself to country pubs. However, consideration has been given therefore to the fact that it was it was last owned by a Wing Commander RAF and it is reasonable to assume the vehicle had been so conditioned before the lessee took over the lease. The fact that the lessee is an infantry subaltern—and we know predilections their flesh is heir to—it is expected therefore that the steering tendencies of a racy Alvis driven by such a one, would, to some degree, be aggravated. My advice is that this must be given generous consideration, sir. It is my considered judgment, sir, that the lessee Lieutenant Roddy Mckenzie has fulfilled the spirit and legal requirements of his lease.'

'Dammit, Freddy, you've given me no room to haggle.' Whereupon he withdrew from a trouser pocket twenty-five pounds which he passed to Freddy. 'Having fulfilled the requirements of his lease in such an exemplary manner, I believe he is entitled to the return of his deposit and I'd be obliged if you would be so kind as to pass this money to Mr. Mckenzie.' The weighty legal transactions completed, all could return to the pleasures of the pub.

'I'll store it with much more care than before, Roddy, and see that it's ready for your use whenever you come back to visit us and I hope you'll do that, and I'm sure, the others do too. If you don't mind, I might offer its use to the dramatic highlander and his delightful lady.'

'That would be perfect, sir.'

'I won't let Hugh near it . . . drives his own car like a tank . . . thinks he's still with the Scots Greys. Going from the foot guards to the tanks was his ruination. D'ye agree with that, Hugh?'

'No, I do not,' Hugh responded emphatically, 'Don't forget, we could have a brew up while you had to have a platoon out foraging for firewood.'

Then spake the captain. 'My intelligence network has to be as good as Whitehall's, and through it, I learned that you had booked a tourist-class passage. As a serving commissioned officer, even without a travel warrant, you must travel first class. I want you to take this chitty and present it when you board. It will confirm that, at no additional cost, your ticket has been raised to first class, and that you will be occupying a port-side single cabin on A Deck for your voyage to Sydney.' I called upon the help of one of my friends, an old chum who has a bit of pull at McDonald and Hamilton since he'd been their chairman for many years. He was very pleased to be of service to a friend of mine. You have become a friend of all of the men here and

I hope you will never hesitate to call upon such friends when you may need something done.' From the breast pocket of his navy blue jacket, he drew a slim wallet of a size suited to holding unfolded one hundred pound notes and taking from it a flimsy sheet, handed it to Roddy, saying, 'Bon voyage, young friend, a wish from all of us.'

'Permission to feel embarrassed, sir,' he jested, in an attempt to diminish the reality that his face was blushing red. 'That is very decent of you, sir. I'm sure I shall remember your kindness every day of the voyage and long thereafter. Thank you very much for your thoughtfulness.'

'My pleasure, dear boy.'

This was the opportunity for Roddy to make his own little speech. 'Thank you all for your good wishes. I'm sure you can recall from your own experiences the feelings a man has when he enters an old well-knit society in an environment where they and their families have lived for many years. You took me into your group and made me warmly welcome. But you will never be able to imagine how much that means to me. I want to thank you all for your generosity of spirit, your tips for young players, and your cheerful good company. I will never be able thank enough my proponent Major Hugh Verney who allowed me a slice of life which I shall cherish forever. Thank you again, Hugh, and thank you all. Please join me in a parting drink.' He drew the barman's attention and asked him to pour drinks all round.

To say farewell to the people of Ranelagh with whom he had spent fulfilling work, he arranged with Hugh to have the barn one evening after work for a bit of a 'knees up'. A firkin of cider and a firkin of Speckled Hen were picked up from the Barley Mow, and since Ovington was no great distance away, reserves could easily be drawn upon. Mollie Trevarthen, the cook at Ranelagh, found it more convenient to cook at home her planned contribution to the festivity than to use the kitchen at Ranelagh offered by Miette. There were seats of straw bales and hay bales and fruit sorting tables on which covers were spread and drinking pots and glasses and jugs could be laid—many of the men would bring their own favourite pewter's. Cedric made an announcement to thank Roddy for giving him and Dolly the chance for weekends off and how the milk was never better tasting or more plentiful than when Roddy did the dairy. The head gardener said Roddy should take up horticulture; he had a genuine enthusiasm and an instinctive understanding of the plant world. The horsemen who bred the Percherons, and kept the leisure horses, praised his skill and horsemanship and declared that the polo ponies had never looked so fit and well.

So Roddy had to make his own speech. 'The story I'd like to tell had its beginning long ago, and under circumstances, that would take too long and would be too difficult to explain. But I want to say that getting the opportunity to come here to work at Ranelagh was the greatest piece of luck—apart from a Chinese bullet which went right through me without stopping—that I've had in my life. The bullet has long gone and left nothing but a fading scar. The good luck of my being here, working with you folk for Major Verney has shaped me for the future. That luck will last me forever. You shared with me your knowledge and skills, you taught tricks and knacks that may have taken you years to learn. I'll never forget them. And I won't forget your friendship and generosity in teaching them to me. I'm off into the unknown now, but I've got a strong feeling that over the years to come I'm going to be using every bit of what you've taught me here. And just in case I don't see some of you again before I go, let me say cheerio now and thank you again for your friendship and generosity.'

It was a roistering good evening and his acquired capacity for beer stood him in very good stead. A good time was had by all.

His departure date was rapidly advancing, but from the afternoon of their last weekend, they had stolen an hour to be alone. The little Alvis was driven up to Butser Hill where they walked to, and a little over, the crest arms around each other's shoulders, companionably, as you see little boys do. Roddy had taken a travelling rug, tucked under his left arm from the dickie seat locker, and spread this on the grass. There was a cool breeze sweeping the hill, so they had to snuggle up for warmth. They looked across a spread of rural Hampshire soft, rounded, and smoothed by the ages, the soil and the autumn trees all in the tones of Tuscany and Umbria, hedges, copses, lonely giant trees, woolly sheep, and cattle red and white. Constable and J.M.W.T. would have loved the cloud formations and the lights. What they were seeing was England in great heart.

'It's how I always think of England,' Roddy said.

'Me too. I live with it every day but never for a moment forget my good fortune to be surrounded by its gentle beauty. I could never take it for granted.' There was a silence whose cause may have been respect for the scene; perhaps their feelings of being who they were, where they were, and what their futures may be required no voice. Their closeness perhaps transmitted more than physical warmth.

Quite softly, as if telling an ongoing dream, Jane spoke.

'Whenever we shall meet again, who we are, what we will do then, and how we will love then, will never be the same as now it is. Even people who never part—as we are about to, move on through their lives leaving behind memories altered by that movement through time, which means nothing mental, emotional can be repeated. Even our memories of past events will be transformed by that passage through time. There shall be new and different joys, but we never can recapture that first fine careless rapture. I'm so glad we are living our love and our joy now. I can't guess what will happen to me when I see you leave. I know only that I shall be saying farewell to this wonderful time of our love.'

When Jane had gone home, he had returned to Ranelagh for the last night in his cottage.

———ooo❦ooo———

In what was becoming a matter of hours before departure, Miette wanted Jane and Roddy to come to Ranelagh so that she and Hugh might have them to share in the warm pool of their affection. Miette had prepared a meal of 'comfort food', hot and easily eaten from a fork. They sat in the special ambience of that small summer house lounge where they had sat with Isabelle and Tearlath about whom they now all talked with affection. The Verney's spoke about the pleasure that having Roddy at Ranelagh had given them and how much they would miss him. They had to thank Roddy for bringing Jane into their lives, a delightful recompense to fill the void of his leaving. This would be Roddy's last night at Ranelagh, and to save using his kitchen further, he had been invited to breakfast in this same room. It was appropriate that the loving four should be together for this time. They knew that whatever the future may hold, their bonds would continue, and however long for either of them that future should be. Hugh and Miette made their farewells in the little lounge, and Jane and Roddy parted on the steps of Ranelagh under a full moon.

They would meet in Fearnas, but neither knew what the manner of that meeting might be.

On the next day, Hugh and Miette were to drive him up to London to take his train for Fearnas; he was not to feel embarrassed or spoiled, because they had much that they needed to do in London and would have to spend a few days there.

In the morning of departure, Miette called at the cottage door.

'Roddy, your sister Jane telephoned. I told her I would bring you now. If you come *tout de suite*, she will be there. Come now.' On the way to the house, Miette explained she had just had the telephone connected to the Lodge. '*Elle est tres gentille.* She speaks Canadian French. She is very excited. She wants to be going to a ball with you.'

When Roddy spoke with his sister Jane, she explained that the burden of her call had been to see if he were interested in partnering her to the Christmas Highland Ball. He agreed at once to go. Jane would immediately make the reservations and book two rooms at the Caledonian Hotel.

After the call, Roddy told Miette that Jane thought it would be a nice part of the process of his farewell to Scotland, and a bit of Scottish fun for her. 'Without me, it is unlikely she would ever in her life attend a Highland Ball. My god, by now she will be having a gown made. My major concern is that our Jane may be going too. But what can I do? Either way, I'm going to disappoint someone. It is one of the perils of our situation which would plague any chance of peace and happiness in our lives. There will be so many people there that if our Jane bumps into me, surely we can play it down?'

Miette was quiet. She walked slowly towards him then embracing him, clinging to him, she could only say, 'I am so sad'.

Because it was a white tie affair, he immediately thought of how he could borrow a mess kit and asked Miette if he might make a phone call. He telephoned Geoffrey Lancaster's service telephone number and he was put through.

The drive to London is not long, and Miette had decided that life should go on and was her normal, happy interested and interesting self. The pair dropped him at Euston where he could organize his baggage and go to see his bank. They had made their big farewells. Miette cried. They drove away: two of the most wonderful people in his world.

He would go to his bank now as planned into their travel from Ranelagh and arrange to move his account to the Bank of New South Wales. At his bank, the teller enquired which of his accounts he wished to transfer to the Bank of New South Wales.

'Do you wish to transfer your Salary Adjustment Account as well as your cheque account?' asked the bank officer to whom the teller had introduced him. Roddy was puzzled; he knew nothing of such an account. The bank officer went on. 'The account has deposits up to last week and was then closed. Have you ceased your employment at Ranelagh?'

'Yes, I have, just yesterday. I leave for Australia on New Year's Day.'

'Because transactions on such accounts are usually known through pay slips, we don't send out statements unless an issue arises.' Roddy was stunned to learn that the account balance was an amount slightly more than he had ever received while on reserve service.

The teller went on organising the opening of a cheque account with the Bank of New South Wales and discovered that a personal reference was required. Roddy explained the circumstances. Too late to try to get in touch with Hugh, and

Erik was in the Med. Everyone was keen to help. His bank
then spoke with the Bank of New South Wales who cabled Jill
Lowing. Her response, which the bank would act upon, would
be telegraphed immediately and his documents would be sent
by mail to the Lodge, Woodend, Fearnas.

Only a short time remained before he must be at Euston
Station. Nevertheless enough time for a noggin at the Naval
and Military. There he had a pleasant blether with an Indian
army bloke, a hale and hearty fellow of ninety who was joined
later by a bloke of the same vintage who had been a pilot in
the RFC. They applied themselves with gusto to pints of beer,
and since they were going to be staying in the club, they were
within a secure perimeter. They were both tall and thin as
whippets; which blows the theory that beer capacity equals body
mass. They were both widowed and living in retired officers'
establishments, of which they spoke very highly, one in Kent
and one in Wiltshire. He left their jolly company in beer-assisted
high spirits. Mind you, there would still be a little time, when
he got to Euston, and good heavens, didn't he owe it to Erik to
have a drink in respect to and in memory of their last drink
at the Platform 13 bar? How different were their moods when
last there. They neither could have imagined how much their
lives would become so entwined, nor could they have imagined
the connections and interconnections that the primary bond,
which had sprung up between them, would produce. Certainly
they never could have foretold the events in which they would
become involved.

Just for fun, and because he saw it on the drinks list, he
had a small bottle Tenants lager to flush the flues and to give
the steward time to get ready the wine which he had promised
himself and had selected to have for dinner. Living in the
company of Hugh and Miette, he had been a student in their
private-tuition finishing school. On their part, this had been
totally intentional, but its design never detectable. He was
helped to learn about French and other continental wines, food,
cultures, and social protocols. He scrutinized the list and the
menu and made his selections. The steward opened the wine

of his choice so he could relax and let it get know the world free from the confines of a bottle to where it might reach the fulfillment of its life cycle.

At Fearnas, it was the middle of the morning and he walked the short distance from the station to the Lodge with his portable kit in a Bergen rucksack. It was a wintry day. Wordie's horse-drawn lorry, not far behind him, would deliver his trunk to the Lodge. In the highland vocabulary of detectable emotion, there were only grinding lows of agony and silent tears hidden out of sight. He certainly wasn't expecting a rousing welcome, so there was no disappointment.

His mother was looking at him indirectly, keen to assess how he looked, yet pretending not to be so anxious to know whether he was healthy, happy, or sad. Jane had been to other places and had no longer those highland inhibitions to prevent her giving him a cuddle and a kiss on his cheek and pushing him back to have a good look at him. 'Gee, you're looking really well, Roddy,' she announced, with a Fearnas accent which had succumbed to the influence of the vernacular speech of her adopted country.

The days were spent in gallivanting. One of these was a drive along the southern shores of the Moray Firth to visit the fishing villages, towns, and harbours as far as Buckie and Peterhead. They returned inland through the rich coastal farming land and, on their way back, penetrated the inner winds of the Avon valley to the magnificent old Dalwhinnie House. Here they would pick up from James Murray-Grant, Geoffrey Lancaster's Royal Hampshire Regiment Mess Kit to wear at the ball, which was suitable, not only in size but with parachute wings already sewn on, and James would take it back after his Christmas leave. At one time, it would have been at least a maid who answered a caller at the front door, now it was Jamie himself who greeted Roddy on the step. 'Roddy Mckenzie, I bet, how are you? You've come for Lancaster's mess kit, I presume, are you going to come in?'

'That's very nice of you, but I've got half a platoon with me; my father, mother, and sister.'

'On a cold day like this, I bet they'd like a sherry.' He came down the steps with Roddy to the car, and Roddy organized the family to get down from the car to meet Jamie. He welcomed them. 'Do come up and have a sherry. That wind is coming right down the valley off the snow.' Jamie's parents, Brigadier Murray-Grant and his wife, were in a large drawing room where a fire was burning merrily. Mrs. Murray-Grant was looking mother to mother at Flora Mckenzie. 'We wouldn't normally be in this room, but we have a crowd of youngsters up for their Christmas break. They'll be back down from the snow shortly and this room will be full of young folk and noise. It's a lovely time for me, Mrs. Mckenzie. You would know well, you have your daughter and your son home.'

'It's just wonderful,' responded Flora warmly. 'I try not to think that it's for such a short time. Jane will be going back to the bank in Canada and Roddy leaves for Australia on New Year's Day. Of course it's what our young ones have always done.'

The ladies shared more of their lives as mothers. The men talked of military matters and Jane was an interested party to all of that. Before he joined the staff, the brigadier had commanded a battalion of Gordon Highlanders. Sandy mentioned that he had on prominent display a print of piper Findlater, who, seated on a rock, both ankles shot, kept playing as the Gordons stormed the Dargai Heights

It was all very pleasant. Warmed by the sherry and gracefully refusing another, they took their leave. Roddy took charge of the mess kit which would be brought back after the ball. Geoffrey had insisted, Jamie said, that he must not have it dry-cleaned before returning it. He had a favourite dry cleaner in Hampshire who was used to uniforms, and their care was his specialty. It could well be, that in Hampshire, their being so many air force and military establishments, an entire industry might be founded on that service.

He and Jane had entered the huge hall with the colours of tartan service mess kits in reds and greens air force and navy blue, white ties, and shirt fronts against rich deep black ladies in long white ball gowns with long tartan sashes, sparkling jewellery in their hair and pendants, a packed host meeting and greeting each other, happy reunions after long periods apart in many places distant, dangerous, exotic. Groups were forming which had been organized long before. Jane and Roddy feeling great excitement, thrilled by the sight they were taking in, stood just to the right of the door so as not to be in the way. They were soaking up and revelling in the impact of the scene. To their right of the door, a group had gathered and was in the throes of coming together for the night of dancing and revelry.

They would have hesitated no more than a second or two to view the exciting scene before them when a very tall, handsome man who was busy meeting his friends turned to look at the pair, and a very attractive pair they were. Roddy, the epitome of military elegance, and Jane, a superb example of style and poise, her chestnut brown hair enhanced by the green tone of her ball gown. She looked taller than she actually was and her natural posture was quite regal. As she looked around, her face reflected pleasure in the man she was seeing.

'You haven't found your party yet?' he asked.

'We haven't got one, sir,' declared Roddy. 'Our being here was the inspiration of my sister Jane,' he said, turning to Jane who was close beside him looking at the tall man as he spoke.

'Well, I think that was a fine idea, Jane, if I may be allowed to address you in such a familiar way. I'm pretending your brother introduced us. My name's Roderick Fraser of Fortrose and you are?' he asked, looking at Roddy in friendly enquiry.

'Roderick Fraser Mckenzie, Royal Hampshire Regiment, sir.'

The earl screwed up his eyes in mock scrutiny and asked, 'Where did you get those medals, the Hampshires weren't in Korea?'

'I was with 43 Highland then, sir.'

'Well, I'll be blowed. D'ye know Erik Barron?'

'Yes, sir, he was my company commander. We were both in the two Hook battles.'

'Well, I'm very pleased to meet you. It won't really be a surprise to you to know that my name is Roderick Mckenzie Fraser. How d'ye like that? Now look here, if you don't have a party, why don't you join us? I guarantee we don't harbour any boring old farts. I made this spot our HQ so that we can come

and go between dances and "circulating". We're right by this
door so no difficulty in keeping bearings. Jane, come and meet
some of the ladies,' he said, offering her his hand. On the earl's
introduction, and not least because they were a very attractive,
yes, striking couple, their evening as for the others, opened up.
It was soon easy to hear laughter and bright badinage. Fortrose
had taken the wise precaution of bringing two servants and his
own siege-defying cellar.

As the jolly evening went on, there was continuous changing
of partners for the Scottish country dances which most people
had learned to elegant proficiency. It was an energetic business
and those returning from dancing were particular targets for
the staff so no one ever stood without a drink.

Jane Mckenzie had been readily embosomed by the men and
women of the party and understandably so. It would be hard for
her to be aggressive, but to be assertive was natural to her. She
spoke clearly and plainly without prevarication or obfuscation
always in direct relationship to whatever may have been the
subject in question with no conflations or category errors. She
had no fear of saying no and was never mealy-mouthed were
there a point with which she disagreed. In all of her negotiations,
her face never showed malevolence or some wish to overcome.

Groups drifted past the earl's stronghold in the process
of forming and reforming after dancing. From one of those
drifting groups, Jane Dugal happened to turn her head. There
was Roddy Mckenzie, hobnobbing with the earl of Fortrose and
his party.

A sharp, shocking feeling struck her to the core. She hated
the feeling. What is he doing here? And what was his so friendly
relationship with the earl of Fortrose? Some idea was making
her shake. Here was the son of a household whose rights would
ensure that *her family's lodge* would be their residence so long as
one of the direct family was the occupant.

'What right has such a person to be at a dress ball in the
company of Forbes of Fortrose? This is not his place!'

She recognized the thoughts that caused such ugly feelings.
Those thoughts had brought the function of her brain to a halt

and all feeling had fled. At that moment, she had crossed the border.

As in Milan Kundera's observation from his *The Book of Laughter and Forgetting*, cited in his 'The Art of the Novel',

'It takes so little, so infinitely little, for a person to cross the border beyond which everything loses meaning: love, convictions, faith, history.'

Jane Dugal had crossed that border.

She was speechless, incapable of uttering human sound, not a word—any word.

Roddy was in the process thanking his last partner and they were next to the earl who had made some kind of joke about their dance and they were laughing together.

He was looking past the girl's shoulder and across the small space which separated their groups. His eye caught a glimpse of Jane Dugal. He saw her face, from which all colour and visible emotion had drained, staring at him.

He turned to the earl and those nearby and asked, 'May I be excused for a moment? I must just acknowledge someone I know?'

He stepped towards group said good evening to them. There was no one he knew except Jane and they were all about her age.

'Good evening all,' he said, 'are you enjoying the dancing?

One of the females responded. 'I certainly am. Don't you think the ballroom's splendid? The mood of the people seems just totally super for Christmas festivity.' She sounded very happy and enthusiastic.

'I'm Roddy Mckenzie,' he said, offering his hand to the speaker. 'My sister and I are in a group over there,' he said, gesturing vaguely. 'I came over to say hello to Jane,' he said, turning towards her. 'Hello, Jane. There must be a dashing white sergeant on the list. I wondered if when it comes you might favour my sister and me by making up the three?'

She was trying to pull herself together and was appalled at the difficulty she was having to do so. Her brain began to function again in a limited way. From somewhere inside her, she heard sounds like words, and possibly serious was someone saying, 'That would not be appropriate.' Her group looked at her and at Roddy. Something going on here between these two; they could only guess what it might be.

Roddy knew that now was not the time to attempt problem solving, so attempting to incorporate what he was about to say into the lightness of his air and the party spirit, he said to her, 'I'm very sorry.' He bowed slightly from the waist to the ghostly Jane and turning to the rest of the group said, 'Do have an enjoyable evening,' and left Jane and with whatever her problem might happen to be.

Addressing one of the young women in the Fortrose's group standing next to him, he enquired, 'May I borrow your programme for a sec, please? Apart from checking up on you, and seeing who's getting the most mentions, I want to find when it's going to be Dashing White Sergeant time.'

'No, you may not!' she said in mock severity and coquettishness, clutching the programme to her breast. 'I won't have you peeking into my private life, but I'll look up the dance for you and I'm bearing in mind that you haven't asked me for it.'

'Alison, when I dance with you, I want to have you all to myself alone. Pray tell, is there a Scottish waltz? If there is, may I have the pleasure?'

'Smarm, Mr. Mckenzie! Yes, there is,' she said, pretending an examination of her programme. 'But of course it's already booked.'

'Hey. Just let me see that programme, Alison,' he joked, then pretending heart-hurt seriousness, and feigning an attempt to seize it. 'You just want to break my heart.'

'Well, just to avoid a human tragedy, I'll make an excuse and write you in.'

'Ah, sweet Alison, how I wish it could begin now.'

They both had a giggle and blended again with the others all close around them. He turned to Jane and said, 'If we can get someone to partner us, would you like to do the Dashing White Sergeant?'

Eleanora Forbes, who was right beside them, said, 'What about me? I haven't heard from my Roddy yet. Will you hold the place for me while I check?' She was back in seconds and, playing the innocent, said, 'Thank you for your invitation to dance, sir, I accept with pleasure.

She warmed to his sincerity as, looking at her and into her eyes, he said, 'Eleanora, you are doing us a great honour. I'll have to watch my steps.' Like all country dancing, it was a great mixer of people. Roddy's partners were decidedly the belles of the ball. They came back to the group smiling, laughing at their breathlessness and flushed by the effort. The earl came back with his partners, one younger and one older woman, equally happy, and they chatted as they 'compared notes'.

Inside Jane Dugal, the turmoil of hell continued. She had observed with incredulity the trio as they danced so gaily— Lady Eleanora Fraser of Fortrose, Roddy McKenzie from their Lodge, their gardener's son; Jane Mckenzie successful Canadian banker, their gardener's daughter.

The ball drew to a close. 'I'll have to watch my steps.'

When the last dance was over, thick brown soup, a buffer against the freezing night without, had been served from large steaming cups brought by passing waiters. As it was being served and sipped, the last bits of conviviality and friendship were being exchanged. There followed a wholehearted rendering of 'Auld Lang Syne'. Inside the earl's party of guests, good nights and farewells were going the rounds with Jane and Roddy warmly included by every single person in the group.

As Alison came to say good night, Roddy said, 'Thank you for your friendship. I'd still love to see that programme, Alison.'

'It was great fun, Roddy,' she said, smiling. He shook hands with her escort with whom he had chatted during the evening. 'You look so lovely, Jane. I do hope you enjoyed the ball,' Alison said to Jane Mckenzie before they parted.

The earl had been much impressed and happy to see that Roddy was the paradigm of a dutiful, entertaining subaltern. He had danced with every lady of every age and made sure the stewards kept them well supplied. The men took to him and could see why the earl was so impressed. Roderick Fraser was pleased to hear of Roddy's friendship with Erik Barron and fascinated by their sailing escapades. He had remembered Erik from the Chindit days and knew that Erik could read men.

When Roddy was leaving, the earl shook his hand and said directly into his eyes, 'Roddy, you'll never be friendless while I'm alive.'

It was ironical that at that moment Jane Dugal and her escort should pass by within earshot. It might be wondered what might have gone on in the conflicted mind of Jane Dugal could she be hearing this.

'When you visit Fearnas, make sure you come up to see me, and, Miss Jane Mckenzie, that applies to you,' he said, looking at Jane, 'you're a very talented woman, but you're so charming most people would never notice.' Lady Eleanor Forbes was the kind of wife the earl would have to have—bright, intelligent, and apparently very capable and a great organizer, a no-nonsense straight shooter (rather like another woman he knew thinking of Miette). They were a good team. She was standing with the earl while he was speaking and added, 'I'm so glad we caught you at the first throw of our net,' she said, 'it was a prized catch. Thank you for staying around with us. Take heed of what my Roddy said, but if you don't want to come up and see him, come up and see me. We sometimes go to Canada, Jane, may we visit you? My Roddy and John Buchan are pals. Roddy, you're a fine young man and I know that my saying that will not go to your head. I know you will do well for yourself in Australia. I'll give you my guarantee. We have some contacts there, so if there's just anything we can ever do to help, please just ask. And, Jane, you have already made your mark. I don't want to sound pompous, but I do wish you all the success in the world and I do mean it when I say we shall visit you.'

Jane was an adept speaker and her words were centred on their coming to Canada to allow her, in all fairness, the opportunity to reciprocate their kindness.

'I don't want to steal what Jane has said, but I shall never be able to thank you both for welcoming us so warmly into your party. I've had the most enjoyable night. On my way to Castle Fortrose when I call to do my devoirs and re-bond our friendship, which began this night, I'll pick up a bottle of Glen Moranjie's oldest—simply to support local craft of course. Should I leave it behind, don't send it after me, sir. Thank you both.' He stood to attention in salute.

As the earl's staff brought their cloaks and capes, Jane and Roddy moved away to jostle with the friendly, merry crowd at the cloakroom, pulled on their warm coats, and with all the pleasantest of emotions, walked the short distance across the Ness Bridge to their cosy rooms at the Caledonian Hotel.

Jane Dugal stepped inside from the cold frosty morning to the warm hallway of Woodend House. In the sitting room, her parents had left a glowing fire to fade safely away behind a spark-screen. Her room was warm from the equally protected grate in her bedroom, the room softly lit by its soft red-gold glow. Before it, she slipped out of her dress and her underwear, letting them fall, uncaring where they fell. The bed had been turned down a little way. She slipped into its warmth and felt the soft, hot water bottle in its woolen cover. Yet she lay there shivering, shivering that she could not control, shivering the cause of which was not the cold of the night. She did not know whether her eyes were open or closed. She could see nothing.

This is what he had warned her about. This is why he had resisted that emotionally driven sexual urge which had her aching with desire. He had foreseen how tragic, how horrible, it would have been had he responded to those powerful urges. Tonight he had broken no rule. He was in the intimate company of Fraser of Fortrose and Lady Eleanor. Roddy had no reservations about his humble social status. He wanted a clear social field—if his status needed to be known, he would happily declare it. 'He knew I was weak. He knew I would not be able to handle, to cope with, my own reality. I was the person on the first firing line of social division. And I had the enemy within. I am the weak link in our love. Why was I ever imagining, and I know I was, that a boy from the lodge, the gardener's son, would not and could not have insight and perceptive empathy? Which feelings, which ideas are class specific? Am I so shallow, are my values so skewed towards a notion of innate superiority, of exclusive access to certain areas of psychological being, a member of a unique onion layer in humanity's wholeness?'

She was totally unable even for the fraction of a second to seize, and hold for examination, any of these ideas. She could not formulate a thesis for a theory of social values. Wasn't there an algorithm, easily constructed, that could be run though that excluded human emotions? How could you attribute values to create a set of symbols which you could be sure would not defeat the solution you wanted? But what is the wanted solution? Was she fundamentally a sham? She loathed herself for what she had found herself capable of thinking. Does she operate on the external surface of an inner delusion? The questions kept coming and coming. Answers refused to appear. Seeing him to talk to would not be a solution. It would be the exposition of a disastrous moral collapse.

In the Caledonian Hotel, the delights of the evening had been recollected and enjoyed by Roddy as sleep was descending. Now he found himself troubled by what he had seen and experienced of Jane that night. A part of the tragedy, which he had thought to avoid, had evidenced itself in a form more acute than he could have imagined. Yet he sensed that that may on a space marked out specifically as hers. She have been a local defensive barrier thrown up for the event of the ball. But why? He hadn't intruded had appeared like a person in quite severe shock, her voice more from the spirit world than of humanity, her response to the question of dancing much like the pronouncement of the Delphic oracle might have been. He pondered and asked himself, 'Surely this was not just a reaction to the surprise of seeing me there? Was it that Jane and I were in Fortrose's party? Oh god! Surely not! Surely she wasn't thinking I was moving in circles beyond my station!' Then he calmed himself and decided that if what he had just imagined were indeed the case, it was part of the entire social status issue about which he was completely aware, and about which he had no illusions. Had he not described similar and inevitable problems, should they continue their association into the future? He had foretold the hurt that she would be asking herself to bear. 'In all honesty, what more can I do?' he asked himself after considering the situation. 'Our farewell at

Ranelagh wrote the last words to bring to an end a chapter in the story of our lives.'

There were few of his old schoolmates who now lived in Fearnas, and with these few, it was easy to catch up. Christmas around the lunch table at Fearnas was a jolly affair and the two people who were 'orphans', friends who needed a place where they could share in the Christmas spirit, were brought into the McKenzie family. Everyone was involved in the preparation, everyone was involved in the celebrations, and everyone was involved in the clearing-up, which was really all part of the party activity.

There was a pleasant jaunt to Dalwhinnie House again to return Geoffrey's mess kit, but when the young lady who answered the door said she would call her aunt, Roddy declined but wished all in the house season's greetings from the Mckenzies and, as well as the suit box, gave her an envelope for Jamie and the Murray-Grants. They took a meandering route home, stopping to take in the clear views accorded by the dry frosty day which accentuated shadows and lights, and a majestic view of the snow-clad Ben Wyvis across the Firth amongst the distant mountains of Ross-shire.

It had been decided that Roddy would leave from Fearnas station and Jane had retained McRae and Dick's car for the purpose; the important farewells had been said at the lodge. They were not on the platform long but with enough time to have a wee blether with the station staff, all of whom they knew. As the train pulled out, Roddy leaned from the compartment window until the train had crossed the bridge over the Fearnas and he could see them no more.

Jane Dugal had neither said that she would be coming to Tilbury nor that she had contrived to have a pass to come aboard. She knew his cabin was on A Deck and its number, but where might he be when she came aboard? The captain had told her how to fix that. An announcement on the tannoy system called Mr. Mckenzie, a passenger, to the gangway. He hurried through the unfamiliar gangways of this huge ship and descended to the gangway level amongst people coming and going meeting and parting. Then he saw Jane. She was different now from the ghost with face to match her gown, who spoke like some phantom the last words he had heard from her. She was the normal Jane, the woman who had invited him to the concert in Trent Hall.

He looked at her. There was nothing that feeling prompted him to say.

In the moments of his hesitation, regardless of people moving around them, she burst out in a torrent of words.

'I have come to see you for this last time. I had to see you, as I did when our joy was so complete.

'On the night of the Highland Ball, I learned what a fraud I am, the despicable person I found myself to be. I wanted to see you face-to-face to remember once and forever what you are, the junction of physicality with a kind of spiritual purity. Roddy, I realize now the unusual phenomenon you are.' She had fixed him so steadfastly with her eyes. The intensity of her emotion was palpable; it was touching his senses, even his body. He must not interrupt. This was what she had taken pains to be here to say. 'Up till not so long ago, I just loved you to the point which I was sure was the ultimate. I've had a little time to think. I know now that my level of being is not enough. There's a profundity that is in you which is truly, and I believe this, found in few humans. The painful examinations of my delusions has pointed me in directions, which from my knowing you are necessary for me, if I am to improve myself, to become a better human. I will need time to produce these skills until they go beyond knowledge, cognition, till they begin to flow in my blood as they do in yours. I have so far to go. I wish I could do that journey with you. In a way, I shall. You will always be that shining life which makes living exemplary life look so easy to be good at, like skilled musicians and craftsmen make what they do look so easily done. If you ever think of me, think of me learning to be a better human. If I can think that you are thinking of me trying, it will spur me on to try harder and harder.'

The last blasts were being blown, hands were moving to the gangplanks and lashings were being freed. 'All ashore that's going ashore!' was being shouted.

'Please, Roddy, take this, even in this torrent of words, I haven't been able to say all I want to say.'

She thrust an envelope into his hand, looked at him from tear-filled eyes. She turned and ran to the gangplank. She was the last to go ashore.

His eyes followed her to the wharf. The gangplank had been drawn up and was now aboard. The tugs were pulling the hull away. She was there at the point to which his eyes had followed her. They waved. She became smaller and smaller, more distant. He was being dragged away from her. She couldn't possibly see his face now—nor he, hers. The stoic halter on his emotions sundered. He burst into uncontrollable sobbing, and his heavy tears which splashed on the scrubbed timber rail made dark spots on its bleached surface.

At last the sobbing ceased and he remembered he had been clutching like a drowning man a twig, the letter Jane had thrust into his hand. 'Read it now. Don't put it off,' he said to himself. He opened it with as much care as he could. It was written in Jane's very clear and attractive writing. It bore no address, only yesterday's date, ah, but yes, as a footnote was the address of their shared house in Alstorp.

My dearest Roddy,

If you should fall in love while we are apart as well you may, my love, because you are a loving person, I hope it is with someone who can hear that inner song that is you, and find the rhythm that makes your heart a source of love and joy. I hope she will adore you as I do. If those things happen, she will be a very happy woman and you a happy man.

With all my heart,

Jane Dugal.

Had he another tear to shed, perhaps it would have fallen then, but he returned to the rail watching with less than careful interest the low banks of the estuary slip by. He was thinking that there was some symbolism connecting into a unity, the estuary that was bearing him out to sea to a new life about which he had no imaginings, simply faith in his own body and mind, and the constituents of experience that formed him to this moment. The river was bearing him away from unrepeatable Halcyon Days; from admirable, generous people; growthful experiences both social, practical, and aesthetic in a gentle part of beautiful England, gone now into memory for happy reflection and a reminder of goodness to be found in life; the love of a beautiful woman, an entirely new experience, an explosive expansion of sensation, the thrills of sharing hearts and minds, sharpening sensitivities and perceptions, increasing the values of events by shared experiencing drawn to a close in a few lines of tender prose; his venture forth into a new world prepared by knowledge of past and loss, and human social systems and value sets absorbed by children from their growing years. It was through him that these connections had meaning: how could he possibly avoid being such a link? He would carry that trail into the unknown life that mere human survival; growth, development evolution even, demanded he must enter into. Bits of what he would do would be transmissions of Erik, Freddie and Woodie, Lieutenant McRae, Miette, Hugh, Jane, Sir John, 'The Captain' Robert, Jilly and Emma, the Earl and Eleanora, Flora and Sandy. He was now the sum of these connecting elements. He was the actor.

---ooo-}{-ooo---

Life on a liner is great fun for all ages and the passenger on A Deck were having fun. Life could, at your choice, be non-stop activity. Roddy indulged to the full extent, and though his cabin was no means large, it was a palatial expanse just for him—more than slightly different from the Empire Fowey, best forgotten. There were more lovely Australian girls, some who would enter university in the coming years, others like Jilly and Emma returning to existing jobs and careers. There were some tea planters returning to Assam, Darjeeling, the Duars, and the

Terai a man from Binney's cotton mills in Madras—all in all a great bunch of people whose company he enjoyed in the sports and dancing and sessions of drinking and yarn spinning. There were storms in Biscay and even a blow in the Med, but there were no gangways thick and slimy with vomit and no choked lavatories which had to be cleaned out by the troops. Otherwise it was sunshine all the way to Bombay. Ceylon understandably 'Serendip'! Galle and the Galle Face Hotel, the Planters' Club, Mt Lavinia, Newaralia, and the GOH in Colombo, all great fun, great enjoyment, great company. A rough sea-stormy ride down Australia's west coast brought the Stratheden to Fremantle where the first chilly Australian beer nearly cracked his teeth.

He and an English chap from Uganda Post Office took the train from Fremantle to the city of Perth where they took buses to various points of amazing beauty on the Swan River and applied some effort to accustoming themselves to icy-cold beer. This was a scene of broad streets with little traffic and cars parked any old how by broad footpaths covered by shady slim pillared verandahs. It was as if everyone in town was on holiday, they moved with almost languorous ease suntanned and lightly clad. In the shipping offices and banks, clerks looked like clerks in pressed white shirts and striped ties; the women were slightly less floral in their clothing than in other offices, shops, and in the streets. It was very hot but the air was champagne clear. On the shores of the Swan River, under tall gum trees one could stand in the shade and gaze across an astounding spread of glittering, grey-green water which divided the metropolis on the north side from what appeared to a pleasant suburbia on the south. In the city gardens, there was a cooling breeze up from the ocean not far away. Some beautiful old buildings of a gold rush past graced the broad streets of the business city and it seemed that anywhere a flower, a shrub, or a tree could grow in peace, there was a park, spreading and spacious or tiny and gracious. Above it all, was a bright blue heaven. A very attractive place to live, he thought.

Melbourne was quite different; again they had taken the train up to the heart of it and wandered amongst quite magnificent

colonial buildings that spoke of prosperity and good times—
whether present or past, they could not tell. As in Perth, they were
caught up in a kind of spiritual incandescence, swept into a world
of young people in bright colours and bare arms; it was Brighton
at high temperature and even stranger accents, with obviously
large communities of Greeks. Certainly the people in the streets
spoke English. But there was something different about the way
they looked. It wasn't only the clothes they wore, even city suits
worn by men, obviously in the business centre, though broadly
similar, seemed to be of a different cut and more puzzlingly
seemed to be worn differently. There seemed too to be a different
style of locomotion; females certainly seemed to stride out with a
confident air. Except for examples of the every old and the very
poor, there seemed to be fewer older people, and older women
seemed more frequently to wear lipstick and rouge and youthful,
lighter-coloured clothing than their English city counterparts. If a
man appeared as if out for a stroll his whole body and movement
told you so. He wouldn't be wearing a jacket or tie and his shirt
would be open at the neck, and if wearing a hat at all, there
was even a marginally more rakish angle about it than normal.
Barbers must have made a decent living if the neat short haircuts
were any indicator. Everyone looked cleaned and scrubbed, their
clothing neat and footwear smartly polished. They looked like
grown-up examples of good parenting. For all of those charming
differences, there was a strong declaration of Englishness. Leaving
Port Melbourne, the big ship went south across Port Phillip Bay past
shoreside settlements and towns backed by a visibly vast hinterland
out again into the Southern Ocean. It would continue east then
and turned the corner, northward into the Pacific Ocean to their
destination in Port Jackson.

Nothing can prepare anybody for the beauty and magnitude
of the panorama which almost literally strikes and dazzles the
eyes of a person lucky to stand on a top deck of a liner coming
around the Heads and entering Sydney Harbour on a shining
blue-bright midsummer's day.

A gulf of sea stretching ahead for miles, with an arched
bridge of curved iron is the focal point in the distance. Port,
starboard and ahead, sparkling windowed houses, set among

trees, climb steep rocky heights surrounding every bay and inlet (and there are so many of them!) clinging there by some unfathomable magic. That must be the city, the tall buildings clustered higgledy-piggledy to the left of the bridge, glistening, or blackened by shadows, holding each its territory on what must have been a rocky outcrop. It would become identifiable soon. Powered vessels have a tendency to bustle when they get the chance and the broad reaches of Sydney Harbour—Port Jackson—allows them that chance. There are green ferries plying between the Heads, the city, and many of the inlets (bustling). Because it is a large international port, freighters and tankers of every line and flag are going and coming without need to consider the level of the tide (bustling, though seemingly more sedately), yachts bustling (when beating), and every imaginable kind of small craft (a concert of bustling). Oh, heavens, what a sight! A nervous moment, or more, when the certainty of the tall mast being torn out when it strikes the underside of the bridge, as it surely will, is by some legerdemain of the skipper, averted, and the huge towering vessel is turned, with the aid of tugs (bustling) into Pyrmont Harbour docks alongside the low, puny wharf, as gently as a cat lying down. What a port of arrival from which to begin a new life!

He had been in touch with Jill and Emma advising his ETA. They very wisely decided not come to the quay at Pyrmont. Being the final port, getting his trunk ashore from his cabin, where it had spent the voyage, was simplicity itself.

Simplicity was not the scene on the wharf. Derricks with cargo nets hoist were swinging overhead, in directions only their operators and stevedores knew, to designated portions of the wharf where they would swiftly descend and 'wharfies' would move forward to extricate the baggage. There were vans, lorries, cars, scores of people, passengers claiming luggage, as Roddy was his trunk, vehicles doing services for the ship, lines and pipes were being connected an apparent chaos in which each person calmly executed his task. It was only when he had organized himself a taxi and was leaving the dock that he could become aware of all the surrounding vessels, all with derricks swinging and the hustle (and bustle) going on around them.

The sights surrounding him now continued to build upon a different kind of excitement than that which had begun when the Stratheden steamed up the harbour. Now the taxi was climbing up from the dock onto the top end of York Street. There it was! And in quick time despite the traffic, he was on it, and now crossing—the world-famous Sydney Harbour Bridge. What an important moment he felt it to be. Next the taxi was turning down to the left into a little loop from Milson's Point to Kirribilli and pulled up before a square block of two-storied red-brick apartments exactly to Jill's instructions. He paid the taxi driver whose intelligence picture of the arriving Englishman lacked only a few details for completion. Emma had gone to Noumea as part of a work project on a French vessel trading around Noumea, Tahiti, and other French possessions in the Pacific, from the line whose Australian interests her company looked after. Knowing it was unlikely anyone would be home on Roddy's arrival, he went to the apartment next door to pick up a key as Jill had planned. Dawn who was Jill's friendly neighbour, opened the front door and ushered Roddy into the apartment. Having gone down and brought up his trunk, Dawn took him to a broad front window of three glass panels. He looked out to the underside of the bridge, where one of its massive stone pillars with mighty curved steel girders of the structure bolted into it. Just out of sight behind their heads, the Bradfield Highway left the bridge and bore the road traffic northward on Pacific Highway, the tracks of the local passenger railway also to the stations on the North Shore Line. The dark shadows of the bridge were contrasted with brilliant blue sky, and sparkling green water, foamed by passing motor powered craft moving in all directions, this powerful perspective just the width of the local roadway below and a green verge away. While they were at the window, a small ferry craft pulled up at the small river wharf just down there; some passengers alighted and the waiting Kirribilli people stepped aboard. Pulling away from the wharf, the little ferry confidently thrust its bows across the river traffic and headed for Circular Quay on the other side, which Roddy could just fix with Dawn's help.

As they stood there, she suggested that since would be a few hours till Jill got home, he may wish to have a wander about Kirribilli or even take a ferry across to the city.

'You can hardly lose your way; the bridge's a bit hard to miss. Where you get off the ferry at Circular Quay is where you pick it up to get back, but on the way back, before it drops you here, you'll have a harbour cruise to another couple of wharves so you can be a sightseeing tourist for a little longer.' The apartment was very welcoming, and courtesy of the absent Emma, he was to have her room which dawn showed him along with all the other important rooms. It would be very pleasant to go back and meet Jill there. He took the key which Dawn had given him and his camera and he was off—off into something entirely new. Just gazing as he waited was a continuation of the excitement which had scarcely ebbed since much earlier in the morning. Then there he was on the waters of Sydney Harbour with lots of other people doing what he couldn't imagine people in cities do. He had had no experience of cities. He had read Dickens and imagined the horrible lives of people in London and Paris, but Shakespeare and historical study scarcely prepare one for a city. The quiet introductions to Fremantle; and Melbourne where he had for the first time in his life actually seen trams, had not totally prepared him for what he was seeing around him now. Everything was so close together, on top of one another, not that Sydney had many 'skyscrapers' at that time. The noise, in a different, higher register, was like being on the outer edges of a battlefield—clanging, grinding, roaring, pervasive, continuous. What he knew of cities was historical. He knew nothing of this city and its history. For the present, he allowed himself to approach learning of it through eyes, ears and feelings. He knew that these impressions, however briefly implanted, would be with him forever. To confirm its English connections in similar ways to those of Fremantle and Melbourne, the name 'Pitt Street' where he was now walking, was surely a connection with the Younger, or the Elder, of British parliamentary fame.

It was that time of day when a beer and something to eat would go down well. A few yards on, to his right, the Ship Inn Hotel hove into sight. He entered what must be one of Sydney's

older buildings. He found a pleasant bar the walls of which
were covered with original works of art in frames of every style
and dimension hung, touching each other all the way around
three walls; there were oils, acrylics, some sparkling water
colours of harbour and rural scenes. There was a cluster of four
brilliant oils of thoroughbreds, and later, he was introduced
to their artist, Jim Croft, a short dapper man with snow-white
hair appearing, curling from under the rim of his smart trilby,
wearing the dress of that elegance and style favoured by those
connected with the sport of kings, it could easily be believed
might once have been a jockey.

Jim Croft was in one of the little groups along the bar, and
Roddy found a way through between two. When the barman
asked him what size glass he wanted, he gestured to those
the men on his left were drinking from. One of the men by
whom he was standing shoulder to shoulder had observed the
conversation with the barman and, turning to Roddy, enquired,
'Hello, new arrival, are you?' The man was short and round
and the face before Roddy was round too, pink, friendly, and
smiling; his head was shiny, white, and slightly pink around his
throat and neck, totally without hair obviously not the result of
painfully close shaving but some internal element.

'Yes, I am, could scarcely be newer. I came in on the
Stratheden this morning.'

'Well, you don't want to be on your Pat Malone, come and
meet this mob. My name's Les Dixon,' he said, offering his
hand. Roddy later discovered that he was the creator of a comic
strip called 'Bluey and Curley', about the scrapes of the two
archetypal Australian characters.

It happened that 'this mob' was a group of artists, writers
and cartoonists and a few others connected with newspapers
and periodicals who were in town to deliver their artwork and
editorial copy to their various journals. They ritually met here
on this day every week. It was not long before he realized how
ardently they were in love with their country, Australia. While
he was learning about them, they had extracted from him a
good part of his story and that his first priority was to find a job.
In the group was John Wilson, an ex-RAAF fighter pilot now

running a very successful advertising agency not far from the Ship and those present frequently provided copy or art for his clients. He had finished his first beer and heard two of the three women in the group ask the barman for sausage sandwiches. The idea appealed and he asked the barman, 'Could I order one too please?' he asked.

'You certainly can,' he said. 'Cash in advance. Delivery five minutes,' said the barman, putting on the impression of a slick trader. Another barman was setting up beers on the bar and John Wilson handed him one. 'You don't need to join the shout. We don't want to see you cashing cheques in a pub first day on shore. Cheers!' he said, raising his glass to Roddy. 'Don't worry, mate, enjoy it while you can, it won't last. Don't come in here next week, a shout'll cost you half the national debt.'

'Talking of cheque books, I have to go to the Bank of New South Wales to get one. Is that far from here?'

'First things first, we've got to get you a job. We need to get you something that pays well where you can live without spending all your money on digs. D'ye mind what the work is or where it is?'

'Not at all.' And he meant it. 'I agree with your reasoning,' replied Roddy.

'Good, we'll finish this beer and we're off.' John Wilson and Roddy said cheerio to the 'mob' that had been so cheerfully welcoming and interested in his story. Everyone wished him good luck. John Wilson put a large denomination note on the bar, put his hat on, and they left. As they walked, John Wilson told Roddy about a construction plan for a hydro-electric scheme to build series of huge dams on the Snowy River. His friend Chris Paton ran an employment service for companies involved in the scheme; his office was on the third floor of a three-story building in George Street which involved simply walking through a joining street. After very brief introductions, and no suggestion of seeing a CV, he was asked whether he had a current driving license, got Roddy to fill in an application form. Chris Paton seemed happy and lifted a telephone to his ear and heard him say, 'Harry, I've got a good English bloke here who needs a job right away. He's bright, capable, and 'fit as a mallee bull.' There followed a brief period when Chris was listening; he turned to Roddy and asked, 'Are you an assisted migrant? Can you drive a truck? When can you leave?'

'I haven't unpacked. Give me time to get my trunk from Kirribilli and I'm ready to move.'

'Right, Harry, Sunday morning would be fine. I'm going to the Imperial Services Club before I go home. Could one of your girls drop the paperwork and Roddy's joining instructions up to me there? You'll come yourself? Oh good, I'll buy you a beer and you can meet your new employee.'

It all happened in the course of half an hour or less. Roderick Fraser Mckenzie was now an employee of Wood Bagshaw Civil Engineering; he had a job!

John Wilson was very pleased, and Roddy found difficulty in expressing the great gratitude he was feeling towards him and Chris; at least he would have the opportunity of buying them a beer at the ISC.

'Thanks for that, Chris, old son, I knew you'd work the magic,' John said to Chris who had stood up to shake hands with Roddy and to congratulate him on 'deciding to take a role in building Australia'. 'Right, next move, Roddy, is to get you to the bank,' said John briskly, as he just as briskly rose to his feet. 'It's almost next door to the ISC, so come up to the club first and I'll introduce you; you can then drop back round to the bank and get your cheque book. Your first cheque will be my talent spotter's fee. C'mon.'

As they strode up George Street, John was able to relate that Chris had been shot down over Burma and ended up as a POW in Changi. He had devoted his early post-war years to finding work for ex-POWs mainly, but any ex-servicemen in general. He hadn't made a million yet, but he had expanded the business incredibly and the big recruitment programs he was running for professionals, tradesmen, and labourers for the companies involved in the Snowy Mountains Scheme were quite lucrative, so anytime now. Soon they had reached the top of Martin Place where on his right Roddy found himself in front of the mighty marble and stone facade of Australia's biggest bank, the Bank of New South Wales.

'Right, that's where you'll be coming for your cheque book, the club is just round this corner, so we'll turn right here.' In a few more paces, they were into Barrack Street, and on their left-hand side, there were the handsome doors of the old building which housed the Imperial Services Club. Climbing the stairs carpeted in dark blue and bearing the club's crest as a pattern motif, they stepped into a room with deep carpets and a bar whose old carved and finely shaped, dark, polished timber work made Roddy feel instinctively comfortable. The tall windows had long curtains tied back with gold cords on one wall Australian air force blue, on another in navy blue, and the third in deep military red. There were other continuities: the bar was smallish and three sided with a decorative timber panelling coming down all round. On the back wall of the bar there, rows of pewter pots were hanging, many owner-specific, and many others for general use, the rails were of polished brass and timber. Roddy was introduced to Bruce Lockwood, the creative director of the city's and Australia's largest advertising agencies. He was also introduced by John to a senior steward, who looked like, and proved to have been an army WOII, as Lieutenant Roddy Mckenzie, Forty-third Royal Highland Regiment, Korea, two battles of the Hook, wounded but miraculously healed by the sight of his first Australian nurse at the base hospital. The old steward registered this information indelibly and it would be his delight to point Roddy out to others who may further along the bar passing on this top-secret intelligence, to which only he had access. Chris would be arriving later, and doubtless John and Bruce had important business things to talk about, it was appropriate that Roddy could withdraw.

The banking chamber he entered was magnificent yet escaped being opulent or vulgar. The ceiling was high, allowing a gallery on four sides to provide a major floor area for the executive offices. In front of anyone entering, there was a highly polished booth of carved timber with two occupants whose task was to assist enquiring clients the category Roddy Mckenzie fitted. From his inner breast pocket, he took out the letter provided to him by the bank in London and began his enquiry about a cheque book. As in London, he was led to a small ground floor office where the process would be conducted. 'There will probably be a little time involved in the process, so I'm wondering whether I could speak on your telephone with Miss Jill Lowing? I don't want to interrupt her work, but if you could just say to her that I'm here for my cheque book and that if she's got a minute, I'd like to speak to her?'

'Certainly, Mr. Mckenzie, I'll do that now.' In a moment, he was able to say, 'Miss Lowing would like me to take you up.' Roddy was taken to the lift whose wide concertina doors were of highly polished brass. A small old man in the bank's livery greeted them and glided them up to the gallery floor. Jill's office, into which he was ushered, was rather grand. She could hold small meetings there. When his guide opened the tall door, Jill put down her pen and leapt from behind her substantial timber desk. She came towards him across the space, taking all of him into her examining gaze.

'Roddy. How wonderful to see you again. You're looking well.' With no regard for the waiting guide, still at the door, she threw her arms round him and gave him a kiss on the cheek. 'I'm dying to hear your news of Ranelagh and Miette and Hugh. Sit down for a minute or two while your cheque book is being organized.' She turned to the guide at the door and said, 'Thank you, Elaine, would you ring me when Mr. Mackenzie's cheque book is ready or if there is any other information you need?'

'Yes, Miss Lowing. Nice to meet you, Mr. Mckenzie. Welcome to the Bank of New South Wales.' Roddy said thank you and she was gone.

'Roddy, I can't wait to get all your news, what an evening we're going to have!'

Then she realized she may have been a bit presumptuous. And her face saddened. 'That is unless you have planned something. Such a pity Em's away. She was so looking forward to seeing you.'

'Jill, of course I have nothing planned. I want to celebrate seeing you again. Oh, and I've got something I want you to celebrate with me. What would you like to do this evening? I'd like to take you out somewhere. So much has happened to me today. You couldn't possibly imagine. When I've done the account administration things, I have to go to the Imperial Services Club to meet two people who have been the genies of my lamp. When are you going to be free? When can I meet you?'

'I can't meet you at the ICS because women are only allowed on special occasions. However we have an executive bar here which really is quite nice, why don't we meet here and we make a plan?'

'Sounds splendid; am I suitably dressed?' He was in his 'general purpose officers' walking-out rig' of blue jacket, grey trousers, and brown trilby.

'Perfectly; when you've finished at the club, ring this number. That will alert me and the doorman that you are coming. The door is on this Barrack Street side almost opposite the door of the ICS. If your friends would like to come, please bring them.'

Jill's telephone rang. The banking process had been completed. 'Oh, Roddy, it's so lovely to see you.' She took his hand and led him to the door. As he descended in the lift, he was still trying to sort out the luck, the people, the rapidity of events, seeing Jill again, and—oh my god—a job!

When he rang the bell at the Barrack Street private entrance to the bank, an elderly man in bank livery let him in and showed him up a broad flight of stairs to the staff club. 'Miss Lowing is expecting you, Mr. Mckenzie, let me take your hat, it will be on a rack inside.' Jill was delighted that he had come, she introduced him to one or two of the nearest managerial types, and their meeting at Cowes was quite a story. There were attempts at describing Ranelagh, Hugh, Miette, and the polo, everyone listened with avid interest especially those who had not yet made the European *hajj* and were keen to pick up tips for travel.

'When are you going to tell about this event that has made you so excited?' she was keen to know.

'When I've bought a cold bottle of champagne and we are sitting in your lovely apartment looking at that great view or we're in your favourite restaurant under sparkling chandeliers,' Roddy suggested.

'Let's do both. Now that we've met and are ready to move, why don't we leave after this? We can buy the champagne on the way.'

'Splendid.'

The evening sun had begun to dip, so the view out of Jill's window should be perfectly lit.

'People who've had a hard day in the city must find this ferry ride home perfectly relaxing. I can't imagine a better way of going to and from work,' ventured Roddy.

'You're right. When I've had to go to other cities, I always find it difficult to imagine putting up with their daily travel. Mind you, not all of the Sydney suburbs are as ideal as this. That's why Emma, Verity, and I just can't imagine us moving. We have easy access to anything we want to do, although keeping a car here is a bit of a problem. When these suburbs were established, there were very few cars, so houses were built without garages and were so positioned on the building blocks, there was not enough on the sides to put one—even sewers are something of a novelty in these parts.'

They had arrived in the apartment, and Roddy felt drawn to the window at once.

'Don't know about you Roddy, but I'm going to change into something more relaxed and prepare for the champagne. There's only one bathroom which you'll find is a bit girly. I'll use it first if you don't mind. Won't be long.'

He went to Emma's room and opened his trunk. He had now begun to think of re-selection and storage and buying the extra kit for 'The Snowies'. Tomorrow was Friday, so he should have plenty time to fix that. He had just finished his share of the bathroom and was wearing a soft shirt, light woollen trousers, and some old soft shoes when Verity arrived home. Jill did the introduction.

Verity had been to RADA, had studied acting, and had in fact had a few parts before going back to study stage production; she then joined TV Channel 8 at Gore Hill not far from where they now were and where she produced Australian drama. She was tall, very slim and 'rangy', dark haired, and Spanish skinned with dancing dark eyes. Now that Roddy's entire audience was seated, it was time to pop the cork and pour in celebration of—and he made them wait for his announcement—'I start work as a navvy on the Snowy Mountains Hydro Electric Scheme on Monday!'

'Congratulations!' the girls cried.

'How on earth did you manage that!' asked Jill. 'Was that because of the genies from your invisible lamp?'

'Exactly,' he replied, 'I wish I had Verity's drama training because it is an amazing yarn.'

'Tell it like it is,' said Verity, mocking a film director.

He went through the story of his day beginning by saying, 'If you don't believe me, I won't blame you, and if it weren't for the employment documents and my bus time for Sunday morning now in the room of the Polynesian Emma, I wouldn't; and almost still can't believe it myself.' He went on to relate every detail of his day almost as much to check its actuality for himself as for the girls who appeared to be sincerely fascinated, but no suspension of belief or particularly vivid imagination were required. They lived in Australia, in Sydney of the fifties where the incredible was the norm.

It was decided that they would do something more interesting on Friday and Saturday evenings and do a low-key meal that evening with some wine and a bit of folksy music which was all the go. Presumably the group was very good.

They simply walked up the street to the Kirribilli Hotel which was as welcoming, or more so, than Sydney pubs generally are. The vernacular decor was ceramic tiles up the walls to head height with 'grano' work cement and broken stone floors. It seemed highly likely that when the last patron had staggered out, the entire interior would be hosed down like an abattoir. The room they went into was pleasant enough. The decor was everywhere in pure colours even the wood work which, when installed, would have been varnished, now was the richest red ever recorded by a spectrometer; all around not a shade or a tone was in view except for the window curtains which attempted to compensate for this lack by being of every insipid characterless shades and tones and with line designs of every geometrical shape possible to be imagined. The effect was on the eyes caused a screeching noise in the brain. But it was all about people really, wasn't it? If you chose not to stare at the curtains all night, date a better-looking sheila. The food was steaks, chicken, Wiener schnitzel, or roasts all palatably 'home style', with three 'veg' and boats of thick sauces. Their choice of wines was Penfold's Dalwood Hermitage and a Marsanne from Pokolbin. The music program was pleasant enough, mainly folk from a religious base, which wasn't by any means 'blues,' almost totally strummed on acoustic guitars. There were one or two slightly Latinized numbers, but the guitar playing couldn't do much for them, which rather let down the amazingly good singing by the guitarists. They listened while they ate, and then moved to another room where they could talk. And that's where they really began to enjoy themselves because they had lots of stories. At a point in the evening, Roddy's need for rugged clothing, including work boots, was touched upon and he was given instructions about how to go to a big store by 'the railway', that is, Sydney's central railway station, where they had all of the kinds of items he would need, including another bag so that his trunk could be left behind.

Friday was an ordinary Sydney summer day, the usual clear blue skies which gave the water the opportunity to dance in the breeze, making patterns, constantly splintering, fleeting away to form a sheet of glittering glass which rapidly tired of its orthodoxy, broke up and rushed off to disappear in white shards. The trees were greener than they should have been and stirred restlessly in the good sailors' breeze that was coming from the south-east. Getting to 'the railway' was literally straightforward. He took a tram on George Street at the Quay and rode it all the way to the central station. He enjoyed the grinding, sometimes jerking, and rocking ride. The street was not particularly broad and the buildings seemed at certain points to hang over it. Nevertheless there were two tramlines in the centre and a motor vehicle lane on each side. Unless the cruel world had overwhelmed one, the stepping off the kerb would not result in just a 'jaywalking' fine under the strictly policed laws, it would be final. The pedestrian footways were crowded with humans who, like sailors on warships kept to their own side of gangways, seemed equally rigidly drilled in pavement practices. There were shops of every kind on his side, their merchandise offering to satisfy every human need from a fruit drink to 'a bag of fruit' ready to wear.

The girls were right. This was the store he needed. Selection was simplicity itself. In no time at all he had secured all he needed, including some heavy elastic sided work boots which he had never seen before, however, as luck had it, he was able to observe a big rough bloke try on some new ones to replace the battered pair lying beside him. Surely this was recommendation indeed. His purchases included a tough army-surplus Commando rucksack into which he could stow the lot, and while still in the store, he was able to try on his pack to make a first trial fit of the straps: it felt good. Right.: now the day lay before him.

At the Quay, he had picked up some tourist brochures from which he had found out, while the old tram ground and screeched its way up George Street that the art gallery was a nice little walk away. He was able to fold his jacket carefully across his pack under the closure flap and snug it firmly without creasing. The walk was particularly pleasant. He put himself onto Elizabeth Street and headed back in the direction of the Quay. Soon he was off the road and walking through Hyde Park, and when he left that, he could continue on grass, under beautiful indigenous, native, and exotic trees right to the gallery. He had to thank St Ninian's Academy for his first very basic introduction to art and painting, however, it was to Jane Dugal that most thanks was due for she had introduced him to galleries, to ideas of classical art, and through that approach to the artists and the histories of their intentions when they had created their works. Jane had that lovely capacity to make her knowledge so pleasantly accessible. He had then acquired one or two books, now stored at the Lodge in Fearnas, to help in his study because he was eager to know more. 'One day I shall attempt to paint,' he had told himself many times, often recalling having had a painting shown in a St Ninian's student art exhibition, and he knew that when he did, his medium would be watercolour. With that in mind, he always searched galleries for watercolour works and felt elated when he came across a Russell Flint, or indeed any watercolourist whose style appealed to him because he had chosen the style he wanted to influence the work he would do one day... one day. Lots of other things were to be learned; and to be done first.

The Art Gallery of New South Wales stunned him, thrilled him; it was full of riches beyond belief, the work of artists who were even now drawing him into the love of Australia that Les Tanner, Eric Joliffe, Peter Harrigan, in fact all the group at the Ship were so fervently in love with; John Wilson, and Chris with his hut at Khancoban, Bruce Lockwood at the club, each had his own expression of this spirit. He could feel his blood already stirring, and soon he would be going out into that great Australia: The Bush. After three hours, he was saturated, reeling—and dying for a beer.

With that in mind, he withdrew his pack from the cloakroom at the gallery, and pack shouldered, he was off—off on a new tack now, but heading for an old mark. He went across the park to its limit; crossed Elizabeth, Castlereagh, and Pitt Streets; and marched up Martin Place where he stopped, turned to face the cenotaph, stood smartly to attention, and bowed his head in respect, his hat held on his breast. After two minutes, he took a pace to the rear, put his hat on, turned smartly, and continued his march with the magnificent Bank of New South Wales, and Jill. Before him, the sensual prospect of a cold frothy beer awaiting him not far away. He asked Dudley, the warrant officer, where he could stow his kit. In the cloakroom, he removed his well-folded jacket which had a Hampshire's tie in the pocket, from below the buckled flap on his pack, and went to the bathrooms where he could freshen up and put his tie on.

The club was packed with members and their guests were beginning to practice for the weekend. When he got to the bar, Dudley, the WO, was quick to note his arrival and got to him immediately. 'What can I get you, Mr. Mckenzie?' he asked. When Roddy had a cold pewter of beer on the bar, Dudley asked, 'Would you like me to introduce you, sir?'

'That would be very good of you. Dudley, yes, please do.'

He turned to two men, both in business suits, who were just beginning a practice round. 'Gentlemen, may I introduce Lieutenant Mckenzie who has just joined us from the Naval and Military Club UK?'

'Thank you, Dudley, yes,' said one who was a nuggetty dark-haired man with some energy who introduced himself as Lawrie

Badge; his companion was tall, slim, and fair and was called Peter Tracy. They had been out of the city all week, Lawrie in the wholesale timber import business and Peter had a small paint manufacturing business. They had been to their individual offices, done all of the things a week away in 'the bush' required, and saying to their staffs, 'Have a good weekend,' they left for the club. Monday would demand an early start, so they had decided that for a couple of days, they'd be at home in a different world and this seemed like a good way to start. Of course the military connections were the launching point of their chatting with Roddy. These two knew each other because they were both platoon commanders in the reserve Thirtieth Battalion Royal New South Wales Regiment.

Roddy had to explain his tie and how he had become entitled to wear it, having begun his story with Erik Barron's encouragement and as much as brevity allowed of the rest of his story to this point, and his Sunday morning launch into the wide blue yonder. They sensed that he had become infected with the sunburnt country bug and he told them how it had really begun in Korea with his Third Battalion contacts. Their questions prompted new enlargements to a further infection by Mick Lowing in Kenya which led to Jill, the bank, and how he had met her and her friend Emma in Cowes. He wanted to ask them about their lives, their Australia, and so when they sat on the carpeted stairs and ate the delicious oxtail, which was the choice of many who hadn't arranged to be in, or didn't want to be in, the overbooked dining room, they had switched to red wine and returned to the bar. Roddy was beginning to think he should store some capacity for the evening, so explaining his position, he thanked Lawrie and Peter for their hospitality, cornered Dudley and thanked him, repacked his jacket, which would not have taken well to being under the shoulder straps of his pack which he slung on, and made his way to the quay for a crossing to Kirribilli.

Leaving his pack in the apartment, he set off to walk the peninsula up into the Neutral Bay area following the water where he could. When the girls got home, he had showered and changed and had a bottle of champagne chilling in the fridge.

They were in a Friday evening mood when they arrived at the Kirribilli apartment, and the bubbles they were now merrily sharing had been preceded by Friday afternoon's mandatory drinks at their offices. Through Verity's web of connections, a table at appropriate proximity to the stage had been organized for the Music Hall Theatre Restaurant at Neutral Bay. The 'new' theatre, fresh from its conversion from a Hoyts cinema, would accommodate five hundred patrons. Some would be seated at dining tables where the stalls once were, where Verity had booked a table, the rest would sit in theatre seating around the hall. All were invited to boo and hiss the villains, sigh for the tragic maidens, and sing lustily in the choruses. Their night was to be special, not just because they were attending, but because the planned bill of Victorian bellow drama would not begin until Monday with *East Lynne*. Tonight's bill would comprise skits, excerpt scenes, stand-up comedy, and songs. It all sounded appropriate to their mood. And so did the whole mock Victorian scene. The atmosphere in the dining area was jolly and a very pleasant meal had been enjoyed. Verity spotted and acknowledged quite a few stage personalities and people from the television stations on Gore Hill. Some came over to say hello, and later, as the evening passed and the acts had effectively livened the audience, moving from table to table became the thing. Roddy was loving it. As the acts on the stage had changed, so did the people who were at their table. Barry Creyton had ceased being a despicable villain in black tie and tails, opera cape and top hat, and of course, black 'pencil' moustache, and became a very personable bloke who joined the table's chat and talked about his experience of London and drifted off to another table. Others, some who were appearing on the night, and some not, collected at their table sometimes in twos or threes, and it was when this happened it was especially pleasing for Roddy because there was talk among them of their stage experiences in Britain, Europe, and Australia. They were, each of them, normal people sometimes with very mundane things to say about where they were living, problems with lovers, offers of parts, auditions which didn't work, families that they missed who lived in distant Australian places, doing country and interstate tours. Roddy was fascinated. During the course of the evening, he had met and spoken with Noeline Brown, Gordon Chater, Carol Raye, Johnny Ladd, and the man and wife whose theatrical venture *The Music Hall* was, George and Lorna Miller. The world which offered him life offered him fascination and novelty, and even in the midst of its happening, his awareness focused on his good fortune and the meaning for him of the spate of new experiences on which he was being swept along, his head, confidently, well above the flow. Among these ruminations, just rarely, and only momentarily, he wondered about the possible answer to the questions: where might his landfall be and whether he would recognize it? Right now, in these present days, did the questions and their answers matter? Tomorrow, yet another treat was in store. He was going to crew in a *Jubilee* at Royal Sydney Yacht Squadron.

The fact that he was going to sail on a *Jubilee* was conditional upon their being a crew vacancy. The Jubilees were eighteen-foot wooden boats with a crew of three; frequently *in extremis,* two hardworking, skilled sailors could race one. Jill had suggested they walk cross to the club, so after a late and leisurely breakfast, that's what they did—and a most enjoyable walk it was. The leafy suburb of Kirribilli functions on narrow uphill-and-down dale, twisting, little streets. The old houses of red-tiled roofs, red brickwork, and generally, woodwork of startling whiteness settle into the earth and rock behind low walls under the trees of great variety . The houses are surrounded by the most beautiful, much-loved, long-cared-for gardens behind the stone walls low or high. Every turn of street seems to offer its own painting subject of the harbour, framed in foliage tossed in the breeze, and always that pale cerulean, or sometimes, cobalt blue swatch of sky visually pushing the foliage towards you. The club was an assemblage of old buildings following a promontory height, down to the jetties where some of the bigger yachts were moored. .

Jill had given Roddy a briefing on the eighteen-foot wooden boats whose design had its birth after a disastrous, destructive storm in Port Phillip Bay, across which Roddy had but recently steamed into and out of Melbourne, and a tough, handy reasonably priced yacht was needed. A Victorian named Charles Peel undertook the design, and on George V's Jubilee year, 1935, the first yachts were ready, and as Jill pointed out, one of those first boats was still being raced on Port Phillip Bay. She showed him the fleet, lined-up side by side on their rail track 'siding' from which they were launched and retrieved. They climbed the steps to the sailors' bar where the major, very noticeable, activity was a mass of crew members around high tables demolishing meat pies and quaffing beer. Since their late breakfast had scarcely been walked off, they contented themselves with a beer while they investigated the crewing situation. One of the much-raced boats, with a much-raced skipper and crew, was minus its third man. It was agreed amongst the skippers but mainly by Mauri Perrott that 'Jilly' should race with him and the 'new chum' should sail with Winston Pratt and Bob Whitney partners in an architecture practice, with whom she normally sailed. When asked about his sailing experience, he had to be somewhat political and thought it best to approach his description without mentioning things like Fastnet and Biscay; he kept it brief and said he had operated winches, trimmed genoas, hoisted and trimmed spinnakers, but realized that each yacht made its own demands and that he would do as he was told unless the occasion demanded otherwise, and thanked them for taking him on. They noted that his sailing whites appeared to have been worn at least once or twice before and that his shirt bore the name *Fear Naught*. Upon their observations, they made no comment.

The start was a short beat to a mark close to the clubhouse, and then there would be a series of spinnaker runs, or reaches depending on the opinions of skippers, and sometimes crews, and a reach to a mark near Quarantine. A spinnaker run or a reach to one more mark near the Sow and Pigs marked the turning point for three more marks and a beat to finish.

They had a little scull around before the start when he saw that *Ilsa* had runners to tension the shrouds on the mast each time the boat changed tack; on, on the windward, off on the loo'ard sides, he found it would be one of his jobs to tend to these—he would also haul and lower head sail and spinnaker halyards. The start was good because Winston had positioned himself on the outer end of the line. As they rounded the first mark, Roddy had the spinnaker smartly to the mast head and the halyard made fast to a horned cleat down by the centreboard casing. Bob had the pole in the clew and the guy clipped on to the mast. Roddy hardened on his windward runner crossed and freed off the loo'ard. Seeing the sheet lying ready on the port side, he unhesitatingly clipped it on seeing first that it was clear and outside the shroud which he had freed off. The down haul was on the guy pulled on, and Roddy turned it on the winch. With a sweet snap-crack, the big red-and-white-striped spinnaker broke out of its rubber tie bands setting without a waver or a ripple or a sag, and set like the wing of a large exotic bird. Bob took charge of the guy, and Winston passed the sheet to Roddy. He was obviously going to be the trimmer. He passed the sheet around the empty port winch and went up to sit on the loo'ard side. Bob tidied up the head sail and its sheets. They were up and running. They rounded the next mark like an Olympic team and were crossing the harbour to the next and a decision was to be made about what to do with the tanker which was moving very rapidly up the centre of the stream towards the bridge. Winston was calculating the angles and *Ilsa's* speed. They were speeding closer to towering fast-moving hull. The harbour rules are 'sail gives way'. Winston decided, Bob did not dispute. They were up wind of it. There was nothing in their way. They had just come under the towering bows when there was a 'ping' and a crack. The spinnaker began to fall. Rod leapt to the mast, seized the halyard as high as he could. Hand over hand, hauled with all his speed and strength, his arms blurring in the action. The sail which filled immediately would pull his arms out. Bob went aft and rapidly took up the slack behind the deck block. Roddy took both the guy and the sheet; the trim needed was minor. *Ilsa* had picked up speed. The skyscraper bow was feet away, and *Ilsa* was on the edge of its bow wave surge. 'No! Let's just get past that!' they were thinking. A surge now would toss their boat about, push the wind out of her sail; they'd lose the set and damned near stop her. They'd lose speed. Second, mere seconds. They missed the wave. Their track was kept by Winston, the trim was perfect. They were through. *Ilsa's* momentum was rapidly leaving the big vessel's wave in the wake of her own gurgling transom.

The spinnaker halyard had been found a belaying spot. Away back in time and the reason for it forgotten, a ring bolt had been put through the keel abaft the dagger plate housing and halfway to the transom. No one knew quite why it had been put there, and often it had been cursed when accidentally trodden on, or a toe was stubbed. Today its presence was being worshipped. It was transformed into an artefact of rare beauty and utility. The shoot under the bow of the tanker had been one of those bonding moments that builds teams, crews, and platoons. Incidents exceed months of planned but featureless training, leaving it far behind.

Leaving things far behind is what their shoot had done to Mauri Perrott who week after week, with his crew, were first and fastest, so much so they could not possibly be handicapped further, without having to drag an anchor. Mauri had had to bear the wind turmoil of the tanker's bulk in addition to having to sail away from the mark. *Ilsa* was now innumerable lengths ahead. But there was a long way to go, and *Ilsa* had to continue faultless. Winston, Bob, and Roddy were acutely conscious of this, and if anything, it increased their focus. Getting to about halfway, another tactical decision had to be made. The mark at Quarantine Beach had been cunningly placed leaving very little space between the mark and the northern promontory. To approach that, flying a full kite would require spot-on positioning and timing of the necessary gybe, few had done it successfully, so a broad reach had become the norm for approaching and turning this mark because then yachts sailed to the next mark on another broad reach. Today was going to be different.

Their spinnaker was carrying beautifully, but it required the utmost care, because, really, they needed a reaching kite of a different cut, a bit flatter and a bit narrower; also with a narrow steel drop keel, there was every danger, as with a dinghy, that you'd trip on it and fall into a fatal broach. Anyway, they were approaching the mark. Should they douse the spinnaker? A board meeting was held with a new member at the table. 'Okay, Roddy, you first,' said the chairman (and skipper). 'Well, *Ilsa* sails very well, that spinnaker has done us proud, if we can keep the pole just off the forestay and put the keel down and aim for a spot to gybe above and shoreward of the mark, there being no other inshore hazard of course, we could round and come out the other side with our spinnaker pulling for the next mark. With due deference, suggestion only, gentlemen,' offered Roddy. The other board members silently looked at each other. As in a string quartet, out of the silence of mutual trust, came the first note: 'We'll leave the centre board down on the gybe.'

That gybe was another incident, another team success. From then on, it was roses, roses all the way. In the end, it was they who were embarrassed. They felt it disrespectful to be over the line 'first and fastest', a full three minutes before Mauri Perrott. It was light labour to put their boat on the cradle and wind it ashore on the rail, up the steep pitch, push it off on the transverse line, and hose it down inside and out.

That deference they were feeling was real, so there was no ebullient expression of emotion over their win. The two architects who very rarely stayed behind after a race, not only stayed behind but in violation for their reputation as 'tight arses', they bought Roddy a beer. It's a matter of degree, isn't it? The two, in their terms, may have been wildly celebrating. When Mauri, Jill and his crew, Tony Scarsdale (eventually) reached the bar, they came over at once to congratulate the *Ilsa* crew. Jill was so pleased that Roddy had been in a winning crew. Winston and Bob were wide-eyed when they heard Mauri Perrott say, 'Bit tame after a Fastnet and the Biscay, Roddy. But I'll bet you enjoyed it.'

'Mauri, I can't tell you how much!'

His sincerity and enthusiasm were so evident. 'When you sail with blokes who really care what the game's about . . . and God almighty . . . to sail on Sydney Harbour . . . on an Australian-designed and -built boat with a history? I'll never forget this day as long as I live. I'm only sorry that it was you we had to beat. Let me buy you a beer. Mind you, you'd have been further behind without your brilliant crew. Jill? D'ye like a beer? Mauri, what about you? D'ye like a beer? Winston, Bob, a beer?' There were beers and, of course, a post-mortem of the race, about what happened where on the course, and when. Roddy hated them. Now, he was interested, because this was about Sydney Harbour sailing.

She looked the very exemplar of a wonderful woman. That an executive in a big bank could be so 'down to earth', so totally unassuming, so perfect as a hostess, so caring that he experienced things that would contribute to his love of Australia, and then he stumbled against a newly arisen question in his mind, 'And her?' Well, let's see. It would be so easy. But he had much to do yet. Also, the ephemeral qualities of his love for Jane were still deep within him, but yes, ephemeral, part of that dreamlike world of possibility and impossibility, of match and mismatch of desire, the dream and forbiddance? What was that going to mean for his future? What was it going to mean when someone like Jill came along? 'Not now, not now,' was sounding somewhere within him, 'get on with what you need to do: get a well-found boat or build one, get your boat well provisioned, well set on its course, set, steady, trimmed, your finishing line known. Yes, there's much to be achieved.'

Just that little apart from the rest, Jill and Roddy could overhear about his quick-smart hauling of the halyard, his making the course decision for the Quarantine mark, his decision about the centre board, his sail setting. They didn't need him there to talk about that. And it would have made him very uncomfortable to be there.

He and Jill had begun, without any consciousness, to create a little subset of the post-mortem group. He got a moment, and he said quietly to Jill who was flushed by a day in the sun and so excited about Roddy being on the winning boat and Roddy being 'hers', 'You didn't know that before the race I went down and hung a chain from your transom. I happen to keep one in my pocket when I'm going racing against top-shot crews.' She knew that he knew, that it was weak humour, and she sensed where it was fitting into what was happening between them.

He had clearly in his mind that Jill was an Australian woman from 'the land', a farm-owning background; she had been to a very good school and had done brilliantly at Sydney University, she had reached a level in the nation's biggest bank long before many ever did, and a woman had to be exceptionally good to do that. She had already begun what would be a solid career of success. She was living in a wonderful social environment, she had good friends working at similar professional levels, and her future would be secure. Should she advance no further in any way, what more could she want? How could someone like he was, a beginner in every possible way, an ingénue with a future, and a capacity for success totally unknown, find a place alongside a woman like Jill?

But now there were feelings working between them; feelings he was enjoying but didn't want to have—not now.

She looked at him and he felt and saw her eyes search his face. 'What would you like to do on this, your last evening in Sydney?'

'Jill, I'm so mesmerized by you, and what you have been doing for me, the joy that you are to be with is indescribable, this place, this life and these lives around me have, quite honestly—and I mean this—literally, set my head spinning. All of what is happening is so new to me. I really am not capable of forming an idea about what we might do tonight.'

Suddenly they were brought back to the present when Winston and Bob announced their intention to leave. They were emphatic about their pleasure in sailing with Rod and that he was a 'bit of a dark horse'. 'Come down to the club again when you're back in town. Best of luck in your venture to the bush.' And they were gone.

Next, Mauri Perrott said he was going, and when he offered them a lift, they accepted. He came up for a drink on Jill's invitation and they sat on the small balcony overlooking the harbour drinking beer. 'Look, if you two are going out, I'm happy to wait until you're ready and I'll give you a lift to wherever you want to go—anywhere. It's a madhouse in Sydney on Saturday night.'

Roddy said, 'Look, I'm as free as the breeze. This all so beautifully new for me. You can't believe all the good things that have happened for me since I stepped ashore. Why don't

I continue with the flow of good fortune? Jill, whatever you decide, we'll do that and I'll claim to have thought of it.'

'Two thoughts flashed into my mind', Jill. said 'I thought of the absolute singularity of Doyle's at Watson's Bay and how everyone should experience that. Then I thought of you as a young soldier after a horrible war and how you might like to see the bright lights and I thought of the high-kicking dancing girls at the Chevron. Actually there's good food and wine and there is usually a very good cabaret—but we'd have to take to take potluck on that.'

Then Mauri added: 'Well, your potluck could be good luck. Dave Allen and Eartha Kitt are double billing, mm, and I think they could be more than double billing. Joking apart, the dance troupe is incredibly good and the band is amazing. Doris and I loved it. I'm half tempted to see if she'd like to go again tonight, but I wouldn't like to cruel your pitch.'

Always expect the unexpected, as they say. 'Roddy, what do you think?'

'I think the famous line was "Include me out". But in this case, you can include me in.'

'Wonderful. But how on earth are we going to get a table at the Chevron at this time of night?' Jill asked.

'That doesn't present a problem, you can have our table. It's a permanent booking,' Mauri offered.

Jill looked at Roddy. Roddy looked at Jill. What on earth was happening?

'Okay, Mauri, on one condition: you get on the phone to Doris now and ask her to come. I want to speak to her too, because I want know all that's going on.'

'I'm not surprised you're a leading light at the bank,' he said

'Roddy, you can go and get scrubbed first,' she said, going to take over the phone.

She waited while Mauri called Doris. He talked and, after a few words, passed the phone to Jill. 'Here,' he said, 'you girls can sort things out.'

'Hello, Doris, Jill.' And they went on to arrange the evening and the night. They knew each other from the club, Commodore's Balls, dinners and special occasion nights, and after sailing drinks which sometimes flowed on to dinner at the club—and they understood yachties. She would bring some clothes for Mauri and he could change at the Chevron. They were to come there as soon as they were ready; she most probably would be there before them, but if not, they could have drinks at the bar and she'd meet them there, whatever, they were to use Mauri's account because it was his idea so the night was to be on him and he'd like to buy the race winner a drink. Mauri took them to the Chevron's glamour bar where Doris was waiting, very well groomed and very tastefully dressed for an evening out, exuding confidence, totally relaxed. Mauri kissed her and said, 'I'll let Jilly introduce her champion sailor, love.'

'Hello, Doris,' said Jill and kissed her. 'You look great. I love your outfit. Doris, I'd like you to meet Roddy Mckenzie who has come to help build Australia. He's off to the Snowy Scheme tomorrow.'

'How d'ye do, Roddy? I'm delighted to meet you.' She had risen and, shaking his hand, went on, 'I'll confess to having heard a bit about you before, and how you met Jill and Emma in England. I can see why they gave you a rave review. Welcome to Australia.'

'Thank you, Doris. It's been a whirl since the morning I landed. It's incredible the good luck I've had and the generous people I've met. I'm mightily impressed with the little I've been able to see so far. Although I've heard it's pretty rough, I'm looking forward to getting to work in the Snowies.' Mauri returned in a tasteful dark suit and tie. They were chatting pleasantly when a nuggetty young man with a red face came alongside. 'Doris, Jill, Mauri, how are you?' he greeted them. 'Will you be dining with us tonight?'

'Yes, we'll be going in shortly, Len. Len, I'd like you to meet our guest Roddy Mckenzie.' He and Len Evans shook hands. Len Evans turned to Mauri. 'When you have settled at your table, I'll drop by and see if there's any way I can help with the wine. We need to make sure you and your guest have a night of fun and enjoyment.'

'Len Evans's came to Australia with nothing, but he's got a good job here as beverage manager. He's made a lot of good friends and he's living a great life. He'll get there in the not too distant future.'

Mauri seemed to be conscious that very soon the evening would become one of interest, fun, spectacle, music, and the enjoyment that it was meant to be—conversation about practical things would be put aside. So there were some things he wisely thought ought to be fixed now. He asked, 'When does your train leave in the morning?'

'Eight o'clock. If there's not an early enough ferry, I'll take a taxi.'

'Too dodgy. I'll get a car to pick you up at quarter past seven. Now, when you get to the Snowies, you'll be in a part of the world that's about the most beautiful on God's earth. Ye're going to get some time off: you need to see it before you travel on. You'll want a car. Now, take this card. There's a bloke up there I want to help out as a dealer. Now, I'm personally not available all the time, but this bloke is. Ring him when you want a car in the Snowies. I'll have worded him up, so anything like cars, hotel rooms, business kinds of things, he's the man. Pity you haven't got a chance to meet him. He's a great bloke and infallible. You may have to get to Cooma to pick it up, but I don't think that will be necessary. You'll have to keep it sparkling bright and make sure everyone sees it wherever you go. Now, I suggest you leave it with the bloke in Cooma and he'll take you back to work and he'll keep it like grandma's hankie.

'Roddy, I've got a feeling that we'll know each other for a long time. I'm not doing you a favour and I'd be disappointed if you ever thought I was. I don't do people favours. I just do what I want to do. Now here's my card as well. If I'm not there, whatever you think you could tell me, you can tell Doris. Now, I don't know if you and Jilly are on with each other, but it would be great if you were. I bank with Jilly. She knows more about me than anyone but Doris. Stick close to her, she's better than diamonds. But you can't just come up from the Snowies and assume you can lob into Jill's house. You can have a room here any time you want to come to Sydney, just call Richard; on the first card I gave you—don't call him "Dick", he'll thump you.

'Doris, sorry to interrupt, love, but I'm just wondering what we need to do for Roddy in the Snowies. When we go to dinner, we'll all get carried away with the show and won't think about it.' She mentioned all the things Mauri had covered, so she said, 'You can tell him not to bring his dirty washing, but apart from that, if I think of something else, I'll stop the band.'

The Chevron Hotel at King's Cross was new and the bar was styled with flat-featured surfaces of glass and solid oblong panels in subdued shades of blue-greys and blacks, lights on pillars and pendant from the false ceiling, were tubular and lit softly to add to the comfort and intimacy of the scene. The furnishing was the latest—clean lined, flat surfaced, with many comfortable, low-backed tub chairs round glass-topped tables. The large room was filled with people standing, sitting, holding drinks, men in suits and many women wearing long gowns; everywhere was bright strong colour painted into the visually perfect spots amongst the mass of grey day-wear suits or black dinner suits; and everywhere bright chatter and laughter. Doris and Mauri suited snugly into this city evening scene, as if natural constituents of the expected social world in a top city hotel on a Saturday night. Their life stories may have begun quite differently from this city world in which they were successful, proficient participants, but this was where they were meant to be, where they wanted to be, and where they quietly, and quite unostentatiously, thoroughly enjoyed being. The dining area was white-covered sparkling tables, only a few occupied but the crowd was beginning to follow behind Mauri's lead.

A woman in a white evening gown sitting under a solo spotlight at a white grand piano was playing Ivor Novello, Noel Coward, Cole Porter pieces with a lovely touch. The spot lit picture in white was an island afloat in shadow. The tempo of the pieces was varied and seemed designed to build until the stage events would take place when the diners were seated and vice had begun. The mood which had developed in the bar had begun to be felt in the large softly lit dining room.

The head waiter came immediately to Mauri's table. 'Mr. and Mrs. Perrot! Welcome.' Louis was Hungarian, had come as a child with his parents, arrivals from Europe in the period between the wars, in time to have to endure the bitter depression of the thirties. His position as head waiter in one of the older hotels, now gone to the demolisher's swinging ball, had been built by him into the equivalent of a seat on the stock exchange. He, like Mauri and Doris had become, was a proficient city dweller. He knew his work, enjoyed it, and loved the relationships that had arisen out of good service to his 'guests'. Between him and many of them had grown mutual respect; and with some, fully developed friendships and sharing of free time pleasures.

After a designed interval, a waiter came up to discuss their order. Roddy noticed the prominence of various cuts of beef, steaks of different cuts and variations around cooking methods for beef and lamb from steak tartare to beef stroganoff and lamb in Italian tomato puree with pasta and lamb kebabs. Fish was fresh and in varieties he had never heard of; every fowl of the stable yard was on offer cooked in different modes. When they had made their selections of fish dishes, Len Evans came along, and when Mauri was consulted by him on his ideas for the night, he turned to Roddy and said, 'Anything special in mind, Roddy?'

'Well, as part of my enjoyable immersion in Australian life, I'd like to have Australian wines and what better than to taste some of your favourites if that suits you and Doris?'

'That'll suit us, what about you, Jill?'

'I'm all for Australian and I'm sure Len's got a white to go with my John Dory.'

'Mainly with Roddy in mind, I was thinking that perhaps rather than have him try wines he may not be able to buy as he travels, we should let him try some good wines that he should be able to get most places he goes.'

Len Evan's advice was taken, and once he had established what they had chosen to eat, he selected two Seppelt's whites A 'Rimini Chablis' and an 'Arrawata Riesling', a Gramps 'Orlando Shiraz', and a McWilliams Shiraz from the Hunter Valley.

'That sounds good, Len, and even rough young Snowy Mountain navvies wouldn't be ashamed to drink those. Anyone like a glass of fizz to prepare the palate?'

'Doris? Jilly?'

'I'd love one,' was the simultaneous pronouncement of the ladies.

'I see you've got some Romalo from Adelaide. We'll have one of these, please.'

'Thank you, Mauri. I'll get that on its way and come and check with you later. Have a great evening.' With that, he summoned a wine waiter and gave him his selection list and went off to get the champagne himself.

The dishes turned out very well, and as they progressed through the wines, Roddy was happy to say that although these wines were new to his palate and had their own style, he found them very clean and palatable. The dinner went smoothly; everyone was relaxed, the Perrotts were perfect hosts and stories of Australia were brought out, not just for Roddy's benefit, although that had been the original intention, it turned that these were new ones from different parts of southern Australia that kept everyone involved. The dessert was on its way to digestion with the help of a Rutherglen Tokay when the floor show burst onto the stage to the music of the show band which had a really good sound.

'There you go, Roddy, what you've been waiting for, the dancing girls!'

'Drat, I haven't brought my opera glasses!'

The famous Australian dancing girls were worthy of their fame. They really were beautiful; their precision in the quite demanding choreography was perfect. Who couldn't get into the party spirit? Roddy led the applause. Later two of the girls, who seem to have been special friends of Doris, came down to the table. Roddy had no idea what he had expected but they were just very bright, naturally intelligent 'girls next door', their beautiful hair was 'legally blond', but what was amazing was how short they were. On stage, kicking mile-long legs, they appeared to be a minimum of six feet tall. In reality, standing alongside them, if they were five foot six, he would have been surprised. Nor did they stay all night drinking free champagne to which I'm sure they would have been welcome, they wished everyone good night and Roddy good luck and left for their suburban homes. An Irish comedian called Dave Allen sat on stage and, pretending (?) to sip whisky (whisky), had the primed audience in fits with his skits and gags. When he had finished and gone off the stage to change, he came down to the table. His behaviour with Doris and Mauri proved to be not much different from what he had been giving the audience.

In the period between the two major performers, the show band became a dance band. Roddy and Jill excused themselves and went up to dance. They were launched into a quick-step and Roddy was delighted to have Jill in his arms. 'You're a lovely dancer, Jill,' he said, looking into her face then quickly, 'That was a prime example of Scottish economy; two statements in one. One, you *are* lovely, Jill, and the second, you're a divine dancer.'

'Being a profligate, spendthrift Australian, I'll make two separate answers. To the first, thank you. To the second, thank you. And add, I think you're being bedazzled by the evening.'

'The evening is splendid and I can't deny that. It's a continuing part of this mesmerizing Australian experience and you: you and who you are, are a big part of that. When you and Emma appeared in the Solent and we spent some time together and you came to Ranelagh, I'd never dreamed that girls, women, like you two could exist. You were sweet, fresh, youthful, bright, and beautiful. Now I see you as a competent executive in Australia's biggest bank you're still sweet, fresh, bright, and beautiful, and I'm dancing with you. And you're in my arms. Can't you imagine how difficult it must be for me to accept all this as reality?'

'I assure you it's all real. Life is responding to who you are, Roddy. Things have been happening for you that I assure you would not happen for anyone else. All you have to do is stay sweet as you are.'

He brought her closer into his arms and found that they were still dancing. 'I must have a split personality. My brain tells me I'm still dancing but my heart is in another world altogether, totally detached, with my arms close around you.'

While Dave and Mauri had been joking together, Doris was observing the dancers. She turned to the men. 'Excuse me, Dave. Mauri, look.' And she nodded her head in the direction of Jill and Roddy on the floor. 'Ah, that's lovely,' he said, smiling, 'they make a good pair, don't they?'

Dave chose that moment to say that he must go, thanked them for having him in their group, and said, 'You'll enjoy Eartha again, believe me. We'll see if we can drop by and see you after the show or in one of the breaks.'

Out on the floor, a foxtrot was being played and the music the band had chosen deepened their emotional mood and moved their dancing to a dreamy sensuous, sinuous flow of two bodies in harmony. He had put his head against Jill's and pressed his cheek to hers. She kept her face close to his and danced on until the number ended.

The dance that followed was a samba, and whether Roddy was just not much good at it, or the spell had somehow been broken, they looked at each other; they knew the question and they knew the answer, so with his arm around her waist, they went to the table.

Eartha came on stage—lithe, like a pale jaguar, her years with the Katherine Dunham Dancers could not be concealed. She walked, if that's the word, to the microphone as if her form was made of oiled silk, frictionless, without a skeletal structure. A piece of sheer textile material covered those parts of her body which, at least by Australian standards of public decency, were forbidden to be exposed. The split-length gown showed a firmly shaped leg all the way from a flimsy high-heeled shoe to a point where, in a normal human skeleton, the leg is fixed to the upper body by a large joint. There was no evidence that something so banal existed here. A shape of hemispheres and hollows followed, at the higher ends of her legs accentuated in their forms tightly as skin, was followed faithfully by the material of the garment. Her silky brown back was totally exposed and some magical apparatus was holding the gown over her breasts to the titillation of the males and the envy of the females both observing with the same power of intensity. She spoke into the microphone to welcome her audience with that dark brown voice. The magic had already begun. She had chosen to open with Cole Porter's 'Let's Fall in Love'. Which male could decline the invitation? Number after number followed with seemingly tireless energy. She was suspended in a spot lit space with darkness and invisibility all around. The audience was herscompletely.

The band was under control and direction in sympathy with the moods of her numbers, allowing the emphases, inflections, and tones of her voice full value. The show was working perfectly. Just as well they had done their talking beforehand. It would have been sacrilegious to utter a word—even of praise. Applause was loud as each number counted out the moods of this performance as if it were a story set to the poetry of song. It was understandable that she and Dave did not come down during the brief breaks which gave the audience time for only a few words of praise for the bravura performance.

When the call for the last encore, and the applause had died away, they talked together about her remarkable performance. 'Like to wait to see whether she will come down?' Mauri asked. 'What would you folks like to do?' They looked at each other questioningly. Roddy waited to feel the direction of the wind. The response was being left to him. The three were looking at him. He had to make his decision. He said, 'For me, the performance was what she is about. It was marvellous and I think I'd like to leave it just like that: which doesn't mean I'd be unhappy if any of you wanted to stay.'

'That decision suits me. I was soundly beaten at sailing today and I need to go home and lick my wounds,' said Mauri. 'What if we just go to the bar, and we can have a last drink while we wait the few minutes for the car to come?'

In the bar, they sat comfortably in the tub chairs and put up little resistance to the thought of a last glass of Mr. Morris's fine Tokay. They talked a little, but just a little. Doris as 'household accountant' excused herself to have their account brought, checked, and signed off. In the conversation, Mauri mentioned that they were going to Scotland later in the year.

'Oh god!' exclaimed Roddy. 'Do you have to go then? It'll be cold wet and miserable. Can't you put it off till May at least?'

'I suppose I could,' he said, 'I want to see if there any agencies or dealerships that I could work with alongside my Fusan franchise without conflict. I'm very interested in Land Rover, for instance, maybe a long haul truck prime-mover line for Australia. I don't want to wait too long.'

'If you can wait till May, you'll find it a lot easier to get around and do business. And you really should see a bit of Britain while you're there.' Roddy suggested.

'Doris's family were McLachlans from Scotland, so she'd like to do a visit and some family tracing if she can.'

'It would be wonderful if you two could go up and see my parents in Fearnas. My mother would love that. Roddy sounding excited at the possibility went on. 'It's a pleasant part of Scotland just near the battlefield of Culloden, it's where Shakespeare set part of his famous *Macbeth*, and Speyside has more distilleries than you could shake a stick at.'

The drove them along the harbour to the Perrotts' house at Pott's Point. Even in the darkness, Roddy thought he could pick out the shape of the harbour by the lights on the shores. They stood in the front door lights of a large house high up amongst trees on a shoreline cliff, the dark harbour with its navigation lights stretching out before them.

'Mauri, I don't know how I will ever be able to thank you for what you are doing for me. Even when I do well materially, there will be no material things I could give you that would show the meaning of my gratitude or would talk the right language. Thank you, Mauri, for everything and the great time you showed us tonight.' Then he turned slightly to concentrate on Doris.

'Doris, am I allowed to give you a wee cuddle?'

'I'd be very upset if you didn't.'

'I'm so lucky to have been able to meet you. I know you're complicit in all the good things that are happening to me. Thank you so much.'

Jill got a peck on the cheek from Mauri in response to hers. She embraced Doris and kissed her cheek. 'Thank you both for a lovely night and the transport. See you both at the club on Saturday.'

Once again he was crossing the bridge, not for the last time in his short stay. He thought out loud, 'This bridge must be worth so much more to the city of Sydney than mere toll fees could ever pay for. It's part of Sydney life in so many ways.'

They stood in the lounge of Jill's apartment, the dark window glass like a sky hung with bright, coloured stars against the blackness. Here and there, rippling water was lit from large lights on the bridge.

They stood side by side close together and, in silence, stared out at the night.

'Jill,' he said, touching her hand, 'thank you for the lovely day that this has been. It's been a day of your creation filled with delight of being with you—and that super evening dancing with you—sheer magic. Here I am, my head spinning with sensations, emotions, images—crowded, unsorted.'

He squeezed her hand just a little tighter and turned towards her. They looked at each other in silence till he moved closer and gently put his arms around her. Her arms complemented his, and as he held her more tightly, so too did she hold him, and her arms were strong. His face was on her cheek and in her hair; he kissed her ear. Their faces moved and they found their lips touching for moments in a soft, caressing kiss. The embrace that had been so intense was reluctantly, simultaneously eased as they allowed their arms to relax.

'Roddy Mckenzie,' she was saying as her hand explored every contour and plane of his face, 'you're not the only one whose head is spinning.' Then they were back in the not unpleasant reality of the present, the recent past of the day on the harbour, and dancing cheek to cheek.

'Just before you say anything, I want to say that it will be bright in the morning and that I'd like to sit with you on the balcony and have a cup of tea together before we set off for the station.'

'*We* set off for the station?'

'Yes, I want to be sure you get on that train.'

He imagined that there may be some chaos with a mob of men on the platform under RTO's orders, but admitted to himself that it would be the perfect way to leave for 'the bush'.

While Jill disappeared to the bathroom and bed, Roddy sat and gazed. 'What a view! What a day! What a night!' Not much sorting had taken place before he heard a *sotto voce* 'Good night, Roddy', and softly a door clicked.

As Jill had predicted, the morning was bright and so was she in sandals shorts and a tee shirt.

'Morning, Roddy', she said gaily, 'ready for the plunge into the great unknown?'

'Yep! Just recently, each day seems to present a new unknown, so I'd say I'm about as ready as can be.'

'Here', she said in an attractive air of domesticity and familiarity, 'take this plate of toast and marmalade; I'll bring the tea.'

The old view was a new view as it must always be on the harbour—splendid, sparkling, and stunning. He'd decided that for a long train ride and an arrival at who knows what kind of environment, he'd wear his brand-spanking-new working duds. Since they were khaki drill, they looked and felt familiarly 'army'. There was something, incredibly, indescribably pleasing about sitting here in the morning sun with this rather wonderful woman. It was yet another visual and emotional sensation, another emotional snapshot, to add to the crowed mental album of amazing experiences.

Mauri's car driver was bright and breezy as he greeted them and opened the boot for Roddy's rucksack. 'I heard a rumour ye're off to the Snowies, Mr. Mckenzie. They tell me it's pretty rough and I don't mean the mountains. Aw, but you'll be right; you look as if you can look after yourself.' It was a view held by Jill too, formed from Saturday's sailing, later holding his body in her arms and experiencing his lightness as they danced, all of that was further substantiated by the added transformation of his appearance wearing his work togs. She was a country girl, she understood men, and she knew there could be the occasional stoush.

At the station, a sign had been put up at the end of a platform that indicated the Snowy Mountains Authority train and a small sign next to it said, 'Wood Bagshaw Personnel'. A man in railway uniform, with a 'civilian' beside him, was checking identities and travel documents of each man passing through the expanding gates which had been pulled close to admit only a person in single file.

'It appears you're not the only one heading for the hills.' Then, with a grin, she added, 'It means you'll have company and someone to talk to.'

The uniformed man called out to Roddy, 'If you're goin' to the Snowies, you'd better get on.'

He held her by the arms at the shoulders and, looking at her eyes, said quietly, 'Good-bye, Jill. Thank you for being so wonderful. I'll look forward to seeing you on my first leave.' He kissed her very quickly on the lips and stood back, his arms extended. She did not move.

'Thank you for being who you are, Roddy Mckenzie.'

He picked up his bag and sprinted to the gate.

———∘∘∘─❯❮─∘∘∘———

'Click', he was saying to himself, 'new world now, change frequencies, change codes, pick up the new quiffs.' Further along the platform, a sign gave the number of the carriage and 'Wood Bagshaw'. His warrant, as on a troopship your pass gives you your berth number, seat numbers were allocated so that numbers and names could be matched and questions of 'Who's missing?' could be answered. They had to get into their allocated seats and make no move until the train was moving. He found himself in a widow seat back to the engine. His good-luck genie was still awake and working and looking out for him. 'Did this link back to the fact that Chris had rung's employment officer? When was that? A month ago, a year ago? No, that was less than a week ago!' The answers to his internal questioning astounded him. Outside, there was a world of building on either side—domestic, commercial, and industrial. Look, there was a tram! It was not at all like Kirribilli. It was darker, dirtier, and there were remarkably fewer trees. But the houses were not packed tenements like those that flanked the railway lines of central England and the irrepressible sky shone blue and the sun poured light on them. Mostly they moved quite slowly with now and then a few minutes burst of speed so that the clickety-clack sounded more purposeful. It seemed a long time before the train began to leave the metropolitan levels and to shake off the binding ribbons which tenaciously, almost desperately followed the roads and the rails leading somewhere to broader, brighter perhaps more hopeful horizons. That may have been the false impression of its appearance; the truth may have been of happy families holding together and gaining yard-by-yard improvement of means and hopes. Had he lost his grasp of the real? For so long now he had been living in the wonderful fairyland of Ranelagh, the world of Hugh and Miette, the friendship and the luxury of the Stratheden, Jill's apartment at Kirribilli, sailing from the Royal Yacht Squadron, the conviviality of the Ship Inn, the ISC drnks at the inner sanctum of the Bank of New South Wales, and dining at the Chevron with Mauri and Doris. Which would be his world?

'That, dear boy, is entirely up to you.' And on that thought, he closed the book of speculation.

The track had begun to climb slowly and steadily through farming country over bridges on rivers, streams, and roads. Often the roads paralleled the rail and often they led over a huge vista of agricultural land over which the rising heat of day was forming a distant blue haze. Then they were climbing round great sweeping bends in what appeared to be a huge, slow, spiral of railway track, and sometimes a point would be reached when a track would be seen below; it would be their track which they had steamed over shortly before. Now they were amongst trees with sometimes red-brown trunks or sometimes white which had burst through rough rocky ground and waved their dark red-green or olive green leaves in the mountain breeze, often on ridges they be waving that blue sky with which Roddy was becoming familiar. He had had been silent and ruminative this long while, as had the man on his left. Now Roddy spoke because the effect of what he was seeing had captured his thoughts. He looked left and said, 'There's something very beautiful about this country, don't you think?'

'Yes, there certainly is, and I'm looking at the rocks and wishing I knew a bit more than school geology. I have reason to do so, but I'm imagining it must aeons old. Do you know anything about geology?'

'I'm possibly at about your level. If you named me three or more periods, I'd likely have heard of all of them, but I'd have no hope of putting them in order.'

'Do you have any special skills that you'll be using up in the Snowies?'

'No, not a thing. That's why being a navvy on the Snowies scheme attracted me when someone suggested it. I went straight from school into an infantry battalion, and apart from learning how to kill a few offending Chinese soldiers, nothing more. Far from zeroing me in on an objective for a life career I couldn't think of anything attractive except farming, and having no funds, which seemed out of the question, except here. I'll possibly still have that idea in mind after I put a few pounds in my bank from my navvy work. I haven't been in Australia a week yet.'

'Except for your idea about farming, my situation parallels yours. You were in an infantry battalion killing Chinese—must have been in Korea.'

'Yes, 43 Highland. Two Hook battles.'

'I've given up thinking that coincidences are rare. We were your support artillery regiment. I've actually been out with some of your people in Forward Observation Positions.'

'Then you were in Twentieth Field Regiment?'

'Right first time. Ex-lieutenant Mike Harty at your service, sir.'

'Ex-corporal 43 Highland, now Lieutenant Royal Hampshire Regiment Roddy Mckenzie.' They laughed and, getting up, shook hands. Mike was Roddy's height and a little less muscular, dark hair, dark brown eyes, and the skin of a dark Celt. He had extended his service, principally because he had no idea what the hell he would do when he got out. His engagement ran out just a bit later than his affection for continued military service. He was out now, just as confused, and with no binding connections in England or Ireland, taking up the offer of a cheap fare to Australia seemed the thing to do. Now here he was. Although his mess bills had not exceeded his pay, the paucity of his subaltern's emoluments had led to the conclusion that only the misery of enforced thrift would ever avert dire penury. Hopefully, there would be 'gold in them thar hills'. They chuckled very cheerfully as they talked about these sad economical truths.

The other sad truth was that although this was not in the smallest way understood by them, military service is not necessarily the kind of activity which inspires the young mind to a sense of career direction. Those people who went on from school to university chose courses where their past good marks seemed to indicate a way to follow. Most often, evidence suggests that, that choice did not lead to a blissful, fulfilling maturity. Very few school leavers, whether proceeding to university or the armed forces, ever sustained any previously held ideas of being airline pilots, arctic explorers, science or literature Nobel Prize winners, foreign correspondents for the *Times*, took themselves off to the deserts of Arabia to unravel the mysteries of Islam, or went forth to stand upon a peak in Darien. Perhaps there is a hypnotic charm in ordinariness to which, if you succumb, will provide with a peace which passeth all understanding. For Mike and Roddy, Damascus lay in the distance, they were on the road; the purpose of their journey was yet to be made clear to them.

Therefore, like their train on its track, they must continue.

As the day wore on, the mountain landscape became even more impressively beautiful and there were times when they would look down into green floored valleys with a winding stream in the bottom, magical as it came into view, stayed for a while to be enjoyed, then the train, speeding on, left it out of sight behind some lofty rock spur. At about mid-day, the train came to a stop. Perhaps because it was a 'special' train, they were forbidden to get down. Small vans were on the platform, and from these, a box was passed up to each railcar. The packets in the box were one for each person in the carriage, with it and a can of 'Simmons' Beer which, except for its bright red colour, looked the same as a 'Brasso' tin. After a verbal warning that the train was about to move, the very slow *click-clack, click-clack* of the restart picked up until the earlier clickety-clack rhythm had been resumed. They passed a country of vast rolling grasslands with belts and copses of tall trees, the grass, which had been plentiful, dried out now by months of hot summer sun. They followed the valley of a river until they reached Goulburn. Here some shunting took place and it sounded as if further trucks were being added. They began climbing again, and from the position of the afternoon sun, they calculated that they had turned south. Sometimes they reached a high point where the loftier peaks formed a ring around the plateau across which they found themselves travelling and they could see for miles towards these ranges of much-higher rounded mountains clothed in low trees. They crossed streams and rivers with rhythmic regularity the crossing their bridges altering the song of their train. Off to their right at one point near the end of their journey was the nation's capital, Canberra. Over everything was blue sky and clear bright sunshine.

The sun was slowly moving to the point of setting when the train stopped at Cooma, the little station in the tiny town spread lightly over the hilly pastures where it had grown up. They didn't spot anyone who had more than hand luggage, and for most, this comprised one small suitcase. There were buses waiting; each assigned to a contractor with whose company one had signed on. About forty people went towards the Wood Bagshaw bus of whom, as was found out later, twenty or more were returning from leave. At this time, the people of the world who came from different countries looked as if they had come from different countries. It may not be possible to establish from which Slavic country a man came, but if you said it in a Slavic language, that would immediately be clarified. Even Spaniards and Frenchmen and Italians could be differentiated, except if they were gypsies, which made guessing their country of birth nigh impossible, and of latest residence, totally so. It was a bit like identifying people in the army who had just arrived in a training base and those who had been in that base as little as a month. Mike and Roddy would have been identifiable as new people and they could guess who of the others was returning from leave. They were deposited at a wooden hut which they all entered together, and once inside, those returning from leave reported at a designated desk. The new group was called to one side where they went through a brief process of documentation. They were asked to follow a man who seemed to be in charge of the new draft who took them to a very large building the size of a small aircraft hangar the main area of which was the mess hall. Even now there were people eating, and a number going past the serving counter choosing food. The other end of the building, which they had to go out and walk round to, was the wet canteen which seemed to be enjoying good business. From there they walked to what would have been called in the army 'lines'. These were more civilized than they had guessed they might be. They were long lines of very army-style wooden huts, however, they were divided into two-bed rooms for each four of these rooms, and adjoined in the same line, was a mini ablutions block of showers, toilets, and wash hand basins. There was a laundry at each end of every long line. It seemed that not all units were vacant for new pairs some would have to take up a share with an existing resident. Roddy said to the guide, 'We two met on the train and it turns out we were in Korea together, not in the same unit, but in the same engagements. Could we have a hoochie together?'

'Who were you with in Korea?

43 Highland,' answered Roddy.

'Twentieth Field Artillery Regiment,' said Mike.

'Small world. I was in3 RAR, Kapyong. I think we can fix that.' He looked at his mill board on which a sheet had been flipped over the clip. Leaving the others to follow, he went further along the line. 'There you are, gentlemen', he said, 'your new hoochie, and you didn't have to scrounge for stuff to build it with. Welcome to the Wood Bagshaw battalion. When you get settled in, we'll go to town one day and have a beer. I'm Martin Musgrove.' He shook hands with each as they introduced themselves. 'If there's anything bothering you, come and see me, I'm a personnel clerk and I'm in the Personnel Office in Bullshit Castle—over there.'

What he indicated was something not different from any of the other buildings except that it was not part of a line. The first thought of the wily soldier sinners was that they may have a friend in camp.

Their room was basic. A bare timber floor supported two wooden bed frames on which the folded bed clothes had been piled, straight from the laundry. Each bed had a little table with a drawer, and a small light. There was a tall plywood wardrobe each, and at each side of the central door, there was a window below which was a little writing table and a chair. As hoochies go, it wasn't bad. Their minds fleeing into the past of recruit days caused Mike to say, 'Shouldn't we be blancoing webbing?' The first thing they did was make their beds.

Immediately, without saying it one to the other, and without wanting to think it, they burst out laughing, not that the remark was so greatly humorous, but because they both realized and saw themselves being drawn into a system, which just as the army had, would consume them.

Without consuming the humans it uses, systems of such magnitude cannot, by the very fact of their existence and objectives, function and achieve what their mass has been contrived to do. Again, they had committed themselves to spend their lives physically and mentally involved in the achievement of tasks in pursuit of the organization's objectives. This would be involved every minute of their operational days and consume much their free time in thinking about how they would solve their immediate operational problems of tomorrow. There would be risks and men would die. Their universe would be their work site and this camp their locus in it. At least here, the bigger philosophies of the project and its benefits would be known to them. If they had no faith in the philosophies, all they had to do was go to Martin Musgrove and say they wanted out. It was up to them to find time between working and sleeping to think about their futures. What inspiration comes from wrestling with a large rock-laden truck on a narrow twisting track twelve hours of the day, or trudging over heath land dragging a surveyor's chain? They were about to learn how to create a system for themselves within the larger system of which even Wood Bagshaw was only a smaller part. Their first parade was an assembly of newcomers in Bullshit Castle.

Mick Musgrove had already pointed out Bullshit Castle whither they had to report at 07.30 on Monday by which time they would have breakfasted. The briefing, by Mike Musgrove, was brief, almost perfunctory. Its content was wages, where when and how people would be paid, how many hours they would work and when there would be time off. There were no orthodox weekends; the breaks would come by an accumulation of hours worked or when jobs were completed and new jobs began. Most workers worked seventy hours per week, many only forty.

When finished with the briefing, someone from the work area to which they had been allotted was there to meet them and take them to the start point of their Snowy Mountains two-year work contract period. By the end of the day, Roddy would have spent, first on a 'watch me' drive, then six hours driving a Thorneycroft six-by-six tipper truck. He would be hauling rock and spoil from a road cutting to a rock-fill dam site. Mike had gone to join a team of geologist—engineers whose work was to calculate volume of a creek catchment area.

People going out to work were supplied, at the canteen, by what was called, from an old English miners' expression, a 'crib' which would keep from hunger until their shift had been completed. Major meals were eaten in large twenty-four-hour operational mess halls where Roddy's overall policy was to have minimal, limited-range conversations—often where his French and German came in usefully—eat enough food, and get out. Almost every day or night there was a brawl. At first you thought it must be about something that happened at work, that perhaps something had gone wrong that only physical conflict could resolve. Often it was later found that the fight was not about a work event that could have happened any day, any time, even several times. No, what it was about was often about some story of long ago, a story told by a grandmother to a granddaughter, or a grandfather to a grandson about adultery, a marriage, a theft, a lie, a slight, from generations before; or even a story about a historical event when the wrong alliances or wrong religion had been chosen; perhaps a loss of political power waiting, waiting, kept fresh by some representative of those people aggrieved in the distant past, for the day when it could be revenged by a representative in the present time. Then there were memories of much more recent creation: in East Camp, Cooma, a major conflict broke out between Germans and Poles which was quite dramatically resolved by a German engineer, in a vocal appeal, where after stability improved. There were knifings, shootings, and beatings with steel bars. When a brawl broke out, anyone could be swept up in it, and could sucked in, to trade blows in self-defence. In this Roddy found himself in a game where he was not necessarily better skilled in simply slugging it out. But he survived and seemed to have gathered a reputation for knowing what to do. That 'what to do' by the way was not some attempt at psychological resolution! No, it was combination of psychomotor and cognitive skills. He punched economically; he knew where to hit and when. He could put himself very quickly in punching balance and deliver a blow which would put his attacker out of action. Perhaps he could operate better because he had no emotional involvement in the issue. His objective was to survive—undamaged if possible. When this did not work and he was in danger, he resorted to judo and kung-fu and the long-ago-acquired unarmed combat skills, which were seen to work effectively in disabling armed attackers. It made the idea of going to the canteen for a beer not at all attractive; certainly no way to spend his scarce free time between his shifts on a machine.

Free time became a cherished hour or two of the day. In the morning, just before the car arrived and he was about to depart Kirribilli, Jill had thrust a book into his hand. 'I'd have got you a new one, but there wasn't time. I'd like you to take this one. I've had it for years.' It was inscribed, 'To Jill from dad, Xmas 1951. Just in case you might be forgetting the bush! And both saw

Because they were in different crews doing different kinds of work, getting breaks together was hard to organise. When it was possible, for the first time, Roddy phoned Richard using the public telephone installed in the camp. The first time they had this opportunity, Mike Musgrove drove them in. On later occasions, they managed to get a lift. On other times when they themselves had advance warning, someone from Cooma Fusan would drive out, pick them up, and bring them back to the camp!

Neither Mike nor Roddy wanted simply to go to Cooma then sit around, eat, and drink. Immediately they had access to the car they wanted to be off into the magnificent landscape that surrounded them. The little car proved a great boon. They drove every curve and bend of every road in Monaro and the Snowy Mountains, climbed every hill and height, crossed every river and rushing stream. The landscape filled Roddy with feelings of amazement and joyful affection for its variety, beauty, and power and the library provided access to the history and the lore. They drove in lashing rain, in moisture-laden sunshine, and with care and chains, over ice and snow to the snowfields and the flights and falls of learning to ski.

Already, their ways of perceiving it had taken shape. For Mike, it was about topography, its physical shape. He wondered, and wanted to know, what kinds of forces and when, through infinite time, had brought it to the forms that he was seeing now. Although Mike's thoughts were included in Roddy's, the emphasis of his enquiry was seeking detail of a different kind. Not for a moment did that mean that he was not concerned about the changes that volcanic turmoil and the ice ages had brought about. It was almost as if the land were presenting itself to him and asking, 'Well, do you love me, or don't you?' It was as if the land could respond; react in some way, to whichever choice he might make. It could be hard and cruel or benign and beneficent on its volition, but not at the whim of man. He was growing towards the land; he was preparing to form a relationship with the earth, offering care and respect in exchange for a contented existence. He needed that information to help him to understand how things may have been when, only forty to perhaps sixty thousand years ago, humankind may first have come to these lands.

'As we dynamited and scraped and shifted layers, were we removing evidence of those early people? If there had been family groups, communities, or even just a few travellers, they would have laid down stories in the sensual memories of their successors? If we as people had only heard of "Clancy of the Overflow" from the poem, the marks of Clancy would be embedded in our self-perceptions until transformed and absorbed into succeeding layers of our human experience with all the other tales we had heard. Our present, however fresh, will still be the sum of our past. In their limited time, and their limited contact, there was little that Roddy and Mike could gain from the local communities in terms of knowledge, yet these local people, unconsciously held in their store, the effects of the past experiences on their predecessors.' These were some of the kinds of questions thoughts that the land evoked in him.

One day, on an excursion, Mike was driving as they went through the valley where Talbingo was. Roddy was free just to gaze and marvel. The road wound through green farms to left and right, across little bridges where water flowed to the right and into a larger stream. Each of the farms had its own little bridge leading from the roadway to cross the larger stream. At each bridge, there was a cluster of weeping willows or a mix of European trees, often poplars, but there were birches and elms, stone fruit trees, and apples and pears. The farms were not large, but they looked rich and it was easy to imagine what life might be like in the painted wooden farmhouses and what might be stored, or housed, in the old bleached grey parallel-planked wooden sheds under tin roofs surrounded by their shelter of willows or fruit trees. It was a sight of such beauty that he experienced a physical movement of his heart; never had he seen anything so appealing to the soul, and he was sure he never would again. Suddenly there was an echo in his inner ear: 'Talbingo.' Yes! This is what Bruce had said at the ISC that afternoon when he had learned that Roddy was going to a job in the Snowy Mountains: 'Talbingo which is the most beautiful place on God's earth.' In ways like that, he became a willing captive of the land of Australia.

Whatever else they did in Cooma, they visited the library. Usually there were borrowed books they had read, to be returned, and with some excited anticipation, requested books from the State Central Library to be picked up. There was a bookshop in town, which they always visited, but it would have been unfair to expect that it could provide for their needs. Except that Roddy had ordered the best bound editions available of a book each of Henry Lawson and Banjo Patterson. They always visited to check any changes in stock and for the simple purpose of exchanging pleasantries with the couple who owned the shop.

Their real urgency was to explore this spectacular land where they had the good fortune to be.

Meanwhile in the days of work, each found different forces influencing his thinking and his imagining: forces, in the sense that the kind of work in which each was involved during the day, gave rise to thinking about those matters concerning only their tasks. For Mike, the volumetric capacity of a stream valley and the data required to make that calculation possible was the occupation of his mind. Roddy found himself wanting to increase his skills in machine handling over as many different machines as were available at Wood Bagshaw. He was interested to consider the time economy in tackling jobs. When they made an excursion in the little Fusan, he could not avoid observing how much earthmoving work was being done in all directions, work which had nothing to do with earthmoving in that other world of the Snowy Mountains Scheme. Influences were at work of which, to this point, he was unconscious.

Within three months of being on-site, Roddy had been transferred from the old Thorneycroft to a bulldozer, operators for which were more difficult to find than truck drivers. He was happy about this because he needed more skills, new skills. One day when they were blasting out rock to open a cutting for the road, it was thought that rather than having to bring up a specialist rock blaster, it would be sensible to have one of the site gang capable of blasting. Roddy was pleased to be the one selected for training as a shot firer. After the training and testing, he was deemed capable of holding a 'powder monkey's' ticket. The road they had been constructing was nearing completion, and the next task was to create a road surface, to the point where a new tunnel would begin. The job to bring this road to finished surface seemed the perfect opportunity for Roddy's boss to have him trained up as a grader operator. Although the overall scheme was highly unionized, there had been no strict operator demarcation codes in place, so multi-skilling was not uncommon. This was perfect for Roddy's personal development plan. He had by no means decided that road building or earthmoving was going to become his work life in the future, but these were the skills he had now where before he had none. His next immediate goal was to operate the front-end loaders which were additional pieces of plant being used in his gang—perhaps he could wangle it when they moved to their next new job.

The first time he borrowed the car, he contacted Mauri and Doris, not to organize the borrowing—that he did with Richard—but to let them know that he was availing himself of their offer and to attempt to express his gratitude. When he called, he was particularly pleased that it was Doris who answered the phone. It was easier to form words to speak ideas and the feelings of gratitude to Doris. She would have a way of letting Mauri know the real happiness he was experiencing from having the car which made possible an exploration of the beautiful countryside around.

Horace Nelson, Mauri's Fusan agent in Cooma, could not have been more helpful and enthusiastic. His car with his advertising on it was seen all around the area. Roddy and Mike had struck up a good relationship with him and was quite happy to drop them back to the camp if there happened to be no site transport around when they returned from a jaunt. When they had accumulated sufficient work hours to take a three-day break, and it could be organised between them, they planned to drive to Sydney, upward by the central route and back by the coastal route. Horace was all in favour.

In phone calls made from time to time, he had kept the girls, Mauri and Doris, aware of their plan to make visit to Sydney when the job allowed it. Wood Bagshshaw had now completed its work at Happy Jacks and was going to move lock-stock-and-barrel to the Geehi site. This transition provided an opportunity for leave. Unfortunately their actual release was only confirmed the weekend before they could actually leave.

Roddy felt that there were important arrangements to be made with his friends in Sydney before he and Mike set off, essentially with Jill, Mauri, John Wilson, and Chris. He had wanted to ring Jill first to arrange an evening with her and Emma, she was not available, but Verity happened to be there and on the point of going out. She was able to tell him that Jill would be there after eight p.m. Doris answered the phone when he called the Perrotts and he told her his plans and that they were dependent on what transpired with Jill, and he asked if he could have a word with Mauri.

'Hello, Mauri, how are you?' he greeted him. 'You're speaking to a number one Australiaphile! I have no hesitation. I'm going to join.'

'You'll have to get your application past me first, so don't take it for granted. We're pretty selective about what Scotsmen we take. McArthur was fine, but I'm not so sure about some of the rest of your mob.'

'I'll enter a good-behaviour bond until application date. I'll ask Horace to vouch for me. Ask him how many miles that little car of yours has done . . . which leads to why I'm ringing. I've been talking to you about coming to Sydney when I got the chance . . . well, the chance has just been sprung on me. You've also heard me speak about Mike, well, we plan to come up together.

'We've logged up more than enough work time to get three days off and we thought it would be part of our education to drive up to Sydney through Kiandra . . . then I've got to see the Dog on the Tuckerbox and then go back east down the coast. We plan to arrive in Sydney late Friday afternoon. That would give us Friday night, when I'd like to ask Jill and Emma to a concert if they're free. Do you have any free time on Saturday after sailing? I'm free all day Saturday and Saturday night, then off at sparrows on Sunday morning for work on Monday. I want to have a yarn with you and Doris and tell you all about beautiful Australia. So what chance do I have of seeing you two?'

'Do you want a sail on Saturday?'

'Definitely, if you can organize a berth. If any of the Jubilee boys will have me that would be great. But I'll sail on anything. Mind you, I'll have my best whites on, and I imagine we might hang around for a beer, so no wet-arsed sailing if possible . . . yes, I know VJs are great, but I'm a bit more sophisticated since I've been down in the Snowies and I like to keep my sailing gear dry. What about an old Folk Boat? Then I can have a beer when we're running.'

'It's about time you left the Snowies cobber. The blokes down there have turned you into a poofter.'

'Okay, I'll ignore these pleasantries and get down to the next item of business to wit— accommodation. Now, since I want to meet the blokes who put me on my path to the future, and because I'm going to meet them at the club, and a girl I know works in the bank next door, I thought I ought to give my club a bit of patronage rather than take up your very fine offer of the Chevron. No hurt feelings, I hope?'

'You've broken my heart. Whatever else, turn up for sailing on Saturday. If your mate doesn't sail, see if he'd like to come down to the club for a beer after . . . or during the sailing. I'll speak to Jill and see if she can organize Emma and Verity; we'll all come back down here to the house and have a meal.'

'Well, I'll swallow my pride, and anything your more gracious wife puts before me, and accept your invitation to dine.' His voice then changed from the bantering tone he had been using. 'No joking now, Mauri that would be splendid. That would put the cap on the weekend.'

'I'll be speaking to Jill after eight tonight, but I won't mention your plan unless she comes up with her own plan for Saturday. That is, if she's going to be free anyway. Shall I tell her to expect a call from you?'

'No. You get Friday evening organized. I'll have spoken to her long before you go out on Friday.'

'Right, all further communication between now and the week end via Jill . . . or failing that, Doris . . .' Returning to his bantering tone, he said, 'she's nicer to speak to.'

'Just get those damned dams built. Leave the social niceties to the experts. And keep my car clean.' With that, Mauri hung up. Roddy was very happy. That had been a very nice conversation with Mauri. Now, to see if Jill was home.

He waited for his turn at the phone box and finally the user left the booth and it was Roddy's turn. Jill answered when the phone rang at Kirribilli. Anticipating the call, she said, 'Hello, Roddy, how are you?' Her voice was light, warm, and vivacious. 'Lovely to hear from you.'

'Nice to hear your voice, Jill; you sound very well and very bright. I don't think I need to ask, how are you?'

'I've just put the phone down from another caller. You'll never guess who.'

'There aren't that many people we both know, so I'll guess it was brother Mick.'

'No, keep going.'

It had to be, so he said, 'Doris?'

'Yes, and she was a bit excited. I had to tell her to get off the phone because I was expecting a call from you. She couldn't resist telling me you were coming up. Am I going to see you?' Her voice was full of enthusiasm, expectation, and a sense of excitement away beyond what he had anticipated.

'Of course you are! I rang to ask if you'd like to come out with me on the Friday evening we arrive. I was imagining that you, Emma, and I might go to a symphony concert, if I can get seats, then go on for supper somewhere chic for supper.'

'Oh, I'd love that, Roddy.' She sounded elated and went on, 'I don't know what you and Mauri talked about, but Doris reminded me that if we wanted to go to a concert, she was a patron and could arrange for good seats, she also reminded me that she knew lots of folk around town if we wanted an after-the-show dining spot.'

'She's a gem, isn't she? I'd made up my mind that if you were free and were happy to come out with me, I'd ask Doris if she'd make the bookings for me. So now I will. I've no idea what the concert programme is, but I'm happy to take potluck if you are.'

'I've never yet been to a concert I've been really disappointed by, so I'm perfectly happy. Now I want to ask you something and I know I'm being a bit selfish, but first I'll tell you something. Mauri has planned a do at their house after sailing that you and I are invited to. Emma and Verity are being invited too, so we'll be having time with them, and your friend Mike will be invited so he might be able to squire Emma for that evening because it's certain Verity will be squired by some theatrical male. Now the difficult bit. I'd like to have you to myself for the concert and supper. Is that woman executive boldness?'

'If it is, I like it . . . and your plan. I'll be in touch with Doris tonight if it's not too late.'

'Would you like me to ring her on your behalf in the morning?'

'That would be good of you with regard to the concert seats. Please ask Doris to choose the supper spot, but no cheating, she's not to tell you what she chooses. Can I trust you two?'

'Of course you can. I think that's fun, and Doris would love a game like that.'

They went through the details of meeting at the bank board's guest room entertainment bar on Friday evening and that they would take a taxi to the town hall.

'I'm so looking forward to seeing you again, Roddy. The weekend sounds exciting, doesn't it?'

'Well, I'm excited, and I'll be interested to find out what Doris has chosen for our supper spot. I have every faith in her imagination. I bet we will not be disappointed. And remember: she is not to tell you. I mustn't keep the mile-long queue for the phone waiting. But I just quickly ask you a favour?'

'Of course. What can I do for you?'

'My trunk is at the ISC, and Jeff, the secretary manager, has the key. Could you please ask him to take my light grey suit to the dry cleaners and have a white shirt laundered and tell him I'll need them when I come up on Friday afternoon?'

'Easy. Consider it done.'

'Jill, you're a gem, thank you. I'll have to let the next poor bloke in or I'll be lynched. Good night, Jill. Look forward to being with you.'

Her voice was warm and soft and, as if attempting to comfort herself, said, 'It's only a few sleeps. I look forward to Friday. Good night, Roddy.'

He told Mike about the arrangements and that he had accepted the Saturday evening date on his behalf.

They had no difficulty getting a lift to Cooma very early on Friday and were there when the garage opened at six a.m. The territory around Cooma and south and west had been gone over thoroughly on their days off. At Gundagai, they would begin to cover new ground and would circle wide around the nation's capital to its west. They planned not to spend time exploring on the way but to get to Sydney with all speed on this occasion, and simply enjoy, and try to get some feel for the country, as they passed through.

Between telephone calls, letter writing, and cables to England, Mike had been accepted as a member of the ISC, which simplified things so far as operating together was concerned. Another benefit was that there was going to be a little welcoming ceremony for him on Friday evening, which would mean that

Mike would not be left out on a limb when Roddy was otherwise engaged. The worst that could happen would be that he might spend the evening at the club, though doubtless there would be an invitation to something social.

They had approached Sydney by coming in through Ryde and crossing through Epping to Pacific Highway entering the city at the right end for access to the club, dropping their kit, and housing the car at a garage not too far away in Day Street. They had made good time on the trip, at the expense of expanding their Australian historical experience, by avoiding stops at many a pub that is famous in story and which would have afforded rich historical background. This sacrifice meant there would be enough time to nick down to the Ship to slake their punishing thirst, to rub shoulders with the mob, and to get dressed for the evening.

Mike had landed in Sydney a week before Roddy, and although his reconnaissance had been thorough, finding accommodation in a boarding house called Stortford Lodge on Cremorne Point, finding a job, exploring Sydney University, galleries, the museum, and the Mitchell Library, he had only the short evenings to reconnoitre the broader streams of human life and, although he had included glimpses of the sleaze of King Cross and some city pubs, had confined his searches to his area of domicile and had made the Oaks at Mosman his area HQ. The visit to the Ship was an essential inclusion in his orientation. Damned nice of Roddy to have thought of it. It was time then for two very tanned, fit young men, glowing almost, from showering suds, attired in evening finery to present themselves in the lounge bar of the Imperial Services Club.

A steward was serving them when Dudley appeared at his side and across the bar welcomed Roddy.

'And, Mr. Mckenzie is this Mr. Harty?'

'Yes, Dudley, let me introduce Lieutenant Mike Harty, Royal Artillery, WO Dudley Moore who attends to all our comforts.'

'Pleased to meet you, Mr. Harty. Welcome to the ISC. I hope you will enjoy your stay. Please don't hesitate to ask for me if you need something. By the way, you are expected. I'll make it known you are here. Mr. Badge is here and Mr. Wilson, so you won't be on your own while Mr. Harty does his first parade, Mr. Mckenzie. Enjoy your beer, gentlemen. Excuse me.'

Dudley returned, bringing with him the evening's orderly officer who was appointed to greet guests, and newcomers, introduced him to Mike and Roddy, and left. While they were still engaged in introductory chatter, John Wilson bowled up and, almost immediately, Lawrie Badge, so the orderly officer, his duty taken over, confirming the welcoming wishes of the club, went off to other duties. It was clear that it was time for Roddy to leave, Mike would not be high and dry, and as Lawrie was a bachelor, they might possibly share an evening together. Chris Paton was next to arrive when they were talking about their stay in Bruce Lockwood's hut at Khancoban where Roddy had filled the kitchen with trout and Mike had done some pencil and some water colour studies, a couple of water colour paintings one, of the old hut which he would like to give to Bruce. Roddy was quick to say, 'The water colour of the hut is exceptionally good. Mike has a real talent. I don't paint, but I'm a student and lover of the water colour genre. He's captured the mood; the weary bones of that old building and its confirmed place among the tress that it seems to have shared life with. You can even feel the mountain air. I'm sure Bruce will be very pleased.'

'Mm, well done. I'd like to be there when Lockwood sees it. I find it interesting to think that quite a number of estimable painters are ex-sapper and artillery officers. Some from the eighteenth and nineteenth centuries are amazingly good. I wonder if you'll get the time to paint some "men at work" scenes. Cameras have done some almost artistic work, but I can image the human story would be all the richer, more perceptive and evocative from an artist. Let me know if you do any. I promise to buy.'

'Ah, touting for business in the club, Harty. I'm sure there's a regulation forbidding it. Okay, we'll have a subaltern's court. That leaves you out, Wilson. Gentlemen! Harty should be fined a round!' declared Mr. Badge.

'Hear, hear!' said Mckenzie and, of course, Paton.

Then it was time for Roddy to make his exit, join the money changers across the road—and Jill.

In the bank's dressing room, Jill had changed from her garments of executive toil and, in a short, square necked dress of black linen which followed every muscle of her strong firm body, showing from just below mid-knee her long finely moulded legs, greeted Roddy. Her black leather shoes were light, stylish, and elegant but somehow spoke supple comfort. She wore scant make-up, leaving her fine face to glow of nature and oestrogen. Her bright eyes were twinkling delightfully as she stepped forward from her group to welcome him. The bank messenger still had his hand on the door handle. She had been waiting and watching. She strode forward, and just a short pace away, something soft yet eager took over her eyes and sotto voce, yet clearly, she said, 'I want to kiss you.' He pulled himself more erect, into rigidity, and stated into her eyes, 'We're on parade.' Then he smiled and quietly said, 'Wait till stand down.'

She ushered him into the group of mixed executive-level people; the high regard in which she was held by its members was evident in the way they pulled themselves more upright and focused their attention on her and her guest as she rejoined their company. Even the bank's clients in her small group caught something of the mood and turned to take in Jill Lowing and her handsome young guest. Waiters, in what was almost tropical mess kit, were moving through the gathering which may have comprised thirty people, dispensing food and drinks. The clients, perhaps thinking the bank owed them a little more for their overdrafts, had been rewarding themselves, one might guess, and were continuing consume heartily.

The conversation ranged across matters affecting the economy; the huge drop in wool prices since the Korean War, import duties, protection for Australian goods and manufactures, shipping and wharf strikes, equal pay for foreign crews working round the coast, advertising since the advent of television, migration, and inevitably but not because Roddy was there, the Snowy Mountains Scheme, how Holden was expanding and building a new plant at Elizabeth near Adelaide. It was a source of education for Roddy, and he not only listened to every word but how the subjects were being spoken about, the feelings they aroused and what direction the views of this group appeared to be taking. Jill listened to his questions and how he clarified the responses. She noticed that people, not knowing he was a machine operator on the Snowies, gave respect to his intelligent, diplomatic questioning. Strangely no one had asked what his position was. They reacted to his accent, his demeanour, the fact that he had just come over from the ISC and the slight sense that they were being in some way assessed and to be inquisitive might not be a fruitful approach. And it was clearly evident that he was under the protection of Jill Lowing.

Soon it was time to go, and Jill mentioned that they must leave to attend a concert. None was any the wiser of Roddy's status, and they were gracious in their farewells and wishes that they enjoy the concert.

They had scarcely got round the corner into George Street when Jill stopped him. For a second, she stood before him as passion shaped her face; she drew him into her strong arms and fervently kissed him. Roddy succumbed and responded, quite amazed at the intensity of the moment. She pushed him slightly back and, holding him by his arms, said, 'Oh, Roddy, I've been dying to do that.' He didn't want to lie. He raised his hands to hold her cheeks and gently kissed her lips. 'Jill . . . that was thrilling,' was all that he could allow himself to say. It was naive, it was boyish, and it was virginal. Jill read all of these things, and she was happy and knew she must take care. He could scarcely confess that he had actually felt fear—fear that this was not a time to be falling in love. The freedom to build a future first would vanish; and the practicalities of employment, income, and the attached social status would again 'rear their ugly heads'. He must not allow an escalation of feeling. He was probably at the peak of his sexual prime, packed with the driving force of testosterone. But he must not fall in love with Jill, and he must not mislead her.

She sensed that she had unbalanced him. Perhaps he was already in love with someone? Yet that was not what his eyes, his face, his body were telling her. 'Calm down, Jill. Be fair,' she was saying inside. Outside she said, clutching his hand and in girlish mood, 'C'mon, let's cross over and jump on a tram.' Roddy could feel some harmony in the rattling of the tram and the rattling in his body. Jill's mind was flicking over Roddy's suspected virginity which seemed confirmation that he had never been to a university. It was not part of Jill's fleeting thoughts, but it would appear that there is a popular, though not assessable unit in the subtext of every university's curriculum—Coitus Heterosexualis 101. Perhaps there would be fewer 'Failed' results in marginal cases were this unit compulsory. 'Cave! Cave!' she was whispering internally.

They stepped off the tram in a kind of a square, a space, in front of the town hall which was categorically a late-nineteenth-century British colonial town hall building seen in variations from Malaya to Rhodesia. The crowded square foyer, with its varnished panelled walls where the audience had gathered, was densely packed. Its high ceiling was hung with chandeliers by floral and leaf patterns in stucco, at its cornices in plaster castings of leaves and rosettes. There was an Australian and a State of New South Wales coat of arms with flags on varnished staffs, and a picture of Her Majesty the Queen. The people were well dressed and there was a good mixture of age groups but tending to be at least over fifty and many more in the sixties. Soon tubular pipe tones called the audience to its place. Their seats were in a box looking right into the orchestra so that they could see every instrument. Well done, Doris! They looked at each other happy to find themselves there—together. Neither had seen the programme.

Roddy burst out excitedly to say, 'Oh, look! The Rossini string sonatas! I love them. I've only heard them once at school and on records and I remember how much I liked them. The Tchaikovsky I heard at Southampton not so long ago. What do think, Jill?'

'Everything, everything and I'm sure you'll love the Mozart. Do you like bassoon music?'

'I didn't have any experience of it except recorded examples, but I did like what I heard in orchestral concerts when I was at Ranelagh. Mind you, I had to spend most of my time on army things, so even there I couldn't get as much music as I wanted. I'm getting so much joy out of my learning life. I know it really began at school but you have no idea how much Ranelagh and Hugh and Miette and Jane Dugal have done for me.'

Jill had a mental flash. 'Oh? Jane Dugal? That's new. Didn't hear her mentioned at Ranelagh. Leave that one for the present.'

'Roddy, we're all learning, all the time, you are no different from anyone else—except those who seem to learn nothing.'

'Yes, I agree, but I'm very conscious of having spent two very important development years in a different world—a separate world—with other people of my age, learning very important things for us at that time, which aren't at all usable in normal society.'

She turned to face him squarely with sincere surprise, the astonishment showing in her wide eyes. 'Good heavens! I don't think I've met anyone of your age who is so socially adept!' His face flushed red with embarrassment. He quite sheepishly said, 'You're very kind. Oh, look! They're coming on.' He was saved from further embarrassment by the players taking their places. And Jill was asking herself how he really could have doubts about his social competence. 'Insecurities? Rubbish! Never seen such confidence.'

They went down the broad staircase at intermission where they joined everyone there in talking about the first half. 'Did you enjoy those pieces, Jill?'

'Loved every note? How did you like the bassoon as a solo instrument?'

'Oh, boy! Wonderful! You do hear it in the back, but it seems to get a bit lost if you don't follow it almost specifically. Ah, yes . . . splendid. And what a player! Would he have controlled his own phrasing, or would the conductor have imposed that?'

'Dunno, Roddy. I suppose it would depend on their relationship and whether the conductor felt the player's interpretation was better than his. I'm guessing that you're guessing it was the instrumentalist, and if you are, I must say that would be my guess too.'

There were no pre-ordered drinks awaiting them at the bar as there would have been in England, but they needed no diversion. Jill did not take her eyes from Roddy's face. Her learning was centred on this man, this 'rough navvy from the

Snowie Mountains', whose showing in the group at the bank this evening would indicate him decidedly as diplomatic corps material. His level of discussion and his questions about the music were incisive and perceptive. She became quite excited, infected by his enthusiasm, telling her now of a performance he had heard of the next piece, the Tchaikovsky Number Four by the British National Youth Orchestra at Winchester; he had been so excited about it.

'The energy of those kids, the exuberance just thrilled me, I tell you.'

The lights went down. It was difficult to settle. The anticipation was powerful. All was hushed. The conductor raised his baton. She reached for his hand. He took it in a firm hold.

From those unforgettable opening bars, the Number Four was thoroughly enjoyable. Staying close, he followed Jill down the crowded staircase, through the foyer, where they became part of the audience cascade descending the town hall steps.

'We'll get a taxi,' Roddy said.

Taking his hand, Jill suggested, 'Let's walk down a little this way towards the Troc. We'll catch a cab on its way up.' She was right, and Roddy directed the cabbie towards Taylor Square to the restaurant of Doris's choice. 'Any particular place?' asked the cabbie. 'No, just right in the square please, south-west corner.' Jill's guess was immediate. Dimitri's was not brilliantly obvious and she could see Roddy's eyes scanning the facades when they left the cab. But she said not a word. He soon spotted it. 'Ah, there we go,' he said and, when they entered, found that they had to climb some stairs. These led into a large pleasantly lit room with a leg off to the right. Although there were larger parties, the number of tables for two was quite noticeable. There were lots of vacant tables for a Friday night which made Roddy wonder. Dimitri approached and introduced himself and gave them a friendly welcome. 'Yes, Mr. Mckenzie, we have reserved a table for you. Please come.' He showed them to a corner behind the back of the stairwell where they could see all the action in the restaurant and out of the window beside them the lights of the square and on to Oxford Street.

'It would be trite to say this place is cosy, but that's the feeling I get. There's a nice atmosphere. I'm just surprised that at this time it's not packed. The people, I see, seem very happy with their evening.'

'Our show being so close by, and finishing earlier than theatres, means we're here first. Just wait.'

'Have you been here before?'

'Oh, yes,' she said, many times. Dimitri's was popular with the Uni crowd, but all sorts of theatre and concert goers have been coming here for years. As you settle in, you may get some idea of why it's been so successful.'

'Good old Doris.' And then with a spuriously serious attempt at interrogation, he said, 'Heh-heh! Or did you connive and collude?'

'Cross my heart, I didn't speak with Doris about it. But don't think she and Mauri don't come here often. They don't go to the Chevron all the time and they go out a lot. Mauri loves anything in a theatre, concert hall, or music hall. They're Sydney people. Their house is not their only home. Sydney is their home.'

Shortly people began to arrive in a rush, and Roddy noted that Dimitri greeted them all, many by first names. A waiter came and offered the menu and wine list. Jill asked Roddy, 'May I make a suggestion? And if you try the dish I'm going to recommend and don't like it, I'll eat it.'

'Nothing to lose. What is it?'

'The garlic prawns. They're famous. After that, you're on your own, mister.'

So that was how they both began their meal. And before he was halfway through, he said, 'I'm glad I took that enormous risk of taking your suggestion. These are delicious!' The Seppelt's Arrawata Riesling was delicious too.

They discussed their enjoyment of the concert in delightful detail from the conductor to all the instrument groups, the skills, and most importantly, the interpretations. They discussed the restaurant, the food, and the wine. Jill was steering towards questions about Roddy's plans and was trying to lay down a conversational path. She began with the Snowies and hoped she could get him to talk about his thoughts on Australia. That might lead him to 'what's next'.

He was loud in praise of all that he had seen since he and Mike had driven out all around the Snowies, and he was excited about what lay further out awaiting their exploration. He was greatly taken by what they had seen on the way up to Sydney and was looking forward to the drive back down the coast. The car that Mauri had put at their disposal was a boon for which they were unendingly grateful. Until he left the Snowies and moved west to see and experience more, they would make use of it to the fullest possible extent.

'Does that mean I can expect to see you in Sydney more often?' (*Wrong question, Jill.*)

He knew exactly the portent of her question. 'I hope the answer to your question is yes. I don't really know what the near future brings because the jobs move in stages, but I can tell, having completed a finishing run on the road I'm doing, we'll be moved to another job. I can only guess what that may be and I don't know where. Time off will depend on the job.

'If I give Wood Bagshaw a year, I think I'll be able to move on with a reasonably clear conscience. I want to work on a sheep or cattle station as part of my Australian absorption, so I may talk to brother Mick about that when I go to visit him on the way west, which I'll do immediately I finish at Woods Bagshaw. Then I have my army reserve time to do, so who knows what demands might arise there. What I've read about the big, broad, rough Western Australia makes it mighty attractive. I have the really big questions still to be answered—where will I put down roots, and what'll I choose to spend my life doing. I think I know the answer to the second part, but not the first. It's a very self-centred tale, I know. But I've got to get that bit tidy or I won't feel I've done what I should have done before my making lifetime commitments.' He was about to say, 'I don't know how that sounds to you?' then realized he didn't want to hear an answer. He could see that Jill was following every word and was quite solemn. Throughout he had made no mention of her.

In a kind of summary, she said, 'I'm interested to see that your plan takes in your practical needs and an emotional preparation. This is such an important juncture in your life. And really, the unavoidable demands of the world put you in it. For the most of us, we just flow on from being children to adolescents and the flow simply continues through young adulthood. Yours wasn't like that. There was a break in the flow and some horrible things filled the gap.' Hers had been a sad solemnity as she listened. It continued as she had spoken, and now the moments weighed silently on time. Before them everywhere in the room, everyone's evening was getting into high gear—except for some couples whose preferred mode was dreamy slowness. There were obvious cases here and there of short-sightedness, the affliction causing the couple to see each other only if their foreheads were touching. Roddy and Jill seemed to have been left out, left behind, left by the current in shaded backwater.

'I ask myself whether I have the courage to ask you what you're thinking', he said, then very softly, but audibly, slowly, and gently as he watched her eyes, 'so I'll ask you. What are you feeling now, Jill?'

'I'm having feelings that of course I have every right to have. If feelings of any kind can be right or wrong, I think mine are wrong, because I was building a little dream for myself which was becoming bigger. I know what was happening inside me: I was feeling love for you.' It seemed as if for a moment the clear-minded, thoughtful Jill was stepping outside her emotional self and putting herself under an objective inspection. 'You appeal to me so much, Roddy. Just being the person I met on the Solent water, the incident on the polo field, seeing how you fitted so naturally into the Ranelagh set, and how much Hugh admired and respected you, and Miette flagrantly loved you. I would have wanted to be part of that world—not the Ranelagh world—although those people are so genuine and make life at Ranelagh wonderful; no, I wanted to be part of the Roddy Mckenzie world. You have just let me know that that is not to be and I'm saying to myself in consolation: at least not yet. The past has irretrievably gone. The future? . . . Well, in truth, who knows what will happen in the next moment? But I do know I am with you here, now, having captured you from everyone else: Carpe diem! *Egestas est. Gaudeamus igitur iuvenes dum sumus.*'

'Consensus est! Gaudeamus', he cried, then much less energetically and quietly asked, 'Shall we take a ferry in the moonlight?'

'Yes, let's.'

Roddy called their waiter; settled the bill, leaving the money, the bill, and a pourboire in the leather folder on the table; thanked him; and with Jill, went to find Dimitri to tell him how much they had enjoyed his restaurant. Dimitri bade them a hearty good night.

This end of Oxford Street was very active; people leaving early and people arriving late were moving to or from restaurants and people walking hither and yon. They took a cab to the quay and on the ferry sat on deck in the moonlight enjoying the lights, the water, and the clouds hanging down where they had been placed in the arch of the sky, their underbellies illuminated by the lights of the city. They were sitting on the bench seat side by side. She turned to him and, as if self-questioning the rightness of her request, asked, 'Roddy . . . may I hold your hand? I feel somehow that I need to.' His response was to turn towards, take her hand from her lap, lift it to his lips, and still holding it, laid it back where it had been in her lap. He looked into her face—shaped, lit, and shadowed by the moonlight, where a wisp of blond hair was being stirred by the breeze. The feelings that were exerting demands on his resolve were showing in his eyes, and in the set of sadness on his face, he softly said, 'Thank you, Jill. Oh, you're a deep, rich, caring, wonderful woman.' And after a pause, added in a different tone, he said, 'There seems to be a sadness in our rejoicing.'

'It seems that our sadness is impossible to evade. I feel I could devour you; I care for you so much. And you feel that you will never achieve completeness if you don't do what you must do next. I'm imagining what you may be feeling. Because of me, you are unhappy about having to make your choice, the choice you have every right to make—and must make. And while your unhappiness tells me a story about your care for me, I don't want anything to do with me ever to make you unhappy. I think we're going through a grief at the moment. But people grow out of grief and those words, depending on the way we might say them, still apply to us.' She turned further, briefly and lightly kissed him.

'Look!' she said, almost brightly. 'We're just about to dock.' At that moment, the ferry's motor changed its tune.

They disembarked and, hand in hand, began the short walk to Jill's apartment.

'It was so good of you girls to ask me stay with you here in lovely Kirribilli. There was a lovely naturalness to coming here, like a happy extension of our Hampshire meeting.' It was sweet sorrow strolling to her door. They stood there in the moonlight on the steps. 'I won't ask you in,' she paused, looking, taking him all in. Quite suddenly, she seized him in her arms so tightly that he had to push his ribcage out to breathe. She clung to him, kissing him in an exploding passion, her pelvis pressing against his. Her whole body seemed to shudder and she let him go. 'Oh, Lancelot', she said, her face recomposing, 'get thee hence! Take ship in the moonlight for the other shore. Let there be no madness of farewells.'

Holding her shoulders, he kissed her lightly, at the same time recognizing these moments' significance, struggling to avoid saying the things that needed to be said, trying to suppress the underlying tremor in his voice. 'The garlic prawns were a good tip.'

She knew he knew. She turned quickly and went in. The night was over.

At the club, he unlocked the door and went up. There was a low light in the bar. He put his head round the door to find Harty and Badge at a low table where there was a basket of dry biscuit varieties, a stand with cheeses on it, and more significantly, two glasses and a decanter of port which looked as if it had developed a leak.

Mike looked towards him and said in a cheery voice, 'We have a guest for the night, Rod. Mr. Badge flannelled Dudley and got a room.'

'Great wisdom in one so young. Aren't you going to offer me a drink?'

'What do you think, Lawrie?' asked Mike of his companion in serious enquiry.

Mr. Badge pondered, screwed up his eyes, and examined the decanter in which he found the liquid level to be dangerously low.

'I shall exercise the club's honour system', pronounced Badge, getting up, 'and on behalf of Thirty-second Battalion Royal New South Wales Regiment, select a bottle of Penfold's Grandfather port from which we can offer a tot to a visitor just arrived.'

'Well done, that dashing young subaltern', hurrahed Mckenzie, 'regimentally wearer of a kilt of barrelled pleats—but not at the moment.'

So it was, that under the swinging lantern, that they sat in the comfort of the club bar, yarned, and told 'warries', and in gentlemanly good taste, retired, just before the dawn would rise naked from its bed.

The yacht club was stirring with bodies of men and women hauling and heaving: others, fresh from work, stuffing down a pie and a schooner before rigging. Roddy was badly in need of a hair of the dog and found Mauri at his table pronouncing the order of battle for the afternoon. He introduced Roddy to two men, possibly in their forties, who had not long ago taken up sailing. Roddy was perfectly happy to join them as crew. The afternoon had brightened up a bit after a morning of drizzly rain which had come with the flukey breeze from the south, south-west, and just about anywhere else. They sailed sensibly, adequately, got on pretty well together, and finished up in the top half of the fleet.

From the Kirribilli ferry, a lady dressed in casual elegance strode towards him. The look of the tumbly, wind-blown, salt-sprayed day had been transformed to loose blond hair falling to a collared blouse of crisp white, a gold chain at her golden tanned throat. A tan skirt with free pleated movement from above the knees, a tan belt with a crafted gold buckle, light shoes with open tops of leather tanned to match the skirt and belt; a small leather purse with gold trim and a light shawl was all she carried; a small gold watch with a narrow tan leather strap brought everything together.

He walked towards her, the posy held forward in his hand.

'Is this beautiful, elegant woman I see before me the wind-blown sailor girl I left on the doorstep of a house in Kirribilli? For you', he said, extending further the hand with the posy, 'a humble token of my affection. I threw away the armful of roses from the florist: too trite, too cliché.' Taking a step forward, she turned her face up a little and he kissed her lips.

'These capture much more feeling', she said, 'thank you.'

Mauri and Doris's was a radically old house on a site where the very first building had been removed over a hundred years ago, the site had for a time after had been occupied by a big shed when the bay had functioned as a busy service entry to the city close behind. The shed had been demolished and a merchant, wanting to be near to the trade and the city, had built a big house functionally solid, Georgian, and in truth, not lacking a kind of grandeur. The area just exactly suited where Doris wanted to make a home. For Mauri, the views, the buildings around them, and the stories of past events, the kinds of activities that went on, and the people who lived round about met all his spiritual criteria. Perhaps there was a spirituality too in the frequently used classic carvel planked motor launch painted in shining deep royal blue moored alongside his own jetty: it was how they came and went to the club across the harbour or visited friends along the shore. So covering up behind them all signs of the modern comforts and facilities they had fused into the structure, they had created a fine, aesthetically pleasing residence which they enjoyed every moment of living in: they were very happy.

It could not have been many minutes after seven thirty when their cab dropped them on Billyard Road in front of a tall iron gate of black spears, set in a high wall of precisely cut Hawkesbury sandstone. There was another piece of wall and then two panels of towering iron gates of the same spearhead design closing the carriageway. Inside the pedestrians' gate, their path led through a dense subtropical garden jungly and dark, yet where blooms, that would be brilliant, possibly garish in daylight, showed colour even now from the path lights and other lights on lampposts amongst the trees. Voices and laughter were heard on the first floor. The doorbell rang with a very old-fashioned beautifully clear *ring-ri-i-ing! ring-ri-i-ing!* which must easily have been heard throughout the house and might even cause alarm on passing freighters? A head, covered in wavy dark hair, appeared almost directly above them over the balcony which ran around the first floor. A deep toned but cheerful voice said, 'I'm Kate Wilson. Leave your swords, pistols, and muskets on the table in the hall and come on up.'

'I'm Roddy Mckenzie, and this lovely lady is Jill Lowing. Don't take alarm, dear lady, I'll just fire a shot to clear my musket and follow your instructions.'

The party was on the front balcony, well, partly, because through the big sliding multiple, glass doors of the house proper, a real party room was dazzlingly visible. The evening was shedding degrees of warmth by the minute. Out there on the verandah broad and wide, high above the water, the guests were spread about. It's not that Jill was blasé about the view because she had frequently been there before, but for Roddy, it was almost overwhelming. He took as much in as he could at a glance, while going with Jill to meet the host and hostess. Doris was not in view, but Mauri was with three others, including their herald, Kath Wilson. Mauri greeted them, 'Hello, Jill and Roddy, welcome.' Jill kissed Mauri's cheek, and Roddy handed over his gestural bottle of Chateau Neuf du Pape and, shaking Mauri's hand, said, 'Very happy to be here.' His eye then refocused on the man and the dark-haired lady standing next to Mauri. Mauri's words of introduction had scarcely been made when Roddy said, 'Well, blow me down! John Wilson! Do you have a surveillance task on me?'

'In defence of the realm, mate. Can't be too careful with foreigners. "The price of safety is eternal vigilance." Best duty I've ever had. My subject spends most of his life in pubs and clubs.'

Mauri said, 'Glad you've got your eye on him, John—always had my suspicions about Mckenzie—looks a bit shifty, doesn't he?'

'You ain't seen nothin' yet. Wait till I take my disguise off.' Then turning to Kath Wilson, he said, 'If you'd heard these two going on about me earlier, you wouldn't have let me in, Kath.'

Huge, dull white, ceramic troughs, filled with ice, looking Spanish-Arabic, with hand-painted patterns of yellow blooms, wispy green tendrils, and green flowers, held enough champagne and cold beer to get the party started and offer a drink to a passing squadron of destroyers.

'Can I get you two something to drink? Jill, what would you like?' asked Mauri.

With drinks in hand, they got down to chatting about how John and Roddy had met and how John was Mauri's advertising agent. Doris arrived beside them and enveloped herself in the group next to her darling Jill and Roddy. Then there was the story about how Jill and Roddy had met, and how Mauri had met Roddy and how Roddy had taken Australia to heart and how his opportunity to get to see some of it and get to know a bit about it was due to Mauri's generous supply of the 'Snowy Mountains' Fusan. So the conversation stretched and unfolded in totally pleasant ease. Whenever politeness allowed, Roddy's eye would turn to the view. Jill could see and understood the attraction. 'Excuse us while I show Roddy the view. I can see he's on tenterhooks to go and gaze. C'mon, Roddy.' She took his hand and led him to the balcony. There, they looked out across and around Sydney Harbour, which from their vantage point was an immense expanse of dark water, glittering flashes, light pools, and activity of ferries and other craft. Roddy found it literally breathtaking. They were at their viewpoint when they were joined by Emma and Harry Ferguson. Harry was a 'mate', that is to say, first officer, the captain's next in command, on a ship of the British Clansmen Line, one of her company's clients. They had met and gone out together a number of times since all the vessels he had crewed on visited Australia in a regular pattern. Mike Harty had arrived, but he had been caught up with Mauri and John Wilson. Later, Verity made her entrance in a sleek black dress with lots of big decorative baubles on every limb, at her throat, and in her hair—Carmen Miranda would look positively dowdy—squired by a very lean, long Englishman with wild blond hair and large black horn-rimmed glasses garbed in bits of mixed tweed and corduroy which neither fitted nor matched: they were the last expected guest to arrive. Doris greeted them and did the introductions. Verity's beau was Erl Finn, an Irishman who had been working in England as a film director, and was a new arrival at Channel 8. They chose champagne as their drink, which Roddy volunteered to fetch from the tubs outside. Food was brought to serving tables at the side of the room and guests helped themselves at will, when they felt like it; it was easily portable, so the idea was to take what they had chosen to a long table in the centre of the long room, at which they could sit where they liked and move elsewhere when they liked. The wines were in little groups of bottles at three or four spots on the table when the dining began, and it didn't matter where they got to their original positions were immediately replenished. Of these, the white wines were in cold-walled buckets without water or ice. There were people standing or sitting, moving and mixing, chatting with whomsoever they wished in loose randomness, joining in or leaving. It was totally relaxed, decidedly sociable. It was clear that each of the guests—business associates, clients, artists, actors, or sailors—was, every one, a friend. They were all people for whom the Perrotts had an attachment of affection.

Amongst the early introductions, Jill and Roddy had met Beverly Nichols, another tall young man, who had come to Sydney from Wagga Wagga to study at the Sydney Conservatorium. Although he played and taught classical music now, he was a jazz addict and had actually recorded two discs of modern jazz piano music which were very highly admired by jazz cognoscenti—he was no mean exponent of trad jazz. He also played swing, ballads, and popular music just right for the ear of the market. Along with him, somewhere in the crowd, were a clarinetist who doubled on tenor, alto, and soprano sax, and a double bass player. While the meal and all the chatter was continuing he, and one of Mauri's men, had drawn open a set of folding doors disclosing an extension of the dining area where, on a small stage, there was a grand piano and room for a half-dozen musicians. He began, very smoothly, to play from the

Cole Porter album. Later, but in no hurry, the bass player had either taken the hint or got the urge to be up there. His arrival was very pleasantly noticeable. Later still, the melody you were sure you knew was taken over by the tenor sax with some very attractive yet very adventurous improvisations that submerged the melody through notes hidden in the complex chords which Beverley had now begun to create on piano. It was 'classical' stuff—what a trio! But through the evening, they smoothly swapped styles without jarring transitions so you may at some time hear Fats Waller's 'Honey Hush', words by the pianist, or even numbers like 'Indiana Home'. During the Jive numbers, Mauri and Doris showed their delight in the sound and rhythm, displaying some great jiving on the floor in front of the band. Emma and Harry were pretty smooth too. Roddy couldn't jive, but he soon got the beat and the message, so he and Jill could have some fun participating. 'Oh, I like this! It's great fun,' he said to Jill. 'I can see. You're certainly getting the hang of it.' Kath Wilson and John with really skilful steps showed every sign of ill-spent youth and war days in England spent amongst Americans. The trio had breaks and came down to replenish their glasses and mingle with the group. There was a feeling of gentle energy, a kind of cohesive happiness in the air. Roddy and Jill could sense it, yet they both felt, much, much more than they would liked, outside it.

Later, Beverly and the trio got back to Cole Porter and Johnny Mercer and to foxtrots and quick steps. Jill and Roddy danced with others in the group, in fact, tried to get around with anyone who wanted to dance. Neither wanted to say that this was the last night and that it may be some time before they would see each other again. They were strangely nervous about dancing together to these slower rhythms. But they did, and their minds were asking the question, 'How did normal couples dance, who were not so emotionally involved?' It was impossible to say, 'It's been an enjoyable weekend.' It was too soon to be talking about skiing. 'What if I went down to the Snowies for a weekend when the racing season finished? How would we handle that? But we've done pretty well tonight.' Such thoughts were passing through Jill's mind.

Roddy had already told himself that he must not, in even the slightest way, mislead Jill. He couldn't suggest that they share weekends of exploration together. How the dickens would they cope with the idea of overnight accommodation? It would have to be day trips. She could easily, and quite rightly, decide tonight that their happy meeting was over. Hadn't he virtually put himself into her past? And that her emotional life must go on? But, 'Damn it, man, you know why you have to do what you plan to do.' And, 'Would it ever be possible to meet someone like Jill again? You may have to live with the memory of this moment, boy. Go on, what about Jane Dugal? Okay, you can rationalize that one, can't you? Huh, that's pretty pat, isn't it? And so you can close up your mind and your heart with adult good sense and logic—facing the facts, eh?' No, his mind was not a happy place. But for Roddy, analysis and logic had to prevail.

Their last turn on the floor was danced in almost complete silence, save some pleasantries about Mauri and Doris, and there was, sadly, some relief for both when the music stopped. It was not the night's last dance and neither, without saying so, wanted to do the last dance. It would be too symbolic of an end.

Through the evening, they had spent some time with the Perrotts—Jill mostly with Doris, who knew there was some sadness passing between the two and explained it to herself as being just the end of a lovely weekend, yet at the same time wondering if there weren't something more. Roddy had talked with Mauri about his last self-indulgence—to work on a sheep or cattle station as his idea of a kind of christening font on his way to becoming a real Australian. Mauri felt the need to say, 'That's a very romantic thought, Roddy, old son, and I can see where you're coming from. But for many years now, the bulk of "real Australians" have never been anywhere near a sheep station, so you could become one without wasting your time going to the bother of getting to work on one. And I can tell you now, you'll be lucky if you earn enough money to pay tax on. It seems like you've been too long in the bush already. You'll be reading Banjo Paterson poetry next.' Roddy did not let what Mauri had said go unconsidered and said as much in response.

'Mauri, what you're saying is good common sense and I know it's right. Maybe I'm just being lazy and not facing the reality of getting what my future is going to be set up as soon as possible. Mind you, I missed the two years when a bloke would normally be trying things out and feeling the wind. The truth is, I see pretty clearly already, where I want to go, much thanks to meeting John Wilson and you. My major objective is to see how to break into the earthmoving business which I've learned a bit about from the plant operating point of view and, should my big plan take longer to reach than I want, would not be a bad way to earn a living. I will admit that I am inspired by your car distributorship. My plan is to build an earthmoving business up to the point where I think I have enough experience running a business, and a good reputation with the bank, to set up an Australian dealership in earthmoving equipment. This means, apart from reading Banjo and Lawson and sitting by a billabong writing poetry, everything that I do will have, underlying it, what can I learn from whatever I'm doing at that moment that will help me sell, or lease to big operators, the products of my dealership. But I want to spend six months crutching merino wethers or knackering steers just to be able to say to myself, okay, game over. I've got to go to work now. That might sound like a dream sitting here today. Let's see what it's looking like ten or so years from now.'

As he looked at Roddy in serious enthusiasm as if they were going to set out on this operation together, Mauri's reaction was to say, 'From this minute on, if there's anything I can do to help, don't you be shy about asking. And you should know by now, I wouldn't say that if I didn't mean it: Anything. Any time.'

After a silent pause, sensitively enquiring, he asked Roddy, 'Would it be all right by you if I began to find out what's going on now in building earthmoving equipment in Japan?'

'On the contrary, that would be greatly appreciated. I just don't want anyone in Australia or anywhere else, from now on, to know, even by inference, what my intentions are. Surprise and security are two important principles of warfare I shall never forget the importance of, especially since there will most likely be a long lead time to my first move. Mauri, you've no idea what it means to me to have heard you saying what you did just now.

I almost feel as if I'm on my way. I've been a very lucky bloke and meeting you has been a great part of that good luck. I'm a new chum and I'm entering into a big hard world that I know bugger all about, I just hope that one day, whatever it may be, I can do something for you.'

'Okay, I'll tell you right now what you can do for me, to make me very happy: get stuck into achieving this plan—unless you come up with a better one—and succeed.'

He caught up with Doris and Jill, who had observed Roddy and Mauri in what looked like a very serious discussion, and when they ended it, how pleased they both looked. 'Perhaps I ought to be thinking about getting on a ferry,' Jill said. The Perrotts wouldn't hear of ferries and said they had planned to get them home by car; they just had to say when. They talked happy 'good night' and 'thank you' things with Doris about her great party and to Mauri for having them on the premises to share his total care and hospitality. The car was organized when they were going round the other guests and the musicians to say farewell especially to John and Kath Wilson, who were super friendly and great fun to be with, they suggested to Mike that he may like to come with them.

The driver dropped Mike at the club, and when he got to Kirribilli, he said to the pair as they got out, 'I'll just go and turn the car.' They walked to the door. They stood facing each other, and he put his hands out. She put her purse under an arm and they both took each other's hands. 'Jill, I want to thank you—for being you,' he earnestly said.

'I should thank you. I understand what you need to do. I want everything to go well for you. Perhaps I shall see you again before you leave for South Australia. Thank you for returning Banjo Paterson, I'm so happy that it has meant so much to you. It has always meant a lot to me: I was glad that you should have it. It will be infinitely more valuable to me now.'

The car pulled up in the road. It had taken quite a while to turn it round.

He took her in his arms and they kissed. She turned and unlocked the door. He turned away and took two paces, turned to her again, and said, quite quietly, 'Oo-roo, Jill.'

When Roddy had free time again, Jill was pleased to hear that he was coming up and enthusiastically suggested that, since their Jubilee racing season had ended, they could consider spending the day somewhere away from the city. Roddy was very happy with this idea. 'I'd love to do that. Mike told me wonderful tales about what he saw during his day out with Lawrie Badge.'

'It's amazing how many wonderful natural sights there are to enjoy without going very far from the very spot where I'm standing now. Shall I plan something?'

'Would you, Jill? That would be grand. What can I do for the venture?'

There was nothing required of him. He suggested that she select from whatever there may be on stage Friday night and, highbrow or lowbrow, make a choice, buy the tickets, which he would repay on arrival, and book a supper spot—and if her choice just happened to be Dimitri's, he'd be delighted. He suggested further that she may like to do the same for Saturday, but if she got any other sociable ideas, he would still be happy. The phone call ended on an enthusiastically happy note, and his heart pounding with feelings, he left the lone phone box on its corner of the road through Jindabyne—the disappearance and drowning of which he was labouring hard to bring about. 'My god, she's a wonderful girl,' he thought while another level was straining to contain feelings of love, joy, and happiness. There was strange sensation too, mixed through the others, of living in two different or even among three worlds in which he was sustained in oscillation by a metaphysical power.

Metaphysical powers apply their forces capriciously. A child, looking forward to some delightful event, will find days cruelly dragging time slowly, painfully out. For an adult, so in Roddy's case, time to an event packs itself in smaller compass. In the days between that phone call and picking up the Nissan at Jindabyne, time had deserted its Mckenzie-related duties and fled elsewhere perhaps to prolong the pain of an invalid. It was as if he had put the phone back in its cradle, then turned the ignition key in the little car.

With its headlights on, and watching where it put its feet, the Fusan ventured out on a day of drabness and drizzle covering all in low wet cloud from the heights above to the very bed of the Snowy River. The road out of Jindabyne required attention at the best of times: today it required concentration. From Cooma onto Queanbeyan, it was better with the thick fog thinning then left behind and, thereafter, really enjoyable. He had left in the pre-dawn, the first light taking some time to become distinguishable. He would take the shortest route and drive as fast as he could to expand the free hours of Friday in Sydney. His kit was minimal, so when he arrived in town in the afternoon, he garaged the car and walked up to the club. Such was his welcome at the ISC that he could well have imagined himself a white-haired old chap with a strictly trimmed white moustache, comfortable in his old tweed suit which, which, were it animated, would be pleased to find itself in a place it knew and loved from many previous visits.

Roddy was beginning to see himself as a regular visitor. He felt the welcome, enjoyed it and the warm feeling it gave rise to. After putting his gear in his room, he went down past the bar, looked in, saw no one he knew so continued with his plan to go down to the Army Disposal store to find a heavy jacket, trousers, and another shirt; oh, and he must remember, more thick socks! There would be plenty time to do this and have a beer after dressing for the evening. Mind you, he fancied one now. Sydney was sunny and pleasantly warm as he walked up Martin Place before taking off down Elizabeth Street.

Back in the club, he was scrubbed and dressed; ready now to have that painfully postponed beer. He waved to Peter Tracy there in a small group, but John Wilson collared him immediately.

'Ah, the Man from Snowy River, I'll stand down my man at Jindabyne and take over the surveillance personally. You're looking well, but there's the look of a recent battle about you.'

'I'm really well, thank you, John, but I've been working my arse off on overtime trying to build the kitty for the last of my swanning around before I get serious. How have you been?' He had seen Doris and Mauri, Mauri a few times on business;

Bruce had told him Roddy had been over to the hut; Chris Paton should be in any minute. He'd just won a very big client and was going really well. Although he was in a state of severe drought, Roddy had to take care; he had an evening with Jill to look forward to. He bade his friends bon soir went down the stairway to Barrack Street and crossed to that special door in the wall of the Bank of New South Wales.

Jill had invited him to the bank for after-work drinks. She welcomed him at the door, her face glowing with health and the emotion with which she welcomed him. Her light kiss transmitted her warmth and vigour.

'Welcome back. Come and have a drink.' They joined the small group that Jill had just left and then, as seemed to be the pattern, the others departed one by one to join other groups. Jill and Roddy had a little time to themselves.

'You look as if you've been working very hard,' she ventured, and he explained that the hours were long because winter was approaching and the road had to be heavyweight ready before the snow came; the ground was rocky and steep so—and he laughed—'I'm working like a church organist, hands and feet flying.'

She closed her eyes and turned her blank face to his. 'I'm picturing you at the controls—in an academic gown—fluttering and streaming behind you in the mountain winds as you push giant stones out of the way with your big noisy machine,' and she laughed as she opened her eyes.

'Mauri has said I have to take a day off sailing because he has a young potential crewman to try out. The trophy's in the bag, so it's a good opportunity. But I think he's becoming conscious of your time running out. So am I. Your Australian Assimilation Assessment will be coming up too, so I've set up a weekend of Subject Absorption. This evening we go to a suburban hall where we'll see a musical based a poem by a local poet and writer, C. J. Dennis, called "The Sentimental Bloke". Tomorrow we shall have a day out on and beside the Hawkesbury River, which I'm not going to spoil for you by saying anything more about. In the evening, it's back to the theatre again, this time in town to see another Australian written and produced piece of theatre *The Summer of the Seventeenth Doll.* Do you think you'll cope and not drown?'

'Fear not, I'll more than survive, even if I have to make copious notes to swot for my exams. I think what you have planned is super: and remember Wood Bagshaw is paying for this. Can you tell me now? I'll write a Bank of New South Wales cheque on the spot.'

'That would be a bit embarrassing and cause eyebrows to be raised. Wait till tomorrow. I didn't bring the car and I think it would be pointless getting yours. It will be part of your testable learning to go to and from the theatre by local rail. You will be observed purchasing the tickets and getting us there and back sans faute.'

'Oh god, I'm getting sweaty palms already.'

After some light chatter with Jill's colleagues in different groups, they bade them their good wishes for the weekends and went off to nearby Wynyard Station where Roddy's 'practical' would commence. With no trouble whatever, even the line change at Central with no assistance whatever from the examiner, they reached Hurstville as intended where, quite appropriately it seemed, they were to see a professional production of *The Sentimental Bloke* at the town hall. Roddy took immediate delight in mixing with the suburban audience in the foyer, dressed up feeling their sense of anticipation in enjoying a Friday night theatre show. He could feel their light mood and sense the jocular pitch of their chatter. He could hear some, who knew the poetry well, allocating roles to the people in their group. Jill's point of observation was Roddy and a good part of her enjoyment came from it. In situations such as this, his pleasure was always a kind of respectful enquiry about people's feelings, their expectations of delight, and what about this event was causing that? Whatever these were, he seemed to become infected by the ideas and feelings in the air. Entering the auditorium he was, like them, ready to enjoy. He was not disappointed. The themes of course were universal, across cultures and classes, and each social degree in each culture had its own view of how the protagonists should handle the problems that life had confronted them with and in any human event, tragic or comical. All had their preferred ways of seeing how the heroes and heroines tackled their fates. He and Jill were two of the happy people who tumbled out of the Hurstville Town Hall on that Friday evening.

'I have no erudite way of making a critique of the performances. Actors on stage act their idea of a person's life in the story to the best they can. Perhaps we just think, "Oh, a real person would have been more positive than that when, da . . . da . . . da." The actor within is still a real person, he's doing what a person is "actually", if you like, doing in the story. If the character is a bit "weak" in the role, the stage action, we just have to like it or lump it, just as in life people don't necessarily meet our performance standards. I just felt happy with what I saw, I think that however the performers played tonight, there were no jarring notes for me, and "what did you feel about it?"

'I'm in your school of thinking, there were some parts of the character that were almost annoying—I felt like giving him a push. But that was exactly how the producer and the actor wanted me to feel. I just thoroughly enjoyed it.'

'I would have been very sad if you hadn't. And you know, in terms of my preparation for the pending examinations, I do believe it has done something towards my Australian metamorphosis. It makes me happy because you had to make the choice about the show. The plot could have been shifted to Hampshire without change, but it would have been an "English" production. So if I'm imagining and comparing, I could recognize that this performance was Australian, mm, perhaps influenced by accents, but I think there was an inexplicable Australian dimension. If you'd brought English actors out to Hurstville, the performance would still have been "English". I doubt that the best Australian producer could not have made an Australian presentation with them.' The conversation followed mainly these lines all the way to Central Station where Jill said they would get out.

Then they were on the platform at Central Railway. 'Right', she asked him, 'if you were taking someone out to supper after a show, where would you take her?'

'Oh, I'd take her to a magic Greek place that she'd never been to before. I wouldn't tell her what it was. She'd have to puzzle and wonder and wouldn't know what her "new chum" escort could possibly choose. She'd be very nervous.'

She caught her breath and gasped, 'Ah! I'm very nervous.'

'Do not be afraid, *chere demoiselle*. My rapier butt's atwinkle. I would fight off all lecherous louts.'

Dimitiri's was packed to the gunnels, but someone had booked them a table. Dimitri approached. 'Jill, how nice to see you. Roddy, I've reserved your table. You were happy where you were last time, so I've put you there again. I hope that's okay?'

'You read my mind, Dimitri. You could not have done better. Mind you, if there are no garlic prawns, we're leaving.'

'Mr. Mckenzie, the chef has kept the last four pints for you.'

'Well done, Dimitri. That may just be enough. Jill may have to share.'

The atmosphere was lively and maybe noisier than last time; there were certainly many more people. They'd had the truly magnificent prawns and were pausing as they awaited the next course when Dimitri came to the table. He looked a bit anxious.

'You can see how busy we are tonight. You can say no to my request and I'll certainly understand.' Then he nodded in the direction of the door where a forlorn young pair stood looking around at the happy crowd of diners. 'That young couple there are not from Sydney', he said, 'they've never been here before, would you mind if they shared your table?'

Roddy looked at him sternly. He spoke seriously, 'We will consider your request. It will mean that you have to ring Government House and advise Her Majesty's representative that you are commandeering the places that I had reserved for him and his wife. On your own head, be it. Bring the poor waifs, we shall give them succour.'

Dimitri turned to Jill. 'Cor! He does go on a bit.'

'Never mind, Dimitri, his bark's worse than his bite. You worked out which of us to pick though, I would have said no.' Jill, Roddy, and Dimitri laughed.

He brought the couple who were possibly two or so years younger than Jill and Roddy, and after introductions, returned with a champagne bucket and said to the new arrivals, 'Miss Lowing and Mr. Mckenzie thought you may like a welcoming glass of champagne.' Smiling, he bowed like an obsequious old-time waiter and left without another word. Dimitri had read his game well. They turned out to be a delightful duo feeling at first very shy and were to be good conversationalists throughout. They were both from wheat-farming families from the Forbes area on the Lachlan River. The man's parents had retired and the pair, now married, had inherited the farm. This was their first visit to Sydney and had driven down for a week's holiday. The conversation centred on life in rural Australia every syllable of which Roddy was soaking up. He was pleased to be able to say that knew of the Lachlan from Banjo Paterson's Clancy of the Overflow and the pair showed their delight that he had taken that kind of interest. Roddy was happy that the conversation was in the main about life in rural Australia, the flooding of the Lachlan, droughts, relationships with aboriginal populations, and how much better off they were in Forbes compared to Walgett where the population was almost even numbers of blacks and whites. There was constant conflict, bitter animosities, drunkenness, and fights. They'd seen little of Sydney and were making plans for their week. Roddy and Jill left the couple when Jill announced ferry time.

It was cool, cold almost, on the water, and they sat on the loo'ard side holding hands. They strolled up to Jill's apartment hand in hand, not talking very much. At the door, they gently embraced and just as gently kissed. They said good night, and Roddy waited while Jill went in.

At an early hour next morning, Roddy was at the door again. He very boldly kissed the beautiful smiling woman who stood there announcing that he had come to meet a Miss Lowing who was to be his tour guide for the day. 'Very forward, you foreigners. Do you kiss the tour guides everywhere you go?'

'Ah, yes', he said in lyric tones, 'one of the great joys of travel. All part of the mind-broadening experience.' Closing the door, she said, 'Do come in and I'll introduce you properly.' She put her arms round him and they kissed. She looked at him smiling and said, 'Good morning. Have you had breakfast?' she asked. He hadn't, so they shared eggs and toast and promised themselves a slap-up lunch. Emma appeared in a tracksuit and had a cup of tea with them, and after just a short exchange of conversation, Jill wanted to get the day's venture into the interior begun. They boarded a North Shore Line train at Milsons's Point not more than a couple of minutes climb from the apartment. As soon as the train pulled out, Roddy's next educational period began.

On the rail track now, which had just crossed the bridge they were on its level, high now above the harbour on the rocky escarpment wall that basically ran all the way around and into every part of Port Jackson, often visibly, sometimes less visibly where over many years the wall had slumped, broken up, and formed little headlands and bays and beaches. Old rifts and ancient rocky water runs had created an irregular topography on which the pleasant, leafy, north shore suburbs provided a congenial natural world in which humans could happily settle. And settle they had, from their Milson's Point start line to their planned destination at Brooklyn on the Hawkesbury River. Station after station marked the progress of settlement on this pleasant land north of the growing city, Artarmon, Wollstonecraft Gordon, where Jill's aunt had a house, and Killara, and it was as if the further north, the higher the status of the inhabitants. Roddy loved the greenery; he liked the possessive, statements of comfort, made by the attractively designed houses fitted into this irregular treed land. In minutes, they were at Brooklyn station.

From the station height, the river before them in a left-to-right traverse was a view across the river to irregular treed shores, wooded hills with shoreside settlements, moored yachts strewn along the stream, skies with scattered cloud allowed sun to make the water sparkle and sometimes cast cloud shadow over the water and trees making the water brown and the trees deeper shades of greens, accentuating forms and heights. Walking down, they entered the pleasingly irregular little township where although roads were mainly disciplined in their direction the house builders had minds of their own placing their future homes where they wished which created a coherence of differentiation. This irreverent view of council landscape was abetted by the different levels on which the houses stood. Here was a friendly feel to the place as if no one had settled here with any intention of taking life too seriously—any aspect of it. Despite the ideal climate, there did not appear at first glance to be many dedicated 'cottage gardeners', but there were those with fond hearts which have been broken to part with some wild art objects, placed by design perfectly in the composition brushed in rich iron oxide contrasting with tall straws of dried-out grass around them which obeyed all the rules of camouflage.

'What did you think when you saw this first, Jill?' He was unable to conceal in his voice his own surprise.

'I couldn't believe it; couldn't take it all in. I'd been to Bobbin Head, so I should have had some idea; but this was a bigger, more spread out, scene. No. That's the point; it was much more than one scene. Wherever I turned my eyes, I found a separate commanding scene; hundreds of separate scenes all day.'

They strolled around just enjoying being there before boarding the old wooden Dangar Island mail boat whose paint coats of green and white weather had bleached away to pale grey woodwork. But wasn't that the way it should have looked? It looked from its small heavily timbered rugged design as if it had been built to weather Pacific Typhoons—so what's a sissy coat of paint? From island to island, they went until they drew up again at the home port jetty.

'That was a brilliant idea, Jill. We couldn't have found a better way of seeing so much of the river—and at just the right speed. Imagine how it would spoil the entire effect to dash around where we've been in a fast boat?'

'Oh, I agree. We did that the same the first time I came. I hoped you'd enjoy it and I'm so glad you did. Now we have to climb up to the station again, because we have a picnic lunch appointment back along the track.' She took his hand and they set off upwards. In the return to Sydney direction, the train stopped at the first station—Berowra—where who should be waiting at the station to greet them but Verity and Erl Finn. Surprise for Roddy, laughter and greetings, and without hesitation, they bundled into "corporate car" which Verity had driven down from Kirribilli and would now take them down to the river and the launch. It was spot-on organization. From the park, there was only a short walk to the point on a wharf where Verity showed them aboard and introduced them to their host and hostess, the owners of the launch.

The owners were Neville and Joan Jefferson who had become friends of Verity through Neville's business connection with the station as a market researcher; they were coincidently clients of Jill's, who had helped them with funding during an expansion period. The story about these two, which Roddy picked up as the day went by, matched entirely their bright, engaged conversations with him and all the others in the little sextet of guests. They had both studied psychology at UNSW, and Neville had added a major in statistical method; they had stepped out into a world in transition where statistics had ceased to be 'damned liars' and become valued tools in market research, consumer and audience analysis, product development studies, and in another part of their organization carried out retail and production stock takes and measurement of media advertising volumes. These were aspects of the larger world, a business world that Roddy had never heard about before and, therefore, while hearing what was being said, learned that these were services businesses would pay for. It was building different kinds of roads with different kinds of equipment, instead of selling cars like Mauri, they were selling quick arithmetic and explanations about what people preferred or why they chose to do some things and not others. 'Incredible!' he was thinking. They established the business and growth had begun very quickly. Their clients had found these people much as Roddy was finding them now—keen, enthusiastic, sincere, and as he learned, hardworking, efficient, reliable. None of what he was experiencing and hearing was wasted on Roddy; it convinced him as being the formula for success and that the application of these characteristics to any business in the developing economy was bound to lead to a good income and an enjoyable lifestyle.

And certainly that lifestyle was enjoyable on their afternoon on Berowra Waters. The Jefferson's launch was a handsome

Halverson of about forty feet white with varnished oak woodwork, berths for six were concealed in a very clever, roomy fit-out, ideal for party cruising on the rivers summer and winter. Today, it would not be used to its full cruising on-board entertaining capability, immediately they were aboard they slipped their lines and going about from the jetty went a short way downstream to the private jetty of the old Berowra Waters Inn where the others of the party were already seated at a big table in the indirect sunlight at a window right above the river. The level of warmth of feeling in the people was immediately felt, and there was no reticence about including the new arrivals in continuation of existing conversations. The inevitable question 'How did you get to know Jill?' and its answer opened up the direct route to who and what Roddy was. From there were the natural diversions to shared and similar experiences, people, and places and what was going on in Britain, and it turned that apart from Jill, only Johnny Bryan, first as a cadet and then as a deck officer with a British shipping company, had been there. Johnny led the telling of risqué yarns from what was almost certainly a copious repertoire, Sue Lawrence was not far behind, Erl contributed his particular genre, and Roddy managed to select one from his collection: the others just didn't stand a chance at inclusion. So it was a non-stop vocal affair over a flavoursome rustic repast spliced with wine to follow the earlier beers. A short cruise was all that there was time for before people departed for home, and a discussion led to the conclusion that Roddy and Jill would return by train because of their fixed commitment, while Verity and Erl would return in the grey-and-pink, rather dashing, Vauxhall Velox. Johnny and Tanya were going back, and would happily have taken them, but the concern really was about a weekend traffic choke on Pacific Highway. It was a delight to cruise under the steep cliffs where marks of drilling on the rock faces told tales of early days and the building of Sydney's major monumental edifices, cathedral, and churches down to the tenements which would become the ugly slums still in existence, shelter for the often jobless poor. To the berth at the bottom of the steep tortuous road to the top the jolly vessel returned to disembark the homeward-bound quartet. A slight increase in engine noise and the sleek cruiser slid from alongside, leaving those aboard to carry on cruising, their cacophonous farewelling filling the river valley.

Recollections of a day of great fun and literally amazing sightseeing filled their conversation on the train ride home. With a kiss, Roddy bade Jill 'Oo-roo' as she left the train at Milson's Point. He continued to Wynyard Station and the Club to spruce up for their evening out.

Again they met at the ferry wharf, and again he felt the surging feeling inside as he watched that delightful, strong, glowing woman stride towards him.

'Bon soir, chere mademoiselle,' he called to her as the distance between them was closing, and he spread his arms to embrace her. 'Bon soir, m'sieu Roddy', she gaily replied, 'Ca va?' He kissed her and held her for a moment, then attempting to take in all that he was seeing, said, 'You look so beautiful—and fresh—and edible. Where are we off to?'

'The theatre's not far from here; for us, an easy walk. I must want to continue the fun of the day. I feel I'd like a drink, what about you?'

'Do Boy Scouts pee in the bushes?'

And from the look on her face putting much power into thought, he said, 'Gosh, you've got me there. I don't know.'

And he sang, 'What she don't know now . . . she can guess. All day, all night, Mary Anne down by the seaside sifting sand . . .', then sang to finish, 'so, Mama, you—can guess! Hurry up now. Take my hand and lead me, maid, where mead is made.'

'Come let's fly to the nearest grotty grotto or salubrious salon, who cares?'

They found quite a reasonable bar upstairs in a very old hotel at the bottom end of Castlereagh Street which would give them just a short hop to the theatre.

A lightning exchange of questioning glances and they had decided to stay. Roddy wanted something clean and fresh, and by strange coincidence when he asked Jill, the bar order was two gins and tonics, 'Tanqueray of course.' The mood of two was tingling; the joy of being out together, the anticipation of play, the funny old nineteenth-century bar, with not a piece of furniture or wallpaper changed, and the curtains had been shaken last spring.

That exciting feeling of a foyer crowd immersed them as they joined it moments before the first ring for the curtain up. The person who booked had arranged for stalls in that row where the floor changes height in an upward slope, so their stall seats allowed them to see the whole stage and wings.

At interval they stood, looking at each other. Who would ask the question first?

'This is truly the first big Australian play most of us here have seen. What did you think?'

'I'm enjoying the Australianness of it. It is pretty authentic, isn't it?'

'Oh yes, even down to the detail on the sets and certainly the story of canecutters—mind you, I've only read about their lives and learned about the sugar industry through economics, but what's happening on stage matches what I know.'

'It is interesting to see how, over a period as long as seventeen years, the characters have chosen to continue that disjointed life. Too soon for me to say too much, eh? I think it is good theatre and I really am enjoying it. But it's new for you too. What are you thinking?'

'To this point I'm thinking much the way you are—it's good theatre—the characters are developing well—lots of portentous dialogue with threats of change to come. It's keeping me involved and I'm enjoying it. Yes, it is Australian.'

Roddy was looking very serious as the pair became part of the foyer crowd and went out into the street.

'Where can we have some supper and talk about that great play? My god, there was so much in it!'

'I've organized a hotel with an upstairs supper room to be brought to a spot nearby, c'mon,' she said, taking his arm.

The Wentworth Hotel to which they came was a classical nineteenth-century monument in grand stately style with curving brass rails to guide patrons up the sweep of broad steps to massive baronial doors wide open and the foyer behind lit by a chandelier. The decor did not let the exterior down and to go up by a carpeted inner staircase to the gracious supper room was a pleasure alone. The pianist on a small stage in a corner was playing the kind of music you hear pianists playing in supper rooms; he was playing noticeably well and at perfect sound level.

The play was still much with them as they settled at the elegantly laid table, and even while waiters were doing their services about drinks and menus, they were eager to start the discussion though that wasn't indicated on Roddy's face. He was looking as if he had a problem that he was wrestling with.

'Taken overall, wasn't that a great performance?' asked Jill, seeking the confirmation she wanted to hear.

'Oh, aye was it!' he responded in idiomatic Scots. 'In every regard, there should have been great cries for "Author! Author!" There were so many ways and at different levels that, that work of Lawler's can be thought about. While I was conscious of and storing up others, the most striking forefront aspects were the characters' approaches to life and the idea of the effect of change on their lives, and it struck me that the change was a message for individuals, for me; but at the same time he was saying it would affect the whole nation. I think the author's idea of the kewpie dolls was absolutely brilliant. So . . . so . . . celluloid, so ephemeral, so intrinsically valueless tat, yet what huge power as the symbol at the centre of the story. Maybe he was saying we're going to have to give away, or at least think about, some of the things we are going to give away which we value now but which are just "celluloid dolls".'

'Gosh, I hadn't got to thinking about it that way yet—maybe I never would.' Jill said. I Iwas interested in how the audience was reacting the plight of the characters. Some of the time they appeared to be looking on their behaviour as a comic commentary on the characters and their foolishness in letting such a life situation arise. At the same time, some did seem to see a mirror view of things that happen in their own lives, like losing leadership through failing performance as your physical ability diminishes, and I'm sure some were thinking how, as physical workers, such a fate would come to them, if not at just any time, it ultimately would—their faces changed then. What then?'

Roddy responded. 'Of course you're describing what happened to Roo and how his early prowess supported his ego, now there was no support so his character would disintegrate and that was a bit sad. I just felt very sad for Olive weeping over the doll because it had been a memoriam of meaning, of times when she had been happy. It was a ten-a-penny celluloid doll which a child may cast aside, but to her it was more than a celluloid doll and now that memory was being taken away—change was taking away the meaning of her doll— and the meaning and the happiness and the consistency, the expectations—the anticipations of the yearly arrival of the men, which had unfailingly happened for seventeen years. It wasn't going to happen anymore. I was shattered, just getting the feeling second-hand from an actress in a play. There's a spate of things I'm thinking—about fading physical fitness, for example, here it's happening to one character but we can see how it affects others in—in the play and surely in our world— spreading ripples.'

Roddy was delivering this speech with such energy and commitment she was asking herself, and thinking, 'Why am I surprised that he should have seen so much in the play, has had these feelings, and is telling me about them? An unusual man, our Mr Mckenzie—his author certainly wrote him to be understood at many levels.'

The play kept their conversation busy, then somehow thoughts turned to what their next meeting might mean for them. It would be his last before he went away, before he continued his quest.

His quest must now include another grail. The play had driven a point into his searching brain. 'You think now, Mckenzie, that you are just about indestructible. So did Roo. Look what happened to him. It may be a long way away—if your luck continues—but one day it will be more than muscle that will be required to keep you, and maybe, by then, people who depend on you to live a good life. Focus your quest with that in mind.' Ranelagh, the Snowies, Sydney, Jane, Jill—somewhere deep inside, he knew, not by thinking, planning, dreaming, or imagining—there was another place another person that he could not invent, and there in that place, with that person, his quest would end.

Jill, too, had feelings and thoughts about his quest. She knew there was some powerful unsatisfied impulse driving him forward. Sydney, despite all that he admired about it, and the friendships he had made, seemed not to be its end. Nor it seemed, would hers be the love that went with him on his journey. She was sad, very sad that this could not be. 'I have my quest too', she comforted herself to think, 'selfish, as all quests are. My career will take me elsewhere, Britain, New Zealand, even the United States or Canada, and it will be with the bank. A man I can love, shared affection? I will never find another Roddy Mckenzie, they don't make two of those, but I will find a man to love one day, of that I'm certain.'

Neither was conscious of it then, but their evening now, and the time until Roddy went away, would be based on these feelings. What was left to them by time, between now and his departure, would be for them, together, in Sydney, not a celluloid doll time, but a part of their lives which, because its feelings, thoughts, and experiences had grown into their hearts and minds. This time which had posed them challenges that they had faced, had now become, and would be part of who they were—forever.

Martin Musgrove's brief friendly enquiries about their weekend was a prelude to a blast of changes which was a little disturbing, even to hardened homeless nomads with an uncertain future, like Roddy and Mike. Even if minimal, by comparison to house dwellers in a static community, having to leave an environment to which they had become attached, with which they had developed associations and stories of experiences, they did feel some regret at leaving the billet that had become their focus of life when not working. Beyond being simply a place to lie down and sleep, it had been their social lounge where they could enjoy in quietness and calm a beer or a glass of wine while they exchanged thoughts, stories, and considerations, they were in the process of making about their future. It was study, office, reading room, library, wardrobe, and dressing room: it

was the mute welcome they came back to after the day's labour.
Physically their house and its neighbours on the terrace would
be taken tomorrow, holus bolus, to an area above the Snowy
River crossing at Jindabyne. Roddy would go there with the rest
of his current team members to clear the site. With their team
would go accommodation trailers as sleeping quarters. The men
were to have a single room each in the trailers. More men would
be coming to the cleared site, and until a camp kitchen was set
up, they would be rationed from hot-boxes brought up from this
site before that too was moved. The 'geo' team, of which Mike
was part, would be located in another trailer further along what
would eventually become the main road, to a point where the
site of a tunnel had to be mapped, the rock data gathered and
analyses and all levels established. After this task, Mike's team
would continue planning the road that Roddy's team would
work on until winter came when they would move underground
into the tunnel, load trucks with front-end loaders, and haul
the blasted-out rock to a dam site, but now they must build an
all-weather road before the weather broke. It was going to be
maximum effort in speed and competence or work would have
to cease until the snow disappeared and until the roads would
bear the heavy traffic volume to continue working. To stop
would be unaffordable in terms of cost and overall project time.
The main road, to be planned and begun now, would become
the main permanent road to, and through the new township,
after the existing township of Jindabyne had been moved up to
approximately where the trailer camp would temporarily be.
Mike's team would move out of the Snowies altogether for the
winter to work on major improvements of the Hume Highway
nearer the coast. They had to be out of their present billet by
seven a.m. on Monday, their gear suitably packed ready for
pick-up at that time.

To make their world manageable and give them some sense
of continuity, human beings had conceived a concept which
to all intents and purposes was 'time'. This idea would explain
the spaces between events, and after some thousands of years,
or fewer, make it possible to explain the recurrence of events
like sunrise and sunset and changes of seasons. If there were

lots of events with short spaces between them, newer versions of humans, the more sophisticated, realistic, super-intelligent ones would fall subject to the impression that time had speeded up. And if boringly not much was happening, well, surely that meant that time was getting longer. Roddy and Mike now had an immediate target for the events of their move measured by a tool adding a refinement to the otherwise-wobbly concept, a readable man-created instrument designed to measure it—a clock, or a watch. So they could apply that humanly created concept of time to related concepts, none of which you could stick a pin in to calculate the space between the events that must occur; and they could measure and decide what they could and would do between finishing their briefing by Mike Musgrove here, and the event of putting their belongings on the trucks at seven the coming morning. What a challenge to human effort, the creation of that mental concept had become! And now that some marks of events had been plotted others would soon join them. More clever modern humans, because their brains were often confused by their dreaded concept, created within themselves this idea that time accelerates. Some event which, at the present moment, seemed likely to occur at some far distant point of the future would appear to be rushing closer if lots of other events took place between the 'now' and that distant, future event, or that that conscious person was being rushed ever more quickly towards it.

Time, and event points in it, used to pervade the discussion and conversation during the nights in their cabin. Now that there would no longer to be this after-work rendezvous, planning joint ventures would be more difficult. They would need to know who moved between their different campsites and who could carry messages. Perhaps, too, trips that they already had in mind may not fall into sync with mutually free times. If discussion is not necessarily helped by the calming, yet inspiring influence of a wee dram, conversation indubitably is. In conversation, actuality recedes in significance though by no means completely, but aspirations and dreams are allowed space to be aired, viewed, and not too rigorously considered—a characteristic function of conversation much undervalued. This allowed Roddy to say in conversation with Mike that he was now sure he had mastered some skills with earthmoving equipment which would ensure him a way of making a reasonable living elsewhere in the future. He would stay with Wood Bagshaw to experience this land in winter and do his best to acquire some ski skills. That is, if there were to be decent snow falls before the end of June. If not, he must still leave and set out to fulfil another aspect of his Australian assimilation. After that last less serious piece of work as a station hand, he must seriously start to build a future using the earthmoving skills as a relatively stable income base.

'I like your plan, Rod, it sounds good. I can see you meeting its objectives. I don't think going to work on the sheep station will be all just self-indulgence. Being able to speak about parts of Australian life actually experienced is bound to be helpful in getting to know and just getting on with Australians, and I think you'll grow from the experience personally, without realising it. Think of your time at Ranelagh! Okay, it seemed as if it were—and it was to an extent—a Merrie England lark, but be honest, look at how much you have gained from that. I admire your open mind: I don't for a moment believe that anyone else in the same situations would have learned as much as you have. Christ, think about doing WOSB and OCTU! Think of the life you have been able to live here as a result!'

He had been listening carefully to what Mike had been saying and couldn't help but think it was a fair picture. 'Except for the exceptional talent you imagine I have, in reality, yes, it has all worked extra well. Now I'll have to fix my targets progressively and precisely. And I've got to make sure I don't allow anything to deflect me. I know, from recent experience, it won't be pain free, yet even now, in my worldly naiveté, I'm convinced that just about anything that's worthwhile will have some attendant pain. But it seems that life will be a question of establishing successive new bases to achieve new objectives that will inevitably occur.' He knew how he was going to spend at least the six months 'in the bush' after leaving Wood Bagshaw. 'What have you been planning, Mike?' he asked.

'Well, when I left the army, I just flopped about. I didn't even know how to enjoy myself! Something had made me forget the trick. I went to Europe. What that did for me, I honestly don't know. I can't think of anything that was valuable for me. Oh, I could join in conversations about places, and bars, and popular music without appearing totally stupid in groups. That was the sum of my achievements. Coming here was a whim, something to do when you can't think of anything better. But here, in the Snowies, I've found that I now know what I want to do; and I've begun the process. Well, you already know some of my thoughts about that, so there's not a lot more to say, but I found inside me a consuming interest in geology and with that, geography, so mining engineering is the way I will go. I'm enrolled at University of Sydney for first term next year, my application has been accepted and I've got a place. I can sign up for a cadetship with Woods Bagot and that will mean an employment future with them when I graduate and assistance with fees while I'm studying. I'll have to work with them in the vacs. I think that will be half the fun.'

Roddy followed by saying, 'Living in our mountain villa together, has done me good, I've seen you begin your studies, the books you've had the library get for you and the obvious pleasure you've had in devouring them. You will get where you want go and be happy getting there—of that I'm certain.'

Then he was out in the rocky wild again. As he ripped his dozer blade into aeon ancient rock, he knew it was a slaughter of the land, an inspired transformation to build a brand-new nation, and he wondered if it wasn't 'old Regret'. This was the land that A. B. 'Banjo' Paterson had written about.

The Australian poet is much enjoyed in a now-famous poem, 'The Man from Snowy River'. From the high seat on his machine, he could see through the sparse mountain ash and wattle and across the sharp rocky outcrops down, down deep into the valley where the Snowy River glinted with a sparkle from the sun. Now its pure mountain water flowed across a stony ford, low water now, but in weeks, not far in time, it would become an impassable raging torrent. Above that mark, where melting waters rose, and winters showed where homes could safely cling to the Swiss Alp slopes to grow years as years passed by, into a town, a point to stop and inhabit since the days when the white people came to take this rugged forbidding land.

This land, this Snowy Mountains land, this Australian land was beginning to pour its story in his ears, his thoughts, his spirit. How long had he been here for heaven's sake?

It was more difficult now when there was free time, to get to the car, and he would not dream of keeping it on-site. The problem was solved one day when chatting with the garage owner at Jindabyne. In one of those notably rustic conversations which witness an information exchange busier than a telegraph transmitter, he offered to give it secure protective cover in a shed beside his general store which was next to the mechanic's workshop.

Mike was not free to come when Roddy's next break occurred. He took with him in the prospect of solitary silence a newly published book by Mary Durack, *Kings in Grass Castles*, which had been warmly recommended by the bookseller at Cooma. When Roddy would be his guide, his brain and spirit were free now to get on with life and his plans.

His plans were re-energized and would be refined now that he had a less-confusing view of things. He would leave Wood Bagshaw at the end of June, snow or not, and if he did not learn to ski now that was something to look forward to when an opportunity arose. In the meantime, he must make sure that Jill got maximum value from any time she wished to spend with him. Since the almost programmed schedule, stable domestic life at the camp near Cooma, hours days and weeks were much more jumbled. The company's plan was to achieve as much as possible before winter set in. This meant that in the daylight hour, there was opportunity to work overtime every day. Roddy took the opportunity to put in as many hours as his body could stand and bank the increased revenue. Sometimes the breaks would arise during the normal world's working week.

On one of these, he decided to go and pay tribute to his new nation's capital city. It was going to be pleasantly luxurious to get away from the confinement of the trailer which, essentially, was used almost entirely for short evening spells of reading, and sleeping off the exhaustion of the days on hard-lying iron-framed beds. It was a very short drive through his mountains to

Canberra set on an almost level piece of a sheep station's land with the Molonglo River running through the quite magnificent man-created lakes around which the public service citizens of the new suburbs had set up their cottage homes. His reaction was that it was a very pleasant, quiet nouvelle ville which could not, for all its novelty, avoid the air of an Australian country town. What was least like a country town was the layout of its streets which on first reconnaissance he found confusing. He found himself a pleasant motel with a Greek name and thought he should leave the car, he did not want to drive anymore, and have a 'walk into town', but as he had gathered from his first drive around, it was impossible to find a 'centre of town'. Looking at maps of urban areas seldom give any indication of the environment on the ground. He had chosen to stay, as a result of his half-hearted recce, in an area called Kingston which seemed to have buildings slightly less spread about, and it was near the water. He wanted quite soon to settle into the comfort of his motel where the first thing he did was request a bedside reading lamp and wait until he saw one installed. While that was happening, he rang Jill just to say 'hello' and report his latest exploration. Emma answered the phone and greeted him enthusiastically. Jill would be upset at missing him. However, she was going on from work with the bank mob to a restaurant run by Burings, the wine makers. She would be home after sailing tomorrow, could he ring then? A few more cheery words of mutual news and he said he would ring at seven tomorrow.

Next, and becoming more important as minutes passed by, find a pub, then a place that offered good food. He could have a drink and dine in softly lit silence at Cythera, but that's not what intrepid travellers do, is it? He hadn't gone more than five hundred yards when he saw an establishment with a hanging sign which announced an upstairs bar attractively named the Boot and Flogger. Canberra had been built on a sheep station's land and it would appear that the shearing shed timbers had been robbed out to build the stairs and clad the walls: he suspected that if he looked closely and sniffed there would a stain and smell of lanolin. The dark timber had been carried on into the main areas of the bar and the windows, drawing in the dying light of evening, made shapes on the dark brown wood surfaces, a mixture of vertical and horizontal lines and shapes with pleasing artistry of changing, mixed tones. There were a good many happy drinkers around the bar and around tables. An empty stage suggested that there would be music later. In loyalty to the ancient owners of the title to the land—by that is meant not the aboriginal populations, but the State of New South Wales—there was Resch's beer on tap. He chatted with some men and women at the bar who were not identifiable as civil servants, but then he did not know whether civil servants looked different from anybody else. They were pleasant people and he was feeling very relaxed, of course it wasn't, but it seemed years since he stood with men at a bar, people he had never met before, indulging in light conversation. However, as a place to eat, it wasn't what he had first had in mind. Mind you, they did serve food. The band was to take the stage at eight o'clock, and from what he was being told, it could be believed that they were very entertaining. He was part way through a dish of chicken Parmigiana of creditable Italian quality, the Hunter Valley shiraz was drinkable but acids and tannins weren't living in the same house and the fruit had decided not to come home. But with a hearty rendition of Bound for South Australia to set a pleasing tone, he focused on enjoying the chicken and convinced himself the passato—the sugo—was home made from backyard Roma tomatoes and herbs among which the now-cooked chook had spent its working life scratching a soil rich in compost and sheep manure under laden fruit trees. Ah, bucolic bliss! The visions evoked a sentiment of ease which allowed the competing visions of the hard days of flying hands on the controls of a thundering, clanking, bucking bulldozer on hard steep hills and barriers of broken trees and loosened tossed-out rock to light his brain clearly and briefly in antithesis. The roaring diesel engine notes had gone; now a mandolin and two guitars of Lincoln Park, for that is what the players had named their trio, was at the same time invigorating and strangely balmy. Mckenzie was enjoying his leisure: enjoying it to the extent of contributing with great gusto to the room's rendition of 'There's Whiskey in the Jar.' Their repertoire was Irish and Colonial so should he have been surprised to find, when he spoke with 'Splinter', the mandolin player, that he was the most London, London Cockney you could find—except for his brother Philip, who was in the audience, and with whom Roddy had been chatting. The second guitarist, and much more skilled player, came from somewhere in the Black Country whose sobriquet was 'Lizard'. The front man was the tall and beefy, his round, rosy-cheeked face almost completely surrounded by wild black curls, was Sean Joseph Roach. During their breaks, he discovered, as they talked together, that in their other life they operated a leather-working business; tanning the leather, designing the pieces, producing first-class pieces much in vogue. They made sure that in the intervals, they consumed at least a pint of ale and took a full pint onto the stage to keep their digital dexterity at performance peak throughout their lively show. He left their notes and vocal tones filling the stairwell as, having said farewell to his companion Philip and leaving his best wishes for the others, he turned his way on a short tack to his Greek island. Ah, 'the benison of hot water' in the luxurious shower; no 'rough male kiss of blankets' here instead crisp laundered sheets. Before he picked up his book—only to put it down unopened—he tracked again the events of his day; the drive down from his mountains, the motel choice, his chat with Emma and his disappointment in not speaking with Jill, the Boot and Flogger, the taste of Tuscany, Lincoln Park, Philip and his position in the tax office, the walk, the shower, and the sleep advancing upon his eyes. It was as if the shelling had stopped.

He slept a full eight hours and awoke refreshed, put on some shorts, and set off to run up Mt Ainslie, possibly a couple, or perhaps three miles away, which he had seen when looking for his motel the day before. He could feel his body enjoying itself; the physical action of running was so different from work. It was not a difficult or long climb and the view from the top, looking down at the new city and the fine surrounding country, made him happy to be there on what was shaping up to be a pleasant sunny day with just a bit of slowly moving cumulus. The terrain around was getting on with its work of being undulating pastoral and farming country despite the growing city in its midst. In every direction he looked, homes were being built and people actually in the area as he viewed the scene now, would be made up of equal numbers of brick layers, carpenters, and other trades, to civil servants and all others. There was an impressive number of private cars moving in the roads and streets with Holdens, from their first 1948 vintage to the current model, making up at least half the visible estimated total. He trotted back to the motel, showered, and dined on the gargantuan fry-up which comprised the 'English breakfast'. Breakfasting gave a further opportunity to look at the maps and brochures he had gathered. From these he realized that if he spent the day on foot, he would not see much of what he would like to see in this city which did not look like a city: he would need to use the car. This gave rise to further thoughts culminating in deciding to depart when the last of the sites closed and get back into the country, see the coast again, spend the night on the road, and arrive back at his Jindabyne car shelter in good time to organize transport back to the trailer camp. Not knowing just how his day's explorations would pan out he left the motel ready for the longer road.

In ways vaguely similar to Italy, Germany, and the United States, Australia had decided to unify its six states into a Federation. In 1901, after Queen Victoria had signed, the year before, a Royal Assent this Federation was to be known as the Commonwealth of Australia, of which after much debate, and rivalry, between Sydney and Melbourne (which had been the capital), a piece of territory was excised from New South Wales to become the capital, Canberra, that was the aboriginal name for the area. He must see the seat of government later. He was at present on the northern side of that sprawling acreage of the erstwhile sheep station where not so very long ago a shrine of remembrance to Australian war dead had been built and opened. He wanted to see that first. He was ashamed to confess to himself that, really, he knew nothing of Australia's fighting men except of their successes in the North African Campaigns in glimpses he had seen on British newsreels during World War II. After the war, he had read about Changi. At school, he had of course heard briefly a sanitized version of the Dardanelles

Campaign; it was only in recent time that he discovered that the Australians had been there too and called it Gallipoli. Certainly not at school, perhaps through the cinematic skills of Henry Chauvel, he had come to hear about the cavalry charge of the Australian horsemen in Syria. He was overwhelmed by what he had learned today about the Australian army's role in France in World War I.

Perhaps their exploits in Africa and the Middle East in two world wars had made some impressions on the architects. The dome of the main building echoed the Citadel in Cairo, the rows of arches to left and right on the first-level ambulatories, and the water pool on the approach to the front doors of the main memorial building, struck him as being quite strongly Arabic even the plants in large pots at each side of the approach supported that Islamic theme. He had not recovered from that experience when he drove across Lake Burley Griffin by King's avenue Bridge to Parliament House. He may have in fact driven north to south, but from an architectural perspective, it could have been from east to west. In the same way that the memorial had been Middle Eastern, the Parliament House was British; no, as English as could be. He was not much experienced, but in what little of the world he had seen thus far, marks of history, buildings and memorials, had been of a very old world, where year after hundreds of years of events, memorials, buildings, statues, or symbols had been raised to mark, at the time of their erection, the pride of nations—and often with changing world views or memories, the shame. Here there was a memory store of battles whose survivors were still alive. Here, an ancient foreign past was being transposed and superimposed on a site and a civilization whose forty or may maybe sixty thousand years of history upon it had been swept away. These, the only known invaders had brought their national myths and totems to change the mood, the smell, the flavour, the mysteries, the stories, and the footsteps in this land. Perhaps Burley Griffin's layout of the city as a series of circles arose from some subliminal aboriginal influence. Now, Roddy Mckenzie from the distant Scottish highlands, sitting on a stone wall not far from the Parliament House in Canberra, Australia, looked up and around him; he found himself confused and full of conflicting feelings. There was nothing more to see here today. As he went to the car, his head was full of unsorted, uncomfortable fragments. Gripped by these imponderables, he paused for only a moment in the seat, abruptly turned the ignition key, and drove away as quickly as he could.

Driving the little Fusan at the fastest speed allowed, he would distance himself immediately from this new experience physically, but certainly not yet mentally. Memories of Kenya came to mind; and the removal of tribes from their lands justified by hypocrisy and consciously created cant. And here he was, self-invited to Australia, to share in the plunder. Oh, 'Think not upon these things, so it will make us mad.'

He drove through Queanbeyan, then a little north to Bungendore to join a good road down from the scarp through very pleasing scenery to the coast at Bateman's Bay, which he and Mike had whizzed past on their earlier coastal journey. The late-afternoon light on the grand estuary was sublime; 'It looked a good place for a village' he thought, so he parked the car and walked around to look for somewhere to stay for the night. The effects of the morning's mountain of protein and fat had now worn off and his appetite had reawakened. He chose to sleep at the motel, drink at the pub, and eat at a cafe on the jetty. A saunter along the estuary and a stretch of beach and he was ready for bed and book. The sun was just rising when he woke and running across the bridge and the length of Long Beach and back to the motel was good for the soul. He would be leaving early, and with nothing but driving and sightseeing ahead, there was no need to stoke up on breakfast and sit in the car with a full belly. The trip to Jindabyne was sheer pleasure all the way even the last eighty-odd kilometres on an unsealed road. Skjyl Nordstrom, the garage owner at Jindabyne, drove him up to the trailer as Roddy had anticipated he might offer to do.

At work, the heavy slogging on the mountain road continued, and Roddy worked the maximum hours for maximum money on a daily—slog, sleep, eat, slog sleep, eat continuum. There were two days when Bruce's hut at Khancoban was free, so he went over to a Walden sojourn of hiking, cooking, reading, and sleeping. It was a different kind of solitariness from the exclusions caused by the location, trailer life, and his work regimen of working hours. He did take time to think. This may not have yielded solutions to all his questions, yet there was progress to the point where he could eliminate some grounds and, having done so, be allowed to move forward without having to bring these back into consideration. His next long break was a weekend, which probably would be his last before his final severance from Wood Bagshaw. When it had been confirmed for the coming weekend, he went down immediately to the box at Jindabyne and phoned Jill.

The further south he drove and the more the road rose in altitude, the more cloud burden that had to be penetrated which meant that all the way he drove in drizzle needing to concentrate on the road. He stopped only once at a 'petrol station–shop cafe' for petrol, to pump bilges, and have a cup of tea.

There was a Wood Bagshaw truck at Sjkel's shop when he arrived in Jindabyne. Sjkel would have been happy to drive him up to the camp, but Roddy wouldn't hear of it. He transferred his kit to the truck and climbed in; they drove up in the truck to join their now, an almost-'finished' piece of the new road which would already ran past the camp. He returned to find that that the old huts which he and Mike Harty had shared had been brought up to this site and re-erected. Roddy had been directed by admin where to go and given a key. The man with whom he was to share a room had was a truck driver who had already taken up residence but happened to be absent when Roddy went to the room. He brought his kit in and went to his last accommodation in the trailer to clear out the rest of his belongings which he took to his new quarters and set them up. After going to the office and returning the trailer room key, he felt it time to search for food. Except that at it was in a different place, nothing had changed of the old cookhouse and mess hall and nothing had changed in the food. It was early, but he decided to prepare his clothes for the morning and get some sleep. He was just settling when his hut companion came in.

He'd obviously had a few beers, but he was friendly, Roddy knew Dave Rodda having met him and seen him many times as they worked in their gang. He'd had a few beers and wanted to talk. He was very excited about a pornographic magazine he had managed to get a hold of and wanted to show him the pictures. 'Not now, Dave', he said, 'I want to get some sleep.'

'Uh! Don't want get randy, eh? Might feel like a wank, eh?' were Rodda's last words. As the days passed, Roddy was to find that sex and the thoughts of shagging were Rodda's life obsession, and in the absence of the real thing, he took to masturbation on a regular basis which appeared rather than to quench the flames of carnal desire aggravated them, to the point where Roddy had to suggest to Dave, 'Rodda, masturbation is meant to be a personal private pursuit, could you find another venue? Hearing you go through the agonies of thwarted lust is like hearing the same crude boring conversation over and over again. I'm getting fed up with it. If you don't find a willing woman or another venue and stop doing it in this room, there's a good chance I might get angry.'

Rodda had a clear idea what an angry Mckenzie might mean because he had seen him in action—for whatever reason the practice in the hut ceased—perhaps he had just thought fair's fair. However, in compensation for the curtailment of his activity, he had acquired, from God knows where, sufficient pictorial pornography to mount a ghastly gallery of quite ugly women, whose faces and bodies had never approached the feminine ideal, to fill the entire wall opposite Roddy's bed. It was almost worth considering switching Rodda to previous practices, but oh well, there's got to be a bit of give and take, he thought.

Rodda's abstention was an improvement, the gallery was truly revolting, but in the remaining time, or ever, there was no hope that the sharing of a room would ever be anything like sharing with Mike. The work grind continued. He managed to get a few opportunities and time to read a little and to write. His mother was quite worried that he should be working on the Snowy Mountains Scheme. She had heard horrendous, true reports of the excessive drinking, drunken deaths in the snow and brawling amongst the men on the Cannich hydro-electricity

scheme in the mountains not that far away from Fearnas. He
had calmed her feelings with stories about how he and Mike
Harty got on well so well together, about his visits to Sydney and
about Jill. He managed two days at the Khancoban hut where
he sawed and split logs did some cross-country runs and hikes.
He read for at least two hours each day—and took some real
thinking time when the fire had warmed the room, he sipped a
glass of wine, by the light of the Tilley lamp on the table, hissing
and gassing away. Ah, Thoreau, was your Walden world like this?
Another trip was across to Cooma. He wanted to speak with
Horace to see if he could buy the Fusan for the travel before
him. Horace couldn't give him an answer directly because it
had been a deal with Mauri, and officially, it was still his car.
'Would you like me to ask Mauri?' 'Yes, if you would, Horace.
I'm down here for another day as you know; do you think you'll
know before I go back?'

'I'll ring him we might be lucky.' He picked up the phone
and dialled a number which put him through to an exchange,
after a few friendly words, the lady at the telephone exchange
said, 'Putting you through.'

'Mauri, how are you going, old pal? I've got a client of yours
here, a Mister Roderick Mckenzie. . . well I think so, and he
looks all right. He wants to buy the Fusan.' Horace listened for
a while then turning to Roddy said, 'He says to give it to you.'

'Horace, can I speak to him?'

Horace spoke into the phone to Mauri, 'He says he wants to
speak to you.' After a moment of listening, Horrie passed him
the telephone handset. 'Mauri... good day! I didn't think I'd be
speaking to you today. Look, I can't be given the car. What you
and Doris have given me in friendship is more than enough—
good beyond description, but buying, selling, or giving cars is
business and that's a different game. I want to make an offer
for the car.'

'Give Horrie the phone.'

Roddy passed the phone and Mauri asked Horrie, 'What
condition is it in?'

To which Horrie replied, 'Appearance?—Showroom;
Performance?—Bathurst.' He returned the phone to Roddy.

Mauri: 'Well, would you pay two hundred pounds for it?'

Roddy: 'That seems very low.'

Mauri: 'Look, Rod, that what it's on our books for, if I sold it to you for any more, I'd be cheating you and my accountant would spend the rest of the year working out what to do with the extra money. Write my company a cheque for two hundred quid and we're square.'

Roddy had a feeling he was being baffled by science. 'I'm not going to argue. I'm just going to say thank you very much for a great little car. I'll be up in Sydney soon for the last time. When I know, I'll let you know. Please be sure to give my love to Doris. And please, officially thank Horace for all that he's done. I'll thank him for his friendship myself. Do you want to speak with Horace? No', Roddy was responding to Mauri, 'any instructions to be given to Horrie must come from you. No', he continued, 'I'll leave and let you speak to Horrie. Okay, all the best to you both. Remember, love to Doris; Oo-roo.' And putting his hand over the mouthpiece, he said to Horrie, 'I'll come back around five. Oo-roo', then passed the phone back to him.

When he went back to see Horrie at around five, it was to learn that the sale and taking possession of the car could not take place until sometime towards the end of June, the cheque could be handed over and the transfer completed when he came up to Sydney. 'In the meantime, we just carry on as normal', Horrie said, 'the warranty service has been done and she's filled up ready to go. Are you off now?'

'Yes, Horrie, all ready to go back to my home in the mountains. Thanks for doing the service at such short notice. I do appreciate that.' Roddy had been down to the coast and arrived back that afternoon. After farewelling Horrie, he began thinking of Mauri and saying to himself, 'That cunning old devil is going to have me carry on the loan arrangements with all their benefits until my departure, God bless him. They're embarrassing and worth much more than the huge amounts of money I've managed to save because of them—and they gave Mike and me an access to the country which would have cost us so much that our saving from pay would have been minimal.'

Winter was beginning to bite, but there was no snow yet, just intermittent rain and short dreich days. A central heating system had been contrived for the line of adjoined cabins where he was quartered and these did break the sub-zero chill of their room. The rain was beginning to cause more damage to the roads: more damage than they were yet able to bear. Facing the inevitability of snowfall, the work had been transferred progressively into the tunnel. Work was carried out under lights so, as a continuo to all the varying intensities of roaring mobile plant, there was the constant drumming of electricity generators and air compressors. The Italian company responsible for the precise work of tunnelling carried out their preparation for blasting during that sixteen-hour span of machine work and blew up the rock front, the roof, and the walls during the night. At the start of shift in the mornings, the day's work of rock removal lay before Roddy and Dave Rodda and his truck operator mates. So huge was the scale of the underground workings that it was like working outside, inside, all activity carried on within a noisy galaxy where the scattered stars, constantly moving, tracked erratic orbits.

Then one day it began to snow, and snow, and snow until two or three feet had fallen rising to ten feet or more in wind-built drifts. Their work had been brought inside just in time; outside, effective work had become impossible.

There was nothing very sophisticated about the snow sports in the area around Jindabyne, although it was said that a chairlift was planned. A bright entrepreneur had quickly set up a ski-hire business in Sjkel's shop. One day before, the snow had crusted; Roddy had a day off during which he managed to organize an hour with a Norwegian ski instructor. The result was that by dogged perseverance, at the end of the of the day's full extent of light, he had just about mastered turns and stops. The next day the snow became unusable.

It was important, he thought, to start up the separation process form Wood Bagshaw (at some time he had heard that the Wood, of Wood Bagshaw, was a Scotsman). 'Had he done his early training at Inverurie Locos? And was he a relative of his late hoochie mucker Woodie?' He needed to have his final leaving date fixed and to have official documentation and confirmation of his competency on the machines he had operated. He put these matters into the capable hands of Martin Musgrove. The results of Martin Musgrove's endeavours was that, he now held 'signed off' documents of competency for his machines and trucks; and all of these matters had been finalized on-site, obviating a call to the main office in Sydney. Taking pro-rata annual leave into account, and some computation about number of hours worked, he would finish officially with Wood Bagshaw in the Snowy Mountains on Thursday, 20 June 1958.

And so it came to pass that he farewelled Rodda and the others in the crew as and when he saw them. Finally, he must bid good-bye to Martin Musgrove. He had seen very little of the affable and thoughtful administrator during his months on-site because of work patterns, and access to the little car which allowed him to leave the site at the slightest opportunity. Roddy had a spare day and Mike Harty had been able to swing a day from his team (a pretty relaxed mob at any time) which was now working down on the coast. They spent a day at Bermagui on hikes and eating and drinking, sharing plans, and deciding how they would keep in touch. They dined right royally that night and parted after breakfast.

As he drove to Sydney, he reflected upon his Snowy Mountains experiences; his friendship with Mike Harty, all the different kinds of men he'd met in crews, the frequent early brawls, how—in some ways—their lives were like being in the army. He thought of how he had come to be there, the Ship Inn, the fateful meeting with John Wilson. And seeing Jill again—yes, seeing Jill. Somehow thoughts of Jill seemed to belong better to a different thought environment, an account kept in a separate, private ledger. Jill was for special thoughts; and he realized that soon he would be seeing her for the very last time, not to be seen again in the foreseeable future.

Sydney. He felt comfort again in being back in the club and liked the idea that a new Argosy, for a new voyage, would leave this, the port of his first landfall, where he had spent his first night on the landmass of Terra Australis. Jeff and Dudley were now bound into a friendly relationship with him. He was not going to dally here—here in Sydney. Time—that non-element, that non-force, the ineffable—was not to be neglected in his considerations of the journey towards his goals. Within that concept, all the events of his life to come would be played out. His mind was plagued by a feeling of restlessness. He knew there would be in them the human feelings associated with the departure of a friend and with them would be enacted the rituals and ceremonies of departure. But those people who were to remain in their own place, among their own people, in permanency, would have feelings different from his. There seemed relevance for him in the words from Shakespeare's *Macbeth*, which came to mind. Even if not an exact match of the play's situation and intention (and certainly no planned assassination!): *"If it were done when 'tis done, then t'were well/ It were done quickly."*

Finer thoughts and feelings were there, present within him, but they were being pushed and pulled around the spaces and corners of his mind, their value diminished by the compelling wish to be moving. If he could maintain activities and diversions throughout the period, it would be over and gone the more quickly, and he would be on his way. The time table, already fixed, made him feel that action had begun.

The culmination of his stay was already fixed: there would be a farewell party at Mauri's on Saturday night. He had planned to leave on Sunday morning and take the less direct route to Jerilderie by driving over the Blue Mountains which he thought he ought to see in daylight, and see now, for he may never pass this way again. Jill was going to be engaged on Thursday evening with training for, and helping in the organization of a swimming carnival. They would have a Friday evening together for a concert after which they had agreed, they must have a farewell meal with Dimitri.

As to Thursday night, he had decided that there was little appeal in wandering Sydney so he would be happy to stay at the club, have an early night, and read. He'd make his mind up depending on who happened to turn up at the club for after-work drinks; a bit of conversation with a good companion and a few drinks would go down quite well. Thinking of which, a drink now would go down well and a loosening up walk to the Ship would do harm. At the Ship there were familiar faces in a group he spotted immediately, so he joined them and was welcomed back.

When he returned to the club, he found Badge and Tracy with a third more senior man in uniform. He was Lawrie's company commander from Thirtieth Battalion down from his country property to go out on a weekend exercise for which all three would form up at Victoria Barracks on Friday afternoon whence the unit would be transported by truck to a military training area south-west of Sydney. Lawrie, Peter, and the major, who was introduced as John Blair, were going to be dining together that night at the club and Roddy was invited to join.

While they were together before dinner, Dudley bowled up, 'I hope you gentlemen don't mind me briefly interrupting. I shall be leaving the club early this evening and I wanted to be sure that I did not miss Mr. Mckenzie before I had the opportunity to say farewell.'

'Not at all, Dudley,' said John Blair.

'You've been an exemplary guest, Mr. Mckenzie,' said Dudley 'It has been a pleasure to be of service to you. I hope you will have a successful life in Australia, which I'm sure you will and that you'll come and visit us all again at the ISC.'

'Dudley, that's very kind of you and I do appreciate it. You've been a great help and done a lot for me very happily, which was far beyond the call of duty, you made this club a very pleasant place for me, thank you for all of that. Whenever I have the shortest time in Sydney, be sure I shall play the guest member again and look forward to seeing your friendly face.'

The dinner was going well right from the start with the conversation not unnaturally on military themes. John had been at the last landings at Buna Beach before the final defeat of the Japanese forces. From John, they managed to elicit tales from his experiences of his war. They were informative and amusing, especially for Roddy, The dinner ended at a seemly hour.

He devoted Friday to historical exploration. Equipped with maps, brochures, and his notebook, he began first by exploring the Rocks area and, after going as far as possible on Dawes Point, turned and following the water and the bays and permissible roads through and around the docks skirted them back to Darling Harbour, got to the Iron Bridge, a monument in itself, and crossed over into Rozelle and Glebe, which were typically old, grimy closely settled run-down port-side suburbs. At Balmain, he turned about. There had been no shortage of historical battered old pubs where refreshment could be had, and the native populace studied at close hand. The day was getting on, and he was feeling the need for a change of scene. He came from a side street out onto a busy main road where trams were running. He took one which brought him the central railway station. He took another tram, and as soon as he saw Hyde Park, he got down and walked through the greenness of the grass and trees. After a good scrub and a change of dress, it was time to meet Jill.

The process trail of farewells begun at Jindabyne continued, when, after he and Jill had been at the bank for a while that evening and had spoken to two or three people whom he had talked with before, he bade them farewell.

At Doris and Mauri's, there was no Kate Wilson on this occasion, commanding from the balcony giving them instructions, so they went to the front door, which was closed on this occasion and rang the bell. Now Kate did appear, to welcome them warmly, and principally the principal guest but not until Doris and Mauri had greeted them. Cars in the narrow street in front of the house indicated that some of the guests may already have arrived. Those guests who had arrived were John and Kath Wilson, Bruce and Amy Lockwood, Chris and Cynthia Paton.

Doris had set the mood in a tone that was more intimate than a party and you got that feeling right away. Doris had chosen the large room upstairs, and it was laid out with the tall dividing doors drawn closed and were now acting as a wall against which furniture pieces had been set—small tables and comfortable chairs. There was even a selection of paintings from their collection, all of them Australian, all of bush or seascapes, and two powerful, richly coloured city streetscapes by an artist whose name had Slav origins. She had arranged the table as a large square so that the twelve diners seated

around, it could see all of the others and converse with them
directly. Doris and Mauri knew how to enjoy fine things: the
glassware was Edinburgh crystal. Roddy wagered with himself
that they would have Waterford and continental crystal in their
collections, but that for tonight; they had specifically selected
the Edinburgh because of him. This was proved to be correct.
When Emma had complimented Doris on the fine crystal, she
said she had put it out tonight especially for Roddy.

All the guests had gathered first in a downstairs sitting room
where tall windows looked across a leafy green garden whose
plants had deferentially kept their height low so that the bay
could always be seen as it was now, again by moonlight, with the
working lights of moving vessels and navigation beacons on the
harbour. These were tall windows of the Edwardian period, with
broad profiled architraves painted a tone or two lighter than the
wall colour; they were dressed with padded pelmets and heavy
curtains, held in folds by broad 'cummerbunds' of the same
material, skilfully cut. Here they could sip champagne, stand or
sit around, and chat. This was not that kind of group which found
it difficult to open up a conversation. Anyone arriving would
enter a group of quite noisy people: the noise was of greeting,
friendship, exchange of news, and pure revoir. Mike Harty and
Emma arrived, and with when Chris and Cynthia Paton came
minutes later, they made the dinner complement complete.

Roddy, pre-occupied, was staring, at the animated people. He
was feeling the significance of what he was seeing and realized a
sense of burden as he realized that all these people had gathered
because of him. He was moved and nervous, fearful almost. For
that moment, Jill and Roddy found themselves on the edge of
the group. He reached for her hand and held it quite firmly as
he turned to look at her. 'I met you at Cowes, on the water of the
Solent, and gave you a lift in a dinghy and you have brought me
all of this. It's through your agency that people here have become
friends. This dinner tonight is happening because I met you.'

'Roddy, you have to begin to think of your own role in
what's happening here tonight. It's happening because you are
the man you are. I wouldn't be here holding your hand at this
moment if, when we met at Cowes, you hadn't made such an

impression on me, then at Ranelagh, then here. Why do you think John Wilson snatched you from the Ship Inn and took you to Chris? And why did Bruce let you have the hut at Khancoban? And Mauri lend you the car? If you weren't who you are, none of those things would have happened.'

Finally Chris and Sylvia Paton arrived. After they'd had a chance to mingle and pick up the beat—and have some champagne of course—Doris invited everybody to come upstairs to the dining room. Her tactically sited place cards were not simply to make finding one's place easy. The Perrot's considered a degree of formality to be appropriate; after all, it was a dinner with an important and particular purpose. So when all were seated, Mauri rose to address their guests.

'Friends, Doris and I welcome you here tonight for this very special dinner to say farewell to our cobber Roddy Mckenzie. I'm not sure I like the word "farewell" because we seem to have attached to it the idea of "forever". I will bet you London to a brick that we will not be seeing or hearing the last of our friend Roddy Mckenzie and we are all pleased by that thought. He's going because he must go. He goes because he is at that age and point in his life when it is imperative that young people do what they feel needs to be done to get themselves positioned to enjoy all that this wonderful life holds for us to share and that provides for our ease and enjoyment. That is the course that Roddy is now continuing to follow. Let's follow the language of other nations who express wishes on parting in a more optimistic way. From Doris and me and on behalf of your dear friends who are here tonight we all wish you; *auf wiedersehen*, *arriverderci*, and *au revoir*. Let us drink a toast to Roddy and his journey.'

John Wilson led the group in standing up and called, 'To Roddy and his journey.'

They had barely sat down when as if by response to a starting gun, the fish course of John Dory fillets was laid before them. These had been removed after cooking, complete, on the bone with head on.

While the fish was being enjoyed, Mauri said sotto voce to Roddy, 'If you want to say anything wait till after the meat course or they may start to fall over.'

'Thanks, I will and, Mauri, thank very much for what you said.'

The sirloin steak was served—seared, pink, beautiful, and splendid. It was served with a new shiraz from Penfold's called Grange Hermitage. Mauri had decanted it early in the morning to allow it to expand and flower; now it proved to be full of flavours and subtleties layer upon layer. It was greatly enjoyed by all to the extent that even Mauri could not provide further decanted wine, and bottles had to be opened. This resulted in proving the old adage that good wine, especially when it is a little aged, is improved by breathing time. Nonetheless the fresh wine had its own charms.

Mauri stood up again. 'Friends', he said, 'our principal guest would like to say a few words, you'll notice that he waited until even the grumpiest of you had come under the benign influence of the Grange. Friends all, our guest Roderick Fraser Mckenzie.'

'First, thank you, Mauri, for allowing me this opportunity to address you, Doris, and these wonderful people who, all of you, are my friends, friends by any definition. I want to say thank you to you all, but I'll blowed if I know how to do it. I'll say the words—and I will mean them with all my heart. But when I consider what you people have done for me'—and he paused—'and the care you've poured over me—how pitifully weak they surely are. The story of these six months that I've been in this great land has been about learning. I needed to learn skills that would make me a good living while I developed my plans for a future. John and Chris jump immediately into the picture here. John who took me by the lug and marched me off to Chris's office where he immediately had me employed by Wood Bagshaw Civil Construction Contractors. They were a good company to work for, and I have left their employment with their good wishes and certificates of competency in the operation of four different pieces of plant and equipment—I'll always be able to make a quid. The Snowy Scheme is hard work; there can be no disagreement about that. What made it bearable, and the short breaks enjoyable, is the fact that Mauri had put at the disposal of Mike and me a magnificent vehicle which appeared to be self-cleaning, self-maintaining, and run on one part petrol to two thousand parts air. In six months, it used two quid's worth of petrol that we paid for. I am now the proud owner of that fine vehicle bought from the world's unique car dealer, the one that I had to browbeat into taking any money for it at all. Bruce, I don't know if you recall having said to me that the Talbingo valley was the most beautiful place on God's earth? Well, due to our car, Mike and I have both seen it and driven its length. I agree with you. For us the Hut at Khancoban was a rare treat of a retreat. We used it to its maximum, and every time on leaving it, to quote the words of the song, "came forth strengthened and renewed". Thank you. Bruce.

'Erik Barron's brother owned a yacht called *Fear Naught*. I was on board alone on it at in the Solent at the time when I was hailed by a French yacht and was asked by the Frenchmen who sailed it if I'd take two delightfully beautiful and very lively young Australian ladies ashore. The French yacht did not wish to berth and needed to sail on. These two ladies were Jill and Emma. I held them up a bit on their trip to shore because I had to go in a hurry to the toilet on board *Fear Naught*. I had a bit of a problem with a seal and a blocked bend', he paused and announced reassuringly, 'but all's better now and functioning superbly. They came to the ancient estate in Hampshire where I was a bit of farm hand, roustabout, groom, and polo team substitute player. It was there that my conscience affliction with indebtedness began. My boss Hugh Verney and his brilliant wife *la douce* Miette, whom Jill and Emma met, were unbelievably kind and helpful to me. There I learned so much about how life may be pleasantly and generously conducted with neither pomp nor ceremony. Our troopship bringing the battalion from Korea to UK, was redirected to Kenya to help stamp out a rebellion. There II met and became friends with a young Australian officer in the Kenya police.

His every second statement was about Australia and why I should go there. I'm looking forward to reuniting with him the day after tomorrow. That Australian was and is . . .'—and he stopped to introduce the possibility—'I should give up now, because you're not going to believe anything I'm going to say aftcr this . . . I'm going to tell you, the bloke's name is Michael Manning Lowing . . . and he's Jill's brother.

'My big Australian learning programme could never be complete and probably never will be, but I'm loving the experience and study of it, and I'll do so for the rest of my life. I wanted to, and needed to learn about Australia. Here my luck was in again. I found the perfect caring coach. She gave me my first course textbook, *The Poems of Banjo Paterson*, which had been a gift from her father—I didn't know this until I later opened it up and saw his inscription on the fly leaf. She had treasured that book from adolescence . . . and now, she was giving it to me! The first thing I did, when Mike and I went into Cooma for the first time, was to buy a copy. I'm happy to tell you now the beloved book is back the rightful owner's hands. Australian, I'd like to pay homage to Banjo Paterson who helped in my education and whose poetry I have greatly enjoyed and also to the Snowies and to what I've learned to love about them. As I'm probably under assessment in Australian 101, I'll to take this opportunity to demonstrate that homage. For your delectation and heart-warming delight and hopefully gain some marks in my course', in theatrical declamation, he announced, 'I shall give my rendering of *"The Man from Snowy River".'*

This he did, with great feeling, vigour, and the right spirit. Had there been rafters in the Pott's Point house, surely they would have rung to the spontaneous applause. His way of showing his growing love for their country, to which they were welcoming him, made the gathered friends genuinely happy.

John Wilson rose to say how happy he was that Roddy had got through the bruising experience that working on the Snowy Mountains Scheme must have actually been. Looking around the group at the table, he went on to say, 'Thinking about this dinner, I wanted to see if I could find out something about Scotland which I could aim at Mckenzie as a really witty remark', and he paused, 'with only minor malice, of course, Mckenzie tells us he's from the highlands and the best I could do on that track was that everyone says, "you know when you're in the highlands when you reach Inbhirness. The train goes into the station backwards". Now tonight, the aforesaid Mckenzie has been piling upon us, coincidence after coincidence. Perhaps I can trump his ace. I was telling my mother about this dinner and the purpose of my research. She recommended caution, she said, "Remember, your grandfather was from Scotland and his father before him. Your grandfather immigrated to Australia before the First World War. So look out, you're nearly Scots yourself." My mother went on to tell me the name of the little highland fishing and farming town where my grandfather had been born; now for the trump coincidence card.' He was stretching the pause to build suspense. 'My grandfather was born in a house on Society Street in- now, wait for it—in Fearnas!' Roddy looked at him in amazement, exclaiming 'I throw my cards in! We'll have to talk about this later because my history teacher at St Ninian's Academy, and the man who also trained me in sailing yachts—I recommend to all of you now hang on to your seats—his name was Hugh . . . Wilson! . . . and some of the family still live in the old house on . . . Society Street!'

Around the table, each turned to other in shared amazement.

Doris stood and asked for a moment to interrupt. 'This discussion of the unbelievable coincidences will go on, I imagine, so what I'm going to suggest is that we leave the table and have our crème brulee downstairs. So, Mauri, would you like to close the formalities?'

'Yes, Doris, good idea,' and he stood up. 'John and Roddy have certainly stirred the possum here and I'm sure each of you has a coincidence story you've been dying to tell someone else. I want to thank you for joining Doris and me in sharing in this get-together to wish our friend Roddy a happy healthy future and that his journey to inevitable success is enjoyable and leads to great personal satisfaction. Please charge your glasses and we'll drink another toast.' Mauri observed as the glasses were poured and said, 'It is'—he emphasized

—'a journey, Roddy, so I'm going to suggest to your friends that we join to wish you Bon Voyage.'

There was an enthusiastic call of 'Bon Voyage!' and when it died away, Roddy rose. His face was showing emotions of humility, joy, and from somewhere, a hint of sadness; it could be seen that he was very consciously controlling his voice. His tone was measured, so were the words and the pitch of his voice sounded all the feelings. 'I'll say once more, thank you, for all that you have done for me. I can't tell you the humbling feeling it is to have to experience what has been happening to me tonight. I hope you have all enjoyed yourselves in your own being together as friends. Doris', he kissed her and looked at her, saying, 'you're a darling. Thank you for everything.' Then turning to Mauri, he took his hand firmly and said so that in the silence all could hear, 'I'll never be able to thank you and I've got a strong feeling that through a long future there will be many more times, and for new reasons, when I will need to say this again and again.'

Gripping Roddy's hand even more firmly, and taking hold of his arm, he said to him, 'You are my "thank you", Roddy.'

When they went downstairs, there was a delightful milling of people, sorted, unintentionally, by a young lady who circulated with a tray of little pots of crème brulee, and they split off in her wake as she handed the pots out. Chris was speaking with Bruce, saying, 'He's an amazing bloke, Roddy. I was talking with Mike Musgrove, the administration manager at Wood Bagshaw on the Snowies job. He said, "Send me up another Rod Mckenzie, he's unstoppable—got really stuck into learning and doing—glutton for overtime, and wouldn't put up with any aggression from the mob. He should get a Lonsdale belt for his performances here. It only needs two big stoushes where he handed out some real, damaging thumping's to big ugly blokes and the hard men left him very much alone." Then, look at him tonight. You'd never know.'

Roddy and Jill were, never far apart as he moved around to say 'thank-you' and cheerios.

Mauri and Doris had insisted on having their car take them home. So Mike Harty and Emma came too and they bade the party people good night. Mike and Roddy were dropped off at the club and the good nights were of few words and brief kisses. In the morning, they would meet again at Kirribilli for a 'stirrup cup'.

After climbing the stairs at the club, Roddy found himself excited still by the events of the evening and wanted to reflect on them before going to bed. 'Don't know about you, Mike, but I wouldn't mind just sitting down for a little and just letting the tide ebb before I sleep. D'ye fancy a last port?'

He wanted to keep at bay the thoughts that would fill his head. He was saying to himself: You have been through all of this in detail again and again. 'For heaven's sake, why are you thinking like this now? You knew the final parting with Jill would be sore. Well, hurt! But you're a fool if you start destructive brooding—it will only aggravate and prolong the situation.'

Roddy took a bottle of Grandfather from the shelf and put a 'chitty' in the tin. He rummaged around to see if Dudley had secreted some better-than-ordinary glasses—mind you, the port glasses in daily use were really not too bad, a bit heavy and soldierly, but many an enjoyable taste in good company had been had from them. They were soldiers in good company: the standard glasses would do.

'God, Mike, d'ye realize it's only six months since we came here for the first time?'

Mike laughed. 'I know precisely what you mean and this club feels as if it's our mess, our home, as if we've just been at the front for a while, and we're now in reserve. I'm glad and grateful you thought of making me join.'

'Anyway, here we are, Mike, let's toast to our friendship which began on a train into the unknown of the Snowy Mountains of New South Wales in Australia in which land neither of has had before set foot. As they say in an old Scot toast, "Here's tae us, wha's like us."' They drank, and Roddy said, 'I think because we've both served and we're here in this club, and can be here in this club, the toast fits us, at the very least because we are "like" in these shared experiences and in in the Snowies we found much to be complementary in each other.'

'You must feel happy about your dinner tonight. I bet there's a whole crowd of feelings that was playing on you during the evening each with a different name, all affecting you now. But they must all be feelings about good things—there were no sour notes, nothing jarring. And we have had no jarring episodes in our shared months in our cabin in the mountains, have we?'

'It was a stroke of good luck being thrown together on the train. My whole Snowy experience would have been much different had you been some other person from amongst the blokes we worked with up there. I got an idea of how much different life could be when I had to share a hut with Rodda. I'm glad that took place when I was grabbing every hour of overtime I could get, and my stint was nearing its end.'

They recalled the experiences of their time off in Sydney; at the Hut, and beaches, their first drive to Sydney, coming down along the rugged cliffs of the east coast on the way back. They drank their port and nursed their friendship.

In the morning, they walked together to retrieve the little Fusan for the last time. All Roddy's big gear was already aboard and Mike had his weekend minimum. 'This will be my last crossing of the bridge for a long time, I think,' said Roddy, coming out of a silent muse.

'I was wondering whether I will,' said Mike. 'I'll have to find lodgings nearer the university next year.'

The girls at Kirribilli welcomed them warmly. People, engaged in minor chit-chat, glanced from partly turned heads and averted eyes to see Roddy and Jill embrace. They were sharing a little of what these two must be feeling, and guessing about the meaning of this day for them. The air around the kitchen was subdued. The abble-gabble that was typical of this group whenever concerned with a task was; news exchange in loud words in exclamatory tones, questions, interrupted answers, part sentences, a quick flit from within a topic off to another quite different one, yet somehow with complete understanding. There was none of that today.

Neither was there bubbly wine. There was just coffee. Verity, whom one might wrongly guess to have no great concern about this major event of Roddy's departure, was watching carefully how Jill was faring. Her world of hope for love with Roddy was going to become one of hearts apart. Yes, that could be love, but what kind of real life would it be? Roddy was not in search of a heart: he was setting out to seek an invisible star. An invisible star instead of a ready, loving heart? His love for Jill was not enough to make him stay. Wasn't that selfish, cruel, stupid? She felt herself making a judgment. She didn't like that judgment. She was changing her opinion of Roddy now. She must not let Jill know.

Dawn and her husband gaily waltzed in to give their farewell wishes and twigged immediately that today's mood was far from the usual, so they gave their good wishes to Roddy, declined a cup of coffee, hitherto unknown in the history of knowing Dawn, quietly greeted the others, and quietly took their leave. Breakfast became almost an 'eat and hurry' busy business day event that it is for many people.

Between the principal two, the emotion was building to a point that would soon become unbearable. Someone would break down. It was Verity who said quite coldly, 'Well, Roddy, the sooner you leave, the sooner you'll get there.'

'You're right, Verity; I really ought to go.' He looked at Jill. 'Verity's right, Jill. I'd better be off.'

'Yes, I suppose you should,' she said and came round the table to where Roddy, nearer the door, had stood up. Before she reached him, he had bent down and had taken from his bag a gift-wrapped, hard, flat-shaped package of large dimensions, a card in an elaborate envelope under the coloured ribbons. 'I hope you will enjoy this always, Jill.' She took it, paused silently to look at it, gently laid on the table, and threw her arms around him. 'I know I shall. Thank you, Roddy.'

He picked up his bag with his left hand and took Jill's hand with his right and walked to his car at the kerb. Diane's garage door was open, they and their car had gone. The group from the kitchen followed down. There was a brief huddle, farewells, good wishes, a last embrace and kiss for Jill, he drove the car a little down on the narrow road, turned, and drove slowly back past the group on the lawn edge. He slowly passed and waved, and looking directly at Jill, called out: 'Oo-roo!'

He abruptly turned his head to the road and quickly drove away.

———∘∘∘❧❧∘∘∘———

The short drive up to the Pacific Highway needed a little attention, so he was well on his way before he shocked himself by demanding, 'Oh my god, what am I doing?' Nothing that had been done could be unwound now. He knew that. And he knew, not for the first time, that there are situations where there is just no going back. 'But damn addition, you will block learning, you won't have the joy of learning—and you'll have wasted the pain. If you think you're in emotional trouble, what about Jill? And you won't be able to help her either. Think of what's going to happen today and think how Mike's geological mind would envy your seeing the 470-million-year-old Silurian sea beds thrust up through the earth's crust as limestone beds split and washed out into sheer ravines by ages of water flow. Think what it is going to be like for you to go to Norman Lindsay's studio, maybe even lucky enough to see the artist himself. What about the new country you'll be seeing? In another day, after four years, you'll be seeing Mick Lowing again. How will he be since last you saw him in Kenya?'

As he drove on, and found himself studying the terrain and townships, his spirits did begin to lift. In a short time, he found himself at the point where he had to turn off the main road before Katoomba and back-track a mile or so to Lindsay's studio. It was an old world that Lindsay had let grow up around him perhaps without his being conscious that there were no trends that he wanted to keep up with. Lindsay was sitting in the garden with a pad on his knee, pencil in hand, he looked up. Roddy spoke immediately. 'Forgive my intrusion, sir. I'll leave immediately,' and he turned to go. 'No need to rush off,' cried Lindsay. 'You must have come here to see something. Perhaps I can help you.'

'That's very generous of you, Mr. Lindsay, I'm sure you must be Mr. Lindsay from the photographs I've seen of you in some of the books I've acquired since I've been here.'

'Pull that chair over and tell me a bit about yourself, if you've got the time. There's a bit of sun here.'

And so it was that Roddy Mckenzie sat with old Norman Lindsay and related the brief story of his life as requested of him by the artist. Lindsay was interested, interrupting with questions. He invited Roddy to walk with him to his gallery. There Roddy was overpowered by some of the works of voluptuous ladies all of whose names Lindsay mentioned with memory sketches of his painting experiences of the women snippets about their character and personality, the stories behind the complex drawings such as *Where War Ends.*

He left Lindsay; his head spinning with what he seen of Lindsay's art that he had been attracted to since he had first seen his voluptuous ladies, and the drama of the huge watercolours of Lindsay's in the Sydney gallery. Amongst the native trees all around, the deciduous trees had shed their leaves; it was their expression of winter and they were going to make it southern hemisphere or not. Afternoon; and the low clouds would have to precipitate soon.

The prospect of rain pressed him to find a hotel and establish himself before taking advantage, of what time remained to scout the town before the dark wet evening set in. The Carrington Hotel, in Victorian majesty, stood on the highest point in town and looked not the least out of place in the Blue Mountains setting of Katoomba. A quick recce which confirmed its attractiveness also confirmed that such grandeur was outside the scale of the expedition's exchequer. Although it seemed that some hotels and guest house had closed down, it was not long before he found an old pub with not only a more suitable tariff but appeared to offer robust country food in an attractive but quite small dining room. The room he was offered was very pleasant and country cosy, really not a lot different from the bedrooms at the Lodge in Fearnas. Its window looked out onto a mossy bank at the side of a narrow road which rose up as a wooded brae on which there were fir trees growing. This little snapshot view was decidedly Scottish. The bathroom on the first floor which he would share with the occupants of two more rooms had a bath on clawed feet and a shower rose above. He took his touring atlas and some brochures and a rolled-up oilskin top in his knapsack and set off down the stairs to explore. He could hear guitar music and a girl pleasantly singing a folk song. Her voice was coming from a lounge dressed in the decor of Victorian times, Edwardian, First and Second World Wars, art deco, with no other vogue excluded. 'Now that's what a hotel in Katoomba should look like!' thought Roddy.

About thirty people of varying ages were spread about sitting in comfortable easy chairs dividing their focus between a low stage which the singer was just leaving, guitar in hand, and a roaring fire in a huge fireplace. 'I must come here when I get back,' he told himself and made his way back across the hall to the front door. Without, the sky was dark and all was dismal. The rain seemed to have decided not to make a decent downpour and be done with it, but appeared to have every intention of dragging the misery of drizzle through the coming night. He closed the door.

'This side of the door is the place to be. There is no valour in striding the streets, saturated, in the half light of a descended mountain sky. It would be unfair to Katoomba to form impressions under such conditions,' he was saying, making decisions which pleased him well. The lounge was crowded, but from a group of different sexes and ages, a man beckoned him to join. 'There's room on the end of that settee,' he said and, seeing Roddy looking ready to accept, stood up. 'My name's Wally Friedman, my wife Ilsa', he said, indicating the lady next to him,' the rest you can meet as we go. Don't be afraid of the mob. No shouts we're all buying our own.'

'Thanks, Wally, Ilsa; I'm Roddy, Roddy Mckenzie. G'day, everyone!' and he was in. The pervasive mood was jollity boosted along by piano, violin, various guitarists and singers, a sax player, a tenor horn player who turned out to be an excellent performer of classical a music hall solos. The programme ranged from 'The Road to Gundagai', 'She's My Ladylove', 'Lily of Laguna', 'Michael Row the Boat Ashore', and Scots and Irish ballads sung and performed more than adequately by male and female artists. The audience was enthusiastic and in fine voice. In the short breaks between performers, he was quizzed by the interested people in the group. They were very pleased to know that he'd just finished working on the Snowies and one man asked, 'Isn't it a pity that so many beautiful, productive places will very soon disappear like Jindabyne where you were last and the Talbingo valley? I can see the logic in what's going to happen in the engineering sense. I just wonder what thought was given to the distant future and what the effect of the Murray diversions will be.' When Wally and Ilsa left for home, the group broke up and Roddy picked this as the time to go and have some dinner. There had been no ceremony about the performances; musicians had decided who was to play next or perform again, left when they felt like it, and shifted out to the bar so that when he came back from dinner it was all over. Well, he had revelled in the whole affair and sang with gusto on the occasions when he knew the words, listened and enjoyed when he didn't. He would go up and try out the tub, get an early night, and read. Before bed, he took a last look out the window and saw only misty blobs of street lights in the clouds which had folded over and wrapped the Blue Mountains township of Katoomba. He sat up in bed with Eleanor Dark's book on his lap unopened while he sat there and thoughts of the day poured back into his mind. Jill's face as they went out to the kerbside, and as they stood there in the final moments, the effort which had to be commanded to make the necessary motions of physically going away, getting into the car, driving past after he had turned the car. He realized—it was done—there was another, a new beginning. He knew what he was going to do, but plans are made by people, humans. The circumstances affecting their progress and outcomes are thrown to the phenomena of randomness, uncontrollable movements of events and the planner's reactions to feedback from the world. It is the kind of world that all living things have to accept, and humans have to learn to accommodate or go mad in the mind's last attempt to escape unpleasant reality. Roddy was fortunate that he faced the unknowns with confidence without fears or doubts. This meant that he could turn to the day's events, experience the sadness of having fallen in love again, yet turn to reason for comfort. He put his book on the bedside table, dowsed the lamp and turned in.

Dark as the evening had been, dark was the dawn—if dawn it could be called. Katoomba still had its head in the clouds and his view from the window did not include the slope of the hill just across the narrow road. Any hope of seeing the Three Sisters and the falls and views across the karsts, this landscape of chasms and cliffs would remain for him, at least for this occasion, between the pages of his travel guide. No point in tarrying, he would have breakfast, and travelling as fast as visibility and winding roads would allow, he would head west, get down from the misty tablelands and out onto the sunlit plains. What he saw to his left and right, even now in the atmosphere of grey obscurity, was rich, green undulating land. Very soon he was in Lithgow, which he knew from his books and pamphlets was a coal mining town. He never in his life had been in a mining town, but from what he had read in Cronin and Lawrence and Lewis Grassic Gibbon, they were places of hill-high grey-black slag piles running their anthracite scree down to nudge against the walls of the nearest row of terrace houses in the town which were grey and black, all in their clothing of the ever-surrounding coal dust.

But it was not like that here. Despite the greyness of the day's weather, the orderly little houses, and the buildings which spoke of law, incarceration, and judgement, whatever the town may have had to say was not lost but muted. The holiness of the place manifested itself in church spires on high ground where one would choose to place a gun. There were guns in town, reminders about soldiers, whose actual doings on the ground of war could never be understood by some of those who had raised the memorials, yet felt about them nonetheless as humans do feel, about loss of a penny or a life.

Once through the town, and as the valiant little car did its best speed across a line of longitude every sixty-plus miles, it hurried away from the dingy weather system he was hoping to leave behind. Perhaps he would reach dry conditions where trucks going off the bituminized ribbon no longer threw blinding mud on the windscreen which was impossible for the wipers to clear away. After the first experience, Roddy had acquired a can of tap water and a couple of big cloths so that he could pull up and clean the windscreen and regain visibility which was almost completely lost by the mud splatter. It was necessary to keep well behind a truck to avoid a mud splash, but he would inevitably get a splash from the slower moving vehicle on any attempt to overtake, in which case the attempt had often to be aborted. There were numerous trucks. After Bathurst, which he did not stop to explore, the skies did begin to clear and at one point a burst of sunlight, sustained for some minutes, washed the undulating, rolling landscape in bright green which made Roddy think that what he was seeing—except for the tree species—was not unlike parts of Hampshire.

Because of the slow going, he would arrive in Jerilderie at an awkward time of the day and he had to decide where best to stop on the way. The day had not been pleasant. He hated to hear a namby-pamby self say it, but the idea of a hot bath, a good dinner, and a warm bed had a strong appeal, so West Wyalong was chosen as the night's stop.

There was enough time to make a recce of the town. He needed to find a hotel and somewhere he could have the car washed—so that he didn't have to change clothes twice—before setting off for the day. A nearby garage was happy to wash the car in the morning which was very convenient so that he could have a walk around in the meantime. Tatterstall's Hotel won the selection with the Globe a close second, the others nowhere in the race. The hotel was comfortable enough, although there was a walk to the toilet and a cranky shower.

Everywhere in the town, there were indicators that flooding was a frequent, extensive, and disrupting event. While strolling around, he was making mental pictures of bullock carts loaded with the tall trees felled from the flood plains, turning the laden drays in these broad streets with the bullocks struggling to change over legs and find new places for their hooves as they jostled to make the turn and still exert a pull so that the bogie would never be in a position to cause the whole load turn over. He doubted that in the early days, eucalyptus oil had been extracted from the monster trunks of these huge trees, but now eucalyptus oil was a profitable export. He learned that gold had been discovered in 1893 but was now no longer profitable to mine. Wheat had become the major income earner. Just to indicate that the little town was not entirely culture bereft, it might be noted that the author Dymphna Cusack had been born here.

It was time to collect the car. The washing job had been well enough done: but what could give the little champion the lustre of Cooma motors, or the Jindabyne garage? Prettied up, she was a mini-wagon ready to roll west. But not directly; it was necessary now to go southward on what might be about a two-hour run to Narrandera, a major road junction for travel to all points of the compass. If all went well, he would reach Jerilderie in the late afternoon in time to find the offices of Goldsborough Mort, Stock and Station agents open, and therein, Mick Lowing.

Mick Lowing was in the office, anticipating his arrival. The *chakula* in his Australian world must have been more palatable than in Kenya and combined with fewer sleepless nights and possibly a happy married life and a job he enjoyed had combined to fill out his frame from the lean form it took when Roddy had first met him four years ago. He still had the keen twinkling eyes, the ready mischievous smile and now rounder, ruddier cheeks. He thrust out his hand to grab Roddy's. 'Jambo bwana, Rod, u hali gani?' Surprisingly, Roddy responded from subconsciously stored Swahili, 'A santé sana, bwana, Mick.' Mick's response was laughter and, 'Well done, Roddy! You probably picked up more Swahili than you think. You're looking fit—must be from pulling the Snowy Mountains apart. That's what Jill tells me you've been doing. Come and sit down and let's hear what you're up to now.' They went into Mick's office which was Spartan and decorated only by maps and some framed stock sale posters now historical documents. Roddy told Mick very briefly about his conviction that to be a legitimate member of the Australian community, he needed to feel that he had done, if only briefly, some service in the bush and that, on a sheep or cattle station. He wanted to get a picture of that part of the Australian life which, if not near the surface seemed, something to be lying deep in the Australian genes. 'So what I need to do quickly is find a station in South Australia where I can get a job, otherwise the necessity to get my life started will force me to abandon the dream.' Mick rose from the chair behind his desk, saying, 'Let's have a look?'

They went to a long waist-high cupboard on top of which were file-stacks of the leading stock and agricultural journals from all over Australia. He selected the pile of the South Australian Stock and Station Journal. 'The job advertisements are in here.'

They began at the top of the pile and in the most recent issue found an advertisement: 'Station hand wanted, single man, able to ride, milk, kill experience of droving, stock work sheep and cattle, fencing. W.D. A. Taylor, Rising Star Station, South Australia.' There was a telephone number and PO Box number in Renmark.

'What d'ye think of that?' asked Mick. Roddy read it again and felt very doubtful about his matching the skills described. 'Oo-oh, I dunno, Mick,' he said doubtfully. 'This bloke has probably got a very clear picture in his mind of the man he wants I might have to bullshit a good bit without telling lies if I'm going to change the picture in his mind.'

'Have a look at this.' He slid open the cupboard door and drew from a pile of large flat sheets a detailed map of South Australia and pointed to a large blank space with nothing on it but the sites of location homesteads, bores, dams, dotted lines denoting tracks and a few scattered hills off to the west getting higher as they went west with a lot of space between them. 'Rising Star covers about 700,000 acres. On all of that, they run about eight thousand sheep and about a thousand cattle. There's a bit of grass but blue bush and salt bush that are the main feed. You'd certainly see an aspect of Australia that would put you in a very small minority. It might be a good idea to give him a try if for nothing but the experience. He can only say he doesn't want you. I'll get him on the phone. It's a bit early to ring, but he might just be coming in after work.'

He happened to be at home and in his station office where telephone was presently connected. Mick rang and introduced himself then told him that he had a man here in his office who wanted to speak to him about the advertisement. 'What kind of a bloke is he?' Willie Taylor, the station owner, asked Mick.

'Well, he's a solid citizen I met him in Kenya when I was with the Kenya police. His battalion was at sea on the way home from Korea where he had just been in two battles of the Hook. They were diverted to Kenya to take action in the Mau Mau emergency.' Mick's tactic in playing the military card seemed to have been right. There is always a soft spot in the Australian heart for an ex-soldier, especially in the country. 'Yes, Mick, put him on, I'll have a word with him,' responded Willie Taylor, the station owner.

'Good afternoon, Mr. Taylor, my name is Roddy Mckenzie. I would like to speak with you about your advertisement in the *South Australian Stock Journal* and to apply for the position. I'd like to tell you briefly what I've been doing in the last six months. I bought a steamer ticket to come to Australia with the idea of beginning an after-army future here. I arrived in Australia in January and on the day of arrival managed to organize a job with Wood Bagshaw as a truck driver. I have completed the six months' work agreement with them and now hold documents of competence on dozers, graders, and front-end loaders which were the machines I was operating at Cooma and Jindabyne, oh, and I have a powder monkey's ticket. I have employment references from Wood. I've ridden ponies and all sorts of hacks since childhood and have played polo.' Willie Taylor pricked up his ears at this mention. 'I have also hand milked and machine-milked cows. My most recent experience of fencing was putting up wire in front of defensive positions and before that being a boy assistant to Jimmy McGillivray putting in five wire fences with larch posts and timber strainers. We were not allowed to kill our own stock during the war and that prohibition went on afterwards I believe. So my last efforts at killing were to stop people who wanted to kill me and my comrades. I think if one can survive the climate on the Korean peninsula and keep operationally fit in the conditions under which we were operating, hard lying on a station property has no concerns for me. I'm in Jerilderie now; I need to buy a swag then start for Rising Star tomorrow morning.'

Willie Taylor listened to the confident manner of Mackenzie's concise speech, delivered without hesitation or qualification. As he listened, he was sorting the information he was receiving. The man had no experience of droving, but he wouldn't be droving on his own. From what he said about the Snowy Mountains experience showed, he could learn quickly. If he'd played polo, he was horseman enough for Rising Star. He wouldn't be wanting a career as a stockman, so he may not stay long. But then you never knew how long any employee was going to stay—or be wanted to stay. 'Roddy, you don't sound like the kind of man who'd settle for a life as a stockman. And as a station hand here, you will not be earning very much money although there is a little house as accommodation which you would not have to pay for.' Was Willie Taylor signalling some enthusiasm for Roddy's application?

'In all honesty, Mr. Taylor, I have no plan to do that, but I feel I'll never be able to call myself Australian unless I've spent time working on a station. I have a plan for my long-term future forming now which will involve my Snowy Mountains experience; and nothing I learn on your station will be wasted. There is another subject I must mention. I do have army reserve time to do—and want to do—but if you allow me leave to go on weeklong camps and weekends, I will not want to be paid for that absent time. I'm used to the army twenty-four-hour-a-day service system and I did as much overtime as I could get on the Snowy, so on your property, I'd happily do odd hours anyway and longer than usual, which might help to compensate for army reserve time.'

'I have served myself and understand army requirements. I give every support to reserve soldiers and I'm o/c D Company Twelfth Battalion Royal South Australian Regiment based in Renmark. What rank do you hold?'

'Lieutenant, sir.' Willie noted the immediate change to military address.

'What position did you play in polo?'

'Four, sir, but because of my work situation and social level, I couldn't play in competition teams.'

'Ah, understood. There's not that problem here, so you might get a game. Do you know where Rising Star is?'

Roddy could feel his excitement rising. Surely this question really meant, 'Do you know the way here?'

'Mick Lowing has pointed it out on a large-scale map,' he answered promptly.

'Okay. Get something to write with and a bit of paper.' Roddy asked Mick for these and Mick's action was immediate.

'Ready, sir,' he snapped.

'Go north through the town of Renmark. Cross Ral Ral Avenue in front of you a sign points east to Wentworth Road and another sign showing Chowilla Station and above it a sign pointing to Rising Star Homestead, below it an arm indicating Canopus Station. Keep going straight past the turn off to Canopus. About two miles on you'll cross a cattle grid and in front of you is the signed entrance gate to Rising Star. The river will be on the right and that's where the house is. Except on Army Reserve duty, call me Willie. We'll expect you tomorrow evening. My wife's name is Bess. See you tomorrow.'

He had time only to try a quick thank you and confirm the arrangement before Willie put the phone down. All that needed to be said had apparently been said, and he was now about to become a station hand in South Australia. He was looking at Mick and delight must have been showing in his face as he exclaimed, 'Mick, you played the trump card, won the application game, and got me a job. You're a genius. Well done, thank you. On the strength of that, I'd like to invite you and your wife out to dinner. A woman with an active child must need a break now and again. Can it be organized?'

'I know Alison's mother would love to have David unless she has something on. She'll just about certainly suggest leaving him there overnight. I'll ring Ali now.'

Mick's house and property was five miles out of town. Roddy parked the Fusan behind Tatterstall's after removing the gift for the little boy, which he had bought at Dymock's Arcade in Sydney, and packages for Mick and Alison. Mick drove his car through broad fields of irrigated crops of table grapes, onions, and mung beans getting to even larger fields which Mick said would be sown to canola. Mick and Alison's property was quite visibly different. It was divided into smaller paddocks, the preferred Australian word for what British people called fields. In no time they drew up in the driveway of a house whose front garden came right to the roadside. This driveway ran around four garden beds chockfull of shrubs, roses, and annuals, all of them apparently enjoying the company of the others in their bed, the house remaining mainly visible through this screen and the plants to left and right. The house was easily concealed because it was low and presented its wider aspect to this garden. It had been built after the First World War and any alterations, if any, were not visible a glance.

The tiled roof would have been terracotta when first built, but now the surrounding trees, which had grown old with the house, had printed a pattern dyed into the clay from the thousands of leaves and twigs which, over the years had fallen, and by sunshine and rain, heat and cold had adhered, dissolved, and integrated into the pleasing patina of the present; they swept down in one continuous roof, forming the broad verandahs which ran round the house. The tiles had replaced the long gone rusty tin whose need for replacement must have coincided with a couple of good income years. From what he could see, the front walls at least, were of a dressed, split stone in thick, flat slabs of blues, greys, ochres, and almost reds and some almost greens, each slab a mixture of these colours with one of them predominating. The house looked much larger from the outside than seeing it from the inside proved it to be. Alison showed Roddy through saying, 'This is the house where I was born', and as she showed him the largest of the three bedrooms said, 'and this is the very room. I was most likely conceived here too, almost certainly, since I am the second child. My brother is a biologist and works and lives in London. Mick and I bought the property from my parents.' Most Australian houses have a separate dining room and a separate 'lounge' or sitting room as this one did but, as is inevitable in Australia, they gathered in the kitchen. Little Davie was a ball of atomic energy and non-stop three-year-olds' speech which was delivered using an amazing vocabulary. The indestructible books with huge bright-coloured pictures pleased him a lot and he began to flick over their few pages immediately. His trip to Grandma's appeared to be an acceptable norm for him as if simply moving to another room in the same house. 'I'm going to show Grandma my books,' he declared, after having thanked Roddy for them on a cue from Alison. Alison's mother was a handsome woman possibly in her late fifties and her husband had obviously not given up his farm because he was unfit. He was a live-wire in every farming political group in the state of Victoria, Jerilderie, and the lands around. Roddy was given a cheery welcome, but Mick and Alison had arranged a flexible, non-static position and tactically withdrew before her father could seize Roddy in his conversational mesh. The Globe Hotel was the chosen venue where, in period surroundings, they enjoyed Mick Morris's Ovens Valley wines. The conversation tripped lightly over Mick and Roddy's Kenya experiences and spread in fascinating topics of Australian farming, politics, what people of their ages were doing and the direction the country seemed to be taking. Without probing or the intrusion of advice, they listened with interest to Roddy's planning and how his Snowies skills would be his start base. The talk quite naturally returned to the event of the day: getting a station job and why he had this obsession with wanting to have it. Then it was time to say good night and thank you. The pair had given him an evening of delight; in conversation and sincere interest in his plans all, stirred throughout with the good humour and wit of both.

On return to the hotel, he sought and found someone with whom he could settle his accommodation bill. At six a.m., it was still dark and he drove the first miles with headlights on. There was a choice of roads of which he chose the apparently less interesting, but there being only two major settlements to negotiate, it was quicker and a bit shorter. His line of advance would become almost direct from Hay to Mildura, but exercising either of the routes, he would have to begin by sailing away from the mark. First by going south-west and away from Jerilderie to Deniliquin then turning almost due north to Hay whence it would be ever westwards. The stores of the merchants in Deniliquin were still closed in the hour it took him to get there. He wanted to have a stoke-up breakfast and buy a swag. Hay was not exactly bustling when he got there, but the petrol station had a cafe where the thinness and toughness of the fried steak may have been an indicator that he was in sheep country and the eggs would have been first-class puncture patches. There was a Dalgety's farm supply shop where he purchased what he estimated to be the Rolls-Royce of swags, a water bag seemed like a good idea, as did a hank of light rope with which he could tether a tent or hang washing on. He didn't need to buy tools. He and Mike had put together a formidable toolkit, which included an axe: Mike had suggested he keep it since varsity students had no great need for such impedimenta.

On this highway, with a reasonable surface, no great inclines, long straights, and almost imperceptible bends the little Fusan seemed content. He bowled on at what he considered maximum comfortable speed of seventy-five miles per hour and ruminated about Mick's present life. After his overseas adventure and his stint with the Kenya police, a good job with a stock company, Mick would have been an obvious candidate for matrimony, a stable married life in the Deniliquin-cum-Jerilderie world and the prolongation of the Lowing family line. Roddy had not the faintest thought of marriage or children. Would the future hold that picture of a happy family for him?

While he drove on, and those reflections exercised his mind, he decided that, quite clearly, the quintessential requirement to bring about any of these conditions or, even thoughts about them, was the need to be in love with a woman who was in love with you. He was saying to himself, 'Yes, I'll have to have a base situation established that'll be secure for everyone I'm responsible for. That makes it all the more important for me to keep my eye on the ball—remember the first principle of warfare, "selection and maintenance of the aim!" and this means there could be another Jill situation before I'm ready. That would be no good for the person I might fall in love with. And what about my objective then? Would I be able to continue the necessary concentration on it? If pursuing the objective hurt the one I loved, I'd miss the objective and lessen the chance of a good life like Mick's. That would be no good for either one of us, possibly even disastrous.' He thought of Jane and her own realization that a mixed caste marriage would be impossibly unpleasant for her. No amount of financial and real estate security, fame, or good reputation would make them secure against the horrible cuts of snobbery. Jane was a love lost.

Jill was a love lost too. How could she live life as a rising executive in Australia's largest bank while he was still climbing towards his goals? How would their life together be—their intimate personal lives, their close social lives, their broader social cultural lives? 'I can't expect to live in Sydney and be a perpetual guest. I've got to achieve my goals by myself or I'd get littlc satisfaction, I'd lose belief in myself, and then in anyone else.' He felt sorrow as he realized that he had cast Jill aside. It was a painful realization.

'God, how Jill must have been wounded by that rejection!' No matter how practical and how pragmatic a view she seemed to have adopted about his need to get out and establish himself, that wound must have been very deep. How wonderful she had been in those last days and hours. 'But aren't these the kinds of decision I'm going to have to make as part of maintaining the aim? There will be many others I'm sure. Well, present pain for future pleasure: remember that. If I drift off course, I will have wasted Jill's pain, Jill's love.' And, 'Will sadness pile up? What lies in the future when decisions have to be made and someone gets hurt—and I get hurt? Is it a question of losses for gains being inevitable?' There was as sadness surrounding him and at the same time going through him. He was finding it difficult to get out of this fog, but his resolve remained firm— even strengthened. 'I must do my best to avoid loss for others. Ultimately my aim is selfish and I'm going to have to accept that. Just don't shilly-shally and make everything worse.'

Mildura came as a bit of a diversion. The mallee trees that sat on bare red ground mile after mile provided a well-designed backdrop for the faint flush of green showing on the vast paddocks left and right where not a shrub could be seen from the road to the distant horizons. He had left the river red gums of an anabranch of the Murray River far behind and the trees of the Murrumbidgee at Hay had long dropped into the distance, and most likely he would not see more river gums until he reached Balranald. If he could sustain this seed for long periods, he should reach the station go to whoa in twelve hours. He would aim to be in Mildura about 13.30 hours when a pint and a feed would be most welcome. The old river port of Balranald could reward him only with a cup of tea and a comfort stop. Local history would have to come from books to be read some time in the leisure of the future. The future was to be seen somewhere within a plan where the pictures created were flicked through and replaced as when new thoughts and new experiences influenced his mind as days passed on.

He thought about Alison, Mick, and wee Davie. Their lives were part of a major plan completed. Alison had most probably decided upon married life, and raising a family in her early adulthood as the way she wished to live her life. The patterns of her own family must surely have had a subconscious influence.

Now he was driving through rows of grapes which engulfed the town. Now there were exotic trees from Sicily and Abruzzi and Val d'Arno; and there was houses and sheds, people were working and moving about and the skies above were of the palest blue. He had to call in his Fusan hound. The gruelling emotional tasks of the drive required some release. The immediate aim became finding the most attractive pub. Ah! Look at that. Just what the doctor ordered. A quick look at his travel guide had led him to famous old Grand Hotel on Seventh Street and Langtree Avenue. VB at its best was being pulled from the tap. How did he know? He was up to his ears in a pint of it. The dining room was old grand and the cuisine matched, in taste and portion. He asked the waiter to keep the cork from the bottle of wine he ordered when he had requested the reddest, bloodiest bits of the roast beef he could possible get. No time to linger, just don't rush. After lunch, he found a grocer's shop where he bought rice, tinned tomatoes, spaghetti, dry beans and lentils, sardines, potatoes onions, and garlic— and some more matches. The camping gear which Mike and he had always kept in big square biscuit tins had become, as had the toolkit, part of his inheritance at severance. Rising Sun, here we come before first you set! Outside Mildura he shortly reached the mallee again which was as sombre as before, but the invigoration of the beef, the red wine, and the anticipation of arrival at his destination seemed to have lifted his spirits. Just as well that his spirit thermometer had risen. Much of the road to Renmark was quite dense mallee scrub for mile after mile on both sides. Before he reached Paringa and crossed into Renmark, it could be imagined that many years earlier the land had been cleared. There were wheat paddocks on this flat plain that was edged, off to his right by high, ancient red clay cliffs which bordered the river close to the road. The geological pre-historic story was completed by the water level lands and numerous billabongs which shaped the other side, the River Murray's northern shores; there were tall river red gums to landward of lignum flats and little sandy beaches that were statements of character in the story's evidence of regular, and often major, floods. His eyes frequently on his map, a hand-drawn extract in smaller scale, he was too pre-occupied to get more than a very general view of a town with buildings scattered amongst trees, table grape orchards, and miles of citrus groves where, all around, the only building higher than the residential bungalows were drying sheds, warehouses, and a pub.

Behind the fence, all was the lush green of shrubs, trees, and clipped lawns roses seen through the church steeples. Willie's description fitted his drawing. Through gaps in the grey-green thin-stemmed lignum bushes, he could see water, beach sand, and some tall rich green grasses on islets; and grey sands where the highest water had borne a flood which had stayed a while and left them to dry out and bleach, leaving dirty brown-stained water marks at each pause.

It seemed odd to be driving to a sheep and cattle station homestead along river beaches two or three miles out of a town. That's not what he had seen in books! It was all wrong.

But there he was driving through a broad entrance in a white post and rail fence on which there was a sign which clearly announced *Rising Star Station*. Through a screen of boughs and over shrub shapes was the house of white-painted brick. There was a verandah all round like Alison and Mick's, and windows with glass panes like any fine English house or cottage *d'un certain age* in jolly old England—quite disappointing really. In truth it was a very beautiful sight, a picture of rare, soft, cool beauty, and deserved to be thought of more highly, and appreciated. Yet here was the antithesis of the homestead of an Australian sheep station one would have imagined. Even the noun 'homestead' didn't seem to fit.

The sound of the arriving car had been heard in the household, and by the time he had pulled up on the earthen roadway at the end of a broad stone-flagged path to the front door, two people were out, standing on the verandah looking towards the new arrival, examining this person that Willie had just employed. As he began to approach the two very tall figures, a man and a woman he called out, 'Hello, and good evening', and when a little closer and still approaching announced, 'I'm Roddy Mckenzie.' It was a cheery, self-assured voice not quite what one might expect from a station hand meeting the owners for the first time; or any time. There was nothing diffident in his demeanour or in his confident stride. When closer, he smiled as he put his hand forward towards the male, the man who, on the phone had told Roddy to call him Willie. The man put out his hand. He remained on the edge of the verandah step. From her higher position on the step above the woman seemed to have decided that shaking hands was not what she planned to do.

'You haven't worked on a station before, Willie tells me. There will be lots to learn. If you've been used to a softer life, you will find it a bit hard. You will be paid by the week, so if the work doesn't suit, you need only give a week's notice.'

'I'm not averse to learning and I've been having a bit of it to do.' The chill had struck him. He did not let his smile die: he kept it on his face and in his voice and looked right into her eyes. 'I'll do my best and hope that I shall the meet the required standards. If I prove to be a bit dull and I'm not picking up the needed skills, I'm sure you'll point that out to me. I'm not keen on failure, but in that worst case, I'm sure you will terminate my service. I would expect that.'

She seemed not to be able to respond, so she said, 'Willie, will show you to your quarters and tell you what your job will be.' Roddy's quick reading of the situation was that they had decided to treat this unusual applicant 'cool and hard', and indeed they had, but there was something unexpected in the new worker's attitude that seemed to have been missed in their tactical plan. If there was a strategic plan, it may have been somewhat amorphous, waiting to take shape when what they were doing was not working.

All Willie Taylor could now say was, 'Yes, I'll show you down to your house.' At which he stepped of the verandah spacing himself from Roddy's side. Roddy watched his move then turned again towards the woman on the step. 'Good night. . .'—pause—'Mrs. Taylor,' he said, still smiling and with a question in his voice which seemed to ask whether she was indeed Mrs. Taylor. 'Thank you,' he said, looking at Willie Taylor but not using the invitation to call him by his first name as offered when they spoke on the phone. Things seemed, somehow, to have changed.

'To begin with, we'll need you to work close to the homestead to do the milking. The weekly ration killing is done after work every Friday night and I'll show you how to do that. You'll also have to start up and shut down the diesel power plant, shift the irrigation lines on the lucerne paddock, and look after the horses up here. These jobs have to be done every day. Whatever else has to be done will be subject to day-to-day needs and I'll let you know these each day.' By this time they had reached the house. With the fading light and the trees around it, the interior of the house was almost dark when Willie Taylor opened the door. He operated the switch on the door jamb, and a solitary, unshaded globe suspended by a piece of cable from a rafter in the centre of the room lit up. Roddy took in the cold, empty scene. 'If you come and get your vehicle, I'll get you some milk from the house.'

'Thank you,' said Roddy. 'That's kind of you,' he said lightly, 'but I picked some up in Renmark and I should use that first.'

'Fair enough,' responded Willie Taylor. He turned to leave the house and Roddy followed. It could hardly be said that there was a conversation on the way back to the main house. Willie Taylor simply stated that normal start time on the station was eight o'clock, but the person who did the milking had to make sure the milk was at the big house by eight o'clock. He also let Roddy know that the house he would be using had been occupied by a married couple and the wife had done the milking and looked after the cows. They had retired to the Barossa Valley where all their relatives lived. With them, they had taken all their possessions. It was customary, he said, that station workers brought all their own stuff with them and took it away when they went. They had reached the main house and he said, 'I'll come down in the morning at half past seven and show you the milking routine', and turned to go.

'Thank you. I shall be ready at seven thirty.'

It looked as if forms of address were not in use today.'

So against all instinct, Roddy followed the example while maintaining the lightness of tenor and simply bade him good night.

As he drove to his house, his first thoughts were: 'Well, you can be a good officer or a bad officer, and you can be you can be an officer without being a gentleman. This could be a hearts and minds campaign.'

On reopening the door, he thought of accommodation past; the relative sophistication of the billets on the Snowy, including the trailer; the great set-up sharing with Mike; Bruce Lockwood's tattered timeworn shack, a humble haven of warmth in the freezing winter—and this. It had been built from cement blocks, most likely made on the station and put up by station labour. They had been painted over sparingly in a pale green. There was a window on each side of this space, but there were no curtains. All the wooden rafters were exposed and they too were the same pallid green. Above them the inside surfaces of the corrugated iron roofing sheets remained the same pristine zinc grey as when they had come through Messrs Lysaght's mill. The floors were cement quite smoothly trowelled. On the same wall as the only door of the building, and as if on exhibition at the Better Homes Show, solitary in space as if to highlight its significance, stood a *Kookaburra* woodstove with two iron hotplates, cast-iron discs, which fitted smoothly into circular openings on the flat top of the firebox below. The layer below the firebox had a slide-out grill. The oven was below that, its door emblazoned with a cheeky-looking eponymous symbol of this cast-iron and porcelain green and cream enamel masterpiece, a Kookaburra; perched perhaps on the curved, grooved, stubby, mighty cast-iron trees which bore the whole about a foot above the cement floor. The door appeared long since to have lost its closure fitting but a skilled artificer had bent a fine piece of fencing wire from the hole left in the door to hook over the latch fitting on the body of the stove. Roddy immediately worried about future soufflé making. The window on that wall was naked of curtain or trim. During the day, it would provide excellent light and sunshine for the housewife when washing up in the tub below. The tub was built of stout sheep station service stuff—moulded concrete—so too were the shaped symbolic arches of the stands, but these were of a ruder rougher cast expressing rural ruggedness. He left the Ideal Homes exhibition of the kitchen dining area to explore the bedroom. Neither was this room cluttered with furnishings. A bed frame of cast-iron tube had an assembly of small coil springs tensioned by joining wires to put a mattress on—that's where he would spread his swag. The lighting followed the same decor design as the sitting room and he noticed there were no power outlets on the skirting boards. There were no skirting boards. He imagined the cement block walls being laid and built then the concrete for the floor barrowed in and spread. The shower and toilet were in separate cubicles, side by side on the end wall to the right of the front door. He thought, 'Must make a sign for the front door, *Home Sweet Home.*' It was a blank canvas waiting for the brush of a creative genius.

The bud of his creative flair would have to wait some future moment to burst into bloom: now he had to apply his more practical thoughts to unloading gear, establishing a base, and feeding himself. He brought in the portable icebox that he and Mike had bought for carting essential beer: if there were spare corners, they put in chops, sausages, butter, milk, and such items of lesser importance. *Tuborg*, and one or two other sensible brewers, put their product out in half bottles, ideal for folks on safari. Mind you, they were inevitably at the mercy of suppliers of ice. He opened a bottle of beer not bothering about a glass which was in another box. Mike, who refused to study maps on the ground, spent long periods poring over maps of different data, so he had insisted that they fund the purchase of strong table with folding legs which fitted snugly up against the backs of the front seats of the Rolls. Roddy had been forever grateful and demanded his share of its use for food preparation, and he would use it now. They had been self-reliant on their journeying with no fewer than two primus stoves (necessary when banquets were being prepared for itinerant royalty) and two Tilley Lamps so that they could be at separate sites while they undertook different study, or reading, or fly winding tasks .

Although he could still hear the chatter of a distant diesel engine, which he assumed was the power generator, he extinguished the abomination of the single light bulb in the void of the room and lit a Tilley Lamp which created immediately a more cheerful atmosphere and a companionship in the sound of the burning gas. He had prepared a luxurious one-pot meal first of instant mashed potatoes in the bottom and, when ready, tipped can of meat and vegetable stew on top. How wise he had been to put a bottle of Mildura shiraz in the famous 'picnic box' from which he and Mike had drawn luxuries many a time. A glass of wine, continuing after a meal, is ever conducive of thought. But now he was puzzled. Had he misread Willie Taylor's voice tones during the telephone call from Jerilderie?

Bess Taylor had not been consulted and was not pleased with her husband's employment decision. The man seemed to have the basic capacity to do what was needed around the homestead, but that was a separate, different issue. They needed a man who could quickly learn Steve's job so that Steve could be shifted up to the cattle at the north of the run. Their attempts to recruit a sheep stockman had been unsuccessful to date. Also there was the unanswered question of how long a man aiming to get station experience would be prepared to milk cows and shift irrigation pipes? What kind of man was this who was willing to accept the kind of work he had been given? She was thinking they could buy milk and butter and cheese from Renmark. They could get someone out from there, daily, to do the irrigation. They could do the ration killing out at the shearing sheds. It would be no time wasted for Willie to fetch it when he was out on the station. Why take someone on who couldn't fill the bill and who was at best temporary?

Another, and completely different, suite of thoughts ran through her mind. Was he a handsome 'ten-pound pom' on the make? He certainly did look like good stud material, and with that beautiful smile and confident manner, he could easily win the gullible daughter of a station owner and he would be set for life. Was station experience part of the plot? He was a wartime officer; he didn't have the bloodline of a Sandhurst man. Nor was he like Australian officers who were drawn from the best families in the land. What a shower of no-hopers the English WWI wartime officers turned out to be. She had read about them in books and magazines. Well, she wasn't going to be taken in. She would show him his place. He couldn't take Australian society as a bunch of 'she'll be right, mate' colonials, all brawn, no brain oafs. She wouldn't be deluded by an accent and a posh veneer. She wouldn't share all her thoughts with Willie. He would not be able to understand. She would keep her discussion to the practical consideration required.

Roddy was making a reconnaissance of his domestic domain, the area within the wire fence which surrounded the house when he saw Willie approach around the trees from the main house. He greeted him, as he came near with a hearty, 'Good morning, Willie!'

'Good morning, Roddy,' he replied quite pleasantly. 'Ah, that's a bit better,' thought Roddy. He was carrying a shining galvanised pail and broke step for no more than a second at the gate where Roddy fell in alongside. They walked down a roadway bordered by tall old pepper trees where there was a shed backed by tamarisk trees and two more peppers one of which shaded the two stalled shed where the milking was done. 'You can do the milking', said Willie, 'Daphne's the one with milk. As you can see Mabel's in calf.' They were two pretty little golden Jerseys with dark brown, dished faces, and they knew who went where to wait for a feed of oats and chaff, their paddock was subdivided and watered so they always had fresh grass and clover to eat. Daphne was oblivious to the unfamiliar hands and the milking took just minutes. 'If you come up to the house now, I'll show you the dairy drill. The wife of the couple who lived in your house would do the separating, any other cheese or butter making and do the clean-up. You won't be doing that. We've been advertising for another couple, but we haven't find anybody suitable yet. When we get them, you'll move up to stockman's quarter's by the shearing sheds. The yards down here are mainly for drafting and loading sheep. The cattle yards are further up again, and we load cattle out to the Morgan Road which runs up roughly south-north to meet the road that goes to Broken Hill. We'll just leave the

milk here. They went in by a side door along the north wall of
the house into a square room totally white washed, fitted out
with stainless-steel sinks, zinc tables and work areas, a wooden
churn and cupboards with fly-wire doors and sides. They walked
then to the pumping shed where an old Fowler diesel engine,
started by a firing cartridge, was housed. A pump drew water
from the river through a foot valve to water about ten or twelve
acres of Lucerne for haymaking and to troughs and tanks as far
as two miles out. The lines of aluminium pipes, with overhead
jetting sprinklers mounted were uncoupled at ball or socket
joints on either end of the ten foot lengths, picked in man's
hands and marched out to the next area to be watered. It was
a laborious job, though not heavy lifting, carried out by the
husband of the couple who lived in the station quarters, now
Roddy's accommodation.

'You take a break and have a cup of tea about ten o'clock and
stop for lunch about twelve. We only take half an hour for lunch
and take the other half off at the end of the day. I'll leave you to
do this and I'll go and have breakfast, then we'll complete the
shift and I'll show you the horses and how to start the engines.
You shouldn't have any problems while I'm away.'

It was a day of dull light, no sun, no individual cloud shapes;
the kind of sky that makes a day long promise of rain which
never comes, so at lunchtime with the additional shade of the
trees, his residence was quite gloomy. He was munching toasted
bread with big Spanish anchovies when he heard footsteps.

Bess Taylor thought she would give this newcomer another
look-over. It was workmen's lunchtime: he would be at home.
Roddy was at the door as she approached.

'I thought I'd better tell you about the water,' were the first
words she said.

'Oh, good afternoon, Mrs. Taylor.' To his greeting, she made
no response. She continued by saying, 'That's river water in the
sink tap, so it's better to boil it for drinking. The shower water
is heated by lighting the fire under the drum.' This was being
said as she walked round the end of the house with Roddy
following uninvited to where a forty-four-gallon fuel drum had
been encased in cement blocks holding sand around the tank

for insulation Two one-inch iron pipes ran from the drum and penetrated the gable end wall just above head height.

'Willie will show you where to get the wood.' What she was saying was automated surface noise. Her brain was elsewhere. She was trying to make sense of what this good-looking very fit man with such a confident bearing was all about. She fished he statement and actually looked at him.

'Willie said you didn't want to make station work your life.'

'Yes. We talked on the phone about the job, and when he said I didn't sound like someone who wanted to do that, I confirmed his thoughts'—and continuing in the light, conversational tone—'I can see he's talked with you about our conversation.'

'At your age, I imagine you will be thinking about getting married.' This she delivered as a bald, colourless statement.

'Oh, I won't be able to indulge in such pleasant thoughts for quite some time yet.' He chuckled as he spoke then returned to a more serious tone. 'I'll have to get myself well and truly established first.' She was almost staring, gazing at him as he was speaking. For a rare moment in her adult life, she felt uncertain of herself. 'How could she ever know this man, who seemed so unaffectedly open; and who, in some way, was making her feel challenged? Challenged about what? What was to be gained or lost?' In her uncertainty, there was a feeling of loss of power. 'Whose would be the successful outcome of this conversation? What had she really set out to discover? Why was domination of this conversation being lost to her?'

Suddenly she was overcome by a feeling whose form she couldn't grasp, so vaporous, so infinite—yet known. She felt quite girlish. She did not ask herself why. She just knew she recognized the feeling. She hoped her face gave no sign of what was going on amongst her feelings. She could see in his face a sympathetic silence. 'God, I wish he wouldn't look like that,' she told herself.

'I just wanted to tell you about the water.' She turned quickly and almost ran away. 'I won't spoil your break any longer. I'll leave you to your lunch now,' she was saying into the air in front of her.

'Thank you for the information about the water,' he was beginning to say. 'I'll take your advice.' He was calling out his last words to her back as she quickly disappeared from view around the trees at the roadside.

Mrs. Taylor was not to be seen for some days during which he saw Willie when there was instruction to be done such as for the ration killing. The killing process was really straightforward, and Roddy found no moral problems in the execution. The ration sheep were good animals, not necessarily chosen because they were poor specimens, big two-tooth wethers. Laying a sheep on its side requires a simple knack no different from jiu-jitsu where you use the weight and energy of your opponent to defeat him. How else could he have thrown the big, horned, black-faced sheep in Jimmie Munro's highland flock when he was still in primary school? The sharp point of the killing knife's blade, held vertically, is put in behind the jaw with the back of the blade against the spine, quickly thrust down into the neck, and in the same movement, thrust forward immediately cutting throat and arteries, a knee is put behind the base of the head and quickly and forcibly pulled back to break the neck and shut down the nervous system. Skinning is an art in which the knife is used mainly just to open up the 'points' where the thin fleece-less skin joins the legs. Willie had a clever 'twist' to the gutting by first sliding piece of the skin down the oesophagus and tying a knot in it, thus ensuring that there was no backward flow of any gut content. Hoist on a gimbals which spread the legs and positioned a hook into the space between the ligament and the bone at each hock the fleecy skin was the peeled off by a downward pull; where there were sticky bits, a fist was put in and rolled so that skin and flesh parted without tearing. The gut, lungs, liver came out in unison at a pull downwards of a hand round the windpipe. A piece of muslin cloth was loosely slung over the hanging carcase and left to set to be butchered the next day. Willie did the first sheep, Roddy the second, and all others on the days thereafter. Roddy was happy to have learned another skill. Mind you, he had killed and skinned rabbits and hares; and sheep were, in some regards, very large hares. Killing and plucking hens or pheasants were also in his skills bag: not to mention catching, scaling, and gutting fish.

When he went to Renmark on a Saturday, he made a point of buying fish which he ate from his icebox in the early days of the week. To have a change from his total mutton diet, and just to be different, he would dine upon roast beef and drink Angove's, Hardy's, Lindeman's, or Penfold's 'hermitage' or 'claret', he would eat all of the available vegetables roasted or boiled and inevitably end up with the, inevitably on the menu, apple pie. Angove's didn't make a bad port either although it didn't have the frequency to become a part of the ritual. Because he was free from lunchtime on Saturdays, he would drive in to Renmark on a rationing, resupply, and admin trip. His first call for the afternoon was to the Bank of New South Wales where except for housekeeping and his reckless expense in the township's fleshpots, he would deposit almost all of his pay, which would have been left for him to pick up from the zinc-covered work bench in the 'dairy' when he carried in the meat. He was an official borrower at the library which he found to be extremely good and scanning the shelves convinced him the needs of Renmark's citizenry were well met. When he wanted something not on the shelves, it was speedily acquired for him. The bookshop was pleasingly rich in backlist volumes and the staff wanted to work there and be amongst books. Then the lure of the flashing lights (Where? There wasn't even a set of traffic lights!) would draw him to that den of iniquity on whose wall, if he craned his neck, he could see the recorded height of the recent Murray River flood. The boisterous arguments as to which of the Australian Rules drowned out any mention of Sturt, or Norwood, or Port Adelaide. Where did they get their best players from any way? Though not in season here, the skills of wily leg spinners and ace batsmen of the touring Australian side were being discussed in erudite detail. Encouragement and praise, powered by enthusiasm and adoration alone, were transmitted across the ether to the other side of the world. What was different here from the Barley Mow?

Yes, there was a decided difference: the beer was almost freezing. It had shades too of the Ship Inn and so far as the cricket conversation was concerned he felt entitled to wear the colours of Hampshire. He became a piece of the Australian Riverland which would be, for the next few beers at least, 'forever England'. Thank the gods of cricket for my education at the Barley Mow, he was thinking. 'Could do with a bit of the rain they're having in Manchester,' stated a man in the group. 'Ah, just a lovely summer shower,' Roddy responded.

'Stone the bleedin' crows, mate, the game'll be a jolly washout! I wish you poms could get your seasons adjusted finer.'

Another voice added, 'Nah, s'all part of a plan mate. Conflict of sporting highlights—they don't want cricket on now. The Homing Pigeon Fanciers are having the Midlands Championship and the Shove Ha'penny elimination rounds are on, all the locals'll be packed. They should get *Wisdens* to draw up the sporting calendars.'

'That's a brilliant idea', said Roddy in admiration of such genius, 'I'll write another letter to the *Times*. My last one ended the Boer War.'

But they were serious about their cricket. They worshipped their Constantine's, Hutton's, Sinji's reserving their most reverential tones for John Arlott, on whose every far away word they hung, savouring syllable by syllable, descriptions of their sacred game. When they found out Roddy was a new chum at the Rising Star, they observed that he would 'be living in the lap of luxury out there'. 'Yes, and when you live like that it gets a bit boring. That's why we toffs like to go slumming now and again.' They all had a chortle.

'So where are you going slumming, Rod?' someone asked.

'I'm going to eat roast beef in the dining room. It's not that I don't like mutton: it's that I've heard a change is as good as a holiday. And I believe it's one of ours—hit by a truck on the Broken Hill road.'

'Sure the poor blighter didn't die of hunger?' Someone wanted to know.

'It' six o'clock. I'll be late. It was great having a drink with all of you,' he said, looking around the group and raising a hand in gesture, 'Oo-roo!'

On Sunday morning, the sprinklers were set up and pumping. He would shut them off at four o'clock. He was hanging his dhobi on the line, after which he would have lunch, when Bess appeared.

'A family has just turned up to take the homestead job they have all their furniture with them and nowhere to go. We would like you move up to Birthday Hut this afternoon. I'll ask them if they could go somewhere while you packed.'

'Yes, I can do that,' he said, cheerfully, for in fact there was not much involved except for his wet washing, but even half an hour would make a difference to that.

'If they don't mind, they could stay here and begin to move in. I don't think I'll be in the way. My packing is scarcely a private matter. I should be fed, packed, and ready to go in half an hour. It will make it a bit easier for them I hope, and help them to feel that they have arrived.' Then he said, 'I haven't been on the Birthday Hut track before. Do you have a track map, I could use?'

She managed to say, 'That's very kind of you'—and incredibly, to say—'Roddy.'

The emotion involved in allowing herself to say these words was clear in her face, her eyes, her voice. Had there never been the other thoughts, those emotions and that stirring feeling before her parting from him last time, she would have had to demand even more of herself now. The conditions of his own arrival were furthest from his mind and she was sure this was so, but felt red guilt for her bad behaviour when he had arrived. She was blushing as she said, 'I'll go and tell them.'

She came back to add, 'Yes, we do have maps, and Willie will give you one and route instructions. He's getting the Graham truck ready for you and suggests you leave your car here in the implement shed. There's a canvas sheet we can put over it.'

She left, walking quite a different way from the woman who had disappeared around the trees on her last departure.

Willie provided an inch to the mile OS sheet which covered all of the station area plus a good bit of the South Australian state to the north and west and the border of New South Wales.

A well-worn Standard Vanguard utility pulled up at the gate. The sight made Roddy feel sad. What he was seeing was straight from an American movie of farmers having to leave the land which through ignorance had turned into desert. The load on the ute had been selected and arranged by stage properties managers; the husband, wife, and child were straight from Central Casting. He gave a friendly call as he crossed the yard to the gate, 'Hello! I'm Roddy Mckenzie. Come on in.'

Not knowing the storyline of this film, he accepted the evocative skills of the casting and costume designers' art. He was a thin young man whose blond hair had been cut in a jagged brevity. The light shades the prominent bones of his face had allowed hollow cheeks to form so that the tanning by the son made it easy for the camera to exaggerate the hollows of the cheeks and temples. He was wearing blue bib and brace overalls—and yes; one bib button was missing, so the shoulder straps hung loosely down his back. His white shirt had once worn by an office wallah, had been cast out in favour of a later Christmas or birthday present. His wife's name was Mary-Belle and the little 4-year-old girl's name was Chloe.

'I haven't eaten yet', Roddy said and asked, 'what about you folk?' to which Mary-Belle replied, 'No, we haven't yet.'

'Well, I've cut some slices from a leg of hogget which I planned to grill. Would you like to share some of that? I haven't done vegetables, but I've got bread and butter', and looking at Chloe, he added, 'and jam too. While I'm making lunch, you can start bringing your furniture and things in. After we've had lunch, I'll pack up my kit and gear and be gone quick-smart.'

He didn't add the detail of having cut only two slices, which he had marinated overnight in tomato passato, garlic, rosemary, thyme, pepper, and salt and some basic Angove's red. One had been planned for a leisurely, luxury lunch today at home the other to have for lunch wherever he may be tomorrow. Anyway, things change. From his icebox in his horizontal larder, he quickly cut and sawed two more big slices, rubbed in salt and pepper, made little slits and filled them with garlic, rosemary, and thyme and slathered them in olive oil. He had to cut and juggle to get the four fair-sized hogget slices onto the grill pan under the fire, which was going just nicely, with lots of embers and bits of wood yet to burn.

'I'm a bit short of plates and forks. D'ye happen to have some handy?'

'Not real handy', said Mary-Belle, 'but I can get them.'

Their table was lying flat on its top at the bottom of the load, so all the other articles had to be brought in first and laid approximately where they would take up more permanent positions at some other time.

The lunch went down well if empty plates are evidence, and the only question or comment during or after the meal was, 'Is this really hogget?'

Now he could pack up, so he began with the dishwashing which he was allowed to do without interference from the family who seemed to be in a state of awe at the energy and activity and perhaps the trauma of travel, arrival, and now having a job and a house.

Taking up not very much space on the floor, Roddy's gear had been put together as if for a pre-embarkation kit inspection. Willie arrived driving the old Graham truck on which was loaded two forty-four gallon drums, bales of lucerne and wheaten straw, a coil of fencing and barbed wire some star pickets and other gear to take up to Steve.

'G'day, Roddy. Sorry, no *Movement Order*,' he said as he stepped down and came to the gate.

'Mrs. Taylor came to tell me that I'd be moving today, so I've got all my gear together. I just have to put the car in the implement shed where she told me I could put it, load this lot, and after a route briefing, I can set out.'

'I'll come up with you and show where you can put your car. I've pulled out a bit of soft canvas which we can put over it and there should be nothing going anywhere near it when you're not here.'

Having put the car carefully away in a corner of the implement shed, Roddy spotted amongst the all sorts that filled the length of the shed, a grader. 'D'ye mind if I have a look at your grader? I didn't know you had one.'

'Yes, we use it for keeping the tracks in reasonable condition.'

His examination of the grader showed that it was a very flexible machine capable of varying blade angle and tilt able to do a bit more than just keep track surfaces reasonably level.

Back at the house, it didn't take more than ten minutes to load all Roddy's possessions which were everything from the car, and this time, including his trunk. Along with the Ordnance Survey sheet Willie gave him a hand-drawn route map with significant topographical features and track junctions highlighted in darker penciling. He'd even put in GRs for the road junctions.

Willie had not acknowledged the existence of the trio of new arrivals since he had brought the truck, and Roddy had loaded it with some assistance from Willie. Roddy turned to the family. They had been watching in silence all that took place, with no discernible feeling nor wish to participate. Their eyes must have been taking in all the events while registering no sign of anything actually having been observed. Roddy said cheerio to the wan trio and wished them well. 'Thank you, Willie,' Roddy said. 'If I get lost with this lot, I deserve to die in the desert. Right, I'll get going. It is said "the sooner you leave, the sooner you arrive", which is sometimes the case.'

Roddy jumped up into the cab of the truck, which allowed easy access since there were no doors; advanced the ignition and the choke by instinctively measured fractions and put a foot down on the raised metal dome of the starter device which poked up through the bleached wooden floorboards. There were sounds, simply expressions of feeling by the mechanism, that the fact that it was going to make the engine start was something it did with bugger all to do with you. The old engine had a happy philosophy of life; all it wanted to do was to run. It reminded you of this when you switched it off. It stopped running only when it had made its point. You had to love a truck like this, so in good friendship and recognizing each its own role in the things that were to be done, they set off. With one hand on the little wooden steering wheel, and knowing that any moment, he would need another hand for choke and timing adjustments, he stuck out an arm in a brief wave, and loudly enough to be heard, yelled, 'Oo-roo!'

He was happy to be on the road. It looked as if what he wanted to see of station life was about to come into view. He hadn't gone far from the homestead perhaps about five miles through dead, dry grass, small copses of low blue-bush and scattered mallee when he noted that the track was getting worse. There were scoured-out gullies in what had once been the centre of the track which would remain forever, no matter how many times they would be filled unless something was done at the point where the water gathered and came in increasing volume to this point then flowed on to the other side of the track, and extended almost out of sight in the paddock. He was very glad he didn't have to drive the faithful 'Fido Fusan' with its low-slung body over the unavoidable ups and downs of the track. Flat flood plains are never precisely flat and there were signs of places where there would be ponds and pools which would lie on the clays of rain and evaporate. There were big areas between and around the mallee trees, which were getting sparser as he drove on, where the water was slower and wider in its flow and had left the sun to dry out and blow away the sand that its slow flow had shifted. The water, sand, and wind had caused long stretches of bone rattling rhythms for humans, and nut and bolt loosening for machines. The driving skill required was to find the vehicle speed, which happened about the safe limit for driving, to match those corrugation rhythms with the bounce of the vehicle. When this was achieved, life became amazingly more comfortable for flesh and bone but a terrifying test of driver reflexes and eyesight. All good things must come to an end, and after the second fence after following a lazy loop in the track, he spied some tall trees and what could be the gable end of a low building and the end one big, very high one, on the northern horizon. What other buildings there might be were visible only as shapes and shine. He travelled the last few miles through the scattered blue bush and some saltbush free from corrugations. There was one more gate on a long east-west fence stretching out of sight in each direction. Now here were athel pines at the sides of the track and huge pepper trees where he could see under their shade two houses, about a hundred yards apart, each with a fenced yard. One of the houses was newer and clad in never painted, weathered board. The nearer was much neglected and made of unpainted galvanised iron which was rusting around the skirts and had a big red-brick chimney construction on one end: the windows were opaque dull and dirty. The shed in the yard, likely the laundry, would very soon collapse entirely, the henhouse might hold out a year or two longer. But the surrounding pepper trees were classics, big sweeping shapes, perfect subjects for the many Australian water colourists for whom they would be inspiring subjects. One could imagine how an artist would enjoy the contrast of the deep, in places almost black shadows. The foliage in places was almost lost to sight, the colour bleached out by the glaring sun.

A man had heard the truck approaching and had come down to the last gate in a ute and had opened it for Roddy's truck. 'G'day!' he yelled as Roddy drove through and pulled up. 'Hello!' he shouted back. 'You must be Steve. I'm Roddy. Show me where to go, Steve—don't want to stop her now, she'll blow up!'

'Park in front of that house,' he called, pointing to the nearer house on the left of the track: Roddy kept moving. The old Graham was ready to boil over the moment the fan stopped turning. Once pulled up in front of the house, he quickly took a rag at extended arm's length and, keeping ready to jump back, unscrewed the radiator cap, leaving it to fall immediately and leaped away. A moment or so later, a geyser erupted. The old truck had made its opinion of the day's slog quite obvious.

Steve drove up from the gate, put his ute under the cover of an open shed, itself under the cover of one of the huge peppercorns, and came round to meet Roddy. Putting his hand forward, he said, 'Yeah, bit of a surprise to see you.Willie rang up this morning to say you were coming up. Anyway, welcome. I'm Steve. ' (The station had its own internal telephone lines. Put in by Willie's father, it was modelled on a system installed in a station in Victoria possibly a first in Australia. Powered by batteries, the user had to crank a handle on the box which had the mouthpiece fixed and listen through a hand piece attached by a piece of cable put to one ear.)

'Hello, Steve, Roddy Mckenzie, good to meet you. It was a surprise for both of us. Just as well I don't have much gear to move,' he said, laughing, and looking at the back of the Graham, nodded towards his few possessions lashed on behind the main load.

'I'm going to suggest you come and stay at my place until we can organize your house. That's the old one on the other side. It hasn't been used since the shearer's cook was in it last shearing. I have a spare bedroom that's seldom used, so you're welcome to it until you're sure you're ready to shift. Let's take some of your gear in as we go. Once it's all in, we can have a beer that I brought up from Morgan yesterday.'

'Steve, that would have to be one of the best suggestions I've ever heard, thank you.'

The gear was at the back of the truck, lashed down since the truck had neither sides nor tailgate;possibly for many years.

Steve Ward would have been about the same age as Roddy. He had an open face, deeply tanned, and his clear eyes, round which weathering had already formed wrinkles, looked directly at the person he spoke to; and out from that well-formed face, they scanned a world that they seem to have assessed as being generally good.

'That's jolly decent of you, Steve. Thank you. I'll try not to get under your feet.'

It was dark now, and while they prepared a meal of grilled chops and boiled vegetables on Steve's fully operational *Kookaburra* by the light of one of Roddy's Tilley lamps, they drank some beer, they found themselves pleasantly sharing conversation.

'What do you think of Willie and Bess?' Steve asked.

'I must say I found them a bit cool. I didn't expect them to fall all over me, but the message I got was that I was a station hand, as yet unproven, and I'd better know my place. There was certainly no chit-chat, and when Willie and I worked together, he only talked about what we were doing—never even mentioned the weather unless it related to the reason why something had to be done. I brought the subject of the army because I have an obligation to do some reserve time. He accepted that I would have to do that and told me that he was a reserve officer himself, in the unit I would be going to, and that there would be a week's training camp soon; and no more.'

'I've been here three years and I can't say I've ever had a conversation with either of them that wasn't about work, but I've never looked for, or expected, anything else. They mind their own business and just expect you to do your work and I've never had any criticism there. I like station work, and apart from three years' droving, it's all I've ever done. I've had bosses and bosses, and I've found the ones that don't bother you, the best. So I might have my own ideas about how they could run the station and make more money, but what they do is their choice. Any kind of stock rearing or farming has risks. Nature and the markets make sure of that. Yet there are some ways of doing things that are better than others. One day, when I see the opportunity, I'll put all my savings into a place of my own— somewhere with decent rainfall!'

'Well, you've certainly built up a lot experience and you have an objective. I wish you every success. I think there's a very good chance for a bloke to do well at just about anything if he truly wants to and gets stuck in. I've met a few blokes since I've been here that came out of the war with nothing and have built themselves successful businesses of different kinds. I've allowed myself just six months just to get the feel for Australia that comes from station life. That life seems to be part of the spirit of Australia's beginnings. It seems to me that even city dwellers hold a reverence for the outback and the people of the outback, even if they've never been there, and never will go there. Mind you, I can understand that feeling, because as I have driven through the country, I have seen that the outback is just at the other side of their garden fences. And I have the idea that many turn their backs on it and look instead into their towns and cities. Fair enough when I think of it. That's where their life and work is. I know it's a very short time and you'll probably laugh at me—and I wouldn't blame you—but I don't think I could live the rest of my life in Australia without knowing, at least a little bit, about what has made this country what it is. And I can't let time go by just finding out. Once I've finished here—and the Taylors know I don't plan on making station work my life—I'll immediately start getting the first parts of my plan moving.'

'Good on you. From what I hear, there's many that think they know it all as soon as they get off the ship. In five minutes, they're ready to tell you how backward the place is and make you wonder why they've come here.'

'Maybe, deep down, they didn't want to leave. Maybe they are having some doubts about why they did leave. They may be missing people they left; and things they used to do that were habits they never realised they had, and maybe there were some things that were better for them where they came from. And maybe they want to make an impression on Australians that they're not here because they couldn't do well enough at home. I don't know.'

When Steve asked him the inevitable question, 'What about you, Rod? What made you think of coming to Australia?' He found himself wondering how much differently he would be answering that question now than how he did answer it before he left Scotland, Britain, when his first landing in Sydney, on the Snowies or on the day he left Sydney to travel west. The person who was Roddy at any of those times would now, unquestionably be influenced by his freshest experiences to form a new truth that would hold only the unconscious indefinable of its birth as an idea.

'Steve, I'll give you as honest an answer as I can, but there are some things about my answer I'm not sure of myself. I could say the army unsettled me and that would be true. But I had ideas of getting out into the big wide world as a boy. If the storybook I was reading was about the jungles of the Amazon I'd want to be there, if it was about Hudson Bay, I'd want to be there, or the deserts of Arabia, or the North-West Frontier. I don't think I ever read any books about cities, and even now, a visit to a city is plenty for me. Then events, and that restlessness I still had, and the yarns I'd had with Australian soldiers pointed me in this direction and Australia was big enough for a bloke to have a go. Now, the great people I've met, life in the Snowy Mountains, a little bit of road travel and I'm hooked. I just need to choose the place where I want to settle with my plans. I'm not sure what sense all that will make or whether I've answered your question. But, Steve, it's the best I can do.'

In the evenings of the nights that followed, they would have such yarns and many subjects all ground for a growing friendship. Steve argued well and stuck to centre of the subject. Of people he was totally non-judgemental save in a situation of sheer evil. The conversations of their days were different: then they talked about the work in hand, the trees and shrubs and plants and weather, dogs and horses and flocks, and the economies of stations. Steve was a patient tutor and Roddy a willing pupil.

There were three fine horses at Birthday Hut and the tack was in good order, kept that way by Steve. They would not be using them on the first day. They unloaded the truck and put the bales of lucerne, just brought up, in a fodder space next to the stalls and the small horse paddock. There seemed to be some sort of principle here: 'If there's space on a vehicle, put something on it'. Anyway, it saved bringing bales down from the huge open-ended shed was stacked to the high roof with lucerne hay and straw, just to fill the stable mangers. The two fuel drums were rolled off the tail of the truck to land on two old tractor tyres from whence they bounce-rolled to a soft landing on the ground. The star pickets and the fencing wire were left on the truck and were later added to by two thick wooden posts and other various fencing tools, their water bags were put aboard with their bags of food for smoko's and lunch, old lemonade bottles of cold tea which station hands found mighty refreshing. Leaving the trees and the buildings behind, they set off in the old Graham for the point in a fence line nearly a jogging and bumping hour away, where a strainer and a gatepost had to be replaced and some fencing restored. This was land of scattered mallee diminishing northwards to very few, there was some bullock bush randomly or in small stands, here and there a sandalwood, some mulga on sandy ridges, and forever the bluebush and some salt bush almost forever. The sun was visible in the sky through a thin layer of low stratus cloud which spread over all horizon to horizon and dulled the day yet caused the riders in the truck to screw their eyes a bit. Coming into view were some drafting yards and it was here where four paddocks met that their task lay.

Having tasks to do before leaving; gathering materials and tools and loading up then checking a windmill and a trough on the way, it was smoko time when they reached their job site. It was a logical spot for the drafting yards. Both gate posts on one of the gates had been so worn by sun, rain, desiccating heat, and the pressure of surging mobs that the day was near when one more mob would knock them over. Before they sat down to eat their bread and cheese and fruit cake from the baker at Morgan (and Renmark) and drink their tea, cool, brown, and without milk, Steve had shown Roddy what they would have to achieve in the rest of the day. They sat down in the faint shadow with their backs against the truck wheels and talked as they ate and drank.

'This is where we'll be driving the mob to tomorrow. They're in the paddock behind us now. We'll get away early and bring the horses up in the horse float. We'll see if we can get the mob here before dark without pushing them. Next day we'll draft out the ewes here. The day after that, we'll drive the drafted wethers down to our yards rather than bring a private carrier up here.' Steve rolled a smoke and Roddy got his pipe going, but they didn't linger. Still smoking, they set about their tasks. Having dropped off two posts for the gate, Roddy drove the truck out for a distance indicated by Steve, where his job was to put in a new strainer post which would become the end of the replacement star picket fence line and the joining up with old fence. Where Roddy was to work, there was a good deal of sagging slack on the old fence wires, so he was able to take up enough of it by putting a picket vertically against them and making temporary wire ties round the wire of the old fence to the picket at the same spacing's of the old fence and running a rope from the centre of the picket, now holding the fence upright, to the towing hook on the back of the truck and driving very slowly, he moved the truck sufficiently to pull the old wires away from the fence line where he wanted to drop in the new strainer post in a new hole on the same line. The new post hole had to be dug into the ancient clay now exposed by wind and rain. Years of compaction in years long before the present meant that he had to drive a long steel hexagonal bar, of about his own height, into this solid mass. Raise, drive down; raise again, drive down again; heavy lift, driving fall; chip after crumbling chip, until it was possible to bring the material he managed to loosen from the mass out of the hole, which had to be little more than the width of the blade on the long handled spade he was using. At last, he had reached the two and a half feet depth he needed and was able to slide the heavy log the edge of the hole, and as if about to toss the *caber* raise it and position it in the centre of the space. Next he scrounged nearby with his spade to gather fine sand together and place it like a collar just away from the edge of the hole. Then having set the post in the middle, eying up the fence line and judging the vertical of his new post against thin air and his innate spirit level, pushed some sand with one foot, so it flowed into the hole then with his left foot as nearly opposite as he could: he let some more sand pour in and so on around the post, just enough to allow him to make the post remain vertical. The he took that same long iron bar and raised and dropped it at its own weight all around the post while moved with it holding the post vertically, adding sand evenly around little by little. He repeated this, never allowing too much sand to pour in. Round he went so that the particles of the sand met and bedded with each other. Before he had half-filled the space, the post was straight as a die and immovable. But he kept the slow pouring and tamping action going until the collaring sand could be compacted no more. (It's at this time that one finds that the post is sadly skewed or not on the required line, or both! Fortunately it was neither—in this case.) He went back to Steve who was progressing well with both old gate posts taken out. He had split these with the axe to see what he could save to use as supports for Roddy's new post before they strained the wires anew. Time for lunch; the cold chops that Steve had grilled in the stove the previous night. As they talked while eating, and for a little after, and as they spoke during their half-hour break, Roddy was comparing immensities—the Snowy Mountains and the land of this sheep station. It was a comparison in which the term dimension had lost its meaning. Yet they swapped experiences of lands which neither had seen and trusted each other in the truth of their accounts; Steve's descriptions of the Channel country of Queensland where he'd seen a collection

of homestead buildings and an airstrip, clustered like a small
village with nothing but vast space all around: and Roddy's of
the Snowy Mountains and the south-west of New South Wales.
Before they left for home the straight, newly hung gate, and the
evenly strained wires, the straight black pickets looked like gold
teeth in the mouth of a rat.

Even Steve's house with the stove going and the lights on
was a different world, a star's distance from where they had
sunk points in the vast space of land and marked them with
puny posts, an endeavour of man. Clean working clothes, saved
for their role as the week's 'dinner suits', added to the idea of
difference from the world without an aperitif of Southwark beer
(it's better in the bottle) topped by the Mckenzie bringing out
a bottle of Angoves' wine to have with their mutton stew, slow
cooked on the hob while they were away.

'I know you'll be wanting to get to your house, but cleaning
up a house is not the kind of thing you want to be doing after
work. Put up with staying here until the weekend and we can
get your house fixed no bother on Saturday or Sunday, I'd think
Sunday for preference so that we could go to Morgan, Waikerie,
or Renmark for rations and a beer off the tap.'

'I wouldn't have you wasting your off-work time doing my
housework, but I know you mean what you say. Sunday it is and
you can choose where we should go to take on stores.'

Before light, they took down the tack they needed, saddles
and blankets, bridles and hung them up in the positions in
the horse float, put down the tailgate cum ramp and loaded
some oats and lucerne, a nibble for the nags, and walked the
horses up the ramp from the loose boxes where they had been
shut in for the night before Steve and Roddy had finished for
the day. The dogs knew there was something afoot and were
barking with excitement. Steve took four off the chains under
the pepper trees, and for a few moments, they rushed around
like mad things stopping here and there for the bliss of a piss
on fresh ground. This was not a truly ruly drovers' truck so
rather than going to dog cages in the open, fixed under the
floor of the truck, they ran up the ramp and joined the horses.
With lights on, they drove out the track to the back end of the

paddock where the mob was. As the dawn light was coming, Big Red 'roos standing on the track, their eyes flashing red in the remaining darkness, moved off with a leap or two as the truck approached. They were travelling west on the *Flash Jack* track in the direction of the road that ran from Morgan through Burra to Peterborough where it turned east to Broken Hill, the Silver City, home of Broken Hill Proprietary Limited, miners of silver, lead, and zinc, the same company that owned the steel works that Roddy had seen in Wollongong. They turned north where a sign pointed to the old homestead site of *Hypunna* now absorbed into Rising Star, and followed a fence for a bit until they reached a fence junction and gates where they stopped then turned the truck into the paddock and closed the gate slipping the ring on the short chain round the post and onto a dome-shaped steel ball on the end of a steel pin bent upward at a right angle, driven into the post.

'We'll stay together to start, Rod, and see what we find they'll just be beginning to move now. Watch where I point'— he indicated—'almost dead ahead, keep that first bushy bullock bush to your left, go right keep looking at your horizon, d'ye spot a windmill?'

'Seen,' said Roddy.

'They'll be starting to move now and might go for a drink. We'll keep fairly close together to start so you can just hear me if I shout. You cover south and I'll cover north. Look out for fresh tracks as well as sheep. Give me a hoi if you spot something. Take Spot and Jackie with you.' Steve and his dogs spotted sheep first. He called Roddy over and instructed him in how to ensure his wing was clear of sheep and to keep his dogs working out on the wing. If he found sheep, he was to keep them on his left hand and move them along at Steve's speed. Soon the sheep that Roddy was gathering put their heads up and saw where their flock was and, still going forward, drifted towards it. The mob began calling and odd sheep would run towards the call, but Roddy had to continue to make his priority the wing and keep his dogs spread out. With the dogs holding the mob gathered thus far, and on a rough count, nearly the whole flock Steve joined Roddy on the wing, sending Roddy out to make sweeps along the fence, so they were both covering an extended curve of ground and only picked new sheep up as they got nearer to the main mob. When they were back behind the mob and the dogs were keeping a nice pace, Roddy rode up to Steve and asked him what was to be done with the float. 'One of us'll ride back and bring it down at smoko.'

'You know I'm in the active army reserve. Well, I've got to try to keep fit and I haven't been doing much in that regard recently, so I was going to ask if every couple of miles or so, if the mob's steady, I'd like to leave my horse with you and run back and get the truck, bring it along by the fence track and run back in to where you are.'

'Always had the idea you were a bit of a nutter. But if that's what you want to do, I'm happy.' And that is what was done. Before they reached the yards, he had done about ten miles because the run-in from the fence was getting shorter each time. At the windmill, there were two enormous reinforced cement tanks fed from a pipe piped all the way from the river by the homestead engine, the windmill switched on and off by a ball-cock mechanism in the long trough. Most often, the function checks were done by Willie himself as he went around the spread. They took off the kangaroo-proof canvas covers from the lucerne bales they had brought up the day before and split and spread them around the yard where the sheep would overnight before tomorrow's drafting.

When Steve answered the telephone extension in his house that evening, it was Willie speaking, and when they had discussed station matters with Willie, he asked to speak to Roddy. When the call was over, Roddy said to Steve, 'Well, I didn't start my training too soon. The week's army bivouac I was expecting is confirmed for the week after next, so we'll just have my house ready and I'll be off. We'll be going down to Adelaide, form up at Keswick Barracks and go by truck to a military training area at Alamein near Whyalla.' On this coming weekend, they would go to Morgan on Saturday for supplies and a beer or two and fix Roddy's house up on Sunday.

The drive out to the Morgan road was on an old track which went across country of a topography and vegetation that Roddy was already becoming familiar with. They went west a few miles to begin then turned almost due south, until they reached a junction still inside Rising Star, and now the single track ran them the short distance right to the boundary at the edge of the town. There were buildings in the town, institutions, to which visits were necessary, inevitable, yea, mandatory; the Eudunda Farmers' Co-operative Store, and the Terminus Hotel, each from its peculiar resources, able to satisfy quite different needs, for the welfare and satisfaction of the rural populace. Before the urge to drink beer overwhelmed them, they loaded into the back of the ute; sausages and bacon, brussels sprouts and potatoes, washing powder and socks, apples and bananas. Ice and beer would fill the cold-boxes before they finally took to the track for home.

The terminus hotel was a grand building built at a time when apart from Port Adelaide, because of its wharves busy with steamers plying up and down the Murray River and transfers to and from the railway at the new railway terminus, Morgan, was the busiest port in South Australia. On this Saturday mid-day, they added their transactions to the much-reduced commerce of the place once so vital to the river land and even more so to the outback. Now dull, washed-out grey, timber bones of long-dead mammoths which once had towered as living things in waving, high foliar glory above the red soil of the flood plain, once full of strength and utility became those high wharves, hewn from the land around, that had stood above the floods stood yet, in a sad neglected retirement. The big sheds that protected the bales; stored the merchandise; or housed in- transfer products, en route to far-off stations, bought from American mail order catalogues. A Briggs and Stratton engine for instance, or a pump made on the Clyde, or in the dark wet smoky midlands of England with other goods in transit up from Goolwa at the Murray river's mouth, were tersely addressed, 'Knox and Downs-Wilcannia- per own steamer.'

It was meet that station men should breast the bar of the Terminus, now wearing the character which accrues from a hundred years of existence, and mingle with the Saturday mob from the district all around. There were exchanges of greetings with those, a few of whom Steve had met before. Before they became fully engaged in the serious, yet joyful, business of thirst slaking, Roddy suggested to Steve, 'Because you have so kindly volunteered to help in the setting up my residence, would you allow me to buy you lunch? I'd really like to do that, Steve.'

'Totally unnecessary, Rod.'

'Necessary or not, I want to do it. Now have a beer and no argument.'

As they talked, a tall young man at the bar addressed them.

'Hello, I don't want to interrupt you blokes, my name's Archie McCulloch, I was doing a bit of eavesdropping and I was trying to work out whether you were Scots or English?' turning his look from the two, towards Roddy.

'Well, I'll give you a clue, my name's Roddy Mckenzie and this is my mate Steve Ward, and as far as I know, Steve's dinky-di, aren't you, Steve?'

'Fourth generation, originally from Cornwall,' said Steve. 'I've never been there and haven't even heard much about it. I suppose things get forgotten as time goes by. The future becomes more important than what's behind.'

'Let me shout you two a beer,' insisted Archie. 'You're just about finished, and I can follow up the clue and share Steve's story because there may be similarities, Steve,' he said, addressing him.

When he came back, distributed the beer, and wished them good luck, he began his story and the explanation of his interest in Roddy's accent.

'I went on a six-week trip to Britain last summer, I went mainly because a few blokes I play polo with wanted to go, they wanted to see English polo and the Argentinean team was visiting and they wanted to see some of their games. That was the start point: but my mother, who's the family historian, said I should investigate the McCullochs, which I duly did, and that's another part of the story.'

Roddy did not want to intrude on a story just about to be developed, so he simply asked, 'What did you think of English polo?'

'We were following international sides, and except for one day at a place called Ranelagh in Hampshire, we didn't see normal club polot.' Roddy still refrained from intervention, this was Archie's tale. 'What was so great about the fair at Ranelagh was that you could actually speak to anyone around you, there was a good atmosphere; a great feel about the place. Otherwise, it's a closed circuit. Jesus, they're a snobby lot. You know, if you're a player, you like to speak with other players. Not in England, except that day at Ranelagh.'

'Steve, you must find that hard to believe', he said, turning towards him, 'but that's the way it is.'

If he was going to describe his life at Ranelagh, even here at the bar in the Terminus Hotel on the Murray River in South Australia, he had to be somewhat circumspect because the snobbery game—although he didn't think Archie was the type to play it—can be played as hard and as cruelly from the other side. It could be doubted that Archie would have mentioned in Australia a recent trip to UK in other than well-known and chosen company. He would have been cut off at the stumps and what he last had said would most likely prove to be the last that he would say from then on that would garner the slightest response from the group in which he found himself. 'Bloody skite', 'Bunging on side', they would be muttering to themselves or actually saying it, softly—or not so softly—to a person alongside.

Before he spoke, he looked very steadily at Archie, not because of the power of amazing coincidence that he may introduce, but because he was sharply conscious of the need to begin the story from an acceptable level, he said, 'I was working at Ranelagh last summer.' He paused to see where the discussion would go.

'Good God! You must have been somewhere around when I was there.'

'There are Fairs and Fetes and functions at Ranelagh as often as they can be organized. Although there's a very well-managed profit-making farm, it makes enough to fund the upkeep of that grand old house and give Hugh and Miette the income they deserve. There's only one Fair at which Hugh puts polo on, so if you were watching that year's game, you've seen me playing.

I was playing four for Ranelagh.' Then, quite naturally, most of Roddy's story of Ranelagh, that particular game and Hugh's invidious social position, could not but be told. He certainly did not mention Jane Dugal nor did he mention the Australian girls.

Roddy said to Steve, 'D'ye think we should ask this bloke if he wants to have dinner with us?'

'I think we'd be bloody rude if we didn't. D'ye want to come in with us, Archie?'

'I would be very happy to join you', Archie pronounced with evident enthusiasm and vocal stress, obviously keen to have more conversation, 'thank you very much.'

And so it was that, Archie McCulloch, graduate of Urrbrae Agricultural College, manager of a big spread that was once part of the old Mt Mary station, joined the men from Rising Sun: the story of the second objective of his visit to the land that was the birthplace of many Australians, or their forebears, was told.

For the hogget fed men of Rising Sun, their quest was for beef, glorious beef, and at least in the Mackenzie's case, red wine. The Terminus had all of these. In a matter of minutes, they were seated and another round of beers had been ordered.

Roddy raised the question, 'What made it difficult to decide whether I were Scots or English by my accent?'

'Well, if it was Scots, it didn't sound like the Scots language or dialects I'd heard up until now. And there was a very English turn of phrase and the way words were chosen to express ideas. Maybe my experience of Scots people in Australia is too limiting. Those I had the chance to speak to in Scotland sounded a bit more like those I know in Australia.'

'You mention dialects and that's important in this case because only the small number of people who are natives of the wee county of Fearnas speak this peculiar way. The other thing is that I had a powerful influence of Mrs.Laidlaw for "proper" speaking in primary school . . .' Then he went on to talk of his immersion in England, living and working there, spending so much time with Hugh and Miette, being in their circle, and of the men at the Barley Mow, and of course the many hours he'd spent with Mike Harty. 'As a little boy, I was a bit of a parrot and a mimic. It won't take too much time and I'll be speaking "Dinkie-Di"; and we want to hear about your ancestor hunt.'

'Well, my mother told me that my great-great-grandfather emigrated from Craigellachie, in Scotland, so I thought I should start there. I travelled north through Edinburgh. There I thought all the mighty effect of the Castle, the statuary, and the classical residential squares were very striking—and there's no point in misleading anybody—all were completely nullified, ruined by the cheap, pseudo-tartan rubbish plastered everywhere. It was bloody awful for a city potentially majestic. I was glad to get on the train for Aberdeen. The ancestor search from Craigellachie was easy. I started with graveyards and churches and the local registrar. Not only could I find the precise links to the South Australian McCullochs, but I found there were living relatives of our branch of the family within easily reachable road distance. The father of the current vintage owned the tourist hotel in Craigellachie, quite a magnificent Victorian building, which was operated under management while he resided in his Forres Hotel. His family was two boys and a girl the senior boy was a regular army officer, a graduate of Sandhurst, the daughter a professional artist of some high repute. The second son a bit younger than his sister had been to school at Loreto in Edinburgh and, having his sister's love of the arts, combined them in training as a chef, and studying music and art design by serious personal application and love of these subjects. This son, for the expression of his talents, bought a very big Victorian house on a hill right by the beach looking across the firth to the northern mountains . . .' He would have continued, had he not been interrupted by the voice of the Mckenzie saying, 'Archie, I'm sorry, old son, but I can't contain myself a syllable longer. May I butt in? I think you will forgive me when you hear', so Roddy went on and Archie did not appear to object. 'That big house is in the town of Fearnas . . . where I was born and grew up, until I went to the army, and where the folk have the odd accent that I use. The house is called *Tigh na Mara* which, in the Gaelic means, "Near to the Sea". The name of your relative is Murdoch and he has become quite a hero of the Fearnas community. His hotel enjoys the highest reputation, and many people of fame, seeking seclusion, come there on repeat visits. I don't know the man myself, but my sister Jane does: they're of about the same vintage. I just can't believe this latest coincidence. That's what caused me to be so rude as to intrude on your story.'

'You're decidedly forgiven. What an amazing coincidence! I can vouch for the high quality of the hotel. There is no detail, of any aspect, that has not been thought through, or on the other hand, benefitted from his spontaneous original flair. And he's quite an imposing character to meet and talk with. When you talk, he listens; when he asks a question, it's because he wants to know the answer.'

The meal went on, the wine was drunk, and the range of topics included a return to station life, farming properties, and stock and produce prices. Steve was able to express his views and ideas very clearly. He and Archie had interesting exchanges so that, at the end of the meal, Archie asked Steve when it would be likely they could have a beer together or dinner again and gave him his telephone number.

They were home in good time with no fatalities, certainly not theirs, and luckily they did not strike a roo, although there were many of them on the way. They sat down for a minute or two before going to bed, and while the day's effect on both of them was still being recollected and enjoyed, Roddy said, in a moment of silence, 'You know, Steve, since I left home to go into the army, the number of people I have come to know, or bumped into, who have either directly come from Fearnas, or who have connections with Fearnas or visited or who have been influenced by someone from there, I still find hard to believe to be true. Then there were the two Australian girls, the brother of one of whom I'd met in Kenya; or someone who was in the same war and the same battles, whom I met afterwards for the first time in a completely different environment. Is the world so small? What is the important power of this little Scottish town? Are they all just spread seeds of Alder, our ancient native tree?'

Steve was intent on what Roddy had been saying, and his last few words made it all the more difficult to respond. What he had heard, he wanted to take away to think about. They both knew that the real response to the moment was silence. To bid one another good night were the last few words they could muster.

Sunday. After breakfast, there were a few hours of house preparation facing them and they tore into it with method and good cheer. 'It is done . . .'. Kitchen sink cupboards were scrubbed out, the massive amounts of furnishings had to be moved about to allow scrubbing down of the walls, windows, and floors, that is, the table and the two chairs were put out on the verandah to be washed down out there and the sideboard press was pulled out from the *'Canite'*-clad wall, the kitchen curtains, faded to the extent that what was probably once a floral was now a dirty mono colour—bonfire fuel! The washroom had two systems of hot water supply; the same as Steve's, but either before or after that installation, a 'chip heater' had been mounted on the wall above the end of the majestic cream-coloured art-deco porcelain bath whose faucets with shaped moulded handles would require a cleaning effort on their own. To complete the glory of this luxurious bathroom suite, there stood, on a tall, tapering pedestal with moulded flat vertical faces to match the horizontals around the bath a wash hand basin. The bath's exquisite taps were matched in the extra-large rectangular basin. 'Ye can come over here to clean your teeth, Steve. I dunno whether I'll let you use the bath, 'jested Roddy.

'How the hell did these pieces get here? Why? Who would have carted them here? It looks as if they had to build a cement block to stand the bath on. Who would have done the installation; and if they were locals, what would they have been thinking? Who was going to live here?' Steve's incredulity was stupefying; and it could be seen that he was visualizing some of the practicalities and wanting answers to his questions.

'It's incredible it could be a detective exercise for you to find out. You can keep me on tenterhooks by sending your investigation reports as a serial,' said Roddy.

By beer time that afternoon, the barrack was immaculate, and the Mckenzie had installed his shabby possessions.

'Mr. Ward, I'd like to invite you to join me for drinks before dinner, and as my first guest in my majestic mansion, to join me for a meal. Could I expect you at five thirty p.m. latest?'

'I'd be chuffed no end to accept your invitation Mr. Mckenzie, but can I come earlier? It's Sunday, and I don't think I could hold out for a beer until half past five.'

'Neither could I! Let's have one now!'

He would have to get used to living alone again. Breakfasting was a much-different event on that first day in *Taj Mahkenzie*, and there was no shared task of packing the day's food. It was new to be reporting to Steve for duty outside the houses. Duties filled the days with droving, drafting, dagging, a bit of hand crutching: the calendar pages blew, fluttering to Friday as if in a wind.

The Citizen Military Forces were Australia's volunteer reserve force. From its bloody history in battle from the Boer War To Pozierres and Hamel in France, Gallipoli in The Great War; Crete's Evacuation,The Seige of Tobruk and El Alamein and the Western Desert to the Kokoda Track The Australian nation had taken its armed forces into its heart. Employers, many of whom were ex-servicemen were, with some exceptions, pleased to release employees for reserve activities. Apart from week-end exercise bivouacs the annual camp was important for officer and non-commissioned officer training. For Other Ranks, in the carelessness of youth, reserve service was a paid holiday, a time to be 'with the boys'. For Roddy and the other officers it was a challenge to make the training meaningful for them.

It was a long from haul by truck from the Batallion's assembly point at Keswick Barracks in Adelaide to the vast training area of El Alamein near Whyalla.

After the exercise and dispersal, there was another long drive in little Fido back to Rising Star. always so—well, very often—that a return trip

Fido Fusan had waited patiently like a healthy dog, eager for her next run. It took minutes to load his kit and say his brief final farewells. Willie was going to stay overnight in their house at Medindie.

Roddy was looking forward to the pleasant drive back to Rising Star, but first he must go to the market and stock up on fresh fruit and vegetables not generally available at their local shops or from Steve's garden. There would be a specific and special gift for Steve of Cooper's Ale. He would wait until Angaston, where he would buy the world's best *Wurst* and bacon and beef which he would share. He was looking forward to being with Steve again; he would delight in delivering his present and a share of the Angaston bounty.

Renmark had an air of familiarity and he quickly covered the short distance to the homestead. Once there, he had to organize transport to his house and imagined taking up the old Graham Bros. Steve had only a guess about when Roddy would reach the homestead so he had made Renmark his Saturday resupply point. Before going into town, he had told Bess and the family in Roddy's old house that if Roddy should arrive before he got back from Renmark to wait and that he would be coming to take him home.

So Steve was there not long back from town; he was rooting around about the sheds looking for odd bits of iron and wire that he had plans for when he heard the quiet little motor of the Fusan coming into the drive. It was almost a Stanley, Livingstone, reunion with the two facing each other before moving forward to shake hands. There was a moment's hesitation. Neither had the words ready to make the first statement.

'I hope you haven't let the place go to rack and ruin while I've been having a gay old time in Adelaide?'

'Nah! All the stock's gone walkabout, your house was lifted up and dumped by a willy-willy, I won Tatt's Sweep and I'm leaving for New York in the morning.'

'Ah well, if that's all, no worries—and good luck to you. Are we in your ute or the Graham?'

'I've got the ute. I'll bring it over to your parking spot so we can shift your gear.'

When they'd done that, he thought he ought to tell Bess that he was back. It's easy to let yourself imagine things, but he thought Bess looked at him differently when she came to the door; certainly differently from the way she regarded (or disregarded) him on that first day; and the way, certainly sexually, that she had regarded him on another occasion.

'Oh, hello!' she said, welcoming, pleased, 'I've been hearing of your exploits. Willie has been keeping me informed. You certainly appear to have made a big difference to the training week, to the CO, the WOs, and the men and the regulars. There was more, all interesting and decidedly of great credit to you.'

'We had a bit of a problem with a sergeant, but that was fixed, so apart from that, it was another training exercise which the men ended up enjoying. I just dropped by to let you know I'm back. Steve's got my gear loaded and we're just about to set off home.' For Bess, this was not what she most desired; she wanted him to talk about how he had handled the situation relating to an insubordinate, incompetent sergeant that Willie had told her about. She wanted hear it all as he had done it. That would have meant inviting him into the house, they'd be alone, Willie was away which thought sent a pleasing tremor through her, but heavens, after what she'd been hearing about his social graces, his rapport with significant figures from higher command and their very obvious delight in his company, the more that tremor hinted of an attractive risk. He could see her hesitation; could see she did not want him to go.

'I won't keep Steve waiting', he said matter-of-factly, 'must go now.' He left her at the door and he could have sworn that there was the colour and warmth of a blush in her face and an unusual look in her eyes.

As the two men in Steve's ute bumped along up the track to the sheep yards, the shearing sheds, and their homes, Roddy spoke up, 'I've got some beer on ice in that tin box in the back—I knew you wouldn't have any—bit of a nuisance getting it—had to have a beer with Frank

Nichols—didn't enjoy it much—had to have another one—his shout.' And with a heavy sigh, he declared, 'Ah, well, it's what you do for mates.'

Roddy's old shack was as he left although he suspected it had been swept out and the kerosene fridge was cold, and would you believe it? There were two bottles of beer chilling in its door. They both had gear to sort out, but when he'd finished, Steve wandered down. Roddy was pleased to have the opportunity to prepare a meal for the evening and told Steve he was invited to a 'you beaut' breakfast on Sunday morning to share the Angaston bacon.

In Roddy's absence, Steve's days were station days, he said, with no great events to be reported. The next week could be interesting for Roddy because everyone, including Bess, was going up to the cattle station to muster and draft out some steers for sale. That would give Roddy a little taste of cattle work in country so different from the sheep run; they could be on another planet, and then back here for shearing. Willie and Bess were going to bring their horses up in the truck. So to reach a camp in reasonable time, in the ute Steve and Roddy would bring fodder for the horses, their camping gear, including a roomy canvas tent that could be put up by one man, very easily by two. Alternating riding and leading a horse, and driving the ute they would reach a camp in reasonable time to feed and sleep and begin the muster the next morning.

On Sunday afternoon, they loaded up and at dawn the first rider leading the other horse was on his way. Steve drove ahead on an old track which had been used since the days of the division of the runs nearly a hundred years before when there were four stations on the land that was now Rising Star. On a trot-walk, trot-walk system, they were covering the ground in fine style, but it took them all of the day to reach the gate on the southern edge of the cattle run. The track followed the most direct it could, and it was sensible for the rider to follow it than try to cut a straight line across ridge after sandy, rocky ridge littered with rock and old fallen trees, close growing clumps of scrub, and Myall woods. Roddy, riding comfortably on a horse with a longer stride than most polo ponies, was enjoying this day of gentle sunshine under a pale blue sky not dominated by cloud, there was a very light breeze making the total effect more spring like than winter. He remarked to himself that the ground was very similar in some parts to the El-Alamein training area. They both enjoyed meeting for their swaps, but they wasted no time for chat—that keep for their evening campfire and the beer. It was not customary, but Roddy insisted on taking the saddle and bridle off the led horse, so having done that, he had a few words with Steve as he filled and lit a pipe, then depending on his stag, got into the ute and drove or mounted up and rode. When they reached the fence, they went only a little further along the track where Steve had used a spot for camping before. The horses were unsaddled and with their halters on, tethered under some taller Myall, rubbed down, and left with their lucerne and water. The boys had their tent up in a trice. Safe on its small, drained, flat space, defence against any sudden heavy downpour, in what appeared from the cloud formation an unlikely event; they soon had a campfire fuelled by dry dead she-oak crackling where they could sit with a beer while the Angaston Bratwurst was sizzling in a little folding wire griddle. This was their time to blether, to talk about their lives and experiences, places they'd been and places they hadn't, a continuation of nights of conversations shared which had begun in their houses by the yards. For each of them, there was an easy joy in the companionship which had so comfortably and mutually developed. When Roddy had been at Alamein that time, used to being alone for long spells though he was, Steve had looked forward to his return. Roddy, needing to move, driven by the sketch plan for his future, already wounded by loves he had lost so shortly into the journey of his life, had found himself wanting to get back to the easy society of Steve's companionship. 'How far will I have to travel? How many loves, how many friendships will I have to leave by the wayside?' he was now beginning to ask himself. He knew that the losses he had endured had not inured to him to the pain. He was committed now, to this present short period of engagement after which he would have to take to the road again. 'Will Western Australia be the end point of my quest?' He found he could not answer the question, but forget 'fate' or 'the lap of the Gods', he said to himself. 'Only I can make the judgement, only I can make that decision.'

The two men who staffed the cattle station most of the time had spent the days before the arrival of the mustering crew finding and very gently influencing the cattle to gather. This was not straightforward, they were seldom moved, spent most of the time with only glimpses of humans, and were a bit 'towy'. Not only had they their own will, but they had formed their own smaller cliques inside the main group and did not want to be mobbed together. So the two cattlemen and their dogs had to use cattle psychology using influence rather than force to get them into a big group spread in bunches over a wide area. It would need the additional people and dogs to guide them closer together, moving in the right direction, head for the funnel of fencing that would then make it possible to drive them into the tall yards. There was water on the way, there was water at the yards, and there would be the smell of lucerne which they come to know and enjoy in the bleak dry days, when natural food had been eaten out. Roddy and Steve had broken camp early and now, with both horses saddled, moved out, and joined the cattlemen under whose direction they would continue the slight pressure on the wings of the herd. They did not want breakaways, because as in the human herd, it would unsettle the bigger herd and even be disastrous if the breakaway was, bull, steer, or cow, or in the human herd's equivalent, a leader.

Yet with all the care and cunning in the world, there were breakaways. They had to be brought back into the herd again as quickly as possible, and the herd had to be nursed back into a settled state.

Roddy's mount, a fine old polo pony, was nimble on his feet and sensitive to rein, knee and heel. They had worked together before with sheep and had developed an understanding. Now it was a question of how best to handle a runaway steer. The thing to be avoided was letting him get away into the wild where he would have to be left, since it would take all their resources; energy of horses and riders, and too much time, during which the herd would break up. Here was Roddy's chance to earn his spurs, which certainly he did. He and his old pony made the moves which baffled the two or three breakaway steers they had to stop and linked them into the mob again, shaking their heads in amazement, wondering what happened to their plans for freedom. The drovers had got near to the yards but not near enough to get the mob yarded before darkness, so they stopped at the first water and set up camp.

Setting up tents was a cooperative effort because it was necessary to keep a close eye on the herd as it was settling down.

Steve and the two cattlemen found it difficult in the extreme to keep their amazement from their faces and manners—Willie and Bess had bought a tent and were going to camp out with the men! It was a historical first, unsettling. 'How do I handle this?' 'What caused this?' 'Why are they doing this?' These were questions, and surely others similar, that were going on the men's heads. Steve managed to say to him, 'I dunno what's going on, but this has never happened here before at any muster camp. And we haven't even got a labour government!'

Facetiously, Roddy replied, 'Perhaps they thought you needed their guidance . . . or thought you may be scared of dingoes.'

The fire was shared, each team having its own cooking branders and meat. The sheep men had their Angaston sausages, part of the half ton that Roddy had brought back from his trip south. There were cold beers during the preparation and eating, and Bess had brought the makings of gin and tonics—well, we all know quinine is such distasteful stuff and malaria for which it is a prophylactic, so debilitating to say the least, and often fatal to be accurate, that the officers in the mess at Khartoum, forced, for its medicinal effects, to drink the stuff every day, found Messrs Gordon's (not known to be relatives of the general of the same name) distillation a perfect camouflage and with a bit of carbon dioxide gas (or without), or with Angostura Bitters (instead), a quite tasty and slightly (or greatly) addictive noggin. Willie drank beer with the boys. No one knew how to address Bess. It meant one had to be face-to-face with her to bring notice of something specific or ask her if she wanted something or if, during the day, she may have seen something. It would surprise us to know how frequently we have to use a person's name in conversation. As they settled by the fire, the talk was of the day's events; the thwarting of the breakaways, their amazement that a bloke who'd never worked on a station before could read the cattle the way Roddy did and get a horse to do the things his old horse was seen to do. It seemed inappropriate in response to mention polo and Indian soldiers, but he could mention farms in Scotland, cattle on the moors and hills, and Munro's sheep, and so effectively slip from under these words of praise so uncharacteristic of Australian bushmen. If the group had been bigger, he would have been waiting for someone, more characteristically, to burst the bubble, that is, in the unlikely event of a bubble of praise having been floated. There was talk of a 'good night horse' and those that were twitchy and saw ghosts. There was a roster to ride very quietly round the herd during the night. A stumble on a log, or clatter on a rock would have the cattle up and anxious, ready to bolt away from suspected danger.

But the area round the troughs and the windmill had, over the many years, been trampled bare of any vegetation. Now, in the form of seed or suckers, roots, bulbs, or tubers the plant life lay under the sand or in the clay for that special year when the release of a little rain would ignite their latent life into a brief blooming and insemination, when new life sources would have been created to be ground through that destructive cycle again.

As it became necessary for the cattle to come closer and closer together, they liked it less and even the smell of the next water was becoming a less imperative attraction. Their mood could be seen and felt. There were no calves in the mob. They had been yarded, castrated, and ear-tagged months before Roddy had come on the scene. Two or three cows had late calves big enough to travel with the mob, and their mothers needed to keep tabs on where they were so there were calls between them in different octaves. But now there was more bawling of the big beasts, very occasionally further back, but now increasing in frequency. Here and there along the wings, were signs of twitchiness. Perhaps bitter memories of previous yardings were being stirred up. The drovers were getting just a little anxious too. They weren't many in number for a herd of this size. If the herd broke, it would take a long time to put the mob together again and it would be bloody difficult to prevent further breaks. If the mob became really anxious, the low-wire fences of the 'funnel' would not hold them if the cattle at the back began to press up against the rest of the mob in front. Getting them into the tall railed yard was ever the trick.

Roddy was on the wing with Bess, who somehow seemed always to be the drover nearest to him. There was a skirmish on the edge of the mob. The beasts on the side began to run.

There was a break in the body of the mob on Bess and Roddy's side. A bit of the mob broke and a bullock burst out. In an instant, Roddy had gathered his horse and surged after the galloping steer. Roddy must stop this leader going further out. It had to be turned back into the herd. Bess would have to go like hell behind Roddy and, further out, travel with his followers turning them back. Roddy was onto the leader, his knees against the beast's side. A slight back pressure on the bit slowed his horse just a fraction. In that second, he leaned and pushed his horse against bullock's quarters. The bullock crossed his legs, tripped, and fell. Roddy got his horse clear with his right knee, his reins on the neck, and a touch of heel on his offside flank. What a pony! He fairy-danced out of the bullocks' legs before they began to flail. Roddy kept him turning out and away, back round onto the grounded bullock which was having a helluva struggle to get up. When he did, Roddy's horse was pushing right on its shoulder. With the force of Roddy's horse on his body and legs, and in his confusion, the steer had nowhere to go but back into the herd. Got ya! Bess had done very well. The dogs on her left, she rode her horse closer to the runaways on a diagonal. They were already seeing her threat on their left and ran on, at the angle Bess had chosen, back into the herd. Job done. The two successful drovers resumed their positions and got on with drove. There was no doubt everyone was keyed up. They knew what a disaster it would have been if Roddy and Bess had failed. Each of the drovers was keyed up now. But it was not a harmful nervousness. It sharpened their senses, concentration, and sensitivity to the animals and what they may do because of their fears. Every yard was nearer to success: or failure, which would have been utter.

They were into the funnel. Gently, gently. See them all in. Whew, they're in. Still ever so gently, now. A steady, steady stroll. The dogs kept them away from the fences at the rear. The spaces between horses and drovers were lessening now. Together now, Roddy and Bess were riding conversational distance apart, but they didn't speak. The leaders hadn't yet reached the high rails and the wide opening of the swung gates into the flat, red void. There, there was nothing to remind them of their world, only the bare red flatness and strange high trees without leaves, and just a few bare branches that stuck out straight and came down their trunks in even spaces, down low to the ground.

Suddenly it seemed, the herd found no way to go further forward. There was bawling from near the front. The leaders had reached the gate. It was crunch time. Just stop. 'Three of you fall back and spread across.' It was one of the cattlemen, keeping the sound of his voice low and flat without change of tone. He didn't want to wake the baby. 'Roddy, you and Willie and his wife,' he hadn't wanted to send Willie. He was going to send Steve, but that was the only way he could get Bess to go without using a name. Anyway, that trio would work.

Then the lures of the water and the feed at the other end of the yard became too strong. First one, then another of the mob stepped into the void to stop and stare, wondering. After seconds, their heads turned in the direction of the water they began to trot; now a small group, then another. That was it. In no time, the entire mob wanted to squeeze through what were the generous limits of the feared, hated gate space jamming the opening and scrabbling and pushing, their heads high.

The trucks had been ordered to arrive the next morning, so it was another night of camping out. Tonight, the concerto for sextet moved into the second of its three movements. The tone, time, key, and theme had all changed. It was scarcely to be marked scherzo, but perhaps we could allow vivace at one point. After they had got settled and the dream of a cold beer had been changed to reality, but before any intoxicating effect had affected him, the cattleman, who was the commander, said, quite directly to Bess's face, 'You and Roddy did a good job today.'

'Thank you, Jimmy,' she responded. Jimmy Johns had just spoken to a woman other than his wife: moreover, a woman who was his boss's wife. He had offered a compliment, perhaps for the first time in his life, to anybody.

The compliment she had just received had deeply impressed Bess. She knew how rare this was amongst such people. She knew what it must have meant for Jimmy to break the mould of custom and show that evidence of a weakness which could lead to eternal remorse. It was like a Pharaoh sharing the God-given singularity of omnipotence with his wife.

It seems there were compliments in the air: part of the mood in this second movement of the concerto.

Bess turned to address Roddy. 'I had my mind on other things too, but what I saw was an amazing bit of riding this afternoon. Willie told me that you had mentioned polo when you made your application for work. I can see where you may have practiced such skill.'

'Oh, I'm not sure', he said, smiling and laughing, 'I may have learned showing off to impress the primary school girls I was in love with.'

'And were they impressed?'

'Of course,' he said with emphasis. 'They fell into my arms. So as not to break so many hearts, I had to mount up and ride away to escape them,' he added with dramatic vocal modulation to indicate his observation that the questioner may not believe the complete truth of his candid response. Did he see that look again? Was there a kind of fidgety movement of her body? And was there another blush? At this point, Willie came, bringing a gin and tonic for her. Her words were slightly stumbled and in an unusual pitch when she needed to use, saying, 'Thank you,' as a vocal lifeline. 'I was just complimenting Roddy on his riding which he wasn't sure he'd learned from polo.' She returned her look to Roddy and said no more. That was their very small secret. Willie had a choice of which conversation line he would follow next and chose to tell Bess how well she had done.

Round the fire again, the crack went backwards and forward and amongst the little group—and yes, it was vivace.

There were more station and droving yarns, more stories about bush characters and bush life and Mckenzie told of the Snowy Mountains where none present had ever been, and he spoke of Banjo and recited 'The Man from Snowy River' to a rapt audience, an audience that didn't doubt the quality of his horsemanship or that he had been there . . . on the Snowy River.

The drafting was done, it had been 'Truck', 'Truck', 'Stay', 'Truck', and so on till all was all over and the trucks full. Now it was time to break camp and go home. For the cattlemen, it

meant following an old track to the homestead houses of one
of the early stations, now part of Rising Star, where they resided
with their families. The trucks would go first on that same
old track out to the Morgan road which for many years now
had joined Morgan on the River Murray to the south, with the
copper town of Burra, and Peterborough to the north, another
route going south-west to Adelaide and of course splitting off
to go east to Broken Hill, and to Sydney far away on the coast
of the Pacific Ocean.

The camps were broken and cleared away. Willie and Steve
put his and Roddy's horses in the truck. The dogs would have
to jump into their wire latticed boxes on the outside under the
floor. The truck drove away and was soon jolting on the track.
Steve joined the cattlemen at their ute where Roddy was. They
were having their last little companionable blether, possibly
their last for months. Bess was standing by her ute telepathising
to the full extent of her power. Roddy had a feeling in his neck
that he was being watched. He turned round. Bess was standing
there, looking at him.

He should go over and say 'Oo-roo'. Leaving the men, he
went across to her. The scene was Australian outback, wintry
and grey but still the outback trees around the sheds and yards
were at the centre of nothing, just scrubby desert and the red
beaten-out space waiting for some blessed rain: an island waiting
for a sea.

'I've come to say how much I enjoyed working with you,' he
said in an honest, matter-of-fact tone.

She had been nervously, impatiently waiting, hoping for this
moment. She couldn't go on feeling about this man the way she
found herself feeling if she could not be 'Bess' to him. There
was a tremor of nervousness and of appeal in her voice when
she said, 'I wish you would call me Bess, Roddy.'

He could feel the tension pulling at the nerves in her body.
Calmly, in a tone acknowledging and responding to the courage
that her emotional challenge must have required, he said, 'I
shall be pleased to call you, Bess.'

She knew that he knew what had been going on inside
her. It took every bit of her willpower to resist taking him into

an embrace. She managed to kiss him chastely on the cheek. Looked at him again. Then very quickly got into her ute, started up, and as it was moving when Roddy waved and shouted out, 'Oo-roo, Bess!' He wondered whether she had heard him.

The three men at the other ute had watched it all but had turned away. They were confused by what they had seen. What was this going to mean for Willie now with Roddy still on the station? They would hate to see anything go wrong with the boss's marriage. What would Roddy be thinking? He had stood there straight as a die. It looked as if he hadn't started anything. Maybe it was nothing—but my god, it was a big change in Bess Taylor.

During the drove, Willie and Roddy had dismounted and each, on a leg folded under his backside, was sitting together on the ground having a swallow of tea. They had been up with the front of the herd when it was their turn to have a brief spell. The herd was moving quietly, slowly but well; a good chance to take a short spell. They were sitting on a piece of ground that was bare, but for the odd tree and bits of low bush, on an almost-imperceptible slope that ended in front of them in a series of deep erosion gullies that had poured the shifted soil in flairs out on to the edge of the flat area along which the mob was lowly passing. On the other side of the mob, the ground began to rise again, quite steeply, onto a sandy ridge like the face of another sea wave rolling towards the back of the wave that had passed through and under them leaving the two men floating on its back.

'That's quite deep erosion, Willie,' Roddy observed.

'Yes. It's characteristic of this country. We've tried packing fallen trees logs and other rubbish into them. The water just scours round the stuff or gets in below and washes out underneath and deepens the crevices. There's no stopping it.'

Roddy listened in silence; thinking. He stood up and looked at this long slow rise which ran left and right for nearly a mile. At last he ventured, 'Willie, I think we could cure this. Do you have a dumpy level?'

'Yes, we do. We used it to grade the lucerne paddock.'

'Well, you've got a dumpy level; and I saw a grader down in the shed, is it operational?'

'Yes, why?'

'You can tell me to mind my own business and I'll acknowledge that with no offence. But with your grader, I could cut swales into selected contours all the way along and down the face of that decline. They'd hold the runoff, and even with the clay, they'd get water back into the soil. Later, below the berms you could propagate salt bush. No one could accuse you of farming a sheep run; it's erosion protection. A couple of days' work and you could add another couple of steers to your herd. To get maximum benefit, you'd have to rest it for a couple of years to establish the new growth, growth that the way things are you don't have now. It's got to be worth the effort.'

'Nothing ventured, nothing gained', said Willie, 'Let's do it before we get the next good rain—which should be any day now.'

Roddy was surprised and pleased with Willie's quick decision and enthusiasm for an immediate start.

And so it was that at dawn's early light on the day after the sale of the cattle, Roddy was given control of the grader and the topographical project. Willie's enthusiasm harboured no uncertainties.

With Roddy and Willie using the level, Steve pegged out the line at the same time also learning how to use the level which he was very keen to do. No sooner was the first contour marked than Roddy began to cut the swales windrowing the dirt to form the berm. A wonderful sight it was when the gouged line ran the one thousand six hundred yards of the slope. While that had been happening, and with occasional guidance from Roddy, Steve and Willie marked the second. At the end of the day's work and enough light to get home by, there were three contours cut. Just in case there should be sudden rain, they skipped two and cut the sixth and almost having to use lights they cut the eighth. As it happened, it didn't rain or the next day or the next. So let it pour! They had completed the entire incline.

It pelted own rain on the fourth night. At dawn, Willie dashed out in the ute to check the result. It had been a good solid downpour even bigger than the night at El-Alamein. There was water in every swale. In the ravines, there was not a drop, except from direct precipitation. There were no signs of running water. Tearing himself away from that most gratifying of sights, Willie raced back to bring the news to Steve and Roddy and, as soon as he could thereafter, to tell Bess.

Life went on after the landscaping exercise. Two men with skill, energy, and achievement goals were achieving records in fencing repair, renewal, and re-siting. Some of this re-siting, using much old material, would help divide some paddocks, definitely improving grazing and the possibility of resting. It would help immediately in bringing flocks by progressive stages to the shears. Willie had a theory about the benefits of winter shearing; it grew a stronger better staple, it warmed the sheep when they needed warming so improved their condition and food conversion. For the shearers, it was the verge of bliss to work in cool conditions.

Then it happened.

A telegram was phoned through to the homestead at Rising Star. Bess Taylor wrote the words down in her best private school handwriting (although, from the beginning, it was her mother, a stickler for good handwriting which she believed exposed the true character of the writer, whose strict regime had given Bess's handwriting its unchangeable beauty).

The words she heard, that she wrote down and which she read again, struck her three shocks which were amazing, exciting, emotionally confusing, then dismaying. She had to grasp control of herself to continue the practicalities the urgency of a telegram message demanded. On her way out under the verandah to get into the ute, she snatched a canvas water bag, always hanging there summer or winter; cool from the evaporation even on a day like today. Her heart was beating with every kind of feeling and it was the excitement that was running through her now, a thrill engendered vicariously by the message in the cable, battle; command in battle, Roddy was needed, the Roddy of Rising Star Station; she was Rising Star Station, this was about her Roddy.

She knew from talking with Willie what would be going on today and where she might meet up with Roddy and Steve and their flock heading towards a newly fenced paddock where the flock would spend the night.

Even in the winter coolness and the bits of rain, they'd had— big occasional showers which suddenly came and suddenly went, not the usual winter rain pattern at all—she could soon see the low dust cloud that, winter as it was, the small hard feet of the mob as they moved, heads down, raising it and hanging it above the flock. She looked around her from the bouncing ute across the miles, and flat out-flung miles, of the blue bush and salt bush which nourished the thousands strong flocks of Merino wethers which grew to enormous size and weight providing pounds of medium wool and commanding good prices at the Adelaide sales. She drove off the track and bounced over the ground finding little flats of bright red soil washed smooth by the winter rains flooding many years ago—and not so many years ago. When any hope of rain had gone, strong dry winds, that sometimes blew for days from the north and often the east polished the surfaces to the likeness of a sheen. There were open spaces enough for the ute to maintain a good speed. For some reason, she found herself hurrying. Bound with a broad elastic band securely into her office logbook, Roddy's telegram lay beside her on the seat. She knew its content by heart, yet she must give this first written version to him.

Telegram: *To Roderick McKenzie, Station hand, Rising Star Station, South Australia. Need Platoon Commander for six months Congo. Start immediate. Collect air ticket Qantas to Salisbury Rhodesia available Qantas, Adelaide. Confirm availability. Major Barron 8 Commando Elizabethville, Katanga.*

She had to admit to herself that the ideas associated with the telegram had made her excited.

This was a call to arms. Her father had commanded Australian troops in New Guinea; her husband Willie had served as a young officer in Borneo. She was no stranger to things military. Roddy was a soldier too. After all, it was a telegram. And it was a call to arms.

As she drove nearer, she sized up what was the best approach to the mob and to Roddy whom she could now differentiate. She got round the wing of the mob and caught up with Roddy further away on the other side of the mob and Steve, the senior, was on the nearer horse. The dogs took their minds off their work to come and bark at Bess and the ute. One dog had leapt into the back of the ute and was barking and whirling around with excitement at the prospect of a ride. Steve rode up to the ute on his big chestnut gelding. Before he could say a word, Bess Taylor had blurted out, loud and clear over the noise of the running motor, 'I've got a telegram for Roddy', thrusting her arm through the open window. Steve leaned down and took it.

'Right, I'll give it to him.'

Laying a rein on the side of his horse's neck and, with a little bit of heel and knee, spun his horse round and cantered over to towards Roddy.

'Bess has brought a telegram for you,' he shouted as he reined in his horse. Meanwhile Bess was slowly motoring towards them. Steve called to the dogs and began to walk his horse slowly along the rear of the flock while the dogs were whistled back to action gently urging the flock forward. Bess saw Roddy read the telegram, hesitated, then rode to meet her as she approached slowly so as not to create a disturbance.

'Thank you, Bess,' he said, dismounted, and read the telegram once more. She was silent and watched his face as he read, the motor still running. She knew, that if she were Roddy, she would have set off for Adelaide immediately!

'This has come at an awkward time with shearing coming on,' he said after the brief pause.

'You'll have to talk to Willie, but I know what he'll say. No one is indispensable, Roddy, we'll get by. I'll have an excuse to get out of the house perhaps.' Bess had been a child of pastoral life and she loved to get back home to the horses and the dogs, the open skies and the distant horizons and the stock, on the property near Jamestown where her father had taken up three thousand acres after the war. Another shock and another set of feelings was striking her nerves anew. Roddy would not be coming back to the station. Though not completed here on

Rising Star, the year he had allowed himself for the station experience would be over. When the Congo engagement was over, he must get on with his plans immediately.

'Leave your horse with Steve and come back with me. The mob is moving well. They're good dogs and they haven't got far to go. They can easily manage the paddock gate.'

'Thank you, Bess. You're a champ.'

He cantered off to where Steve was coming slowly at a trot across the back of the mob. Bess decided she wasn't needed there and switched off the motor.

She watched them.

Roddy was asking himself as he rode towards Steve, 'Was all of life a continuous succession of meetings and partings? Surely to go at the planned end of his time would be so much less painful than this sudden wrench. Their bond was mutual. They both needed parting time. Time for philosophical appreciation of the emotional dimensions of the event was desirable. Surely it meant that all connection would not be lost? All process of this parting would take place in the next few minutes. That's not the way it should be.' All of this was tumbling through his brain as they approached. He stopped his horse and passed the cable to Steve and dismounted. Now he was going to have leave a man he had shared many deep thoughts with, had shared work with, had shared those short hours of free weekends together with; he had to leave a man whose moral view of life he admired.

As he looked up at Steve, he said, 'I know what I'd like to be saying and I wouldn't like to be having to say it for a little while yet so that we could get used to the idea of parting. I'll keep in touch with you . . . and you must keep in touch with me . . . wherever we are. We have to meet again, and believe me, if I'm alive I'll make sure of that . . . you mean a helluva lot to me, Steve. Keep your plan alive as I will mine.'

Steve in a slow movement passed the piece of paper into Roddy's hand. 'I don't need to say anything, mate, thank Christ. If I had the gift, I'd have said exactly your words.' He leant down and firmly squeezed Roddy's hand. He passed his reins up to Steve, and barely getting it out of his throat, he said, 'Oo-roo, Steve.' He had one last look at Roddy standing there, gathered the reins and wheeled the horses, flicked his own horse's reins, yelled out, 'Oo-roo, Rod,' and galloped away.

Raising a pointing arm, 'Go way back', he called out, and Spot bolted off to the back of the flock. A warm, slow northerly breeze was blowing just strong enough to move the dust cloud from hanging over the mob. He stood back and had a good look at the man, the horse, and the total scene. The sheep close by, their thick wool dusty red on the outside. But that wool in deep would appear in dense fleeces when the shearer's hand piece and comb had run in long blows the length of their flanks, fold smoothly away deep cream and snowy white nearer the body. This wool was the rich product of the arid land. The mob, moving slowly across the watcher's viewed from behind the mounted horseman, was backed to the pale horizon by mile upon mile of blue-bush and salt bush with here and there a small isolated stand of she-oak and maybe an odd, low twisted mallee. The sky, washed pale blue at the horizon's rim, flowed upward, darkening as it climbed but never becoming more than a pale cerulean. There was not a cloud in the sky. He wanted to soak in this scene. He wanted it to be a memory he could retrieve. Whatever Willie decided, Roddy knew he had to go. His time in this kind of land, this kind of Australian 'bush', and the experiences he had enjoyed here and recollections of the people he had met, on and off the property, in mutual friendship, he wanted to keep forever.

As Bess drove back, she was silent for a while, thinking; thinking about the bad start she had got off to with Roddy. She thought of the sudden rush upon her of that warm female feeling for him that became embedded, changing and strengthening. Now he was going and she didn't want him to go. She knew there was a lot more in this man that she wished to draw into her. Even now there was a feeling that something had already grown; something valuable. Was it love in one of its many forms? Love has manifestations in practicality. Had she not been experiencing this visit to her emotions, she would never have thought of what she was going to propose next.

She asked him, 'Have you made arrangements to store your car and kit in Adelaide?'

'No, I haven't yet. I plan to speak to some of the blokes in the battalion to see what ideas they might have.'

'At our house at Medindie, which is on the north edge of the city, part of the stables at the back are used as garages, two have big doors which can be locked. I know that apart from a few odds and ends against the wall you could park your car there safely. Before you actually depart, you could just put the key into the letterbox on the front door, not the one in the gate pillar. You could walk into town from there. When you've sorted out the kit you're going to take, I image you'll stay at the club while you make the last arrangements and catch your flight.'

'Bess, what a great offer. Thank you so much. I'll do that. The rest of what you said is word for word my plan.'

'Fortunately you've got the Graham up here.'

When they reached the house, she got out of the ute and said to him, 'Do you mind . . .', she said wistfully, 'I want to see your house before you leave it.' When he opened the door, she stepped inside and slowly looked round, in silence, letting her eyes linger as if she were taking photographs, pictures she wanted to store in a collection of special things.

'This is not the place you came to. It's a new creation; an extension of you. It says so much about you.'

She saw the bookshelves he and Steve had brought back from a weekend raid on Renmark giving a home to his Australiana collection; joy and reference for his avid study. His reading chair, another trophy. A hanging rack for his uniforms amongst which she noted his Hampshire blue patrols; his *batterie de cuisine* where he made the exotic experimental meals which he had Steve so frequently enjoyed. She felt the ambience of rest from labour and quiet delight in living.

She looked at him and in a soft murmur said, 'Thank you, Roddy', and moving closer took him in her arms, and putting her head on his chest, said again, 'Thank you, Roddy.' She gently left his embrace, extending her arms until her hands at last fell away. 'I want to help, but I know you will be much quicker on your own. You'll need all the time you've got.' They went out to the ute and they waved as she drove away.

Yes. He'd need to get weaving.

A quick note for Steve. *I'm leaving the cooking books and all the spices and herbs. Anything I haven't taken is a gift, old son. You may want to use this house as your kitchen; you can sit in the armchair while you watch the spuds boil. I'll write soon as I can. Thanks for everything, yours, Roddy. PS. Unfortunately I've had to leave some beer in the fridge. R.'* Outside, a last look at his homestead, Steve's up the road, where he could hear his hens clucking, then up into the old Graham and away through country he now knew quite well. When he reached the sheds, the transfer of gear to the Fusan took just minutes and he drove down to the house. Willie and Bess had heard him arrive, and long before that, Willie had taken the cover off the car and stowed it in its pouch. Now they were waiting.

They heard Roddy's quick strides across the verandah. 'Come in,' he heard Willie call. It was a surprise, because in all the time he had been on the station, he had never been in the house yet. He had understood why Willie had chosen to keep the relationship at that social level while he was an employee, just as Steve was.

'Willie, I want to say thank you for having taken me on, giving me a chance, and now letting me go like this. I'm leaving you in the lurch.'

'Employing you here was one of the better things I've done and you've well exceeded a year's work in what you've done here with so much enthusiasm and energy. It was almost literally a tonic to have you here. And you've been a godsend to the battalion. God knows what you're going to face in Africa, but you and Barron will face it and do more than your duty. I'd ask if you'd like a drink but . . . what the hell . . . remain standing . . . a *joch an dooras*, as you blokes say.' He smartly turned to the drinks table and seizing a bottle of twelve-year-old malt poured a very good mouthful into three crystal glasses. 'You too, Bess,' he said, handing her a glass. 'Roddy, we wish you a long life and a happy one, thank you for what you've done for us.'

'Thank you both, *slante!*' they drank together. He looked at them both, and Bess had moved closer to Willie. 'I'll leave you now.' He shook hands with each, and after she had shaken his hand, Bess gave him a chaste little kiss on the cheek. They walked quite quickly across the verandah, and when he had got into the car, he shouted through the open passenger window, 'Oo-roo', and waved out the driver's side as he went down the drive.

He drove through Renmark which was quietly carrying on, in its unhurried way, the business of its day. There was the pub where Steve and he, when favouring Renmark with their precious leisure time, had beers with the locals, and their sumptuous meals of beef when Archie McCulloch would sometimes join them. Now a drive through the citrus groves and orchards of apricots along the wonderful Murray River, which he crossed by punts at Waikerie and Kingston. It was not always remembered, by those it served the best, that it was the sustenance of almost all human and animal life in South Australia. Now past the Clare Valley and soon the Barossa where creditable wines were beginning to supplant fortified wines and 'cheap plonk'. Through the vast stock yards and abattoirs at Wingfield, suddenly he was in the northern suburbs of Adelaide. With a slight diversion, he could go to Medindie now but first to the club to sort his kit down to the bare essentials for Katanga. After that, he would park Fido who had scurried down from the station happy to feel clean air flush his innards and his lungs. But first to the Qantas office to get his hands on that ticket and get any updated information on his flight. That done, there would be less pressure next day to garage the car and attend to any final details. The secretary manager at the club remembered him and welcomed him warmly; all his registration details could be done when he returned with his air ticket. He found he was walking significantly faster than everybody he overtook even taking his urgency into account. Adelaide's colonial buildings were ranked on either side of King William Street which he turned into from Angas Street and where the Qantas office was alongside the Bank of New South Wales at the North Terrace end which had closed its doors to customers earlier in the afternoon. At Qantas the really quite beautiful young women gave him very warm welcome and lavished services upon this tanned, rugged epitome of Australian manhood. Had his performance with these ladies been observed by a film producer, he would have been seized upon by him as a way to a quick few million. It is not to be thought that the Mckenzie did not engage in and enjoy wholeheartedly this delicious game.

To return to the club in his present airy mood, he chose to turn right, round the corner of the bank, and proceed along this boulevard, so in harmony with the Qantas engendered mood. Across its breadth and double tree-lined footpaths was Government House on the corner and behind its grounds, the barracks HQ of Tenth Battalion Third Royal South Australia Regiment. He had no time to go there to pay a call, but he had time to make his return to the club a more leisurely affair: time to relive a little of the last encounter at Qantas. He couldn't help thinking about himself in that most delightful of situations and about himself as the person who had experienced it. To enjoy the increased pleasure of walking under the trees on the northern side, he had crossed over past the powerfully evocative statue of the Light Horse Memorial feeling, vicariously, the tensions, and the muscular demands on horse and rider in battle so skilfully loaded into the statuary by the sculptor.

Walking along this terrace was the erstwhile schoolboy from little ancient Fearnas, who had been lifted out of his boyhood. He was extracted from that world of youth into another world which he could only imagine from the few anecdotal snatches he had heard; or reading that was dated and of limited use in imagining his future. His youth now drifting further behind by the racing current, had been snapped off, leaving him ill equipped for thinking anything of where or why; or even paying much particular attention to the world passing him so swiftly by. In a blink of time, still wet behind the ears, not yet part of adult society, he was in a hole on a hillside, day after day blasted by shells, losing friends to tearing, breaking death, to do battle in a war which he understood only because his country was involved. Knowing nothing of Korea before he went there, he knew only a little more when he left. In those first fledging years little registered on his consciousness of things that, had they been examined and considered, may have widened his world, adding new visions and points of reference, marks on the pathways through information and experience. All the time of this journey, he would have to take the greatest care not allow certain idea-forms to set, to lodge and fix, that would erect a screen, a filter-mesh of prejudice and fixed ideas that distorted pure inflow, leaving him with no more than an accretion, a load, of prejudice and lost opportunity to grow. In his present self-assessment, he could see by how much the content and value of his store had been enlarged since he had left the army. He must now continue to add quality of thought to his journey. Who knows, those experiences soundly considered, altered from mere information to knowledge, at some time perhaps, just perhaps, might metamorphose to wisdom.

No sooner had Roddy embarked upon his Ranelagh venture than Major Erik Barron MC, Retd, had thought of doing some good for society. He had taken *Fear Naught* to the fishing port of Burghead on the Moray Firth to help his old school of Gordonstoun in its work with the Outward Bound Movement. He took pupils from the school on tough sea voyages up past Caithness to the Orkneys, south-west round Cape Wrath through the maritime galaxy of the Hebrides, south and around the Mull of Kintyre until they were sailing up the Clyde. Of course there were pupils male and female from other schools and universities, but the start and end points of each adventure was Gordonstoun. Among the Outward Bounders were students from St Andrews.

The drive to Adelaide gave Roddy time have those kinds of thoughts: then his mind took a natural turn to the immediate future. It seemed years since he had seen Erik. He knew that he had spent much time meticulously searching the owners of the Congo mining titles and in Adventure Training groups. Short letters had been exchanged, but nothing which prepared him for the telegram. What made it stunningly unexpected was that it had come from Katanga There seemed to be no logical connection between a recently graduated Master of Arts in History and Politics (International Relations) and the content and implications of the telegram.

Roddy had been kept informed, in broad outline, of the progress of Erik's studies in his two major subjects for which St Andrews had a notably good reputation. In his work for Gordonstoun and Outward Bound, there had been an invigorating, rejuvenating flow of information and enthusiasm between Erik and the participants on the courses. It was exhilarating to be with bright young people preparing themselves for that big, wonderful world they saw before them. He could enjoy this pleasure forever. But these young folk from every group were moving on. And he realized that what he was doing, although it certainly would be a rewarding life's work, would seem forever unfinished. During a cruise one day, a third-year student asked if he had ever been to university. When Erik replied that he hadn't, but had been to Sandhurst, the student said in earnest tones, 'With all due respects, sir'—and so obviously it was with respect—'that is really vocational training; important, necessary, valuable, but quite different from the university approach to learning and the processes of building knowledge. Why don't you matriculate? Come to St Andrews. You can still do this stuff, or long, ocean races during the long vacs.' It took a little thought and research and he decided. That he had chosen to go to university had not surprised Roddy when Erik broke the news. Famous recipients of the King's shilling had gone on to make good careers in academe. For all his love of freedom and change, he knew Erik valued structure and purpose. That Erik had chosen St Andrews was influenced by reports of the reputations of the teachers of his subjects; the delights of its location, and access to the North Sea and Europe: there were Fearnachan ethnic links too, but mostly, swimming around in the Oxbridge pond held no charm for him.

The persuasive St Andrews student was Wil Klerk, who had been sent by his father, a senior officer in the army of Congo Belge, to study at Gordonstoun as a memorial gesture to the Scottish soldiers whose lives had ended in Belgium during the Great War and the high regard in which that ancient university was universally held, ranking third behind Oxford and Cambridge. Through a link that went back to the founding of the school by Kurt Hahn, an almost natural process had brought Wil to St Andrews to study mathematics and he was working on a Ph.D. when the now, freshly minted master of arts, Erik Barron, took him voyaging again to the Baltic. More than once, he had sailed with Wil to Belgium. It was during these visits that he had struck up a friendship with Wil's father, Colonel Piet Klerk, which was of a different kind and had gone beyond the very firm friendship that he and Wil had made.

In his International Relations studies, Erik had taken a serious interest in the effect of decolonization around the world which was becoming a foremost interest to International Relations scholars everywhere. During his studies, the Belgian Congo was not politically independent; his reading of the journals and his conversations with Piet Klerk indicated that independence was not far off. Belgium would have avoided the shocking wars for freedom that the Dutch had in Indonesia, and likewise the French in Algiers and Indo-China. He was conscious, too, of the potential for internal tribal wars with old scores to be settled to complicate the new political alignments struggling for power. When Moise Tshombe decided that Katanga should go it alone, which he had been thinking about in the late nineteen fifties, he asked for help from the Belgians to establish and provide staff for a Katanga army. Colonel Piet Klerk was posted to the military establishment that went as staff to Katanga. Tshombe had no high regard for the United Nations. He was in no way leftist orientated and avoided Russian interest, but had no desire to fall under the influence of the United States. 'Better the devil you know . . .', made the small, manageable, known quantity of Belgium his prime choice as ally. It was Colonel Klerk who contacted Erik, whose military capabilities he now knew thoroughly, with a proposal that he form one of the Mercenary mobile units that would be known as Commandos. Erik was convinced that he could help minimize deaths and the even worse horrors of tribal/political insurgency warfare that would inevitably arise. He assessed Tshombe as being basically good, and who, with Belgian support, should be able maintain a decent drive for peace and prosperity for the new state. Erik knew that Roddy was eager to try himself out commanding a platoon in serious action, hence the telegram and hence Roddy's scheduled departure for Rhodesia tomorrow afternoon. He decided that there would be adequate time to carry out the thorough division of his kit early in the morning.

Ernie would be at the club at the end of his day's duty. So he let himself enjoy the walk under fractal tracery of the bare branches of the mixed trees, many were London Plane's with pale brown boughs forming an enhancing screen through which to view the architecture of the handsome terrace buildings that told, without words, the story of the South Australia Company, of traders and entrepreneurs who had begun the first settlement venture; and of the progression to Crown Colony, finally to become a state of the Australian Federation in 1902.

After taking a small bag of overnight essentials from Fido, parked behind the club, he walked into the bar to check whether Ernie was there, 'Good', he thought: 'I'll put this bag away.' Within minutes of his return to the bar, Ernie arrived sporting a tweed jacket and slacks that he'd changed into in his office at the barracks. It could have been just a change from one uniform to another judging from the dress of others at the bar who had walked from their homes in North Adelaide, or the pleasant suburbs across the racecourse in Rose Park and Tusmore whither, if they didn't feel like walking, they would return by bus in time to share a drink with their wives before dinner. Adelaide men, it would seem, were not so 'snobby' about travelling on public transport as was the case in other Australian cities. The tweed, the trousers, and the polished brown shows were a little reminiscent of the group at the Barley Mow. In conversation, Ernie had said that a similar group would be gathered in a small bar at the Murrayville Hotel further out on Erindale Road. Soon they were joined by men in suits who had walked from their offices.

The two were pleased to see each other again and fell into easy conversation at about the beginning of which Roddy said, 'And why are you in the big city? I hear you ask. You hadn't, of course, at least not yet, but in case you get impatient, I'll show this. I don't necessarily want its contents bruited about, but it's not classified.' Ernie's face reflected his interest in what he was reading. He looked at Roddy and said, 'I want to know more.' In explaining his motives for responding affirmatively to the cable, he included his desire to prove himself in his commissioned rank in a battle situation before carrying rank became nothing beyond symbolic. So long as I fulfill my reserve minimum, the British army really doesn't care much what I do so long as I don't work for the enemy; just don't make it a subject for general conversation or become the subject of a story in the London tabloids.'

'Well, the best of British luck! Your real objective is to become a boring old fart who tours Naval and Military Clubs around the world boring young subalterns with exotic "warries". Thank God, you haven't been yet, we can have a decent dinner and a glass or two of wine and I won't have to tell lies about having another appointment.'

They did have a decent dinner, enjoying it and exchanging their very limited knowledge of the Congo before moving on to conjecture about the Cold War which was not, in Australia, a topic on the tip of every Australian tongue, except that Russian spies were under every bed. At just about the time that they were so engaged, Willie and Bess were discussing why Roddy, who had already been through the terrors of frontline battle action should elect to go to Africa and face the same, or worse, again. In response to a question from Bess, Willie thought a few moments about the venture, 'He has to do it while he still understands fear, and still can face it, and conquer it. He may not be conscious of it, and I'm pretty sure he won't be, but deep inside him he knows there will be a day when he can't do that. He wants to do this Congo adventure before that time comes. Perhaps, too, there's our cult of the hero, our paradigm of tribal aspiration, a hero who will have faced the fears and perils, who will have gone through them and come out the other side cleansed. The hero figure is attractive to females, the anti-hero or non-heroic male is less so, or unattractive. So males have the thought that if they have not passed over the heroic curve, their mundanity makes them prey to emotional manipulation.'

As Ernie and Roddy were parting, Roddy said, 'I'm not a person who keeps a diary and don't write many letters, but I'll try to make myself write to you, at least now and again.'

It was quite cold and grizzly when Roddy went to breakfast. As he read the *Advertiser*, he found nothing sensational in its pages but that was good, he thought, it was a paper of record, no room for assumptions and the only 'by-lines' were in the feature pages where articles were the information and opinions of the writer whose name appeared above it. The early pages were full of the advertising of city retail stores with John Martins exhibiting ladies' underwear, demurely and artistically, in quite brilliant line drawings. Local Australian Rules football took up all of the back pages, but there was a report of a cricket match between England and South Africa at Manchester from where the summer sunshine was absent, 'left out of battle' in Durban. It had likely been pulled from a galley of pre-set type ready for use in the test season; the headline read, *'Manchester Test. Rain stops play.'*

Following Bess's sketch map of the route, Club to Medindie, he drove north across the park to a very pleasant two-storey early-twentieth century house set in trees and gardens easily finding the large wooden gates which shut the stable yards from a quiet tree-lined side street where the frontages of similar house raised their gables behind driveways and well-kept grounds. He tucked little Fido away in stately comfort in a garage which still had that summery herbaceous odour. Above were staff quarters in one of which Steve said he had stayed. On his way to drop the keys through the letterbox in front door, he could see that there were half a dozen loose box stalls facing through broad verandahs onto the stable yard. The whole effect was quite manorial, a statement to the golden days of the wool trade and a world that moved to a different rhythm. Ernie's words, on leaving the night before, were, 'Pick you up here at 15.30 hours.'

'Time to have a little look at the state capital methinks.' Grey and cloudy it surely was but not dispiriting to the ardent traveller. He walked south now back across the terrace with the rich residences of North Adelaide away to his right, his purpose to explore North Terrace to a little more depth. Following his nose, he arrived on North Terrace at the point where, having passed the entrance to the zoo, a large technical training college occupies one corner and the eastern corner is filled by another big brick building, the Adelaide Hospital. A quick look showed him where he had turned yesterday, on the other side of this broad terrace, to get to the club. He retraced his steps and appreciated the architecture of the public building and the gothic Bonython Hall which may have been a part of the Adelaide University. A little further and he found the Art Gallery of South Australia. It was second only to Scotland's National Portrait Gallery for the size of the rooms so tastefully hung. It was obviously the recipient of rich bequests and the money had been spent on astute purchases of historical works of great quality and charm. The small rooms—compared with some of the European Galleries—were architecturally restful; and movement from one to another a series of treats for the soul. Perhaps he would come again to charge his aesthetic batteries when he returned to pick Fido up for their journey west by unbitumenised road across the infamous bulldust of the Nullarbor Plain.

Ernie arrived a minute early, straight 'from t'mill' wearing khaki battledress. They set off immediately passing Keswick Barracks on the way. At the airport, Roddy decided to get the admin done and perhaps there may be time for a drink before take-off. He presented himself at the desk and his two pieces of baggage were taken. When he was being given his boarding pass, the lady smiled and said, 'You must have influence in high places, Mr Mckenzie, you will notice that, on instructions from the Adelaide office, you have been upgraded to Club Class. This means that you will be able to use our special Club Class lounge where you may entertain a guest.'

'My goodness, who do I have to thank for this kindness?'

With a twinkle in her eye and a knowing smile, she passed the secret information, 'Well, let's just say we hope you enjoyed your visit to our office as much as our booking staff did. You may like to use the club now; there will be time for a drink. If you do, we hope you enjoy it. Have a pleasant flight and come and fly with us again.'

'Thank you. If you possibly can, would please thank the lovely people at the office for me? I must tell you, I'm quite touched.' The way he looked said he meant what he was saying, 'They made this luxury possible.' There was a slight pause and a new facial expression. 'And they delegated the task to a very charming messenger.'

Ernie was wondering whether Roddy was about to propose marriage. He seemed in no hurry to disengage from the conversation.

'Sorry to keep you waiting, old son, please join me for a drink when I can thank you for your patience.' He walked to the room designated, with Ernie in mute puzzlement about the direction they were taking and by the description above the door. 'What's the Mckenzie up to now?' When they were in, settled, and sipping celebratory champagne, he told Ernie the story, starting at the point of meeting with the gorgeous girls in the Adelaide office, with only very minor non-distorting embellishments.

Once airborne, the hospitality of the club missed nary a beat. Even before the motors had been fired up, he was invited, at his choice of course, to continue drinking champagne. They were getting off to a flying start.

It was going to be a long haul to Elizabethville. He would leave his Qantas flight at Nairobi, transfer to a British Overseas Airways flight to Salisbury thence by an aircraft of the Katanga government to Elizabethville.

In mental preparation for his mercenary role in a political state, newly formed, he had absolutely no information to work on. His history of Africa was almost entirely subscribed by his church's teachings about David Livingstone and what he had read of 'Bosambo' and 'Lt. Tibbett' from Edgar Wallace's Sanders of the River. School had taken care to see that he had learned of the heroism of General Gordon's disastrous situation in Khartoum which had not mentioned that his besiegement there was the result of his having disobeyed the order that had sent him to Khartoum: then of course there was Kitchener. His only real information was that sadly enlightening experience in Kenya. The major influences in his undertaking this engagement were, firstly, Erik's notice of invitation, secondly, and equally, this big drive within him to command a platoon in battle. In a normal military service engagement, he could spend all his military years without ever having fulfilled this need. He could never become a regular soldier spending a career in perpetual training, and living in barracks awaiting a pension. Such would not constitute 'living' as far as Roddy was concerned. So this engagement appeared to do two things, fulfill a portion of his happily borne obligation to Erik, and free him from this unrelenting need which, when it was met, would allow him a clear mind to apply himself to the demands of building him a future.

It had been as late as June of that year that Congo had gained independence from Belgium. Less than two weeks had passed and Katanga had split away to form its own independent state. All of this was happening while Roddy was in distant South Australia eradicating another bug from his personal development system, which was to have worked, and experienced life, on an Australian sheep or cattle station.

There was quite a bit of room in his club in the sky. Either Qantas was particularly caring of its club passengers or the influence of the ladies in the Adelaide office permeated the flying crew as well. Care and attention were being smilingly and, with the greatest good humour, showered upon him. He had been seated in a spacious corner of a for'ard bulkhead and the side of the fuselage with a window on his left, and because proximity, continuing staff presence, drink supplies, and the galley. It was the harem system in reverse; he was the possession of the crew, cut off from contact with a defiling world of other passengers. He would not pass a dull moment, not a silence or loneliness; there was always someone there by him, enquiring, informing, joking, chatting, discussing, and pouring drinks, fetching newspapers and magazines, finding radio channels. He thought of Jill and Emma and had to decide that there some planned breeding programme for Australian women, which was proving very successful. At Nairobi, there was an emotional parting. Two of hostesses filled the doorway waving, while the third, stationed on duty at the bottom the alighting stairs, threw her arms round him, and gave him a thorough going kiss which the Europeans among the ground staff, joined by the Africans, thought was a spectacle worthy of a gale of hurrahs. All passenger descent was arrested until Mr Mckenzie, who was first off, had been cleared and had at last turned his back to march off this expansive parade ground to report to BOAC.

Although he still held his rank as a first-class passenger, the BOAC flight, to be fair, but not unkind, was something of an anti-climax. Just as he had arrived at Fort George driven in the CO's car, so he would arrive to 'join up' at Salisbury, first class on British Overseas Airways—then just as certainly, the soldiers' life would begin: noise, danger, hunger, fatigue.

He had to sit with an English-born Rhodesian farmer who, he found out, was doing quite well growing vegetables and stone fruit not far outside Salisbury. As their patchy conversation went on, kept going by the Rhodesian, the theme that always underlay the conversations with British settlers in Africa arose, as it always does. It was that expression of hurt feelings of African ingratitude for all that Europeans had done for them. This great delusion, that the kinds of social change that they wished that Africans would espouse would bring them, eventually, from their childish ignorance, although finally never reachable, to the standards of quality of the British white person, while remaining in servitude. In the meantime with care and great goodwill, they would continue their paternal duty to guide them to that greater destiny. 'How could they possibly be happy being who they are?' When Roddy had been asked why he was going to Congo he had felt shame in resorting to subterfuge; and possibly, but not quite, prevarication when he said he was going to Katanga on a short military engagement with the new government of Katanga. 'I hope you're getting a lot of money. Don't expect any, thanks,' the farmer advised.

'Came out here as an LAC with the RAF on the Empire Air Training Scheme during the war . . . spent my time here till demob in England . . . didn't stay five minutes . . . couldn't stand Blighty anymore after the war . . . place had gone bloody near communist . . . couldn't get back here fast enough . . . I suppose I've got the adventurous spirit.' Roddy responded by saying yes, meaning that he acknowledged that what the man had been saying was his truth.

In the small terminal building at Salisbury, there was a man in a khaki cotton uniform of an army lieutenant, for those arriving for service in Katanga; there was no requirement for questions to be asked: they homed in on the khaki-clad figure.

Those who had come on the BOAC flight, and there were two, Roddy and one other, had their names were ticked off on a sheet on the lieutenant's mill board. He explained in English and in French that he was expecting another recruit on the next incoming BOAC flight which would arrive any minute now after which they would proceed to their aircraft to join the others. No more than ten minutes of idle standing were rewarded when the noise of a landing BOAC aircraft filled the air. The Route Transport Officer Wil Goris and Roddy stepped out to meet the expected arrival, where on descent from the aircraft, they beheld a magnificent sight which became clearer to inspection as it took the square shape of a six-foot male figure—square head, square face, square shoulders, and square knees of red hairiness showing between khaki hose tops and a kilt of regimental Gordon tartan. The British khaki battledress blouse was he wore was emblazoned by a colourful line of medals on the left breast, on his left arm between the elbow, and a Gordon tartan patch were parachutist wings—it was later learned that he had been in the Arnhem air landing and ensuing disaster, above the cuff bands of both sleeves were the sewn, khaki crown badges of a Warrant Officer Class II. On this sunny African day, in the thin air of Salisbury Rhodesia, the sheen on his boots not only damaged the sight but took the breath away. His kit was in the square-shaped FSMO Field Service Marching Order) webbing equipment; large pack high on his back and a small pack on his right hip. This webbing had been stowed assembled on the aircraft's luggage rack, and they had witnessed the deft movement of fitting it on and securing the web waist belt with glowing buckle and sliders. On his head, there was now, securely pulled on and positioned, with the hat band the space of a thumb to the first joint above the eye sockets and the wild ginger eyebrows, an officer's Tam o' Shanter (bonnets highland). Another liberty had been taken by wearing an officer's cap badge with a stag's head in relief above the word 'Bydand'. He marched up to the Belgian lieutenant and, observing the polite three paces, slammed to a halt and saluted. His eyes looking straight ahead at somewhere in infinity with the lieutenant's head somewhere in that line, he clearly uttered the sounds,

'Warrant Officer Class Two, William Mitchell, reporting for duty, sir!' The brief ceremonial over, Lieutenant Wil Goris shook Willie Mitchell's hand and welcomed him to 8 Commando. The others introduced themselves and shook hands. Roddy was able to pack his small canvas carry bag into the top of his Bergen in reserved space, and with the straps provided for that purpose, attached to the side of his pack the military water bottle which he had refilled at the airport. With their kit slung, they made their way at ease from the airport buildings to a lonely dilapidated DC3 parked on ground bare all around, a corner of the airport distant from any building. Sign painters were packing up their tools having just completed painting Katanga markings on fuselage and tail plane and were ready to leave in their truck. The waiting men who had carried their kit down the same internal dirt roadway and were sitting around in the plane's shadow, stood up to greet Lieutenant Goris and the new arrivals. No time was wasted in getting aboard, and once the pilot had done his checks and spoken to the control tower, he got the old motors started, their revs and oil pressures right, and it was taxiing out for take-off on its second haul that day.

The volunteers who would make up 8 Commando had been arriving by Katanga government aircraft and civilian flights at Elizabethville all that day. When numbers were sufficient, Katanga army trucks ferried them the sixty miles north-east of the city to a deserted convent school at Kiruwe, a small settlement on the hilly bush veldt. Amongst the men waiting at Salisbury, Roddy had met Philippe Noiret, now sitting beside him. His lithe body spoke energy and quick movement. His skin was light brown, his aquiline nose suggesting a genealogy which may have included Spanish Moors, Romans, Phoenicians, or the Grecian traders of ancient times, who had founded Marseille and Nice. There was nothing of the Latin languor in Philippe Noiret. His jet-black hair was combed back and under black eyebrows restless black eyes darted to pinpoint changing targets: he was a puma ready to strike. He readily engaged Roddy in conversation in English.

He had been born in a small fishing village at the top of a bay to the south and a little east of Marseille where the old coastal road comes nearly to the sea and where the broken limestone land rises almost vertically upward. As a conscript in the French army, he had served as a second lieutenant in the Algerian War of Liberation. When conscripted, he had opted for service in the navy, but due to the shortage of naval war engagements and the high demand for soldiers as a result of the colonial wars, the powers of the military conscription authority had sent him off to Draguignan there to learn the arts of soldiering and pass through the officers' training school.

His NATO compulsory military service had ended (the French government had approved the dispatch of these conscripts to Algeria) with a result for him not dissimilar to Roddy's. The Algerian war was still raging, and worsening, but Philippe had no desire to continue with the French army's objectives or methods being applied there. He needed time to sort himself out and consider a civilian future. He had not allowed much of that time to pass when, in a cafe in Toulon, he met up with a group of disgruntled ex-soldiers who had served in Algeria. They had got wind of recruitment for a mercenary force for action in the Congo, and among many other political-cum-military subjects were exchanging some thoughts on that. From that discussion and with very little reasoning, Philippe had followed the information trail and volunteered to join Twelfth Commando with a promised appointment as a lieutenant equipe commander. Soldiering, in almost any form, is most certainly undertaken for reasons other than the paltry amount of money that nations are prepared to pay their fighting men; most particularly the pittance paid to national service conscripts. Erik Barron was later heard to say when he addressed his volunteers, 'If you have joined this force for the money, you will have left us and gone home long before you have served out your engagement.'

Major Erik Barron had not had much to do with the selection process and there had been no time to make detailed assessments of the soldiering skills of the volunteers. As a result, allocation of the twenty-four men to each of the seven equipes had been random. The old convent at Kiruwe comprised a set of separated buildings; the chapel, one administrative, and a classroom building were built in mud brick and white washed.

The other buildings, built in wattle and daub, were dormitories, cookhouse and refectory, store buildings, and a little hospital all arranged under shade trees around an open tamped earth square. Slightly apart were some buildings in the same style, which housed the lay staff. Parallel to the chapel was a long building with shady verandahs and inside, a series of cells, nuns' bedrooms, and at the end, a common room and a washroom. This virginal accommodation would become the temporary home for the equipe commanders.

Since 8 Commando had not yet formed, Belgian officers and NCOs of the Katanga Army were undertaking the administrative duties. Queues of arrivals had formed and troops were already being checked off the lists and, after their identities had been confirmed and they had signed on, were given the number of the equipe, they were to join and the identification marks of their billets. Subalterns were directed to another room where Erik Barron's Belgian adjutant and two clerks were one by one doing the checks and giving basic information about the camp and a warning order about a meeting with the old man sometime before the evening meal. Roddy decided that, much as he would have liked to call on Erik, he should not endanger relations with the other subalterns. At their 'nunnery', each name had been put up on a door. His room, almost as palatial as his room at the trailer camp in the Snowies, was the last numbered, near the end of the corridor, and was number 7. He had thought of changing into uniform, but they would not be undertaking anything military until the next day. What he must do right away was go see how his men were accommodated and what needs they might have. He found their 'house', for that's what it had been, for resident students at the Catholic school which was a part of the convent: a card on the door bore his name and Equipe 7. It would have housed a number of pupils with quarters for a house mother under the same roof. There were six rooms which, with four men in each, gave space for kit and reasonable room for movement. As he looked into each room, he checked how they were settling in and said he was looking forward to meeting them all in the morning. 'You'll have a chance to start getting to know each other this evening.

I have it on good authority that there will be beer on at the canteen tonight. Enjoy the leisure while you can. I look forward to seeing you all in the morning.'

The room where the officers met was in a separate plaster walled building under some trees and had possibly been some kind of meeting room, but the furniture that was there now was a mixture of tables from army stores and a collection of odd chairs scrounged from the second-hand traders in Elizabethville, scrambled together for 8 Commando. The subalterns who were gathered there now were a fine sample of human diversity from Karl Ackers, Equipe 1, from Hamburg who, after a short stint in the German Army grew tired of perpetual exercises on the Luneburger Heide and the life in barracks at Buxtehude and took to roaming the sea with daring young sailors who bummed around and across the Pacific in two different, ancient yachts with wild and woolly companions who hadn't realized the 'pacific' was a misnomer: when they found out, didn't care. They would voyage back down to New Zealand and pick apples when their coffers ran low, have dentistry done if any were needed, and with surprising frequency, pick up a paying passenger male or female, who having sickened, or inspired themselves with vicarious adventure, were dying to try the real thing. To join this crew would demand the suppression of revulsion on time of seeing them first, assembled in a pub; but once a social step to join them had been taken, their charm, worldliness, and good humour was embracing, overwhelming and satisfying. Let the voyage begin!

Were a continuum to be run out with Karl at one end, Captain Michel Foucault, Armee Belge, Commando Adjutant would be away towards the other. He was a career soldier who had attended the Belgian Military Academy and passed out with high marks his progress was rapid and he later returned to Staff College as a captain where he again performed very well. He found himself posted to Congo at military headquarters and there as a diversion and delight he took to writing spy novels: for which he also got high marks. With royalty cheques flowing into his bank, he found it convenient to fulfill his military contract in sinecure service while his leisure hours provided ample time to write at least one spy novel a year. His efforts at HQ could be spared while he took his annual leave and went to help write the film script for one of his novels. The film attracted big audiences and the critics gave him high marks for that too. He would never be the life and soul of an army mess. He rarely spoke unless spoken to when his responses were ever factual and offered in précis form. He was seen to smile, or on occasion laugh, at humorous remarks or events. He was of middle height, balding, the remainder of his reddish hair kept clipped short, his rosy cheeks supported rimless spectacles and because he knew tropical service well, he took a couple of servants with him wherever he went, so his dress was always sharply laundered. There were a few tall men among them, but Erik Barron still stood out as the prominent figure and that was not because of his rank. His voice had an attractive baritone sound and roundness; its language and speech were delivered from the ground of a genetically installed highland, Fearnas accent and intonation. Anyone, listening to all the animated conversation would not have heard, ever, the question: 'Why did you volunteer for 8 Commando?'

Having spent so many years of the recent past on staff work, it might be imagined that the voice of the parade ground at Koninklizke Militair School would have withered from his vocal chords, but the voice that called the, mostly young, officers to attention was not so much loud as clear and of perfect volume to be heard over the exclamatory babble of the subalterns.

'Gentlemen, welcome to 8 Commando. Your commanding officer, Major Erik Barron, would like to speak to you', he announced, 'but I'd like to ask you if you feel happy that I include in our meeting Warrant Officer Willie Mitchell. Anyone have any difficulty with that?' There was no dissent. Michel said, 'Excuse me, gentlemen', and went to the door, he was absent for a moment or two, Willie dressed, in denims was at his side, 'Major Barron, sir, gentlemen, I wish to introduce Warrant Officer Willie Mitchell, ex–Gordon Highlanders and participant in the Arnhem battle of World War II. Gentlemen, Major Barron.' With those words, he took up a position beside and slightly behind Erik's left shoulder.

After some seconds of silence, while his eyes scanned the group of now-expectantly alert men, Erik spoke to say, 'As I see you all here', said slowly, his eyes roaming around the group, pausing on faces here and there, 'I can see myself, as a young subaltern, being addressed by Ord Wingate', as if he were looking into a clear picture of the past, 'before we set off to go behind the Japanese lines in Burma. There will be other similarities to that time. We shall, almost certainly, spend most of our operational time surrounded by enemy whose first desire in life will be to kill us and our men. And just as was the Chindit situation in Burma, there will be times when we are damned near exhausted, without food, running short of ammunition, and out of wireless communication with our support.' Here, he paused to make sure, that what was going to be said next, would be given serious attention. 'There will be two important qualities we must take with us into that situation. The first is unbelievable physical fitness and endurance; the second, and even more important—much more important—will be mental hardness. We will not have much time for training, so we must train hard. The moment you feel you can't go on—no shame: come and see Michel or me and we will see that you can get away immediately. If any man, especially an officer, breaks down in action, it will mean most likely his own death—but worse, the deaths of those left to carry the burden of keeping fighting ability intact. If I push you too hard and you want to thump me because you believe so—try it—you will have to suffer the consequences, and I don't mean military law.' The firm, strong Erik Barron face, shaped and etched by experience of hard times past, was the perfect backdrop against which his voice spoke the words. 'This is not a pep talk. As the days unfold, you will see that I have said nothing other than ensure that you know the facts.'

Again, there was a pause, for the meaning of what he was saying to find some internal register. In a changed tone and pitch, he asked rhetorically, 'Will there be no joy?'

'I cannot know what you describe for yourself as joy. I only know that I have gone through times when, with my comrades, death, face-to-face has looked into our eyes and, out-stared, passed on. In this room now, is one of the men I've shared that experience with'—again a pause—'more than once. On one of the occasions, I got an MC and he got badly wounded. So far as I know, the major grouch he has is that he was so fit that he was back in action for the second battle of the Hook which denied him the opportunity of gazing into the eyes of the gorgeous Australian nurses in the Kobe hospital.

'This brings me to another point of very great significance. The strength and effectiveness of your equipe is not achievable without the heart and goodwill of your men. Never, ever, forget that. They have to be fit and their brains have to be hard too. These men will need to respect you—you will only gain their respect when they know that you respect them and care sincerely—with no artificial ritual or fakery—by deed, and by visible signs of spirit, that they mean something of great human value to you. Soldiers can smell bullshit from afar off and by the holy Jesus when they sniff it—look out! I want you to get fit. I want you to get hard headed and I want you to get that joy of sharing fear and danger with men like yourself. As we work together, we'll get to know each other. I hope this will be a good experience for you. I know it will be for me. Now, enough said. I just want to leave you with those words I have just spoken. I want you to think very deeply about them. Michel will give you the details of what I want to happen tomorrow.'

Erik turned to Michel and thanked him, adding, 'Your turn now, Michel.'

What Michel had to say to the group was no set of instructions it was simply a description of how he wished the equipes to be marched on in numerical order to form an open box facing the saluting base where Sergeant-Major Mitchell would be posted. Equipes would present their strengths to him. Erik would then march on and take post; after Willie had reported strengths, he would hand the parade over to Erik.

Erik would see the whole Commando on parade. Having carried out their own equipe muster parades, they would march on in numerical order and form, up each right marker halting by a Katanga soldier already in position. Given Michel's outline, the detail of how this was to be achieved had to be worked out by the equipe commanders.

When Michel had finished and had given the 'Carry on please', Roddy made a bee line for Erik. 'Erik! Grand to see you again'—he was looking into, and searching his face and after a silence—'it's been a while. Student life obviously agreed with you!'

'Oh, it did, it did!' he said with delight. 'I'll tell you about it. And by heavens, you're looking well! Your letters told the story and now here's the living evidence.' His voice changed as he said, 'Jesus, Roddy, I'm glad to see you. You've no idea, how glad. We'll need to organise a time for a good yarn.'

'Would after dinner tomorrow evening be any good? I know you can't store sleep, but I want to have as much as I can tonight. It could be the last luxury. Also I want call into the canteen to see how the men are getting together. That was a very good idea to have Willie Mitchell in for your address. I hope he turns out as good as he looks. Is Michel coming into the field with us?'

'Yes, I thought it must help to have him know my views on life; and since we have no sergeants yet, and no mess for him, we mustn't leave him out in the cold and certainly not throw him into the midst of the other ranks. Yes, Michel will be in Commando HQ all the time. I can see myself being needed up front much of the time. It's early days, but I like what he's done so far. I'm looking forward to meeting the men tomorrow. C'mon, let's get a hold of him and see if he'd like a drink with us before dinner.'

The acute sense of what is essential to life, which infantry soldiers seem to be born with, was there, in a corner of the room; an Electrolux kerosene refrigerator crammed with cold beer and, surely, enough ice for the whisky drinkers. It would be senseless to ask questions as to how it had been acquired and came to be there; it indicated that there were people on the team who knew how to wangle things. There was a half hour or so of drinks before dinner was set up. Once it was established that there was beer on hand, its presence was accepted with quiet pleasure; the pitch and babble of their early meeting had gone. The mood in the room was serious. There was a lower

volume of sound and deeper pitch in the voices; and an air of
seriousness intimating a wish to 'get down to business'.

The required deep thinking, which Erik had suggested,
appeared already to have begun. It was clear that the gathering
was taking this opportunity to meet the men, nearest around
them, who were very soon to become their comrades in war.
It was noticeable that the introductions and greetings were
more militarily purposeful than simply social. Questions were
designed to find out what each other's combat experience may
have been in any form of warfare. They appeared to be as keen
to say what they had not done, and so avoid false expectations
when, together, they faced the enemy. Had a man been asked
what he had thought of this short time together after Erik's
address, he would have replied that it was a half hour well spent.
All of them agreed, and said so, that the training they did here
was going to be crucial to their ability to perform. Sitting across
the dining tables further helped the mixing process, exchange
of ideas and assumptions. The high quality of the meal of
chicken and fresh vegetables did not receive the attention it
deserved.

In the OR's mess, the atmosphere was totally different. They
had greatly enjoyed the meal, the Belgian beer was brilliant,
there was the new company of fellow adventurers, there were
yarns galore to be told to a new audience, and tomorrow would
be another day. Roddy looked through the happy throng
greeting people here and there asking for Equipe 7 people. He
struck a pair one of whom said he was a seven man. He turned
out to be an Australian from the Commando Reserve Battalion
in Sydney. Things were quiet in Australia at the moment now
that Korea was over, and he was looking for some battle action.
The training program he followed was of his own design built
around needs in his unit. It included climbing, rappelling,
parachuting, endurance marches, orienteering, karate, and
boxing with a swim whenever he could fit it in, which was quite
regularly summer and winter. He worked for a company which
ran adventure training camps. 'Well welcome aboard,' glowing
with enthusiasm and delight that a bloke with such a way of
living was going to be in his platoon. 'I'm Roddy Mckenzie

and I'm Equipe Seven commander.' The number 7 man was Andrew Denton. The other man was in number 6 equipe. His love was car rallying and had driven from Cairo to the Cape of Good Hope camping out every night of the trip with just one companion all the way. The journey was not just a point-to-point speed trip. They had white water rafted on the Blue Nile, the Zambezi, and others, climbed Kilimanjaro, and just as a small diversion, and for something to brag about, they had made a short diversion to Timbuktu. Roddy was fascinated and said so: he excused himself and said he'd like to meet some more of the seven men. 'I'm looking forward to serving with you in Equipe Sept Andrew,' he said, leaving. Three men were huddling head to head at a small table deeply engaged. The trio turned out to be equipe seven men.

'Hello,' he said, in a breezy greeting. 'Anyone happen to be in equipe seven?' he asked in a light enquiring tone. 'I'm Roddy Mckenzie, equipe commander.'

'We're all in seven,' responded a man with reddish hair who spoke. His look embraced the other two as if he had already taken hold of a seven identity. He stood up and, offering his hand, said, 'I'm Cyril Cusack from Southampton, but when I left I was working for the Outward Bound School at Laxford in the Western Highlands of Scotland. I got that job on a tip from a passenger that I was serving in the dining room of the Caronia on the New York run at the time.'

'Pleased to meet you; and welcome. I've never been to Laxford, okay, but I heard about the school starting up.' Following Cyril's lead the others stood, greeted Roddy, and gave their names. One had done his national service as a gunner in the Royal Navy on the very new frigate HMS *Russell* before it had fired that first annoyed shot in the Icelandic Cod Wars. He did his reserve time from Portsmouth and had been working on a market garden growing vegetables. He was still restless and the formation of 8 Commando attracted him. The other had served at sea in the North Sea and the Atlantic on a trawler out of Grimsby. He had spent the bulk of his national service at Tel el Kebir just west of Cairo. The bits of the army he liked best—exercises in the desert—didn't happen often enough.

The other seven people had gathered in little groups, many who were going to be sharing rooms. When he was sure, he had met the full complement, he left for bed and a mental review of the day, and his plans for the morrow.

As dawn was breaking, he put on an old pair of jungle green trousers, his beloved Australian army boots and green US army sweatshirt, and got on to the road for an intended half-hour jog and run. As he turned out of the compound onto the road, he cleared himself through the guard room and got into his rhythm. He came round the first bend and found that he was not the only man with the idea of an early morning run. Ahead of him by about a hundred yards were two khaki figures running side by side. He began to run to catch up. The thudding of his feet alerted the two in front who turned round to note the pursuing figure. Seeing him they faced their front and increased their speed. Roddy twigged that the game was on, so he pedalled a bit faster. The leaders matched his increased pace and surged on. In half hour which the leading pair also seemed to have allowed themselves, Roddy found he couldn't close the distance until one of them slowed: it was Amarjit, whose training life had never been at the level of Andy's, indeed nor had Roddy's. 'D'ye think you can stay with me, Amarjit?' asked Roddy in a non-judgemental tone. 'Dunno, I'll see, but if I drop behind, leave me to it, I'll still have to run the half and we're about . . . oh, look . . . Andy's turning we must have reached half time.'

'Okay, Amarjit, why don't you turn now? I'll go the spot where Andy turned and see if I can make it back in the half hour.' Roddy was really driving himself: and like running to bring up the truck when mustering on Rising Star, he would have to run as fast as he could drive his body.

Andrew was waiting at the guard room still heaving breath when Roddy ran up shouting, 'Good game, Andrew. Well done!' gasping and grinning as he clapped Andrew on the shoulder. 'Thank you, sir. I thought it was worth the risk to see how you would react,' said Andrew. Roddy gasped aloud, 'I'm glad you did. Believe me, I enjoyed the idea—and the contest—all good stuff and in a good cause. Ah, here's Amarjit.'

'Well done, Amarjit,' Andy and Roddy shouted together. As they made their way to their billets, Roddy asked Andrew, 'How's your drill? Can you go from a bunch of men on the edge of the parade ground, get them to form threes, then open order for inspection and close order?'

'I reckon I could handle that,' said Andrew confidently.

'Good; I'm going to announce that, as of this parade, you are appointed Acting Corporal. I'll tell the boss and Willie Mitchell. I want the men ready for inspection by zero 7.30 hours on the space outside your billets. I'll be watching the performance.'

He did watch the performance and mightily pleased he was. Andrew had obviously done all the right team leader things. When he had given the 'open order' command, he fell in behind Roddy as he inspected the ranks. Roddy shook hands with every man and faced each one keenly as he came to attention before him. He tested himself on remembering the names from the previous evening and his attention, repetition of the name and the associated story, secured him a complete recall. When the last man in the rear rank had been addressed, he and Andy took up their positions in front of the squad.

On Erik's instruction, Willie Mitchell had moved the parade to a piece of sloping land, the lower front of a hillock near the flat space of the parade ground. Erik drove round in a half-ton truck and pulled up. Standing up in the back could see all the men of 8 Commando sitting at ease, spread along the face of the slope. He began, 'While we have the opportunity to sit down and I can be with all of you at one time, I'd like to say a bit about what's ahead of us. War is almost as old as mankind. Though there are principles of warfare that have stood the tests of time, the principles remain while the warfare changes and takes new forms. For many of us, what we are going to experience will be a newer form of warfare. There will be a lot that that we have to learn together while we are achieving our strategic and tactical objectives. We're all in this together which means that we have to be sure that we share our learning amongst ourselves in Twelfth Commando. In the heat of the moment, we will be locked into the action. As soon as we get a chance after an engagement—success or failure—we've got to sit together in our equipes and work out what happened and why. Any man may have something to say. We'll all have to listen and hear what his understanding means for us. This should mean that the new tricks are spread around so the next engagement will require less effort, lessen risk, and get better results.

'The point is that we'll be engaged in action almost immediately. We will not have done all the training that would have been ideal. Whatever training we have time to do, we must get as much out of it as we possibly can.' His speech was direct. He knew that among the kinds of men who sat there on that sloping bit of African ground were honours graduates of Toulon taverns, London or Dublin pubs, from legitimate academic universities, students of much critical personal reading, and would have seen about as much of the world as Marco Polo. Now sitting there at ease, he did not forget to thank them for their parade and their turn out. What followed was not much different from Erik's to the officers on the previous night. He talked about his belief in the ritual of shaving with a tale about the below-freezing conditions of Korea when men took pride in shaving and how much better it made them feel; cleanliness and order in billets and the absolute need for hygiene in the tropics; parading to take their *Camoquin* when in this training situation and the corporal's job to remind everyone when they were on operations. 'One of the most important aspects of operational soldiering is caring for others. Sort each difficulty out the moment it happens or as soon after as you can. Sorting out personal problems is a high priority part of making life worthwhile. You should be able to solve them within your equipe. If it's an admin problem, your best bet is Sar'major Mitchell then Captain Foucault.

'I'll leave immediately to go to army command for an intelligence briefing. I will know more when I come back. Be sure I will let you all know. In the meantime, get cracking in your equipes. Thank you all. Sar'major, the parade is yours.' The men were called to attention and Willie Mitchell and Erik Barron saluted each other.

Roddy took his men away for issue of clothing, equipment, and weapons. After issue, they set about putting together and getting the feel for the new straps, belts, and pouches of their webbing equipment. Roddy told them, that to get used to the need to move with this kit on and loaded with its battle contents, they would from now on, for every hour on duty, unless otherwise commanded, wear this kit. Next, they were issued with Belgian FN self-loading rifles and FN9UZI sub-machine guns which they set to stripping, cleaning, and learning about before proceeding to range firing practice later in the day. When it was time for the mid-day meal, they doubled down to the canteen-cum-mess-hall where they were allowed to take off their webbing to eat.

After a quick lunch, Roddy appeared at the mess room wearing 'battle order', the kit that had been issued to the men that morning, and walked along the tables asking the men about the meal. When he had gone the rounds, he went back to stand near the door. He called out loudly and clearly, 'Listen in!' The men looked towards him in silence. 'This afternoon we'll pick up some hard rations which you will carry in your packs at all times. Then we'll go out on the ground to get used to fire and movement again.' He said this clearly and loudly, taking in the men with his eyes as he spoke. 'We'll move to a range we've rigged up and we can have some practice in using these brand-new rifles. In a very short time, I'm going to give the command: "Fall in outside." You'll have washed and packed your mess tins and stowed them in your small pack and you will have refilled your water bottles. Right; last man out in two minutes owes me a beer.' Then he paused and watched the action as the men scrambled to get to the wash-up troughs. Then he called the command, 'Equipe! Fall in outside!'

Immediately after his talk to the men, Erik drove to HQ at Stanleyville on the rough road through scrubby, rolling grass land where sometimes there were groves of mixed trees; and lone trees of different kinds choosing their sites on the flats, or on the slopes of the many hillocks, sometimes to be near the angular rock formations which had thrust through the skin of the earth where disappearing seas had left them exposed to heat and cold, wind and rain through thousands of years, till their flesh of soil and softer rock had been worn away. The briefing was conducted by a Belgian captain. The Kaluba tribe was in revolt, they were holding meetings of clans, and larger groups were forming. They were going through a psychological indoctrination by the witch doctors who, with the assistance of *dagga*, were working the tribesmen up to what would become a conviction of invincibility. Once aggregated and ready, the massed tribes would be looking for a target, and the first most likely was the town of Kyunzu which would, right away, require defence and for which a convoy of troops, ammunitions, supplies, and a medical team would be ready to start in a matter of hours. One of the Commandos would have to provide a convoy escort. In the meantime, the other Commandos would have to mount rescue missions for Europeans and Africans who staffed schools, hospitals, and civil service posts scattered across Katanga. There would be other Europeans moving around Katanga whose exact locations could not easily become known and would therefore require search. He made the statement to the commanders, his understanding of their reasonable reaction visible on his face, 'Alas your plans for training may have to become learning by doing. You must become operational at once.' There was no time for sociability. The commanders would be given time to seek answers to their immediate questions; they had to take what steps they could to get any needed supplies and equipment— right now! He pointed to group of officers and men sitting in the seats to his right in the group and asked them to stand up. 'These men will do everything possible to meet your needs. Sandwiches and coffee, writing tables and maps are over there ready for use.'

As his driver, Erik had taken with him to Stanleyville, Tommy Farr from Equipe 6. When Erik went to the staff meeting, it was time for Tommy to go on a bit of a scrounge. He took a clip board with the jeep's running sheet on it and, in the hand of his straight left arm, smartly set off, knowing from experience that, if he moved around in a soldiery manner, he would be ninety-nine per cent immune from interference and enquiry. 'Lay an iron filing to a magnet. . .' Something drew him towards a roughly lined-up collection of mixed types of military vehicles. In seconds, he spotted a Wehrmacht half-tracked troop-carrying vehicle. His eyes brightened with interest. Clambering aboard, he examined the instruments, found what looked like an ignition switch, rattled the gear stick, found neutral, and turned the switch. To Tommy Farr, the responding roar followed by quiet, even rumbling was a melody by Gershwin. Inside him, his motor mania was insisting, 'I want it. I want it.'

Erik had joined with the other three Equipe commanders to pore over the maps and plot the areas of enemy activities reported by intelligence and to divide the combat area into zones for which each Commando would accept responsibility. The numbers given to the equipes confused the truth that there were only four; Mike Hoare, an Englishman who had spent a bit of time in Africa and Erik Barron were two of the commanders and two Afrikaner South Africans, Piet Groose and Jon Sanders, one each. It was odd that these men had come from a country in which *Apartheid* of blacks and whites was very rigidly maintained. As they planned and discussed the challenges before them, Erik envied the Afrikaners their knowledge of Africa absorbed and passed on to them by generations of forebears multiplied by their own life experiences and their love for and deep interest in the land of their birth. To this could be added a more than rudimentary knowledge of the land over which they would be warring. They were enlightened men, much in the cast of Col. Lawrence van der Post. As he listened, Erik read them as being practical, pragmatic, and at the same time, philosophical and not insensitive. They admired Jan Smuts in many of his parts and they had great delight in having given the British such a hard time during the Boer War. Now here they were, in units called Commandos, a term and a military structure they had invented. If it is sometimes said that the Dutch South Afrikaner is stolid and humourless, certainly these two were not. In the short conversation they shared despite its concentration on the military objectives, Erik gleaned some strong impressions of the qualities of these men. They had taken their wives and children to Rhodesia and were contemplating and researching a move to some other place and were being persuaded by some other South African friends—among the many who were already there—to come to Australia. The Intelligence briefing over, they were joined by President Tshombe who came while they were poring over a map spread before them. After a welcoming preamble, he said, 'You already know, with your experience and trained eyes, what you are up against in terms of the enemy and terrain. We will give you all we can of ammunition and supplies which you will need for your military tasks. I believe your skills will do much towards solving the problems of creating stability. Fighting the political problems is my task and my government's. Yours is the hard and dangerous job of fighting on the ground. Fancy trying to tell men like you how to do that? I think the Belgian military staff are very good men and they will help you every way they can. Our army is made up of some old soldiers and mostly new volunteers and all just newly formed. They will see what you do; and learn. I find it hard to ask you to be patient with them when all that we need to do must be done in haste. There are people spread throughout Katanga who, though not native to this country, have done much to help to serve and improve it. They will now be in some danger. They need our protection. Thank you for joining us. There is much that is worthwhile to be achieved.' He shook hands with each of the commanders and said, 'Good luck,' paused, looking on the group of eager, alert, committed men, all now standing erect, Commandos, and the Belgian staff, on all of whom so much depended, and with his aide, turned away.

Moise Tshombe had left the Commandos with a general impression which confirmed their decision to have joined his force: the thought was encouraging but not to be dwelt upon now: there was much to be done.

Much was being done by Tommy Farr. Seeing towing hooks fore and aft on the half-track just begged for a trailer: he wasn't long in finding one. Soon he had collected jacks, steel ropes and winches, camouflage nets, fuel cans, shovels, a pick, and an axe. 'Now, what about weaponry?' he asked himself. The boss would be doing something about that, but he thought he better do an independent search. He was convinced of the virtues of the FN rifle, but it had a tendency to rise when firing on automatic. A light sub-machine gun would be the ticket. He had found the small-arms store and ventured in to chat-up the storemen from whom he successfully oozled six, slender lightweight air-cooled German automatic weapons which used the common .76 ammunition of which he was given a generous supply and even got some help in having it carted to the half-track, which he now organized to take to a refuelling point, to have it filled along with a dozen ten-gallon cans. He was very pleased with his day's work and decided that he'd better check with the boss. Major Barron was on the point of having Tommy brought in. 'We have a Katanga driver to give a lift to, he's just gone to collect his kit,' was among the major's statements and questions as was finding out whether Tommy had managed to get the stuff on his list which Tommy had been pleased to see included a couple of grenade launchers for the FN rifles, two-inch mortars and ammunition, a Very pistol and flares, whistles, military pattern, camouflage nets, ropes and cordage, and blankets. Erik appeared to be so pleased it seemed to Tommy to be an opportunity for a gentle introduction to the story of his prizes, so when Tommy said, 'Could we make that driver earn his keep, sir?' the major simply asked, 'How are we going to do that, Tommy?'

'Well, sir'—and Erik guessed that a yarn was likely to begin— 'while working on your list, I just happened to walk beside a park for old vehicles and believing what a senior officer once told me; that "time spent in reconnaissance is never wasted", I decided I ought to examine this trove of vehicular treasure. Time spent to good purpose, sir. I decided that the OC of our equipe required the services of a safe versatile command vehicle. I therefore undertook to acquire a German half-track troop carrier, for which, in addition to your own personal needs, sir, would have no end of assault roles to play. Now, as regards the spare driver: going at the same time was the German equivalent of a jeep which is a small nippy vehicle; a must-have for a mobile force. The spare driver could drive that, and if you wouldn't mind taking our jeep, sir, I'll bring back the half-track.'

'Trooper Farr!' exclaimed Erik, choking on a laugh. 'You've got it all worked, haven't you. I'll take the German jeep to see whether you haven't been sold a pup.'

'A soldier has to have a plan, sir, which I made after I'd made an appreciation of the situation.' He too was struggling with chuckles, while feeling totally chuffed at the boss's reaction.

'Come with me', commanded Erik, 'I have legitimate stores to collect from HQ, and we'll get a hold of the driver.'

'Sir!' responded Tommy crisply to the order and fell in alongside his commander. 'Since we'll probably be doing everything tactically from now on, I've placed a German sub-machine gun in the weapon clips above the dash board in your jeep, sir. I tested it and it's in firing condition, and to alert, sir, it's loaded with the safety catch on. I also acquired a radio for the command vehicle, sir, which I'm sure could handle a brigade net. We may find a good wireless op. in 8 Commando, if not we'll have to advertise in "positions vacant".' In less than an hour, three vehicles and a loaded trailer behind the half-track, with all stores lashed up and stowed, left for Kituwe.

When the mini-convoy arrived at Kituwe, it was late in the day, but Erik knew that he must call an O Group immediately. The day's field training in ambush drills had gone pleasingly well for all, each equipe having demonstrated that the men were thinking about what they were doing; watching, and working in cooperation with their mates. The subalterns were particularly grateful for Willie Mitchell who had gone from equipe to equipe, his experience in Malaya being clearly evident to men and commanders; and when it came to the analysis and summing up afterwards, all were enthusiastic in their expression of their pleasure in working with him. 'Yes, we were understanding more, thinking and responding to commands quicker,' said one trooper. 'I think we'll be better when we have corporals,' voiced another of the men, looking around the group for agreement as he spoke. The positive response to his words was a consensus.

Roddy chose to respond to the mention of the appointment of corporals. It seemed that by natural process, perhaps because he could speak French, perhaps because of his performance in the training exercises, perhaps because he seemed to relate to troopers and commanders alike, he had become the unofficial 'Analysis Group's' chairman. 'About the appointment of corporals', he said, 'you will understand that we have no time to prepare candidates for selection or to give NCO training so we will have to do the best we can and'—he looked at the other officers—'we'll announce the appointments on first parade tomorrow. I have no idea what news the CO will bring back from HQ, but I have a feeling in my bones that we've had just about all the training we're going to get.'

Immediately on arrival, Erik had a brief discussion with Michel who would take over all matters related to the convoy's arrival on the morrow and plan its ongoing road journey, leaving tactical aspects of the plan to Erik. Now the O Group. The equipe commanders, gathered in the mess, writing boards and pens ready before them, were eager to know what news of action their CO would announce.

'Gentlemen, we start tomorrow. Our first task will be to deliver three civilian trucks of supplies to two small towns and a mission station to the north of Lake Mweru on the lower hilly country on the western edge of the Mitumba Mountains which you will see on these maps prepared by the intelligence boys at HQ from ordinance survey maps, with added information from their gathered intelligence. There will also be two trucks of the Katanga forces, one with personnel aboard, one with their ammunition and supplies. These troops will augment the small force already at Kiambi. My intention is to intersperse these vehicles with ours, where they will be placed will be in the convoy plan Michel will provide us with, based his knowledge of the terrain. There will be no movement order. At any stop planned or otherwise, we will without hesitation take up tactical anti-ambush positions around the convoy. The Katanga troops in these events will be under our command. The next important issue is that we must give ourselves this last opportunity to practice the approach to, and the assault of an enemy occupied settlement. You will have to organize enemy and own troops as you have done in your training to this time. It may mean an early reveille, so you will need to give your troops a warning order now. Before I leave you to your planning, I must tell you I've had to make a decision about the appointment of a 2i/c. I have given each of you equal consideration in the selection process. With immediate effect, Roddy Mckenzie will become acting captain, second in command of our Commando.' There was an immediate rumble of assent and congratulations. That natural process had been made official without objection. In this mercenary situation, there were not the usual career, or time-dominated influences found in regular soldiering, where seniority envy, disagreement, and future prospects can cloud or affect the issue. Tomorrow was going to be a busy day. It was up to Roddy, now, to take command of the planning which would have to be done that night. Immediately the men must be told.

There was indeed an early reveille next day. While all the major activities of the Kiambi convoy were being carried out, and Commando HQ was working at full speed, all the people involved had to ignore 'an invading *enemy* force' which had 'occupied the settlement' and were involved in their own 'aggressive, murderous activities'. Working on intelligence reports of an escapee from the settlement, a force of 'counter-insurgent forces' was approaching with the objective of trapping and destroying the invaders, taking prisoners, liberating the villagers, caring for casualties, and establishing a defence of the area. The exercises provided many invaluable lessons for all the troops involved. Swapping roles on the same day in the same situation was not ideal, but did have a few advantages; neither was it ideal that the numbers in the three equipes which would normally form an attack force had to be intermixed and combined, forming larger-than-normal assault parties so that all troops might take part in the experience. The shared learning from the shared experience, however diluted, would prove to be invaluable as events would unfold.

The convoy from Elizabethville arrived late in the evening and was immediately inserted into the positions in the convoy formed according to the route plan. The number of vehicles planned had been at the last-minute augmented. Michel had persuaded HQ that the convoy size had increased beyond what 8 Commando could support so an LAD (Light Aid Detachment) had been provided in the form of a large four-wheel drive truck with winching cables fore and aft, a small crane mounted on the back, two mechanics, and its own wireless. Another addition was a vehicle with *un Medicin sans Frontieres* and a nurse, French and English-speaking Italians, bound for Kasongo. The stopover at Kituwe was treated exactly as a night stopover en route. 8 Commando personnel had spent their last night in the luxury of buildings; along with the new arrivals, they slept the night in the open, which provided excellent training for their future.

The road onward to the final destination at Kiambi began quite well on packed clay and angular gravel with washouts and old track ridges which could be astutely dodged. Roddy led the advance in Tommy Farr's German jeep followed by Equipe 1, whose commander Amarjit Singh was in the cab of the first troop-carrying truck. Behind this equipe came Erik in his jeep, followed by the magnificent half-track with a mounted GPMG, the big wireless and its newly recruited radio ham operator, Michel, Willie Mitchell, a driver from Equipe 2, trained to amazing skill by the expert tutor Corporal Tommy Farr, and five troopers from the same equipe. The three civilian trucks were alternated in the centre of the convoy with the Katanga military trucks behind them. The Commando 'vehicles one ton', which carried stores and supplies, each had a GPMG mounted in the normally canvas-roofed cockpit. At times the convoy reached exhilarating speeds of forty miles per hour which brought the average up to just less than thirty miles per hour. Erik wanted to spend their first night away from the vast swamplands around Lake Mweru. The convoy would strike through between Pweto and Kalamata going in an almost straight line from the river to Bodoma.

Normal traffic to Bodoma would have made for the major town of Pweto at the head of the lake. However, taking a convoy through a town choked with pedestrian crowds, donkey carts, laden trucks, and buses, was sufficient reason to find an alternative route. Were the convoy to be attacked when in the middle of town, it would be trapped; and should the troops fight their way out, it may well be with only the remnants of their fighting force and none of the supplies it was their job to deliver. There would inevitably be a slaughter of the town's populace, a subject for extremely bad

The crossing point was a small cabled ferry powered from a diesel engine housed on the upstream side of the flatdeck; the cable ran round a large wheel firmly fixed on each bank in an almost continuous loop wound onto big wheels by the engine. On the right bank, the operators and their families had formed a makeshift village on the edge of a steep beach, in the shade of

tall trees a little inshore of the bank. On the upstream edge, they
had cleared a bit of forest for gardens, and poles had been raised
up and over the stream where men could perch to fish; there were
also two big canoes drawn up on the sand. It crossed in calm, but
steadily flowing water upstream of where the current stalled at a
stony shelf edge before boiling on, creamy white and tan, through
a stretch of rocky rapids. To cross, one laden vehicle at a time,
the cable was wound onto the wheel by the engine; to return the
winding was reversed. The ferry was parked on the convoy's side
of the river when Roddy's lead vehicle pulled up.

The ferry people could speak French, and when some
money changed hands, shipping began. The first vehicle across
was Roddy's 'Renard' (a name the ex-German scout car had
mysteriously acquired) meaning advance HQ, comprising the
forward scouts and a wireless set. In its cramped back space,
a GPMG had been mounted on a stand allowing, with some
balletic footwork by the gunner, three hundred and sixty
degrees of fire. Leaving the bridgehead to take shape under
Amarjit's direction, Roddy set off to reconnoitre the route. Away
from the convoy, the scout vehicle made good speed.

There was some space on the ferry's flat deck, so most
of Amarjit's men, standing and crouching, came across with
mortars and GPMGs to form a bridgehead. Next, came HQ
in 'Tommy's Half Track' with as many of Equipe 2 as possible,
followed by the trucks of Equipes 1 and 2 and men of Equipe 3.
Priority now was bringing over the balance of the troopers of
equipes one and two so that the advance could continue.

A third troop-carrier truck loaded with troops was on the
ferry when the rope leading back from the far bank to the
motor on board snapped. The ferry immediately swung on the
strong quiet flow to come up with a crunch on the stony ridge
above the cataract. The motormen on the ferry attempted to
draw it back to its start point. The ferry remained firmly stuck
on the rocks.

While this was happening, Erik had been called to take a
wireless call. The call was from Roddy.

When the scout group had reached a point about two or
three miles distant from their estimated location of Bodoma,

they picked out a plume of black smoke rising against the sky. They drove up onto a bald hillock and through the field glasses confirmed that they were seeing smoke from a large fire, and by calculation, it must be at Bodoma. As they scanned the ground from the hilltop, they spotted, in the bush below, two men moving away from Bodoma, parallel to their position. They swept down from the hill to intercept them. Hearing the engine and seeing the vehicle bouncing towards them, the two men stopped. Both could speak French and told how they had been outside the town when the raiders arrived in two trucks. They said they could hear screams and shouting and shooting. They had run away.

Roddy radioed Erik at once.

'Erik, we're at—'and he gave a map reference'—three miles out of Bodoma. There's a plume of black smoke rising. We have two escapees who say two truckloads of raiders arrived about two hours ago. They heard shouts, screams, and gunfire. I need troops immediately. I want to make a three equipe attack. I'll go in the centre with Amarjit's equipe one, equipe two will take the left and three on the right. I will control the attack from this HQ and keep in touch with you. RV [Rendezvous] will be at—'he gave the grid reference—'And could we have an interpreter please? Over.'

'Roger. We're being delayed by ferry breakdown. Your requested force will be on the way to the RV within one hour.'

At the crossing, what was needed now was some power on the other side of the river to pull at an angle from the ferry's bow in an upstream direction to get it off the rocks and to hold it there while the main rope was rejoined. Upon the scene of the ferry's—and the convoy's—plight, an engineer to take command suddenly appeared: Lieutenant Amarjit Singh RE. Using radio, he called the other bank and arranged for men to take the heftiest ropes from Erik's stores and take them across in a dinghy. With a party of men from his equipe and the ferry men, the separated broken tail was joined up to two twisted-together ropes from Twelfth Commando's supply. Enough tail end of the broken ferry rope was available to be pulled ashore by Amarjit's men on the right bank. The part still fixed on the ferry end was made fast to a strong point near the engine house. The other end, hauled to the shoreside, with a loop spliced into it, was attached the towing point of Tommy's half-track after being passed round the bole of a stout tree to come nearer to the required angle of effort and still allow the half-track to move along the shore. The LAD on the opposite bank was at a much-bigger angle on its shore also pointing upstream, its cable made fast to the ferryboat three quarters of the way along the side of the ferry to another steel ring bolted into the timbers, its purpose was to bring the front end of the ferry away from the rocks. The two troop trucks on the right bank, side by side, were roped up to the front of ferry. On maestro Singh's beat, all four vehicles steadily pulled along their appointed directions. Slowly but surely, with much engine noise to begin with, the four vehicles followed their tracks, putting the theory of a parallelogram of forces into effect, until the ferry was safely landed. With Tommy's half-track reversing while taking up slack, thus sustaining direction, it was easy for the LAD, with the purchase point of its rope moved aft on the ferry, to bring the ferry back for reloading, which it did with all haste. The priority troops for the attack were brought ashore on the far bank at once along with an ammunition supply. The two equipes mounted up and set off *a toute vitesse* for the RV.

Amarjit of number 1 and John Sparrow of number 2 spoke with Roddy over wireless, received and confirmed their orders. The cast of that rather jumbled dress rehearsal at Kituwe was going to face the music.

In a situation of this kind, niceties are kept in mind, but by necessity, they have to stay there. The nature of the conflict demands a tactical approach of its own, so the equipes made their way into the little town with as much yelling and noise as possible and all guns blazing. The concern the men had about the danger of killing civilians was satisfied in the worst way. It looked as if there were no civilians standing. Those on their feet were wielding pangas on already fallen bodies, the others, goading them on holding rifles which were now pointing at the oncoming troopers of the equipe. The Commandos moved from target to target in sweeping arcs, from weapons locked on automatic. The wing equipes, as well as following the main clearance plan, wanted to find the assailants' trucks to cut off escape; if possible keeping the vehicles in a working state; if not, too bad. From the central area, only one or two escaped the first onslaught of the Commandos. They would run into the arms of the surrounding equipes. The Commandos had to work in close cooperation with the centre equipe to avoid the great and real peril of being killed by their own fire. The trucks were found not far from the centre square of the hamlet settlement, with those intending flight already on board or still clambering on. After a treatment of hammering heavy machine guns, hand grenades were lobbed into both. Now, all of the force could be concentrated on clearing the village from the outside in.

There was not a man in 8 Commando who was not aware of the atrocities human beings can inflict on other human beings in degree of horror and scale. Most would have seen historical documentary film taken by photographers entering death camps like Belsen and Auschwitz. They would have read about the calculated starvation of Russian farmers who would not cooperate with the Russian communist regime. Some at least would have seen shocking photographs taken here in the Congo of workers with a hand cut off for 'slacking', not bringing in enough rubber latex. Shocking and sickening as those visual experiences may have been, they were removed, distant in time and place. Those experiences and their associated feelings did not prepare them for what they were seeing around them now in this shattered Congo settlement on a steamy summer day, under a tropic sun, dusty already after recent heavy rain.

How could one ever imagine seeing the steam of warmth rising from a corpse; the corpse of a man hacked to bits, a piece at a time, each piece after perhaps two or three hacks of a heavy machete; with its lifeblood still running out forming a puddle on the sand; the last feeble movement of its lungs stopped only seconds ago. No help to think that you had managed to kill the slaughterer, now lying dead by the corpse his evil machete still in his hand. Your bullet had caused his immediate death, and his pain would have lasted a fraction of a second. There were other bodies hanging from trees where they spent last hours hanging from trees by their wrists in perhaps their last phase of the torture begun in the hours before. All these murderous activities were going on while the screams and wailing of women locked up and separated from their children mixed with the wild shouting of the killers and torturers. The old Portuguese chaplain was hanging from a tree, his neck at a strange angle: blood from his head had run copiously onto the dirty white of his cassock which now looked fresh, laundry-clean in contrast with the drying blood. From the strangely distorted positions of his pendant arms and legs, it was agony to imagine what had been done to him before he was hoisted to spend his last minutes of life hanging by his fractured neck.

Doors bashed open by the Commandos revealed women, huddled together in darkness waiting for their fate of rape and death; or transportation for continuing use by the frenzied, depraved men. More reason for destroying the trucks. The male children who had not been killed were retained for recruitment to bear arms, or slavery, or simply death. The female teachers and the nuns were prized plunder, locked up and used for multiple raping by any killers who wished a change from the delights of the marihuana augmented, mad massacre. *Le Medicin sans frontier* and his nurse had moved amongst the stricken, selecting through a process of triage those with the best chance of survival. Those chosen were treated where found; there was no time to spare to move them and nowhere better whither they might be moved.

Meanwhile Erik had kept Etat Major in Elizabethville informed of events at Bodoma. By the time the restructured convoy arrived there, Roddy could report that the settlement was now secure and prisoners were being held. Unless the enemy wanted the deserted village for a camp, there was no longer anything left there for the enemy to return to. The church was still burning, as were several other buildings, the acrid smoke and all the smells hanging in the hot still air under the canopy of the trees standing round, themselves now bearing wounds, mute witnesses to the havoc.

A situation report was relayed to Etat Major. HQ now had transport on its way from Pweto to bring in the survivors and take care of the dead.

Pending the arrival of relief, equipes 4 and 5 provided a perimeter defence and rear guard while the convoy was reformed. When ready, the convoy was eager to move away from the horror that was now the charred charnel house that had once been a school for happy children, a hospital where the sick found succour and the chapel where Christians sought the goodwill of their God. Bodoma as once known was no more.

The next objective of the convoy was to deliver the new Katangese troops to Kiambi, so its route was northwest taking a twisting track along the hill slopes. Clearly they would not reach Kiambi in the remaining daylight and the scouting party had to look for a suitable piece of ground where a harbour for the Commando could be set up before darkness. A piece of ground, clear under the canopy of mixed, spaced trees, free of lianas, and thorn bush with laagering ground for the trucks around, and within it, low scrub and further scattered trees allowed a meagre fifty-yard field of fire all round. Immediately the convoy halted, the light vehicles and two troop carriers strung out in a line swept the area right around the laager. Across the track, at its edge, the Katangese soldiers were given machetes to clear a strip of growth to minimize enemy concealment. The trucks, positioned under the aerial camouflage of the trees, had easy access to the track. The equipes each took a segment of the perimeter posted sentries and dug in. The young Katanga Sous Lieutenant was very pleased that his troops should have a role in the preparation and duties of defending the laager, literally side by side, with the men of 8 Commando. It would have been lunacy to imagine that enemy did not know the whereabouts of the convoy; it's what the enemy would decide to do with that knowledge that was important.

In a way similar to Kenya freedom uprising, the general Kikuyu population, including their leader Jomo Kenyatta, had planned a pathway to independence along more orthodox lines. But Mau Mau arose amongst a small minority of people who believed that more extreme measures involving, murder slaughter of the whites, and terror, would lead more quickly to a better, final outcome. Mau Mau used witch doctors, and rites of beliefs in the power of magic that would give immunity to their terrorists who, except for pangas and rudimentary weapons, were unarmed in the normal military sense. This was the case in Katanga with the Jeunesses, angry, radical young men who did not want fall in with Tshombe's idea of Katanga independence within a federation and its amicable relations with whites. It was these people that the mercenaries were fighting.

While the laager and its defences were being established, even over the noise of shovelling earth to make weapon pits, and latrines, everyone was conscious of the noise of continuous drumming. Blocks of the rhythm would change and sounds would change. The Katanga officer was able to tell Erik that these were messages telling warriors to gather: he said that when they had smoked enough *dagga* and drunk the water of invincibility administered by the witch doctor, they would attack. The Jeunesses may already be on the way and that we should listen for the sounds of their approach which would not be silent. Darkness had had fallen, so that ideas that native warriors did not attack in darkness, seemed misguided. Erik ordered stand-to. First there was a murmuring which grew louder and louder. Then there were the first loud yells. So close. Then the noise became louder and hellish. Each equipe fired its Very pistol, launching a ball of glaring light into the sky, a lingering, eerie brilliance, almost stationary, each flare lighting a good fifty yards all round rendering every man in silhouette. The equipes poured fire from automatic weapons into the area before them, selecting targets when appropriate, taking careful aim to kill. Visibly the bodies of the crazed attackers were falling in bundles in front of them. *Pour encourager les autres*, two-inch mortar bombs were fired, so close to their own lines that the troopers had to keep their heads down on firing. The noise had died; there were a few voices left to make any; then a haunted silence. The troopers continued to fire at the slightest sign of movement: no move was made to ensure that the enemy had gone. It would be inviting loss of life to venture troops into the scrub to check, so it would have to be fifty-fifty stand-to all night.

Erik and Roddy, as in similar situations, alternated with each other—two on, two off—throughout.

It was a relief, when daylight came, that the Katanga officer said that the enemy would, most likely, prefer to bury their own dead. It would have been a hell of a task; and none of the Europeans had any experience of burying the dead in the customary crouched position of the local people. So the one hundred bodies, with due care, were brought onto the clear ground and laid side by side. While carrying the feet of a dead Jeunesse to the line, a trooper bent to lower his burden at precisely the right moment. A thwack sounded as an arrow struck his backpack, an immediate action by a corporal who had seen the arrow's swift flight. Instinctively spinning round and aiming up into a tree, shattered its foliage and branches with 9 mm. shot. After two or three seconds, there was a rustle of leaves, the sound of snapping branches. The body of the sniper, following gravity's law, fell in with a dull, soft thud on the hard ground: an explosive gasp of air from his lungs, and a little puff of powdery earth silently settling, another life had suddenly ceased.

The troops were keen to leave the site and asked to have breakfast somewhere along the route.

Bringing the Katangese troops to Kiambi completed the Commando's second objective. There was time now to clean thoroughly all the weaponry, have a major sort out and re-stowing of the Commando's gear, do a 'make and mend' on their own, and for a proper rest, while they awaited orders.

Etat Major was concerned about the safety of any Europeans who may be anywhere in Katanga. A voluminous sheet of orders was sent to Erik at the Kiambi garrison station by light aircraft.

8 Commando would be required to sweep the area to the east of Kiambi as far as the shore of Lake Tanganyika and to the head of Lake Mweru and north to a line south of Albertville. It was to rescue endangered people, gather and feedback intelligence, engage the enemy in battle, and take prisoners. It was not required to enter the high forest-covered Mituba Mountains. Mobility would be enhanced by two Land Rovers and wireless sets. The LAD was not mentioned—certainly not

by 8 Commando—neither was Tommy's Truck nor the Fox. Another trailer was requested and supplied without demur.

On the very day that Erik had received his orders, there arrived at Kiambi Garrison the most amazing man in an almost equally amazing truck. The man had brought concerning news. On his travels, he become aware of the Jeunesses gangs roaming wide in the countryside and asked the garrison intelligence officer whether two European survey geologists had reported their whereabouts. They had not: the garrison was unaware of their existence. They army immediately sought reports by wireless from all stations. Nothing was known of the geologists. Mr. Herbert Entwhistle, for that was the name of the amazing man, was directed to speak with Major Barron.

Herbert Entwhistle was short, lean, with bright twinkling eyes set deep in glare-furrowed sockets. He seemed restless like a clock spring ready to strike the hour. He spoke truly to the Tottenham type that he was, in a pleasant voice that hinted knowledge, experience, and literacy. A couple of weeks ago, he told Erik, he had welded and machined a broken part on the test drilling rig of two Belgian geologists and their African drilling team. He indicated the location on the map Erik placed on the table. Erik asked Michel to recall the O Group which he had dismissed not more than two hours before. Asking Herbert if he wouldn't mind staying with him while the group assembled, they engaged in discussion which Erik found militarily and socially rewarding. Michel, Willie Mitchell, and the subalterns arrived very soon, and Erik was pleased to introduce Mr. Entwhistle. The upshot of the meeting was that Erik pointed out, 'This falls within the scope of our orders. I see no reason why we should not make this our first search and rescue objective. We'll leave at sparrow's tomorrow; no offence intended, Simon. Michel, Roddy, gentlemen, I'll leave it to you to make your plan and the movement order. Let me know soonest when I have to throw off my eiderdown tomorrow. On your behalf, gentlemen, I shall invite Mr. Entwhistle to be our guest for dinner this evening.'

'Major Barron', Herbert spoke up, 'I'd like to make a request. I think I could be of help in your operation. I have been all over most of Africa; I speak Swahili and bits of this and that. I've been in Eastern Congo for about five years doing bush engineering from Kivu to Kasai and down into Rhodesia. I want to come with you; on my own responsibility, but under your command. I think you'll find having my vehicle an advantage.'

Erik looked around the assembled group. There wasn't one man who couldn't see some advantage in having Mr. Entwhistle with them. 'Herbert, it looks as if you're on. I know you don't think it will be a Kenya safari. Roddy, you may wish to invite Mr. Entwhistle to part of your planning meeting? I'm also going to suggest—if he agrees—that Herbert should be up with Roddy and the Scouts. Yes, his vehicle would be an asset and I know just the man who could handle it.'

Roddy volunteered, 'I think we all know who you mean; Tommy Farr?'

'Herbert, what do you think of that arrangement?' Erik asked.

'I agree. Tactically I'd be best with the scouts; and I have a notion that you understand how important my truck is to me and that you're sure you've got the right man in your Tommy Farr to handle it.'

To take full advantage of daylight, the Commando would need to be moving by 0630 hours next day, make as much progress as possible, so that, all things being equal, they could harbour and be dug in before dark. Immediately, each equipe commander must hold a briefing and issue the warning order for next day. Part of the reorganization on reaching Kiambi was to make the Commando ready for whatever the next action may turn out to be; vehicles had been serviced and fuelled up, rations and water for ten days had been loaded, and the equipe commanders had done kit checks. The order of march had been decided: with men and their weapons aboard, they could start at once.

'Right; Michel, gentlemen, any questions?'

Michel looked around: heads wagged a negative. 'No, sir,' responded Michel.

'Very good, I'll leave you to your planning. Herbert, if you'd like to come with me we'll go and find Corporal Tommy Farr.' So the long and the short of it went on their quest.

Tommy knew from the sounds of a different motor that there a new vehicle had come on the premises. To see it, with its owner, and later learn that he was to drive it operationally was stepping into a world of dreams. Erik Barron would have been quite amazed if these two had not struck the right notes at first meeting.

'Tommy, I'd like you to meet Mr Herbert Entwhistle, the owner of this mighty GMC.'

'Pleased to meet you, Mr Entwhistle That's a mighty rig you have there,' Tommy responded with obvious enthusiasm.

'And I'm pleased to meet you, Tommy. An' if everyone around here keeps calling me "Mr", I'll come out in a rash. My moniker's 'erbert.'

'Right, I'll leave you to get the instruction done. We're for the road tomorrow, Tommy. Your equipe commander's on his way to tell everyone. You will be driving Herbert's pride and joy.'

That night in the mess, Herbert Entwhistle was the cynosure of all. One question after the other was asked of him; each brought a clear and ready response. Where it might add to, and not cloud the issue, he would colour the facts with enhancing detail about terrain, tribes, people, situations, and sights. Unavoidably his own story became intermingled, to the added pleasure of his listeners. He was one of that breed which turns up from its ranks men, and more often that might be imagined, women, each on his or her own, an individual of the species, in odd places, at odd times, anywhere on earth; or even at sea. They are often hard, sometimes humourless, but mostly quite the contrary, rich with experiences and capable of doing most of the incredibly diverse deeds that travelling on one's own demands for survival. Herbert was one of these. He was recruited to the RAF and had not homed to his Tottenham tenement since that day when he left RAF Uxbridge for the dream posting to the Empire Air Training Scheme in Rhodesia. He had taken full advantage of his time in the air force; completed training as machinist, fitter and turner, motor mechanic and had ended up as a flight sergeant. Africa held him in thrall. He took every possible opportunity to be in the wild; hunting, exploring, on safari, and learning about the peoples in open-eyed, unprejudiced wonder. He had contrived to have himself demobbed in Rhodesia when his service came to an end. On release, he set out to travel Africa from north to south and crossings east to west at various points. It was in Casablanca that he came across what he considered would provide him with the basis for a future way of living: it was a huge five-tonner, ex-GI, GMC, four-wheel-drive truck. He had transformed the area behind the driver's seat by opening the bulkhead to fit out a kitchen–dining–sitting room–library–bedroom with showering services. Behind another bulkhead was a fully fitted-out workshop complete with lathe, compressor, and generator—the smithy and its forge had to be outside under an extension canopy. He was living a continually happy present with a never-ending supply of work and happy customers, most now friends, who looked forward to seeing the massive yellow leviathan bursting out in front of the following, swirling sea of its dust cloud.

It had been a hot night, but each man under an issue mosquito net (demanded of Q Store, with joint voices, by Erik and Michel) had slept the way each different man would, who was going out to God knows what in the days to come. But they now knew what they were doing in action and felt that their team play was improving.

The military vehicles were making long moving shadows that crossed and mingled with the shadows of the roadside trees as the column began to move one vehicle after the other taking up its designated spacing behind the one in front leaving behind the strong smells of petrol and motor exhaust concentrated around the vehicles which had been awaiting their move with engines idling. The mechanical snake stretched its vertebrae to equal spaces and speed until its whole body took on the purpose and direction of its hunt. The brain and corpuscles of this snake, the officers and troops of 8 Commando, were feeling the tingling excitement of imminent striking action. Ahead of the body, the snake's long flickering tongue would guide the body's direction and sense the whereabouts of the prey. Roddy, driving his Fox with Herbert at his side, a wireless operator and a gunner in the back, were the alerting nerves of the 8 Commando snake. The Fox would move further ahead out of sight of the main body, eager to find the quarry.

About noon, the main body stopped for a slightly extended comfort break; sentries posted, the men stretched their legs, and consumed their packed lunch ration of fruit, sandwiches, and hot tea from an urn in the LAD. They dispersed around the area in maximum groups of their tactical fours, their weapons lying ready, their eyes watchful as they spoke with each other. With perfect timing, the last swig of tea was swallowed, the last fly button done up when Willie Mitchell's voice shouted out an urgent, 'Mount up! Mount up!' The command was relayed by corporals along the line. The troops scrambled. The hunt was on.

Herbert, looking around sensing the terrain while recollecting the little-used track they were on, said, 'Roddy, we're getting close now. This little breeze will help us, we're up wind of the site, but we'll have to keep engine noise as low as we can. We might be as little as six hundred yards away. We should stay this side of the rise ahead and get out and have a look.'

'Right, Herbert, I'll do my best.'

Herbert had brought his own rifle, a Holland and Holland .375 that regularly filled his larder, and made him very popular when he turned up at a big village with a freshly killed eland or wart hog in the back of the GMC. He was no slouch in the gentle arts of field craft. Taking what cover they could on the edge of the crest, they looked ahead. Before they had properly begun a visual search, the light wind was bringing them sounds of shouting from about a mile away. Simultaneously they faced each other with the same thought in mind. 'I'll signal Erik,' Roddy said tersely and ran down to the Fox. 'Danny, are you onto our OC?'

'Yes, sir', said Danny, handing Roddy the mike and the headset, 'he's waiting out.'

'Erik, we're a mile away from a raiding party at the geologists' location and going to move in immediately to engage. Suggest main force follow the planned track. Urgent support needed.' He had almost gasped out the telegrammatic words in hoarse clipped tones. He knew that time was the essence.

'Roger. I'll come up myself with your equipe. Good hunting, Roddy. Over.'

'Look forward to seeing you. Out.' And Roddy and his Fox were off and hunting.

Erik's words had also been clipped and minimal. He too knew the need for speed. He took his HQ forward in Tommy's truck and brought the Land Rovers with guns and grenade launchers forward with him. He ordered Philippe to take command of the column, to make haste, and to follow the drills when they reached the area of the fire fight.

Herbert was in the back of the Fox now while Danny drove. Between his knees, he clasped his own rifle a Holland and Holland .375, bolt action, five-round box magazine, 'V' sights set for one hundred yards; across his shoulders, a leather bandolier of Holland and Holland ammunition, the rifle's eight and a half pound weight was comfortable for him because, for a short man, his power to weight ratio was amazingly good. He was well used to his weapon: capable as it was, with a suitably aimed shot and the right ammunition, to bring down big game, he had only ever used it to feed himself and others.

They drove the Fox down off the track to their left and turned to face a manageable hill covered in scrub and huge boulders and made their way to its crest.

'Danny, watch the rear and the Fox, Cyril take the gun up. Spread out. We'll have a look over. Fire when you see a target. C'mon.'

They reached the ridge and chose their cover. The scene below was a vicious industry of hacking and killing and men hauling other men, sagging from huge wounds, up into the iron web of the drilling rig to hang them where two already hung. Staked out on the ground were two Europeans being given the rough surgical opening up, intent on taking from the victims their beating hearts and the starting seeds of life. Already the chest of one was being hacked open to disclose, and give up, its living heart. A hail of automatic fire disrupted this depraved ceremony and the surgeons of unearthly powers folded in bundles across their sacrificial subjects. Herbert moved off to one side of the ridge very quickly and found a tree and a rock to break his shape with their shadows. Nothing on or near him would shine. Bent on one knee, without fumbling, he pulled from his bandolier five rounds and laid them on a piece of cloth from his pocket, he drew his rifle to his shoulder flipped up the backsight, took aim on one of six men in the mob who had a rifle, and standing up, were beginning to return fire. He fired. One man with a rifle fell. He pulled back the bolt of his rifle in a fluid movement, another round slid into the breech. He fired again. A second later, he dropped another man. Twisting his body over his left foot, reload, aim, fire. Third man down. In under eight seconds, all those who had been carrying rifles were dead on the ground. Except one. Now, with a speed of movement that couldn't be called haste, he refilled his magazine with the rounds from the cloth by his knee. He then stopped enemy rifleman six. A man ran in to retrieve the fallen rifle and turned to run: two paces into his flight, he appeared to leap forward headfirst, stretched flat on the ground. He was dead.

Roddy and his group could not go down into that space now. Remember the archer? How many of the enemy were out of sight when the firing began? Don't be impatient. Wait for the supporting troops to arrive. Make this a defensive position and wait. What can you do for those down there now? They harboured. They reported to the boss on the wireless: and waited.

It was not as long as it may have seemed to those waiting before a mobile squadron of the half-track, the Land Rovers and a troop carrier of Equipe 7 arrived. Very close behind, and already seen to be taking independent routes around the objective to form a net, were the tactical troop-carrying vehicles of the column. Tommy's truck with Erik and his HQ, guns ready, descended to the geologists' camp and the strewn bodies on the ground. They went first to the bodies of the staked-out Europeans mutilated their genitals crudely removed, one with his chest cavity gashed open, his sternum cleft by panga blows, his heart exposed on the rough edges of the smashed ribs, his torn shirt saturated in his blood. Troopers cut the geologists' wrists and ankles free from the stakes which held extended their bodies taut. The slaughter had kept the raiders engrossed; otherwise they would most surely have set on fire anything combustible. There was an open-sided tent with a table on which contour maps with colours indicating rock types, held down by heavy slabs of metal a tube with a sample had been opened on the table its contents exposed for examination. There was a trailer which served as office and sleeping space for the two geologists. Was it disdain for paper documents that reminded them of childhood days when they had been beaten as they laboured to learn the white man's French language? Was it to ridicule the white man's obsession with paper which could stare at for hours on end, flip it over leaf by leaf from stacked piles? Whatever the reason, someone had perhaps delighted, when everything paper was seized from the office in casting it on the ground where the light breeze would now and again set a piece to flutter away, a little at a time, across loess soil.

The geologists' research could be valuable information for Katanga, so Erik, Roddy, and a trooper set to, to gather up the littered documents. Erik was stacking them for packing up to hand over to HQ when his eyes lit upon a half dozen documents of heavier paper clipped together. A brief flick through them indicated that they were claims for mining tenements, unregistered. He did not add them to the growing pile, for which the trooper had gone to find a receptacle of some kind. Erik folded these and thrust them into the map packet on his trouser leg. Roddy looked at him enquiringly. Erik understood the look. It told Erik that Roddy knew he was doing something not quite kosher. Erik said, 'Roddy things are politically becoming very complex in this conflict. There is a growing struggle amongst the political leaders. Who knows what the outcome will be, and who will protect the interest of these dead men? I see, and understand, your concern. But we are not normal soldiers, and this is not a normal political situation. Who knows who will uphold what laws? Who knows how many of the current political elite will not seize what they can and flee? No, it is better that these men's efforts be in my safekeeping and care.'

'I understand what you're saying and I trust you, Erik,' said Roddy evenly, looking directly at his eyes.

In blankets, taken from their beds, the shattered corpses of the two Europeans were wrapped and laid out behind the cab in a troop carrier. HQ had instructed they be taken to Stanleyville.

The circling equipes had killed more enemy and taken four prisoners two of whom were wounded. They were secured and made fast to an inside rail in the troop-carrying truck where the wrapped bodies were lying. Herbert was to choose the best and quickest way to Leopoldville.

The men of the Commando now deserved some relaxation. They were quartered in barracks an easy stroll from a luxurious swimming pool, bars, and restaurants. Apart from having to book in at the guard room before 2200 hours, they were free from 1300 hours when all regimental duties and training were done.

The weeks of their six months were speeding by filled by similar heartbreaking engagements. Clearing a small town without much practice in street fighting, losing two men really affected the feelings of the whole Commando which by then had become tightly bonded. The emotion translated to anger, a dangerous mood when fighting men must not let that sentiment impair impartial, professional combat skills and self-control.

Enemy activity, which took place on a whim, was difficult for intelligence to anticipate, until once when intelligence had got wind of an attempt to land a big supply of weapons and ammunition on a beach on Lake Tanganyika north of Albertville. There had been movements of enemy groups to camp on sites near the coast from which, quite quickly, they could assemble to tranship the weapons and provide a defence against a possible Katanga gendarmerie force. Intelligence updates indicated that as well as armaments, the enemy had intended landing foreign forces assembling across Lake Tanganyika. It was to be an invasion. It was to be the task of 8 Commando under its own command, but in conjunction with Katanga forces, to blunt the attack from the landward side and damage and destroy the arms shipment.

Erik called 8 Commando together. It was an open meeting, out in the sunlight, on a chosen sloping spot with officers and NCOs mixed through the group and equipes blended into the one whole body that 8 Commando had become.

'Every man must know what was in store and what the implications are. Whatever else, this is going to be a big one for us,' Erik told them. 'We have never worked in conjunction with any sizeable Katanga force; nor indeed has a Katanga force ever been in a major engagement. We are going to have to be even more flexible than we have proved to be before. Bear in mind there will be casualties. Our planning will carefully include detailed *casevac* drills. We have only just received this news and our orders. Our planning starts now. Obviously we must prevent the enemy creating a beachhead or getting any of the weapons ashore. There will be an opportunity to damage a major enemy force. You might like to think along these lines. When you've done some thinking, talk with your corporals and equipe commanders about your ideas. Get your usual readiness drills done while you're thinking. I can't give you a warning order now. Be as ready as you can to stand-to. Now what I'm going to say is an inviolable principal of warfare; security. Do not talk about this to anyone outside of 8 Commando. Careless talk costs lives. Do not give any sign in your behaviour that you are excited about a pending action. I'll ask the adjutant to arrange for the canteen staff to have the evening off, so it'll be self-service and you'll be free to talk amongst yourselves. Out-of-barracks leave stops from this minute. No one can leave these barracks until further orders. Thank you all. Get weaving.'

A mood of excitement pervaded the planning when the officers got together. This would be a different kind of engagement; it would require different kinds of plans: different kinds of plans required different kinds thinking about plans. The period of their engagement was running out; let them go out in a blaze of glory; this might be their grand finale. Michel got in touch with intelligence: it was imperative, he urged them, that they know what kind of craft the enemy was going to use in the transfer of the troops and ammunition across the lake. What kinds of heavier machine guns 8 Commando could be provided with? Was there any small moveable artillery they could avail themselves of? Even as he was talking new information had come from the Belgian contacts in Tanganyika. An old lake steamer had been acquired on lease. It was going to be taken down to lie off a point out from Mpanda rail terminal. Armaments would be trucked to a point on the beach, transferred to small craft to be loaded onto the steamship. An old Belgian naval vessel with a two-pounder gun was lying at Albertville, serviceability unknown. On hearing this news, a sub-plot was quickly devised to check the vessel out. Herbert, the naval gunner John Sparks, and Danny Boulter, the trawler man, would go to the Stanleyville port just round from the main town disguised (!) as civilian tradesmen and would be seen to be, very obviously, working on the refurbishment of the old trading vessel rafted up alongside. These tradesmen had taken up residence in a far from posh hotel on the dock where they made sure that everyone on the staff knew what they were doing and their dreams of future fortune working for any, and all, the belligerents who would pay their rates. Comms with 8 Commando HQ were by wireless from Herbert's GMC. It was found that the old gunboat had not been totally neglected, and from what John Sparks found on examination, it could do all that it was meant to do after Herbert had thoroughly gone over the traversing gear. Short of actually running the main motor and firing the gun, all looked well. Michel had checked the availability of ammunition and secured ten charged rounds which, when cunningly concealed in a bundle of planks, were delivered to the old trader by Katanga officers in disguise. To test the motor on the gunboat, the motor on the old trader had to be made to run. Under the cover of darkness when no could be sure where the exhaust was coming from, both motors were run simultaneously, and after easing the rafting up lines a bit, they even moved the gunboat a yard or so ahead and astern. It was 'O Jubilate!' on board when Herbert rang 'Finished with Engines' on the engine room telegraph. After a call to HQ, they celebrated with a few beers on board while the motors cooled down, then, all closed and secure, they went to their hotel.

L'Etat Major had appointed Erik Commander 'Operation Rose', with Operation HQ at Leopoldville Captain Foucault would be the staff officer and liaison officer between L'Etat Major and 8 Commando. Captain Mckenzie would be 2 i/c 'Operation Trasimeno'.

In very basic terms, the plan was to intercept and sink the troopship steamer and its cargo of weapons; to encircle and destroy the enemy beachhead force.

To support 8 Commando, there would be a company of Katanga troops from Kabala and Kongolo, both being on rail links; leaving the more highly endangered garrisons and posts fully manned, and capable of providing support should the enemy mount further assaults.

Would the enemy to choose to carry out their operation by the light of the moon or take advantage of the darkness of a moonless night four days away? The enemy chose the moonless night and, to reach their landing point on the other side would have to leave the eastern lake shore before dark. In the days before the moonless night, the old naval gunboat was seen to make small sorties out on the lake crewed by what appeared to be Katanga men in Katanga uniforms there were one or two bearded Europeans in casual civilian clothing. The drinks which were being continually passed around when they were seen on deck, and their attention being drawn to beauty points by the extended arms of an officer or two seemed to indicate that there was a bit of a jolly going on aboard. One day only the tradesmen were aboard when the vessel sailed out. Once well clear of land, it turned north and went to take up station behind a northern promontory at the head of a sweeping bay. An observer looking south from a vessel on the lake would not see the gunboat.

The enemy ground forces were gathering inland of the lake in groups of hundreds scattered in the scrub, creek beds, and undulating land. Katangese forces were ready to move by companies, a mile or more behind in a tactical advance, as the enemy groups each got up to move and concentrate above the shoreline.8 Commando would take up the southern sector and they too were lying in wait spread out, camouflaged, motionless, silent. At dusk, a light breeze began to blow from the lake, only stars lit the land and lake through gaps in the moving cloud.

The gunboat rounded its headland and made its way north: ready in the breech, a high-explosive shell with an incendiary round ready to fire immediately after. The .5-calibre Browning M2 mounted on the for'ard corner of the bridge on the starboard side, on a stand of Herbert's construction. The first belt had been filled with two high-explosive rounds followed by one incendiary. Two 'Able Seamen' had been recruited from the Commando volunteers; when they were not loading in the gun turret, they were passing ammunition belts to the .5 cal gunner, or applying GPMG fire on the enemy vessel.

Aboard the gunboat, Sergeant Denton had calculated his steaming time and made a guess about the enemy's speed, calculated their steaming time. He checked his watch and had Hebert shut down his engine. In the almost absolute silence, it seemed as if they had spirited into another world. There was the soft lapping of wavelets against the hull. Danny Boulter seized Andrew's arm. 'Listen!' he said, just above a whisper. Andrew turned his face into the breeze. 'Yes! Yes!' His whisper showing the excitement. One of the AB's whispered, 'I've got it.' It was the enemy's vessel steadily approaching.'

'We'll stay still,' said Andrew in a soft voice even with the knowledge that they were upwind, the dominating idea was that sound travels far across the un-obstructing surface of calm water. Aboard the enemy ship, its engine noise would drown out all but an even louder noise. 'Okay, Herbert, let your engine idle and with just enough power to hold our position and let's work out where they're going.'

'Aye aye, sir,' said Herbert.

All available eyes were focused ahead. An hour passed. Milo Stoic, Croatian AB, pointed ahead and almost shouted something in Croatian which most likely meant, 'Look!' Everybody followed his pointing finger. 'Yes, just a blob, you could only guess it's a boat,' Danny announced. The blob was becoming larger, its lower part now appearing broader than the upper. 'Right, Herbert, let's advance to contact full speed ahead.'

'Aye, aye, sir,' he replied. Immediately the gunboat began to surge; a bow wave breaking, a bone in her throat, and a wake-gurgling astern.

'May I have the pleasure of taking down the garden shed from over my turret, Sarge?' asked the gunner.

'You may remove our for'ard camouflage, Gunner Sparks,' replied the ship's commander. Andrew took a bearing on the object ahead its bulk increasing by the minute; the front view of an approaching hull and superstructure becoming clearer. More rapidly it became a Lake Tanganyika cargo vessel. Then it turned to starboard presenting its port side. Andrew called below, 'Give her all she's got, Herbert!'

'Aye, aye, sir!' And the canny engineer gave out his engine's valued reserve power.

The gunner was now in his turret, a HE round loaded. 'Use your sights and ranging. Have you enough visibility to engage. With the breeze and the distance, I wouldn't chance the Very pistol yet. Danny, when your range is right, fire with HE. Get their controls. ABs, clear their decks.'

'About to engage.' It was John on the voice tube. Then, brusquely, 'Engaging now!' The gun roared. The blast blew back on the bridge. There was a hell of a crash on the trader as the top of the wheelhouse blew away in wood splinters. John lowered his elevation and put a round below its water line.

Andrew sent up a Very light to signal H Hour for the ground forces.

The rocket had exploded. Now a brilliant, quivering light hung in the darkness from the floating parachute flair that appeared spotlight a war drama from Ealing Studios. The .5 cal was making a hellish noise, while its heavy HE rounds punched holes in the timber hull. The sea around the trader was a mass of bodies dead and alive jostling and bumping each other. There was no more enemy fire from the enemy vessel. Next John struck it below the water line with an incendiary round. There was a flaming explosion immediately and the old timbers began at once to burn. The trader lost weigh and steerage. 'No point in taking unused rounds back,' the gunner was saying to the AB who now, having no targets for his GPMG, had returned to his role as 'gunner's mate'. John was determined to sink her. He did. But to make it convincing now; and to complete their mission, it took two additional rounds before they saw her fill up and go below the surface of the lake.

When the first Very light flare lit the sky, it signalled H Hour for the troops on shore. They would cross their start lines. They would advance upon the enemy. The land battle would begin.

Major Erik Barron had devised a three-sided moveable 'fence' of advancing troops, the lake shore being the open side. 8 Commando had taken the southern side and lapped around to form a part of the western side. The remainder of the western 'fence' and the entire northern fence' down to the beach was the assault responsibility of the newly formed Katanga force. All troops were to keep closer together than is normal and make sure that no one part of the fence get too far ahead, causing the fence line to show a gap and potentially fall victim to their own fire. The enemy must not be allowed to break through the fence.

The wondrous brightness of the Very lights hung in the black sky, the loud explosions of the first shells, the loud fire of heavy machine gunning would already have caused alarm and awe. All eyes were on the lake, the source of these threatening effects. Now, random fire of two-inch mortars into the enemy groups, beginning close to their start lines and ranging forward by 8 Commando and the Katanga companies would cause confusion and add to the element of shock from the loud firing and the glaring lights in the sky above the lake. The general purpose machine guns on the western wing of the 'fence' were applying heavy, waist-level fire to their front, while the north and south wings were concentrating on the areas closest to the beach. Tall leafy trees were given special attention by the GPMGs.

Erik had left 8 Commando to get started under Roddy's command. He had positioned Tommy's truck with the big wireless on the face of a hill undercover of some trees and scrub from where he could see the whole battleground out to the lake, visible in the darkness only as a flatter form of darkness until the battle of the vessels began their engagement. No one could see the beaches and what might be happening there. The Katangese had their mortars going quickly and began their move forward keeping together very well at the controlling commands of their NCOs and officers. He roved along the rear of the troops assessing progress and what needed to be done. Some lone members or twos and threes of the enemy had lain down hidden in the patches of scrub and had not been flushed out as the troops advanced. When they thought all of the Gendarmerie had passed, they leapt out and ran. But the troops going forward had been trained to watch their backs and most evaders were gunned down. Some were rounded up and made prisoner. As the wings of the 'fences' were coming closer together, men could be spared to round up and guard taken prisoners.

The truth is that the fenced-in enemy force was annihilated. It was a massacre which very few had avoided, and of these, most were foreign troops who had swum ashore or been rescued from the water.

Major Barron, Operation Trasimeno Force Commander, could speak by wireless to Etat Major and report the operation had been completed with all objectives met.

With congratulations from HQ still in his ears, he spoke to the captain of the battleship and asked if all aboard could hear. 'Thank you all for a magnificent performance. Essentially, the real battle was yours. You have done very well. All steam ahead for your home port. We all look forward to meeting you there.' Having posted pickets, Erik gathered all together: 'Well done, everybody', he said, and then announced, 'I can now tell you that Operation Trasimeno is completed with all objectives met. Thank you for a perfect performance. With not a single casualty. Make ready as quickly as possible for an immediate return to Leopoldville. I'll wireless ahead to get the beer on ice.'

The erstwhile battlefield was now under control of the Katanga forces whom Roddy had gathered in their companies and, addressing them in French, thanked them for their effort and wished them well in their future and for a successful future for their new state.

The gunboat was going home in triumph, the sun about to appear on its port beam. A growling of engines announced that the convoy had begun to roll as the eager snake pulled its body into line, heading for its lair.

Throughout what had been, until only very recently, the old Belgian Congo, the digestion of the new freedom from colonial power was causing much gas and growling in the body politic and amongst some of the populace. The creation of Katanga was one of the events which would be part of a transition to something else not yet known. Inevitably, although a progression to Belgian control had been conceived before the event, there was impatience and disagreement that culminated in a ghastly civil war. External forces of China and Russia saw opportunity in the vacuum of departed colonial rule to further spread their own political dogma to counter and prevent the successful installation of the amorphous, pious, pretentious fantasy called liberal democracy.

Erik Barron and Roddy Mckenzie were at the point of stepping out of the kind of world they had grown up in and in whose values they had seen much sense. Their time in Katanga was up. Their time to make any decent contribution to a well-run stable sovereign state was past. The battle of Lake Trasimeno was an example of that past.

'We had the weapons and they had not,' said Roddy, corrupting the poem of Hilaire Belloc.

'Aye, but there will be weapons. And their introduction will be much more sophisticated than the Trasimeno effort. There will be various warring factions with equal weaponry. What will happen then doesn't bear thinking about,' responded Erik.

Roddy, sadly and bitterly, said, 'Bigger and better massacres for all factions. And old long-healed tribal wounds will be torn open again: discovered weaknesses, to be turned to their gain by people greedy for power, status and the fortunes in money that goes with them. Oh, we're a bad lot.'

'Perhaps not all of us, Rod. Even if it's just some us, we can try to do good for the folk around us. And that must be something worth trying for,' said Erik hopefully.

'You're right, Erik, and you know, it makes me feel that *I* have to do well, so that I'm in a position to be helpful?'

8 Commando rolled into Leopoldville, parked its trucks, and got down to the business of relaxing, glad that the episode of the massacre was over and hiding it under the merriment of relief, and burning off the detritus of the adrenalin that rattling back to base in trucks had merely left inside the men to clog the channels of feeling. There were no separate messes that day: it was one in, all in. Time, circumstance, and sharing ensured a high feeling of camaraderie.

The next day was devoted to one of the Commando's mammoth sort-outs and cleansings.

In mid-afternoon, a muster was called. Erik addressed the paraded troops to say, 'I have received our new orders from Etat Major. We are to start for Elizabethville tomorrow *ack emma*. When we get there, I want you to be totally regimental and give any and all who see you, civilian or military, a true picture of the good soldiers you are. You all know what scallywags there are in Highland regiments and you know tales of the Foreign Legion, but if any you have seen of these regiments put on a bit of bullshit, I know you would have felt proud just to be looking at them. Now, I'm not saying that any of you are rascals, and I'm sure you can put on a bit of regimental bullshit. We are going to have to do this in the barracks at Leopoldville.' He turned to Roddy, handed over the parade to him. He ordered the officers to fall out, and when they had marched off, he gave the parade to Willie Mitchell.

The return to Elizabeth was carried out tactically with high regard to security. Just in case unfriendly people anticipated that they would move on the main road, Herbert offered an alternative to Michel Foucault when asked. Harbouring, as in territory of enemy activity, they followed all the drills with the utmost diligence.

After only two nights out, for all their dislike of barracks, they were happy to be in Elizabethville. Next day at muster parade, Erik made another announcement. 'You realize of course that our contracts of service are about to expire. Due to international pressure on the government of Katanga, the termination will be brought forward. However, the good news is you will be paid up to the actual termination date. The day after tomorrow, we shall mount a farewell parade to receive the thanks of the colonel who is commandant of Etat Major; he is the highest-ranking officer in the Katanga army. I want you to prepare for a parade of a lifetime. I want you to do yourselves justice. There will be no issue of dress uniforms, but Captain Mckenzie and Sa'r Major Mitchell will help you to turn the sow's ears of your baggy denims into the silk purses of Savile Row suits. There will be strictly no leave until we march out and are officially dismissed. Good luck with your square bashing.'

What Erik did not tell them was that their Trasimeno Operation had been described in local and some international press as a massacre of innocent people by a rabble of foreign mercenaries. Etat Major was not prepared to allow Eighth Commando to leave in shame, yet they had to make their departure the least public possible. After the farewell parade, they would be dispersed across hotels in the city and taken by arranged transport to join their departure flights bookings for which would be fixed up in the intervening time, and even if it meant taking unusual routes, they would all be out of Elizabeth the day after the parade.

It was quite surprising how the whole body of troops took to the square bashing; the improvements to be made to attire, their pleasure to pull themselves up to stand erect, and the last rehearsals on the huge and sacred parade ground of Elizabethville. They had even achieved to damn near perfection, forming nine bodies of three equipes, for the 'Advance in Review Order'.

The Commemoration and Marching Out Parade took place at noon. Tropics or not, this was the hour. A dais had been raised on which Le Colonel de la Gendarmerie Katangese and his staff would stand. There would be not one political figure present.

There was no military band or the concerted male singing voices as of La Legion Etrangere in slow measured parade. It was up to officers and NCOs of 8 Commando to give the whole parade life. Their demeanour and quips during training, such as, 'My god, Stoic, if I weren't married, I'd make you an offer', and in response to a fart, from somewhere in the lines, Willie Mitchell asked, 'Did someone blow me a kiss?'—the whole readiness drills were peppered with this kind of banter. A tension was building, almost, but not quite, like going into battle. Willie Mitchell called his parade to attention and gave the parade to the 2 i/c,(Second in Command) Capt. Mckenzie. There after they completed their final rehearsal. Erik was there, watching with pride, then to participate in his own role. They were ready.

The colonel inspected the troops passing through every rank of all the equipes, looking into a man's face when he addressed one taking disciple time to look at each man on parade. His words of gratitude to the officers and men of 8 Commando sounded across the vast African parade ground with tones of sincerity. He talked of his staff and the true pleasure they had had working with such competent professional soldiers. Then, on Erik's Sandhurst voice of command, the Commando marched off, three equipes in turn, snapping into an eyes right on a subaltern's command. On that parade ground of very mixed military history, 8 Commando's day of glory was over.

The men then went to a barrack hall and morphed into civilians, swapping their uniforms of glory for the best civvy duds they had arrived in. There were buses waiting where they had to line up in order of the route on which their hotels lay. Perhaps hotel bed space was at premium. The hotels were far apart. Was this to discourage the entire equipe getting together in the city?

(Note: Herbert Entwhistle marched shoulder to shoulder with Tommy Farr in his equipe. He found where Tommy's hotel would be. He had a quite regular berth for the GMC when in town, so he parked it there and joined up with Tommy for the celebrations.)

Michel had arranged for Erik and Roddy to be in the same hotel and to travel out together on a Sabena flight to Bruxelles and on to London. From the moment he had left Australia to join 8 Commando, it had been Roddy's plan to leave Congo immediately at the end of his contract and get back to Australia where there was so much to be done to create his future. Now this had happened; he didn't feel so bad about it. He wanted a little wind-down time with Erik and knowing very well that setting up in Australia was going to take concentrated attention for two or three years—or more—he ought to have a little time with his mother and father. Erik was going up to Fearnas to see his father and the lady whom his father, much later, had married and who, because she was delightful, had happily come to call 'mother'. They would have some time in Fearnas together.

Despite any negative publicity potential and despite being located at every point of the city of Elizabeth's compass, a full muster swarmed at a bar. It was at the docks, it was a bar, but it was more like a jolly good pub. How was it found? Well, hadn't Herbert Entwhistle earned membership of 8 Commando? Did they sing like a chapel choir? Well, not quite. Did they sing badly? Certainly not! The soloists had the most amazing repertoire of naval, military, air force ditties gathered from Sebastopol to Cairo, Armentieres to Madras. In between songs, there were the solo performances—magicians, pianists, guitarists, mouth organists—and 'The One Armed Fiddler' sketch by Willie Mitchell brought the house down.

It was difficult during the evening to find the few moments he wanted to say how much he had enjoyed soldiering with Andrew Denton. He hoped that one day, although he couldn't imagine when or how, they might have another adventure together. What a great crowd! People were constantly mixing within the group, each realizing that this maybe a last time. They had to say farewell. During the night of consuming gallons of beer, some were becoming thoughtful, asking themselves sombre questions about themselves, and about others and asking, 'What's it all about?' In all the laughing and leg-pulling, there existed differences, and ways of approach to one another, more particularly so, and arising somehow, from the differences between the civvie dress of the officers and the men the ways they spoke and often how differently they might approach the same subject. But as Erik quoted Robert Burns to a soldier who found the differences confounding, "We're a' Jock Thomson's bairns."

Michel came to their hotel to see them off. The three spoke in French. It was a *tragedie* that they should part like this. He had enjoyed, so much, sharing their professionalism and more than that, their personalities and their humanity and the hints of their broader philosophy. 'Please let us meet again.'

When they were back in their hotel sitting quietly on the verandah, gazing over but not seeing the city, before moving finally to bed both were silent, Erik said, 'Aye, Mckenzie, it's no' the first time we've flown away from a horrible situation together. I hope it's the last. An adventure in pitting our skills with an enemy of equal or not more advantage is one thing, but what we have just experienced is another. I feel guilty of misleading you.'

'Erik, we're Fearnas boys, you have been my military commander, we've had our lives at risk at the very same spot together, but what you are to me is indefinably more than those things. You could call me one morning and say, "There's a game on. Do you want to be in it?" I'd not ask you what the game was. Why ask? I'd know that my logic would be lost in your enthusiasm and sincerity. For any sake, don't feel guilty. Remember, I'm a sane person. I make the decisions.' So thinking, they took flight.

—ooo-)⊗(-ooo—

Erik said: 'I don't have a place to stay in London. Why don't we kip at the club?'

'Except at the club, nor do I. Good idea.' There, after being well fed, they slept in luxurious warmth on a freezing winter night in London, with Africa still on their minds.

Euston station again; a beer in the travellers' bar; Scots voices around them; and sleepers to Fearnas and with that rare, uninterrupted sleep at the club was the heavy dark mental cloud of Katanga slipping away? Contrasted against a New Year's Scottish present, would the experiences begin to be consumed into a best-forgotten past?

The cosy smallness and the wood fires of the Lodge; meals with mother and father and Jane, visiting friends dropping in, with cheeks and noses red or blue from the frosty air, for a cup of tea or a dram: truly Christmas. He had walks by the beach with his mother and Jane; and by the river with his father, old Sandy Mckenzie, where the Fearnas River rattled to the firth from tea-dark pools that contrasted with the snow at their edges. There were snow-covered rocks and the glittering gems of icicles hanging from the boughs of conifers where snow was caught melting by a sudden bite of Jack Frost, hearing in the clear air with all other sound muted by snow, the surf breaking on the shore of the Moray Firth. They would look up now and

again and see the ducks' egg blue of the cloudless sky through
the bare brown branches and leafless twigs of Alder trees that
would hold the banks of the Fearnas together when in spring;
mountain spates filled the valley with the noise of wild rushing
water.

There was a 'Do' one night, a dinner, organized by the
former pupils of St Ninian's Academy who were to take over
so much of the hotel's main dining room that the guests had
been banished to the lovely sunroom where the moon would
shine on them through boughs of the tall, magnificent, ancient
Scots pines. The meal was organized around tables for six and
a menu of small courses after each of which, two people from
each table would move to another thus, was the process of
mixing and meeting achieved. It was in one of these transfers
that Roddy happened to come to sit at a table where there also
sat a ravishing girl with the blackest wavy hair that could almost
be, and very often was, called curly. She looked up at his face
as he stood, with the other joining diner to announce himself,
taking him in with tiger yellow eyes bright with vivacity.

'Hello', she said with the most engaging smile, 'and I'm
Jessica Innes. I had Erik Barron at a table where I sat earlier. He
talked about you. He said you're not going to be staying long.'

'Oh, you'd better tell me what he said so that we can be sure
our stories match,' said Roddy warily.

'I think that would be impolite and unfair to Mr. Barron.
I shall just listen very intently; and correct you if you're off
track on any point,' she said through squinting eyes. 'So'—with
sinister cheekiness, and going on—'I won't tell you what he said,
and let you flounder in a deep bog of awful lies.'

'Oh?' was Roddy's reaction. 'Well, I'm not worried', he said
haughtily, 'I can tell better stories than he can.'

'Go on then, tell us one!' demanded one of the girls at the
table.

'Yes, go on then!' prodded another and, catching the teasing
mood, implying doubt that he could.

'Well', he sighed and seemed to be settling himself to deliver
a lecture, 'there were these two Irishmen outside a chapel—'
but he was cut off.

'Hey, that's not about YOU!' cried Jessica emphatically.

'Anyway that story's been around so long there's no one who doesn't know it,' someone said in the greatest derisory tone.

'Well, it would seem to leave me no option but to tell of my fame throughout the state of New South Wales for my role in building the Snowy Mountains Scheme, but it would take too long and Erik must have told some truth. It's right. I'm leaving on Tuesday, back to Australia. I'm part of that great historical Fearnas Diaspora.' The chat then fell to sweet reasonableness, but not before they'd had a good laugh while they'd played their game.

He turned to look closely at Jessica and said quite softly, his face as if in fear, 'There's only one more course to be served.' A slight pause, then he ventured, 'I've just realized that I could be stuck with you for the rest of the night!'

'Well, I was going to move on', said Jess, feigning a move to get up, 'but I'll stay just to ensure you spend all that time being miserable,' she stated, sitting again, in winsome devilment that only lightly veiled the loveliest of smiles and the softness of those amber yellow eyes. The dining part over, there were calls for music, and since there was a piano, Les Cameron played. Jessica was called to play her fiddle, so they lent her rich soprano to execute two of Burns' ballads with great skill and touching interpretations. There was dancing; Scottish contra folk dancing both the energetic and the graceful.The few not dancing at any time bunched in chatter groups around the floor.

'Twas a merry night. There was wine and whisky and coffee and roaming from group to group. Jessica, Margaret, and Erik ended up speaking together at just about the end of the do. 'Are you going back to Ballycrochan tonight, Jessica?' Erik asked.

'No, I'm staying overnight with Margaret who's kindly offered to move over the bed a bit and let me in.'

'Well, that's uncommon decent, I must say. She knows you snore?'

'Erik Barron, did you tell her that? I thought it was our secret.' The acting was so good that Roddy was amazed to hear the words.

'It's only when she's in bed with men that it happens,' said Margaret.

The teasing of the earlier part of the evening was apparently on again. Anyway, the last event before pulling on big coats and going out into the clear frosty night was the traditional event of drinking a large cup of steaming, brown, oxtail soup. Out they went, from the heat of dancing and the roaring fire, into knife-edged still air under the light of a nearly full moon in a nearly cloudless starry sky.

Jess took Roddy's arm, and Margaret, Erik's, and off they strode in the most irregular manner along the road, set into the hillside, that followed the shore by the swashing, thumping waves that sounded so loud in the clear, dry, silent night air. That sound would follow them all the way to the Fishertown where Margaret and Jessica would go to their beds.

'Hey, anyone feel like a little sail tomorrow or Sunday?' Erik called out from the leading pair.

The couple behind looked into the faces the one of the other. Their eyes wordlessly agreed to sail, so Roddy asked quietly, 'Which day?' To which as she looked at his eyes, promptly replied, 'Sunday.'

'We'd prefer Sunday!' Roddy called out to the leading pair and felt a cuddlesome tightening of Jessica's arm. They bade a chaste good night to their charges of care outside Margaret's smartly painted blue-grey Fishertown cottage. Of course there was light touching of cheeks with lips and an arms-around squeeze which was almost a cuddle.

The men walked back past Erik's family house on the edge of the Links, and with no more than a parting wave and '*Oidhche math*', Roddy strode on and away to the Lodge at Woodend with warm happy thoughts in his head that to have stayed for a blether would have ruined. Among the pleasing musings, was the amusing thought that his mother and his sister would be waiting up, impatiently, to hear all about the do.

On Sunday, Erik went round from the Links house to collect Margaret, the two picked Roddy up at the Lodge and with him hampers of supplies, including thermos flasks and wines. Then it was off to the hills and Ballychrochan to gather up the lovely Jessica.

Jessica must have been alert to the arrival of the car. She stepped out and closed the front door. Roddy got out of the car to greet his guest who wore a camel hair coat like a British army 'warm' worn by officers. Jessica put on a smile to greet him, and he perceived a changing of mood from some other state to a happier mode appropriate to meeting and being with friends. Once in the car, the greetings and talk and the plan for the day occupied them immediately. Roddy, while listening with half an ear, was trying to sort out in his mind the impression of the unkempt dilapidated farm buildings, of the dour stone farmhouse standing bleakly on a patch where once a garden may have been, but which had for years been left to nature to overcome, to grow, and to die away, making its own selections of what should dominate. How could this charming cultured young *mondaine*, of great musical erudition and skill, bubbling vivaciously with her friends, walk beautifully clad, out of that kind of place?

Erik chose back roads through the hilly wooded south of Fearnas and lands of small farms with small fields enclosed by dry stone dykes, stone farmhouses, and stone out-buildings all roofed in grey slate. Some had pleasant cottage gardens and some even vegetable plots and quite a few with fruit trees and a few with decorative deciduous trees. They swept down in the smooth comfort of the Barron family's Wolseley to Forres and on to Burghead where he had left *Fear Naught* in the care of Gordonstoun School.

All was found well aboard when the old lady had been inspected, and they were under weigh within minutes of getting aboard into a gentle nor'easter on a low swell coming into the Moray Firth the sky had a few sketchy clouds and a cold brightness. Behind the white shape of Ben Wyvis on the other side of the firth, dense grey cloud hung low: it could well be imagined that snow was falling. Passengers and crew had put on the storm gear provided, which soon warmed to their bodies.

'What course, Master?' Roddy at the helm called to Erik.

'I think we should take a quiet, gentlemanly reach on a starboard tack as far as we want to go, and then do a reciprocal. I find we spill less wine when we don't get too ambitious.'

'Hear, hear, sir! And Aye, Aye' as well! Starboard tack it is.'

'I'll just get these landlubber passenger to trim the sails for you coxswain,' said Erik.

He got Jess to tail for him as he cranked the head sail to a perfect curve. 'Right, soon as I shift this traveller a fraction, we'll pipe spirits.'

'With respeck', master. Permission to speak?'

'Speak up, Cox.'

'What say we drinks the cold stuff first, sir, to wit, the bubbly French liquor and we keep the Spanish mulled wine for later when the winds may be gnawing at our bones?'

'Passengers, ladies all. Do you hold with the Cox's sentiments?' enquired the master.

'Brilliant!' shouted one. 'Hear! Hear!' shouted another.

The flutes were not the Lodge's best, but Flora was adamant, despite Jane's demur, that she would not see her best in the hands of 'rough sailors'.

Margaret and Jessica poured for the master and crew, and the quality of the glassware proved to have only the very slightest effect on the champagne. The whole of the day was a delight. The backseat passengers on this return trip were speaking rather quietly of subjects of their own.

The Mckenzie talked of possible return trips. She talked of her plans to join an orchestra. They vowed to write letters, and he must not address any to Ballycrochan, only to her Edinburgh digs. He must write first so that she could have an address. When soon they would reach her house, she turned her face close to his and whispered, 'Kiss me now, before we get out.' It was gloaming when they arrived back in Fearnas.

'Was this going to be it? This Fearnas woman? This seed of Alder?' In happy puzzlement, he asked himself the questions. As he wondered, he felt some subtle auguries.

In all of that beauty, the quiet companionship of family and the civilian society of his great friend Erik Barron, and now this new impact on his feelings, his mind was far away: he was twitching with unbearable impatience which Flora Mckenzie sensed and saw in the face and the bodily movements of her son. He wanted to be away, off to Australia.

———————ooo-❧❦❧-ooo———————

It was a gentle irony that the Qantas flight from Heathrow to Sydney touched down first in Perth, where Roddy so eagerly wanted to be, and stopped over only long enough to replenish its fuel tanks for the long haul to Sydney, a distance equivalent to that from London to Moscow. The next leg would land him in Adelaide where his car and all his worldly possessions awaited in storage. He had cabled the Taylors immediately as he arrived in London. A key to the Medindie stable should be waiting for him at the Naval and Military Club.

The flight approached Perth from the north, giving a view of the miles of beaches which seemed to run from horizon to horizon down the Western Australian coast of the Indian Ocean. The city could be seen only in the distance from this northern approach, marked by one or two tall buildings around which the suburbs spread all around, and before the steep descent, the view of an immense sheet of water at the city's edge. At the airport, he bought a street guide, a city and suburban map sheet, a roadmap of Western Australia, and a copy of *The West Australian*, the city daily, these, so that he could begin his search for somewhere to live immediately. Perth was part of his basic, overall research of what was quickly reachable in this vast and varied country. He had no self-commitment to end his travelling, to bide forever there. His mind was boiling with the idea that there was no more time to waste. He had to begin to build a future of substance and of more than mere financial worth.

When he re-boarded the plane again, it was to find that the window seat next to him, previously occupied by a turbine salesman from General Electric, Cambridge, was now occupied by a very nice-looking dark-haired young lady. 'Hello', he said to her cheerily, proffering his hand before sitting, 'I'm Roddy Mckenzie, on my way from London to Adelaide. Are you going there too?'

'Hello,' she replied brightly, looking up at him and having to perform a slight contortion to use her right hand to shake Roddy's. 'I'm Lynne Appleyard . . . going to Sydney to visit my company's head office.' When the aircraft took off, it climbed as it crossed leafy green suburbs to a point where it had the city on its right. Across the fuselage, Roddy could see, for a few moments, a broad expanse of water, a large lake beyond which there were more trees and the ocean; the plane was now turning west, flying over forest and rocky ridges. He turned to Lynne, saying, 'I'd have loved to see more of that big lake and picture of the city setting.'

'That "lake" you saw is actually the Swan River. On the weekends, it's a mass of sail; of keelboats and dinghies. I sail a *Cherub* from Nedlands Yacht Club on the north shore of Melville Water. That's what the big lake's called, it's part of the Swan River and it winds out to the ocean from there.' She could not help noticing his intelligence trove clutched on his lap. She was smiling as she asked, 'Are these your souvenirs of Western Australia?'

'Well no . . . they're my research documents . . . intelligence materials. Perhaps I should explain. I'm going to Adelaide to pick up my car and my belongings which I've left there. Immediately I pick them, I'm going to drive over to Perth, find myself a flat and a job, and settle down to having a thorough look at Western Australia. I mean to settle in Australia, but I haven't decided yet just where. These maps and the paper are to help me in the accommodation and job hunting in Perth. Would you like to help me in my investigations?'

'Will you stay in a hotel while you look for a flat?'

'I'm going to stay at the Naval and Military Club, which I'll have to find, all I now know is that it is right in the city at the top end of the main business street. Will it be difficult to find a decent flat in a pleasant neighbourhood?'

Lynne was taken by his manner, the sound of his voice, his mention of the Naval and Military Club, and the easy openness of his explanation.

'Would you like to live right by the beach?'

'Yes, I would', he said unhesitatingly, 'That would be grand. Perhaps you could point out where I should look on the map, and then I'd know where to be looking in the newspaper ads?'

'Okay, may I have your street directory for a moment?'

She opened it at the page on which all of the city and its environs indicating the 'lake', where her sailing club was, where she lived in Dalkeith, and then she put her finger on a seaside suburb called Cottesloe and pointed to a spot on the street called Avonmore Terrace. 'How would you like to live there?'

'Blow me down, that's right on the beach!'

'Right at the moment, my friend Ann Bancroft lives there. She has, for about four years, and goes up to work with American Express on St George's Terrace by train. She has just bought a house in Nedlands not far from the sailing club . . . she sails a Cherub too. You may like to contact her to see if her flat is still vacant. It really is a beaut flat, I've been there many times and gone surfing from there.' She took a small notepad and pen from her bag and wrote down Ann's name, street address, work address, and two telephone numbers. If you like, I'll give her a call when I get to Sydney to say that you will be in touch.'

They talked non-stop all the way to Adelaide covering everything from the dirt road that ran from Ceduna all the way to Kalgoorlie; about the potholes deep with 'bulldust', the talcum powder-like dust which rock and sea shells had become after eras of heat and cold, wet and dry, and sun and wind; corrugation strips of broken rock that ran for miles on top of the cap rock beneath, which rattled the fillings from your teeth to say nothing about what it was doing to your car. They talked of sailing and sailing clubs, fishing, Rottnest, theatre, and the coming Festival of Perth, and they wined and dined. He was feeling great enjoyment in hearing a woman's voice again in close conversation, noticing that there seemed to be a female way of phrasing a thought; the natural fresh body smell of a woman, so different from the best scrubbed male; the way a woman had a more natural instinct to look at your face when she talked to you, practicing her unconscious art of listening, she wanted to know what you were feeling about what you were saying. These responses made simple dialogue something deeper, more animal, satisfying, pleasing. They had promised to meet again in Perth and sail a Cherub. Their time together had been utterly enjoyable, and they told each other so as Roddy picked his kit bag from the rack and disembarked.

He took a taxi directly to the club. Another lair, another nest, another home, a warm familiarity, where he could take up where he had left off. 'Mr. Mckenzie', greeted a steward, 'welcome back. There's some mail for you. I'll bring it. Would you like a drink in the meantime?'

'Please. A Glenfiddich would go down well right now. I'm very grateful that we have Murray River water, Henry, but I don't think the gods would be hurt if I asked for the soda siphon. Thanks, Henry.'

The garage key was in an envelope with a note from Bess. All was well at Rising Star, they'd had a good clip, sorry, they were not going to see him this time. Steve Ward had left for Western Australia. The other piece of mail was a letter from Steve Ward to say that he was camping on a thousand-acre block which he got through a deposit and a loan from the R and I Bank of Western Australia. The land was part of thousands of acres cleared, and seeded to lupins, by an American millionaire. He had sold up and got out. Steve had one of the parcels which had a dam on it and good rainfall. He'd bought a small flock of ewes. He was carting second-hand building materials up from Esperance to build a house for himself, all pretty basic. 'But my dogs and I are happy as Larry. The future's all out there waiting. Come down and see me as soon as you can.' That letter from Steve lifted his spirits further and injected even more energy into his resolve to get out there and succeed. This is what it is all about, isn't it? Start. Rough it. Work. Plan. Isn't that what hope really is? If you just sit and 'hope', you'll sit forever and your idea of hope will die. I'll go and get the car right away. There's still light. It will be worth another hour in the morning. He took a taxi out to Medindie (an approximately ten-minute drive).

At first light, he had already had breakfast, paid his bill, and was moving in the quietness of the hours before the major work-a-day world began its introductory rhythms. His soldier's box was in the boot, he was wearing a comfortable, old pair of jungle greens, he had all the long haul gear he needed, and Fido seemed contented to be on the road again. He could feel even now that it was going to be a hot day and it had been a very hot night. Tonight, having skirted Port Pirie, and having left Whyalla, of recent memory, off to the south, he would be in Ceduna, with Adelaide five hundred miles, there would remain one thousand five hundred or so miles to go. He had heard from Lynne who, so as not to discourage him, had made light of the very rough state of the so-called road, which was in truth just a track. Her joke about not sinking in a pothole because you could get across on the roof of the car that was already in there was just short of hyperbole. He rapidly found that he had to recalibrate all his estimates of time over ground that he developed from driving in southern New South Wales, his drive from the Snowy Mountains to Rising Star station in South Australia then down to Adelaide. The conditions on the track were even worse than even pessimists were ready to relate. In so many ways, it was a return to Katanga and a role more suitable to the Fox. The fact is that in Perth Western Australia, where the concentration of such people would seem most likely, it was just as rare to find someone who had been round the Horn or driven from the Cape to Cairo as had driven across the Nullarbor; relatively few had done it. A year's vehicle crossings of the Nullarbor in recent times would number low hundreds. He had to depend on the word of locals whom he questioned early in the afternoon, at the widely spaced stopping points on the way, whether he should attempt going on. To know the distance was not enough to base a judgement on. The condition of your vehicle and the state of the track were the limiting factors. On that first afternoon, he realized how hellish it was to be driving in the late afternoon with the sun in the middle of your dusty windscreen; to drive for hours against a westerly wind in a temperature of a hundred degrees in a car designed for temperate motoring dictated a frequent need to stop, turn the car around so that the back was to the wind, lift the bonnet, and let the motor idle so that the fan could cool the engine a bit. 'Do not attempt to remove the radiator cap!' There was no merit in attempting to drive in the slightly cooler darkness. At dusk, kangaroos on the road were a hazard. To hit one of these big-boned creatures, at even a modest speed, could inflict disabling damage to your car and it was on some occasions lethal to the driver. The track surface spread to phenomenal width where drivers, wishing to steer clear of rock base extrusions, the broken-up or dust-filled centre, sought new ways around even if new ground had to be broken. To reach your night's accommodation was to allow the rattling of your bones to stop and allow joints and sinews to creep back into place. Market forces influenced the quality and availability of overnight accommodation and an inverse ratio of price to quality was in effect. It was just as well that travellers were, in the main, a hardy lot and were equipped with enough cash to purchase their share of paradise. It was not one of those motor tours where you drove along communing with nature in a cloud of pleasant dreaming. Concentration was required to avoid disaster and the clouds were not in the sky, where there was never a single one, but in blown dust. When he arrived early at a decision point about whether to risk another leg before dark, he was glad that there was always cold beer and that in his box a book he could read until night fell and the weakness and location of the light in his room made attempts at reading an agony; better to diminish the number of agonies and face the last, the unavoidable—the bed. Nevertheless he loved living in the hours of the cooler dawns as they turned into days when another two hundred, sometimes more miles were taken from the debit side of the ledger and with gratification added to the credit side. Mind you, he had real concerns about what must be a speeding depreciation of his treasured asset; Fido Fusan. He agonized as it rattled for miles on corrugations, or bottomed it's suspension on invisible bumps and imagined a spoor of nuts fallen from the bolts that held the invaluable machine together. But there were times of other wonders. He marvelled at the way nature provided soil types where certain plant species could make a living and where, in some areas, others seemed to prosper, leaving a demarcation where competing types had given up any demand to shift the borders of their inherited domain into that of their age-long neighbours. He wagered with himself that animals would be doing something similar. Petrol, water, oil were the primary requirements wherever they were available. Each of the six and a bit days it took to cross the Nullarbor had a tremendous sameness of routine and call on concentration. What excitement he felt when he went through the rock passes at Eucla and Madura, lying two hundred miles apart, where the track had very short stretches of a bitumen seal: the contrast between the bone shaking, and the noise, seemed like an exotic massage and a heavenly silence. Fido seemed to coast on a limpid lake. Beginning at Norseman where he stopped overnight to gird up his loins for the conquest of Perth, and on through the gold-bearing regions of Coolgardie, where he turned west, and Boulder and Kalgoorlie which he left to the north, he felt, as on his first Qantas flight, that he had been promoted to club class. His trials were over. The winds and seas of the storm had abated. He didn't want Fido to be reading his mind, but he was thinking, 'Wouldn't this be fun to do in the Alvis?' The terrain was changing now as he drove; forests, wheat stubble paddocks, granite crags and boulders, iron-stained soils, despite their well-defined edges, all standing in counter melody to give the landscape a unity. While sitting in the shade at Northam on the verandah of the pub, he was deciding that he liked the local lager, and a final examination of his directory confirmed that from this point, it was plain sailing to the club; no serious tacking required.

There was a small laneway from St Georges Terrace that he had to look out for and the picture of his target was imprinted on his brain. He parked Fido at the back of the club promising the faithful one some rest and rehabilitation and went into the club by the clearly signed back door which gave access from the car park.

He was welcomed by a steward at the small bar in the sitting room. As steward, Andy Stewart was general factotum; he did the very minimal clerical duties required of Roddy's registration. Andy showed him to his upstairs room where there was an austere group of mid-thirties furnishings, a narrow military bed, a wardrobe, a chair. A tall sash window gave a splendid view over the bishop's cottage garden below and further out across the broad waters of the Swan River to the opposite shore, where pretty red-tiled suburban houses sat amongst their trees. It was comforting, and somehow appropriate, that the oblique marginal view to the right of the frame disclosed the assuring, bulky mass of a brewery.

'I'll just show you where the toilet and the bathroom is, sir, an' when ye come doon, I'll show ye roond the club.' On Roddy's descent, he found the club premises to have a similar austerity to his bedroom. Its tall walls were sparsely adorned with photographs of the queen, other royalty, general Wavell and Bill Slim. Dressed from his box, which he had carried up to his room, now scrubbed to shining cleanliness, he was in appropriate rig to make his first entry. It was a rule of the club that ties must be worn and he had selected his 43 Highland. It is not always so, but in most cases, as now, the members took a bit of friendly interest in the new arrival. The Nullarbor crossing was the natural first topic, and although all in the little group would allow the impression to be had that they had at some time crossed it, none actually had. This seemed the time to ask where he might find the main service workshops of the Fusan agent. It was a company called United Motors on Adelaide Terrace, which was the eastern extension of St George's Terrace. That was going to eliminate the need to find his way around unfamiliar territory; indeed he had glimpsed that name on a large building and showroom as he drove past it earlier on the way to the club. Then the topic became military, and when he mentioned having served in 43 Highland, someone said, 'Ah! That explains the accent. I had taken it that you were English.' He explained the peculiar characteristics of the Fearnas accent and his last few years in the concentrated company of Englishmen as giving his accent its confusing tones and pronunciations.

The men in the group he was chatting with were on their way homewards and he bade them farewell. There was a dining room at the club; nowadays it was reserved for specific functions and the monthly Friday members' luncheons on the first Friday of every month. Andy told him of a very grand hotel just along the Terrace where he might choose to dine; he also said that he would be closing down at ten o'clock; there was no breakfast served in the club and asked when he would like him to bring him tea in the morning.

'That would be very good of you, Andy, but after being in a car for days, I need some exercise so I plan to go for a run and then go out for breakfast. Thank you just the same. I'll probably need your services for a beer during the day, so I shall see you then. Good night now. Until tomorrow, Andy.'

The Adelphi Hotel was only a matter of yards away on the corner of Mill Street (a story of the early colony in that name perhaps?) and the Terrace. It dominated the corner. As the height of the verticals of its fronting walls increased and window heights diminished in size as each floor went upwards the impression of height and dominant mass was exaggerated. Roddy guessed that the architects may have been influenced by the strong forces of art deco which seemed to have captured the hearts of Australians, and perhaps there were hints of Rennie in the narrow verticals and the window shapes: maybe its erect posture and illusion of height and strength were unconscious symbols of Australia's intention to be strong and to grow and to recover stature after the sad, hurtful financial depression from which it had just, at the time of its building, struggled free.

The same influences had modelled the interior. When he entered the dining room, he had only a moment to look around before he was greeted by a swarthy, possibly southern European or Levantine man in white tie and tails.

'Good evening, sir. Are we dining tonight?'

'Yes. I'd like to have a table. I'm travelling on my own, so a small table would be fine.'

'When would you like to dine, sir?'

'Not too late but I'd like to go to the bar and have a drink first.'

'Of course, sir. When shall I send someone to tell you your table is ready?'

'Oh, half an hour?'

'Certainly, sir, please give your name to the steward who serves your drink. The bar staff will let you know when your table is ready. Enjoy your relaxation, sir.'

Even in this more pretentious hotel, the staff treated patrons with an easy familiarity well short of being intrusive to which, if one reciprocated, time and service with no hard edges was prompt and pleasant. He noticed that stiffer behaviour by patrons brought stiffer responses and, though satisfying to some, took the vivacity from this human intercourse. He was very happy at the bar where, were this England, the staff in a hotel similar to the Adelphi would be thought of as appallingly familiar. Yet Australia was fundamentally a conservative country despite its having given birth to the Labour party and a 'Jack's-as-good-as-his-master' philosophy. Composite families all based their training of the young to the view that in all human society there was an unspecified limit that it was an affront to exceed and therefore an invasion upon other people whose way of life, like their own, had social virtue at its core.

In the last thirty years, there had been a world war when Perth had been thronged with American servicemen; Catalina flying boats had taken off and landed on the river just downstream of the Adelphi and the club, to set off on the long noisy flight for Ceylon; Fremantle port had berthed and serviced a US submarine fleet; the latest in Swing music and jazz was been heartily taken up, with remarkable prowess in performance, by Australian musicians. In the sixties, their music, and the associated dancing, was still evident as a large element of evening recreational activity. The dining room at the Adelphi was a calm interpretation of the social moods of society and their choice of popular music. The ensemble providing the light music had not slimmed down to the quartets and trios that were to come; and there were still violinists in the personnel on stage. There was a small dance floor for the diners.

All was crisp white napery and reasonable glassware. The food was 'silver service', brought to the tables on silver salvers, served deftly by uniformed male waiters who at any table, were responsible for all of the food and wine, putting together a steak 'tartare', flaming the very popular 'crepes suzettes' on burners by the table, or bringing the cheese trolley. As Roddy dined, he could observe from his vantage point much of the dining room and could feel the general air of good heartedness and joviality appropriately echoed in the popular music from the band.

After dinner, Roddy went back upstairs to the bar which was now filled the young and not so old people of Perth many standing, all in groups large and small mostly dressed in suits or jackets and slacks, but all wearing ties. The girls were in colours of mainly pastel hues; the current vogue. A bigger band was playing dance music and good crowd was jiving to some traditional New Orleans jazz about which Roddy knew at least a bit but could not dance a step.He liked the beat, and when the jazz group from the big band played *ensemble* during their number, he really liked what he heard. He was standing in touching distance beside a group and was so obviously on his own that one of the girls asked him, 'Are you on your own?'

'Yes, I am, I just arrived in town today from South Australia.'

'This bloke's on his own,' she said, turning to her group. 'Just got into Perth today. He's from South Australia.' Then turning back to Roddy, she asked, 'What's your name?' then announced to the group, 'Hey, folks, this is Roddy Mckenzie.' She left the natural process to take place; the men nearest Roddy shook his hand and announced their names. The introductions swiftly done, the questions began. 'What brings you to Perth Roddy?'

'I'm working my way round Australia, and tomorrow I'll begin looking for a job here,' he replied.

'What do you do?' another man asked.

'I'm a construction plant operator; bulldozers, graders, and other machines.'

They looked at this well-dressed, clean-cut man, the way held himself and how he spoke and thought there was something strange here. He didn't look or sound the part. 'Where are you staying?'

'Well, until I can find a flat, which I hope to in the next couple of days, I'm at the Naval and Military Club just along the Terrace.' This answer bought visible puzzlement to some faces.

'That means you were once a serving officer in the armed forces then?' queried a young man who actually had heard about the club. 'What's an ex-army officer doing driving a bulldozer?'

He laughed as he replied, 'I think you'd be surprised at some of the things ex-service officers turn up doing. I met Australian soldiers in Korea who convinced me that this was God's own country, so when my full-time army service ended, I bought a ticket and sailed for Sydney. When wars are over, there isn't always work that ex-soldiers can do so I had to learn how to do something to earn a living. I got a job on the Snowy Mountains scheme and learned to operate construction equipment. So that's what I'll look for here.'

He was making this conversation when one of the girls said to him in a jocular imperative, 'You can gas bag later'—then smiling at him—'We're wasting the music. Do you want to dance?'

'I'd be delighted,' he replied, returning her smile. Off they went to the crowded floor and slipped into a foxtrot for which only a few bars of the music had been played. She was a good dancer and they went well together. Her conversation was light, without being an interrogation, about where he came from, parents, married or single, what did he think of Australia and he told him about her job in the office of an insurance company, the suburb where she lived. There was only a short break between the dances and a quick step was announced. He was asked to dance again. Every girl in the group wanted to dance with him and he was given his first lesson in jive. His partner was a good teacher and began with the basics and stayed with them helping him to see how like all dance it was beat driven and the progressions of steps were influenced by and depended on listening to the music. He was enjoying himself thoroughly. Each time he returned from the floor, he could sense that the mood amongst the males in the group was changing, some of the warmth was fading, there was laughter but it was of a different kind. Sadly it seemed to be infecting the girls. Time to make a tactical withdrawal. He chose a moment and took the opportunity to say. 'Folks, thank you for inviting me to join you. You have made a great night for me. I enjoyed the music and the dancing. I must be off now. Thanks again and all the best.' Particularly the girls wanted to say good-bye and wish him well. The men were quieter and none shook hands. He raised his arm, looked around the group, saying, 'Oo-roo!' and left.

As he walked back to the club in the warm night air, he recalled that although his mentioning the Snowies and New South Wales arose in response to their questions, he had the very strong feeling that they heard what he said as skiting about something far away, exotic, about which he knew and they did not. Perhaps mentioning catching trout at Wee Jasper was not taken as praise for the bounty of this wonderful land? Perhaps it evoked envy of the water-rich state where the wise men from the east were bred? Or was he just skiting about himself? He had felt uncomfortable. Anyway, back to his Fort George bed, a good kip and a trot round that beautiful Melville Water in the morning. Then, first things first, from the top of his list; he would take Fido to the laundry. He opened the curtains and fastened them back, raised the window, and knew that the sun would wake him.

He had imagined, before he turned over went to sleep, that he would wake before dawn and with eye on the sky, he would watch as the elision of night with day took place, and when *"the sun's first rays had fled and Phoebus from his ocean bed through ether wings his flight"* he'd be up and off for a run.

Phoebus beckoned the Mckenzie to join him. He leapt to the invitation, pulled on his 'shorts PT' and his old khaki US undershirt, trotted down the stairs, greeted Fido good morning and asking him to be patient, loped off to experience the tantalizing view from his window now spread wide before him.

Choosing the high ground as he left the club was simple. It took him first away from the water, but soon he was jogging uphill where he entered a curving avenue under tall eucalypts their silver grey trunks bare of branches until, very high, they burst out, in whippy branches at the top, into a leafy canopy. He would lose his rhythm, but Wordsworth's accusing finger was threatening his heart. *"Dull would he be of soul who could pass by a sight so touching in its majesty."* He had to stop and stare. Below, in front, around him and spreading across before him was all that expanse of Melville Water made magical by the sun ascending the sky-track line of its new day—*his* new day—in *his* new world. Now still in shade, the escarpment of the Stirling ranges made a horizon to the east.

Green treed foothills flowed down to the flat river plain where the city had grown. The sunlight, gradually spreading through the trees and rooftops of the suburbs, in the space between, were selecting their own effects of sparkle, and dark leafy shade to highlight or obscure the buildings, public, ecclesiastical, domestic, which suggested a comfortable symbiosis between them and with the land, where humans with sick skins had chosen to place them. The present warmth could be felt increasing: it foretold a scorching day to come. But he had to serve both soul and body so began to run again, just before he did, he noticed that of these well-grown trees, each had at its foot, in moulded relief on a sturdy cast-iron tablet, the number rank and name of a serviceman lost in WWI. When he came down from the height of the park, which had been retained in the indigenous bush state in which it had first been seen by the settlers, he found himself facing the campus of the University of Western Australia. Turning east, he ran along the water's edge, full of the feeling of enjoyment in this beautiful place and the prospect of a productive day. He increased his pace.

At United Motors' large servicing department, he was given a pleasant reception from personnel who had the air of white dust-coated efficiency. He was confident that he was leaving Fido in good hands. When her registration was done and Fido had been whisked away, the service foreman asked him whether he needed transport and offered a car for the day. He explained his situation and needs, declining the offer of a car at this time instead, asking whether he might use a telephone to make a local call. 'Most certainly,' was the response, and he was led away to a small sitting room where there were comfortable chairs, facilities for making tea and a telephone.

He dialled American Express and, at his request, was put through to Ann Bancroft.

'Ann, hello, good morning, my name is Roddy Mckenzie. Your friend Lynne gave me your number . . .' but before he could finish the sentence, a warm female voice interrupted.

'Roddy, yes!' she exclaimed. 'Welcome to Perth. Lynne rang me. When am I going to meet you?'

'Whenever you wish to, Ann. Perhaps if you're free, and you'd like to come, I could take you to lunch? You would have to choose where, I'm afraid.'

'That would be fun. Would you like to call and meet me here, on St George's Terrace? Would one o'clock be a good time?'

'Excellent, Ann, I'm looking forward to meeting you. By the way, did Lynne mention anything about your flat?'

'Yes, she did; we can talk about that at lunch, eh? You're in the centre of the city, so it's possible anything you need may be right there. If not and you need help, don't hesitate to come to the office and see me.'

'That's very good of you, Ann.' And she would certainly have recognized the sincerity in his tone. 'I haven't begun to job hunt yet, but I'm going to begin when I've checked out the newspapers. If I don't come wailing at your door in the interim, I'll look forward to our lunch appointment.'

The drift of walkers was west from Adelaide Terrace to St George's, only one single, anxious- seeming soul scurried, some force of urgency speeding her steps; the gently flowing stream walked on, unperturbed around her. He joined the slower flow. A newsstand at the doorway of a restaurant where patrons appeared to be having belated breakfasts gave him two reasons to pause. With a copy of the day's paper under his arm, he took a small table amongst them. Bacon and eggs? Why not? But an orange juice to begin, and a cup of tea. He scanned the 'Situations Vacant' and there was—horrible thought—with all due respect to those in the calling, it looked as if, had all else failed, he could become a shop assistant. In the Tenders and Contracts column, there were found only three items. Of these, could he tender for painting a new retail store inside and out? Or gas appliance maintenance in council flats? Keep looking!

Stepping out into the sun and the hot easterly wind, he walked westward and soon came upon the State Governor's residence set in European gardens behind excellently executed brick work walls of no less quality than were those of the presidency itself.

Within yards of each other, he found the art gallery, the museum, and the presses of the State Government Printer establishing almost at one scan of an eye the heart and expression of power of the State. The city's hospital was at the ready nearby.

He went first of all to the gallery and enjoyed the works evidencing early history and a jumble of later works. In the museum, the skills and art of taxidermy had shaped a more flexible future since the works he saw had first been displayed. Perhaps unfairly, he thought—and chastised himself for having had it—he had taken the view that the presentations in the buildings looked as if, after the first day, and having declared *his rebus actibus,* the presenters of the exhibits had turned their backs on them and walked away never to return. Now on the wrong side of the tracks, it was time to hike himself thither back to the Terrace and his meeting with Ann.

Her company's office was on a glass-fronted street level, and he entered an open airy space between the front doors and the business counter. A young lady behind the counter quickly glanced at the wall clock and asked, in pleasant enquiry, 'Good afternoon. Are you Mr. Mckenzie?'

'Yes, indeed I am. I have an appointment with Miss Bancroft for one o'clock.'

'Yes, Mr. Mckenzie. She's expecting you. I'll let her know you're here.'

In a few moments, Ann Bancroft appeared. It is sad and sinful to call a certain colour of hair 'mousey'. At the same time that it could be said that the colour of Ann Bancroft's hair was mousey, it had to be emphatically stated that Ann Bancroft was emphatically attractive. The sun must have allowed only its gentler rays so softly to tan her skin. Was it the sun that gave her the tan, or did her obvious health and vigour so accept the sun's rays? The Mckenzie was stricken. How long does it take neurons to signal thought processes that result in your brain saying to itself, 'Mckenzie, it's happened yet again. Do you often and only meet women who express life in such an aesthetic way?'

Military training? Rubbish! He really had to control at least what his voice was uttering and realize that like the bullet that hasn't hit you, it's too late to duck after you've heard the shot.

'Ann'—and taking her hand and looking at her face— 'Roddy Mckenzie.'

'How are you? Welcome to Perth.' She turned then and said to the envious lady behind the counter. 'Thanks, Sheila.'

They looked at each other again, and before they left the office, she said, 'I've chosen a place nearby. Shall we go?'

They hadn't needed to look at each other so intently or take so long to do it; but they did.

Ahern's was a quality department store in the next parallel street, the beneficent bastion of a family whose fortunes had grown with the growing colony. For the benefit of their many loyal patrons who came from the furthest corners of the vast state, they had created on their first floor a commodious restaurant where diners could find themselves in proximity to other solid citizens of their kind, some even famous, at least within and not infrequently from without, the state; genteel people all. What a mood there was between these two. This was excitement! What was causing it? Don't ask questions!

'Lynne told me what you'd talked about on the plane. I bet there's quite a lot more. You gave her only chapter headings; I want to hear the verse.'

'You're inviting yourself into a bog of boredom. If I were ever to tell my story, people would begin with expectations just like yours and before long suddenly remember a forgotten, urgent appointment.'

She did not respond immediately. She looked at him in silence for a few moments, then, 'Somehow I don't think that would be the case', she said, wagging her head. They ordered wine and food and settled comfortably into the atmosphere of the restaurant.

'Lynne said that she'd mentioned to you that I've bought a house and that I'll be leaving my flat at Cottesloe?'

'Yes, she did, and it sounded exactly what I was looking for. Is it still going to become vacant?'

'Well, no, it isn't. Flats of that quality in Cottesloe are never vacant for long, and by the time Lynne rang, Mac, that is Mr. McGillivray who built and owns the whole block, had accepted a new tenant who had enquired about a possible vacancy some time ago.' She saw a change in Roddy's face. 'I told Mac about you, and although I didn't know about it before, he told me that the very quiet follow, who was my next-door neighbour, plans to leave in a few days' time to a job promotion in Melbourne. I asked him to keep it for you and that I'd bring you down to see him. When will your car be available for collection?'

'They said by three o'clock.'

'Right. Now, if it suits you, as soon as we've finished lunch, I'll go and lock the safe at the office—not really—but clear up anything that needs my attention and meet you at the Adelphi corner. I'll be wearing a grey trilby, a red carnation in my lapel, and a folded newspaper under my right arm—not left arm, most important.'

'Will you or will you not be smoking a cigar?'

'If I am, don't hesitate for a second. The game will be in jeopardy. Keep moving and take likely tailing precautions.'

'It's a grim business, Miss Langhorne.' The full weight of its grimness and with both of them in jeopardy coloured his voice when he said with determination, 'I shall follow your instructions to the letter. If you have had to remain concealed for any reason, I shall with the greatest care go round the block and repeat the pick- up procedure.'

'Excellent. Hunter, for a new recruit, you seem to have the hang of the game.'

'I just do my loyal duty, Miss Langhorne,' he said, and the forward thrust of his firmly set jaw caused near disaster to the gladioli in the heavy vase on their table.

'Good. Let's return to the pretence of humour and long familiarity.'

The agents tried not to giggle, the new recruit was just holding together, then exploded in laughter, sotto voce Langhorne said, 'You really have got the spirit for the game.'

At United Motors, the service manager greeted Roddy, 'Mr. Mckenzie, we had been tipped off by the chief that you'd turn up one day soon, but you slipped past our radar. However, please expect a message at the Naval and Military from Mr. Rhys Jones, our managing director. He has had to leave the office today; anyway his message will most likely explain everything. The report says your car has done amazingly well; timing has been adjusted, new fan belt fitted, new exhaust system all oil systems drained and refilled. So your car is ready, Mr. Mckenzie.'

'Right, thank you very much. I must settle up and must move very quickly.'

'Well, there's no administration to be done, the car's been road tested and fuelled up; you can go right away.'

'Are you going to send me the bill then?'

'There is no bill for you, Mr. Mckenzie. Our policy is that every Scotsman who crosses the Nullarbor in a small Fusan Sedan gets a free service.'

'Oh-ho! I smell a rat. Mind you, a very generous rat that I can take care of myself. Thank you very much to you and your men. Doubtless I shall be seeing you again.'

It can now be disclosed that the two agents met as planned, although Langhorne appeared as a smartly suited city executive lady. She gave instructions to the driver the moment she entered the car and they drove off towards the riverbank. They were not followed. Their tail had been shaken off.

From the Adelphi corner, they followed, in reverse, Roddy's waterside run, and where he had come upon the UWA campus they bore left following the river past Royal Perth Yacht Club and keeping close to the river passed Catalina Landing. Just as they turned past some houses to get still closer to the river, she pointed to a street named appropriately Hillway, which climbed up and away from the river. 'That's where my house is,' she said, pointing up the hill. They came to Nedlands Yacht Club its low-roofed cub house on the sands, Hobie Cats and keel boats parked behind and down its sides. In front there was a jetty where larger craft were berthed and up and downstream boats on buoys were moored off.

'This where Lynne and I sail our Cherubs,' Ann said, pointing. 'We really haven't got time now but you can be assured you will be here again. We'll hang you out on a trapeze.'

'Looks like I'm in for some wet-arsed sailing.'

'You sure are!'

A few yards further on the two-level building of the Perth Flying Squadron looked out across a lawn and a little sandy beach to a number of jetties running straight out into the river. It too had boats on big area of hard-standing, amongst them he could pick out *Solings* and *Diamonds*, Yachting World Keelboats. Keeping close to the river, they had to climb steeply up to the roadway, and as they went, Ann said, 'This is Dalkeith and Lynne lives, just'—and she raised her arm, hand ready to point an indicating finger—'there.' She pointed to a sandstone bungalow spread out below and amongst tall trees on a front lawn where there were beds of large hibiscus bushes and paths edged with magnificent roses. Further on they passed Claremont Yacht Club seeing only the roof of the clubhouse which clung, out of sight from the road above, against the sheer cliff. A very old and beautiful Scots Pine at Christchurch College for boys marked their next turning point. There was yet another yacht club on this shore of the river. Saying that it would not add much time to their trip, Ann directed Roddy to turn down again to the river to Freshwater Bay Yacht Club. The clubhouse occupied a grand old house on a rock knob above the river enjoying a wonderful view back up to Perth. There they turned away from the river again back up to, and across the main road into Eric Street and towards the ocean. As they drove on, she announced, 'And this is Cottesloe! There, on the right, Mac is going to demolish these old depression years' homes and build a shopping centre and some more accommodation.'

South Australia had introduced him to infinite horizon boundaries yet this view impressed. The Indian Ocean, for heaven's sake! It was not exactly blue but an opal green with accidental sweeps of wet brush blue, inshore, the water over the yellow sandy bottom was bright yellow-green, blinding white where curling noisy surf broke up and pushed waves up the beach then rushed back to leave the sand at first glistening then leaving the wetted sand umber dark. A low island on the horizon, a larger one to the south and a couple of smaller rock outcrops in between, one with a shining sandy beach, coaxed the eye to scan the entire panorama. 'That's the OBH, surfing headquarters and sub-branch of the chamber of commerce,' she said as they passed a hotel with big glass windows all along its front, framing a seascape, the epitome of a seaside resort, for the many beer drinkers at the bars and tables. Fewer than a hundred yards on, she pointed and said, 'That, as you can see, is the Cottesloe Hotel famous for its beer garden. You can't see it from here. It's round the back; packed out for the Sunday afternoon sessions.' Turning left, at right angles to the seafront, away from the beach now, up a steep hill, they then turned right turn into Avonmore Terrace, past one or two bungalows then pulled up alongside a one-level block of orange brick flats. Ann pointed out her flat, the second door of six on the front facing the street across a piece of open ground. Beside each house door, there was a white-painted wooden double garage door. There was a line of trees along the tall wall at the southern, left hand, end of the flats where, with trees and shrubs all around it, as if hidden in a thicket, nestled a shop, a house attached to and running back behind it. As they slowly drove along, she pointed. 'You see that little shop? It's a gold mine and it's from that, that Mac made his fortune.'

After passing three more dwellings, they arrived at John McGillivray's house. It would have been considered a mansion when built in the period after the First World War. It was attractively handsome set on the highest point of the ridge that ran parallel to the sea; both ground and first floor rooms must have enjoyed, out of their large windows, the most magnificent views for three hundred degrees all round. Its architecture was of uniquely Australian design executed in local lime stone, the low-pitched roof tiled in terracotta. The broad front veranda had a low stone wall of the same stone with a broad opening allowing access to the heavy double doors. A driveway ran in a crescent from the road past this opening and excited to the road through one of the two openings in the garden beds and lawns. Ann guided Roddy to drive up to the front door.

There was a loud, clear ring from the doorbell, and Janet McGillivray's sunny, open face welcomed them.

'Hello, Ann', she said, 'and you must be Roddy Mckenzie. How d'ye do?' she asked. Roddy touched his hat and shook her hand. 'I'm Janet McGillivray. C'mon in.' Roddy removed his hat and followed Janet and Ann into a large reception hall. Not all the McGillivray's tenants were on naming terms, or house visitors, but Ann Bancroft was rather special. They followed her for quite some distance down a broad passageway out onto an extensive roofed patio, similar to those you might see on planters' bungalows, where John McGillivray was replacing a telephone in its cradle on a tall table made for the purpose.

'Hello, Ann, you've brought Roddy Mckenzie, I see. Welcome to Cottesloe. I'm John McGillivray. Can we offer you two a drink?'

'That would be very nice, thank you, John. Friday night hospitality as usual.'

The four sat down round a low table looking out over the ocean. The surf could be heard but not seen when seated, the house being too high upon the ridge. John had, had a call from the tenant who was leaving for Victoria. He would not be home until later in the evening, but John was welcome to allow Roddy to go in to see the flat. There would be an advertisement in tomorrow's paper to announce his furniture for sale, so if Roddy spotted anything, he wanted was to leave a note to say what he had selected and he would mark it as sold.

'So let's just have a welcoming beer and I'll take you round to the flat,' said John.

'Thank you, John. That would be great.'

When they walked down to visit the flat, Roddy was well pleased with what he saw: two bedrooms, a nice little kitchen with a small dining area, a separate bathroom and toilet. It seemed, just right for Roddy's needs. Full-length glass double doors opened out onto a balcony of usable size, separated from Ann's flat next door by a full height brick wall. The tenant moving out was an accountant. Perhaps Roddy had in his mind some stereotype of an accountant: there were only good quality, functional necessities, in good taste. Also in very good taste and looking very desirable was what identified itself as a high-performance hi-fi Marantz sound system.

Roddy turned to look at John who had been wondering what may be going on in his mind. He looked in silence for a moment or two, then said, 'John, these furnishings would do me perfectly!' he exclaimed. 'I can't believe my luck in being able to get this flat. Thanks to Lynne, Ann, and you. I should be buying the drinks.'

When they returned to the McGillivray house, John asked, 'Janet, Mr. Mckenzie wants to buy us a drink and we shouldn't disappoint him. What say we bowl up to the OBH and introduce him to his local pub?'

The Barley Mow, the Ship Inn, and now the Ocean Beach Hotel: would it carry on the pattern of contacts and great good fortune that seemed ready to make a hat-trick?

'If we're going to the hotel, I'd like to go home first and change into something more casual. I'll drop down and meet you later,' said Ann.

'And I'll go with Ann and come down with her,' Janet immediately added.

'I just want Roddy to meet the blokes at the corner. Wouldn't do any harm if he's going to become a local.' Janet and Ann knew exactly what John McGillivray intended. There were people in the group who could help him get Roddy a start in Western Australia. John wanted to get the process begun right away.

'What if we all come back here, Jan, and I'll throw a few prawns on the barbie, eh?'

'That's becoming more Friday night sensible. I'm going to suggest an improvement. You two go to the pub, introduce Roddy, and have a beer. Ann can get changed and we can come back here and get some food organized to have with the prawns and anything else you might cook. So if you'd like to bring anyone back with you, we'll be ready for them.'

The main saloon bar of the Ocean Beach Hotel was barred to surfies who tended to wear only board shorts, and on their feet, rubber thongs mimicking Japanese sandals; they had their own extensive salty, sandy bar, down at street level. The top bar was where the huge windows he had seen earlier were filled side to side with a stunning view of sea and never-ending sky which would later turn pink, and shortly after, fiery red and orange before fading to darkness after the sun had touched the horizon line and, as if being dragged down by some incredible force, slid out of sight. Up in this 'posh bar', the noise from the surfie crowd below was scarcely louder than the whoosh and crash of the surf breaking on the beach.

It could hardly be claimed that those who ritually gathered at 'the Corner' came to see the sky, the sea, and the surf. They were gathered round the last turn of the bar at the back of the big room, a dead end, which wasn't even all that well lit. Just as in the other two pubs, this group noticeably received a dedicated service from the bartenders male or female and sometimes Mike Mahoney, part owner and licensee, came down to concentrate on serving the Corner patrons: and wasn't he one of them himself?

Harry Plumrose was there, retired features editor of the *West Australian* who had begun his career as a cadet on the *Melbourne Herald,* went off to fly Short Sunderland sea planes on cold and lonely flights far over the Atlantic, hunting and killing German submarines. He went to the *Advertiser* in Adelaide after the war and when the *West Australian* needed an experienced features editor, he moved west again. Here he was, living less than a hundred yards up the hill and swimming, *"just down there"* every morning in all seasons and all weathers. Claude Hill was there, a tall lanky lawyer with a patrician look, who specialized in commercial cases and who, by the appearance of his attire, had not been in court that day; mind you, it was just as likely that he had. Frank Dalby, an old-fashioned accountant in an immaculate suit, with linen of the same standard, who had removed his hat from a head of wavy, greying, black hair, joined. The fifth member was a broad, nuggetty man of just above middle height, who was a senior engineer in the Department of Main Roads, very interested to hear about Roddy's fresh experience.

'You may have seen the beginnings of road works between Norseman and the border. The piece we are engaged in now will be a completely new road; a new alignment.'

'Yes, I saw works going on, but I couldn't be certain they were for a road. They were quite a way off the existing track. I was very interested to see it, whatever it was, because starting with tomorrow morning's paper; I'm going to be looking for work on earthmoving equipment. When I was working for the Snowy Mountains Authority, that's what I did. I operated big trucks, dozers, and graders. So with references and Plant Operating tickets, I'm ready to go.' He laughed and added, 'I've even got a powder monkey's ticket.'

Bruno had been listening with increasing interest and his question may have seemed unrelated to the topic. 'Are you married?' he asked Roddy. When Roddy's reply that he wasn't, he followed, saying, 'Well, you've got experience of being in the bush: do you like the bush life?'

'Yes, I certainly do. On my way across, I had six months' contract on a sheep and cattle station north of Renmark, which was a great experience. I had just finished when I got a telegram from my old company commander in Korea asking me to come to Africa to be 2i/c of a Commando he was forming at the request of the new government of Katanga. When that six months' engagement ended, I went back to Adelaide, picked up my car and my gear, and here I am ready to find a job and start my future.'

'That new road is one of my projects,' Bruno went on. 'Would you like to bring all your documentation and come into my office on Monday morning? We'd need to get you down there before the week's out. Here's my card with the address, come in as soon after nine o'clock as you can.'

In Roddy's brain, there sounded a 'Bang!' He was dumfounded, 'It's happening again! Three balls, three wickets.'

There was a new tack to the conversation now, questions about; his current accommodation, the army, his future accommodation, Sheffield Shield cricket, fishing. John McGillivray could see that this conversation would not end after many sunsets. 'What are you and Alice doing tonight? Jan said when we left to ask if anyone wanted to come down, we're just going to barbeque something, it's not going to be a dinner. Anyone else want to be in it?'

Bruno and Alice, Frank Dalby and Jennifer, Harry Plumrose and Joyce came along, not for the first time, to be with John and Jan on a Friday evening. The prawns had been brought down 'from up north' by a friend, John had caught the King George Whiting from his motor cruiser. He kept it at the Swan Yacht Club a decidedly unglamorous fishermen's club on the left bank close to the rail and traffic bridges. An evening breeze from the east was just filling the house through big open front doors while the back of the house (or was it really the front?) had already been tempered by the sou'-wester which had been blowing from about ten thirty that morning and had died now. Everyone involved in the totally relaxing evening was socially, comfortably at ease. Roddy was too, he had been warmly embraced by the people in the group: he found them attractive, friendly, interesting characters. Ann was not in the situation of having a new male friend for introduction and assessment; she too was not going to be begin with anxieties about how her friends accepted this new male.

There were sounds of the sea to provide a romantic background to the volume of continuous conversation. He was becoming conscious of time and the pitch that the party had reached. Later in the evening, he had had an opportunity to have a moment alone with Ann.

'This has been an overwhelming day for me. Meeting and sharing that lunch with you, your tourist guided introduction to this very appealing piece of my new world; organizing my new home and introducing me to such charming, friendly people. And can you imagine this? I think Bruno is going to fix me up with a job on Monday! I've loved being with you. Now I feel I ought to go, leave on the crest of the wave. That's part of my surfie-talk. Pretty good, eh? If you feel like going now, I'd love to drive you home.'

Ann had been watching while he was speaking; tracing his feelings while he was attempting to express in words what his face was telling her. She saw excitement, happiness, gratitude, and yes, even his feeling of being overwhelmed.

'Roddy, all I did was take you to meet John and so that you could arrange to lease a flat if you wanted it. That doesn't seem very much.'

'You make it sound less than the delightful miracle it turned out to be, and all because of your kindness and care. I don't know how I'll ever be able to show the gratitude I feel for what you did', he said in gentle emphasis, 'because it was your care, your feeling, your kindness that led to everything. If you were not the Ann you are, you would never have the fine relationship you have with Janet and John. Oh, look'—his words stumbled and hesitated—'it seems so inadequate just to say "thank you".'

'Roddy, what you have said is beautifully adequate. Now don't you worry about leaving. I think I can understand a tiny bit of what you may be feeling. I want to stay and help Janet; and Plum and Joyce will drop me on their way home. I'm feeling very happy about what has been happening for you. You go when you're ready.'

There were hearty good nights and a confirmation of Bruno's Monday appointment. He was given Paul's phone number to arrange a meeting and takeover of what was to become his new home, his Western Australian HQ.

From that meeting with John McGillivray, the consequent events took place in a time flow of physical spaces and experiences, ideas, inspirations, and the powerful one, needing a formula of complex physics mathematics including a significant symbol of its own that told of the energy value latent within the almost immeasurable power of human aspiration. Roddy Mckenzie was accepted by the men of the Corner at the OBH not because there was a triumph in his getting an insignificant job as a grader driver. His almost powerful, palpable aspiration, his drive to go beyond, that drive which would push him upwards in the hierarchies of esteem and *ipso facto* of caste, was the key that unlocked the door to that minor elite's embrace. Small though it may have been in social or monetary terms, his start as a 'for-the-duration-of-the-project contract worker' with the Department of Main Roads was destined to be atomic fuel for something whose fission cycle never ceased to produce power.

Following the simple route instructions given along with the good nights at Avonmore Terrace, was so easy, that while driving back to the club, he could begin immediately to review the day's events.

'I wonder what Rhys Jones will have to say? Ann's a delight, isn't she? How like Jill and Emma she is. John McGillivray? Smacks a bit of John Wilson: Hugh Verney too, when you think of it. It seems men who achieve, want to help other men to achieve without putting them on the spot, directing them or taking away their own initiative. Paul—whom I must see tomorrow—is ready to leave. The furniture will suit me fine. Wonder if the sound system is included? I wonder when people start responding to advertisements—I'll ring at eight o'clock. Ann has her house-move chores tomorrow and doesn't want me around. She'll be going to the yacht club, but only for the competition races she said: "Two-man crew—dinghy club—not much chance of a

casual sail—race starts at two o'clock—drop down to watch if
you like—introduce you around after".'

At the club, all was darkness. Knowing where the switches
were, he lit himself to his room. There was a letter on the pillow
of his turned down bed. Dear old Andy. A nice touch. He took
it to the little table where there was a lamp.

Dear Roddy Mckenzie, Welcome to Western Australia.

*Please phone this Rottnest number at 1300 hrs Saturday to confirm that
you have read this. If you would like to come for a day cruise, I will pick
you up at East Street Jetty Fremantle at 0930 hrs on Sunday and return
you to Swan Yacht Club at 1900 hrs approx.*

Regards,

Rhys Jones.

'Well', he thought, 'more action.'

Perhaps a few seconds before eight o'clock, he rang Paul.
'Good morning, Paul, Roddy Mckenzie.'

Paul agreed that Roddy could have all of the house contents!
Roddy was invited to come down as soon as he liked, and Paul
would show him how things functioned at the flat. When he
said he would come down immediately he'd not had breakfast,
Paul asked, 'Why not come down here and have breakfast at the
beach. I haven't had breakfast either. I'll meet you at the cafe
on the corner opposite the Cottesloe Hotel.'

The Surfside Cafe had its back to the climbing sun. The
morning was already warm aggravated by a hot easterly wind
which meant a super hot day before the benison of the sou'-
wester would be felt. The ocean was a green-blue glittering sheet
of glass, flat, all the way to the low line of Rottnest Island where
the sandy beaches below the cliffs stood out as pale yellow ochre
below the low line of scrub on top.

He found the black-haired man with the large black-rimmed
spectacles seated at a table for two with the day's *West Australian*
open before him. Paul Behrens stood and, with a pleasant smile

on his thin dark face, greeted Roddy and asked, 'Will this be all right?'

'All right?' he exclaimed, looking around at the setting and the ocean view. 'This is super!'

There was nothing 'tropical' about the breakfast menu. They chose from the combinations of items from a British diet; but they did have delicious orange juice, squeezed out by hand on a glass orange juicer. Roddy had to trust that Paul's price was fair. They discussed the sound equipment separately, and a price was struck with Roddy having no reference prices from which to deal. But what Paul said sounded good and he told him about the sound specialist dealer in Mosman Park where he had bought the equipment. When they went up to the flat, there was a furniture removalist's van at the front. Paul stuck his head into the open door of Ann's flat and called out, 'Morning, Ann! Anything I can avoid doing to help?'

'Yes. Go and play in the sand pit. Or see if you can catch an earlier flight.'

'Just thought I'd ask. I'm a bit caught up in a business engagement with an overseas buyer.'

A lovely shape in short shorts and a T-shirt came to the door. She surveyed both and said to Paul, 'Oh, is this your overseas client?'—then turning to Roddy—'Count your fingers after you shake hands with him. I can't really be sociable now. I've got impatient loaders who need direction. Catch you before you go, Paul?'

'Sunday evening maybe? If the deal comes off okay, I might bring the buyer along.'

'Sounds good. We'll have to work out where to meet. Let's all keep in touch. Here's my new number.' She gave him her new personal card. 'The phone's on. I could be there.'

'We'll work on it,' said Paul, looking at Roddy for agreement.

The deals were made to mutual satisfaction while listening to the answering machine answering potential buyers that all had been sold. Having learned on what day he should put the rubbish bin out, what he should do about paper and milk deliveries if he chose that method, but suggested it was more painless to just use John's that is Harry's shop; it was open from eight till late, and before he left, Paul took him down and introduced him to Harry, the long-time lessee.

After leaving Harry, a bit of the morning remained, enough to reconnoitre the East Street jetty. He followed the coast and onto a manmade promontory which ended with the red navigation light on North Head. Going back, he followed his directory map to the jetty clearly marked Rottnest Island Ferry. 'Good', he thought and saw where he would park Fido, 'that's fixed.' As he passed the university on his way back to the club, he saw a group practising jiu-jitsu on a lawn under some cork oak trees. He pulled up and got out of the car to watch. When, shortly, they stopped for a break, he crossed the lawn to talk with the coach who told him that this was a university club and that they practiced on Saturday mornings. He rummaged in his kit bag and brought out some paper and handed Roddy not only the year's calendar for that club, but a list of all the judo clubs around Perth. They chatted a little, and Roddy told him that he was keen to keep his skills up to scratch. He had then to move quickly to the club to make his scheduled call.

Rhys Jones had to be called from the bar to answer the telephone. Roddy was thanking Rhys Jones, apologizing in anticipation of his having to come back over from Rottnest to meet him and pick him up. 'There's been a change of plan, but it will mean that you'll have to move a little earlier. If you could go to the Flying Squadron Yacht Club at Dalkeith at half past eight and meet Graham Knight on his motor cruiser *Smerelda*, he'll be happy to bring you over and we'll meet up in Geordie Bay. Don't bring anything with you except personal things including bathers. We'll have everything else.'

Sunday held pleasing prospects and what was left of the day was left for discovery.

At Perth Flying Squadron, there was some activity of people—men, women, and children—all dressed in minimum clothing, loading rubber-tyred wheel barrows with supplies to take down the jetties for a weekend at sea. It was warm and would become really hot soon, as the sun climbed above the warm easterly breeze. The sky was a clear pale blue dome which Roddy had already become accustomed to, though he still could not believe that it could be like that day after day after day.

One of the men transferring supplies from car to wheelbarrow directed him to 'A' jetty where right at its end was the large white motor cruiser with *Smerelda* scripted in blue on its side. A dark-haired man and a dark-haired woman were there doing 'shiply' things and looked up when Roddy's figure loomed at their stern.

'Good morning', he said and asked, 'Mr. Graham Knight?'

'Good morning, yes. And this is my wife Jacinta. And you would possibly be Roddy Mckenzie, our passenger to Rottnest? Come aboard.'

Roddy removed his heavy leather sandals and came aboard through the transom gate, his action not going unnoticed by Graham and Jacinta.

'Everything is stowed so we can start up and cast off.' Without asking whether he had ever been on a boat before, he said not really in the intention of a question, 'Roddy would you like to do the bowlines? You'll see pegs on the pen posts; just hang them on to those. The tide's on the ebb so we'll let go the shoreside line last.'

There was a skilled manoeuvre of ahead and astern required in the limited way between the pens made to look easy by a skipper who'd obviously done it before. The *Smerelda* slipped out into the stream, the motor gurgling quietly as she gathered a little bit of speed before settling at the sedate limit allowed on the river. He and Jacinta went up, and joining Graham on the bridge, he was able to appreciate the full beauty of the view of the shores where comfortable looking houses large and smaller reached down to the top edge of the beaches and up in steps on the steep banks. They were arranged on stretches of the tree and bush-covered land, their orange Tuscan tiles, and the sandstone walling here and there contrasting with foliage of every tone of green, brightened by flowering shrubs, bougainvillea, hibiscus, and a host of others from planted gardens, individual in their creation.

Now he could see Claremont Yacht Club in its river bay under the cliff. On a short point, butting a little way into the river a little further along and around the bay side, from its height, the Freshwater Bay clubhouse guarded its pens of yachts and cruisers arranged below it. Past the club, the water then narrowed to enter the cliff-enclosed Blackwall Reach and widened as it left the reach to a broader water on the left bank of which lay Swan Yacht Club. They cruised slowly under the traffic and the railway bridges and into the harbour with the main part of Fremantle city on the left bank. Huge cylindrical wheat silos filled the harbour side on the immediate right bank, their wheat storage function explained by Graham. Left and right now cargo vessels from Britain, Europe, and the East swapped cargos hauled out from the deep dark interiors by the ships' cranes and dropped on the wharves to be freed by the dockside workers and reloaded onto rail wagons or waiting road trucks. Bales of wool or skins were dropped by shore cranes, or manhandled into the big cargo nets spread on the wharves, raised then by the ships' cranes and lowered into the deep cargo holds; rising later slack and empty to repeat the performance.

Travelling downstream, towards the sea, past the green South Mole light on their port side and, a little further, the North Mole with its red light to starboard, away from the river's speed restrictions, Graham put on speed and the bow of the forty-three-foot Northshore rose up, sending white waves rushing off port and starboard across the blue water of the Indian Ocean, while astern a densely bubbling wake tried to keep up. The compass swung to two seventy degrees, their course for Rottnest Island.

The island was a low grey-green line of scrubby vegetation with a few humps and the white stalks of two light houses, one apparently in the centre and one at the north-eastern end. The sun was lighting the entire shape of the island, white rocks making the sand of the beaches and exposed land surfaces truly sparkle. Breaking water on shores and rocks gave an idea of life to the scene, but in truth, it was scarcely a flourishing tropic island. As he looked back towards the mainland, the coast was not dissimilar. The lovely trees all through the city and the green parks were invisible. How disheartening it must have been for Vlamingh and the early Dutch sailors who, after a long, wild passage, made their landfall here in desolation, amongst rocks and reefs, and freshwater not easy to find.

Yet the people of Perth were leaving the green heart of their lovely city, going offshore to enjoy this desolation on an island. *Smerelda* had not been alone coming down the river. There were boats of every kind, large and small, clinker and carvel, sail and power, and they were around her now, the keel boats with colourful balloon spinnakers filled just nicely by the easterly breeze. Roddy could see them all very closely as *Smerelda* passed. They were not glamorous craft and none appeared new. The crews were young and old and seemed to know the rhythm of their craft and the character of the waters that bore them well, fitting the shape rising to the top, and seeming to slip down, out of sight, in the troughs of the smooth-rolling swells. They seemed to be vessels that the everyday working man had saved up for, and could afford. He felt that there was a kind of healthiness in what he was seeing of this happy fleet of adults and children enjoying their leisure. For Graham and Jacinta, this was an almost weekly event, most often to Rottnest, sometimes to Garden Island nearby, or down the coast to Mandurah or simply out to sea fishing. Though there was no one besides Roddy aboard today, they were pleased, at any time, to take friends, business contacts, interstate or overseas visitors, or friends of friends, for a sea trip.

As *Smerelda* approached the island, Roddy could see that if they maintained this course, they would pass the end of the island. Graham said, 'Where we're going today is around this end of the island to Geordie Bay where we and Rhys have our own moorings. The most popular spot is Thomson Bay where there is a settlement which people enjoy. It's behind that rock, Phillip Rock; you'll see a bit more of it as we pass. We'll keep clear of rocks and reefs and go round Bathurst Point where that lighthouse stands.'—he pointed out Longreach Bay—'We used to go into that bay most weekends when we had a smaller boat, but *Smerelda's* too long to get round the rock shelf and nigger-heads into the bay, so now we use the mooring we put down in Geordie Bay where we're going now. They came in on leading marks towards Armstrong Hill: Oh my goodness isn't that something?'

Roddy exclaimed when he had a view of the whole bay nestled in high natural rock walls showing little sandy beaches here and there, and then they slowed swinging to port, going further into the bay where there were moored yachts and motor boats. As the three had talked on the way over, Jacinta had asked whether Roddy had had any experience of boats and his reply was, 'Only of yachts.' That was all the information they needed. 'Jacinta, you can have a day off. Give Roddy the boat hook. Roddy, go up to the bow and, as I come onto that yellow mooring, pull up the rope, take it in under the rail, and put it on that deck cleat, would you?' Roddy was on the bow in a trice. The easterly breeze had no effect on them here and when a sou'-wester blew they were in the lee of the island; in northerlies, the towering rocks sheltered hem; it was very snug anchorage. Made fast, and the motors stopped, Graham and Jacinta drew fenders from a long lazarette in the after deck and lashed them at points on the stanchions on the starboard side, that done, it was in a minute or two that a slightly smaller power cruiser of American design slowly came alongside, and a line was thrown to Roddy who was positioned on the bow. He passed the line under the fence and put a turn round the cleat and waited for the next command.

'You've got working crew I see, Graham,' said a sandy-haired man at the wheel of the arriving vessel. 'Hello, Jacinta', he called out, and, 'Come aboard when you're ready.' The two vessels securely and comfortably rafted up, the three from *Smerelda* crossed into *Cymru*. Once on the afterdeck, Rhys, a little shorter than Roddy, hastened to grasp his hand. 'Welcome, Roddy, Welcome to Western Australia, Iris, and I've been looking forward to meeting you. Iris has your life story from Doris Perrott.'

'Oh, golly, I'm in trouble before I can even get started.' He laughed and scanned Iris's face, checking the effect of what he imagined may have been Doris's description. 'Iris, how d'ye do?' he asked, taking her hand. The deck had been set up for entertainment with chairs and a table. After she'd kissed Jacinta and Graham, she said, 'Do sit down, folks.'

'It's past twelve o'clock Sydney time, and if Mauri and Doris are having a drink, let's join them in spirits and splice the main brace. What would you like to drink? Jacinta, what can I get you?'

'A gin and tonic would be nice, Rhys, please?'

'Iris?'

'Yes, I'll have a g and t, but I'll get them, you look after the blokes.'

The men had beer—Cooper's Ale from South Australia was Rhys's stock favourite. When all present had a drink in hand, Rhys, raising his glass, said, 'Welcome to WA, Roddy, and the best of luck in whatever you choose to do, and here's to Mauri and Doris for introducing us.' There were words of welcome all around. Then Rhys said, looking principally at Graham, 'Iris and I caught the lunch this morning; squid and sand whiting.' Roddy asked about the fishing, and before the conversation broadened to the larger topic, Rhys said that they had caught today's lunch over the side of the boat right here and, that if they all felt like it, keeping in mind that the sou'-wester would be in, they could try for King George whiting at their favourite spot on the windward side of the island, or they could be satisfied with some Skippy from this side. Inevitably Roddy had to tell bits of his story again, particularly about meeting with Mauri Perrott and Doris. The subject of fishing led to the question of boat ownership when Roddy described his impressions of the size and variety of the fleet he'd seen on the way here, and even in this bay. Both Rhys and Graham explained that it wasn't beyond the possibility of an otherwise frugal working man to get a boat of some kind if he was serious about it. 'If you're sea minded, and one day you want to buy a boat, Roddy, you will; but you'll have to decide whether your real love is sailing or cruising and fishing. When you think you're ready to buy, speak to Graham and me, we both have contacts amongst yachties and motor boat owners and keep our eyes and ears open for deals in the market. Ask Graham about how he bought *Smerelda*.'

'I tell you, Roddy, that's a real Australian story,' he said in introduction. 'A bloke, whose family members were first settlers in the colony got a settler's grant of a large piece of vacant land that later became Adelaide Terrace just up from Rhys's operation. On this piece of land, which would be near the growing city, the great forebears of the chap I bought our boat from had built a row of quite smart terrace houses for people who worked in the growing city. Like much of London real estate, they were occupied on long-term leases, heritable in the lessee's family. In addition to this city real estate, the Mckillop's owned a cattle station up north in the Pilbara, so it wasn't illogical to become fell mongers down in Fremantle near the abattoirs and the port: they're still the biggest in the west by far. Kevin, the present head of the Mckillop family, saw that the old terraces had reached a point where there was no profit in spending on refurbishment. With Australia growing and more gold and other minerals being discovered every day, he could see that one day soon there would be a need for a modern hotel and where his terraces stood was the perfect site bar none. Kevin Mckillop knew there was no one in Australia interested. Europeans were a possibility, but the poms and the yanks were the most likely for a hotel deal. Rhys, in a conversation with Kevin, who he'd sold a Cadillac to, because he is an agent for some General Motors brands other than Chevrolet, learned that Kevin needed a boat to do the kind of financial wooing people in hotel ownership would require. In his quasi disinterested way, he asked, "Would you like me to see if I could get one for you and I may be able to arrange the sale of your present boat."

'"That would save me a lot of time that I could spend better doing something more important," says Kevin. Rhys got in touch with Mauri and between the two of them negotiated the purchase of a super modern American boat of fifty-two feet, and although very pretty, it had an after deck perfect for game fishing. And it was made of fibreglass, finished in dark blue and white. So Mauri made a couple of quid, Rhys got the price of a beer or two; I got a boat that had been cared for like a baby all its short life for a very reasonable price. So what's the moral in that story, Roddy, eh?'

'I'm going to take that as a serious question, Graham, and I can see it's an extension of my story so far. Success is very much a question of establishing chains of contacts, using them, looking after them, and seeing that everyone gets a share.'

Graham turned to Rhys, scarcely able to hide the delight in his face, and asked, 'What do you think of that, Taffy?'

'I don't think Mr. Mckenzie is going to be a grader driver for too long.'

On Sunday morning arriving back at the club about noon after exercising and exploration, Roddy went to the bar where Andy greeted him and said that a Mr. Behrens had rung earlier to say the he had effectively cleared out and would be staying in a hotel overnight to make catching his plane easier on Monday, so he could move his gear in today and that he'd leave the keys with Harry.

'Thank you for passing that message, Andy. It looks as if we are going to part company. I have to come to town to have a meeting with Mr. Brunsden at Main Roads tomorrow morning, could I come in and settle after that?'

'If you come in about one o'clock, Commander Chalmers, the secretary, will be here and he'll do your account for you.'

'Will you be here, Andy?'

'Aye, I'll be here. I'm always here when the commander needs me; but I'll no' be here on Tuesday and Wednesday.'

'Grand, Andy, we can say a proper farewell before I go. I'll go and pack up and see you next on Monday.' Taking a notebook and a pencil from his pocket, he wrote down the address and telephone number of his new abode, bade Andy cheerio, and hastened upstairs to pack.

It was a moment he would never forget. He walked through the front door at number 6 of 36 Avonmore Terrace in Paul's immaculate apartment, now his, and framed in the glass doors beheld the enormous sky, the horizon line of Rottnest Island, the opal green-blue of the Indian Ocean, and heard the pounding waves. Another beginning. He brought his gear in with all dispatch, dashed down to Harry's again, and picked up essentials for Monday morning. Giving him the keys, Harry said, indicating a drawer under and at the end of the back counter, 'Even Ann has at some time lost her key. There's always a spare key here so you'll never be totally locked out.' He took his stores up, stowed them, and adding a precious new key to his key ring, drove off to Nedlands Sailing club to see Ann race her Cherub.

The *Hobie Cats*, the club's most highly reputed interclub, nationals, and international winners, needed the water to themselves so they had sailed in the morning and had now all but finished stowing away boats and gear to the back of the club building.

Out on the water, the Cherub Fleet, the Gwen 12s, and ones and twos of other dinghy classes (he was told by a spectator) were on the far side of the water where they had to round a mark, visible but not identifiable. It's a bit of a sadness really, he was thinking, which means that sailing will never become a great spectator sport: the exciting action takes place too far away. The agility, the skills of handling sheets and guys and halyards, and all the knickknacks of tuning gear, the cunning of skippers, the strength, the stamina, not seen, cannot be understood. If spectators could see the sport, they would soon learn the rules and observe the skills, and enthusiasm would grow. In this wonderful sailing venue, people were free to walk their dogs or bring their small children to the beaches without restriction. Surely they must gain an indefinable pleasure, quite unconsciously, from; the entirety of sky and water dashed to foam, tall white masts and shorter brown ones askew at all sort of angles some unbelievably impossible, sail with stripes of all the cardinal colours, bright reds, yellows, blues, greens, and some indigos and violets, dashing and weaving against backgrounds of high cliffs and banks, low beachy coves; trees with bushy tops or slender branches holding their leaves in bunches at the ends bending, dancing, buffeted by the strong sea breeze.

Later, when the fleet came past the club, he was mightily impressed to see the trapeze crew member unhook her trapeze wire on this side, make it fast, duck under the very low boom (that barely cleared the gunwales!), hook up on the other side-stretch her body full length, go on sailing on the new tack. At the same time, the Cherub skipper while controlling the jib sheet and keeping in mind; course, strategy, tactics, and rules of the road had to do all of these among the fleets of numerous keel boats from two other clubs thundering past them, overtaking them, crossing in front of them on port or starboard tacks! Meanwhile, languid ladies on long lounge chairs on the high rock-steady decks of mighty, modish motor cruisers sipped champagne, while the wash from the screwing surge of their ship's propellers caused, for the sailors in dinky dinghies, feats of gymnastic balancing as they were heaved about in small tsunamis of cruiser-caused wakes. All this in twenty knots of wind!

After the race, Roddy helped to haul up and lift the hull onto the lawn, stripping off the rigging, washing down the hull, folding the sails, Roddy helped the sailors to put away their boat under cover in an open-fronted shed, while many others put their boats on trailers to tow home. There was a chattering noisy jumble of sailors, children, mums and dads, and venerable elders filling the crowded clubhouse with sun-hot bodies. The officials were totting up the scores and while waiting for the announcements, leaving Roddy with people they had introduced him to, Ann and Cheryl showered and changed into dry shirts and shorts. Ann, and Cheryl her crew mate, were later announced first and fastest in *Angel*.

At the river end of Broadway, a young man called Garrett, with a bit of flair and imagination, had opened a restaurant which, from the day he opened the doors, was a raging success. It later became a local institution, especially with sailors, and after racing days, it was packed with noisy laughing young men and women, eating extremely tasty dishes from a limited menu. So tightly packed was the old building, never foreseen as becoming an eatery, that to occupy a seat at a particular table one had to get up on it and walk across it (the tables were of robust heavy timber) to reach the small corner amongst your companions to drink your wine, bought from the bottle department at Steve's. There were some people who even knew its actual name—the Nedlands Park Hotel. But people who had been drinking there for the years since the Second World War when Steve returned from war service would scratch their heads if asked directions to a hotel of that name. The food, the people, the wine, the joking, the snatches of almost sane conversation in this tumultuous pack, condensed under the low ceiling and into odd-shaped rooms torn out of the old house, leaving just sufficient internal bricks and mortar to hold the roof up, combined to transform

into a writing knot the humans therein. The result? Feelings
of fun, enjoyment, sharing, release. Ann had taken advantage
of her residential proximity to the heart of 'the village' and had
carried her little kit bag to the yacht club and had intended
to walk home. However, one person in the pack, a resident of
Cottesloe could, very easily, drive up Hillway on his way home,
offered her a lift. She gladly accepted this gallant gesture, saying
that this would afford him the opportunity of seeing her newly
acquired residence.

Ann's house was a bungalow of the between-wars years,
made of stone and brick with a very workable layout, bigger
rooms than the norm for Nedlands. The rooms that did fit the
Nedlands norms were the bathroom and the 'pokey' kitchen
with its vintage gas stove and a hatch through which to pass
food to the dining room. He could imagine Ann turning it into
something very comfortable. 'I think it's great you have got your
own house already. It's a great achievement. From this base, you
can grow even more. You can settle in to living now. I feel you
will be happy here and I certainly wish you that. You must be
happy right now, and very excited.'

'Yes, I'm enjoying the feeling of excitement and I am happy.
An aunt of mine passed away and left me some money with
what I had saved and my work history the bank was keen to give
me a mortgage. I'll be paying it off on principal and interest at
amounts which I can handle comfortably. Everything has come
together so well.'

'But essentially it's about what you have achieved; and the
choice that you made about how you would use your aunt's gift
is part of that. I've got the idea from what I sensed about you
that you will live and achieve and what you achieve will need
no other contrivance on your part, just your way of being in the
world. Other people may have thought of different things to do
with the money; that would have been up to them of course,
but I think your happiness will not just be momentary. You are
another good example for me.' He was sincerely happy for her
and shared her joy: and with the expression of these thought
and attendant feelings, he left her for his flat at Avonmore
Terrace.

At ten minutes to nine on Monday morning, Roddy
Mckenzie, handicapped a little by a fine quality tweed hacking
jacket and grey trousers, a fine shirt, military tie, brown trilby
and eye-blinding shoes, stepped through the main door at the
HQ of the Department of Main Roads, Western Australia, to
apply for work as a grader operator. He was shown to Bruno
Brunsden's large office on the first floor. Bruno stood up
immediately behind his big timber desk and came round it
to greet Roddy warmly with a smile and a firm handshake.
'How are you? Come and sit down. How was your weekend?'
he asked. Everything in the room was large scale; a big window
looked across North Perth back towards the city, the walls
were covered with maps of roads and big working drawings. In
front of his desk was a finely polished heavy timber table for
meetings, at which he and Bruno sat. Bruno was interested to
hear about his new flat and every detail of his weekend with
Rhys and Graham. He described the work that he would be
offered, that it was in the bush and that the work would last
until the final grades for road laying had been completed in
a planned time of two months. 'It will keep money coming in
while you are getting yourself orientated and your plans under
way. There will be other work most certainly. I want you to be
in a position to choose what you think is your best way forward.
I'll just ask Jack Johnson—he's the chief employment officer
for machine operators—to come and get you and do all the
employment administration. You'll be leaving this weekend,
but hopefully I'll see you down at the OBH before then.'

Jack Johnson was a friendly bloke who had been a machine
operator himself in his younger days and was now happy in his
role which kept him in touch with his past. He was impressed by
Roddy's papers from Woodshaw and the reference from Willie
Taylor which mentioned the contour work and his exemplary
military contribution. He was shown a map of Perth railway
station where he would join a Main Roads' bus for Norseman
at eight thirty on Sunday morning. Roddy was impressed by the
amount of pay; it was equivalent to working on the Snowies. He
would be paired with another grader driver, and when dozers
had finished, they would have to rip, level, and clear beforehand

then spread the road material dumped by trucks to a surveyed, cambered form on the road bed.

The bus dropped some men at Norseman and those remaining would go to a trailer camp at Cocklebiddy, Roddy was one.

Cocklebiddy, the trailer camp at the edge of a track in semi-desert land, affected Roddy not at all. But there seemed to him to be two major difficulties to be overcome: capital and communication.

Simple sums showed him that at the end of an entire life's time earning wages, he would not have sufficient capital to begin his realization of dreams: however well he may use his skills, however many hours he could force his body to work would never be enough. How could he become a contractor and make a financial margin significantly greater than wages? The more he thought, the more he realized that he could not become a contractor, even as a very small version of Wood Bagshaw without men, machines, and an organization. He had to struggle with, and overcome the fixed idea that his visibly physical contribution through hard, skills application on a machine in the field was essential to success.

His capital was meagre. He did not want ever to live through a totally fruitless day, a day in which he was not measurably making steps towards the achievement of a goal. Yet he had, what was almost a fear, that he must not make any such transition too perceptible because he wanted whoever he employed to have a vision of his application of skills, his bearing of the physical load and delivering work of high standards to impress on them a conviction of the need to apply maximum skill, effort, and dependability. He wanted to breed trustworthiness, which resulted in people pushing to achieve goals they had set for themselves. He wanted to reward them well so that they could enjoy happiness and create good lives for themselves and their families. Goal number one was to begin profitable contracting right away.

Yet he had to invest time in solving the second major problem—communication.

He had to find lines of communication; an information web. What were the ducts that joined the information flow in the worlds of heavy earthmoving equipment? How could he find opportunities for contracts in earthmoving works? What new machines would be used? What kinds of work problems in earthmoving were being faced day to day which needed solutions? Who were the major people—the users, workers, buyers, the sellers?

At Cocklebiddy, Dave and Roddy followed each other in echelon formation on their machines, dust distance apart, concentrating on getting every stage dead right, never ever having to go back refine a shape: it demanded concentration—all day—every day. So the days passed. Before sleep, the nights went by in talking with Dave whose professionalism Roddy admired and in whose views of living there was so much in common to be shared.

He managed to read a bit. He began to experience many thought-jumping moments, insights, or descriptions of life episodes that took him out of the mundane. He had views of mundanity as it had existed in those other worlds of fiction; he read of heroes and heroines their trials and tribulations their successes and failures. The dramas of these fictional lives and events gave him shots of vaccine against false gods and popular fantasies pretending truth. He became annoyed, impatient, frustrated, trying to understand: he needed to read more, he needed to be more largely informed, if he were to make valid of assessments about what he was reading. Why was it that what was being said then, warnings so sharp, so clear in their meaning, so far back in the past (and so many horrifying times into the present), were so largely ignored? Why, if we know of the existence of the warnings, do we fall into the same traps again and again? It is as if our populations and politicians have never known of the happenings? Don't we know from early Greek drama alone that empires arose, never by virtue, and fell, their nemesis written into their creation? And how many mighty empires have risen and fallen since? Yet, he thought, the people in those ancient times were really very much the same as we. If there should be such a phenomenon as fate, then it was unavoidable. He had found from novels, dramas, and histories that humans brought about by their own thoughts and deeds the troubles that befell them. It was up to him, he told himself, to live by what he had learned. Until now his instincts had served him well, now he was moving into a world of new, bigger challenges, responsibilities, and obligations. While doing so, he had to put aside those ideas that would inhibit progress; ideas likeable but impractical such as needing to be out in the physical field being the untiring best worker. He must be sure to keep intact the ideas and beliefs he valued most. Essentially, he must still keep his core, spiritual muscles well exercised.

—————∘∘∘━◖◗━∘∘∘—————

His return to Number 6 Avonmore Terrace, which he had known so briefly and had left so abruptly, filled him with delight in its truest definition. Although he well understood the idea of delight and the word had a place in his lexicon, he would never use the word to describe a feeling he had, and it would be further unlikely that in the third person he would use it, except to describe a feeling experienced by a female. It was his flat now, where he could experience the sight and sound of the ocean. He was very happy to have been able to buy, 'just like that', from Paul such tasteful, appropriate furniture. He wanted to rush away now and buy some music and browse a bookshop. Surely he would soon see some local art which appealed to him, which along with his music and his books would clothe with comfort, his domesticity. He was happy to have a close relationship established with Mac and the social exchanges with Harry in the shop. Then there was the group at the corner in the OBH, a friendly mob that he should catch up with later in the day when it was their hour for gathering. There was Ann; and Lynne coming back soon, and Dave Oliver. (Now, wasn't the sum of *that* delightful?)

He purchased a newspaper as soon as he had helped Harry and the waiting newspaper boys to open up the bundles to fold the papers for delivery in the Avonmore Terrace store's patent origami. There was nothing at all of work interest in this morning's advertisements.

Fitness next: he ran north along the sands sometimes rock-hopping. He was feeling good and could only estimate how far he'd run. He would have a swim before breakfast, so he turned back to a beautiful piece of truly local beach. After the swim, he had a flat-out run up to the flat to shower. He decided to go to Cottesloe town, edged by Stirling Highway to the south and by the Perth to Fremantle railway on the north, to see what there was to eat there and to find somewhere he could have secretarial work done. There was no knowing what he was likely to bring back from the day's sortie, so he would take Fido as load carrier.

There was no choice about where he should eat in Cottesloe. The only, and tiny, restaurant open for breakfast was exotically, excitingly, away ahead of any trend: it offered Swiss muesli—imported from Switzerland! Considering the exchange rate of the Australian pound, perhaps the scrambled eggs and tea and toast he had to accompany this international novelty were actually free. As he stepped out, he thought it better not to yodel.

Next he found a secretarial service run by a tall thin Irish woman with red hair. He asked if he could see some of her work, and as he looked at some tender documents the agency had prepared for clients, the idea of what a tender presentation might look like was a confrontation with just one tiny part of what his future may hold. He'd seen his share of military documents and orders, but the format, the headings, the changes of typefaces, the numeral and letter systems, amazed him. 'You look a bit shocked there,' she said, observing his reaction. 'Indeed I am, Miss Gaunt, you have shone a light onto a world that existed until now in the dark void of my ignorance.'

Claremont, a larger town just further up the line, was a small criss-cross pattern of little streets and low buildings, the tallest, at the Stirling Highway end, was an old picture theatre surrounded and suffocated by Drabbles Hardware store, a rambling maze of rooms, treasuries of every conceivable article of hardware. He found the newsagent and bought the most recent copy of *Punch*. He found a well-stocked bookshop where his eye lit on a Maurice Walsh book, *The Spanish Lady*, which he hadn't read and which he knew, if true to the author's style would nurture his romantic soul, and Lewis Grassic Gibbon's *A Scot's Quair* to bring him down to earth. A music shop was close by. From its rich range of recordings, he chose a foundation stock to satisfy his present needs and upon which he could build a collection; a boxed set of *The Nine Symphonies of Beethoven*, Karl Boehm conducting the Vienna Philharmonic; Josef Suk, violin, playing the *Beethoven Violin Concerto* with Adrian Boult conducting the New Philharmonia Orchestra; he had to have some Paganini and chose Arthur Grumiaux with the Orchestre de l'Opera de Monte Carlo playing *Concerti per violino N. 1 e 4*. He was full of good feeling, very satisfied with his purchases, and stowed them in Fido, under the passenger seat, out of the sun and drove off to find the *Highway Hotel* where he had arranged to meet Dave Oliver. They had lunch in the dining room which by the date of its structure, its furnishing and decor told the stories of two world wars and the growth of the Claremont, Nedlands, and Dalkeith localities. During the week, it attracted quite a few locals, mostly older people and a few businessmen. As Dave and Roddy dined on roast lamb and vegetables, they talked more about working together. After lunch, they drove out to the industrial suburb and railway marshalling yards of Kewdale where there were two or three plant hire establishments and some used equipment dealers where they introduced themselves and sounded out the operators of the businesses, found out about prices for the hire of specific plant and pieces of second hand equipment. Roddy later drove Dave back to where he lived in a little stone cottage by the railway at Swanbourne. When Roddy arrived home, he decided to leave the arrangement of his treasures until later. He had gauged from the position of the sun in the sky that it may be the time to walk down to the Corner at the OBH.

The sun beginning to move lower, its rays now shone directly into the top bar of the OBH, yet the Corner was still, frankly, gloomy. At the bar, on which stood a sealed jam jar full of some dark matter, Claude Hill and Plum were in conspiratorial conference about its contents, a product of one of Claude Hill's amateur joys, making Indian curry pastes. The two were dedicated cooks and among their coterie renowned for the splendid spicy, aromatic meals they presented. They produced other delights too, which their group shared—preserved lemons, olives and capers, tomato passato, marmalades, and many other exotic European and Asian novelties. Plum, whose labour was available during the day, was the prodigious fruit and vegetable gardener.

When Frank Dalby arrived needing an audience for his fury about a disallowed catch in the weekend's local cricket match, the conversation switched immediately to their other primary love—cricket. Roddy was politely ignored, as would be the king were he present. He was enjoying what he was hearing nevertheless. Then came Bruno, accompanied by a very tall young man with copious curly reddish hair in wild confusion all over his bespectacled head, his rosy-cheeked face had a cheery smile which looked likely to be perpetual. 'Howie', he said to his companion, 'I'd like you to meet Roddy Mckenzie.' The two shook hands. 'Howie has not long qualified as a surveyor with a very good report from his master. You may need a surveyor sometime soon. He's a bit of a bushie, so just like you, he wouldn't mind out-of-the-way jobs. By the way, I had a good report from Leon Williamson about the work you two did at Norseman. There's another bush contract coming up, but there be a "Request for Expressions of Interest", this will later be open to tender. It could be up your street. There are culverts and drains to be installed, so you'll have to think about how you're going to handle that. It would be another good job for your development as a contractor. You could think about it. You'll need a surveyor. It will be advertised on Saturday and the documents will be available on Monday morning.'

'Thanks for that, Bruno; you can imagine I'd certainly be checking the paper. That was my dawn task today. I had to help open the bundles and fold the papers with the newsboys before I could get one to take away,' he said, painting the picture of the stir and bustle in the little space that was free of packed shelving and produce on the floor in Harry's little shop. 'Dave and I spent the afternoon at Kewdale looking at equipment hire and second-hand plant, so that that we could meet the local dealers and get to know what's available and costs.'

Then turning to Howie, he smiled and chuckled as he said, 'Here's my card with phone number and address.' In turn Howie took out his wallet and he passed his card to Roddy and in jest about its novelty, said: 'Be careful, the ink's still wet,'

It was at this point that Mac came in and joined the conversation. He told Roddy his young tyro, in whom he had taken a personal interest, about his plans for a shopping centre on Eric Street and another on Broadway at Nedlands. Roddy was becoming excited about the challenges that these projects presented. He told Mac and Bruno that, on Friday afternoon, he was going with Dave to the Highway Hotel to meet a father and son who were plant operators whose reputation for dependability and good work was well-known, who might be interested in combining with them on contracts. Mac and Bruno were pleased with what they were hearing. 'Would you like to come down home afterwards?' Mac asked Roddy and Howard. 'We'll most likely be having a few folk in for a barbecue and a few beers?'

'That's very kind of you, Mac. I'd like that very much,' was Roddy's ready response.

'Thank you, Mr. McGillivray', said Howie, 'When should we come?'

'Well, after you finish at the Highway. Any time after I get back home from here. About six o'clock?'

During the week, Roddy diligently applied time to his correspondence with the treasured people that he wanted have told his news to had they been here; with his parents, his sister Jane, Erik, Jessica Innes, Mauri and Doris, Jill, Hugh and Miette, Nora and Ninian.

At the Highway, Dave was there to greet him in a crowded bar where he was silhouetted against a window where leafy plane trees allowed light to send bright shafts of sunlight onto the noisy gathering of men. With the wave of an identifying raised arm, he called out, 'How are ye goin'?' The mass was made up of a number of smaller groups not always identifiable as being separate. With him were a burly man possibly in his late fifties and a very handsome well-muscled young man with dark wavy hair in his mid-twenties. The older man was introduced as Bill Gray. It was no surprise that the younger, a pea from the same pod, was Billy Gray, his son. They both shook hands with Roddy and the elder said, 'Good to meet you, Dave's been telling us about you. The Snowies scheme must have been interesting work?'

'It certainly was, and believe me, I'm glad I got the job. I was very lucky in more ways than one. Have you ever been over to the Snowy Mountains, Bill?'

They talked a little about the Snowies and about work the two Bills had done, farm dams to big dams for irrigation storage, clearing, preparation and site work for hospitals, hotels, demolitions. It was a great range of experience: if they worked together, there wouldn't be much they couldn't do. As he spoke with them, he realized that young Billy was a bright live-wire who had operated almost every kind of earth moving equipment. Amongst the larger group which flexed into changing sub-groups, Roddy was introduced to two geologists, a draughtsman, and a civil engineer. He thought that it must be unusual that they were all talking about work, about what they were doing, what problems they were wrestling with, what major projects were being mooted, and what mining exploration was being done. There was talk about raising capital for ventures, about working with lawyers and accountants about what was happening in prospecting geology; there was a driller there, too, who had worked with them. Were people seeing the amazement, the enthralled look on Mckenzie's face? This was an intelligence gold mine. Without leaving the Billies and Dave—and he did not really have to—he wanted to speak to, and register attention with as many of these other men as he could. This would not be his last Friday at the Highway.

At a certain hour, Bert McPartland, the publican, put on a free drink for everyone in the bar. Bill Gray introduced Roddy to Bert who came from behind the bar to say hello to the men in the groups when he had finished helping with the rush to pour his free Friday round.

Before he left, Roddy made sure to say to each of the people he had met that 'he had to go' and 'Oo-roo'. He said to Dave he would give him a call when he had read the advertisements

in Saturday's paper and said his good-byes to the Grays, saying,
'I'm sure we'll all be on a job together in the not too distant
future.'

The present suburbs of Nedlands, Claremont, and
Swanbourne had all been part of a sheep station when Perth,
the present capital, was struggling to grow in the difficult early
days of the colony. But grow it steadily did, there was no rush,
just a steady, almost continuous increase in settlement housing
from the day in 1829 when the first blocks of land were being
sold. The manner of their slow growth engendered from the
start in the population of these suburbs a strong feeling of
interdependence; for indeed, if there were no feeling of it, it was
a fact of early colonial life that their situation demanded. They
had become so well knit, so comfortably together, so fervent
in their attachment to the local institutions which they had
created that there was a sense of felling that they had been there
forever. There were big houses and smaller houses managing
directors and worker all mowing their lawns or painting their
sheds all speaking in the same vernacular and using the same
colloquialisms. As time went by, there were primary schools,
secondary school, and colleges; Methodist Ladies College,
Presbyterian Ladies College, Christchurch College, and John
XXIII. There was a church for every conceivable variety of
Christian belief just a comfortable distance apart; cricket and
football clubs, sailing clubs and tennis clubs, And of course
there had to be pubs like, the. Highway, the Swanbourne, the
Nedlands Park, the Shenton Park.

Of the men who had gathered in the Highway that night,
there would have been an equivalent gathering in each of the
others. Amongst those men, there would be very few who lived
as much as five miles away. And there is significance in the suffix
'park'; throughout and around them there were dedicated parks
and sports fields. There were tall, ancient red gums, trees of
varying eucalypt varieties, melaleucas, and amongst them, the
imported European trees, the most beloved and most successful
of these, the London Plane.

As he drove back to Cottesloe, he marvelled at the experience
he had just had. When he next went there, he must make sure

he missed nothing; he must hear what the geologists were doing and for whom. Mining meant haulpaks, shovels, front-end loaders! And for Mauri, light vehicles, trucks, even cars. 'Get going, Mckenzie!'

He went home, showered, changed, and got to Mac's at about half past six and found his way through to the gathering, leaving on the hall table a bottle of Veuve in a carton, with a card for Janet. The small group of guests was on the lawn having spilled out from the verandah. The sunset evening was warm and the women were in light bright dresses. A barbecue was sending out mixed Asian aromas of fish and meat from different plates and open grilles on the barbecue. Claude and Plum wearing stout, very professional aprons appeared to have control of one end of the fire where they were grilling kebabs which each had marinated and skewered at home. He went to meet Mac by the barbecue, excused himself after a few words of greeting, and saying he would be right back, went to greet Janet. Ann would not be there tonight she told him, she was going to the airport to meet Lynne which, in fact, he had known.

Mac was interested to know every detail about what he had been up to. When he heard about Bruno's next likely contract, he said, 'Roddy, you've got to get yourself a good accountant, and for your kind of business, as well as mine, you can't get a better one than Frank. We'd better get a hold of him tonight so that you can get something organized next week. You'll soon see that while you're out there and doing the work, you will find—and there's many blokes who've gone wrong at this first stage—that there just isn't time in the day to look after the business accounting. You just wouldn't be able to get a full knowledge of tax laws and using your bank, before you got yourself into real strife. He called to Frank who was nearby. 'Frank! Any chance of a bloke getting a beer? And one for Mckenzie too while you're at it.'

'I'll give him a hand,' said Roddy and went over to Frank. 'G'day, Frank. How are you? I'll give you a hand and find out where the ammunition's stored.' They returned to the cooking site where talkative, but attentive, chefs also required the service of runners to fetch beer, to keep them in the fun of the gathering while bringing their kebabs to readiness.

'I was just hearing Roddy's story and suggested to him that he should talk to you tonight about getting an accountant with a view to getting himself set for a start so that he doesn't get off on the wrong foot,' Mac said to Frank.

'Well, it just so happens that's what I do for a living. Can you come in first thing on Monday morning—say, nine o'clock?'

'That would be great, Frank,' Roddy said with enthusiasm.

These men were drawing him into their society of quiet, solid success. He was conscious of this privilege and its strengthening effect. He was beginning to belong. He was being pointed in the direction of effort and its reward of success. He was also seeing that there was space for a good life of firm friendships, contented marriages, and sharing of recreational interests and activity.

At first light, Roddy joined the paperboys and Harry down in the shop on Saturday morning, did not spend much time helping to fold the papers ready for delivery, seized one and went quickly up to his flat, squeezed some orange juice, and opened up the classified advertising section.

Under 'Tenders and Contracts', there it was. "Expressions of Interest …are invited by The Main Roads Department… interested to tender for an improved roadway to run from Marble Bar, for twenty-eight miles, to Big Beauty proposed haematite mine site'.

'My god!' he exclaimed to himself, his head dazzled by the star burst of possibilities in this venture. The roadwork was just a start.

What about the mine site preparation? And the trucks needed to take the ore to the port, the possible trucking contract; the heavy equipment to operate extraction from underground and to haul it when up top? This was huge!

On his excited first reading, the Main Roads contract was quite specific, he thought, and was confined to the road improvement which was only becoming a Main Roads project because the state government had succumbed to the honeyed persuasion of the miners that a road would be a 'long-term asset' to 'opening up the region', 'serving cattle stations', and 'attracting future tourism' giving 'access to a valuable mineral'. Yes, the road was the primary target. But he had to get working on the plant and equipment aspects immediately. The establishment of the Australian agency for earthmoving plant was becoming urgent, urgent!

While this blast was still thundering in his head, he had to continue to examine the tenders. There was one other. The Shire of Collie required a road to be built from an existing public road south-east of Collie to a point where the Collie Coal Company was going to tackle the Hebe seam from another, more productive angle. This had an earlier date for receipt of tender and a start within the month. (Roddy fervently hoped that the rumours were right which informed him that it may be an open-cut project! Think of that, he told himself.) He would have to go for that too. He thought of the people he could draw upon to man this job and maybe leave him a bit of time to get the plant agency preparation begun. He was tense with excitement. Seizing a notepad, pens, his gazetteer of Western Australia, a state sheet map, and after a memorized rereading of the tenders and while his head boiling about to burst, he stuffed them into a small rucksack and set off for the Cottesloe Beach Cafe and breakfast.

'What a glorious day,' he thought, looking around, and down at the ocean where a few surfers bobbed, waiting for waves. 'Isn't it great to be alive?' he asked himself.

He wanted to phone Mauri immediately and had to bear the frustration of waiting until he would get back from sailing and when he may be at home before inevitably going out with Doris for the evening. He wouldn't be too late to go and collect the Main Roads contract documents after his talk with Frank. He would draft a letter requesting a set of tender documents to take to Miss Gaunt for posting to Collie Shire before closing of the mail at six p.m. on Monday. It would be there for Tuesday morning. What he wanted to think about now was Marble Bar and get his thoughts targeted on all the elements of business opportunity, set up a time/activity plan, and chart the interdependencies of events. Time would not lie heavy between, but he had to practice calm control for two days until Monday.

Doris answered the phone when he rang the Perrotts and the chit-chat was limited to the basic question, 'How are you?' She knew Roddy would not have rung for a social chat; most unlikely anyway. 'I know you want to speak to me, darling, but I'll get Mauri for you. I'm getting dressed to go out with another man. *Au revoir.* I'll get the dirty details from Mauri. Saw Jill today, she's well. They won today. Hang on.'

Mauri came to the phone, and Roddy gave him a situation report and strategic summary.

'Can Dave Oliver and the other blokes do this Collie job without you if necessary?' he asked right away, as if he had something already in mind.

'They're all very experienced and dependable. I'm sure they could. Though I'd like spend at least part of the time with them to get to know them better through working with them and to get a spirit of interdependablity developed. Why do you ask?'

'I'm going up to Japan in a fortnight and I think you should come. In the meantime, I'll get one of my contacts from Fusan to airmail, directly to you, everything he can gather about *Ugojim* who are making very good haulpaks, and they may already have begun to think of Australia as an export market. We could help with their thinking. The Japanese have been impatient about our restrictions on exporting the massive amounts of iron ore they know we have. The embargos have just been lifted. The government will be looking to an enormous inflow of foreign capital to take up and develop the tenancies. There will be a little bit of lead time, while the investors get organized and begin to put men on the ground. I think we should begin our first moves. Look, I'll send you all my Japan flight details; just arrange so that we fly together, I use the bank to handle our travel arrangements. You've got one successful WA job you can brag about as well as the Snowies, which, let's face it, is not a great deal and isn't the essence of being an agent and marketing very big-value heavy equipment all over Australia, me boy! Post me, in less than a page of a letter, the headings for the steps you will take to represent them here. Be prepared to make a presentation when you get to Japan to convince them why a big Japanese plant manufacturer should choose you to be their agent in Australia. You seem to have gone down well with Rhys and his mates and he has a high regard for the other blokes you've met up with, so it looks as if you're settling in on the right lines. We'll have to organize financial backing. Needless to say, and I'll tell you now, I'll stand behind you. I'll have a yarn to Rhys, and if he's going to be available, I'll come over to Perth next Thursday and we can meet on Friday to see if we can all work together. Your friend John McGillivray with two shopping centres on his mind will probably not have too much financial leeway at the moment, but I'd like to speak to him anyway. After I've spoken to Rhys, expect a call. Keep checking your answering machine. Talk to John McGillivray to see if he's got any time on Friday and tell him that you've got Rhys and me coming to talk about giving you financial support. After I ring you about Rhys, set up a meeting place. Do a good job of your Collie Shire tender. You must get that one. See you on Thursday.'

'How much spinning can the human head stand?' he wondered. His thoughts ran on: 'Mauri had stepped right in close. There was no doubting his enthusiasm. He obviously had a picture in his mind of what I would need to do and he knew that to try for this very big deal he would need all the help he could get. 'And what was a network of friends for?' Mauri seemed to be asking. 'One day it would be my turn to be in there helping and I will have some experience to draw from when that time comes. Boy, so much is happening so quickly: I must get myself organized and get started.' He had also detected in Mauri's conversation another very important dimension in business planning that was completely new to him—Australia's national, political, economic interests and directions. Mauri was aware of this influential element. Roddy could only see from newspapers and wireless short unconnected descriptions of circumstances which seemed very distant from his present needs. He could see only that he had to get work here, now, and take every practical step to build a company as his savings grew.

In 1960–1961, Australia was not doing so well. The recent glory days of merino wool selling at a pound Australian per pound weight had ended. The press had labelled the last national budget as 'the Panic Budget'. Inflation was high. Allowing increased imports to energize the internal market was not working; and exports were low. There was no great interest in iron as an export commodity. It was thought that if it were mined and sold, Australia would be left without iron for its future needs. Even when massive deposits were discovered, the embargo on its export had remained until 1960 nationally, and 1961 in Western Australia. The increasing industrialization of Japan created a high demand. To bring the iron ore to the market would require huge volumes of capital which had to be found overseas. The government would welcome such an inflow of overseas investment. Australia, particularly Western Australia, could be about to undergo a time of growth and wealth creation. He may not have realized it quite yet, but the change of thinking and worldview that this brought about in Australia was going to have to happen—and for Roddy Mckenzie too.

He could put thinking about the tenders aside until he got the Main Roads documents on Monday, then wait for the Collie tender. He must immediately compose the page for Mauri; and Miss Gaunt could send it by facsimile. He would now begin to sketch a proposal for the Japanese company Ugojim, with a completion deadline ten days from now (!) and draw up a strategic marketing plan. Tonight, he must write that one-page summary of marketing points, ready for Miss Gaunt to send by fax to Mauri first thing on Monday morning. From his intelligence gleanings, from newspapers and radio, his mind had settled on the idea that WA would the precise place in Australia to start. In their regular phone conversations, Mauri and Roddy had been able to talk about gathering intelligence on Japanese manufacturers and the dearth of such information in WA. Mauri's contacts had gathered valuable information about a company called Ugojim. This had come to hand on Friday and was being sent to him by airmail and special delivery. It should reach Roddy on Monday.

In his appreciation, Roddy did not omit to consider that the companies that took up the tenements and put up the bulk of the capital would be big organizations. They would be mining companies: if not, then purely investors. The top levels of the men who would be entrusted with the development of the mines and extraction of the ore would inevitably be battle-hardened mining campaigners who had done it all before all over the world. Among them would be men who had bought heavy equipment before, and who had operated it before. Their first thoughts would be to buy products they knew and sellers who had cultivated them over years. They would place their orders in the very early days, long before any dust was stirred in the Pilbara ranges. Ugojim's products were not yet widely known. These men would need to be shown on the ground that Ugojim products matched the criteria of all the others on offer and had something unique, something extra in utility, power, and technical backup. They would have to be sold the idea of achieving mining targets in a 'partnership' of Ugojim and Mckenzie Earthmoving.

He worked on, and on Sunday too, until it was time to go to Nedlands to watch the Cherubs race and to welcome Lynne back. He wanted take her and Ann out for dinner afterwards to thank them for all that they had done to get him established in WA.

They chose to go to the Cafe Greco where Ann had taken him. It was where everyone went after sailing in all their noisy numbers. It was the same rollicking fun as before and the same enjoyable food. There was a gush of the sailing banter then other topics like work, cricket, and personalities, and a new topic about a product that may come on the market soon.

A pill to prevent conception had been tested and found effective; so much so that it looked likely that it would be available sometime soon and may even be sold over the counter. All the lurid possibilities of frenetic frolics in fornication were seized upon immediately to much ribald imagination and laughter. Then conversation settled around the more practical benefits of motherhood by choice, and the long history of female sexual self-restraint being likely to continue into the future for reasons other than the fear of pregnancy.

He did enjoy seeing Lynne again and realized that apart from being a very attractive female she was very bright, quick witted, her charm being an emanation of the totality of her abilities and personality. He imagined that her emotions and feeling of sexuality would have to find a particular, special respondent.

When he returned on Sunday evening, and simply because his head was abuzz with thinking, imagining, supposing, his nerves were twitching, searching for insights, for information. He checked his mailbox. There was a note card from the PMG to say that there was an express item at Cottesloe Post Office. The office would be open from 8.30 a.m. on Monday. Good, he could pick it up before he went to meet with Frank.

Frank's office was on the second floor of a two-storey building, which he owned, right next door to the post office on Stirling Highway.

There were warm greetings, and when Frank asked whether he had had an enjoyable week end Roddy told him all about the phone conversation between him and Mauri, which had to include a concise description of their relationship. 'You are very fortunate to have made such a friendship, but I can see that you realize that. It is going to be very important to you, I think. Our meeting now will have to be influenced by what Mauri is proposing and we have to decide to do things now that we could have kept for a future date when developing events dictated direction. We will need to create a company and we will need to get you the supporting troops that all companies need to have. The first appointment you're going to have to make is an accountant. Sitting here together now, you may feel obliged to make me that person. Roddy, I assure you: you must not. If you have other plans, you should follow them. You'll need a lawyer and you'll need a banker. There will be other things or supports you will have to think about and your lawyer and accountant will help you with that.'

'Frank! I was presumptuous enough to think of this present meeting as being with "my accountant"!'

'I was hoping that would be your choice. I liked the cut of your jib and how you've handled those older men at the OBH. They're all solid successful men that you can trust, they trust each other and what you may or may not have twigged, they haven't said it and there's been no need to, but they have brought you into that circle of trust. You told us the story of your good fortune in Australia. I believe it's just about to begin.'

'You're going to go to Japan with Mauri Perrott as a well-documented Private Limited Company. We should have that achieved by Thursday when Mauri arrives; if your lawyer can hurry the Companies Office. You may actually have to sit down with your lawyer and that could possibly need to be arranged for after hours. We'll see. But tell me now whether you would like me to suggest a lawyer?'

'Certainly. Did you have Claude in mind?'

'I would be doing you a disservice if I didn't,' Roddy readily assented.

'Good. I'll see if I can get him on the phone now. What will you call the company?'

He really hadn't thought about it but instinct and deep conviction made him declare, 'Mckenzie Earthmoving!'

'Claude, g'day, Frank here. I've got Roddy with me'—Roddy felt elevated to hear that there was no need to use his surname—'and we're forming a company for him, would your firm agree to being his solicitors? I hope there's not another Mckenzie Earthmoving because that's the name we've chosen. We have a major meeting this Friday, so we'll need to have been through the Companies Office by Thursday.'

'We've always tried to avoid taking on Scotsmen as clients. You can tell him this is an exception which we're approaching with caution. How long is your present meeting going to take?'

'We'll be finished by half past ten at the latest.'

'I'll brief my clerk. He'll be waiting for Roddy at eleven o'clock.' With that, the arrangements amongst the client, the accountant, and the lawyer were decisively in place.

'This will get the legal framework in place. We need twenty shareholders but a minimum of two. Neither Claude nor I can be shareholders. They will be one pound shares, but yours will be founder's preference shares to ensure that the other shareholders can't outvote you. So who've we got?'

'Well I'd like to offer shares to Mauri, Mac, Rhys, Bruno, and some special people; Erik, Jill Lowing, and Ann and Lynette, my mother, father, and sister Jane. There are another three very special people.'

'You can stop there. The share register needs to be sufficient to meet the requirements of the Companies Office now and other decisions will most certainly have to be made very shortly. In fact, before you go to Japan, I'm sure it will have changed. Let's meet Thursday's deadline. I'll need the names and addresses of just some of the people you want to include. Can you do that now and we'll get them typed up so that you can take into them in to Claude's office? I'll tell you where that is. It will be useful to make this your registered office for all company correspondence and we will act as your company secretary and you can use our fax until we get further down the track. I can see that you'll very soon need an office of your own. Now, take this,' he said, passing Roddy a slim quarto accounts book. 'You will need to enter here every amount you spend on Mckenzie Earthmoving down to the nearest Ha'penny. If there's not a heading to cover it, put it here'—and he indicated a 'journal' page—'and keep all your receipts. Now, who do you bank with?'

'From before I came to Australia, I've been with the Bank of New South Wales and one day I'll tell you the story why.'

They discussed fees for service and Roddy happily trusted that those agreed upon would be appropriate. They also discussed Mauri's visit and the meeting with Mac and Rhys. 'I'm sorry I can't fix a time for the Friday meeting of Mauri and Mac and Rhys. From the business point of view, I feel I must have you there; and I'd like that personally too. Will you come if the time suits; please? Naturally, that would be a legitimate fee.'

'I'll make the time suit,' he said positively.

As they stood up to part, Frank took his hand and looked at him squarely. 'Well, Roddy, you're on your way. Things are moving for you and pretty fast by the sound of it. You know I wish you all the luck in the world; and every other good wish.' He put a hand Roddy's shoulder, adding, 'You've got good friends and they'll be right beside you.'

'It's a pleasing feeling to have great moments in your life with people you admire. That's the way it has been for me. *This* is a great moment. You have my respect and admiration, Frank, and great appreciation for what you are doing for me.'

At Hill, Fox & Company, he was introduced to the senior clerk who was indeed senior. The tall, slim, white-haired man wearing a pleasantly loose-fitting grey serge three-piece suit gave Roddy the impression of kindly old uncle. He was perfect for his surroundings which were exactly what Roddy imagined a solicitor's office would look like, he had, after all read Dickens and this was Dickensian: mind you, Claude too was a suitable fit for a Dickensian character. With all his placid friendliness, Mr. Derek Jacobs was the epitome of business exactitude. He knew exactly what was required by the Companies Office and they would get exactly that with the minimum inconvenience to his client. 'The papers from your accountant are very well presented and complete, Mr. Mckenzie. We can do our part and they will be in the Companies Office this afternoon.' Within half an hour, Mr. Jacobs had ushered him out into the brightness of Pier Street where Fido was waiting, baking in the dry scorching heat, exposed to the many demure yet watchful eyes of the cathedral's tall leadlights and the glaring, dominating eye of the sun.

The position of the sun clicked a switch somewhere amongst the whizzing turmoil of his brain and he knew at once what he must do. He must seek some shade for Fido. No, he couldn't bear the self-delusion: it was time for a beer; and yes, there could be a bit of shade behind the club. But first he would go across to the Association of Mining and Mineral Development on St Georges Terrace and see what intelligence bumf he could pick up. Maybe there was a bulletin issued on latest events in discovery, tenements, and licenses? There was indeed a news sheet and some interesting mining-specific maps of which there were copies available. Carrying what he could take away, he got into Fido's scarcely bearable heat, took some old leather gloves (memoria of the Snowies) from the glove box, without them, it would have been impossible to hold the steering wheel, then up the hill above the city to the government office near Parliament House to pick up the Main Roads 'Expression of Interest to Tender'.

'Now you may have that beer!'

'Guid aifternoon, Mr. Mckenzie, an' fou are ye dain'?' greeted the smiling old Andy when he arrived at the club bar.

'I'm very well, thank you, Andy, and how are you?'

'Ach, no' that bad. What'll ye hae, sir?'

'A very cold beer please Andy; in one of those glasses with a handle, please.'

Roddy said hello to a trio at the bar and let them hear him say, 'I've got a bit of work to do, Andy. I'll just go out to a table.'

He was not in conversational mode. He wanted, quietly, to go through all that had been happening, must happen next, what more needed to be done, and read the government tender. He sat down with his back to the direction of the bar and the front entrance and spread his material on the table. For a few moments, he ignored it, while he recapitulated the events of the morning and took a hefty swig of his beer.

Some significant elements jumped out from the Main Roads 'Request for Expressions of Interest to Tender for Marble Bar Eastern Pilbara Road Construction'. First was that the contractor who did the clearing and preparation for final road making was to supply, transport, and install all culverts and drains. The area maps provided from Ordnance Survey Sheets were simply main guides to the positions of these. The precise locations would be decided by the contractor; detailed surveying for location of drains and culverts were to be surveyed by the contractor. He thought immediately of Howard Treloar, went to the club telephone, and left a message on Howard's answering machine to ask him to phone him at his flat or meet him at his flat any time after two that afternoon. He finished his beer and automatically stood up with the intention of having another. 'That's enough of the good life, Mckenzie, just one more as you scan the other material and you're off!'

'Yes, sir,' was how he replied to himself.

The phone at the bar was ringing. Andy had to stop pouring Roddy's beer while he answered. 'Good afternoon, sir . . . Naval and Military Club . . . Colour Sergeant Stewart speaking, sir. Aye, he's right here, sir. Wait, one'—and turning to Roddy—'A gentleman to speak to you, sir, would you like to take it in the booth?'

'No, it'll be fine here, Andy, if that's all right with you. It won't be a long conversation.' Andy handed over the hand piece. 'Howard, that was quick. Can we meet sometime today? I've got the documents here for a Main Roads "Expression of Interest". There's work for a surveyor in it. You may be interested, I hope. When I leave here, I'll go down to my flat. Could you meet me there? You've got my address. Two thirty? Fine, see you then. Oo-roo.' He gave the phone back to Andy to cradle it. 'Thank you, Andy.' He took his new beer and went back to his table. Now he wished he had not been so self-indulgent. Hurried or not, he forced himself to enjoy the cold refreshing beer; collected his papers, farewelled Andy, and went down the back stairs to Fido.

Howard arrived at the flat right on his tail. They got to work immediately, but it wasn't long before a big bowl of fruit and dishes of nuts appeared on the table amongst the papers.

The first thing Howie did was to seize the maps. 'We're going to have to go up there and look at this site to see what's going to be involved in placing these culverts and drains.'

'Strewth!' he exclaimed. 'There's mobs of them! And "marble" may be a misnomer, but there are going to beds of that hard granite and basalt material traversing this planned road line at nearly right angles just about anywhere, we'll have to hope that they're, deep down, covered with old gravelly wash and clays. I fear they might appear on those inclines though.'

Roddy could see this may not be an easy project to undertake. 'All this means we have to go as soon as we can—immediately almost—but I've got Mauri Perrott coming over here for a meeting that is going to be critically important for the future of Mckenzie Earthmoving; and within a fortnight, he wants me to come up to Japan, also about the Mckenzie Earthmoving future. And tomorrow I should get the tender papers for Collie Shire. I'll need to see these before I go anywhere. I can see that my car won't be suitable for my new way of life. I'm going to have to buy a ute. Surely I'd get a good trade in with Fido?'

'Don't bother about that now we're going to need a vehicle that's run in: I'll borrow one of Dad's utes. My father's company is Treloar Haulage and Transport. We might put the hard word on him to get a good price to shift the equipment and pipe and culverts up to Marble Bar, eh? Hauling that kind of stuff, big equipment, boilers, turbines; that's what they do all the time.'

Roddy laughed as he said, 'With those connections, we'd have to get the best deal going! As soon as I've had a look at the Collie tender, I'll need to work out how soon I could leave. What about you, Howie? Do you think we could leave on Sunday? I guess we'd need two full days at least on the site, don't you? I've got the meeting with Mauri, Mac, and Rhys on Friday, so I've got till then to work on the Collie contract which will involve a trip down there. Mm, things are going to be a tight fit. I have to be ready to go to Japan only a week after to make a bid for the Australian distribution of Ugojim earthmoving equipment. How are you going to be situated for time?'

'I'm more available than I'd like to be. The roads after Newman are even more horrible than they were before it, so we will take damn near two days of shared driving and maybe a six-hour kip at Capricorn Roadhouse.'

'I'm worried about a time for "jollies" with the inter-staters who have done, and are doing, so much for me. If you knew them, you'd know that they never stop working really. If you go fishing, you may catch a fish or two and enjoy that, but mostly, you'll be talking, planning, deciding, agreeing, and making deals. They're all fiercely independent, but they all know they are depending on each other. But if I tell them, even before we meet, that you and I must go north because of Main Roads contract, I know they'll accept that, and work round it. I'm not taking that for granted Howie, but you know, I've already got a feeling for these men. They'll respect my need.'

'Fine. Well, I'll get a ute from Dad and get it ready for the road. We'll just keep in touch for the details. If you ring home and my mother answers, you can tell her any details; she'll get them all right and pass the message one hundred per cent. She may also ask you questions. Answer them thoughtfully. You may be surprised that what she asked you is something important you hadn't thought about.'

'That's great, Howie, I'll keep opening my answering machine and keep alert for the phone. Knowing that you know Bruno and some of the others at the OBH, if there's any after-hours eating and drinking going on when Mauri is here, would you like to be involved?'

Making the whole idea of such an invitation ironically minimal, Howie pitched a voice as unemotional, as if uncaring, and said, 'Oh we-ell, all right then.' Roddy had the feeling that another member had just put his thumb mark down as crew on the as-yet-unlaunched vessel of Mckenzie Earthmoving.

His afternoons' work on the Ugojim paper found him at first floundering, almost hopeless. He could not help but list the negatives, the realistic view of his position. His experience of earthmoving equipment was short and shallow, he had no money, he did not yet know anything much about the country in which he was proposing to represent Ugojim, even to the very word 'marketing' in his mind, he had attached an adscription: 'There be dragons'.

When he first wrote, in a brief introductory paragraph, a very short sentence on his front line action in the Korean War, he could not know what a powerful influence those few words would play in his entire future with Ugojim. Yet as he wrote, he had not really known why he had included it, other than to explain activities in time. He had learned as a junior officer, ten principles of war. They had captured his imagination and he had mused on how they applied to any purposeful goal-centred human activity. He drew upon them now. His proposal was all about: Selection and Maintenance of the Aim, Maintenance of Morale, Offensive Action, Security, Surprise, Concentration of Force, Economy of Effort, Flexibility, Cooperation, and Sustainability.

Of course, he used none of these words in any way discernible as military, each was incorporated in newly formed phrases of civilian purpose and their original military purpose camouflaged in civilian terminology. Offensive action had now changed into the strategy master Clausewitz's hated 'intelligence' and had become Roddy's declared intentions of finding out about the new company, about its structure, who would decide to buy equipment, how to convince that person or those people of the advantages of buying Ugojim products. Finally he wanted to have convinced Ugojim of his personal ability, his strength of character and the power of his aspiration to do everything in his power, with dedicated energy to put Ugojim on the Australian map. With him and Ugojim sharing the same need for success, they would cooperate to capture a profitable, continuing market for their products across Australia.

From Miss Guant's office, in the sun suffused, life shaping, socially tribal culture of Cottesloe; from Western Australia, the nation's least considered state; the inexperienced new-Australian sent off, by facsimile, to Mauri Perrott in far distant Sydney, a brief message—the required page—about a matter that affected Australia and Japan.

'I can't see how I could do better than that. I'm sure Mauri won't take long to respond,' he mused, as he drove back to his home. 'I'll go for a run and a swim then toddle up to meet my mentors before I cook dinner,' he thought. He had just had a shower and was changing when Howie phoned. Howie, sounding very excited, launched into his story. 'I asked Dad about the ute, no worries there, but when I told him what we wanted it for, he said we were a pair of suicidal lunatics, and Main Roads would never allow two of their own blokes to do what we planned to do in this season. Typical Dad', he said, 'you'd better bring him over here for a feed, would you be free to come over for dinner tonight?'

'Of course I'd like to,' he said honestly. 'And listening to what your father said, I think I'd better. You'll need to tell me your address and the time.'

'Dad's going to be home about six so any time just after that. I'm glad Dad wants to see you and I'd want you to meet my mother as well.'

———∘∘∘▪◈▪∘∘∘———

What on earth could he bring for Mrs. Treloar? The shops were closed. Would Harry have something? Something for a senior lady whom he had never met? No, he'd have to fall back on the old reliable. Opposite Frank Dalby's building in an old limestone warehouse a young enthusiast called George Formby had opened a wine store he had named the Wine Cellar. He had already bought wine there and knew he stocked Veuve Cliquot.

The Treloar's house was on View Terrace on the highest point in East Fremantle, and when the water tower, with which it shared the eminence to the east, was discounted, it had a view of river, ocean, and Rottnest Island to rival all others. It was tall and handsome, a three-storey tower of skilled masonry set in a garden of native flowering shrubs and low trees on the downward slopes where an ornate Victorian 'bandstand' created a pleasure point. Howie answered the door bell and took him through the elegant house of high-ceilinged rooms their off-white walls clad in tastefully framed original paintings, mounted as if by a sensitive curator of a permanent exhibition. Of course there was a roofed verandah broad and wide, giving an extensive view, and of course, it was the place where the Treloar family spent much time. A tall rangy chiselled man with greying curly red hair came forward and took Roddy's hand. 'I'm Freddie Treloar.'

'And I'm Ethel,' said a smiling woman of middle height who with tight, lightly tanned skin looked very fit and strong. She had represented Western Australia in hockey. 'This is our daughter Gwen,' she said, and a fine-looking girl made a lithe movement forward to shake his hand. 'You'll have missed the session at the OBH tonight, so I imagine you're ready for a beer, eh?'

'Thank you. Yes, I would like a beer, please.' He was still clutching the champagne which he now moved forward to present to Ethel. 'Just a way to say hello, Ethel. If you're a teetotaler, you may have less-ascetic friends.'

'Thank you, Roddy. I've never had a friend of that kind, but I won't mind sharing.'

'Now what's this bloody business of going up to Marble Bar? I can just see the headlines in the *West*—"Young English migrant perishes in Pilbara sun". Even the lizards stay at home when it's like this. I got the paper and I saw that at this stage it's just calling for expressions of interest. When they see who's serious about doing the job, they'll send them the tenders. In no way will the work start before June, I can tell you. So you can show your interest then just calm down and wait for the tender, but if you need a ute for something else, give me a shout any time or tell Howie.'

Freddie Treloar had worked for his dad from when he left school and had built up a very big trucking and haulage business. From his father's lowly start to a growing fleet clearing and delivering freight from the docks, Freddie had pushed further and had built a major company, which in many cases was the only operator with the capacity to deliver anything that could be put on any conceivable truck to absolutely anywhere around the state where it was possible to take a motor vehicle. Treloar Haulage now delivered anywhere in Australia. Even houses had changed their location on a Treloar truck. From a pretty Christmas package by a little van, to a turbine for a power plant on a low loader. The family stayed together throughout a very pleasant meal of roast beef and burgundy. Each was interested, participative, involved in every part of the evening's discussions.

As the talking went easily on, a natural process was drawing from Roddy sketches from his past. He related how incredibly fortunate he had been and how so many people who became firm friends had given him so much help and were prepared to stand to support him as set out for his next objective. He told him about his relationship with Mauri Perrott and how he was coming over here for meeting this Thursday; and how he wanted Roddy to go with him to Japan to meet with Ugojim with a view to making a bid for the Australian dealership. While participating in every conversation and questioning Roddy, he was watching and listening to this young man and feeling the pulse of his ambition. He knew, and still did know, about setting goals and going strategically and tactically, with concentrated force, to achieve them.

'Roddy, you're making me more than just interested to hear what you plan to do and the stage you're at now. There's a bit of excitement here. I want to be in. I'd like to be part of it. And I think there's at least there's a couple of ways I might be able to help you. The Treloar Haulage company is a success and I'd be a liar to say I'm not proud of it. People like to be associated with success. If Ugojim got a brief look at the Treloar company's story; and if they knew that I was backing you with not only money—though I'd want to be in that too—which means I think you could make me money, but advice, guidance, and support that would surely help to overcome the possibility that they may think you don't have enough runs on the board.' Everyone at the table, and Roddy especially, could see, hear, and feel that Freddie Treloar was excited.

'My god, Freddie, what am I to say? I think what you suggest would have a huge positive effect on Ugojim, and being here tonight with you and your family gives me a strong feeling that we could work together.'

Ethel spoke up, 'All this family is total Treloar: we all think and feel Treloar. You've heard what Freddie has said and we've heard what you've been saying.' She looked at Gwen and Howie, at each face for a second or two, like a concert trio waiting for the beat they would see and sense in the eyes and the faces of the other players, continued, and said, 'And we want to be with you too.' He knew what Mauri and Doris would feel having Freddie Treloar aboard. Apart from being a local business hero, Freddie Treloar had captained East Fremantle when it used to win the premierships that Claremont did not win. Mac, Bruno, Claude, and Frank would all want Freddie in. He could count on the group at the OBH. What a team! Ugojim was looking like a decided possibility.

When he rang Mauri first thing in the morning, his reaction to Roddy's description of the previous evening was enthusiasm for Freddie's inclusion. Freddie seemed to be the kind of man and his company the kind of operation that the Australian Ugojim should be associated with. Rhys was similarly pleased. He had already suggested to Mauri, and was now confirming with Roddy, that his board room was the most appropriate place for the Ugojim planning meeting. As he said, 'And we've got all the showbiz abracadabra, chart stands and overhead and a film projector. I can have a lunch brought in so we can work on. You can confirm place and time with the other blokes now and tell them it's most likely to take all of the day. You can now draw up the agenda, we can talk about it and get it to the others so that they have as much time as possible to think.'

Again Roddy was somewhat stunned; Mauri and Rhys were clean, clear, and concise. They did not know that he did not know about, nor therefore had even considered, an 'agenda'? What was that? As with 'Expression of Interest', 'fax', and others, these were new terms coming into his essential vocabulary every day. He'd have to consult his most trusted companion, bought from that treasure cave, Claremont bookshop, the mighty tome of an Oxford English Dictionary. Maybe the old army idea of 'Making an Appreciation' would help him? So he went through the headings in his mind replacing 'enemy' with 'Ugojim' although he could never consider them in any reality as such. It seemed to work; and when he had listed his 'considerations', the definition of agenda as defined by the OED, took form. A quick visit to Maude's office (Miss Gaunt and Mr Mckenzie were now on first-name terms), and the message was off to Mauri and Rhys asking for their additions/deletions before circulation. Before the day was out, the alterations suggested by Mauri and Rhys were incorporated, a finished version typed up and faxed to all concerned. A separate note was faxed by Mauri to say that he and Doris did not want anyone at the airport. They would go to the Adelphi; he would come to Rhys's office on Friday morning; they could meet up socially with the ladies after work. Mac called Roddy after the agendas went out. He asked if Mauri would be bringing his wife. 'Right. Bring up all the fax numbers and Janet can invite everyone for dinner up here on Friday night.' So he did. Janet said she would invite all the Corner boys and asked if there was anyone else he would like to be there. When he mentioned Ann and Lynne, she said, 'Oh, good, I didn't know if they were yours or mine—and Howard Treloar, that's good too. Do the Treloars have any more family?' And he said, 'Yes, they do, a daughter called Gwen who's about two years younger than Howie.'

'Good, we'll invite her too.'

'I'm glad you suggested that. They are very committed to each other.'

'We'll do it on the verandah because that mob likes to blether.'

The tail of a monsoon cyclone was spreading down the coast and the wind was moist and north-westerly so Perth could look out for a bit of a blow and showers of heavy rain. Janet knew this, but it was of no concern, the verandah was roofed and there was plenty of room to come inside. Anyway, it may not come or it could have come and gone by Friday night.

Friday morning began hot and humid. Bits of cloud on the front of the breeze had drifted in from the north-west in which direction, on the very edge, very low and just distinguishable, breaking the even line on the far horizon, there was a long bumpy ooze of white, foaming cloud like cream being squeezed from a bun whose top and bottom were ugly dark grey-black.

Before the men took their seats at marked places around the oval table, in Rhys's board room, Roddy Mckenzie, the meeting's chairman, had allowed a total of five minutes just for shoulder rubbing and for him in his elegantly-cut, grey-tailored suit to move among the men to make the introductions informally. Along with the agenda, he had issued mini biographies of those present.

At the table, he chose not to stand. 'I am very proud to be here for our purpose today in the presence of men of your calibre and life success. And I am humbled to think that you have left your important daily tasks to come here . . . to help me.'

Roddy's voice was clear and confident with an evidence of solemnity. There was neither the least tinge nor the very slightest tint of bullshit in what his words meant. How the listeners felt, he couldn't tell. Nothing of any emotion or effect showed in their faces as he looked round.

'Your presence leads me to think that to anchor the whole of Ugojim's Australian activities in a company that we shall form and operate is a worthwhile venture . . . with potential to bring us all considerable financial returns . . . and great satisfaction in the work of making it succeed and grow. 'That means that this meeting will be important to that objective.

'However, its importance is increased because today . . . we will have to go further and faster in our decision making . . . and planning for risk management . . . than we might normally prefer . . . because . . . in ten days' time . . . Mauri and I will stand before Ugojim in Hiroshima making your pitch for their Australian representation, sales, and distribution.

'I'm certain you are all dab hands at meetings of this kind . . . I'm equally conscious that apart from Platoon O Groups, I've never chaired a meeting in my life! I know you will all give each other clear air to develop and expound arguments and at their ends, when questions are asked. Those clarifications or explanations will be brief and to the point and can be assured of objective attention.

'With all that preamble done, we can start with the first item on the agenda . . . and because he was a major instigator of this scheme, I'll ask Mauri to address it . . . Mauri, would you like to begin for us please?'

The meeting should have been filmed for posterity and circulated as a management training tool. Such a demonstration of a productive meeting would be wasted on politicians who are not purpose oriented or disciplined in their approaches to ideas or objectives. They at least have one only crystal clear objective: to be elected, regardless of the national virtue or value of any argument that will achieve that primary goal.

It was agreed that it should be the major objective of people going to Japan on behalf of, and representing this group, to have Ugojim become a major shareholder in a company to be called Ugojim Australia Pty. Ltd.

Rhys had two shorthand/typists at the meeting who took turns in recording, and in breaks typed up, as if a Hansard report, everything that was said.

Having present, owners of two companies with national ramifications—Freddie's and Mauri's—was seen as extremely important. Because of the high quality of their relationships to their superiors, these people in every state would become excellent sources of national intelligence and aids to travelling personnel of the new company. For example, if it was needed to be known what the beating of native drums was saying in Kalgoorlie or Mount Newman, there would be one of Rhys's or Freddie's men on the spot embedded in the local community. Mt Isa or Darwin, and similar far-flung places, would be on the network too; and flowing from all of them, their own local networks.

It was agreed that Roddy, Mauri, and Freddie represent the group in Japan. Freddie's film was great stuff and would be cut and re-edited to suit the argument to be presented and the purpose to be achieved. Plum would be asked to put together a maximum two-page piece with mini biographies of all the present members of the group. Existing Japanese intelligence of the iron mining situation was up to that available to Australians, including this group, and apart from the lifting of the embargo on ore exportation the future would to a great extent depend on the whims of politicians. However it seemed right to include photographic slide material and maps to illustrate the terrain where it was most likely to take place and where new harbours may be built. Freddie would be able to let the group see his deep knowledge of conditions at these sites and illustrate photographically the capacity of his vehicles to deliver Ugojim equipment to them. It was going to be part of Roddy's job to sell the advantages of the solidity, harmony, and cooperative abilities of the members of this group to Ugojim. Mauri of course was their source of experience in business and cultural protocols with Japanese people; as in different ways was Freddie.

The sandwich lunch at twelve o'clock was a stand-up, around-the-table affair everyone eager to keep up the pace. At four thirty, Roddy was able to tick off the last of the agenda items and ensure that nothing germane was left unsaid. It was agreed that they had, each and all, achieved his and their objectives. The chairman, having praised the quality of the meeting's endeavours and the detail of the results they had achieved in so short a time, spoke more personally, 'I'm not at all sure that it is appropriate for me to say that this day spent with you men has been the most rewarding day of my short life so far. I'm glad that none of you had asked me whether I had ever chaired a meeting before. It may have given me cause to think and time to go into acute panic. However, I must confine myself to thoughts more relevant to our purpose for being here. It has given me a powerful feeling of confidence that we shall reach our Ugojim objective. And it has made me believe that as men, we have found ourselves to be of the nature that will bind us to go on together to such further achievements as we may wish to set our minds to. Thank you all and each one of you. I can now declare the meeting closed.'

At the end of the meeting, Mauri was handed a message from Doris to say that she was already slaving in the kitchen at the McGillivray's. There was a similar message from Iris to Rhys which was given verbally by his secretary who said, 'I have to tell Rhys to see what he can find in the fridge. I've been invited out to dine.' Each was now scheduled to meet at Mac's. 'Anyone want to go to the OBH for a beer first?' a voice enquired. So that's where they all went.

Roddy dropped Fido Fusan home and walked back to the OBH—a purposely tactical break in contact.

At the OBH, there was a wonderful mood of contentment about achievement from the group. Spirits were high, indeed euphoric. This kind of relaxation would allow a natural ebb to the tide of adrenalin that even these hardened sinners had felt flowing. It would allow them to enjoy their mood and let some of the major ideas from the meeting sink in. When they got to the pub, and climbing the steps making for the bar, Rhys said to Mauri, 'Christ he's a bloody winner that bloke. I've never seen anything like it.'

As they were settling in at the corner and facing their first beers, that's what all of them wanted to talk about and they were glad that Roddy hadn't arrived yet. It was like the eager talk after a football match that your team has just won. Roddy arrived and someone thrust a beer into his hand, it wasn't someone who'd been part of the meeting but had been involved in listening and hearing about their new chum. It was Freddie who had given himself a role of thanking the chairman; 'I don't know how many chaired meetings I've attended in my life, but I think, Roddy, you had the horseman's touch giving us the bit when we needed it, reining us in when you required to. You took ideas we didn't know we had in our heads and made us express them; you trained us to listen objectively when people expressed ideas and led us to work back into them or work out from them. Whatever you might call it, chairmanship or leadership; you knew what you were up to. I thought it was a masterful demonstration of ideal chairmanship and we were too involved to twig what you were doing.' The others called, 'Hear, hear', and each seemed to have an extra word to adorn the praise.

As part of the conversation, Freddie declared that right away he intended to make it a task to sort out all his mining industry contacts, people that he had done work for, and ask a whole lot of different questions now, and he would work on how he could broaden the network further for this new purpose.

And Roddy reminded Mauri of his asking if his men could handle the Collie job on their own. 'I was just thinking that to get this Ugojim operation going, I'm going to have to concentrate on that virtually full time. Another thing I have to think about— I'm going to have a word with Frank and Claude about it—and that is whether Mckenzie Earthmoving as a company goes into Ugojim, or if I go in personally. I'm not sure whether financially I can keep building Mckenzie and get Ugojim operating at the same time. Things are moving a whole lot faster than I could ever have imagined. All of it will require deep thinking. Also I'm thinking that I may have to rob Mckenzie of Billy Gray. There's a lot of moral as well as mental wrestling ahead.'

'I think that's going to be the case for all of us and some of us will go back nearly to living on the edge for a little while until the first cheques start coming in. That depends on the mining market but it will depend a great deal on the deal you and Freddie and I can make with Ugojim.'

There was a wonderful scene on the verandah at Mac's when the men arrived. As they walked through the house to the verandah, there was before them, vividly prominent against a black and threatening sky, a tableau of beautifully dressed women in strong colours; some in stark black were lifted out from absorption into the dark mass of the cloud by skin tones, dressed hair of gold and grey and brown, and the sparkle of jewellery: lovely, vivacious women happily engaged in conversation. There were welcomes, kissing and an immediate merging. The women knew immediately that the mood of the men was not the result of their visit to the pub but rather that their time at the OBH had rounded and softened what must have been a very high level of energy. They also knew that the men were still 'up there somewhere' about their meeting. As man talked with woman an observer every now and then could see a female head turned in Roddy's direction.

Roddy first went to meet Lynne and Ann allowing the husbands to greet their wives. When he could, he felt comfortable to go to Mac and Janet who seemed for the moment to be alone, then Claude Hill came to speak to Mac leaving Roddy to greet his hostess. In their conversation, Janet said, 'I hear you did very well today, Roddy.'

'Janet', he said very earnestly, 'I am very glad to have been in the company of these men today. I find it totally humbling to see the extent that they're prepared to go to, to support me. It makes my plans for success even more demanding of achievement. I have an obligation to *them* now, and I must meet that obligation in every way.'

'It's much bigger and more demanding than representing the state in a sporting competition', Janet responded, 'but it has similarities that I think Ethel would share with you in that you're not just playing for yourself and your pride, you're playing for your whole state, your team, and your supporters and their pride.' Politeness and honour served, he excused himself and made a bee line for Doris.

She greeted him in a big squeezing hug and still partly in her embrace Doris said, 'How's my darling boy? I hear you won the hearts and minds of all present today.'

'I'm happy that they're all as pleased as they have been telling me they are, of course yet I find it totally humbling. You can imagine how clearly I realize that now, to succeed is not just to fulfil my personal dream: I must succeed for all of them. The onus is on me to come up with success. Once the meeting began, I had to keep calm, keep my eye on the objective and do my best to keep everybody's effort on the track.'

Still holding him in her arms, gazing, as might a passionate lover, into his face, softly and with soul-felt conviction, she said, 'And what you have just described is essentially what you will be doing from now on. And, just as it did today, success will result. I know it will.'

As if to add exclamatory punctuation to the passionate strength of her words, the whole sky went mad with flashing wriggling beams of uncontainable energy. Overhead an explosion deafened every ear and shook everybody. Human forms were lit in an eerie flickering brilliance of unimaginable light. They stood stock still, stunned. Yet their black shadows flickered all over the verandah space as if on stage, in jerky exaggerated movements like puppets in a Hindu shadow play. Searching cobra tongues of glowing yellow lit their way to earth disappeared on penetration never to leave it again. Long trembling wires wriggled and flashed light from uncontrollable energy. Dense ungainly cloud, obese villains lumbered towards the back stage to the lit proscenium. In the orchestra pit, cymbals, thudding bass drums, rolling ripples from a battery of tympani signified the drama of heavenly events. On cue, the electrician cut the lights. The unseen conductor's baton waved its final command. There was silent blackness: and the rains came. There was a new sound; water battering down, its volume huge, its weight in tons, falling down in absolute cascades, shooting sheets over the gutters and far beyond the roof's edge. The concentration lasted for ten minutes then steadied to the heavy rain of a normal summer shower. The people who had watched in awe could converse again in raised voices.

Roddy was happy to be at Mac's. He knew so many people and in even so short a time as he had known and been with them he felt as if he were in the company of old friends. As the party went on, the rain's noise diminished and the volume from the men rose and the sudden mighty storm reminded them of the climate and weather in this wide brown land of theirs and how their forebears had to struggle to come to terms with what they couldn't change. Soon there were stories of characters from memory, and men women they had known whose gameness and fortitude they admired. There were some tall tales and while the theme was being enjoyed. Mauri said, 'C'mon, Mckenzie, let's see what progress you're making in your Australianisation programme. What about giving us "The Man from Snowy River"?' It really wasn't his mood this evening for another performance after the day's experience. He was already becoming more than a little uncomfortable with the continuing focus on him. He was going to be put in the spotlight again. A refusal may be seen as a kind of snub and could have a spoiling effect on everyone's happiness. He had to get a grip of himself. Standing where he was, he pulled off his jacket and waistcoat and carelessly dropped them on a nearby chair off which they immediately fell to the floor, as he stepped forward, ready to ham it up, one of the ladies picked them up and almost reverently arranged them carefully on the chair.

He stepped forward and made his body tell of a man ready to relate a yarn. Everyone was on him. Each listener had his or her Australian myth evoked, some vision of the land and life that was his or her own; the idea of mountainous rugged land, The Australian Light Horse in their famous charge at Beersheba, skill pitted against danger and courage to overcome all.

For some seconds after his last dramatic diction ended, there was utter silence. Suddenly the entire verandah was filled to its still rain running roof. 'Hooray!'; 'Where did you say you were from?'; 'Well done, Mckenzie!'; 'We'll get you to do the *Geebung Polo Club* next time.'

When the crowd had sorted themselves out again, he moved to take comfort with Doris and Mauri. 'You bastard', he said to Mauri, 'You set me up!'

'Roddy. It was a lesson for everyone. I think everybody knew how you were feeling and they got an insight into you; a person, doing what he has to do and doing it well, with full commitment, even when he doesn't feel like doing it or plainly doesn't want to do it; he does it because he must. No joking, it was something for all these folk who want to be your friends. It's as if you had clearly decided to cross into being Australian with them. I know I was bloody proud of you.'

The excitement of the evening had peaked, the bodies and minds clogged with the detritus of burned-out adrenalin, delicious food, and good wine were beginning to wind down, and the braves, all tired and sleepy, wished to return to their little tepees, Rhys announced his duty and pleasure to drive the Perrotts to their hotel. Everyone had enjoyed herself or himself. It was time, after queuing up to thank the hostess and host, to go off into the still dark and raining night.

Saturday's dawn burst onto the stage bright, sparkling, and calm. For those who had rigid weekly work commitments, the banal necessities of housework if not attended to on the weekend would hang around their necks and mar the week and spoil their enjoyment of it, so both Lynne, and Ann who had to be in her office on Saturday morning, declined the invitation to picnic off Herring Bay on Garden Island as almost all the others had had agreed to do the previous evening. As religiously as to a mass, Plum, Claude, and Frank Dalby were going to a Sheffield Shield match at the 'Waca' Oval. Freddie and Ethel would have liked to go too but decided that they had to be with Mauri and Doris.

For those on the picnic cruise, there was no requirement for an early start. The two vessels would leave their own clubs at their own times and arrive in Herring Bay to pop the corks around one o'clock when the sea breeze, surely back to its normal cycle after that rainstorm, would cool down the central hours of the day. The term idyllic to describe the summer days off shore in Western Australia's summer is sadly cliché, sadly, because it remains ever appropriate. Freddie pulled his big, workmanlike Randall cruiser alongside Rhys and rafted up. Now that Freddie had committed to a business relationship with Rhys and Mauri, he and Ethel felt they should ensure a good supply of all that would make the day enjoyable for the picnickers which would have entailed probably only the addition of extra champagne to their beer and wines locker. There would also be food galore for boarders. Mac and Janet hove-to alongside Freddie and with Howie's and Gwen's help rafted up.

'Have you washed all the glasses, Janet?'

'I'm glad I'm not a publican's wife,' she called across in reply to her question from Doris.

Like a quietness before a pending military engagement, the day was made sacred to ease though not all mention of the coming engagement could be averted.

As they sat side by side at one point, Roddy asked, 'Doris, have you ever heard the Scottish Symphony Orchestra?'

'No, I haven't, not even on record or the ABC, but I've read and heard about them and that they are very good.'

'Well, I think you should make a small effort to hear them.'

'Oh. You seem suddenly very concerned in my cultural development. What brought that fever on?'

'Well, you are coming up to Japan with us, aren't you?'

'I haven't been asked. But there's no show without Punch, so naturally I'll be coming. Is the Scottish National going to be playing there?'

'No, it isn't, but it's got a season booked in Hong Kong and it just occurred to me that if one or two of us wanted to hear it, we could make a detour via Hong Kong on the way. It would just add a day and a bit to the trip depending on what demands to stay in Japan come from Ugojim. A very good violinist from my hometown will be playing, so I'd love to take this chance to see her again and hear her play with the Scottish National. I think would enjoy meeting her.'

'Ah', thought Doris, 'a musical disguise for an emotional motive. Let him have his game.' Then, 'That's a nice idea, Roderick. It's sweet of you to have thought of me. I'm sure I could persuade Mauri to take the extra time. Now, it would be sad if Ugojim's time demands go past the season. What about your time?'

'It looks possible and I think I should take this opportunity as it presents itself. I've got a strong feeling that I'll never have much time to spare, for a long time into the future.'

'I'm sure you're right, my darling. We had to wait a while for a breather after we started.'

Roddy promised Doris to fax her Scottish National's Hong Kong programme.

This afternoon was a farewell to the Perrotts. They had fitted into the West Australian, Cottesloe, cruising, work, and social milieux as if they had been friends and neighbours for years. Mauri and Doris were adamant that tomorrow they would follow their usual pattern of making their departures on their own. So the glorious day of swims and drinks, and even a catch of whiting, happily went on, and it was well into the evening when all the vessels were back in their own club moorings and an invitation from Freddie and Ethel's balcony to watch the sunset was accepted by all. 'It doesn't bucket rain at our place,' said

Freddie. The sentiments in the farewells were almost sad, yet through each person there, the approach to an adventure sent a frisson: both feelings were consciously controlled. They knew that they would all be involved in creating the future.

—⸰ₒₒ⸰≫◇≪⸰ₒₒ⸰—

During the past week, Roddy had been to meet Mike Harris, the man whose outfit had done the big Cocklebiddy job for Main Roads to ask whether he was going to tender for the Collie Shire work since Collie wanted to deal with just one contractor for the complete job. Mike had planned to do so and was happy to speak to Roddy about getting a price from Mckenzie for the preparation. Dave, Howie, and Roddy would go to Collie on Monday to see the site and make their plan after which Roddy would calculate a price to supply to Mike Harris. They met and set off at sunrise on Monday from Treloar Haulage in a Treloar crew truck. Their goal was get all the needed information and return in one day.

On arrival in Collie, they went to meet Harry Jewell, the shire engineer, at the shire office, and tried to keep the usual country-style conversation to a polite limit steering it gently back to the purpose of their being there and with him, drove out to the site. Mike Harris had said to Roddy that if Mckenzie did the same quality work as at Cocklebiddy, he wouldn't bother coming down, he would just quote on dimensions, and he'd pay Mckenzie surveyor's fees. The principal work would be the preparation. A narrow fire access track through a bit of mixed forest would require the removal of many trees before inclusion in the new road. There were immovable rock extrusions which would have to be demolished by explosives, old natural gullies, and little hillocks requiring filling and levelling. They talked with Mike about choosing the most economical road line. It was very important to be making this visit and Mike Harris, who had watched their approach to the assessment and had no illusions about what was involved. No detailed survey of the proposed road track had been undertaken. The tendering party would have to undertake the survey—a specific cost. There would be a major role for Howie in this project and he would have tender a price to Roddy. Mike had no illusions about the kind of work that would be involved and was prepared to be faced with a large expense. Then Dave and Roddy had to make their considerations of the nature of the terrain, then choose the most suitable plant—machines which would come on-site once and be flexible enough to carry through an effective role from start to finish. The deadline for submission of the Collie tender was to be three weeks out.

Five days remained to prepare for Ugojim. Roddy had been interviewed by Plum and had provided a *curriculum vitae*, as had Mauri and Freddie, and stories of the success and solidity of the additional supporters, Mac and Rhys were also included. Special studio photographs of the five were taken by a reputed photographer selected and engaged by Plum. A strong yet elegant, introductory information sheet had been produced which could be circulated separately from the main promotional document included in the presentation folder. Plum had chosen a local graphic designer who had produced a work of great aesthetic appeal, itself a message of good feeling, quality, integrity, care, and honesty, and after informed research, aided by the Japanese trade commissioner. Reo Ito, whom Plum, and all who had contact with him, found to be charming, erudite, realistic, relaxed, and humorous, guided Plum and his design team in choosing very subtle inclusions of Japanese motifs that they had wished to embody. A set of these context-setting documents had been sent to the male 'secretary' of Asahi Ishikawa, president, chief executive officer of Ugojim in Hiroshima.

Roddy and Freddie sat down and created the document which clearly stated the offer made to be presented under the banner of Mckenzie Earthmoving Pty. Ltd. It detailed, to the extent possible, their desire to form a company in joint ownership to be named Ugojim Australia Pty. Ltd. It detailed how they actively demonstrate to the Australian mining industry the Ugojim 'haulpaks' and bulldozers. Where there were gaps in the Ugojim range, and there was a particular demand from miners, equipment from other manufacturers would be purchased and sold by a third marketing company owned by Ugojim Australia rather than Mckenzie which would be dedicated to earthmoving operations. As soon as Ugojim manufactured competitive products, only Ugojim products would be offered to Australian buyers. Demonstration units provided by Ugojim Japan would be held in Australia as assets of Ugojim Australia Pty. Ltd. There were further details included, covering marketing, sales targets, market development, public relations, advertising and promotion, technical and operator staff training, servicing, and showroom premises. Faxes and phone some calls fired along the lines between Mauri and the two 'offer' designers at Freddie's office in North Fremantle. They took their notepads and pens to the lunches that Ethel and Howie prepared and brought over to the office. When they could not possibly read that document one more time and synapses blocked when a Ugojim code came near, they sent their masterpiece to everybody. 'My god, if anybody quibbles, they'd better have bloody good case!' said the leader of the deputation to the co-creator of the document which had to be approved quickly so that it could go to Plum's man to be dressed in its christening robes.

With Reo's help, precise dates and timings of their first visit to Ugojim had been confirmed, and accommodation booked. All the major pieces were in place. Ethel and Freddie were booked on the same Qantas aircraft as the Perrotts and Roddy; accommodation in the same hotel had been arranged. A business meeting had been scheduled with Jill at the Bank of New South Wales; first, with Jill and her bank people, Roddy, Mauri, and Freddie, and a meeting augmented by the Japanese trade commissioner immediately flowing on.

Departure from Perth would be at nine on Thursday morning. Plum had earlier offered and arranged with Mac and Ethel to take them and Roddy to the airport while the Treloars would be taken out by Gwen and Howie. On arrival in Sydney, there would be two cars waiting to take them to the Sheraton after which, at a comfortable time, they would be collected and driven to the Perrotts' at Potts Point.

At just about six thirty, they rang the melodious bell at the Perrotts', and in seconds, it was opened by a cheery, welcoming Mauri. He was happy to give Ethel a welcoming kiss and shook hands with the men. 'C'mon up', he said, 'I'll lead the way.'

Doris had assembled some guests, hardy annuals who bloomed across the years since the first seeds of friendship had been sown. Newer seeds had set, and there were links to Roddy. John and Kate Wilson were there, Mike Harty and Jill. Doris did the introductions and immediately those were over, and amidst the gathered group, Jill and Roddy moved straight towards each other. They closed each other in an embrace and kissed. She took his hands in each of hers and, holding out his arms by his sides, stepped back and looked at him. As her heart observed them, Doris was sad in her love for them both: and now she was wondering if there were now another element of influence.

'You're looking wonderful, Roddy,' Jill said in a joyful admiration. Then, because there was too much feeling to express, she resorted to the mundane, 'Work and Western Australia seem to suit you.'

'And you are charming . . . and very beautiful,' he said, keeping their arms where she had set them.

There was a long pause where they gazed at each other, each feeling the same barrier of his aspirations causing and maintaining their emotional separation. Inside Roddy, a signalling spirit commanded, 'No! Not yet!' Jill knew that she would know when, at some time, sooner or later, a new emotional force became stronger than the restraining bonds of Roddy's reasoning. Her love would become free, new, different, valid. Was this venture to Japan the beginning for them of a possible future together?

Of course there were drinks on the balcony. Although the Treloars were certainly no strangers to Sydney, it was a delight to look out onto Sydney Harbour from there, making no attempt at impossible comparisons with their own sea view. John Wilson knew of the giant western haulage company and its strategic locations around Australia. Mike Harty had topped his first-year geology course at Sydney University and was very enthusiastic about his subject. If he could keep up his part-time earnings, he planned to follow a line taking in all the steps—honours, masters, doctorate—then go out into the field of professional consultant geology, wherever on earth; high in the mountains or deep in the sea.

Doris had arranged a seated dinner round one of the removable sections (Kath Wilson knew, because she had asked long ago what on earth she did with the other bits) of her dining table where each had elbow room and could see and hear the others without having to crane—she had no anxieties about odd numbers.

Were these overtones, or undercurrents of tension that infused the range of subjects and interests of the discussions? Whatever, tension there surely was. For Doris, there was an extra-curricular tension manifest when, describing their intention of going to Hong Kong to hear the Scottish Symphony Orchestra, she nearly blew the gaff by mentioning Roddy's special interest in a female violinist. How terrible it would be inadvertently to set a cat amongst the doves of feeling between these two.

The tensions that seemed to be spread amongst Freddie, Mauri, and Roddy were as much an eagerness to be there in Japan now making this win-or-lose pitch for a future; for a fascinating, financially rewarding time to come as contributing participants in Australia's destiny. The very brief intervening time between being here and facing the Ugojim people in Hiroshima was too long.

Perhaps the tension was a cause of briefer than usual explorations of the topics of discussion which arose, and why fewer opportunities were taken to deliver the frequent polemics that were a norm and why the dinner was drawn to its close at an unusually early hour.

Jill held the meeting in her own office, the office where Roddy had called upon her when he was hours new to Australia. Now, at once, that seemed like minutes ago and years ago.

The major purpose of the meeting was to demonstrate their plans for a Ugojim venture and the form they desired such a joint venture with Ugojim should take; to make clear arrangements with the bank for access to funds by a line of credit until the structure of such new company, likely to be named Ugojim Australia Pty. Ltd. was in place; to regularize the promises of financial support from Treloar Haulage, Fusan Australia, and Mckenzie Earthmoving. Jill decided that she would take overall control of dealings with the Ugojim venture as they had hoped she may. When the Japanese trade commissioner arrived, it was clear the he and Jill had, had dealings before. The purpose now was to allow him to meet the trio personally and to confirm that he was au fait with what the delegation was setting out to achieve. They also needed to know what arrangements had been made for their reception in Japan the time, place and with whom they would have their first appointments what news he may have of the mood of the Ugojim people about their wish to meet with them. He told them that Reo had been in touch with Ugojim directly and had kept him up to date. As Reo had told them in Cottesloe, Ugojim was pleased to welcome them to have discussions. Arrangements on the ground had been made and the Japanese trade department had appointed one of its staff to be with the delegation, and to look after its needs while in Japan. When the meeting ended, all parties were pleased with the results. All thanked Jill for her guidance of the meeting and thanked her for undertaking the role of overseeing relations between them and the bank.

When they reached the pavement on George Street, Roddy turned to Yoshinari and said, 'Yoshinari San, I was going to suggest to my companions that we go to my club, which is just round the corner, to celebrate what I think, and I hope you do, was a successful meeting, if they agree with my suggestion, would you like to join us?'

'Thank you. I shall be pleased to join you. I like your idea. While we are in Australia, please just call me Yoshi?'

There was a healthy lunchtime gathering at the club, and when Roddy oozled his way to the bar to order the drinks, he was warmly greeted by Dudley Moore.

'Mr. Mckenzie, pleased to see you back with us. Are you going to be staying?'

'Not this time, Dudley. These gentlemen are going to whisk me off to Japan tomorrow.'

He introduced his guests, and when it came to Yoshi, Dudley immediately extended his arm across the bar saying, 'Yoshi San, pleased to see you again.'

'Thank you, Dudley, my pleasure to be here again,' Yoshi replied warmly, shaking Dudley's hand.

Freddie had been freed of any requirement to look after Ethel because Doris had swooped her up during the morning to take her out to the Arts Club at Woollahra, which on Fridays was always well attended by mainly women, lovers, of theatre, music, painting, and other creative arts particularly because of the acclaimed luncheons. Doris, without domestic responsibilities that evening, was feeling free too: she had planned dinner and the show at the Sheraton for their evening and a reasonably early night before their flight to Japan on the morrow.

The dinner at the Sheraton was a pleasant affair, a good choice by Doris. Jill and Yoshi had come along, so in a very relaxed way, it was a time just to confirm that each thought the meeting had satisfied everyone's needs and that now was a time to allow friendship to develop. Ethel Treloar was a social asset. She and Doris had had an enjoyable day in which they found that they were both realists, were very close to their husbands, and were very close their husbands' work in knowledge of it and shared enthusiasm for and about it. Their relationships with their men were beyond the normal where often a man and his work were contained in one world separate and a man and his family in another. Work was something that had to be done and often an attitude was developed to smooth its harder edges and find ways within it to make its dullness or discomforts tolerable so that dislike of it did not let a contagion from these aversions become mixed up with the other world, giving rise to thoughts of being a prisoner of both work and matrimony. In the cases of Doris and Ethel, Mauri and Freddie had chosen and developed their own economic and social worlds and the women were included in the goal of living their lives of achievement in which it could be said that, as couples, they hurt no one, were generous of spirit and pocket and people thought well of them.

Roddy was seated between Yoshi and Ethel and finding it totally pleasant while Ethel had Mauri on her left. Jill with Mauri on her right was in 'home' waters, and on her left, Freddie, the classic 'sportsman' in virile good looks and manner, an enormously successful businessman. While conversation ran between and amongst table neighbours, Yoshi and Roddy had opportunities to find out more about each other. When sport seemed to be the topic being shared around, Roddy asked Yoshi whether he had a favourite sport.

'I'm not sure whether judo is classified as a sport or not, but it's the nearest to sport that I come to. I took it up when I was at school when the idea of spending hours fielding on a baseball ground appalled me as a waste of human mind and body. I've enjoyed it ever since and love the trickery of, it's portable and through it I've met a mix of people and their motives for learning it. I like it because it uses all of your body and you spend all the time thinking very quickly. I have no interest in martial arts as martial.'

'I'd call judo a sport and I took it up as a progression from boxing which I began in my secondary school years. When I had the opportunity, I took to jiu-jitsu and karate and I'm afraid it was with martial intent because I went straight from school to the army. I saw more possibility for karate helping me to survive than a straight –left delivered Bulldog Drummond style.'

'Oh, I know Bulldog Drummond! I caught up with him when it was too late for any youthful enjoyment, but it gave me an insight into aspects of the English values system—it was a half-facetious suggestion by a friend when I was studying politics and history at London University.'

'I'm fascinated. I wish we had all night to talk. I'd love to hear every detail of your experience of English university life. Wouldn't it be great if you had to come over to WA for some reason we could do jiu-jitsu, swim, sail, and you could see Freddie and Ethel and some other good chums of mine in their natural habitat? When the Ugojim venture is up and running, I'm sure I'm going to have to pass through Sydney from time to time. You must have a great story to tell.'

'You've just signalled me your confidence about a Ugojim deal. I've been listening and watching today—and right now—and sincerely, I think you and your colleagues would do a first-class job for them. And I think it would be good fun to get together again. I want to know the process that moulded the man I'm talking with now.'

Yoshi cabled his superior in Japan to recommend the delegation from Mckenzie Earthmoving.

The delegation flew from Sydney to Tokyo on Saturday where they changed to a Nippon Air aircraft and flew on down to Hiroshima.

At Ugojim, Asahi Ishikawa, the chief executive officer, chose to see Roddy first, alone.

Mauri and Freddie were made comfortable with a Japanese guide who spoke very good English, and a production engineer who spoke none, in a pleasant little room, business like but looking onto a manicured garden, seeming to demonstrate that a calm life could be enjoyed, where flashing arc welders and banging steel-shaping presses were mixing lights and noises into a boiling broth of sound which hung like a greasy almost tangible atmosphere over the enormous, ugly sheds.

Asahi Ishikawa was sitting behind a large desk of Japanese clean structural line, colour and design. Before him, the only item on the surface, when Roddy was shown in was Plum's brochure. Immediately, he rose and stiffly bowed. Roddy returned the gesture from where he stood before the desk. Asahi Ishikawa came around and when quite close to Roddy bowed again. After Roddy had bowed, he greeted him, 'Good morning, Mckenzie-san', extending his arm and shaking Roddy's hand. He was of slightly shorter height than Roddy, with the appearance of muscular strength, and what had been to Roddy's great surprise on first seeing him, rosy-red cheeks on a tanned face: his bright, dark eyes and his greying hair complemented this attractively.

There were two European chairs and a square mid-height table in the centre of the room. The walls were of a buff material, possibly bamboo, divided by stained wooden verticals; possibly masking steel structural studs beneath, these divided the surfaces into large panels. One wall was totally glass; screened by bamboo in horizontal and vertical weave not unlike a tartan, their clever spacing, while subduing glare, could be looked through as just a fine film. The view was an expanse of white gravel raked to follow selected and sited plants forming miniature under- and middle storeys as if the vegetation cover of small islands in a white sea. Some islands were rocky, the lichens, green grey and buff, were the flora clinging to cliffs. Others had forests of tall trees, which further out cut off the sky. Roddy found it distractingly striking. It was contained peace. This peace, designed to lie in the midst the noise and clangour of manufactory, was perhaps an intended counterpoint to the industry's role. That was to make powerful machines to rip, tear, and move volumes of the earth from a place where it had fallen or poured from the unimaginable heat of a volcano or as sediments of shells in shallow seas or as grains from rocks, fine grain after fine grain, or leafy growth condensed to carbon, at the very beginnings of earthly time to another place where it would take on another form.

Roddy was invited to sit in one of the fine chairs which he imagined may be antique Dutch. As they sat facing each other across the politely symbolical protection of the table, Asahi Ishikawa began the conversation.

'You have been leading a very active and interesting life, Mckenzie-san, and still a young man; you have come here to see me to ask if I will allow you to represent my company in all of Australia. Do you not think that is somewhat bold?'

'He delivered these words in immaculate English like a narrator, say, Richard Dimbleby, describing a coronation.

'To achieve success, one must inevitably use some degree of boldness, Ishikawa-san.'

'Indeed, Mckenzie-san. I agree.' Roddy left him that last word. Asahi Ishikawa let the silence hang.

'Part of your story tells that you served in war action as an infantry soldier.'

'Yes, Ishikawa-san, I served in Korea with the Forty-third Royal Highland Regiment part of a United Nations Force fighting the communist Chinese.'

'Reo San has researched for me this part of your story, and I learned that you were wounded and that you were awarded a

Mention in Dispatches decoration. I too have been an infantry soldier by necessity. Our family manufactured weaponry and tanks. I was in a tank regiment but in the part of Burma, at Kohima, the terrain was not suitable for the use of tanks and we faced a stubborn English force on Kohima. I was made an infantryman overnight. I was engaged in trying to dislodge your Royal West Kent Regiment from the ridge at Kohima. I failed. You won. I greet you with honour. I think you would fight boldly and tenaciously for Ugojim. If we were to look at a graph we would see the success lines of your colleagues continuing on the ascendant. I look forward to talking with them. Every man has a story. You three men have special stories. I am told that you are all part of a society of very good citizens. I shall tell my colleagues to make our assessment of your plan shrewd but as accurate as possible. Needless to say our men in the Department of Trade have furnished us with detailed intelligence. To strengthen your belief in Ugojim, we ensure that you shall see all that we are doing in research and product development, what we are doing, and what we intend to do. You must feel free to ask your guides any questions you wish to ask. There is no value to be gained in long negotiations. I hope that all that must be done here will be completed within two days. You will have our decision then. Let me talk with your colleagues, then you may make your presentation to my executives.'

He stood up, faced Roddy at about arm's length, and looked at him for some seconds. Roddy knew these seconds were important. He tried to use them too.

Ishikawa-san bowed to Roddy and offered his hand again. 'While you are waiting Mckenzie-san, my men will look after you. Pease see that you have everything you need. Our people will set up the room so that we may view Mr. Treloar's film. We shall follow your suggested agenda.' He then walked shoulder to shoulder with Roddy to the door he walked through with him. 'Thank you, Mckenzie-san,' he said. He bowed again.

Roddy joined Freddie and Mauri in their room. The Ugojim guide excused himself and left. When the pair asked, 'How did you go?' 'I don't know. But I can't help feeling he'd made his mind up before I went in. And hope I'm not kidding myself, but

I'm sure he's for us. He struck me as shrewd, but a good bloke. I don't want to say anything else. You mustn't be influenced by me.'

It was not long before the guide returned to invite Mauri and Freddie to come to see Mr. Ishikawa. When he had taken them to Mr. Ishikawa and made the introductions, he came back and asked Roddy if he would like something to eat or drink.

'Would it be possible to have some English tea?'

'Yes. Of course,' he said, smiling and enthusiastic. 'I'll bring the makings and I'll make it here. Won't be long.'

'Good heavens', thought Roddy, 'that sounded like a better class of English butler.' When he came back, he chatted with Roddy as he heated the kettle drawing some water off to warm the tea pot while he boiled the rest. 'I do hope you get a chance to see some of our lovely country while you're here and to eat our food. If not this time. Perhaps when you come back you will be able to spare a bit more time with us.' ('What! What is this bloke saying? Am I wishfully misreading his words? Or does he already actually know something that I would like to know?' flashed through Roddy's mind.)

'I would most certainly like to do that, and to get out on the ground to see some of the lovely country we flew over. By the way . . . where, and when, did you learn such amazingly accurate vernacular English?'

'At my mother's knee. She came with overseas volunteers after the war and married my dad. So I'm half English. I was teaching English when the opportunity came to join Ugojim. I jumped at it. This company has exceptional working conditions and is very go-ahead so my services are in demand looking after folk like you. I've made some very good friends through my work. I travel with people from the company so maybe I'll come down and see you one day. I'd love to. I haven't been in Australia yet.' (Not again? What *is* going on?)

They enjoyed their English tea and talked about Ugojim until Mauri and Freddie returned about half an hour later. Sato suggested that they would probably want to prepare for their presentation and that he would leave them. 'If there's anything you want, however trifling, just raise this phone and dial 33. I will come, my room is not far away. If you want to go and get a feel for the presentation room, I'm happy to take you there now . . . or later when you've had a chance to exchange notes. As soon as you want to, ring me. You have half an hour before the presentation. Actually I think you'll find that everything's set up; film projector, screen, chart paper on two chart boards, a projector loaded with Roddy's slides and tested for function, waiting for your finger on the button, chairs in a discussion group set-up, easily moved if you want to so there shouldn't be anything to worry about there. Look, would you just like to go there now, have your debriefing, and be there when the executives arrive?' Sato looked around the group. 'C'mon', said Roddy, 'we may as well be there as here.' Smiling and saying, as he included Sato, 'And I bet Sato will bring some more tea: If that's not straining the friendship?'

'Not in the least. Bring your belongings and we'll go there now.' He laughed and said, 'I thought you might have wanted sake.'

Mauri and Freddie had a conversation with Asahi during which they become entirely at ease. They knew that they were under intensive scrutiny of the most benign kind. They did not for a moment underestimate Asahi's skill and were in a state where they would almost disclose their innermost secrets without resistance. They knew he needed to know who they were, and that in absence of a long pedigree of selling heavy equipment, he needed to know, when he finally decided, that he had followed a due process, that he found these men had pedigrees of trustworthiness, of success, stability in their national community, that they wanted the Ugojim representation as part of their drive for continuing success and that were convinced of the ability of their youthful leader.

The executives were a rigid component of the decision mechanism. This could not easily have been detected in the family slide show atmosphere which pervaded the group. They loved the story of the Treloars and laughed at the days when they, and we, all drove cranky old trucks like that, they were in some awe at the evidence of carting water tanks miles into the bush, the shots of vehicle breakdowns in sand and in mud. They loved

Mauri's showrooms in Sydney; and his Cooma agent, which he
genuinely laughed about, as he explained Roddy's connection
with him. There was a shot of the young man himself, in work
gear, with Fido at the petrol pump, dressed in Cooma Fusan
signage all over her outside. The fact is, they loved it and they
loved the familial intimacy of being there now with the present
head of the Treloar family company. Sato had to be involved
when someone (and everyone) in eager interest wanted to pose
questions to the group about technical or mechanical aspects,
climate, distances, or terrain. The truth is that the executive
team was very happy; happy to be among men connected with
past, present, and future. These men were not presentation
show ponies, previously experienced; they were not talking
about anyone but Ugojim and where they and Ugojim could go
together.

The remainder of the day, after a light, lunch packed with
energizing fruit, vegetables, and fish, was spent by the trio in
an eye-opening survey of the plant and processes. Roddy was
humbled by what Ugojim had to offer. They had been building
battle tanks before the First World War, they made massive
electric turbines and electric motors compact yet powerful
enough to power the driving hubs of their haulpaks. He had
allowed himself to become obsessed by haulpaks, and to an
extent rightly so. But these were for developed mines. To open
the mines, excavators, dozers, and front-end loaders were
needed, and Ugojim had them all. They also had heavy haul
dump trucks! Ugojim's range was a cornucopia.

At the end of the second day, Asahi gathered everyone
together in the presentation room now set in a different
configuration. He said, 'Gentlemen, I want to thank you for
what you have done today. It was up to you, as the people you
are, to convince us that we should entrust our entry into the
Australian market to you. I know that you are conscious that this
is a very important decision for us. I know that this is a critical
time in the future of Australia's iron mining industry. I think

that's why you have chosen now as the time to be here. We would betray everyone who works for Ugojim if we were to make a wrong decision. We should leave tonight with your own thoughts and we spend the night and tomorrow with ours. During the day, we would like you to spend two and up to three hours together with us while we examine more closely how you see the unification could be constructed. That meeting will have its own conclusions. You will then be free to do whatever you have planned and Ugojim will spend the rest of the day deciding. At the end of that day, by four thirty p.m., we shall have decided. Whatever the decision, we can then get together in the evening and dine together as friends to celebrate our having spent, enjoyably, important human time together. At that time, Mr. Perrott and Mr. Treloar, I hope that your wives will be pleased to join us.' The words had been directed mainly at Roddy.

'Ishikawa-san. I am a young man and cannot hope to have your wisdom, but I gain comfort and strength from hearing you speak. While you are making your considerations tomorrow, with respect, I ask that you allow us, in the time of your deliberations, to spend our time in the plant. Whatever you decide, I know that we three and Mrs. Perrott and Mrs. Treloar would be very happy to share your hospitality. Defeat does not mean the end. Evidence shows that it is an opportunity to begin. I am persuaded by the evidence in that belief. Thank you for allowing us to present our case to you today. I hope respectfully that we may say thank you to your staff who, I think, understood our situation and looked after us so caringly.'

When they returned to the hotel and rejoined the ladies, their nerves were still jangling a bit as much with anticipation and high hopes as with the relief of having delivered what had appeared to be a well-received presentation. As group leader, Roddy's room had a pleasant, small ante-room with a bar and it was there that they gathered to discuss their days' adventures. The ladies told of the charming guide that Ugojim had provided who had taken them out of the city to Itsukushima Island where, after enjoying strolling through gardens of magnificent flowers trees and traditional Japanese Architecture of the Shukkei-en gardens, they had a delightful Japanese lunch of raw fish, vegetables, fruit, and Japanese sweet deserts. On returning to the city, they visited the Hiroshima memorial which provoked rather sad thoughts which clouded any wonderment or interest they may have had in the castle. It was the men's turn then to tell their tale which they attempted to do without seeming to crow about their interviews, and how encouraged they were by the kinds of questions the executives asked and by the way they asked them. The presentation had gone really well they thought judging by their participation and enthusiastic interest shown by all four present.

'Well, I think I'd be talking for the three of us when I say we're feeling very positive about all that we experienced,' said Mauri. Roddy could not help but retell from his interview with Asahi that 'he showed how conscious he was of my age and how inexperienced I was in the field of marketing, but he seemed not to lay too much weight on that. I got the impression that Freddie and Mauri had not only that kind of experience, but they were going to give support through that to me. I don't know which was most important, the presentation or the interviews . . . and I haven't checked this with Mauri and Freddie . . . but during the presentation, from the way they were acting, what questions they asked how they put them to us and how they handled our responses, they seemed to see us committed to each other and shared exactly a common mind on our wish to join with Ugojim and make the Australian venture go with a bang.' He looked at the others. 'I think you're right, Rod. They could see that we trusted each other and I think in the whole question of a business venture together, they were looking for the mutual goal of shared trust. They seemed to ask a lot of questions designed to find out if we were going to relate to each other as people. If they found that, I think they would see the practical, the real, challenges of doing business together as a company, Ugojim Australia, would be with people who shared similar personal views and who'd want to share Ugojim's business goals. There'd be nothing shonky on either side.'

The group spent a quiet evening. They shared moieties of their experiences, Doris and Ethel were able to offer more detail of their day while the men seemed to be distracted each by his own rumination lying just beneath this surface of the interesting diversion. Next day the ladies were to travel by train with a guide to explore the countryside outside the city. The men would have their morning meeting with Ugojim at eight thirty.

In that morning meeting, the three confirmed to the Ugojim executive their corporate structure proposal in greater detail and responded to specific questions from the executive who, maybe a shade more solemn and serious, still were sensed to be relaxed and their probing questions directed almost affably. Again, they went through the Ugojim Australia Pty. Ltd. financial structure document which had been drawn up in Australia. Ugojim Australia would be owned fifty-one per cent by the presently proposed Australian major shareholders, Mauri, Freddie, Rhys, and Mckenzie Earthmoving; forty-nine percent by Ugojim Japan. Roddy would be executive chairman of the Australian company, and Ugojim and Ugojim Australia would provide three board members each. Ugojim Australia would provide premises and operating staff. Ugojim Australia would transact sales between that entity and Australian purchasers of equipment sold to Ugojim Australia by Ugojim Corporation Japan at an agreed beneficial transfer price. Ugojim Australia would be the nominated Australian agent for all Ugojim's entire product range. The marketing plan, also outlined at the first meeting, was equally thoroughly examined and now the detailed programme of public relations targets was outlined. An advertising plan would be drawn up and costed and sent to the Japanese partners for examination before any arrangement with an advertising agency was committed to. There was also a major effort to be put in place, combining the efforts of Japanese networks and Australian networks to get early notice of mine projects and pinpointing personnel influential or responsible for buying decisions of heavy equipment. There would also be an intensification and speedy sharing of intelligence regarding capital raisings for mining ventures in Australia. The Australian partner would send to Japan, as soon as possible after the agreement was signed, an experienced plant operator from Australia (Billy Gray) to gain close practical knowledge the Ugojim equipment before demonstrations in Australia. Australia would also send a young qualified mechanic (from Treloar Haulage) to Japan to be trained on Ugojim equipment. By about one o'clock, the meeting was satisfactorily closed and the trio was free until four thirty.

They had another healthy lunch comprising sushi, seafood in great variety, and beef sliced paper thin, which they found enjoyable even in the cold weather. They had already arranged a thorough investigation of all that Ugojim was doing, how it was being done, and what that meant for them. They were very keen, their nerves tingling with enthusiasm, to get out there and with Sato Tanaka's help soak up as much as they could of products, processes, and potential. They had not come to buy, or with intention to sell, electric generators, but they could see applications for them in major mine operation other production settings. Such was their concentration that at about four o'clock, Sato had to remind them that if there was anything they had missed or some product they wished to return to there was only a half hour remaining before the decision meeting. They raced back to its site and had one last look at the new giant shovel project. Echoing a thought that must have been in each mind: 'Imagine selling one of them?'. Now, off to have the fate of their venture decided.

The chairs had been arranged in a circle; Asahi-san's chair was slightly further back from the perimeter and there was a larger space on his left and right, there was a vacant chair between each of the executives. The Ugojim men stood, turned, and bowed to the entering delegates who had been led in by the door where Asahi-san was exactly opposite. The delegates bowed. Sato led Roddy to sit between two men, to face Asahi directly. He returned then led Mauri first, then Freddie to their chairs. Asahi sat. On that signal, the others sat.

'Welcome back from what I hear was your tour of fascination in our Ugojim Hiroshima operations. I hope your keen, intelligent interest was rewarded by what you saw of our products, our production and our detailed research methods in current profit improvement and new product investigations. We are very proud of our products. It is a very short time since you arrived here to present your proposal to represent Ugojim and these products in all of Australia. We have listened very carefully to what you have said and how you have said it. I would not speak now if what I have to say had not been arrived at by these experienced men in total agreement. I am happy to be the person who has to say these words. Ugojim Japan agrees to appoint Ugojim Australia Pty. Ltd. to represent, in the manner you and we have decided upon, Ugojim Japan in Austrialia. We wish to congratulate you on your success and we look into the future and to our going forward in harmony to our mutual contentment and financial success.'

He stood up and took two paces forward towards Roddy. He bowed low. Seeing Asahi's intention to approach, Roddy had risen swiftly to his feet standing erect and took a symbolic pace forward. He bowed deeply—a long bow. He rose from the bow stiffly alert, and tall. 'Thank you, Asahi-san. Thank you.'

He moved, in a smart incline, to Asahi's side, just a little forward of him. From that position, with his back never to Asahi, he bowed to each of the executives in turn and facing all said thank you. This done, keenly observed, felt, and understood, by Asahi, he went forward and shook hands with each. Now Asahi went forward, bowed to Mauri, and shook hands, then Freddie, then all exchanged bows and handshakes. Perhaps in other situations there may have been back-slapping. Roddy could feel an affinity in all of this with his native Scottish highland reserve below which the emotion could be intense. In these business negotiations, Roddy's values from boyhood, and his sense of goodness and honesty, seemed to have been rewarded as they had been so often on the few miles of life's road that he had thus far travelled. Was there nothing beyond the ability of these men to achieve?'

Mauri, Freddie, and Roddy found it delightful, and a great compliment, that the executives risked their embarrassment and tackled the impossible 'Rs' to say Molly-san, Fleddie-san, and Loddy-san. Later, Roddy was to say to them that British people had difficulties even within their own language, and more so in other languages. 'We will never, ever, think badly about how you pronounce our names: you have shown a friendship and care for us that goes far beyond how words in a language are pronounced. That first hour when you used those names minted gold coins that we will treasure beyond their mere face value. Please, always remind us of our friendship in this way. I can assure you of this; their wives will feel and think exactly the same way.'

The Ugojim Australia Pty. Ltd. executives and their wives, dressed and jewelled, as ever in best taste, elegance, and style were more than a little bit proud to accompany their successful men to a Japanese restaurant where it had been decided that the table for their special group should best be set amongst the other tables of Japanese guests in this Japanese restaurant. It was not one of those to which Japanese or visiting foreigners brought their clients or business guests. It was a restaurant where people of Hiroshima, valued by their society for social worth, intellect, or artistic achievement, gathered with special friends of long standing, to share the pleasures of eating together. There were occasions when humorous naughtiness expressed the mood of some guests, or poetry was recited or songs sung or small groups of musicians played. The food was both rustic and refined and sometimes the one was the other, most was traditional but just now and again a dish might be introduced which was a recent invention of an acclaimed Tokyo chef.

The mood of their group could be sensed as a mixed wash which spread, flowed, and ran around amongst them and glazing over and connecting them; euphoria, running into and blending the new friendships with the happiness that the days' events had given rise to. They were filled with the feeling of vigour and strength, physical and mental that comes from the achievement of an objective, the thrill of pride stemming from their decision to come together and work together for a future which began today. Stepping out of the strong background of the world of business, their relaxation came from an inbred security derived from tested behaviour and success. That security ensured freedom, permitted jocularity to infuse brightness and lightness into this occasion. It was a wrench when the hour to end the evening came: proximity of new friends was for a time to be ended here, and carried away by each person as memory.

The Ugojim people mixed with their guests in the cars which took them to their hotel so that on arrival they all stepped out of the cars onto the forecourt of the hotel to make their final farewells and exchange their memorial gifts: the new friends would leave for home tomorrow.

They gathered in Roddy's lounge at the hotel to sort out their thoughts and feelings of this memorable time in their lives. They realised how much *they* had become a team, amateurs, in it for the love of the game, and for each other. It struck Mauri as very odd, paradoxical even, and he voiced this to the others later in the evening, that while Australia's quintessential weekly magazine *The Bulletin* had at its masthead a declaration of support for The White Australia Policy; and remembered enmity for the Japanese was widespread in the nation, that their little group had gone beyond the functioning rituals of international trade and that they had sealed an international deal in corporate cooperation based on friendship, trust, and the shared belief in the merit of 'goodness'.

Their conversation was a bit less disciplined now. They were so full of feelings, so many things they wanted to say; there was such competition to utter their overflowing words. If there were five people, there were ten times five attempted conversations simultaneously vying for a place to have their words heard. It was nervous exhaustion rather than common sense that shooed them to their beds.

It seemed sensible to sleep long without the tension of anticipation to spend a day in the magical, historical Hong Kong without schedule, later to bathe their senses in an orchestral concert; a change of scene, a chance to make a bridge from that hectic Japanese experience before landing again to pick up the step, the march rhythm of their beloved Australian lives; surely that was just what the doctor ordered? That Roddy Mckenzie should satisfy his urge to hear—and see—Jessica Mckenzie from Fearnas play in the Scottish Symphony Orchestra was simply a coincidental cause for this dash of well-deserved rest and rehabilitation, was it not?

The Luk Kwok Hotel on Gloucester Road in the Wan Chai district was a Chinese hotel, and a very good one, that

the bank had booked for them. It certainly was not new, but
constant updates and restructure had changed it—and its
neighbourhood—continuously over the years. One could not
look to the west now with any hope of seeing Victoria Harbour;
and Bauhinia Square was somewhere nearby, or was that just
tourist tattle? When they disbanded for bed the night before, all
that had been agreed upon was that if they all met for breakfast,
that would just be good luck. No time would be fixed. When
Roddy slowly ascended from sleep to wakefulness, he recalled
having noticed from the buttons in the lift that there was a
swimming pool on the top floor and thought a few leisurely
laps would be a good way to get his body stretched. The pool
was not very long, but it allowed bones and muscles to feel some
strength and flexibility moving in them. The breakfast room
was as bright as a cloudy sky would permit and the furnishings,
had not escaped completely from Edwardian English flavours
behind the Chinese design. Looking relaxed, refreshed, and
very touristy, Ethel and Freddie came and joined him. Within
minutes, Doris and Mauri arrived; rested, visibly refreshed. How
would the day be spent? Moving around a throbbing city would
be a challenge for a group of five people unless they chose from
all the possible tours that could be taken one that would suit
all. 'Hardly possible,' they thought; and anyway perhaps they
needed a bit of time to be themselves. There were still reactions
to the last two days which needed quiet reverie; thoughts allowed
to wander off on personal paths. Surely the critical decision to
be made was to decide where they were to meet at mid-day
beer time? It may have been Roddy who raised that question.
Since they all knew where the hotel was, and they could agree
that that it was a pleasant spot, and took into account that any
shopping done would be becoming troublesome by then the
hotel choice was favoured. 'Right here at about one o'clock.
That gives you an hour after the gun goes off,' said Roddy, the
colonial historian.

Maybe he *had* picked up bits of information (misinformation?)
about British colonial history on his way through school and
in undirected reading, certainly not through any rigorous
study. But the unease that he had been feeling since reading

about Mahatma Gandhi, the partition of India, the troubles in Palestine, and most disturbingly what he had encountered in Kenya had frequently been stirred up each time he encountered new information about European colonialism and particularly Britain's. The difficulty was to separate the implanted myth from the historical reality. He wanted to use these hours before the concert to walk this historic ground.

His sortie into history would require some guidance in the form of maps and a guidebook both of which he found in the hotel lobby. Kowloon, apart from being the land on which Kai Tak airport was, had cropped up in yarns since boyhood, and Percy F. Westerman's young merchant naval officer cadets had certainly made adventurous voyages to that clamorous, seething oriental port of Chinese intrigue and danger. After a short walk from the hotel to a quay on Tonnochy Road named after Malcolm Stewart Tonnochy, a short-term acting governor of Hong Kong, he was afloat on a big diesel-powered ferry and on his way to the historic Walled City. There was too much to observe from his upper deck viewpoint to look at his data sources now. The name Tonnochy rang in his mind a reminder note that the history of China and Hong Kong and East Asian Trade was very much as story of the lives of Scotsmen at least one Mckenzie among them. Spread seeds of Alder? He could look out now and see the funnel markings of spick-and-span Clan Line merchant ships still bearing the owners' name, McKinnon Mackenzie; among the many well-known names were Jardine, Matheson, Duncan, Finlay, Yuill, Binny, Lockhart.

He went on foot to the Walled City having briefly stopped for a coffee near the quay to have a quick glance at his guide. He found from it that, when the lease with China had been signed, adding the 'New Territories' to the ninety-nine-year lease it was on condition that there be a continuing Chinese enclave there. That would be okay, said the lessees, so long as they residents don't participate in political activity. So the enclave has been there since the beginning. During the Japanese WWII occupation, the walls were pulled down and the materials used in later land reclamation. The governing body of Hong Kong had never any interest in expending money or energy on this

'Chinese' asset so left it to its fate. That fate was to allow it to grow like Topsy as a home for people finding it difficult to get accommodation under the rule-bound HK they moved in. Refugees from Chiang Kai Chek's China and from oppressive life in China before then moved in. A tiny bit of land on the Kowloon peninsula ceded since 1840 was now of a low order of interest to mainland China. With no one caring, it became a cosy spot for criminals and drug dealers. Despite the vice, crime, no sanitation, electricity, or water, in that tiny confine, so crowded, with a physical shape so structurally squeezed that life could be lived without ever putting a foot on the ground, a very 'normal', cohesive, thriving community took shape. As he made his way through the dark narrow streets cut off from the sky by the joining structures of footways and hanging clothes, where shops were trading and people were going about their business, Roddy found it incredible that people could possibly live there yet dress, look, and behave like high-rise city dwellers possibly anywhere. The slums of Glasgow and Naples looked positively bucolic by comparison. Meanwhile overhead, big, modern, international aircraft were passing, minutes apart, thunderously, dangerously low. There was high-density living all around, existing and in the course of construction, of a kind where he could not possibly ever live. He was glad to have had that learning experience, but he was happy to be leaving it behind, to be able to walk away. On the ferry, he looked back and realized that life had gone on there at least since the beginning of this century, was going on there now, and would be going on there tomorrow.

Back on the island, he entered the sharply contrasting world of the Luk Kwok. He looked into the downstairs lounge but the others were not there. At the reception desk he went to ask whether there were any messages for him. Yes, the others were back and would be down shortly, the clerk said, and there was an envelope addressed to him. He had just thanked the clerk and turned round when the four tourists came down the stairs.

With a mid-day middy in mind, each couple kept an eye open on the way to the hotel. Not far away Mauri and Doris had found a tall building in which there was a terraced bar and restaurant high above the street with a view back to the bay. That would be it: so off they merrily went. The beer was not quite cold enough for the Australians, but 'when you're roughing it abroad, you have to take what you can get'. They sat there in this lofty luxurious setting, relaxed happy, looking across the hectic waterborne traffic of the strait, telling exciting tales of their mornings. 'I ought to open this envelope', said Roddy, 'I'm sure it will be our tickets for tonight.' Along with their stalls tickets, there were three invitation tickets for Mr. and Mrs. Perrott, Mr. and Mrs. Treloar, and Roderick McKenzie Esq. They were for 'a celebration of the Scottish Symphony Orchestra's first concert in Hong Kong', 'Only the bearer of this ticket may attend.' There was a short note from Jessica: *Hello, Roddy, I'm looking forward to seeing you again. There's quite a competition for the celebration tickets. If you, or any one of your friends cannot come, please phone this number and let them know immediately. I hope you enjoy our concert. Very excited, Jess. PS. Ditto the concert tickets. It's a full house. J.*

'That does sound exciting, doesn't it?' Ethel said exuberantly immediately on hearing and looked around the group. 'I can't wait.'

The others agreed, and Doris suggested that they may be wise to have a short zizz later in the afternoon before dressing to go and even have something light to eat somewhere near the city hall. The lunch mood was light and airy and really so were the drinks and the guided selections of Chinese food. Comfortably relaxed once more they set off on foot for the quay to choose a tour ferry for a harbour cruise which slotted neatly into their schedule for the rest of the afternoon.

The foyer of the Hong Kong City Hall Concert Hall was positive evidence of a full house. Had one left it late to join a group, it would be impossible now. The sound of low-volume, vivacious conversations seemed to be the chamber's air, as if apart from, and simply absorbing the black and white figures of the mass into which splashes of bright colour brushed in, here and there, at chosen intervals and positions, helped the eye to sense the nervous life. Even hardened old concert goers would had been mixed into the wash of tension, energy, and excited expectation. Then the first bell sounded. It was time to go in.

The auditorium was lofty and functional. 'Get your silly jitters under control and pay attention,' its broad bare spaces were saying. 'And get all your coughing and fidgeting done now.' The lights went down. Only the stage was lit and the orchestra walked on from the left and right. The second violins and violas took their places before Roddy's expectant eyes. One pace ahead of the leader, Jessica Innes her black dress, like a panther skin, defined the fluidity of her long-limbed stride. Doris grasped him firmly, pulled him over, and gasped, sotto voce, in his ear, 'She's *stunningly* beautiful, Roddy.' She let him go. He could only turn towards her and nod: Doris required no great power of observation to reach her judgement. Jessica now sitting erect, her shoulders square, her curly black hair falling over her bare old-gold shoulders to her dress. At the temple, some concealed device held it back lest vigorous bowing let it fall forward and make reading impossible. The rich black hair framed her perfect face and the nose, long and straight, almost Milanese, gave it strength. Her cheeks were a natural rose pink on the lightly tanned skin that flowed down to her exposed shoulders where small firm breasts, strong and erect, shaped her professionally severe gown. The last scattered notes of tuning stopped. A languid wrist held her bow across her right knee, her left hand held her instrument upright on her left knee; the falling folds of her dress outlined her long thighs.

Andrew Dobson, the Scottish conductor, short and square, strode to the podium as the audience clapped a welcome. He turned to the audience, bowed his acknowledgement, and turned again to scan his players. Up went his baton. The second symphony of Rachmaninov in E minor slowly and quietly rose to life. The symphony takes its time to begin. After all it has sixty minutes to tell its complete story, but tonight the periods of pensive languor and reworking of themes had been trimmed to a twenty-seven minute form. This is enough for all the figures and themes to be presented and bound together into a whole without the stitches showing and each of orchestra instruments and none that is ever played seemed to have missed inclusion by Rachmaninov. Each of these throughout the performance explains its having been chosen by its enhancement of the overall sound.

At the end, the audience sat in silence and then there burst out an explosion of applause; clapping, cheering, and loudly vocal acclaim. It was interval and they kept together as they went from their stalls area up the richly carpeted steps to the exit which led into a room a broad space in which this part of the audience had much more space to itself. Most locals had used the service of pre-ordered drinks and went to fetch them but there two or three small bars where the service was quick and cheerful. So the needs of the group were easily met.

'What did you think, Doris?' Roddy asked.

'Musically they were very competent. All the instruments did great work. The conductor was he especially good. He seemed to be inside the music and his orchestra was right with him in spirit. I don't know it had been written by Rachmaninov but I think the phrasing . . . and the . . . sometimes silences, were the conductor's genius. He impressed me a lot. I've never heard this symphony sound so emotionally good . . . it put a story into the music . . . it was like a ballet score . . . and that was because of the conductor . . . and because of him, by the musicians. They were breathing in time with him.' These words flowed from Doris. Roddy was so pleased for her. 'I'm so pleased you enjoyed it, Doris. I managed to glimpse some of the things you could see so clearly. I put it all down to the composer. But I did enjoy its richness of composition.'

The others, particularly the men, listened to Doris and watched Roddy listening to her. Mauri knew of Doris's love for classical music and admired and supported her dedication to it. He knew he would never understand it as she did, but he had learned much from just listening to what she had to say when she came home about performances she had been to, and from his attendance as 'husband' when she went to concerts of the societies of which she was a member. For Ethel and Freddie, music concerts were something they knew went on but neither had ever attended. This was a first, and they were happy to have had the experience. At least they had broken their duck.

It is almost as if one had to know Scotland, or at least have spent a long visit there to grasp the full emotional mood of this symphony. A Scots person listening to it will readily sense that Scotland had crept inside Mendelssohn and captured his spirit. Roddy could relax now in his attention to orchestration and indulge himself in watching the beautiful Jessica play. He gazed and saw that she had become one with the music. As the mood shifted, or as emotion concentrated, or there was simply, almost a sentimentality, the feelings could be read in her face, her bowing, and the movement of that part of her body which was her violin. He was enrapt. The music dissolved into the distant Scotland and the bows brought the last tone from the strings.

If noisy then, even noisier now, there was even stamping of feet like the last night of the London Proms; there were 'bravos' and cheering. The conductor bade his orchestra stand. The decibels rose. The orchestra bowed to their conductor and began to clap. This was a clear signal not to be denied the audience. Everybody rose. The decibels threatened the roof beams and went on and on. How Dobson must have been feeling then. How the musicians must have been feeling then. 'Encore! Encore!' were the shouts. They sat down and played Annie Laurie. There was not a dry eye in the house. Then to dry the tears, they played 'Kelvin Grove' in which grove there was dirty old city that was their home.

Roddy had been given instruction that they were to come and meet the musicians before proceeding to the big 'Do'. So they went to a secret doorway in the furthest corner of the large space in which the ordinary listeners were milling and talking in delighted reminiscence of their fresh experience. They were going to see the musicians. That gorgeous violinist was a find of theirs. It was all quite melodramatic, especially when they found the door locked. A couple of sharp raps administered by a Mckenzie fist led to a dweller in inner earth or highest heavens opening it enough to see out while keeping interlopers at bay. 'Jessica Innes has asked us to come,' pronounced the Mckenzie. The head disappeared as did the slot in the doorway, but as he was turning; they heard a loud shout, 'Jessica!' Out of their hearing, the head was saying to an advancing female form, 'Jess, come an' see if these are the folks you invited.' The door opened again a little further this time. Two heads and bits of bodies appeared: one was Puck, the other was Aphrodite. 'Come away in,' said Aphrodite with a smile that would melt any human heart. They stepped into the space with the click on the lock behind them. Jessica stood before Roddy, then like a housewife greeting her husband home from his job, she kissed him on the lips. 'You're looking very well, Rod'rick,' she said.

'Aye, ye're not looking that bad yourself, Jess.' The observers were immediately introduced. 'Doris, I feel as if I know you. Roddy's told me so much about you. I'm so glad you were able to come tonight. You too, Mauri. You've done an awful lot for Roddy.'

Doris replied first. 'He's been a great joy to us, Jessica. He's a fine young man. He'll do very well for himself. You won't have heard yet what he has just achieved in Japan. That's for later.'

Roddy introduced the Treloars who had been watching the exchanges with the Perrotts and having a look at what was going on in this crowded noisy room of popping champagne corks.

'Come and meet Andrew Dobson,' suggested Jessica.

Doris was delighted to meet the man whose mastery in tonight's music was unquestionable. They found him in a huddle mainly of men who were talking about selections for the Scottish international football team and a bloke called Frank Hubbard who played for his home team of Motherwell who had been chosen as right half. He smiled warmly on meeting the Australian Doris, who plainly expressed her thanks to him and his musicians. She had enjoyed both symphonies immensely and she told him so, almost in the words she had used in her critique to Roddy. It could be seen that he sensed her sincerity and that she was no newcomer to orchestral listening.

'Ach, I have my critics, Doris, as you can imagine . . . but I think you have to be true to yourself and I've had no conflict with even one of the musicians . . . brilliant players who've worked with well-known conductors. We get on well together . . . there may be something Scottish about it . . . but we're happy and I'm very happy. Thank you for your kind words, Doris. If you'll excuse me. I'd better round this crowd up or we'll all be fu' before we get to the big "Do". Come and hear us in Scotland.'

'Never fear. I'll take you up on that, Andrew.'

The 'Do' was a formal Meet the Musicians Cocktail Party so there announcements from the associated bodies of the Hong Kong musical community and those organizations who had made financial contributions to the funding of the tour; there were to be two concerts with different programs—both fully booked—and a matinee when only a portion of the hall was bookable in advance. The shy young (well, perhaps not all were so very young) musicians were almost too reserved to point seemingly extensible arms to the trays of ever passing waiters whenever thirst became unbearable. Sad, really, when you consider that playing music in any genre is known to be thirst causing labour. The Australian visitors thoroughly enjoyed being with the musicians finding those they spoke with, to be a friendly folk, very easy to chat with, showing interest in subjects away beyond classical music and when the Treloars mentioned that their son Howard was a jazz fanatic, one of the players was able to say that he regularly played in a trad jazz band in Glasgow and suggested that when Howard was in town, he should come and hear them and they'd take him round the other venues or appoint someone to do so if he was unavailable. Roddy, Jess, and the couples flitted off having farewelled those they had met. They passed by the group in which Andrew was engaged and *en passant* Doris wishing not to interrupt quickly said as she continued on, 'Thank you, Andrew.' He could disengage himself only sufficiently to call out after her, 'Come to Glasgow, Doris.'

The restaurant where they had booked a table was high in a commercial building a short walk from the city hall. All of the audience who were not at the 'Do' were at the restaurant. All the tables appeared to be taken. They sat down together in a Chinese restaurant, to eat Chinese food, amongst Chinese people in a Chinese world. It was absurd that they should be at a table in restaurant now famous for its fine food when they had just come from a party where the Chinese food served was of the finest. But for Roddy and Jess, it was an additional dimension to their seeing each other again their first time since he and Erik, Margaret Stephen, and Jess had walked on the links to the Fishertown and he had kissed her for the first time. It was nice to be close to her and to hear her speak. The others were eager to know about them. It was Doris who opened up the important subject. 'And what do you think these three have been up to in the last two days?' Jess looked at each of the men and none spoke. 'Oh, they won't tell you, so I will. They have just secured the Australian agency for all the heavy construction and earthmoving equipment of the big Japanese company Ugojim and have formed a jointly owned company comp called Ugojim Australia Pty. Ltd. I think they have done marvellously well. What do think of that?'

'I don't know what to think . . . it sounds incredible . . . but I know it must have taken a lot of doing . . . and I'm sure it must mean big things for the future. Congratulations you three. Well done!'

'Well he was the one who did it,' said Freddie, looking at Jess, and as he turned his head, he raised his chin to point at Roddy. 'When Mauri and I had our interviews with Asahi Ishikawa, we each had the feeling that he had made his mind up. He had to see how his executives would make up theirs. But our confidence began to rise then.'

'I can't see how I can be given credit for all this,' he was energized, adamant, intent as he stated these words and went on, 'That would be untrue and unjust. It was Mauri's experience and success with and for Fusan Motors; and the growth and magnitude of Freddie's company that gave them the confidence. They knew that you two were behind me and would provide the experience I patently didn't have. I may have helped, and I sincerely hope I have. If I really have made a worthwhile contribution, imagination . . . if I can just be included whenever it might be said, "We did it," I'll be very happy.'

There was a pause while everybody recognized that what was now being clearly exposed was the essence of Roddy Mckenzie; his need to speak the truth, his need to have contribution, even his own, made recognisable. In his very words and how he expressed them, the women could see something of the magic of the Mckenzie and how that might have affected Asahi, Mauri, Freddie, Mac, Rhys, and the mature good men at the Corner.

Jessica felt the power and reality of Roddy's words and the pure gold of his feeling; she would never forget that little speech. She looked at him in awe and feeling that moved in her gut. She was hearing a voice inside her whispering, 'These are the admirable qualities of a man: they are the admirable qualities of a woman too.'

Ethel wanted to know about this little highland town that they had come from.

'Did you two know each other as kids?'

Jess told her about her childhood on a farm about eight miles out of Fearnas, her little school at Bareavan; about Miss MacDiarmid her teacher who played violin and piano and the little organ in the church at Ardclach, how she noticed how true to pitch Jessie's voice was, and how she could pick up and hold a part when they did little three voice choral pieces. She gave her little private tests on the piano where she had to pick a note that naturally followed and a notes that harmonized. And she asked which she liked better, the piano or the fiddle. She had been glad when Jessie chose fiddle because she could practice at home where there was no piano or come to her house where she could learn to play with an instrumental accompaniment. She must start learning immediately. Now Miss MacDiarmid lent her, her own precious fiddle, gave her a scale to learn, and sent her off home across the hill.

'I went on from that day without ever stopping and did music as a university study in addition to history and English. I've always wanted to do mathematics and that doesn't mean I never shall.'

'Roddy had been some years ahead of me and had gone to the army when I arrived at St Ninian's. I met him when he came back. But I'd heard about him.'

The stories of the two came out in bits and pieces with the men and the women asking different kinds of questions, all fascinated by the stories of the short lives of these two.

But then it was time to consider tomorrow, for Jessica a concert and for the Australians departure for home. They vowed that they would all meet again, perhaps not all together at the same time, more than once and knew that there would be no doubt or difficulty in keeping that vow.

'I'll just walk Jess home,' he said to the others who would have expected nothing else. They went down to the street, and after a cuddle from Doris and fond good-byes all round, Jess and Roddy waved them off in their taxi into the traffic of the neon-lit night.

The two were alone together for the first time since they had met. It was like being suddenly naked, vulnerable. This footpath below them; in Asiatic Hong Kong, with a lively night population passing around and almost jostling them, made the exchange of intimate thoughts incongruous, unreal, futile even. And glass walls, soaring sheer above like animate preying monsters with flashing rapacious eyes chilled the blood. Those feelings had to be escaped. 'Madam, will you walk and talk with me?' Roddy sang theatrically, putting out his hand. As she took it, she looked at him saying, 'Thereafter the lyric makes promises neither of us is ready to make at this time.' He gently squeezed her hand and let her continue. 'We're both going to fly off on flight paths of our own for a while. I wonder if they will ever come together?' There they were; the fact and the whimsical fancy in her question.

He turned, with her hand in his, in the direction of her hotel which was only two hundred yards or so away from where they stood saying, 'Neither of us can know. It may sound stodgy and not the stuff of story books, but we both know that our careers need our attention first. You could never write a best-selling love story based on a statement like that. You need to refuse the big Carnegie Hall engagement and fly to my arms. We will love passionately until I have both a company and a personal collapse. We have to live in a Gorbals style room with distant, shared plumbing; surviving on milk loaded with tuberculosis that we would have to pinch from other peoples' doorsteps, and while I'm dying of alcoholic poisoning, you nurse me till I die then, exhausted with travail and caring, succumb to consumption. I've purposely missed out the horrible, agonizing, foul parts, but they'd all be in the book; fiction's preferred world.'

'Right, Roderick, I was just about to weaken. But I shall continue to dedicate myself to my craft. That won't stop us scribbling a line or two to share our experiences. I'll want to hear all the details.'

'If you keep me up to date on the orchestra's bookings, I'll want to come and see you and hear you play again.'

'That's exciting . . . my imagination's making pictures already . . . I can immediately see us having fun and frolics . . . sharing the history and the delights of the great cities of Europe . . . food and wine, music and art . . . maybe the odd matinee. Sell lots of haul trucks!'

'Believe me I'll be putting one hundred per cent effort and all imagination into it. I have a huge responsibility to do that.' They were outside the hotel. 'Look we're there,' he noticed. 'Let's share just a moment away from the lights and all these people.'

They walked together into the large foyer.

Losing consciousness of any one around they stood looking at each other both aware that that whatever was said would be their final spoken words for some time. 'Thank you for coming here to see me, Roddy, I'm so glad you chose to come and now I know something about the nice people you live with: I'll want to hear about them too when you write. You will do well in your new venture. I know that. I also know that being a successful businessman won't change you and that makes me happiest of all.'

'Jess, I couldn't have been this close to seeing you and not come. I had to and I'm so glad I did. You are such a delight. I am so lucky that we can be the way we are and understand our needs to do what we're doing. Doris and Ethel and the blokes have really taken to you and if you get the chance come to Australia for a visit,' he almost pleaded. Ethel will put you up and I live close by. Don't go to Sydney first. Doris would never let you go.' He looked at her beautiful face for some seconds then took her into his arms very lightly and kissed her. 'It's late and you have a performance tomorrow. Good night and good-bye Jess.' He let their hands slip apart. She turned and walked gracefully to the lifts. She raised her hand and waved as the doors closed.

He could have walked to the hotel, but he wanted to get off the street. His thoughts would be better entertained in the silence, solitude, and soft lighting of his room.

There was no requirement for haste at breakfast next morning. There would be ample time to be at the nearby airport for their noon flight. Yet when they came down, everyone had already packed. They had time to make their way down to the park by the edge of the bay, but there was so much construction going on that it was quite unpleasant to attempt.

'Let's go to the airport anyway,' said Doris, looking at the fidgety mood of her companions. Her suggestion was well received. Once at the airport, each of the men got out pads and pens and began writing; calculating dates, making priority lists, asking each other Ugojim questions. An administrative HQ had to be set up for the new company, so they concentrated at one point on planning that. 'The wool store next our place is up for lease. The present owner is winding up the business because of the big change in the market. I'll have a look at that as soon as we get home,' Freddie said. It seemed no time till they were stuffing their papers into their brief cases and boarding.

Arrival at Sydney necessitated a quick transfer of Roddy and the Treloars for their flight to Perth. The Perrotts were met by a driver. There was little time for fond farewells.

At Perth airport the black swans were, as usual, in their pond, but they paid no attention to the return of the natives as they walked by to the terminal hall. Amongst the excited crowd in the rustic, friendly interior, Gwen and Howie were waiting for the Treloars and waiting for Roddy were Mac and Janet. The meetings and partings were brief the travel tales would be told when the travellers were comfortably home, the Treloars having graciously declined an invitation from Mac to drop in for a drink on the way. 'I'll ring you this evening,' were Roddy's last words to Freddie. They had agreed to a meeting on Monday afternoon at four depending on the availability of Rhys, Frank, and Claude. Mac had agreed immediately and said he would be available. The meeting would be important because, in addition to a debriefing of the Ugojim events, allocation of immediate tasks, and roles to be played in the immediate and near future were essential as would be a discussion on the subject of company structures, finance, and staffing. There must be no pause in the momentum.

Janet invited Roddy to toddle along for a meal to save him from having to cook on his first night home, but really, she wanted to hear about this beautiful Jessica that Doris had told her about. Just as Doris was concerned about what this friendship meant for the future relationship of Roddy and Jill, Janet was concerned about what this new woman's appearance on the horizon might mean in his relationships with Lynne and Ann.

She could only surmise that he wanted to put aside any feelings he may have for any one of them while Ugojim was demanding all his thoughts and energy and understood when, in response to a question, he had expressed that he wanted to have his economic future well established before he could allow himself to let his feelings move him to a declaration of love. Having satisfied her curiosity to the extent that she could, she said, 'Well, you all had an exciting time, you and the others enjoyed meeting Jessica and hearing her play. I'll just go and do a couple of things and we'll be able to eat in forty minutes.' Yet both Doris and Ethel had an implicit understanding of what was going on in the relationships between Roddy and the girls. They knew the lure of lust, the drive to bodily embrace, and that misty dream of lush copulation. These were vigorous, healthy young people in whose bodies the blood flowed in a hot tide. They knew that career girls like Jill and Lynne were nor unhappy to wait outside marriage; to forego for a while the inevitable children and a lost career. There would be time enough to enter that world where the male reached for ever higher goals beyond the requirements of the family's financial needs, devoting only a part of his life to the emotional needs of his wife and her children. Married life and a family required more just a part of a wife's effort and care. Yes, Roddy and Jill and Lynne, without any need for analytical contemplation, had drawn a distinction between the innate drive for the voluptuous joys of sex and the ongoing needs of an economically sound, stable life. They must not allow themselves to falter, to succumb.

Much more prosaically, Mac wanted to hear all about the Ugojim events straight from the horse's mouth. Roddy related the facts totally in terms of the team and how they had got the harmonies right and how Asahi Ishikawa had been sensitive to this unison. Asahi and his management team could see that Mauri and Freddie were 'dinkum'. Quickly they moved to agenda items for tomorrow and what he and Mauri and Freddie had talked about in Hong Kong and on the plane. When they touched on the item of staffing, Mac said, 'Ask Graham Knight, Rhys, Frank, or Claude who the most important member of your staff will be and I'll bet London to a brick they'll say a secretary, office manager, call her what you like. Peter Gill's wife Madge is out of work at the moment which normally wouldn't matter all that much to them but as you know when they were living at flat number one in your block, they had the opportunity to buy that house on Broome Street and they would have been foolish not to take it, so they need the mortgage money. Lakribeta, the grocery wholesaler she had been with for many years merged with United Food Wholesalers which has an identical kind of operation. The senior managers retired or took positions elsewhere, the rest were cast adrift. I took some of them, but I have nowhere I can place someone at Madge's level. I've dealt with Madge over the years and have great admiration for her. I think she would be just right for you. She's a shorthand typist, a book keeper and she's first class at dealing with the public. She could look after both Mckenzie and Ugojim for your first few years. Would you like me to arrange a meeting?'

'The sooner the better, Mac, things are going to begin to hum very soon. Freddie says there's a property right next to Treloar that's up for lease and will be available in about a month when the last of the wool is moved out. Freddie knows what we'll need and thinks it's damned near ideal. Freddie and I plan to have a look at it tomorrow. When we have to move plant around it's going to be very handy to be next to Treloar. He also said his people are updating some office equipment and he could give us a fax on loan for as long as we need it.'

When he imagined that people may now be home from their daily activities, he began making his phone calls. He rang Rhys first and it was he who answered the phone. He was going to be available for a meeting and on the subject of a venue said, 'Since you blokes are all down in Cottesloe or Freo, ask Mac if he'd mind if we had the meeting at his house Janet is not to be allowed to cook because I think we should invite her with the other women to come out to dinner with us after the meeting to the OBH or wherever you choose.' With Rhys still on the phone, he checked with Mac who said was a great idea, and that he would arrange it with the pub. When Roddy spoke with Frank and Claude, they both agreed on the time for the meeting and the dinner venue. He also rang Dave and left a message on his answering machine. Bill Gray was next and he sounded exceptionally pleased to hear the Ugojim news. Roddy asked if there was any chance he could meet him and Billy for a chat on Monday morning at his flat if possible they needed as much time as possible to think about his plans for Mckenzie. He outlined the idea that, should Billy be agreeable with the idea, he would like to send him up to Hiroshima, for the minimum of a month, to learn up all about every piece of plant Ugojim produced and that once they had WA going and a bit of experience gained Billy would transfer to Sydney or another location in NSW to sell Ugojim in NSW and Queensland. Roddy was conscious all the time of the Collie commitment the possibility of the Marble Bar contract, Mac's demolition on Eric Street, with Broadway coming up later. He was acutely conscious of the need not only to keep money flowing into Mckenzie but to increase that flow. Mckenzie would need more jobs, and would need to build up a stock of operators like Bill and Billy Gray to call upon. The welter of considerations and the pursuit of work for Mckenzie could blunt the thrust to establish Ugojim. Yet each revenue unit, Ugojim and Mckenzie, must be appropriately resourced. They had exhausted as much as they could sensibly discuss before tomorrow's meeting, when Janet came out to ask if they were ready to eat. She had prepared a delicious fish pie which Roddy enjoyed so, with many thanks, and Janet's blessing, he strolled thoughtfully back home.

He was happy to be back in his flat again. Its acquisition for rental, the deal with the furnishing, and its location were way points reached and rounded on the course to Hiroshima. Out there and ahead were more way points: many of the next marks on the unfolding chart would be plotted here in the still waters of this Cottesloe flat.

He immediately saw Madge's coordinating role for Mckenzie, he needed to shape and define Dave's role in Mckenzie which would also depend on Madge. Billy Gray would be out of Mckenzie with immediate effect and old Bill Gray would have to take a larger, more regular, role in Mckenzie operations. Additional high-quality operators would have to be found. His own role as an operator would have to become 'emergencies only' work. His selling career for Ugojim began in Hiroshima five days ago. 'Remember, Mckenzie. "Selection and Maintenance of the aim", and acutely important: "Maintenance of Morale"! So keep your eye on the ball and your brain clear!'

———∞∞o﹜⬨﹝o∞∞———

The meeting was at the big table on Mac's verandah now decidedly business orientated. This verandah, focused memorably on light-hearted social events, was not only quite visibly different. The sun, the sound of surf, and Rottnest on the horizon was following its own code. But here, on the verandah, the tribal furnishings had been laid out for a new ceremony. The trinkets of joyful happiness had be ritually removed and ritually replaced with pads of blank paper and pens and water jugs and glasses. Stiff-backed chairs had been positioned around the altar so that each priestly face could see any other clearly. The spirits of bubbling festivity had been bidden to depart; now the sterner fate-changing gods had been summoned and were mixing their spiritual odours and influences in the air. The priests wore ceremonial robes indicating their obeisance and reverence for the pantheon of power; as they stood, and moved, they held their bodies differently and their voice tones shifted to that pitch used when power and manhood had to be signalled amongst gathered priests; seeming to say, 'Speak: whatever you say, I shall treat seriously.'

As chairman, Roddy thanked everyone for making this important meeting possible. 'It will be the first of many which we shall have until we settle down to an operational management system for Ugojim after which we shall most likely agree to have monthly board meetings for Ugojim. Mckenzie will be a little different and will require a special kind of attention. Its profitability will be the source of cash to honour our borrowing agreement with the bank. Mckenzie will require great care because it will immediately suffer two blows. I will no longer be a unit of operator labour . . . and . . . I plan to send Billy Gray to Hiroshima for the minimum of a month to get full knowledge of all Ugojim products. This morning I spoke with a lady who will be our first employee, and Mrs. Madge Gill will join us with effect from tomorrow. Frank, I had to make a decision on the spot and I'll send you the details officially tomorrow. The company administrative office will be, for the meantime, the spare room in my flat. But Freddie and I will be exploring the possibility of leased premises for the combined needs of Mckenzie and Ugojim in our formative years. The financial, official address will continue to be at Frank's office and all legal work will be referred to Claude's.'

'Now what does each of us need to do for these companies to achieve the goals we have promised Ugojim? Perhaps I might begin just by indicating one or two aspects of our challenge. To honour won contracts, Mckenzie will have to recruit high-quality operators. Ironically, I took from the Snowies plant operator skills which I will no longer be able to apply day to day. As from only a week or so ago, I have become the salesman for Mckenzie WA and Ugojim Australia. Where am I going to get selling skills? I am going to have to acquire them very quickly and I'll be leaning on Rhys and Mauri for help. Now as Rhys and Mauri will tell you, your best prospect to sell a car to is someone who owns a car and Graham Knight would probably tell you the same about houses. This means that every shire in Australia, every mining company, every forestry operation, demolition companies, dockers, shippers, and more are potential buyers. I will need to know who runs operations and who makes the buying decisions. Somehow I have to get close to these people and let them see how their needs or even aspirations can be met by our companies, Ugojim or Mckenzie. It will be up to me to target those in need and start filling the pages in my order book. The first call I'm going to make tomorrow will be to Bruno Brunsden. He will likely know from his dealings with them, who at Big Beauty proposed haematite mine at Marble Bar was the powerful person that persuaded Main Roads to build the road from Marble Bar to the mine site. Let us hope there has been no decision made yet. If no decision has been made, I want to whizz him, or a couple of his people who will choose the equipment they will buy, up to Ugojim as soon as possible. I will also ring Collie to see how near they are to making a decision about their work. A soon as I know, I'll have to discuss with Frank making Dave and the two Gray's permanent employees and shareholders. Similarly I'll need to discuss with him what I can expect from Ugojim funds as a salary and get into more detail about the share register.'

As they continued to discuss tasks and roles, Claude suggested that Plum possibly wouldn't mind undertaking some desk research saying he'd be good at ferreting out news of new mines, and the people involved in running them. This reminded Roddy that 'we must decide now how much we should pay Plum as a reward for the excellent job he did on the promotional materials for the Ugojim venture'. Frank said that all the providers of material and services had already been paid and then suggested what he thought was an appropriate amount. This was agreed to unanimously, and Frank said he would attend to it and issue a cheque, adding that Mac and Freddie should be co-signatories as required, in addition to Roddy and himself. Roddy closed the meeting when all agenda items had been treated and individual duties and tasks confirmed.

'I think it's only polite and appropriate that there should be representatives of the group at the OBH to await the arrival of the ladies and bid them welcome', Claude proposed and asked, 'Any volunteers?' Those present volunteered to a man.

After that first meeting, the surge of growth began to move quickly, then faster and faster. On the Mckenzie front, Bill and Billy were happy with their terms of employment, and Billy

was tremendously excited and enthusiastic about the future
with Ugojim Australia Pty. Ltd. that Roddy had outlined for
him. He had never been to New South Wales nor did he know
much about it. The local paper reported events in Canberra and
national politics, but Billy found the reports neither exciting
nor informative. Canberra, New South Wales, Sydney were a
world away. He had a great world to live in right in the West.
Nor was the cinema a source of great stimulation. He saw some
similarities of terrain in the many movies of the Wild West
and enjoyed some of the yarns, the comedies were fun, the
dramas of love affairs, and city life left him wondering how
many Americans were affected by the kinds of events that he
knew must have been greatly overdrawn for the purposes of
fiction. He saw them and had an immediate reaction to the
tensions, the dangers, the poverty, the glamour, the fact that
people were very seldom actually working unless on chain gangs
and swinging from girders at dizzying heights. The reality of his
own life was pretty good and he assumed that New South Wales
being peopled by Australians would be more like WA than the
United States. He had been made a shareholder in Mckenzie
Earthmoving, he was moving forward. He had a good boss and
he would be surrounded, even if at a little distance, by the good
men who supported Roddy. He did not yet allow himself to
think of going away, alone to a strange environment and a load
of responsibility of a kind entirely new. There would always be
Roddy. Look what he'd done.

Mckenzie had won the contract with Collie Shire, and
Bill and Billy had introduced two new plant operators whom
they knew, having worked alongside them, were highly skilled,
dependable, and of conscientious attitude.

Main Roads had issued the tender documents for the Big
Beauty road job to those who had submitted Expression of
Interest responses. Howie, Dave, and Roddy set off for Marble
Bar towing a caravan behind each of two pick-ups hired from
Treloar.

They were in the Marble Bar Ironclad Hotel having a beer
before moving on to choose a site for their first camp. Made
entirely of corrugated iron shaped in the exotic design of a

creatively imaginative architect was influenced by his reaction to seeing photographs and paintings of farm sheds left after the failures of the depression. His design certainly achieved congruence with the Australian rural landscape. Apart from the publican and a couple of suntanned men locked in discussion at a rustic table at the side of the room, the Mckenzie trio made up the crowd.

The publican was speaking to a little wizened bloke slumped over the bar. His clothes were rags. Roddy eavesdropped on the publican's words.

'No. No more, Simon, you haven't paid your board yet and that was the last of your dole cheque. There's a bloke leaving for Hedland in half an hour and I'll get him to give you a lift. You're doing yourself no good here. You'll have a better chance of a job in Hedland—if you sober up.'

Roddy could see Simon as a real 'Derro' on his way further down. He'd only get himself into trouble in a wild town like Hedland and that would be the end of him. He would become a hopeless case and end up dying of malnutrition. He was drinking more than his dole cheques could meet and he wasn't looking very good. In fact he was looking very bad. When the publican had moved away, Roddy stepped up to him, looked into his bleary eyes, and put it on him: 'Do you want a job?' he asked curtly and directly.

'Yeah. But there's nothin' about here.'

'Never mind that: what gear have you got?'

'Just about what I'm standin' in.'

'Okay. You start now.'

Dave, Howie, and Roddy were ready to go. He squared Simon's account with the pub and they were off.

Roddy only had a misty idea what Simon's job would be or what kind of character this bundle of skin and bones may prove to be. 'Mm . . . mm . . . yes, Mckenzie, so you've rescued a stray dog that happens to be a human. Wil he be in any way similar to a dog snarling to protect and keep the food offered, have the propensity to go beyond just defensively biting the hand that feeds it?. It was a question now of finding out where, in this human wreck, his heart is.' He must provide this disintegrating human with an immediate purpose. As surveyor's assistant, as a kind of company runner and roustabout, he would be able to see—if he wished to—that he was doing acts that needed to be done. He would have to see. What may happen after that was presently unknown.

There were three berths in each caravan. Dave and Howie were in one. The other was to serve as the office, the main galley, store, and Roddy's sleeping place. It was obvious that a few papers and maps should be removed from a bunk in the second van to provide bed space for the Boss's new recruit.

To make the twenty-eight miles of road to the mine site usable by laden trucks, the building of this road was not just a question of smoothing the top surface and laying bitumen. They had presaged this in their Expression of Interest. They were here now to calculate accurately what man-hour-machine-time would be required for each yard of road that they had described in their proposal. The work was difficult, a challenging mix of geology, geography, and hydrology, the siting of drains and culverts. The finished road would be expensive, and the mine developers had been very shrewd in their move to have the state of Western Australia pay for it. The calculations by the Mckenzie men had to be correct; they must measure accurately the cost of what they had to achieve—for the sake of their client, Mckenzie Earthmoving and ultimately Ugojim. When the three sat down and looked at their final figure, they were astonished at its magnitude. They went back, and back again, to recalculate, reconsider every detail. If their price were not acceptable, they knew it would destroy any other to do it for less.

That evening, Simon had gone into the scrub to puke up the bread and vegemite which was all he would eat for supper. He moaned, groaned, and threshed about on his bunk. He got up and went out two or three times. Roddy had to put up with it remonstration would have no positive effect on the withdrawal that Simon was experiencing. Next day Roddy gave him a filled army-surplus water bottle and said, 'Drink every drop of that before mid-day and more if you can.' He had made toast for him, with the thinnest spread of butter on it for breakfast. 'That's all you're going to get until lunchtime. All day today, you've got to carry Howie's measuring staff and hold it steady while he makes his readings . . . and do anything else he tells you to do.' Slowly over the three days, he made a recovery, but he lacked strength and struggled to carry the tall red and white measuring staff.

It was the third day when a light aircraft which had circled and flown low over the site making a couple of slow, low runs came again and flew over the Mckenzie men in the field. It banked turned again this time coming in very low so that the Mckenzies and the people in the cockpit could be recognized and exchange hand waves. Having gained height, the pilot flew back overhead and 'waggled' his wings as he flew away. The noise of the motor died away and the aircraft disappeared behind a low boulder-littered hill.

Not much more than an hour after the fly-past two Land Rovers hove into view coming in their direction. Howie Dave and Simon were some way away registering the site and direction of a culvert. Roddy was sitting at a field table near his van with a map and documents anchored by copper castings. Had there been a flat-topped mimosa above him, he could have been Blixen—or Hemmingway—or Robert Ruark writing of Africa.

From the leading Land Rover, a very tall, angular man stepped down; he was muscular and lean, but not lank in the Howie style. He had a cartoon character square jaw; he was wearing bush gear and a pair of boots that Teddy Roosevelt would have been proud of.

'Hallo,' he called, as he strode to Roddy's table from behind which Roddy was rising. 'How are ya? You guys gonna build the road?'

'Good afternoon . . . and tell me, sir . . . whom do I have the pleasure of addressing?' It was classic Mckenzie, the smile, the song in his voice, the erect body, and the eye-to-eye address.

'Hi!' he said, extending a long arm with a large, square, dry hand at the end of it.

'I'm Pete van Eisen. I'm chief mining engineer for the syndicate that's gonna develop Big Beauty mine.'

'And I'm Roddy Mckenzie, managing director of Mckenzie Earthmoving. In answer to your question—yes—we'll be building the road . . . when the Main Roads Department accepts our tender.'

'I notice you didn't say "if". You must be pretty confident.'

'Well, Piet, we don't cheat and we don't avoid reality. If anyone quotes lower than I do, he will make no money and probably go broke.' There was every sign that Piet had listened.

'Hey, look; you guys are doing serious work here and I don't want to steal your time. Could you build a landing strip for me?'

'When?' asked Roddy.

'Tomorrow.'

'The impossible we do every day. Miracles? Well . . . we've got a short waiting list . . . so I'd say about a week.'

'Roddy, can you come up and have a quick look?'

'Sure I'll just call Dave.' He let out a loud 'Coo-ee-ee'. The three men in the low scrub looked towards the call. Roddy raised one arm with one finger pointing upward then put his left hand flat on top of his head; with right fist clenched, he pumped his arm up and down quickly. Like a startled gazelle, Dave doubled over to them as they bumped their way in one of the Land Rovers towards him. He was introduced, and Piet registered that this new man wasn't really breathing hard when he'd stopped beside them. The sight and sound of this football player-operator rang true with Piet van Eisen.

'Piet wants us to build him an airstrip next week, Dave.'

'Ah, well, it'll have to be later in the week.'

Mckenzie Earthmoving built that air strip and went on to do most of the site works for the mine. Mckenzie won the tender to build the road on sheer accuracy of estimates, planning, preparation, and recent reputation.

Roddy took Piet van Eisen up to Hiroshima to meet Asahi. Piet ordered a shovel, two big excavators, and twelve haulpaks. When the question of price arose, Asahi quietly said to Van Eisen, 'You must ask Mckenzie-san about that.' During the visit, Asahi sought time to be alone with Roddy. They sat together as they had, at what now seemed such a long time ago, yet what was, in reality, a bit more than a month ago.

'Loddy-san, you cannot know how full my heart is. I am very happy for you. I am happy for me too, because you have confirmed my faith. I am so happy, so happy!' He uttered those words with quiet solemnity, speaking to himself, inside himself. What effect it had on Roddy and the ambient air was a faint echo of Asahi's contented soul.

There was another deal that the wily Piet contrived: if Treloar would acquire trucks to his specification from Ugojim, of course, he, Piet, would talk to Roddy about getting a really sharp-pencil price from Ugojim for his heavy mining equipment, then Treloar could have the road haulage contract to take all the ore from Big Beauty to Cape Lambert for five years, renegotiable, or at the time of complete depreciation of these assets.

Fiery Range Resources was Roddy's next target. He found access to this company, currently in the process of formation, via Claude, whose firm was handling all the legal work for the mine consortium's capital raising. Soon Roddy would be taking the Fiery Ridge people to Hiroshima.

Roddy's frequent visits to Hiroshima in no way altered the restraint and respectful solemnity of his meetings with Asahi.

Back at Cottesloe, or more correctly, at Leighton Beach, the old house which had never been knocked down when the wool store sheds were built but had become, at least its ground floor had become, the offices of the wool brokers. The top of this once-isolated two-storey residence had been simply shuttered, left, and forgotten. This upper floor was given to Simon and left for him to develop as his own residence. Help to undertake any restorative works was provided only when asked for, as were any restorative works on the emerging Simon. It was a work still in progress, but it was quite remarkable to see what the erstwhile Redfern lout and vagabond drunkard had done to transform that space into a home. Save on invitation, neither Roddy nor Madge ever entered his home, which became later to be known as Templar's Penthouse. He was now a regular drinker at the Highway and Swanbourne hotels. Respect for Roddy and recognition of Roddy's need for space to enjoy with his friends, away from work, meant that Simon scarcely, if ever, drank at the OBH preferring his locals, *The Railway* or *The Rose* a short walk from home. He had become a regular, steady and controlled, user of alcohol. While working around HQ and Madge, he became unable to resist the lure of what went on in the office. Under Dave's tuition, he had proved to be a very apt learner and a competent operator of all the machines Mckenzie used. Okay, if 'the Boss' wanted him to be the universal fit-in operator, fine, he would do that till the end of his life—if that's what Roddy wanted. But Simon wanted to be a part of the company's larger scope, of its place in the larger world of earthmoving, its plans, policies, procedures, its goal selection and steady direction to their achievement. His face may still look like a potato kept behind for seed, but the wrinkles seemed more flexible and those little blue eyes seemed to sparkle with life interest and a foreseeable future.

Madge was as steady as the proverbial rock, absorbed in, and very happy with, her life at Mckenzie. Now she had a demure young Dalmatian girl as a very intelligent, able assistant. Tania Vitasovic loved the idea of getting a wage and having to spend only the weekends planting or pulling onions on her parents' market garden over at Spearwood.

To cope with the welter of job scheduling and machine location, Madge now had a 'scheduler', a man recruited through the Highway, who had lost both his legs in a mining accident and destined to be lost to the working community. The Mckenzie heard about him, met him, and employed him. He had a great memory, a brain for systems and organization, lots of imagination and intuition. So really everything was humming. It meant that Roddy still had little time for himself, but he played squash with Freddie once a week when he was free. Freddie stood in the centre of the court while Roddy sweated his way through game after game rushing to get balls that trickled down into a back wall corner, or fell like a lump of lead from just above the line on the front wall. He still ran down for a swim at dawn.

He was religious in his correspondence to Jessica, Erik, the lovely Ranelagh people, Harty—no one was left out, even when it meant burning a bit more midnight oil. The Sydney-siders Jill, Mauri, Doris, Mike, and those who used the Naval and Military, he saw when he passed through en route to Japan.

Then, from an aspect of a world fading from memory, came a telegram from Erik.

'Need you to command an air-ground operation overseas. Total time one month. Good pay. All training in Australia. Means you drop everything. Details when you agree to join. Ike.'

His first reaction was to say a very loud 'Blast!'

This event precipitated the meeting with Freddie, Mac and the others, Frank Dalby, and Claude which was already a planned priority. His frequent absences were going to recur for the foreseeable future. If every tender and contract were kept for him to vet and price, it would delay the process which benefitted so well from prompt attention. He would hand over the tender and contract processing. A system of pricing based on accurate costing of salaries and overheads and all the other fees incurred by a growing business had to be put in place and applied as a basis to pricing jobs. With advice from Dave, Bill Gray, and Simon Ray Robinson was building a core of sources from which he drew plant and equipment to suit the work on each tender. Madge finally put it all together for presentation. Also a member of this action group, who had won his spurs through his contribution of ideas and shrewd questioning, was Simon Fraser. Roddy was delighted to stump up the cost of fees and study materials promised if Simon completed a TAFE course to enable him to sit for the university entrance exam. He had topped the state in his TAFE studies and was in the top two per cent in the uni entrance exam. He would start a commerce degree at UWA next term as a mature-age part-time student. He had an enquiring mind and was the ideal student who looked upon study as a fascinating game, opening up to the further puzzles presented in running a successful competitive business.

At this time, Mckenzie was functioning as the sales office for Ugojim. Simon would switch to the Ugojim payroll. Billy Gray just back from Ugojim would stand in for Roddy. Much was new for all of them and they had to learn quickly.

―――oooﻬ<ﻬ–ooo―――

In the world of Islam, at this time there were two major social thrusts for change—one inward, one outward. The inward thrust was to return Islam to that interpretation of the

Koran which would reverse the entire Islamic world, then the entire world, to Sharia law. The other thrust was to return the Near and Middle Eastern nations, and the nations of the Orient, to that place of eminence in the sciences, the mathematics, the astronomy, the matured philosophies, the poetry, the artistry and song, the outward looking enlightenment and freedom, which, before the advent of the narrowed vision of Islam, they had once, everywhere, enjoyed. Across, within and amongst these major forces there were differing shades of feeling and differing objective foci. There was another factor which clouded the future of everyone on earth.

The Cold War between two 'western' blocs held the rest of the world's nations without real choices in deciding their own fates: powerless, they were held strained on tenterhooks while Russia and the United States decided the fate of the world.

To aggravate the problems in the Islamic world in the Near and Middle East was the daily killing and strife in Palestine and Lebanon. The worse of these was the renewed confection of Zion. The people who came to this land which their god had promised them were Europeans of whom very few spoke Hebrew but many Yiddish, which had been spawned out of German from the lands where many had lived. The confection was a sour-sweet, stirred together by Britons, who like all people, despise those from whom they must borrow to fund their dreams. As a salve for their consciences and the popular view of Jewry, they generously granted the land of a people impoverished by Islam to the modern-day lost tribes—Jews from Europe.

Each of the Oriental thrusts had different sources from which to draw its leadership.

For the Islamists who wished to achieve a universal Caliphate and Sharia law, there was an abundant source of Imams and graduates of Madrassas and those empowered by experiences of mosques. However, to complicate issues, there exists a major doctrinal schism between the persuasions of Shia and Sunni. Deeper within that schism, there were acid-alkaline differences between races, tribes, adherents to potentates, tribal chiefs, war lords—and racism.

The second group was led mainly by academics who saw past the whims-turned-serious of Islamic zealots, who under the Sharia saw a means of progression towards a welcome in Paradise for the faithful. Instead of unearthly joys, this second group saw a Muslim world of the Orient, the Near and Middle East returning to a world in which the populations could walk, heads up, anywhere on earth, with valid pride in their continuing contribution to the science, arts, philosophy, and constantly developing scholarly excellence. The big difficulties lay embedded in their own populations. They knew very well the dangers of, quite inadvertently, shifting, or removing 'faiths' in civilizations. Yet they could see a distinct possibility of those 'faiths' happily surviving in an enlightened, productive, fulfilled society.

Omar bin Ahmed al Sayeedi of Oxford University was one, and a leader of these scholars. He had proclaimed his vision of an eastern, an oriental world, in which enlightenment could bring hope for every person to achieve a better life. The last thing he and his fellow supporters wanted was some imitation of American, British, French, or Russian ways of living. When he spoke to an audience his speech was too calm, too full of reasoned logic, too clearly expressed. He was a danger which would grow, not from a flash of gunfire or howling mobs but through the assimilation of reality, by clarity, even of untutored minds. Such converts would absorb, retain, and would require, demand, an equal logic to overcome their now internalized beliefs.

This man could be seen as a new prophet. He must be silenced now before the sickness spread.

As an enemy of God, and Mohammed was his prophet, this man, Omar, should be killed.

He was seized from a London taxi when visiting Birbeck College. Now, in a lone and crumbling house, an archaeological site, its neighbouring buildings robbed out to found other structures, a single ancient ruin now remained. It was in this hillside house that Professor Omar Sayeedi was now a prisoner of fanatics.

If he were not freed, his certain death would provide impetus for an explosive jihad. The 'West' would have shown itself too dumb, too weak, too lily-livered to rescue this man so honoured in their society. 'Pah! Just what you would expect.' But any overt or stumbled move by a 'Western' power would tip a myriad balances precariously poised. Should some nation grasp the nettle all the others would claim no part even when success was undeniably established. There were whisperings and mutterings in the shadowed political passages of the 'Western', international world. Britain drew the short straw in having to undertake the rescue. Britain would have to tread softly. The Foreign Office and Whitehall said to MI6, 'This is your kind of trick. Of course we'll give you all the help we can [meaning not much].' MI6 had a friendly 'subject expert' whom they summoned at once. He was a certain Tearlath Cumming, distinguished scholar in Oriental studies, who filled theatres in the West End with dramas, comedies, and 'whodunits' when he wasn't dressed in a kebiyeh and speaking different Arabic dialects, sophisticated Farsi and Pashtu, doing errands for the crown in lands where he had become over years, part of the patina.

If modern personnel selection agencies had the skills and networking power of Tearlath Cumming, they would certainly have chosen Major Erik Barron MC, Forty-third Royal Highland Regiment, Ret., to devise and coordinate a little caper to extricate a prisoner from rough people in rough country within a very limited time. He had been a Chindit; he had commanded mercenaries in the Congo and had shown exceptional courage in saving the lives of the crew of a foundering yacht in a Fastnet race. That was the Erik Barron who had been Roddy's company commander in Korea and for whom he had crewed in that horrific Fastnet race, and for whom he had commanded a platoon of 8 Commando in Katanga. The telegram to Roddy was from him.

The Mckenzie replied: *Thanks for your invitation. What next?*

Barron replied: *Why don't we meet for a drink Campbell Barracks mess fourishTuesday next? We can start our holiday next day. You may know one of my chums. Come in your own car. Plenty parking.*

'Well, high diddly bloody dee!' The Mckenzie cursed. 'I don't mind a joke, but I'm a bit busy at the moment. Glad I've had Freddie to run me ragged on the squash court and the sea on my doorstep. I'll have to get him to support Madge and see the troops stay happy.' Everything must be tickety-boo before he left. But sudden departures and being off-site for days had really become commonplace. The telegram was telling him he would be leaving next Wednesday. Where was 'overseas'? Obviously out of Australia—but Africa? South America? Asia? Middle East? Afghanistan? Wherever, if he was going to travel, it would be somewhere nearer UK than Australia. 'Why not add a week and fly on and visit the old folks? Mm . . . might even catch up with Jess?'

He would let Asahi know he would be off station for six weeks and that Freddie would be his contact.

It is possibly not so remarkable that when he walked into the SAS mess, Mckenzie Earthmoving and Ugojim vanished from his brain. First he saw Erik, who sprang up from where he was seated among a number of men mostly in uniform and stepped smartly to meet him with a hearty welcome. He was looking very fit and carrying no extra weight. Roddy was the last to arrive—possibly stage managed—and Erik introduced him to the other fourteen men of the extrication squad. He had immediately recognized a lieutenant in NSW Commando Regiment uniform—Andrew Denton! Erik closed his introductions telling them that Roddy would be in command of the mission on the ground. Then began the briefing.

'The situation is this; a strategically important Arab man is being held hostage. He is being held in a location in the hills of north-eastern Lebanon. Our mission is to get him out alive and deliver him alive to a waiting helicopter just over the border in Iraq.

'The operation's code name is The Heist, it will be carried out by ten men who will take the prisoner alive—I'll say again—alive and march him from the site on a route and direction where a mobile retrieval group in armoured vehicles will be approaching to meet all The Heist troops and bring the freed man back to a helicopter. The assault group will then be flown to Israel, disbanded and dispersed after debriefing. I will command the total operation and lead the retrieval column.

Lieutenant Roddy Mckenzie will command the tactical group
on the ground. We will have radio comms restricted for control
and emergency purposes only, including casevac and air SOS
support tasks. Codes will be disclosed during training.

'Australia was selected as most suitable for recreating The
Heist situation where we can rehearse again and again. We
have very good on- ground intelligence of the enemy force and
its operation down to number and locations of sentry posts
with daily updates. Silence and surprise will be essential. The
approach will be by free-fall parachute and a forced march
carrying only weapons and water. Three of you will be trained in
free fall by an instructor who is part of the force. The approach
of the retrieval AFVs will have begun at H Hour so you shouldn't
have too far to walk back. I won't ask for questions now. Take
time to think. We'll tackle questions tomorrow. Now we can
have a beer, a good feed, a good night's sleep, and a zero six
hundred hours reveille tomorrow. We'll go out for a trot before
breakfast then issue all the kit we need then move out to our
Pilbara training site by chopper from RAAF Pearce. I think we
have a great troop and I can't say how pleased I am that the
Australian and British SAS and NSW Commandos have been
so keen to join in this incredibly, globally important venture.
Thank you all.'

At the training location in Western Australia's northern
Pilbara, a tented camp had been set up secluded in a broad
gully above the danger of being caught in a freak flood. There
was a scattering of shady trees on the sloping red ochre soil and
imposing views wherever one stood. The area all around was
being secured by constant patrolling of 'friendly troops' who
folded this added duty into their own training programme. At
the wide northern entry to the gully, but a couple of miles out,
an almost perfect hill had been found to simulate the Lebanon
hilltop. Examination of aerial photographs brought down from
Lebanon showing latest sentry positions and orientation of the
old house was given detailed study resulting in the creation on
the ground of a good replication.

The conversion from static line to free-fall parachute training
of Roddy and another two of the men, by an Australian SAS

sergeant had to begin immediately so that repeat rehearsals of the total operation could be carried out. In the meantime, they could rehearse the march to the target area once in daylight and then, every night, in the darkness which would be the reality. The vital action of The Heist would be at first light. They therefore had to insert themselves silently into their precise positions and wait throughout that night. As the rehearsals developed, stuffed figures of the sentries were put in their positions. Roddy had to learn the Oman's figure form and shapes in any position with and without a beard, sitting standing, lying. The house assault party practiced again and again the sprint to the door. Every salient topographical feature, every waypoint and compass bearing, estimated time from point to point, was memorized by every soldier.

To extract Omar Sayeedi alive: this was critical requirement of the operation. At the first sign of an attack, the people holding him in the house would kill Sayeedi. Were this to happen, the entire humane, political, strategic value of this effort would have been lost; and the failure perverted to the benefit of the kidnappers. The consequences for the nations who may be accused of complicity in the operation would be terrifying and prolonged.

In London at MI6, Tearlath Cumming had a bed by the telephone in his small pokey office, constantly in touch with Whitehall and the Foreign Office. But the important news would come first from MI6 net and it was on that, that his attention was focused. More important than the strategy and the politics involved, he needed to know that his old friend Omar Sayeedi was safe. Yet he understood the reality facing the men on the ground.

Swift, silent, stealth would be the watchwords. Skill, focus, accuracy; the essentials. All of this could be injected into the operation only by perfect planning, rigorous training, and rehearsal.

They had time for more rehearsal before the planned start time when a radio signal reached Erik to say the it was feared the kidnappers may be about to shift camp. They had to start—now!

Erik came to Roddy and said, 'Get ready. We're off.'

With speed but no panic, they gathered their gear, checked and rechecked at its ready position, and buckled it on and mounted the trucks, ready on standby, and rumbled off to an airstrip where a Caribou could be landed. There was a long noisy air journey to northern Iraq, broken by a fuelling stop, until they reached their assembly point.

Before last light and the arrival of silent night, two civilian high-winged light aircraft, with Australian army pilots, flew through nicely calm air in which the temperature was only just beginning to cause what would soon become rougher thermal change. Looking up, it would be difficult to detect ten dark spots which, after some time, developed into flatter pieces in the sky became larger and twirled downward very quickly until they were lost to sight behind the hills. Ten men under the command of Lieutenant Roddy Mckenzie tilted their canopies and tip-toed down to the ground upon the rocky scrub in the hills of northern Lebanon within thirty feet of each other.

They carried their principal weapons at the trail; the riflemen, their automatic weapons; the archers, their strung bows, quivers on their backs like Masai murani. One man carried a crossbow. Each had a sharp knife in a sheath on his trouser leg. Each took a turn at carrying the wireless. The house and the hill they distinguished in silhouette were, in the gloom of night, different from their training mock up. But because they knew where to look, each pair was able to spot the position of its target sentry. Now began the night vigil. As with watches, he had kept at sea or on land, an hour of sleep and an hour of wakefulness and concentration made the night seem to pass quickly for Roddy whose show this was. Everything that happened now was his responsibility. A gentle tap-tap of his buddy's foot on his ankle woke him when dawn would, in minutes, gently infuse some light into a day to come. He waited until he was sure his men, now all alert, could see his hand signals. He checked his watch and looked towards his nearest trooper's position and raised a hand. A hand was raised in affirmative response. The signal passed to all positions. A hand from the nearest position was raised again. All were ready. Roddy raised a hand with one finger pointing—acknowledgement from near position—his hand raised again . . . pause . . . three seconds on his watch . . . dropped sharply down. Five arrows flew. The armed head of the arrow, piercing the sentry covering the door, did not explode to disperse the silencing, killing drug. A loud yell filled the silence.

'Let's go!' Roddy called out. He and his buddy, Andrew Denton, rose like sprinters from their blocks. Andrew kicked the door open and it fell into the room. Roddy clattered across it launching himself at the shape of Omar rising from the floor, threw him back to the ground, and lay on top of him. The room filled with the hammering explosions of rapid fire spraying around the room and the standing men of the kidnap group slumped almost simultaneously to the floor unable, since the bursting open of the door, to fire one defensive shot. The crossbowman spotted a man appearing on the roof, released his arrow which pierced his chest.

'Come, Omar, you are safe. We must be quick.'

The archers, checking that their targets were indeed dead, turned the shafts of their arrows two turns to the left and withdrew them. The evidence from what may be left in the remains of the exploded charges would be a forensic puzzle.

They seized the kidnappers' jeep and with Omar aboard, the driver with two troopers in support, drove off on a compass bearing to the canopy cache. Roddy radioed to Erik, 'Kwais. Kwais.'

'Gle math,' was the response.

He and the remainder of the force swept the area, then, in tactical formation, by the light of the now appearing sun, they set off to meet the advancing column.

The operation would not be over until they had been debriefed and dismissed. They joy of their success and survival must wait until then. They had risked their lives and used their skills to avert the eruption of a catastrophic epidemic of religious war.

The approaching column reached the cache and the Armoured Personnel Carrier crew picked up the gear. Erik's AFV pushed on. It met the marchers and wasted no time in bundling Omar aboard into the cramped space, wheeled around, and set off on a reciprocal course. It was not exactly luxury in the troop carrier and the combination of speed, terrain, and a suspension system whose design parameters had never included comfort was still a better place to be. They had done what they had come to do. They wanted to be leaving it behind. The flight from Iraq to Israel in the Caribou would be described in a romantic novel as 'bliss'—that is not to say it was—but it was helping to leave the past behind.

In Tel Aviv, it was getting towards evening. It was a good feeling to be landing there. The Caribou taxied to a halt away from the terminal, and before the propellers ceased to turn, two black cars swiftly approached from the edge of the tarmac. Half a dozen men quickly got out and formed a rough circle eyes in all directions. Erik and Omar walked down the tail ramp and, with two of the men from the circle, climbed into one of the cars which sped smoothly away. They and their escort went to a guarded room where Erik officially handed over his charge to British Security Service people and police. That was that. He asked to be taken to rejoin his men.

Roddy and the raiders walked down and climbed into a civilian bus which had just pulled up at the end of the ramp and set off for Rabin Army Barracks in Tel Aviv. They were happy and comfortable to be with soldiers. How unpleasing it would have been to be dumped at an airport into the extremes of difference between their military culture and the ways and habits of civilians. Desirable soon? Immediately, no. Erik knew they would prefer to get the debriefing over before they were shown to their billets. He was taken to where the men were spread around the ante-room of the Israeli unit's mess. Israeli officers male and female were talking with them. They were being circumspect in what they revealed, describing it as the release of a hostage.

Erik greeted the Israelis and said, 'Thank for your hospitality, but we must excuse ourselves for just as short a time as it needs. C'mon, men, let's finalize the business of The Heist. An Israeli officer allocated to the task walked with them and took them by lift to a room in an upper floor. Before anything else, I want to thank you all for what you have done from the day we first got together to the total success that you must be happy and proud to have achieved without one casualty.

'As commander on the ground, I can only say my version of what the Boss has just said. Your execution was stuff for a new manual. I've never, nor will I ever serve with a bunch of men of your calibre. Congratulations. You were magnificent. If there are any loose strands, thoughts you want to get off your chest, please feel free to express them.'

The Australian SAS sergeant spoke. 'When we first assembled, I was full of prejudice and the stories about piss weak Pommie officers and I've served under Australian officers that I'll reserve my opinions about. But it was a treat to serve with you two, the Boss as you call him could not have been better. His planning and organization and training were superb the . . . results speak for themselves. But the most important thing to me is I wanted to do what you wanted to have done and never felt that I did it because of your rank. It was a privilege. Invite me again.' It seemed there were no loose threads. Every comment was positive. They were surprised at 'how soon in the process we had come together in trust and confidence and . . . yes . . . admiration for each other'. Erik was damned near effusive in his praise of the execution of the extrication of Omar, from their total commitment to the training and the tremendous importance of their achievement. Each was given a chance to express his feelings and views of the operation. The spiritual comfort was good. They understood what they had done; 'Was about giving world populations a chance to live their lives in spiritual freedom,' as one trooper said. No point in going on when everyone had mentally halted. Erik ended the debriefing. 'Okay, let's find our billets then down to the mess. I'll put a quid on the bar.'

From an Australian, a split second after Erik's last word, 'Jesus, Boss, I'm just blown away by such generosity from a Scotsman.'

At this puny little gag, everyone burst out into loud laughter. Many an ace comedian's classic one-liner never got such a result.

A number of Jewish mess members joined the group, and possibly on Mossad's information, David Ben-Gurian, Minister of Defence, accompanied by Moshe Dayan, both of whom happened to be in the building, came to see them. The Jewish officers leapt to their feet at their approach, and with no more than a second's delay, The Heist party was on its feet. They knew what Erik's group had achieved.

'Perhaps even you, Major Barron, don't realise the immense importance and value of what you and your men have done,' he said, shaking Erik's hand then, turning to the whole group as they stood round. 'A great achievement, men, I congratulate you, and the free world should congratulate you. Thank you for that splendid military effort. Enjoy your evening with us.'

Moshe Dayan stepped forward to seize Erik's hand. 'Such a success could only come from brilliant planning and already it has been confirmed to me that this was so. I hope your superiors can understand what a great challenge that planning must have been and that you will be suitably recognized. You did not lose one soldier; you got your man unhurt and met every time target. Yes, brilliant. Major Barron . . . on behalf of Israel and everyone alive in the Middle East, thank you to you and your men.' Then he turned to the men. 'Thank you all, each of you.'

Andrew Denton, standing erect, and addressing both Ben-Gurion and Dayan, 'Permission to speak?'

They looked at each other, then both said, speaking at once, 'Granted', 'Go ahead.'

'I think every man in our group would want to say that part of Major Barron's genius was choosing his 2i/c, our on-the-ground commander Lieutenant Mckenzie.' There was a round of 'Hear. Hears.'

'Well done and well said, I have been a soldier all my life; and in occasions in any way similar to this after battle situation, I've never heard such a declaration. Congratulations to you, Lieutenant Mckenzie. You've just had the greatest reward a commander could ever get. Good-bye and good hunting all of you.'

'Before you go, sir, I'd I would like to thank you for what you have said. May, I just add this; we would have an infinitely lower chance of success if your intelligence had not been so accurate and timely. Particularly the field intelligence. We would not have had our accurate plan to base our rehearsals on and use in our assault, or get warning of the move which launched us in time.'

'The pilots who dropped us spot on target and the other pilots who lugged us around and the crews who brought us our personal kit—all of these—and I'm sure there are more— deserve a big share of gratitude. To them, I think I can say thanks from all of us. And our thanks you to you gentlemen for coming to visit us. We appreciate that very much. Good-bye.' There were more cheers from the standing group standing and waving farewell Ben-Gurion and Dayan departed.

'I hope the company comedian's listening. I think I should put up another quid upon the strength of those kind remarks.'

'Give it to me, Boss; I'll take it up for yuh.'

The spirit in the group was already high. Now, with nothing to do next day but get on a plane and fly home they could relax, enjoy the accolades and celebrate. There was no talk about how wonderful they may have thought they had been. Nor was there any detail of any part of the engagement of the kind you might hear after a game of golf or a sailing race. 'I was happy about the preparation. It was a good feeling to find us fitting together.'

'Yeah, when we got onto that hill, I knew I was ready.'

'It was bloody cold, though.'

'I've got to tell yuh, that first free fall was a bit exciting. I'm not saying the second wasn't either.'

'I liked it when I first heard the sound of motors 'way in the distance".'

'I'm not going to admit it when I get back, but I reckon some pommie commanders aren't that bad. Mind you, that was just a small sample.' Their celebrations and farewells had to be cut short. A BOAC flight was leaving for London that night. There was a bit of serious hand shaking and long looks at each other. All the 'Poms', the two English archers, Erik and Roddy, would be leaving. The four Australians would leave together next morning. Roddy could catch the train for Fearnas the following evening. There would just a little time with Erik in London. They would have to make the most of it.

As they talked before falling asleep, Erik talked of a lawyer he had engaged to confirm the legitimacy of the mining claims in Katanga. He was a specialist on colonial Africa, post-colonial legal issues, and how they could best be massaged. He wanted to see him, simply to pick up the prepared documents before he left on a short Outward Bound cross-channel cruise: it would take only a few minutes. Perhaps Roddy could come with him, and afterwards, they might have a last drink before he went down to *Fear Naught* and Roddy went to Euston station and got on the train at platform 13. She had been tied up in the Thames for all the time Erik had been engaged on matters of The Heist, and the patience of the water police was wearing thin. She was being looked after by the redoubtable gnome, Charley Farley who, when the war ended, had hung around his old Burma Chindit 'Guv'nor'. Erik's post-war vagrant gypsy life suited Charley who had a genetic aversion to regular work. He loved doing things like shinning up a mast to fix the navigation light; splicing ropes; driving cars (while Erik was away, he had picked up a few hours' daily work driving to garages around the boroughs delivering for a spare parts dealer); at night he slept aboard.

∘∘○—▷◁—○∘∘

Erik's first appointment was at the Garrick Club where he was to meet with a man called Cumming from MI6. Harry Crossman a mining engineer, who had gone with him to Africa, camped out, and worked untiringly to make a collection of samples to take back for expert analysis, organize a drilling team to find sites for sampling and do some preliminary planning about how the operation might be begun on the ground. As a reward for his efforts, and having funded his endeavours, he would become a quite substantial 'paid-up' shareholder in the venture and continue in employment as chief mining engineer. He would be meeting with Erik after lunch at a pub on Villiers Street near the lawyer's house on Condobolin Street, just round the corner.

Roddy was not immune to a sense of history that seized his mind on hearing the very name. It plucked and sounded all the strings of theatre, art, and music that somehow, it seemed to him, he was born to enjoy, through some untutored instinct and spiritual rhythm. Barron and Mckenzie announced themselves to a porter on the inside of the second set of tall doors which admit the favoured to this delicious sanctum on King Street, Covent Garden. They announced themselves as guests of Mr. Cumming. 'Yes, gentlemen, do sit if you wish, I'll tell Mr. Cumming you are here. I know he will want to greet you himself. Excuse me.' Through an archway on the left, there entered a short square man with the broadest of shoulders, black hair was cut quite short not troubled by too much combing and not disciplined by oil. His face, Roddy thought, had its genesis through a Pictish king. His black eyes sparkled as they lighted on Erik. 'Ceud mille failte!' he said earnestly in a deep soft voice. There was no doubt of the deep affection these men had for each other. His eyes turned to Roddy whose being, he felt at once, was under acute assessment. Those black eyes were registering, as if through his own eyes, into his soul finding more of it than he knew himself. 'Mr. Mckenzie, I'm proud and very happy to meet you this day. Quite separate from that feeling, I have much to thank you for. I shall never forget your role in this last successful exercise. Do come up you two. We'll have a dram or two and a plate of haggis and neeps.'

Tearlath Cumming led them to a dining room beyond a fit for merely regal diners. Roddy was quite enraptured by the quality and sheer rightness of the portrait art, the mood of the room and just a glance at the company of diners. When they sat, Tearlath asked, and looking at Roddy first, 'What are you fellows going to have to drink?'

'I'll have a beer, please?' answered Roddy.

'And you, Erik?'

'Yes, beer too, please?'

Tearlath said, 'Well, I'm in a celebratory mood, I'm for champagne.'

The soldiers looked at each other, and Roddy said, 'Well, it's really a bit too cold for beer. I'll join you in the champagne.'

The noble Erik, rushing to their aid, said, 'I feel it my bounden duty to help you in your endeavour to drink a bottle of champagne before lunch. All right, I'll have some too.'

They shared a bottle of Krug and found it not quite enough. Anticipating that such may be the case, Tearlath had had two put on ice. It was superb and set the mood that Tearlath had wanted for all three; a feeling of completion, a job well done, and the required result achieved. It had helped to free them from the lingering tensions, slackened the nervous strains, and coupled with the reunion of friends, had every calming effect.

As they slipped into silence, each in those moments with his own thoughts, it was Tearlath who spoke.

'You have no idea what a feeling of wholeness and comfort I have to be sitting here with you two men. I'm thinking that it was by the skin of our teeth that we got through this last caper. Despite your impeccable planning, Erik, your execution, Roddy, and continuing accurate intelligence, it needed only one silly minor part to come adrift and we'd have been scuppered. We did everything we could to overcome that likelihood, I'm overjoyed that we succeeded and that Omar is saved.'

'When the arrowhead didn't explode in the front sentry and he yelled out I thought with dread; "They will kill Omar this instant." Andrew and I were desperate when we rushed that door. Too late and all that we had set out to do would have been lost and the political worlds of Britain, Israel, Australia would have been thrown to the jackals of international politics, strategies, and religious darkness, to go on and on and on worrying the world. It's a great sensation now to feel that desperation dwindling. We could be anywhere in London, but because you are a distinguished playwright, we are here in this very special place with you. Erik is known to you as an old friend, I may be something of a psychological study for you and I think you have probably assessed me to the deep corners of my soul. You knew that this was the place to take me with the Boss to effect a cure and allow a bond to grow. You knew that because of your Pictish insight that is beyond mythology.'

Tearlath and Erik listened; they looked at each other and at Roddy. They let him gaze at them for seconds which somehow had been given extended life.

'We are sib we three, Roddy, kindred of hearts and souls. I am very happy to be in your company. I trusted Erik, Erik trusted you, and now I shall always trust you.'

The seriousness of the recent past continued to recede and now the conversation drifted to theatre and Erik asked after Tearlath's wife Isabelle. 'Right at this moment, she is most likely enjoying forty winks. She has a performance tonight in one of my plays, *The Ambassador's Wife*, at the Lyceum. David Niven, David Tomlinson, and a delightful young Australian called Diane Cilento are in the cast, and Wilfred Hyde Whyte has a bit of the second act to himself. He loves the role and wants to do it because somehow he fits it in with filming. When Isabelle is finished tonight, we may come back here for supper or go to the Ivy, it depends what the others are doing after the show.' Although it's been running a while, they frequently have supper together.

From nowhere, Tearlath began to chuckle. 'You know I think it quite remarkable about us three sitting in this wonderful old club, you two with your histories of Korea and Africa, serving and in action together in a regiment which is very much a local affair. Me, with three plays once running in this capital city at one time. And you, Roddy, with that business which you have built off your own back, your own brain, and more especially because of who you are. I've got this club and you two have yours. Now, all of us were involved together in this last episode of enormous international importance. Don't you think it's quite amazing what we little boys from St Ninian's Academy, in little highland Fearnas, have achieved in our lives? In Fearnas, no one knows of us, which I think is pleasing and desirable. And I know we are not alone. Think of Ninian, Erik. What a crop of useful people that little township and wee county have produced.'

'Aye, little highland Fearnas provided fertile soil for us, spread seeds of Alder,' said Roddy.

'When you're back in Fearnas again, you must come up and see us in Darnaway. You may have to lie on the floor. It gets a bit crowded when there's more than four.'

'No. That's when there's more than two,' said Erik.

———ooo-⧓-ooo———

The delights of sharing company had to come to a close. They stepped out of the sumptuous surroundings of the Garrick into a thick, wet London fog, and shook hands again. Tearlath would go to his apartment, and Roddy and Erik would go to the pub on Villiers Street to meet with Harry Crossman and Charley Farley. They had to move briskly: there was not a lot of time. The appointment had been hurriedly arranged and they must not miss it. Erik's previously scheduled appointment in the lawyer's city office had to be cancelled while Erik moved overseas to continue The Heist operation. Bartolemeusz did not seem perturbed by this need for another change and arranged that they should meet at four p.m. Erik said he would be bringing Harry Crossman and Charley Farley since they were going on elsewhere immediately after their visit. Indeed they were; Harry back north to Birmingham, Erik and Charley down the river to join the student crew who were to be arriving about six and clear away before they were impounded, Roddy up to Euston to catch his train. Bartolemeusz's home office was just round the corner in Condobolin Street off Villiers, and all they had to do there was pick up the document confirming the unencumbered ownership of the Katanga leases.

The White Hart was an Inde Coope's house on Villiers Street frequented by the broadest clientele of locals and visiting football, League, rugby and cricket fans, there was a fair admixture of local business folk who fell into two or more categories. Male and female, they gathered about round their tables and talked loudly as they quaffed their Allsop's lager or the red Inde Cope's Arctic Ale. The sooty fog of the street mixed with the dense fog of cigarette smoke in the old room of beautifully timbered bars and tables scarcely seen and appreciated in the crowd and the general gloom of the winter afternoon, despite the ornate, hanging lights. They found Harry, the bulky ex-League forward and the imp of wiry muscle, Charley Farley who, because he had so much energy and initiative, would rise to whatever challenge might be presented. He had been invaluable on Erik's Katanga explorations: he and Harry Crossman had become bosom pals.

Erik stood large and close to the seated men around the table. 'Good afternoon, all. And who's the leading liar to this point?'

'Crossman by three goals!' cried Charley.

'I might have guessed', said Erik, 'It had to be one or other of you. Sorry, lads, if I had a whistle, I'd blow "Half Time". I'm afraid these two won't be coming back for the second half, and my friend and I haven't got time for a drink from the leading liar. We've got an appointment at four o'clock. Okay, you two can ease your jock straps and fall in outside.' There was a scurry of farewells and they left the group to elect a new leading liar.

'Here, Guv', I brought this for you,' said Charley, handing Erik a long weatherproof jacket. 'Don't want you catching your death.'

'Well done, Charley, it is bloody cold.'

Condobolin Street was short, but when rebuilt in the early eighteenth century was wide enough to turn a landau round in. Since the latter part of the eighteenth century, it had provided quiet residence for businessmen and civil servants climbing to higher rank. The house which Bartolemeusz had acquired was not in any major way different from any of the other houses on the street; some were larger and another storey higher, but they all blended, in their irregular way, into a whole that matched them with houses in almost every street in Westminster and Kensington and other suburbs besides. The facade was of a three-story brick house, four if the level below the footpath were included which, with two windows below street level, provided light for what may at one time been the housekeeper's residence—perhaps just one room—the rest of the cellar or basement floor may have been larders and the kitchen. Above the pavement stood the house, the character remaining that its original owner must have wished it to have. It was dressed in two kinds of brick well laid and pointed. The high wide and handsome windows—now that the tax on glass was gone—would on spring, summer, and autumn days fill the rooms with light facing as they did to the south. Erik pulled out the ornate knob from the centre of a solid brass surround and musical tones told the visitors that their arrival had been recorded. The tall wide door was opened by a man of medium height in a well-cut charcoal-grey three-piece city suit. He was smoothly shaven and his greying wavy hair, once obviously jet black, was caringly barbered. 'Do come in,' he said. There were brief introductions of Roddy and Charley, whom Erik introduced as 'field assistant to the mining engineer', which chuffed him no end.

He led them to a door on the right-hand side of a large square reception area of which the only decorative feature was a large centrally hung crystal chandelier lit now to reveal tall walls in very light yellow ochre with thin black framing lines at a perfect distance from their edges defining their space. They were shown into the office where Bartolemeusz went behind an oblong ebony desk, stark black, echoed by black lines as in the hall; and shiny black verticals of half cylinder inset mouldings on the corners of the return walls framing a window behind the desk. The curtains of a fine material in alternating panels about a foot wide in black and the same washed-out yellow ochre as the walls were drawn to hide the drably darkening day without. There were black-and-white line drawings of figures positioned by an expert eye for space, balance, and impact, which the lights, in shiny narrow black wall frames, too difficult to distinguish in detail at the level to had been dimmed.

'Do please pull up some chairs.'

'Thank you; and thank you for fitting in this appointment at very short notice. We won't keep you long because none of us has much time before he must travel off in his own direction.'

Before he sat down, Bartolemeusz took three or four sheets of paper from a desk drawer to his right. He locked it and put the key in his waistcoat pocket. He placed the sheets neatly before him where he now sat. There was not another item on the table except for a lump of rough rock very much like an ore sample placed on precisely the point of medial section on the desk's dark surface.

When all were seated, Charley was out on the left, his back to a wall with Bartolemeusz behind his desk in profile view, Harry was next, in front of the desk with Erik on his right, Roddy was on the right at the corner of the desk looking across the group and Bartolemeusz.

Bartolemeusz addressed the group concentrating on Erik and Harry. Roddy could not see all of Erik's face, but looking across at Charley, he saw the sharp eyes of a peregrine falcon watching every move and trying to read Bartolemeusz from the side.

'The mining claims have all been registered and the tenancies established,' he stated directly. Then added slowly, as he looked in turn at Erik and Harry, voiced in tones of hinted foreboding, 'They have no value until they are physically in your possession.

'Now we can talk about what is going to happen next. When, and at the point when, the company is about to declare its annual net profit another line will be drawn. A payment of fifty per cent of the net profit will be payable to me by cash transfer to my bank. Until such time as a legal agreement to that effect has been signed, these claims and tenancies will remain in my possession. To save you time and inconvenience, I have had a holding document prepared which will serve until we meet again, before witnesses, to sign the formal document of that agreement.'

For a moment, there was stunned silence. Harry jumped to his feet and shouted, 'You bastard! That's extortion!'

He lunged forward, fist clenched, to land a punch on the lawyer's jaw. The lawyer's hand moved towards the papers. Charley's hand had nailed them a moment before the lawyer's. Erik's left arm was thrust up under Harry's to send his blow off the mark while seizing the rock with his right smashed it onto the side of the lawyer's head. Charley, now with papers firmly in his grasp, moved his body to support the unbalanced Harry. The lawyer fell to the floor rolling onto his back. Roddy rushed round the table to the lawyer. There was no blood, but the mark of the rock was imprinted into his skin. He put his hand under the jaw to feel the carotid pulse. He could feel nothing. He put his ear to the chest; there was no sound of a heartbeat and no movement of air from his lungs when he put his check close to his nose and mouth. 'He's dead,' declared Roddy.

The rock, still in his hand, Erik thrust it into the big pocket of the jacket. Charley passed him the sheets of paper which he folded and put into the left pocket.

They stood looking at each other. 'This is my problem', Erik said, 'I think we should disperse and each do what he had planned to do. Charley and I to *Fear Naught* from Embankment tube station and you two to your trains. Go as naturally as you can. For you this has never happened. I shall be in touch as soon as I can.' He paused and looked at his dear friends and said, 'I am very sorry.' Roddy looked at Erik, put his hand on his shoulder, and said, quite evenly, as he looked into his eyes, 'When you've had time to think, tell me what you would like me to do to help.' There was absolutely no action he could take to help now. That would require having a long talk with him first and this was not the time.

He felt deeply sorry for Erik. He had time enough, so he chose to walk to Charing Cross tube station. As he walked, his small bag hanging from his arm, a rush of cascading, flashing, scenes flooded his internal vision. The last free-fall jump into what possibility? He was back on a hill in Lebanon cold, waiting; he and the great Andrew Denton driving themselves, in desperation, towards that door; then Erik stealing Harry's shot; Erik's face and the tone of his voice when he said, 'I am very sorry.'

From the tube at Euston, he made straight for the bar at platform 13.

As he walked to the train, he passed the porter at the sleeping car section and wondered whether he should ask whether by chance there was a vacancy. Over two more paces, he had thought again. He would prefer to sit up. Perhaps more food and wine would help to turn this stupid tide of mixed thoughts and feelings and let it flow out, out across the bar to be caught in deeper ocean's flow.

On the side of the Thames, upstream of Southwark Bridge, there lay *Fear Naught*, kept by her springs as the tide ebbed. The cruise crew had not yet arrived. Charley and he could go aboard and get ready to cast off as soon as the young folk arrived. But first. Erik went to riverside of the yacht and from his jacket pocket took the rock and let it drop into the stream.

The train from London drew smoothly to a halt greeted by Charlie Morrison's confirming call that this was Fearnas. He had expected to have to cross the platform footbridge and walk up Cawdor Road to the Lodge. However, Jane was waiting on the platform with a car in the station square outside. Roddy surveyed the station square which he remembered being filled with tanks during the war, much to his and his pal's delight because they climbed all over and into them.

Today the clear cerulean sky above tall skeletal trees set off the stone walls of the surrounding houses with sloping grey slate roofs in a pale wash. The surface of the yard spread dusty dry form the hard frost. In moments, his ears were tingling and his nose needing a sniff. 'Won't I be lucky if it stays clear like this?' he asked Jane. 'We can take the old folks touring. Can we go up to Dingwall?' He was being recaptured by real, present, enthusiasm.

'Dad would love that,' she said cheerily in a natural American accent that made her attempts to recapture the Fearnas language sounds quite comical. 'Have you had breakfast? No? Well, look out for a "stiver". Mam kept us all waiting for you. We all had a cup of tea though.'

For the two days that he was there, the clouds for snow were gathering and the temperature was rising slightly. They had a glorious day for their trip through Inverness. The long, the narrow bending road followed the shores of the Beauly Firth. He and Jane remembered their night at the Highland Meeting Ball and were tempted to make a visit, but that would be unfair to their hosts. It was pleasing to drive out with Dad and Mam, they had many tales to tell about the country around them often prefaced by: "I mind when . . .". They dined right royally at the handsome stone-built Dingwall hotel. They couldn't claim that the cold had made them hungry. The car was sumptuously warm.

As Jane would be leaving the day after Roddy, it was therefore decided to 'make a day of it' and drive Roddy to Forres to catch his train to London and then to Amsterdam to see Jessie Innes again and hear her play. 'Aye, it's a long way out of your road,' Flora said, knowing damned well she was loading into her words an underlying question. 'Would you not be better going straight from London and not have the expense of a hotel in Amsterdam?'

'Ha, ha,' he thought, 'she wants to know if there's something going on between me and Jess.' He would play her at her own game. 'Well you know how much I enjoyed the Scottish Symphony; this would be great chance to hear them again on my way back [avoiding the use of "home"]. They'll be playing in the very famous Amsterdam Concert Hall, and Andrew Dobson will be conducting. Jessica Innes told me the program and I'd like to hear it. Besides I've never been in Holland before. To come all this way . . . and miss the orchestra just for the price of a night in a hotel?' Flora was bursting to ask more direct questions and she suffered agony in her restraint. Jane, as she drove, was smiling almost grinning at what was going on.

Soon, there were last kisses and hugs and he was looking from the open window of the carriage door at the tiny trio of his family being left behind on the platform at Forres as the steam loco hissed steam power, puffed smoke then smoothly sliding away gathered speed. He kept them in his sight, waving until the curving track hid them from view.

Amsterdam was covered in ten inches of snow. It covered the steeply pitched roofs and ledges of the buildings and defined the edges of the canals. Trees, usually given form by shadow, were now shaped by snow. Turning his head in awed delight, he saw everywhere scenes that had delighted artists since ever the Netherlanders had dyked out Amsterdam from the rising North Sea. Though not in his current view, he knew that before he his brief experience ended he would see windmills whose slow turning sails propelled the salty waters back onto the sea where it belonged. His flight would leave in darkness. Sometime, somehow in this brief day, he must see them. He impatiently waited in the warmth of the *Konzertgebouw* for Jess's rehearsal to finish. She came with a little band of musicians to find him. She ran out from the party to hug him and kiss him then gabbled some introductions to her friends one or two of whom he had met briefly in Hong Kong. The members of the group had their own agendas and after 'See you tonight' being said, the group dissolved. They were alone to extract what they could of the few hours before them. He asked her, 'Will you need to have a wee nap this afternoon before the concert?'

'How could I sleep on a day like this? Most of us went to our hotels to bed as soon as we finished and woke up to find this,' she said, indicating through the window to the trees at the edges of the snow mat on the square marred already by footsteps and tyre marks of many bicycles. 'Have you finished your coffee? C'mon then,' she said excitedly, seizing his hand, tugging at his arm like an impatient child, 'C'mon.' She dragged him, running, out onto the square. She stuck her mittens in the pocket of her coat and bent to skilfully gather up some snow and packed a round snowball which she accurately launched at Roddy who was joyfully watching and had to duck while the missile exploded on his shoulder. He quickly bent and made his own snowball. It wasn't long before their faces were bright red and they were steaming inside their warm clothes. 'I'll put some down your neck, Jess Innes!' It was threat, in memory of childhood, not to be executed now.

'Let's get out onto the canals. Maybe I can show you my Napoleon Hotel on Herengeracht.' It was typically Jess; no reservations. They were Fearnachan; children of the same world, seeds from the catkins of the Alder trees, on their journey down a river of life leading back to the distributary Fearnas so far away.

They took three different ferry trips one after the other. To their delight, one quietly passed by the Napoleon Hotel. Amsterdam was itself a big museum curated by the master hands of people and time. But they did go to the Van Gogh museum and marvelled at his masterful black-and-white drawings. They ate lunch in a tiny cosy restaurant in Oudkerk looking out on a backwater where a wooden house, being transported on a barge, was brushing each side and scattering cascading snow from the boughs it bent and shook en passant.

It seemed that very quickly it was dark and the light of the shops and cafes looked warm and welcoming, the streets sparkling under the lights. They kissed when they reached her hotel and she said, 'Thank you, Roddy, it's been a day of wonders and delights . . . and great good fun.'

'And I saw windmills!' his wish granted.

'Thank you . . . see you after the concert.' A mini kiss and she was gone; upstairs to prepare for the performance.

The performance was rewarding; Sibelius Symphony No. 1; Respighi, Ancient Airs and Dances; Elgar's Cello Concerto. Andrew and his flock were in great form and the, quite staid, audience loved them. When the free drinks and food were gobbled up and they charmed their post-concert visitors, a group detached itself, boarded a tram, and clattered off in the swirling snow to an upstairs restaurant not far from the Rijksmuseum. Here with amazing gusto, they ploughed into a truly magnificent Rijstafel. There were some hearty Glaswegians in the group, full of college-style banter. It was a lively night and it was late when Roddy walked back with Jess to the Napoleon. Their embrace and farewell was the stuff of love and romance, the parting for heaven knew how long, promises to keep writing, 'and tell me what you played and about your doctoral study. You must be tired. Perhaps you should go up?' A last embrace, a last kiss, and the curtain fell on the performance of a joyful day and night in Amsterdam.

━━━━━∘∘∘❈∘∘∘━━━━━

It was bitterly cold at the airport waiting for the, impossibly early, four a.m. departure of the KLM flight for Perth.

Simon was at the airport waiting for him. He was driving the Fusan pick up that Mckenzie had purchased second-hand from Treloar. He thanked Simon who had brought him from the airport. 'I've got the key, come,' Simon said. As they stood before the door, he gave Roddy the key.

'Home again, Simon', he said as he opened the door, 'it's a very good feeling. Would you like to come in and have a drink?'

'No thanks, Boss. You look a bit tired . . . and like you've got something on your mind. You look as if you need to be on your own.' He passed the small bag to Roddy.

'You're right, Simon . . . very thoughtful of you,' he responded, wondering what evidence there was that enabled Simon to be so accurate in his assessment. 'Thanks for the lift, Simon.' He was speaking more slowly now and possibly more softly. 'I appreciate it . . . see you tomorrow.'

To re-enter his clean sanctuary, to be accepted back, he must honour the ritual of cleansing. He quickly threw off his clothes and showered. Clean now and comfortably cool, he poured himself a good familiar Australian Barossa shiraz and sniffed its rich fruit and purity. He knew the wine could only get better, opening up in the glass. Now he could look around, and a feeling of security and comfort began softly to echo Jess's embrace. Holding the glass untasted, he stood on the balcony to inhale deeply the aromas of the world around him, to scan the sea, the sky, and the island. How pleasing it was going to be in his own bed in these surroundings. The chaos of departures and arrivals, dramatic foreign places, high energy training, and explosive injections of adrenalin for competition with death were past. Yes, home again, with all the body bits in place but a mind and spirit requiring to be bleached, washed, hung out and dried, ironed, folded, hung up ready to clothe again a fully functioning human.

His humanity, thoughtfulness, and care had to make fact of the dream; that vast complex vision of a part of the world he was bound to create. The enormity of it, rushed now, too soon yet, to his head. The power of it, despite his idea to slip into peace, forced him against his confused will, to focus on his dream . . . just for a moment then tranquillity . . . his dream of Ugojim . . . successful with a realistically long-term future; Mckenzie Earthmoving fitting a comfortable, flexible, profitable niche amongst giants; in peril of their own magnitude. He must never lose touch with his people, he thought, yet realizing that growth in the numbers of people employed would inevitably mean his presence, over a network that covered this expansive continent, would be less than intimate.

His brain needed to break out . . . and coast . . . especially . . . and even if only . . . tonight. The detritus of spent adrenalin was clogging his system. No, no real thinking now, perhaps he could just allow himself to draw up an outline of what he must think about tomorrow. His mind flipped to Amsterdam, to Jess and the sweetness of their farewell. Slowly . . . fatigue, shiraz, and the sea worked their complex miracles. He watched in some awe the barred cloud shapes become pink, then flaming red. Then the lighting engineer withdrew his services as if sullenly on strike—he even drew a dark skullcap over his head as he disappeared behind the line of Rottnest.

———○○○-◢◣◤◢◣-○○○———

His sleep had been heavy, but not refreshing. He woke with no energy and a leaden blankness of brain. 'Get a grip, Mckenzie! Move!' He jumped up, hastily pulled on his bathers and some old sandals, grabbed a towel, and ran down to the waves. He plunged in and swam fast and furiously.

He put on a khaki cotton drill workman's uniform and safety boots and went down to Fido. As the old double act bowled along the beach road, he knew that he was going to enter a world that had been functioning in his absence.

Madge was visibly delighted to have him back. Inhibition stopped her throwing her arms around him. In the time that she had been in the service of Mckenzie Earthmoving, she has fallen for this man's sincerity, the true ring of what he said and the evidence from what he did. Her husband Peter had taken home stories from the OBH adding confirmation, from the views of these competent, mature men that Roddy Mckenzie was good stuff.

The speed of Ugojim's growth was exponential and Mckenzie Earthmoving marched, in quick time, *pari passu*. Newcastle, city and port, where plant could be received by ship from Japan, with proximity to the Hunter Valley and coal mining, was the selected base for Ugojim in New South Wales. Billy was happy to be there except that he was starved of Australian Rules football, the games, the barrackers, the sharing of opinion and team loyalties, the two-phase conversation in the week's discussion from the post mortems of the last week's game and the forecast and wagers on the next. Would he ever espouse the chaotic scrambling of Rugby League? Mauri made frequent visits and ensured that he made a good range of helpful contacts in both business and social fields. Roddy visited too, now that the base organization was functioning well. They visited potential clients together and once their showroom and yard was opened invited people from far and near to 'demonstration days'—and it was no harm at all to practical men that Billy, the local business chief, was the demonstrator.

To reach distant mining operations in New South Wales and Queensland, they used the air operation of a flyer named Andrew Denton who was growing his own rural airline and who would eventually serve all their ongoing flying needs in these vast territories where it would have soaked up very valuable time to reach clients any other way. It was the commonplace modus operandi for Australia.

In Queensland, there was a neat combination of the Fusan franchise and the operation of Ugojim in that state. A block of inner-city land near the Fusan headquarters, showrooms, and service operation was acquired at a very good price and the Ugojim operation established there. Mauri, Billy, and the Fusan chief in Queensland were the selection panel for Ugojim staff. It was the first time that Roddy was not the principal determiner in staff appointment. Billy also played a role in the sales operation working with the Queensland manager in all the big-value deals. This did not displease the Queensland manager who valued Billy's support and undeniable expertise not only in aspects of machine operation but in dealing with clients—and it affected his income positively.

------◦◦◦─❀─◦◦◦------

It is said that 'all work and no play makes jack a dull boy'. Although work was play to Roddy, there was still the human need for contrasting activity in a different environment to keep focus in one's major labours at the required pitch of acuity. Graham Knight had always kept in mind that Roddy was a sailor and phoned him one day to say a bloke at Royal Perth Yacht Club had perforce to sell his Swanson Carmen class yacht because his organization wanted him back in Sydney. Graham knew the market and confirmed his opinion by checking with others in the know and suggested to Roddy what he might offer should he want to buy and that he felt sure he could organize a pen for him at Perth Flying Squadron Yacht Club on the river at Dalkeith where he had long been a member and where Peter Gill was also a member. Roddy arranged to have a good look at the vessel. He was mightily impressed by the skilled craftsmanship of the timber fit-out, the layout of berths and galley, the Bukh diesel auxiliary, the standing and running rigging, the deck fittings, winches and their locations, and the sail wardrobe. There were two or three others sailing with river clubs and he gathered what he could about the craft's performance. What he found was all good. This began an enjoyable relationship with the Flying Squadron and among its sociable membership made a number new friends. He participated in competitive Saturday afternoon sailing—after his Judo Club sessions in the grounds of UWA just a little way upstream—and Thursday evening Twilight races when Lynne and Ann enjoyed sailing with him. In all, these associations created a rich social bundle which was just what he needed. The Naval and Military Club, the OBH, the Highway kept other business social streams flowing and Perth provided classical music and first-class drama and dance. He was fitting into the fibre of Perth, and Perth was absorbing him. His work took him to every possible kind of location in Western Australia in all its climate ranges in all its seasons and indeed over all of Australia. He was enjoying a life of effort and great reward. He stood on his balcony sipping orange juice after a swim, or nursing a cup of tea in winter and marvelled at his good fortune; never for a moment taking it for granted, or failing to fuel it with contributions to its maintenance. 'What a life!'

On the antipodean equivalent, Jessica Innes was enjoying her work with Scottish Symphony. It was a good orchestra consistently winning laudatory reviews. She had a house in Kelvingrove which she shared with another musician and an organic chemist in a research team at Glasgow University. She found Glasgow life good, it was an excellent base for activities in hiking, hill walking, and it was a hub from which she could easily move to anywhere in Britain or Europe to see or hear whatever was being performed, exhibited or to be enjoyed: she had easily made a circle of friends with whom she could share her interests. She very rarely—hardly ever—went to Fearnas. There was nothing for her there but strained obligation.

Roddy made sure he saw his ageing parents at least once a year. Jane matched her visits so that they could enjoy being together at the Lodge and doing day tours of Scotland—and on occasion even to England. Whenever he made those visits, he made sure to catch up on a concert of the Scottish Symphony when he and Jessica would go out somewhere for 'a lark', eat, see a play, go sightseeing, visit an exhibition. Whatever they did, it was always about laughter, leg-pulling, jest, or quiet satisfaction in sharing. They had last met in Aberdeen.

After the performance, a merry group of players launched out on Aberdeen with Roddy now welcomed as a regular participant in such jolly outings. Jess knew all the haunts: the University of Aberdeen was her alma mater. As they walked back to her hotel, flatness in her mood was evident.

'Something not right, Jess?'

'I'm here in Aberdeen. I can't really come this close to Fearnas and not go and see my parents, but I don't want to. Isn't terrible, I'm dreading the thought? I feel so bad about thinking this way; I feel I shouldn't even be telling you. Anyway, it's a filial obligation. I must go.'

'I don't envy you. But I do know of other people who have the same problem. I don't think love, respect, or caring can be constructed. It's there or it isn't. On that basis, and I know it must be easier said than done, but I believe we don't really need to feel guilty about having no affection for our parents. If we can understand and be honest with ourselves and accept this reality, no one will be being cheated.'

'Morally I can't argue with what you are saying. Somehow I can't clear away the fairy book idea that children love parents and parents love their children. I've always had to create that illusion for myself. From early childhood dependence, I perhaps thought that that's what children had to do in a world that sometimes could be quite horrible. Every child had to create her own happiness and invent a world in which she could be happy. I had to create my own happiness. Maybe this will be my last occasion. I may be about to change other parts of my world and leave the orchestra if I'm going fulfil my personal and professional needs.'

'You've often mentioned moving into small group playing, is that what you're thinking about now?'

'Please don't tell anyone in the orchestra, but I've been travelling around listening to groups and I've found the one I'd like to be with. My next move is to arrange an audition.'

They had reached her hotel.

'This is a very difficult time for you, Jess. Any one of these issues would be enough to have to handle at once.'

'I have to settle everything, but the chamber orchestra is the most important. I'm not much fun tonight. Sorry to have ended your evening on my low mood.'

She did not reach out to him. There was no attempted embrace. He gently took her into his arms and held her. There was no response. Moving her arms around him seemed merely like somewhere to put them. He turned her face up and looked into it, but Jess had already gone: she was here, but not here. She was backing away out of arm's reach, then came quickly back to clutch him tightly in her arms, sought his lips, and kissed him hard. 'Oh, Roddy', she gasped, said, 'Good night. Have a safe journey back.' She turned away again and ran up the steps through the door of the hotel which swung shut behind her.

He stood on the footpath and gazed at the shut door. 'My god . . . there's turmoil going on there.'

He walked to pick up the hire car from its park and set off on the ninety-mile drive to Fearnas. He began to think about what he'd experienced. 'There were three things within her mood which she could not now confront; her low feelings about her parents, her hanging on to her orchestra position while her mind had already been made up to move . . . and saying that we would never more have our relationship. Neither did she mention the name of the chamber group nor the reason why she had chosen it. Why should a change of orchestra change our relationship? Ah, well. I can't have everything. Maybe she thought I was keeping her on a string? Stupid of me to think the relationship we had could go on to that point where we, together, would decide otherwise. But wasn't that how we had created it to be?'

Of the quartets, quintets, and trios, she had travelled around Europe to hear she chanced upon L'Orchestre de Chambre Europa. She saw the oboist around whose brilliant playing he had built the orchestra, and like a teenager for a matinee idol, she almost collapsed on seeing this male vision, this Adonis, and she wanted him. A life with him in a world of music would be a paradise beyond the gods to create. Her obsession became her pursuit, he was her goal.

It was one evening in Berlin that she went to a concert of the Europa Chamber Orchestra. The concert was in one of the smaller but esteemed halls. It was a beautiful building, of which some part of the walls remained from the blasts and burnings of war, faithfully reconstructed.

Each of the pieces on the program included an oboe part, and of the six items, three were oboe solos. She did not have any particular aversion to oboes, but as wood wind instruments had not been on the top of her list. They, and the music written for them, had now become a subject of serious study. The venue and the program suggested a program designed for a special segment of the total audience for classical music. The name Europa had connotations of dedication to the music of a grand Europe, and of old pieces which may have been lost in neglect and that merited being played before such special audiences.

It was time for the players to come on. And so they did the bass, the cellos, the violas, two clarinets, and a bass clarinet, a bassoon, and then the violins. Then he entered the leader, the oboe soloist, the star with the grace, elegance, and pomp of Nureyev. Jessica, enthralled, was in wide-eyed silence. The audience was emphatic in its welcome. He stood there erect, so perfectly made, so appropriately beautiful until the applause tapered slightly. Then he bowed from the waist. Her heart was bursting with the effect of seeing this magnificent creature. There, in this majestic hall, he stood so perfectly made, so appropriately beautiful, in this architectural perfection, amongst these select people who had come to fall at his feet. She was aquiver, panting, skin moist. She had never, no never, seen a man like this who so radiated power and control of self and

others. He was tall. You knew that those movements, that gave
clothing a new meaning, dressed a body of supple muscularity.
You could make no other judgement than that his clothes were
made, by a well-paid tailor, to his design. A panther or a python
would look rigid by comparison. His very blond hair was cut in
a Hitler Jugend style, long on top and short up the neck, back
and sides of the head. His eyes were very cold blue and were set
in such a way that seemed to say: 'The world will be as I see it.'

He addressed the audience and described the first piece
with a voice that was blessed with a tone slightly above baritone.
His enunciation was clear, the accent of his French, acquired
from birth, would have made Charles de Gaulle smile in
ethnic satisfaction. His Hoch Deutsch version was not merely a
translation but how a German would phrase ideas. In English
he used an accent more desirable than the Queen's, washed
tastefully, by intention and astute delicacy, in Gallic tones. It
was joy to the multi-lingual's of the audience to detect in each
version his skill in reflecting the cultural mind habit of a native
speaker in each language. He was a master showman: nothing
was unstudied. She was shaking with the thrill of hearing this
mastery. He was the human exhibitionist par excellence and she
gulped her admiration into her beating heart.

The structure of the concert included the Bach Concerto
in C minor for violin and oboe, Mozart's Oboe Concerto in C.
The first piece in the program was one opened by the oboe
which strikes and sustains a perfect note for five bars before
strings sweep in to carry the structure. This was a piece from
a concerto, which tonight they were not going to play in its
entirety. She paid scant attention to the violins. The oboe may
have been perfect. He was perfect.

The performance ended and the selected members of the
audience moved into a large foyer where tables were laden
with canapés and petits fours, every imaginable confection
of delicious finger food. Champagne and wines were being
brought around.

It was a glittering evening of tiaras and svelte female forms
in long—or very short—dresses; men in white ties and tails
and decorations which now told tales best forgotten; cigarette

holders impossibly long, of finest ebony and gold; and waiters and waitresses, almost equally well dressed, gave the appearance of delight to be given the chance to make it all happen again, do it all again, as if suddenly, a rich, elegant, fabulous, dreamed of world were being remade now; and they were fully part of it. It was a return visit for the Kammer Orkester Europa, L' Orchestre de Chambre Europa, the Europa Chamber Orchestra. For the faithful, it was without question that they would come to worship in the temple. For those who had travelled from outside Berlin or outside Germany even, it was an opportunity to be in the presence and the company of the Creator, Conductor, the Leader, the internationally renowned, almost the indisputably best living exponent of that demanding instrument, the oboist of incredible brilliance: Michel de Mont Savour de Lattre de Sassigny. And in this whole crowd of age and youth and sparkling elegance, he was, *sans doute*, the most brilliant.

Where he looked, he saw. His was not an unguided glance. If his eyes were directed, the object of his view was under scrutiny, however momentary that glance may have been. He moved amongst the crowd with ease and a seeming insouciance. Of course he cared. There is no point in being beautiful; there is no point in having the discipline that leads to excellence, if people do not recognise the beauty and do not appreciate the soul and technical genius that brings music to them of a level high, high above the commonplace. It is hardly possible to believe that these people could realize the special quality of the way he was bringing music to them. He did not mind being there. Adulation was part of the reward for being a special human. It was acceptable and justly rewarding. Energy flowed from him in every direction. Everyone wanted to be in the radiation zone.

He was the living totem of their tribe, the embodiment of their cherished tribal traits. He was of the blood, the present scion of ancient nobility going back to Charlemagne. Warrior power had undergone a metamorphosis to musical prowess, but it was still power. He carried his status, in perfect physique and skin, all part of the sacred detail of their tribal myth; he was the extant Junker. It was right that he should be disdainful, proud, and powerful. He was important to them as trope for their own aspirations to nobility and power, their defiant devotion to a broken dream of empire, now the dross of a glorious Prussian past.

Those svelte young women and equally svelte young men, all of whom had the appearance of being hired to model the evening clothes, be decoratively delightful, and say only the words from the script, were playing their parts admirably, engaging in stereotyped chatter. To counterbalance the svelte, there were more substantially constructed women with portly partners who, though they may have had landed properties throughout Europe, reaped their more bountiful harvests from corporate dividends. They were all Michel's people, cultivated by him to enjoy a symbiosis ever nourishing. When he did relax from performance, Michel would go to any of a number of magnificent houses anywhere in the world to be feted and petted and further introduced. These, even if and when some of them realized it, were Michel's continuing, energetic, committed public relations machine. All he had to do was continue to be his arrogant, above-everybody self, and play the oboe like nobody else.

Amongst this crowd, the musicians, the more blasé, more 'professional musician' members whose lives revolved around the orchestra, performance and travelling, had remained to share this part of music sociability. If they were there at all, Michel was not, nor did he wish to be, aware of them.

Michel's was like a self-functioning galaxy within the universe of concert classical music. There were only a few random spots at any part on the gravitational fringe where any musician from the orchestra might be recognized as having any small, almost insignificant part in contribution to the greater grandeur of their galaxy's brightest star.

God was here but not to be reached or touched, so Jessica took control of her obsession and turned her mind to a more practical closely linked aspect of desire—her career. Having invested in a ticket for the after-concert celebration, she joined the throng in the reception room. She recognized a violinist, a viola player, and two of the male cellists. She approached them and, excusing her interruption, said, 'That was a stunning performance tonight! I can see why you folk have such a high reputation. I play violin in the Scottish Symphony and, while we're having a short break, came over to hear you.' Jess spoke in English because it was what this little group had chosen to speak at this time.

'Hello!' said an attractive young woman with a London English accent. 'My name's Jeudi, this is Jennifer, Wili, and Vlad.'

'Pleased to meet you,' she said as she shook hands all round.

'You don't have a drink,' said Vlad. 'What would you like? It's not flat but I don't think it's champagne. I think it's Prosecco. I heard some people in the group behind murmuring.'

'Oh, that's fine. I like Prosecco.'

'Good, there's a waiter.' He approached the waiter, confirmed it was Prosecco, and took a glass. 'Voila, mademoiselle. Santé!'

She raised her glass to Vlad, the other, and said, 'Salute!' It was nicely cold and moussing beautifully. The conversation was easy, spontaneous, and animated, the subject was music! Jess was effusive in her praise of Michel. Each of the group glanced at the others with a look that was asking, 'Shall we tell her?'

Wili took over, avoided a difficulty, and said constructively, 'Yes, he's a brilliant player. Possibly the best. He pays his musicians more than most in the world.'

Jess described her request, her liking for this orchestra, and went on to say, 'I'd love to play with people like you. I'm so madly keen', and said with a chuckle, 'I have my CV in my pocket all the time so that, should opportunity knock well . . .'

Vlad jumped in immediately. 'Well, let's see if we can make opportunity knock. I'll go and see if Sasha can join us.' Snatching another drink from a passing waitress, he surged off through the crowd seeming to know where to go. While he was on his errand of fortune, Jeudi explained how Vlad would know exactly where to locate Sasha. He would be close to Michel. He had to be. Was he not Michel's 'right-hand man'? The major strategy for the orchestra was Michel's, but it was the young Sasha who put all the pieces together. Sasha knew that Michel paid well, but he chose to recruit a practising genius or one who

would morph into a genius in the next week. Vlad found Sasha
and told him in Russian about this violinist who was already
leader of an orchestra and was a graduate of the Edinburgh
Conservatorium. Sasha knew of Michel's present quest was for
the ace violinist soloist who would make it possible for him to
add more violin /oboe pieces to the existing repertoire.

Shortly, Vlad burst into the group. He had an arm over the
shoulder of a good-looking young man. 'Sasha, this is Jessica
and she would like to join this orchestra. And you won't believe
it; she has her CV with her now!'

Sasha wasted not a second in pleasantries. 'I'm not going
to ask silly questions about why you want to play with Michel's
orchestra. You are here. You have your CV. You came with a
purpose. How long do you intend to be in Berlin?'

'Only until tomorrow evening, I have my Eisenbahn ticket
for Hamburg already.'

'So, *wir mussen schnell machen*! While you talk to these
charming social butterflies, do you mind if I read your CV here
and now?'

'Are you sure you'd like to read it here, now?' She was not
sure that that would be a good idea, but with some misgiving,
took it from her bag and gave it to him. While Sasha turned his
intelligent bespectacled head to reading, Vlad said to Jess, 'Don't
be concerned. This will not be a cursory glance, I assure you.
He knows what he is looking for and he is meticulous and very
quick in making analyses.' The group chattered on frequently
hailing waiters to taste and see whether the wines were of the
same quality as the Prosecco as they discussed career paths that
had coincidentally been crossed, concerts they had put on their
'Wow' lists, incidents, performances and places, hotels good,
bad, and dreadful. Each member of the group had been struck
by her relaxed natural charm, wit, and sense of humour.

It seemed no time at all before Sasha was asking Jess, 'What
are you doing tomorrow morning? Would you be available for,
at most, an hour after eleven o'clock?'

'Yes. I was just going sightseeing and doing history things.'

'Good. Don't move, I'll be back in minutes. Be patient. There's
lots of wine and food. There's a rehearsal tomorrow morning

and an evening performance, but such is of no concern to your companions, they react better to the world after a Jeroboam of champagne'—and he threw the last word over his shoulder as he hurried away—'each!'

Sasha returned with another question. 'Do you have your audition music with you?' And then he said, 'Sasha you idiot. Of course she has! You may have your CV back now. If you need somewhere to prepare, I can arrange that. The audition will actually be on the same stage as tonight's performance. Eleven o'clock'—and with emphasis—'precisely.' Each word was delivered in executive tones.

'Sasha, this is incredible! Thank you so much.' Then she turned to Vlad and threw her arms around him and gave him a big hug. 'Vlad, you are truly the messenger of the gods. It was you who set the fates in motion and set the stars in alignment. Thank you, thank you, thank you!'

'Well now, wasn't *this* a time for celebration?' However, compelling realities such as sleep, morning rehearsal, and evening performance confined their celebration of Jessica's good fortune to hugs and kisses and wishes for success in tomorrow's rehearsal, looking forward to having her with them in the future and hopes that between now and when she joined them in the orchestra they might meet up with her again.

The figure of such power, with the strength and command of the present that had been so sensational, that had made her tremble at the concert, the previous night, was the figure that Jessica saw on the morning of her audition. Thought of her audition piece was furthest from her mind from the moment she saw him. She had chosen a piece from his repertoire, for which she had bought the score and had listened to it on a Deutsche Grammophon recording. It had been selected with care so as many as possible of the violinist's skills would be demanded. The piece had also been chosen to demonstrate lyrical expression, interpretation of feeling, and the tone control required to express the emotion written into the piece. She purposely had not included an oboe piece. Surely he wouldn't play with auditioning hopefuls. 'Just play the music, Jess. Just play the music,' she was saying to herself.

She ignored all the famous violinists' interpretations of the audition piece she had chosen. She had performed it with her heart; with skill, and touch, tone control, and phrasing that was true to just how *she* played. There were eight bars of crisp pizzicato, which in the whole piece would have echoed a woodwind part before an ascending melody created the approach to a dramatic crescendo. She raised her arm and bow on the final note. She looked up to see how he had reacted. She could only attempt to read his face. All she could conclude was that it did not show displeasure.

'That was well done,' he said, looking at her for only a second and quite without emotion. 'I want to hear now your violin in a small group.' What was to happen next was obviously part of his plan for today's audition. Of this, or certain auditions, or was it in all auditions? Jeudi and Jennifer had apparently not expected it. They had been asked to stay on after that morning's practice. 'I have arranged for Jeudi and Jennifer to form the other strings. We have a part of a full score here. I shall play the oboe part. We shall play the part that begins where the solo violin begins after the pause, at the top of the pages I have given you.'

He opened the long horizontal sheets made up of four book pages and gave each a sheet. Automatically they spread them on the stands, looked at the key signature, and found their parts—cello for Jeudi and viola for Jennifer. The mass of the other instruments of the orchestra filled the pages with black ink but had to be ignored. They each noticed the oboe part.

Now Jessica was about to be heard as a first violin soloist, 'in concert' with the kinds of settings that might arise in other works and accompanying an oboe. Jeudi had a very worldly view as to why this bloke was doing this. Jennifer felt that she was also being tested. Jessica, in a cloud, wasn't thinking; everything was going too quickly. She was going to play with him! 'Oh god! Watch the timing!' She looked at the music and had to shock her brain into professional reality: 'Just play the music, Jess, just the music.'

He could never play at less than his best. She had to struggle to stop listening to the oboe part and try to reach a quality in her playing which was equal to what this oboist was playing.

She had never played this piece before. She was a professional, for heaven's sake, whose heart and soul understood music. Read! Play! The oboe was leading the way to the emotion of the composer's intention. Jessica was a very good musician. She had glanced at the musician's instructions on the score, and in four bars, she had seized the magical requirement of time within time. A note has only one value, but the musician's genius is giving the time value of that note internal life. The 'song' was now being felt. She responded to what the oboe was asking with sureness of pitch and volume. And it was here that the demands were being met, of meaning within time. The music had seized her and so she made her violin match the oboe's song. She was giving the performance of her life. The last notes had to resonate: oboe, violin, viola, and cello, at a precise tone and volume.

'That was well done,' he said to Jessica, as if he were looking at a statue from a distance. 'There was strength and accuracy in your part. In a proper performance, it would have sounded well. Thank you, Jeudi; your cello was appropriately supportive. Jennifer, you combined very accurately. Jessica, if you wish, to join my chamber orchestra, this is a copy of the contract document which your solicitor can examine and you can sign.'

Michel was not going to tell her that she was the violinist he had been searching for. She had shown impeccable technical ability and interpretative sympathy. She would be perfect for the oboe violin pieces he always wanted to play in his repertoire. She would complement his playing perfectly. She was the total professional. There would be no need for a long period of talent development. She was ready now. While making his clinical assessment of her characteristics, he included that she was young and exceptionally beautiful. He knew she would sign the contract and told Sasha to ask her if she could contract for the remaining half of their year, to join immediately and finish the year with them.

At this point, he handed—over her music stand—a document in a stiff, figured parchment folder. 'It will require to be answered within one week. I will tell you now that the chamber orchestra takes a number of forms which are not orchestral. We have trios, quartets, and ensembles in which you will be required to play as written in the contract. No one ever misses a rehearsal.' And that was that. He said the last words and left the room, leaving Jessica and Jeudi sitting behind their stands. Jessica's brain exploded. This was a contract for her to sign. She was in! She was going to work for the maestro, the very beautiful Michel de Lattre de Sassigny. She turned to Jeudi and Jennifer and through her shaking excitement almost shrieked, 'Heavens! I'm just trying to grasp what's just happened. I've just been offered a contract to play with *him!*' From what she had heard the night before and hearing this now, Jeudi sensed Jessica's infatuation as she poured out the stunning effect that this man had upon her. Jeudi knew that it was useless to point out dangers but felt prompted to say in her best most pungent cockney: 'Just watch him, duckie. He is so far up hisself that's all he can feel.'

Though Jeudi and Jennifer had gone, Jessica was not exactly alone. The remaining orchestra members were staying overnight in Bern and did not seem to mind if it were spent in the Konzert Kammer foyer or the restaurant. They all had eventually drifted to the restaurant. She was with a very merry group of string and wind players round a table where the laughter level and the noise were high. It had been a hardworking hectic year for all and they were enjoying letting the tension, which they had not until then truly recognized, present itself for release. Swiss clocks had indicated the new day. The svelte and the rubicund still there in good numbers' had pulled on overcoats, and were departing. Michel left t last, He bade them a farewell, turned and approached the table where Jessica was. She had been staying in a hotel just two hundred metres from the Stadtcasino Musiksaal and had planned a late and leisurely breakfast a short and pleasant train trip to Zurich airport for her flight to London. Though he knew what to say, how to say it, and in which language, with more suavete than charm, he had no idea of party chatter. The merry group paid him scant attention. Jessica felt the particularity of his presence. The half year had passed with no personal contact save at rehearsal times.

He never participated in after-concert activities or afternoon outings which some groups of members organised for relaxation, diversion, education, or entertainment. One morning, when she was jogging by the Binnenalster in Hamburg, there he was jogging towards her. When they came up to each other, he said, 'Guten morgen', and passed by without altering pace.

Now he was here, standing beside her. Ignoring the others, and it was apparently mutual, he said nothing more than: 'I'm leaving now and going home. It's just round the corner. You can come with me. We'll walk.'

'It'll be great to be out in the cool air even in this garb.' She did have a long very light scarf of the finest naturally white wool; the rest was her performance gown long, black, and flowing closely around her slim body, shoes low but stylish and only really seen when she walked. Picking up her black purse and her scarf, she said her good nights and good-byes to the group and said, 'I'm going with Michel.'

It was cool, so she threw her scarf around her neck and shoulders. She was tall and had a good stride, so she walked quite comfortably alongside him.

He did not look at her, he just walked on, but he did say, 'The orchestra has had a good year, don't you think?'

'I think you could judge best. But yes, I had a feeling that it was going well. We've had good audiences.'

'Yes. I think we attract very perceptive listeners.'

The silence was awkward, and she was quaking. She had been chosen. What now?

In minutes, they had reached the front of a fine old house whose two-storey facade with a tall window left and right of a large white door; English style, it was perhaps a pace from the footpath. He unlocked the door, stepped through, and held it open while she walked in. He closed the door which clicked securely.

'We'll go in here,' he said, opening a door to the right of the hallway and walking into a sitting room where he put on wall lights set in straight glass frames. The room was redolent of Germany before the Third Reich, and amongst the original paintings, there was the mandatory Gustav Klimt and a Klee in his sombre period. Jessica took in little of what she saw except that every vertical line seemed exaggerated, and there was black and gold and statuary of male and female nudes.

When he returned from the room, he was naked. Her heart was hammering. He paced towards her, taking her in without accompanying expression. He stood before her and put his arms around her body to undo the zip on dress and let it fall to the floor. Then he removed her petite black lace panties.

He placed her seated on an armless chair and stood over and astride her thighs. Her eyes were level with his enormous penis which hung relaxed over testicles, their sac pulled up tightly behind it. He put his right hand behind her head and, holding the soft member in his left hand, briefly stroked its dragon head against her lips from side to side. Suddenly and firmly, he thrust her head forward and his penis was in her mouth. As he slowly moved it back and forth deep into and almost out of her mouth, she felt it grow and harden. He pulled her up from the chair. His left hand was firm and strong behind her shoulder blades and she was close to his chest. His right hand raised her left leg, and her bent knee was held under his arm as his hand spread over and grasped her buttock powerfully lifting her up off the ground. His right hand was guiding his penis to contact the lips of her vagina. Her arms clung to his neck, and her knees involuntarily clung to his sides as he walked with her to the bed. He put her shoulders down and slipped his hands to her hips, pulling her vagina up to his mouth and licked and sucked and thrust his tongue inwards and upwards. She felt the urgent approach of a climax. He put her down, spreading her out, and entered her vigorously, continuing to thrust across that spot which made her scream and groan with sensation. She felt the power of an orgasm which shook her entirely. Still he thrust and thrust until at last with an extra thrust which stopped deep inside her, she could feel the torrent of semen flood around her vagina. Without hesitation, he deftly turned her by her pelvic bones and, holding them, excruciatingly sodomised her. She screamed in agony, but he continued thrusting until he ejaculated again. He let her fall half on, and half off the bed. Nothing had been spoken, and no word was said as he strode away to the bathroom. Jessica slumped against the bed, kneeling on the floor, her body shaking and trembling, weeping in huge sobs. The convulsive sobbing was still shaking her body and her whirling brain sought sense in what had happened while a feeling of utter alienation and degradation seared her inmost soul when he reappeared. She managed to take in his smooth classically styled sports clothes and that elite, superior demeanour which aggravated all the hurt she was feeling, and then he spoke. 'You can have a shower and let yourself out,' he said, as he picked up a bundle of keys from a small table. His last line as he went through the door, with the merest glance behind, was, 'Keep up with practice till next season.' The door clicked shut and he was gone. So that was the male epitome, the masculine ideal; the status of the sexes explained.

In her hurt sobbing abjection, she picked up her clothes, unthinking, and put them on any old how. She picked up her purse and, through tear-blinded eyes, her lovely scarf, and staggered out through the front door leaving it open behind her. Such was the torment and confusion in her brain that she was barely thinking. Only some bundle of instincts directed her movements. Her hotel was only a few hundred metres away in the direction by which she had come. Although the hour was into the early morning lights in the narrow street left shadows broken by the light from the stores which beckoned the few silent, inattentive passers to call tomorrow and buy from their displays of expensive products. It was the longest journey. It seemed to take forever. Hotel. Pack. Bag. Airport. 'Quick! Let me be on that plane. Quick! Quick!' She wanted the cocoon of the plane where the low noise of the engines would murmur: 'escape'. There would be a form of silence, aloneness, and time to sort out what had happened. Perhaps she could try to make a way, to find a way to bring reality back to her world, to replace the destructive horror of what he had done.

She was in the hotel for a very short time. Her packing, thank God, was done. She asked for a taxi to Zurich—damn the expense—while paying her bill. (She had imagined, and had anticipated with pleasure, the train trip to Zurich through the mountains, by the rivers, the pastures, the farms and villages. It would have been the sweet beginning of her vacation.) She had wiped her face but had not bowed before the goddess of make-up. The hour or so to Zurich passed in numbness. She had expected to be tired after the last concert, so she had chosen to fly business class. Thank God, she wouldn't have to spend the hours waiting for her flight in that most miserable of places, the passenger lounge of an airport (even at Zurich).

At last she was in the plane. She kept seeing his face, so handsome, so strong, so really in every way beautiful. She had somehow been absorbed into his power. It was as if she had abandoned control and discretion. She could see, strongly in her vision, the absence of anything sexual in his eyes: no lust, no love, no affection, no interest, only an utter coldness and intent. She could not think of that then. Everything just seemed to be happening. The question, 'What's going on?' and any verbal expression could never describe the swift flow of fear, ideas, doubt that this was good, knowing it was not; what her dream had promised was just an incomprehensible blur of emotion in her mind. Then the rigour and swiftness and the physicality of the events; her body being taken over and moved by strong arms that knew their purpose, began to shriek into her senses: Wrong! Wrong! Wrong!

In the dull drone of the plane, she thought now, in a dreamy horror-fantasy of what Madeleine and Sophie from the orchestra had said about Michel. They were just carping, she had thought, because they hadn't had an affair with him. Now, what they had been saying fitted her experience. She had been a naive fool. At least she could have thought more clearly about what they were saying instead of wrapping this man up in an illusion of human perfection. Her fantasy had been about to become reality; but the reality was not to become desire fulfilled. It proved to be the antithesis; a bitter painful destruction of innocence.

He put the letters from his letterbox on the passenger seat and drove to work. Because business and personal mail was sometimes mixed, he opened the letters when he got to his desk. Seeing a letter in his mother's handwriting, he would normally have left it to be savoured when he got home. As he looked at the envelope and with the increasing rarity of mother's mail, he paused, then decided to open it.

My dear son, I'm not happy to be writing to tell you that I fear your father will not be long with us. There's been a big change in him and I think he's ready to go. If you could arrange it, can you come and see him before he goes? I've told Jane and she'll come, but I know he'd like to see you again before he goes. Your mother, Flora Mckenzie.

This was a letter in the mail! Cripes! Moments later, he was speaking to the bank's travel desk, where his name and bookings were familiar, and said to the girl who answered the phone, and who knew him and Madge well, 'Please book me on the absolutely soonest and quickest way I can get to Scotland by air. Please ring me back as soon as you can. My father is dying. Ring me in my office on Madge's number. I'll go home and pack.' He did and was standing by when Madge rang to say Simon was on his way at this moment and would get him to the airport in time to board the plane which would leave in one and a half hours. 'The bank is delivering the tickets to the airport by bank messenger and Air India has been alerted. I'm so sorry, Roddy. Don't worry about anything here: I've got Simon . . . and Freddie nearby. I've given Simon some money from petty cash to keep you going until you can get to a bank. Give our love to your mother.'

Flora heard the doorbell. At the door was young Willie Forsyth in his post office uniform, his red bike left at the gate. 'I have a telegram for you, Mrs. Mckenzie. Can you sign for it please?'

'I'll have to get my glasses, Willie.'

'Don't worry now, Mrs. Mckenzie. Just put something down. There'—and he took his cap off and put his receipt book on it holding it up for her to lean on to sign—'Ach, that's fine, Mrs. Mckenzie. I'll be off.'

'Wait, Willie! I must get something for you.'

'Next time, Mrs. Mckenzie.'

'Sandy? Roddy's coming over to see you. He'll be here the morn's morn.'

'Ach, that'll be great. It's a while since I've seen him. If I'm sleeping, make sure you wake me before he comes in.'

'Aye, I will do that, Sandy.'

And she did. Roddy had organised getting the De Havilland bi-plane from Croydon to Dalcross and McRae and Dick in Fearnas would be there waiting for him. Jane had flown to Dalcross from Paisley. She arrived at the bedside, pretending not be in haste, and she and Roddy were telling their father their latest stories—in halting bits of sentences and some delayed responses from the old man—and getting him to tell his, to keep his interest, and to amuse. 'Flora . . . what about a wee *deoch an doras* for us all,' he asked in a soft voice charged with what vigour he could muster. 'Aye . . . an, I'm at the door,' he sighed in observation of a seen truth.

'Roddy'll get it, Dad,' Flora replied.

Each with a glass in hand, Sandy, sitting at the slope in his bed, said, 'Slainte math. We're all together at our own fireside. It's gran' to see you all together. I hope you're looking after the folk's money, Jane, an' build you gran' roads, Rod, an' mind you, look after yoursel', Flora . . . I'll not be here to do it.'

'Slainte mhor, Dad,' they said. He drank all of his whisky without cough or splutter. 'Here, Rod, take you this glass'—with not much strength in his movement to proffer the empty glass—'I've been on sentry all night.' Indeed it had been a wakeful night. 'I must hang on until the bairns come,' was the force that delayed his departure. 'Time for a sleep. Ach, it's nice and warm.' He closed his eyes. For Sandy Mckenzie, it was stand down.

Flora was comforted to have her children with her when Sandy, to whom she had been married almost all her life, died. That Jane and Roddy were with her was all the comfort she needed, and in her heart, she thanked her God for that. She had prayed that they would come. And here they were: Sandy's prayer was answered too. Who would she have had if he had been killed in France? What would her future have been then? Who would carry her life and Sandy's on into the future? Now she had these lovely children who loved each other and who loved her, although, even in the lingual currency of her own mind, she never used the expression 'love'. It may have been thought that Sandy Mckenzie was not well-known in Fearnas. Certainly he never held any public office. He did assemble the services' contingent on Armistice Days and parade them to the cenotaph. Beyond that, he simply kept the noiseless tenor of his way and walked his tree sequestered homeward way from the club of the Forty-third Highland Regiment every Saturday night, until a few weeks before this day, to Flora in the Lodge at Woodend. The blood the shit the shells the screams of dying men were drowned in the silence of all but the sea and the wind in the firs, the bonny silver birches, and the Alder trees of Fearnas.

People were standing on either side of the road all the way from the stone gates of Woodend to the open grave in the cemetery on the other side of the River Fearnas. There were six pipers that played every foot of the way save for ceremonial service silences. And a catafalque party marched on either side of a Wordie's lorry draped in black, drawn by Jock Allan's Clydesdale horse 'Darkie' whose colour was black, with a white blaze on his forehead and washed white spats, dressed in blazing black harness and shining chains; his pace perfect; perfect too for old Jock, holding the long leather reins as he hobbled, his left leg shorter and stiffer, saved in a field hospital at Fromelles. The Reverend F. S. Gordon Fraser officiated. Ach, and after the grave was filled and the friends of Sandy Mckenzie dispersed, and the other wifies came to comfort Flora, one could hear here and there, and there again: 'Aye, an' d'ye mind when . . . ?' Roddy had ensured that enough whisky was available at the Forty-third Highland Club to see Sandy safely to his peace. And Gordon Fraser who had been a padre, chaplain to the second battalion in the war, had a dram too. The club president who had been a pall bearer at the service spoke on behalf of Roddy asking to be excused, and to say that it was a time to be with his mother.

—oooᗕ◈ᗏooo—

Two days remained of the time Jane and Roddy had scheduled for suitable flights. He wanted to buy something different, unusual to add *quelque chose d'autre* to their wintry diet. Rose Brothers shop was surely the place to find that something thus on his quest, thereinto, did he plunge. In Fearnas, as almost anywhere in the 1970s Britain, foreign exotica rarely, if ever found a place on a family's shopping list. For those of eccentric cravings and peculiar tastes, there was a treasure trove in Fearnas to wit, Rose Bros.

But first he had gone to see Jimmy Robertson the butcher on Leopold Street to ensure that the primary requirement for the meal he had in mind, some pork and some veal mince, would be obtainable. There was a cheery greeting from Jimmy who was sporting a head of white hair now. 'Have you got more to do?' he asked when Roddy had made his enquiry. 'It'll take me about ten minutes to cut it down from the cool room and mince it?'

'Ach, that's fine, I've got to go up to Jocky's and back to Branders.' Jocky Macpherson's shop, open-fronted from above the pavement, was hung around with a rustic display of rabbits, hare, ducks, geese, hens, and pheasants hanging on hooks from stainless-steel rails. Framed by the pendant game and poultry, on a sloping marble slab, highlighted by a decorative layer of fresh green fern fronds there lay, amongst a rubble of glittering ice, a bountiful display of salmon, trout, herring, mackerel, flounder, haddock, and cod. But what Roddy had come for were kippers, those very special kippers, smoked by the wifies of the fishertown; nine at least, to take for breakfast at 'The Dessert Island Picnic' the next morning. To the establishment of Willie Brander next, the bobby who had morphed into a green grocer and florist. Roddy was after garlic, basil, oregano, rosemary, and two or three bay leaves. Willie was very apologetic. All he could offer was the garlic, and right at the moment, he had no fresh bay. Fearnas wasn't warm enough to grow any of the others fresh, but Roddy would find all of them in dried form at Rose Brothers.

Quite undeterred, the dedicated hunter would return to Jimmy Robertson and the basis of his *sugo Bolognese*. So here he was, in the only place in little ancient Fearnas, where, if good fortune, and the Cameron brothers (who from 1935 were, ipso facto, 'Rose Brothers') could do it, he'd find the essentials for the preparation of his planned meal.

It was one of those wonderful old shops where everything that the structure ever was, still was, and had ever been. Under its old timber ceiling, the long beech wood timber counter was still there on the western side, smoothed by the packing and the sliding passage of many people's 'messages', when pennies purchased pounds, and a stone wasn't just something found on a seashore. Here, before one's eyes, a pound of sugar would be scooped from a fine jute sack to a brown paper bag placed in a copper bowl on a set of balance scales. The sugar from the scoop would flow, measured with uncanny accuracy, into the mouth of the waiting bag. From the scale pan, the bag was placed on the old beech wood counter; two firmly pressed crisp folds would close the mouth of the bag up tightly. From a neat coil of string on a rail, just enough white twine would be drawn to form a loop vertically around the standing bag, a perfect knot tied and then the twine' looped round the shop assistant's finger, with one strong, sharp tug the strand of twine was severed. There like a guardsman on parade stood one pound of castor sugar, firmly sealed. As well as the colourfully laden shelves, the floor was an additional and important display space for open sacks of oatmeal and pearl barley, lentils, peas, beans of many varieties shapes and colours. 'Arborio' rice, back again in supply from Italy with the destruction of the war now becoming distant. There was rice from East Pakistan, no longer part the empire 'on which', it was said, 'the sun never sets', continuing a stream of supply which dated back to the years when the graduates from St Ninian's Academy were first staffing the offices of the Chittagong 'godowns' and the banks which counted the profits. There were open crates of tinned fruits from Australia and South Africa, known well to a spectrum of the clientele. Roddy was enjoying the entire feeling of the shop, the people, the histories, the timbers, and the texture the shapes formed by the spaces, the furniture, and the merchandise. There was colour everywhere and sharp little shapes of light on reflecting surfaces and corners of deep darkness. There were heraldic knightly colours and black-lined shapes of McVitie and Price's biscuit tins; and green and gold tins of Tate and Lyle's Golden Syrup which depicted bees making their hive in the lion's mouth and giving forth sweetness.

Here, in this 'Fortnum and Mason' of northern provincial Scotland could be found the treasures of Lombardy, Jamaica,

Cyprus, Heraklion, and Chittagong. There were chests of teas from Darjeeling and Sylhet, perhaps the produce of estates where men, now retired *barra sahib* planters born in Fearnas, or round about, lived out their retirement in its kind climate. The cooks and housekeepers from the castles and big houses all around came to purchase on account of their employers. Quite a number of employers chose to join in this social status melting pot. It was not rare to see at least one colonel in the throng, and the admiral occasionally, a high court judge, a cabinet minister, or a run-of-the-mill politician and the normal wifies of the town and the countryside doing their family shopping; or in to get something special, like a tin of Portuguese anchovies perhaps. As he wriggled his way along the shelves, he saw before him in the crowd a woman's head with the most beautiful rich black curly hair. There was only one person in the world with beautiful black hair like that. That figure was unmistakably Jessica Innes: perhaps not so upright, perhaps without that energy that used always to surround her. But yes. She was wearing modish, continental winter clothing. That was surely Jessica. He couldn't restrain himself and tried to move forward more quickly through the shoppers. At last he could reach out and touch her. He laid his hand very lightly on her shoulder. 'Jessica?' he said, in a tone somewhere between a statement of fact and the very slightest tinge of doubt. When she turned, he burst out: 'Well, I'll be blowed! Jessica! I can't believe it!! How are you?!'

This was Jessica. But this was not the Jessica he knew and had always remembered. There was something wrong. That particular vivacity that was her hallmark was just not there. How do you hide what you feel? Her smile was sincere, she was pleased to see him, there was recognition, but he did sense a subtext which said that maybe right now she didn't want him there. He kept speaking, giving her space to collect herself.

'How grand to see you! What a coincidence! I'd never have dreamt you'd be here! Mind you, it's been a wee while since I saw you in Aberdeen.' On those words, something like a flush of embarrassment or shame passed quickly across her face. 'How are you?' His eyes were scanning her face. The eyes that always sparkled were not shining. The smile that was always ready in them and, on her lips, flickered as if her inner power were running on low. They were the same height and she looked into his face. She registered the swift change as concern flashed into his open, naturally cheery face. 'I'm fine. Just a bit tired. We just finished a hectic tour.' He sensed that what she had said were probably facts but that there was something bigger and more serious attacking her spirit. 'Will you have time for a cup of tea after you've finished your shopping?' he asked. Here was a woman in need. 'I'll wait for you. Don't hurry.' He looked at her and, with his last words, touched her with a soft grip on her right shoulder almost like guiding a partner in a dance step, directing her where to go. 'That would be nice,' she said with a weak smile, possibly lying, and both quite out of character.

'My god, what's going on there?' he asked himself. Roddy's search took him to the exotica on the shelves of the eastern wall his fervour to meet his search challenge much diminished. His search was successful—tomato passato from Sicily, Italian olive oil, the dried herbs in jars. He was standing on the kerb gazing onto High Street yet not quite registering what he was seeing when a soft voice at his ear said, 'I hope I haven't kept you waiting?'

'Not at all. You didn't give me enough time to do my social survey of this Royal Burgh's citizenry. Let me take your bag. Perhaps I can continue my important research as we walk? I have a car up behind the Regal . . . brought it in for refuelling. Did you have a car somewhere?'

'No, I came down in Shaw's bus.'

'Good girl!' He said, 'It's important to give old Johnny Shaw the business. He's done a valuable service for a long time— beyond just driving. I don't know what the folk in that area would do without him and his bus service for news and the local gossip. Mind you, there are always the commercial travellers. I think the ladies like them better because they get all the gossip from them and they never seem to be in a hurry. When you think of it, there's really very little you can't get from the travellers. Mind you, you have to wait till it's their time to come round.'

'I remember Mr. Shaw from school days', Jess was saying now, 'when we used to come down in the bus from Barevan. I had to come down on the Saturday bus for music. If anyone wanted to go to the pictures, they had to go to the matinee and you could go to see the county play, a home football game, or see a bit of the cricket match on the links. I used to meet up with some of the girls from school and often we'd go to Morganti's for an ice cream. I've had many an ice cream in Italy, but I always imagine Morganti's in Fearnas to be the memorable world beater.'

What she was saying would have been backed with enthusiastic delight in the recollection. Today it was a flat, necessary, conversational contribution. They had almost reached Roddy's car and there was a period of silence, an unusual event when one was in Jessica's company. He let her into the passenger's seat and put her shopping bag in the boot. When he had got in and settled, he looked at her and said, with a smile that he hoped would convey warmth, 'It shouldn't, of course . . . but there are times when my brilliance just amazes me. I've just had great idea! I know where we should go. Let's go to the Firth View so that we can sip and see the sea?'

He didn't want to be frivolous when there was something worrying her, but something had to be done to ease the mood which seemed so heavy. They drove down through the delightfully narrow roads of the seaside suburb past old two-storey homes made squarely and solidly of stone each with a low stone wall in front, bare now of the cast-iron spears which had been cut down and carted off at the beginning of the war to make steel for tanks and guns: very few had ever been replaced. Soon they reached the slope to the sea at the end of Seabank Road and there was the Moray Firth whose waters on the other side flowed through the guarding Soutars of Cromarty into the Cromarty Firth and Invergordon an anchorage often used by the Home Fleet of the Royal Navy. Behind the high cliffs of the shore were the hills of the Black Isle (neither black nor an island), and far behind, Ben Wyvis and the mountains of Sutherland.

They drove into the parking area under the very old Scots firs and parked under them before the handsome doors of the hotel. He left the car and walked round to Jessica's side to open her door. As she folded her knees to get her legs out of the car, Roddy was reminded how beautiful her legs were and how she so elegantly moved them and, feet on the ground, a lissom movement saw her standing erect. He instinctively took her hand. She didn't withdraw but ever so slightly squeezed his. She knew that his was a gesture of caring and friendship which once he had thought he might never experience again. They walked quietly into the internal space, the foyer, with which they were both quite familiar, and Roddy guided them into a lovely sitting area bright now in winter sunshine that painted onto every surface a shadowed tracery from the bare trees in the grounds. The furnishings were chintz-covered armchairs and sofas strategically scattered, and amongst them low tables. Tall pedestals standing on the polished beech floor, visible at the edge of enormous rugs, supported tall vases of gladioli. The back wall had a pleasing display of oil and watercolour landscapes of admirable quality, their subjects were local land and seascapes, not too many, and very well and cohesively positioned. In all, it was an aesthetically pleasing room calculated to give comfort and ease. The master strokes were the tall expansive glass windows which formed the wall on three sides. These invited the eye across a deep rock pond set in lawns, and banks of rhododendrons out to the vista of the Firth. He spotted a table off in a glassed corner at the front where the big windows came together at an angle. 'Oh, look', he said, 'that's a taller table than the others, I'd prefer that. How about you?'

'Perfect,' she said. It was comfortable, the view was superb, and although the lounge was empty now, no one would ever be really close to them should people begin to arrive.

He had to speak; to ease open their way into this unhappiness, to engender some feeling of freedom to expose, to shed the fears about whatever this problem might be.

'Jess, I'm no psychologist nor am I much of a philosopher; but I'm an animal and I sense that there is something not right. I want to help you in whatever way I possibly can. If you want to, you can tell me about this unhappiness that I sense is deep inside you. Say only what you want to, just enough to give

me even a hint as to how I might help you.' He was hunching
forward, taught, speaking with intensity, as his eyes, set seriously,
scanned her.

'Oh, Roddy, I remember you from my schooldays, when
you were one of the senior boys, before you were called up and
went to fight in Korea. I remember how thoroughly delightful
those occasions were when we later met . . . when I was a music
student . . . and later when I was with the orchestra. You were
always so easy, so amusing, so engaging, so interested in me and
my life; yet you never intruded. We both knew our lives were
going along on their own trajectories and how, for each of us,
that was the way it should be. We knew at that time that we both
wanted it that way. Our meetings were so happy, so liberating,
so free, and so much fun; with no hidden agendas.'

At the point where, concentrating deeply, he didn't quite
know what she may say next, what she might be leading to, and
what he could say next to help her to go on; his dedication was
abruptly stopped. A very pretty blond waitress in a black dress
uniform came to their table. She was very neat and sweet. A
white frilly apron followed up over her young breasts and a
corona of white lace with black ribbon woven through the part
which fixed the little white lacy decoration on her head was
dulled to a grey by the brightness of her golden hair.

'Good afternoon,' she said, looking in a way to include them
both. 'Welcome to this lovely place. Is there something I can
bring you?' She said this so lightly and liltingly and in such a
friendly way it might have been someone in your own sitting
room, going, perhaps, on an errand to the kitchen.

'Good afternoon. Yes, please. I'm sure there's something.
But now that I know it's afternoon, that has a huge influence on
decision making. Jessica, when does Mr. Shaw leave?'

'Four o'clock from where you picked up your car.'

'In that case, would you like to have lunch with me? Please?'

His eyes were saying, 'You need to talk. Talk to me.'

Her mind and memory rushed backwards. He was the Roddy
who, when his work permitted, would come from Australia and
hear some of her concerts in Europe. With him as companion,
she'd shared delightful, fizzy suppers in lovely places in Paris,

Amsterdam, Hamburg. Of those nights, she remembered the laughter and a kind of clean, healthy naturalness which began in happiness went through humour and, laughter, often childlike; and sometimes almost erudite conversations. She remembered them wandering home down streets or lanes and, a fond kiss, brief and sweet, before she left him and entered, alone, her hotel or apartment.

She startled herself from this flash of reverie, looked at him and quietly, and said, 'Yes. Thank you. That would be very nice.'

Roddy said to the obviously bright waitress, 'If I said, "The sun is over the yardarm", would that have any meaning for you?'

'I would take it as meaning'—she said in dramatic tones—'that you have a mind to drink spirituous liquors, sir, and that I'd better bring the wine and drinks list toute de suite. The luncheon menu shall be brought at your behest.'

'Brilliant! You'll do me for rough old china. I bet you're studying psychology.'

'No, sahib, geography, but my father was a tea-planter—*jaldi jate.*'

'Isn't she a pleasant girl?' he said, then the frivolity gone. 'I realize that alcohol is no help in the business of problem solving and I'll be guided by you, but just for old time's sake, perhaps a glass of bubbles would be a better aperitif than most?'

'Champagne may not help to solve my problem, but it may help in improving my dismal mood which you must be suffering.'

The waitress returned with the list in a leather folder and offered it to Roddy. He looked up at her. 'May I ask your name and may I address you by it?' he asked.

'Yes, certainly, to both parts of the question. My name is Elspeth and I'd be pleased if you called me that.'

'I won't look at the list, Elspeth', said Roddy, 'you'll know which champagnes you sell by the glass and which we should try. What do you suggest?'

'There are only two by the glass one of which is quite good.'

'May we have two glasses please? But tell me has it been opened long?'

'There's an open bottle in an ice bucket in the dining room being used now. I'll fetch it, and if it's found to be sans mousse,

I'll open another. I don't want a roaring barra sahib in my lounge.'

She returned in a few moments with a new bottle. 'There wasn't much left in the opened one so . . . shall I pour?'

'Please.'

'Thank you, Elspeth,' he said when she had filled two flutes.

They looked at the dense mass of tiny bubbles rising from the centre bottom of the glasses. Roddy raised his and looked at Jess's eyes. 'A toast?'

'Yes, we must,' she said.

Then—and he chuckled, attempting to lift the air of solemnity without degrading the moment, so the chuckle embodied some of the seriousness that underlay the original first few words of the toast—'Here's Tae Us, Wha's Like Us? Damned few, an' they're a' deid.'

'Seriously though, I didn't expect our meeting. I'm very pleased that we bumped into each other, but I'm very sad to see you so unhappy. This is among the loveliest of those places where we've had happy encounters and a drink and a blether,' he mused, as he looked at her and out at the Firth across the trimmed gardens and winding earth paths round the quarry pool. Then turning back to engage her, he quietly asked, 'Are you able to tell me what's troubling you? I'd like to listen.'

'Oh, Roddy, yes, we've had so much fun together and a kind of friendship that must be very rare, if not unique. We've never made demands on each other's individuality. I always felt in our meetings a kind of free comfort almost like spiritually swimming in the nude. I'm just remembering a bit of that freedom right at this moment and already something is happening to the shape of my problem.' They sipped the wine and allowed their eyes to tell the things that were away deep behind mere words.

'Just let yourself speak, Jess, please; and don't worry about how your ideas and the words come out.'

'Well, every story has a beginning, but I don't know where my story begins. The latest most difficult bit is that just today I found out that I'm pregnant.'

In his face, little wrinkles at the edge of his eyes seemed to tighten, an almost imperceptible movement of his head silently signalled acknowledgement of her news. He did not voice a word. His whole body was saying, 'Go on.'

'I haven't told my parents yet. The world has changed me so much that I'm not sure I ever shared their views about life . . . maybe we share the same very basic values . . .'—she paused and added—'I'm not sure? We function and construct our value systems in relation to our world; our world is our context and it's in that context that we respond. Even the horrible circumstance of this pregnancy has to be seen in context, not that I come out of it very well, but I'm sure they may not understand why or how I was such a fool, and how I allowed myself to create a fantasy that blinded the natural instincts that had guided me well and happily until infatuation and thrall possessed me. My fantasy had placed me in an unassailable position to achieve what my fantasy told me was desirable. These were the kinds of things that were happening to me and which I didn't know how to talk about and why I was so horrible when we parted in Aberdeen. What has happened to me thereafter was a kind if hubris. The pregnancy and its effect on the family and their ideas of life, and their contextual society, is the immediate problem. I can only imagine the impact it will have on them. I can see no way that I can diminish that.'

'Your champagne's getting warm. Have a sip while I try to get my head around the problem you've described.' His face had reformed, and while it retained its empathy, something had shifted in his brain and reasoning processes had begun. His eyes now had an eager active look.

'Jess, how preggy are you?'

'Just one month.'

There's nothing showing yet—at least that I can see. Would another woman know?'

'Maybe, but I don't think so.'

'How long had you planned to stay up here?'

'I hadn't really got a plan. I was just so broken . . . and so angry with myself. I know I'm not actually thinking . . . and the world seems full of imagined threats.'

'Now, next question. Do your parents need to know?'

'They are my parents, they ought to know.'

'Mm. Would it cause more harm or more good if they knew now? In the context of *your* life and *your* reality, what value would you put on telling your parents now?'

'I'm just beginning to think that it would do more harm than good. Why don't I just disappear? I've just been thinking of this; I'm not sure that I'd like to be near the family as I raise my baby. All my school and university friends have gone; I'd see more of them if I lived in Canada.'

'If you would think of going to Canada, I can see the attraction in having many school chums and Fearnas people there; but Canada is a big country. You'd be lucky if one or two that you cared for most, lived anywhere near each other or you. You may even be lucky to see them once a year. Mind you, I'm just guessing. You would be a single mother with a very young child for a while, faced with finding and maintaining an affordable place to live. I'm not for a moment saying you couldn't manage. If anyone could, you could.' He was about to go on, but Elspeth appeared.

'Oh, here's Elspeth. Elspeth, I know what you're going to say: "The natives in the kitchen are getting restless, and if we don't order now, they'll be cooking us." Quick, Jess, have a look. Order for me. I've got to get the wine organised. Regardless of what mademoiselle chooses'—addressing Elspeth—'whether it be the best fish, well, maybe not; or poultry, well that depends; I'd like something from Chateau Neuf du Pape or something else from the Rhone. Ah, there we go', he said, spotting Guignal, the name of a maker, a Grenache-Shiraz-Mourverdre, 'however—how much time is there before the head chef comes after us with a cleaver?'

'Not a lot . . . so . . . quick things . . . say fish? Easy. But any steak or veal would be okay. The chef is an Italian who migrated here from Glasgow so many Italian dishes would suit.'

'Oh, did you hear that, Jess? Do you think we could ask him for something like scaloppini alla marsala?' he asked Jess but included Elspeth in the question.

'Another brilliant idea, Mckenzie!' Jess replied. This response gave him a thrill of delight and hope. Was the cloud lifting?

'Right, lovely Elspeth, go at a canter and save us from decapitation. Don't' stint on the marsala!' he called to her back as she scampered off. He had a nice feeling that Jess was rising perceptibly above her problem. Her voice, as she quipped over the menu choice, was in a better-sounding tone.

'Now I've got time to brag a bit about how brilliant I am before we begin chewing. Being a young infantry platoon commander trains you to think of two hundred things at once with the mission still primary. While I was occupied making an excellent wine selection, I had yet another brainwave. All of the things you have been saying today have been bundling up and forming a solution. God, bless me! Here comes the wine! Elspeth, you're in line for sainthood—if you want one—or would you rather just have a Ph.D. magna cum laude? I'm sure you've got a good cellar but a good cellar master? Ah, that's another question. Shall we have a wee taste please, Elspeth? Jess?' And to Elspeth directly, 'Elspeth, we two are Borgias. Take a glass from yonder sideboard and let's see you taste this wine.' On Roddy's command, she brought a glass over and poured three samples. 'Okay', said Roddy, 'eyes and hooters ready? Regard! Sniff! Slurp!' The mess committee sniffed, visually assessed, and tasted. Roddy, looking a bit smug, asked, 'What think ye? If you say what bank of the Rhone it comes from, you get minus points for that. One adjective each will do. Elspeth?'

'Unctuous.'

'Splendid,' cried Roddy. 'Jess, what thinkest thou?'

'Rich. What about you, *maitre de vins*?' asked Jess, pronouncing a beautiful French 'r'.

(Roddy, in a 'bee-u-diful' attempt at an Australian accent.) 'Bloody beaudiful! The Grenache-Shiraz-Mourverdre, but mostly Grenache, that's the magic'—His '*r's*' were beautiful too, thanks to Mollie Bonne, Annie Laing, and a good ear—'I think we have an excellent wine. Well done all. Do we have to go to the dining room?'

'*Pas du tout*. I'll set lunch here. Let's not disturb the atmosphere.'

Only moments passed it seemed, when there appeared through the kitchen doors the chef, clad in artistically splattered and smudged (filthy) apron, three days black stubble, chef's hat askew, and a beam on his glowing face, bearing two large plates.

'*Buon giorno!* Welcome to the Firth View, I am influenced by Elspeth what she tells me; I had to come and see you. I do hope you enjoy your lunch. Do enjoy your stay. *Buon appetito!*' he said. He bowed, turned about, and the large body, feet clad in ammunition boots without laces, swayed off to his domain.

'*Grazie tanto,* maestro, we certainly shall. 'Auguri,' called Roddy.

'I wonder which wine he chose for lunch,' Jess would have liked to know.

They began to eat and there was a saner note in Roddy's voice when he said, 'Thinking about how you described our friendship, I knew that I wanted it to go on like that forever, and whatever. Using that to guide me, I've just had other thoughts, about how you might "disappear"; how you may want to bring your baby up somewhere away from your parents. That's when I found the solution.'

As they lingered on the wine, the tone had returned to seriousness.

'May I tell you about the idea I have?'

'Do tell,' she said, consciously using the favourite phrase in the manner of a gossip urging another to 'spill the beans'.

So he began to outline a suggestion which was rushing to formation in his brain on waves of the typical Roddy Mckenzie excited enthusiasm.

'Well. Let's get the picture sorted out.' Roddy had leaned forward, his shoulders hunched, one hand grasping the other on the table. He was straining to hold his enthusiasm in check.

'I own, and have let the apartment next to mine to a person who only needs it for a fortnight. He is having a house built which is now just about ready to walk into. You could have that apartment. It looks down on the most beautiful Indian Ocean beach.

'Before I go on with my suggestion, I want to make some important points completely understandable for you. How much you are prepared to trust me will be crucial to this issue and, I'm sure, to the decision you choose to make.'

He wanted to hold her hands in his but had to stop himself from reaching across the table. He had to control his feelings at this very important juncture; he did not want to add a confusing emotional weight to what was really going to be a plainly practical suggestion. Composing himself, and the excitement he was feeling about his idea, he went on.

'The apartment next door is furnished and completely self-contained. I would be delighted to have you for a neighbour. You would be completely, utterly independent of me and I would not intrude upon your life. I would introduce you to some very nice people to get you started and I'd love to show you around the place, a kind of orientation programme. There's a very good medical practice nearby and a first-class hospital in Fremantle.

'What is the most important aspect of all of this is that you are not, nor must you ever think so, beholden to me. If you don't like Australia, or the accommodation or Cottesloe or having me next door, you are free to go anywhere you wish, at the shortest notice. No harm done. I would be very unhappy if your thoughts were guided by a feeling of obligation. If you want to pay rent, I can understand that you may feel better if you did, that's entirely up to you. I'm not asking for it.

'Your flat will look down onto an Indian Ocean beach with really good swimming not right in front but just a little further along. Western Australia is actually renowned for its obstetricians and there are kindergartens and schools just everywhere around. We have a very good symphony orchestra and young people aching for violin lessons. I have to go bush a lot, so I won't be a perpetual, neighbourly nuisance. I know a number of really good people whom you may like. I know the current conductor of the WASO and the leader, plus a dazzling redhead viola player. I have a contact in the music department at UWA. Also, I know the bloke in the "I sell everything" store next door. I get steaks from him, which legally, he's not allowed to sell, and all sorts of other SOS stuff if I come back from the bush and the cupboard's bare. Who could live without Greek dolmades or Portuguese anchovies, I ask you?'

All of this was delivered in a torrent of enthusiasm. He paused, as pause he should, if only to draw breath. 'Oh, Jess, I don't want to bowl you over, but here's a solution. Try it. If you don't like it and you decide to leave and go somewhere else, say, Sydney, if you think the music scene is hotter there, or do something else, believe me, I will only wish you well and try to help you do that, and if you don't want me to interfere in any way, I won't do that either.

'I'm a member of a sailing club and I own a yacht. The club is, self-evidently, good fun for so many; mostly very nice people, mostly married, young and old. Say you wanted to come and join in the social life . . . I'd love that to happen . . . but again . . . it doesn't mean that I feel I have some kind of claim on you. Life, and the style of living in Western Australia, is very free and easy. You've heard me boast about the climate every time we've met. When you mentally come to grips with your pregnancy, then motherhood, I've got a very strong feeling you're going to enjoy it. You couldn't possibly make a decision now and I don't expect you to. I'm off back to Australia the day after tomorrow, and if you had decided by then, I'd be really chuffed: if you haven't, no sweat, just phone me or drop me a line and just let me know what you've decided.'

Then his reserve fell and he had to hold her hands across the table, 'Jess, I just want to help', and his voice and his eyes were saying very tender things.

'Roddy, you are the sweetest man I've ever known. I'm overwhelmed by what you've been saying; really I found it difficult to string even these words together. It would be silly and inadequate, quite inadequate, to say thank you. God knows what this evening's going to be like. Can I get that event over first?'

'Of course: you must. Would you like me to come up with you and see your parents?' Then he very quickly said as he was changing his mind, 'No, maybe that's not a very bright idea. They don't know me well enough and you . . . and they . . . need to focus. What say I come and pick you up tomorrow? Let me take you to a Desert Island picnic tomorrow morning? Would you like to come? You can have one of the kippers I bought and taste the marmalade. Who could resist an offer like that?'

Old Bob Shaw would soon be waiting in his bus beside St Ninian's Church. It was time to be off.

'If you'll excuse me, I'll just go and say thank you to the lovely Elspeth, who's too young for me to whisper sweet nothings in her rosebud ears, and then I must take you up to Mr. Shaw. Doubtless you will wish to say your adieu.' This was an awkward time. So much emotion had been shared of life drawn from totally different worlds of living, to be portioned off now by leaving this table and this place to be taken to other places where newer, different emotional challenges would have to be met.

He went in search of Elspeth. When the appreciation of her help had been expressed with warmth, and the kind of banter which had marked the whole affair of being there for lunch, he kissed young Elspeth sweetly on the cheek, and in the seconds of doing so, furtively managed to pass some folded banknotes into her hand. 'Merci mille fois, chere Elspeth, bonne chance! Au revoir, a la prochaine fois.'

When she faced her mother across the bare kitchen table to confide her plight of pregnancy, it was more confession of an unforgivable sin than sharing a confidence. 'You can't stay here! How can we live forever more in this wee place with that shame on us? You've thrown away all that we did to give you a chance for a better life. The neighbours wanted you to succeed. They were proud of you. What you were doing was for them. It showed that success can come from poor beginnings, that we're not just ignorant dolts. Now they will feel that maybe we are, after all. Her father was in no way sympathetic; he shared all his wife's expressed thought; with perhaps a slight feeling of compassion. He knew that if a man wanted a woman, he could have her. She had turned white at that moment of learning that her beautiful, graceful, gifted girl had succumbed to her lust. Now a bitter heartfelt disappointment that had fallen, like darkness, upon her and looked grey haggard and much older than her years. She would bear a child that, even though the fact that the father was known would make it no more legitimate. She would not marry the man. And the man would not marry her. Why could she not suffer a life with a man, for whom she had not one kind thought, rather than give birth to a child with no family name? Neither was Roddy's proffered solution satisfying. Yet in reality it totally was. It met her most important requirement: to exile the loose woman, who would, progressively and soon, blatantly bulge with the result of her lust, out of her sight, and the sight of the people around. The distorted communication system

along the wee roads and among the wee farm hoosies would turn
the tragedy of Jessica's downfall into something worse than the
agony in the heart of her mother.

She could hardly look for support from her brother. The boy
with whom she had happily played rough and tumble tomboy
games and from whom she had learned a little about boys, who
were basically young males whose change of common descriptor
at some post-adolescent point would be from 'boy' to 'man',
who, apart from becoming larger and more certain that there
was innate superiority in their sexual difference, remained
essentially boys. Her brother's first thought on hearing that
she was pregnant, was how she, whom he secretly admired, her
difference, her talent and her success was an 'easy ride', just like
some of the dumb local girls he had screwed? How would he be
able to hide this truth which would become so patently evident?
What would the local loons say about the beautiful Jess being
up the duff, coming back here with a bun in the oven? 'Oo-
ah,' they would gasp as they leered. 'What kind of a fuck would
she have been?' Jess knew that all those thoughts would have
been in the minds of the entire male populace. They had been
denied the right to deflower Jessica Innes. There was a primeval
rancour; there was a biblical abhorrence of a woman who had
broken faith; who had gone of her own volition beyond her own
people, to find satisfaction for her female lust. Jess knew this
kind of thinking. She had grown up with it. Nothing would have
changed. Her mother knew all this too and she would walk in
the shame, which was her daughter's, amongst all the men. 'Just
because it was you who got what you wanted, you come back
here and drag us all in to the shame?'

It was a miserable, sleepless night that she had to spend it
under that roof of the house where she had been born. Would
it never be the time for Roddy to come and take her away?

—————∘∘∘⚬✕⚬∘∘∘—————

The morning of the picnic dawned clear and crisply frosty.
The washing on the clothes line on the back green was as
hard as deal planks; grass was white from frozen moisture

sparkling in the wan sunlight. Roddy had loaded his car with his contributions to the breakfast feast including two Thermos flasks of steaming milky coffee. As he started off for Ballycrochan Roddy was still wondering—as he had been since the evening before—and from his waking that morning how Jess had fared in her disclosure to her family. He drove through the lands where the turned soil was dark, with a white frost dusting on the higher parts of the turned furrows. The soil at the roads' edges was bone dry and dusty. The trees on the hills into which he was driving were being lit in certain parts by the climbing sun the differing shades of green making a pleasing picture. He drove up to the house over muddy tracks, now frozen solid, which would become a quagmire in a thaw. The steading and the sheds of Ballycrochan farm struck him as a scene of desolation and neglect. The people in the house must have heard his approach. Jessica appeared at the door. She closed it behind her and stood before it. She was unaccompanied. She placed two large suitcases and a smaller bag on the ground beside her and awaited the approach of Roddy's car.

Roddy immediately guessed that all had not gone well. Jess had decided to leave Ballychrochan. But had she decided to accept his offer?

He saw at once the desolation in her face. 'Let's get your bags into the car', he said without a pause for greeting, 'we can talk as we go.' The bags stowed, he went round and opened the passenger door and closed it when Jess was seated. They drove along the frozen track, beside a stand of ancient Caledonian Pines, up to the road which would lead down to the edge of the hill line and to the Howford Bridge.

'D'ye mind if we stop for a minute?' he asked when they had reached a dry piece of roadside bank where he could safely pull up. 'Please, let's,' she replied. Once stopped, they could turn to face each other; and Roddy began, 'Things didn't go very well, I'd say?'

'It was all quite horrible really. I knew and could understand that they would be unhappy and feel the social stigma of their daughter having an illegitimate child. I think you have more than an inkling how I was feeling about what social effects it would have on them. I couldn't have dreamt how much this would hurt them. But it told me really how little I mean to them beyond their fear of wagging tongues and some unbearable loss of family and personal esteem. Perhaps the care of families for families is rarer than I led myself to believe. Thank God, you came when you did. I was finding just being there after last night threatening. What the threat might have been, I don't know. I know I would have picked up my purse, my papers a change of clothes and simply stepped out. I was sure no one would follow. I would have walked to Lethen Hill and asked Jimmie McIntosh if he could run me over to Cawdor. There's a bus to Fearnas on Sunday.' She looked at him with a look of defiant conviction. She would have done exactly as she said. Had she not been successfully directing her own life in environments so different from the one she was now determined to leave? It was not a conscious thought; but there was a flash across poles in her core circuitry: she felt a sensation which thought interpreted as meaning that she would care for her baby with love, everlasting, and intense. 'Would you take me to Cawdor, Roddy?'

'No, I won't. Remember what Willie Shakespeare gave Mrs. Macbeth to say to the Thane? *"Nothing is so bad, but thinking makes it so."* I'll not take you to Cawdor but to a magic island just upstream from the Howford Bridge. There you shall talk and dine and enjoy the infectious idiocy of a band of Fearnachan of whom I am one. Thereafter I shall take you wheresover you wish to go. But there's one condition. Cheer up!' He reached across, took her face in his hands, and gently but firmly holding it, kissed her lips.

She looked at him in some seconds of silence as he too was looking at her. He had to say something—quickly. 'That was against the rules of conduct, but what could I do with a poor wee bairn looking so sad and lost?' he asked.

'I'm not a poor wee bairn; and I'm not sad and lost, Roddy Mckenzie,' she said in mock indignation, pulling herself erect. 'It's just that this morning I felt in need of a kiss. And what was I going to do to get one?'

'Well, just don't get the idea that that works all the time!'
Thus spake the Mckenzie with dramatic conviction.

Jess and Roddy were among the group which seemed to be
arriving at the same time. Roddy noticed that there was none
of the wee kisses and wee hugs which would be going on at
such a gathering in Australia. It didn't mean for a moment that
friendships were any less sincere or even less warm: they were
just not expressed in that way. Jess knew most of the people
although they were all of Roddy's age group.

They scrambled down the steep little track to the riverbed
and had to take great care in walking across the rounded rocks
and pebbles to the sedimentary collection of gritty sand and
leafy detritus which had raised a hummock that had, by every
spate, had its top washed away to flatness allowing bits of low
tussocky grass to grow. There were bigger 'islands', longer
hummocks, where Alder trees had sprung up and grown tall,
leafy, and lissom, defying eviction. But they were *tropical* islands,
not *desert* islands. Theirs was an island where, any Friday, quite
astonishingly unexpected and puzzling, a footprint might be
seen on the sand. From all the rounded stones ready to hand, a
fireplace was built. Sticks were easily found and gathered and a
fire crackled into cooking heat when the bigger sticks, later laid,
began to flame and settle to glowing embers. Mrs. Mckenzie's
coffee was doing the rounds and all were cheered by its milky
warmth.

It was a costume event, and R. L. S. would have been proud
to see the extent to which the participants went to create the
atmosphere of his beloved stories. There was even a 'Blind Pugh'
who, except when 'hamming it up', showed remarkable ability
to overcome his handicap. Of course there was a costumed
Davy Balfour and a Catriona. Helen Phillip, who was the wife
of a dairy farmer, provided the massive amounts of butter in
which the kippers were fried, and some for the scrambled eggs
and spreading on Jimmy Ashwin's rolls. On the toast, carefully
prepared on the glowing embers to one side of the fire, the
Seville orange marmalade was a universal success leaving only
the empty jars to be taken home. Although it was a day when
ears were burning with coldness and noses were generally bright

red, the jollity and chat was undiminished as the group bunched
closely around the fire.

Two of the women were on visits from Canada and one of the
men from New Zealand, so it was natural that the Fearnachan
wanted to hear their stories; and many and fascinating the
stories were. They told of differences in the style of living of the
populations of which they had become parts; the social and
political experiences that had only some similarities and many
differences with those of Scotland and certainly the Scotland
they had known throughout their early childhood and the
changes they were seeing in Britain since they had last cooked
stew on this island. It was about the effect of having a childhood
in a nation at war—a war that was not always far away; about
the huge and daring sacrifices of Canadians, New Zealanders
and Australians in that war. Seldom were they given recognition
for their 'out of all proportion' contributions from their small
populations. A question was asked, 'Was the contribution of
Indian forces *ever* mentioned?' There were threads of discussion
about education and change; how young people were looking at
their future; about landscapes and farming and the dangerously
dwindling diversity of living things.

Jess had found herself in a group across the fire from Roddy.
Those nearer her were keen to know her plans for the future
having heard her say that she had decided to leave the chamber
orchestra. Roddy heard the question, 'So what do you plan to do
next, Jess?' and he tuned in intently to hear what her response
might be. Jess looked at her questioner but also across the fire
to others who had the same interest. 'Well, tomorrow I'm going
down to Glasgow to meet up with old friends and hear a couple
of concerts, then across to Edinburgh to do the same. I'll do a
bit of visiting in England and hear some more music. After that
I plan to go to Australia. I plan to settle there; most likely in the
West.' She was telling him, he realized, that she had made up
her mind to come to Australia. He was somewhat surprised to
hear this now, but managed to say quite steadily, 'I'd better give
you my address and phone number. I'm unofficial chairman
of the local migrant welcoming committee.' Coming to him
obliquely as it did, he felt that the importance to him of the

news for him somewhat vitiated. She had been asked a question; she had given an honest response. On the other hand, why should he have been told first and separately? Was she not her own person in the arrangement he outlined to her? He had to remind himself of the non-attachment aspects of his own suggestions. Was this an omen to him that perhaps *he* may be the one who would have to overcome a difficulty in keeping emotion out of the arrangement? Was she hurt to think that he should take her proximity as easily resistible? 'I made the offer, I described the rules. I've now got to understand that there will be many subtleties of feelings and behaviours involved in our everyday lives. This is a sobering realization,' he concluded. Her decision had been in some way modelled to suit the terms of their contract. The complete, hasty confidence of mood in which he had constructed the plan seemed at this moment to have been perhaps a little rash. 'This woman has every right to take me at my word. My god, what an exercise of trust she is undertaking!' he realized. He still did not know whether she would be taking up the offer of his apartment. 'I have to anticipate that she will take up the offer of my apartment on the terms that I laid down.' And he went on, in his advice to himself, 'I mustn't let this little shock, and this realization, destroy what I was sincere in saying.' In self-admonition, he stated emphatically, 'Do what you said you'd do, Mckenzie; and do it in the spirit that you'd intended. Now get on with it!'

All well and good the jollity and interest of the whole event, but it was undeniably freezing, and now a north-westerly breeze was beginning to blow which could be felt even down in the shelter of the high riverbank and the trees; perhaps they should be moving homeward.

The thick, tartan travelling rugs were shaken out and folded and all the paraphernalia of picnicking was put into wicker baskets and boxes. It was agreed that the fireplace in which the last embers had died should be left *in situ* to baffle anthropologists making future finds should it stubbornly survive the power of spring spates. The narrow upward path forced them into a single file reformed as a group at the side of the Kildrummie Road to load up their cars. There were expressions of enjoyment at their being able to be all together again to reunite in their shared past; the sharing of stories of their new countries, about and the fun, the food and the blether of the morning.

All the visitors from overseas, including Roddy, would have returned to their homes, the last of them within ten days. And now Jessica Innes was going to join the migrant flock: another seed of Alder spreading on the flow of fortune. Jimmie Ashwin and his wife Ann suggested that the cold weather had created a need for a warming dram and invited the mass to proceed to their house on Seabank Road to share one. Roddy looked at Jess to ask her what she wanted to do. She quickly put the question back to Roddy as the thought of a bleak and morbid afternoon and evening which lay before her flashed in her mind. 'I'd love a warming dram, what about you?' He could not read her face or her voice or her body as she said, 'I'm game if you're game.'

'Thank you both. Jess and I would like to come,' was his response. It could be seen that the mob *tout entier* would have liked to come, but many had already committed themselves leaving a nice little half dozen in all to accept the attractive invitation.

'I'm glad you thought of accepting the Ashwin's, invitation it'll extend the morning's jollities quite appropriately and get us in out of the cold.'

'I'm glad you wanted to go too. In my present mood, I wasn't looking forward to the remains of the day in Fearnas waiting for a train.'

'I can run you to Inbhirness later on which will cut down the lonely boredom time. Then you wouldn't have to wait too long after breakfast to get a train.'

'That would be really good of you, Roddy. I was thinking of the Westerlea on the Inbhirness Road.'

'Let's see how the day works out; I'm easy with whatever you ultimately decide. Can we just drop in on mother on the way so that I can tell her what we're up to?'

'Not at all, I'd love to see her.'

'Hello, Mum, it's me. I've brought Jess Innes to see you.'

'I knew it was you by the noise. Come away ben.' The joy when she looked at Jessica Innes could be seen in Flora Mckenzie's face. 'Oh my Lord! Wee Jessie Innes. You have grown into the most beautiful woman I have ever seen.' Jessica blushed deeply with the honour of this senior woman's delight in her.

'Mother, this wee lassie is for Glasgow the morn's morn and she wants me to take her to the Westerlea, but I said I'd take her to Inbhirness.'

'Ach, you're mad, but we know that; and Jessie has more money than sense. Why doesn't she stay here in the wee roomy? There's always a bed ready. And there's plenty of time after breakfast in the morning for you to run her in.'

'Well there you are, Miss Innes,' said Roddy like a magician waving his wand over a *fait accompli*. 'Surely an irresistible offer. In your career, you've spent more than enough time in hotels and probably will in many more in times to come. Don't look a gift horse in the mouth.'

'Mrs. Mckenzie that would be great. It's very kind of you. Thank you very much. You've such a lovely cosy house here and warmth that's not just from the fire; and there's such a feeling of welcome. It's more than you and Roddy are offering me now. You can't know how much I appreciate your kindness. With Roddy here on a very sad occasion, I'm sure you want him to yourself. Yet if you're like Roddy, and you're maybe where he got it from, you don't say what you don't mean. So thank you again.'

wJess was right about the atmosphere of the house: there was a feeling of soft envelopment. Every colour was in a warm tone that showed off to perfection the timber work; the beech wood door and its jambs and architrave, the skirting boards and the small panelled dormer window, yet not shrinking the quite limited space. She felt so happy that it was not a hotel. In the minute or so of Jess's absence he told Flora of their invitation to the Ashwin's and a little about the picnic. Jess only put on make-up on very glam occasions or for footlights, otherwise she didn't need to, so there was no make-up session. 'So you're off to Jimmy Ashwin's, I hear. That'll be nice. I'm sure you'll enjoy yourselves. Jimmy still gets up early in the morning for his baking so you won't be late home. We can have a blether when you come back. Jane and I will be waiting for you.'

It was only a short drive from home to Ashwin's and Roddy said, 'What Mother was saying about Jimmy Ashwin rising early is true, but I think she'd just love to have us round the fire.'

'I'm sure you're right and I want that too, more than you could possibly imagine.'

They were welcomed at the door by one of the youthful Ashwin children and guided to a large open room at the back of the house that had big glass doors which, when not winter, would be pleasantly open to enjoy some of the afternoon sun and the sunsets. The others had arrived and there was a jolly chatter going on. Jimmie came over to see what he could get them to drink. 'Jessie, what do you fancy? Ann's having a white from France which she likes, but there's what I think is a nice burgundy open—or just say what you feel like and I'll see if we've got it. Aye, and there's mulled wine just ready. I should have set it up before we left for the picnic, but it's ready now'

'Oh, I'll try the mulled wine please.'

'Fine, what about you, Rod?'

'By gee, I'll have the mulled wine too,' he said with enthusiasm. 'That'll be grand. Show me the ropes and I'll do it while you look after your guests? By the way, found this in the back of the car, McRae and Dick's give one to anyone who hires a car. ' He handed him a bottle of aged Glenlivet.

'They don't put whisky like that in a hire car! Magnificent, Rod!' He winked to Roddy and, conspiratorially, quietly said, 'We'll have one later on, eh? Or you might have a look at my wee collection and see what you fancy. There may just be something different that ye'd like to try?'

'Fine. Anyway put that down with the others.'

Having Jess there in the group seemed naturally to turn the subject to music, add Les Cameron and obviously someone would get them playing. But Jess did not have an instrument. Problem solved. Ashwin Junior contributed, 'Robbie McIntosh always leaves his fiddle here. I bet he wouldn't mind if Jessica played it.' There was a sax on which the young Robert Ashwin had made quite a bit of progress. Her great natural sense of rhythm had attracted Jennifer Ashwin to percussion and the drum kit fell to her. All that was required was to select some numbers to play. When Jess was tuning Robbie McIntosh's violin against the piano, it was clear that it was time for the piano tuner to call. What the hell? Les was elected to make the choice of the first number and since Robbie thought he could handle 'Ain't Misbehavin', that became the first choice, and since it was best for Robbie, it would be in B Flat. Les played a little intro to give the players the start note as he called out the beat which he addressed especially to the drummer, 'Okay, folks; I'll do that intro again and call the time, then one beat and we're off.' And they were. Jess knew the song and joined in, weaving harmonies and rhythms through the melody in the Joe Venuti style of long ago. Les loved it. Maybe they weren't going to pack the Palais, but it was great fun, and hitherto possibly unknown singing talent was discovered. Jess played 'Diel Amang the Taylors' at great speed when requests were made for Scottish music, and since there is only the requirement for a basic plink-plunk-plonk accompaniment, Les left it to Jess. The day's second round of farewells did come early mainly in respect to Jimmie's calling demanding a very early start, but for all, it was school or work the next day.

At the Lodge, Flora was excited to have two youngsters coming at any minute, Jane almost equally so. And there they were at the door with Roddy calling out, 'We're home, Mother'—his pronunciation of 'mother' sounding more like 'mither'—'we all took your advice on Jimmie's early start.'

'Oh, very good. Hang up your coats and scarves and come away in and sit down—or maybe you want to go and put slippers on?' The more comfortable they were, the more likely they may be to sit longer. When the two returned, Jess put on a cotton sweater, some light loose slacks, and slippers. Roddy had a light jumper, cotton slacks, and brown leather sandals with feet bare Australian style. As Jess sat there in a deep armchair covered with chintz of large pink roses sparsely spread, she didn't know whether it was the fun of the picnic in the clear, sharp winter air, the mulled wine and frivolity at the Ashwins', there was now a peace.

In Flora's warm welcome to her comfortable home and the whole atmosphere of wholesomeness that pervaded it, she felt serenity wash over her. I was a response to the sensitivity that she intuitively felt flow from Flora and from Jane too. Here were people, just like Roddy, with whom she could share her fears, her secrets, her hopes without judgement yet at the same time even handed common sense. Flora would not be a 'there, there, dear' fatuous comforter. She had the feeling that she could not, with equanimity, sit together with this lovely woman who had welcomed into her home, nursing, her situation as a secret. She wanted to tell Flora and Jane about Roddy's offer and what she had decided to do.

'So you're off to Glasgow tomorrow, Jessie? Were you ever there before?' asked Flora in an innocuous opening gambit.

'Oh, yes, I shared a house with two other women and lived there when I was with the Scottish Symphony Orchestra. I just want to meet up with them again before I go away. I've been to Edinburgh too, many times. It's a spur-of-the-moment idea to go there now. I haven't planned anything. I just needed to get away from home at once and that just came to mind when someone at the picnic today asked me what I was going to do next. I had in mind too that I never wanted to come back home again. And having that in mind, I thought I would never come back to Fearnas again. Yesterday I was in Fearnas. I'd just been to the doctor who told me I was one month pregnant. I was infatuated by the man who was the leader of the chamber orchestra I was playing with. It was after the last performance of our season and we were all going our separate ways for our holiday. I had been drawn to play with the orchestra because I thought this man was marvellous. He had never in my time with the orchestra made any sexual advances, or even hints of interest in me. In fact he was very cold to me just as he was to absolutely everybody else. That in no way diminished my obsession; rather I saw his severe demeanour as strength. He lives in Basel and has a house there. It was in Basel that we had that last concert. My friends who are Europeans had arrangements made to leave Basel immediately after we players had said our farewells. I was to go to Zurich by train the next day to fly to London. When the orchestra's public party was over, he came to the table where I was with some other musicians and he asked me if I would like to come to his house. It was as if the hand of God had reached down to me. We walked to his house from the concert hall which was near to my hotel. I was totally naive and completely in his thrall. What happened then was sordid, horrid, and degrading. He left the room showered, dressed, and left; his parting words as he hesitated at the open door were, "Keep practising for the new season". As I said, my close friends had gone. I flew from Zurich and came home. But there was no welcoming. Time was passing and I had reverted to being a farm labourer, cook, housekeeper, and laundress for two men; a father who had lost heart, possibly as a result of the war and a poor relationship with his son and a mother feeling hopeless as she saw the farm running down from neglect. Then yesterday I came into Fearnas by bus to see the doctor and got the news I feared. I am one month pregnant. I was in Rose Brothers when I bumped into Roddy. He spotted there was something was wrong. He took me out to lunch and probably for much the same reasons as I felt I must tell you, I told him what you have just heard. The family made it very explicitly clear that they didn't want my shame in their house and amongst the local people. I packed and when Roddy came to take me to the picnic as planned I was going to ask him to run me to Cawdor to catch the Sunday bus to Fearnas. Perhaps, Roddy, you can tell your mother the rest.'

When Roddy had told his mother what he had suggested to Jessica, as he tried to look at both his mother and Jess, and include Jane, he finished by saying. 'But Jess hasn't told me yet what decision she has made about my suggestion.' It was now her opportunity, which there really hadn't properly been until now, to tell Roddy what she had decided.

'Roddy, I can see that is a situation which will bring problems with it,' Jess said gently, rather as if identifying a need for caution. 'It's surely a most unusual situation. You want to ensure my freedom; but what about yours? You're a desirable young man and there will be many girls who would like to spend their lives with you. What are they going to believe about your relationship with me, however chaste? We have been friends— of the best kind—for a few years now, each leaving the one to live without personal ties or expectations of each other. We had, and still have, our careers to follow. The recent events have given me no time to really think about it. It's just five weeks since we finished the concert season. For me, those five weeks have been a lifetime. My heart says to me, "Do it, accept Roddy's generous offer." So, Roddy, if it's still open—and you can change your mind: I'll be sad—and I hope we shall be the friends we were forever, but I won't be hurt. Your plan gave me a powerful feeling of hope when I most needed it.'

'I think honesty and balance will be very important.' Then he told them his reaction to Jess's announcement that she was coming to settle in Western Australia and the details of the lecture he had given himself. Then he looked at her tenderly and said quite softly, 'You've no idea how happy I'll be to hear you say yes.'

'Then I'll say yes.'

Then they turned to look at Flora not asking anything, but hoping for approval. Jane was a silent empathetic listener whose eyes lost no fragment of feeling or meaning in facial, body, or vocal expression from what had been said.

'I'm a favoured old lady to have been present with you to share what you have had to say to each other. I know you will succeed. Who knows what will happen when the agreement has run its term? I'm sure I know. You will succeed and I wish you every happiness. Now, you people may have had all that you want to drink today, but I'm going to have a wee sherry and let my excitement settle down a bit.'

They both hurried to hug and kiss Flora and thank her for what she had said about success and for the blessing of her best wishes.

'If you tell me what kind of sherry you'd prefer, I'll get the sherry . . . Jane, what about you?' said Roddy. 'Mother, what kind of sherry would you like?'

And while he was absent, Flora got up, crossed to Jessica, and in a gesture of emotional display almost unheard of in Scottish society where a kiss was rarely exchanged in public and was delivered more as a salute than a sign of affection, threw her arms around her. She said, very softly as she looked at her from extended arms as she held her hands, 'I can understand perfectly why you don't want to marry each other . . . yet.' Jane was not to be denied her share of hugs and kisses. 'I'm so excited by you two and excited for you. I'm so lucky to be here with you and very privileged.'

Flora was not to be alone in having a drink at this exciting moment in their lives. Jess asked for a fino, while Flora and Jane had amontillado. Roddy opened a big heavy shiraz, knowing it would not go to waste in his remaining time at the Lodge. 'Here's to happiness!' toasted Flora.

'Oh, indeed, for all four of us, and thank you again for having me here and listening to my woes which now seem almost to have disappeared,' Jess's voice pronounced with solemnity, relief, and joy.

'Oh, I'm pleased to hear that, Jess,' Flora said in a tone of sincerity and as if a sadness had ceased. 'As soon as you're into your flat, you'll be able to settle down and enjoy getting ready for your baby. Mind you, you'll need to catch up with your friends before you go because it could be a good while before you see them again. Maybe if you stayed here tomorrow, you could make some phone calls to see what can be organised. Maybe you and Rodd could travel down together, at least as far as Stirling. He's got to travel down on Tuesday because his plane leaves on Wednesday morning.'

'That's a really good idea, Ma, what do you think, Jess? You could waste a lot of time hanging around in Glasgow trying to line things up with someone who may not even be there.'

'Flora, that *is* a good idea, and I think I should do both the things you and Roddy suggest.'

And so it was that Jess stayed on, made her contacts repacked, and was able give Roddy a suitcase to take since he had travelled with minimum luggage. Jane was taken to Dalcross and fondly farewelled. The train tickets were arranged and confirmed so Jess would make the normal change of train at Stirling for Glasgow. There was a weepy farewell at the Lodge and especially for one of the two in the car which was going to be driven back to McRae and Dick's in Inbhirness. To both Jessica and Roddy,

Flora looked so small and lonely as they left her, at the gate of Woodend Lodge. They felt like running back, bundling her up, and taking her with them.

Settled into their seats in the south-going train, Jess was clearly conscious that these present moments were something of major significance in her life, as if in travelling from state to state you crossed a border into a country where the language and the social customs were different you implicitly agreed to live by the rules and regulations of that land and that you must not violate the customs of its society. And you would feel it helpful to acquire its peculiar language. She was committing herself to a contract however Roddy might insist that it was not that. She could not believe that he would not be hurt if she went off to do something that left him out of a future without her somewhere in his life. Would it not hurt him if, when after her baby was born, she were to find and fall in love with someone with whom she paired and go elsewhere to lead a life in marriage? That was a bridge too far to be crossed in conjecture. She had always ever been comfortable with Roddy. His was a happy energetic spirit in which there moved together fun and thoughtfulness and caring. 'Heavens, what more could a heart desire were *he* to go that's where she would want to be?'

In Roddy's silence, fact and affection were harnessed to the same chariot to provide the best in comfort and practical help to enable Jess to 'feather her nest', to be safe, secure, and comfortable and enjoy having her baby and becoming a mother. He felt that, however emotional had been her decision to take up his offer of help, she must have seen the practicality of it as an attractive means to resolving her problems.

Soon they were in Stirling.

Although there was no absolute time limit to her stay with friends in England, they had discussed and agreed that it would be an advantage in every way that she be settled in her accommodation, and her pregnancy under supervision sooner than later. Standing on the platform at Stirling station in the lowlands of Scotland, all of these thoughts and feelings were present as they tearfully hugged and cheeks were chastely kissed. Roddy returned to his train which was about to leave while she had to hasten to hers which very soon would. Although they parted now at Stirling, for both, the destination was Cottesloe, Western Australia.

As he had on a couple of occasions before, Roddy made his way to spend the night at a very pleasant hotel which served good food and wine, just off the runways of Heathrow.

<hr>

He had not long been back in the whirl of Ugojim and Mckenzie when a telegram arrived, giving Jess's flight details and arrival time. He had already given Madge and Peter, Janet and John, Ethel and Freddie a version of Jessica's story. While it was essential that Jess should be the one to tell it, he had to find a way to tell them something about this event in which he needed their caring interest, and to give them some preparation for a new person's entry into Roddy's social circle in which they were the most important players. The McGillivray's and the Treloar's had the advantage of having met Jessica in Hong Kong amidst the glamour and prominence of the Scottish Symphony Orchestra. Doris and Mauri would be the first to hear her story directly from Jess. He had alerted them to her aircraft transfer and stopover in Sydney with perhaps the opportunity to see her, expressing his hope that they could. As might be imagined, Doris was immediately sensitive to Jess's coming to Australia and to her becoming next-door neighbour to her Roddy. He imagined the excitement that Doris would be feeling; and the intriguing undertones to the Jessica story her sensitive ear would be hearing.

Mauri and Doris were at Mascot to greet her with warmth for her and pleasure for them. They whisked her off to Potts Point, and on the way, Jess was already being drawn into Doris's caring world where in Hong Kong she had found a place, and in addition to her own genuine charm and musical talent, she had the additional attraction of being an intimate friend of her Roddy. Doris wanted to be alone with Jess as soon as decorum allowed.

While Mauri excused himself and went to his office to do some Fusan business, Doris chose a small sitting room with a green garden view where they could be in the intimacy of each other's company and sip some welcoming champagne. 'Although I hate the thought of going through the subject of my present problem again, I feel a lot of comfort that it's you, Doris, who are going to be listening my tale of utter stupidity and shame. Of course I can't possibly imagine what you will think, but I'm sure your judgement will be fair and I will accept however your feelings respond.'

Doris regarded Jess, her face expressing the honesty she meant, saying, 'And I can't say what I will feel or think, but when I met you in Hong Kong, I formed a view of what I'm sure is the essential you and I felt very happy with the shape of it. Even if it were to be something dreadfully vicious, I know it would be an aberration for which there were powerful causes. Please, Jess, just say what comes . . . don't worry about the words . . . or the events you have to try to describe . . . just say what comes to you.'

Jess skipped briskly over her desire to move out of big orchestra playing to small, even more sensitive, intimately cohesive groups for which there had been exquisite music written; how it was during her search for such a group to try to join she first saw, no, she didn't *see* Michel, such a figure could only, at the very least, be beheld. Michel de Sassigny, the greatest exponent of oboe music in the world. She felt such a surge within to behold this human figure: the most magnificent male figure; beyond mere handsomeness; the earthly approach to a God. He had a proud grandeur; he knew, she could read from his posture, that his position in the world was in a special ranking of status and perfection. She had never felt like this; she didn't know how to feel about what was going on inside her; she just flashed past any hint of human sexuality, about which, anyway, she only knew about from hearsay; but whatever it entailed, with him it would be magnificent, a surrendering to a God. She described the night in Basel, described how that night in thrall had become so heartless, the use of a human body to celebrate control, power, and superior maleness over lower beings; with all the extra dimensions that only the human mind can construct. It was worse than brutal; no sensual elevation to ecstasy, only a descent to denigration and degradation.

Doris heard, too, of her parent's reaction, which was so tragic because it was understandable. Her Roddy had been expectedly noble, she could imagine nothing else. She was interested to hear of their compact and could say only that Roddy Mckenzie would break his heart rather than break the compact.

Somehow she had managed to say all this to Doris in these words, and Doris, who had viewed the worse aspects of human depravity vicariously through drama and literature, quailed at what she was hearing and felt so weak in her inability to do something for Jess that would restore her to a loving world. She need not have feared for that. Jess said, 'Doris, I have not gone through all the description of that night as some cathartic exercise for my benefit; only so that in our relationship there should be nothing lying in a corner that may come to life one day and ruin our friendship. I know there is a real world, a better, wonderful world of people like you and Roddy and his mother and Mauri and others of yours and Roddy's friends whom I've met . . . and dear friends of mine. And dear Roddy, who is such a dreamer in some ways, felt with me, and stepped forward to offer this contract of faith and wonderful practicality.' They stood up and embraced.

When Mauri rejoined them, the women were still in each other's arms, in seconds they were ready to relax, and Doris with her vivacious skill had slipped the scene from the sitting room, in which they had sat to speak, out to the balcony's shade and the capturing panorama—and the rest of the champagne. To change the scene yet again from the nervous horrors of disclosure, they took her to dine at Rose Bay where there was a good restaurant near the flying boat landing area. There Mauri could explore the girl's future living next to the Mckenzie.

'Don't expect to knock on his door to ask for some sugar or an egg—he's never there. He moves at a hell of a pace, working or playing, but when and wherever you find him, he'll be the same Roddy. You'll enjoy your flat . . . I'm sure of that. It's in a lovely spot. You'll have heard of John and Janet McGillivray . . .

you'll be surprised at how close by they are . . . I hope you brought your bathers . . . the beach is right in front of you.' Small talk continued in which it was implied that Mauri had to go to Perth every month for Ugojim and Mckenzie board meetings so she would have to come along.

The meal at Rose Bay was especially pleasant, and when they had taken her back to the Wentworth and she settled in her room to look out on the lights of the city, she had a sense of ease and gratitude. 'What a wonderful pair the Perrotts are', she reflected, 'she reminds me a lot of Flora.' She slept soundly: the prospect of seeing Roddy again soon had been a silent lullaby.

———∘∘∘⊰⊙⊱∘∘∘———

It was a standard Perth summer day—glaring, blazing. As she stepped from the aircraft, Jess felt the oven-hot blast. Her beautifully stylish Italian sunglasses were being challenged. As she descended the steps and strode the tarmac to the arrivals gate, her tall slim figure made the chic of her Italian Riviera colours speak of elegance and refinement of taste. For Roddy, this was the real, the normal, the natural Jessie Innes he knew. Her career and much travelling had by subtle influence transformed her into an elite continental woman. She simply had dressed for any arrival contingency. She would attract every eye in Venezia. It was no different here. Only the blasé black swans ignored her.

Jess cooed with delight as Roddy followed the Swan River in faithful Fido past the Tuscan architecture of the University of Western Australia, where Roddy indicated the Department of Music building near the road, along the expanse of Melville Water where they could look down from the height and Roddy could point out the Perth Flying Squadron Yacht Club. 'Much more of which later,' he said, as they drove on, his intention being to make the drive to her new home pleasant but as brief as possible. The Avonmore Terrace flats in which he lived and where now Jessica Innes would take up residence were scarcely of imposing architecture but their flat unadorned brick had something honest about its humble simplicity.

'Come, I'll show you where your letterbox is'; he said as she stepped down, 'there you are, number five.' He took her left hand and into the palm placed the key with a pretty ribbon on it. 'And look you've got your first mail!' he gleefully exclaimed, 'That is, if you are Miss Jessica Innes of 5 Avonmore Terrace Cottesloe? Aren't you going to open it?'

'It's rude to open your mail while someone else waits. And anyway, it could be a secret message. I'll take it inside.' Putting the key into the door for the very first time, she was conscious it's being a note in the opening bars in the first drafting of a new piece of music. 'How will the composition develop?' she wondered.

She opened the door which allowed her a view across the depth of the main room out to a small bricked balcony and the brilliant green-blue of the Indian Ocean. The view was marred (or enhanced) by streamers, blazing ribbons of colour in crosses and diagonals from wall to wall of the room, festoons of coloured balloons were everywhere, and on a low polished cupboard along the left-hand wall stood a tall glass vase with a striking arrangement of fresh blooms. A banner from side to side cheered out, 'Jessica—welcome to Australia!' She gasped at what she saw. 'Roddy, isn't this fun? I think it's really sweet of whoever did it. I wonder who?'

'I want you to know I had nothing to do with all this; I didn't even provide a key to anyone. I'll leave you to explore while I bring the bags.' She was pleased it was basically comfortable. In one of the two bedrooms, a double bed had been made up and the covers turned back, there were fresh towels and soap. A small card with flowers, petals closed, and a pale moon on a pillow said, 'Sweet dreams.' The envelope which she opened while Roddy was bringing the bags was from Madge wishing her a warm welcome and saying how she was looking forward to their meeting.

'Have you checked your phone . . . and the fridge?' he asked.

'The fridge is definitely working. The champagne fairy's been and the bottle is just about freezing. Yes, phone's working too.'

He left her to do some unpacking, saying, 'A bit forward of me I know to make a lunch appointment without consulting you, but you must meet the office manager of both Ugojim and Mckenzie, Madge Gill. Madge is more than just the strength of our administration, she is a great person, part of the family and I know she will a great help to you as you settle in. Of course you can have a quick glance at the Ugojim and Mckenzie operations. In my absences, the redoubtable Simon looks after Ugojim so you'll meet him too. The others you'll have to meet over time; at present they are out on work sites. I said I'd pick Madge up at work which is just along the beach, minutes away, before one o'clock. Does that give you enough time? If you need more hangers, just give me a hoi.'

'Could I have twenty minutes?'

'Of course. I'll drop back in twenty minutes.'

In trusty little Fido, looking very polished, they drove the short distance down Deane Street to Marine Parade and followed the beach south towards the port of Fremantle, turned left over the railway track through the industrial area of sheds and huge oil tanks to Bracks Street, and turned right again along a high fence and large iron-clad building emblazoned in large letters with the name Treloar Transport and Haulage. 'D'ye remember Ethel and Freddie Treloar from Hong Kong?'

'Oh, yes, I do, they were a nice pair I thought.'

'Well, that's their business . . . it's a very big national company, and . . . right next door . . .'

The signs on the buildings running along Bracks Street from Treloar's made their own announcements. Tall, square, three-dimensional capitals letters, medially positioned at the top of a high and wide glass front, declared Ugojim (Aust. Pty. Ltd.). Through this glass facade, the hulks of enormous earthmoving machines in bright orange paint work dominated the eye. The forecourt, paved in pink-grey marble slabs was bordered by two panels of lawn inset with tonsured shrubs from the broad entrance in the low stone wall at the street to the foot of the tall glass facade. A broad access road separated the rather grand Ugojim showroom from a smaller rather less-grand two-storey brick building, a dwarfed attachment to a high iron shed with tall, wide sliding doors on its front which continued the same line along the yard. Through these open doors were various earthmoving machines undergoing maintenance. Above the doors and under the eaves of this shed ran a banner of Mckenzie tartan with superimposed white lettering indicating the occupier as being Mckenzie Earthmoving Pty. Ltd. The land space in front Mckenzie premises was a plain, black bitumen surface, which said something about the different purposes of each of the buildings.

Further along the line, but separated by a tall mesh fence, was the yard of 'RentEquip', a totally functional area where serried ranks of bobcats, fencepost borers, post hole drills, back hoes excavators—any imaginable pieces of moveable plant, including electricity generators and lighting plant, were presented for rental. A small tin shed at the back served as administration building. This nicely profitable Mckenzie subsidiary was Simon's idea. Run by a man recruited by Roddy from the Highway Hotel who had reached the age when years had taken him beyond the point where he wished to be out there all over the Western Australian bush in the energy demanding role as an operator.

Madge was the first person they saw as they walked into the neat, orderly office in the small brick building. She was a strong-looking attractive lady of possibly mid-fifties whose fair hair pulled back by a ribbon revealed an attractive square face.

'G'day, Madge. Madge, I'd like you to meet Jessica Mckenzie who arrived here from the old Dart just this morning.'

She had heard about Jessica from Roddy and the Treloar's, and when they now met, she saw that none of their complimentary descriptions had been exaggerated. There was none known who reacted to meeting Jessica in any other way.

'Jessica, I feel as if I've known you for a long time. Roddy talks about the good times you have and about your concerts whenever he arrives back from overseas, and the Treloar's were in raptures when telling me about meeting you in Hong Kong. Welcome to Australia, Jessica. I'm sure you'll enjoy being here and let your career go even further.'

Jessica blushed. 'That's very kind of you, Madge. I've heard a lot about you too. I sometimes think from what he says the sign outside should read Madge Gill Earthmoving.'

'Let's not waste time blethering here Madge, Jess can catch up with Simon and Ray when we come back.'

Madge phoned Simon to say she was about to go, then she phoned Ray who came out immediately to relieve her. He arrived from another room powering his wheelchair with his arms. Jess was surprised to see that for a man who was totally wheelchair bound that he was not overweight. She learned later that so he could go to the pub with the others and drink his share of beer, he put himself under a rigorous programme of exercise and not overeating. They drove along Stirling Highway, and passing through Cottesloe town, Roddy pointed out Frank Dalby's office and Napoleon Street where Jessica may any day now choose to shop.

'Ah! How fortuitous and felicitous', exclaimed the Mckenzie purposely loudly, 'we've caught the two of them together!' Alice and Bert McPartland were at the reception desk poring over their guest register. After Jessica was introduced and welcomed by the McPartlands, Alice showed them to their table in the dining room where the between-the-wars decor had a welcoming, homely touch of shining jarrah wood and brocaded upholstery, chandeliers, and long heavy plum-coloured drapes. There were photographs of local historical significance and watercolour landscapes in gilded frames decorating the walls, crisp white napery on the round jarrah tables, spread around on a rich red patterned carpet which pulled the decorative elements together giving a sense of honest middle-class comfort. Roddy wanted to have Jessica meet people like the McPartlands and to see this hotel which he thought reflected so well the character of the local society. Madge had been here before, as she had to many hotels and to the best of the restaurants in Perth and the suburbs when she accompanied her husband Peter who represented the Penfolds wine company. Roddy wanted to ensure that Jess and Madge have an opportunity to meet and get to know each other and since Madge would be unable to attend the welcoming gathering at the McGillivray's that evening this seemed the perfect solution. 'You've got Roddy to be company for you and I know he will bend over backwards to see the you are happy, settling in and getting to know people and that's grand, but I like to think and there is a relationship that goes beyond Roddy and me and Mckenzie Earthmoving. I want you to know that, because at any time you need another woman to talk to, about absolutely anything, please don't even stop to think, get in touch with me at work or at home or at the yacht club, wherever or whenever.'

Jess was serious as she looked at Madge and responded to what she had said, 'I'm very grateful for that, Madge . . . very grateful . . . and happy that you have made that offer. I'm not always as independent as I'd like to think I am and I suppose I take my old friends very much for granted. They are that sounding board, so easy to use that I'm not conscious of using it. I'm glad we're having this opportunity now . . . and here in this pleasant place. Thank you, Madge.' The conversation went on to include basic subjects such as shopping, about Jessica needing some time to become orientated to her new world, her international driving license, and her pregnancy, the needs of which were an important subject with Madge giving her the address of her own doctor, whose practice he conducted from his house in Cottesloe, and suggested that she would ring him telling him to expect a call from Jessica.

Then Roddy had to say, 'Now I'm going to have to be a bit of a spoil sport but as some bright spark tiresomely said, "the wheels of industry must keep turning", and Madge and I have to provide some of the motive force so we may have to exit left and get back to work.'

They said 'Oo-roo' to the McPartlands and were on their way. As they drove, Roddy said, 'Madge won't be coming tonight, she's going out hitting the high spots with Peter. What I'm going to suggest now is that if you drop Madge and me at work, Jess, you might like take Fido over and use him to drive around the locality if you like. I'll come home in my pick-up and get there about half past six, tidy myself up, and then we can walk up to Mac's for seven o'clock.'

'Oh! That'll be a bit exciting! Thank you. If Fido's not there when you get home—send out a search party.'

Before seven o'clock, Roddy knocked on Jess's door. She appeared, wearing a creamy white linen dress with a flared skirt and deep-blue paisley-patterned bodice. She wore deep-blue low-heeled shoes going back into the flat to reappear in a second clutching a deep-blue leather purse.

'You're looking very beautiful, Miss Innes. I'm very proud to be walking out with you.'

'Thank you, Mr Mckenzie. Very kind of you to be my escort for this evening.'

They walked happily in the evening light the six score of yards to the McGillivray's.

John and Janet McGillivray were delighted to extend their hospitality to a new arrival in Australia, friend of the Mckenzie, reported upon with glowing praise by the Treloar's and Iris and Rhys Jones. Lynne and Ann were there, eager to see this fabled woman. The Treloar's, who had lost the contest for the night's venue, fielded a full team with Howie and Gwen looking forward to meeting this lady about whom they had heard so much. The initial introductions were quite decorous, then the group became a flock of noisy magpies, chirruping willy-wagtails and white-cheeked honey eaters, excited, warm, friendly, welcoming. All of the OBH corner boys and their wives were there, the men were entranced, the wives delightedly curious. Jess had slipped into a variation of her post-concert mixing-with-the-audience mode, radiant, smiling totally charming with the enhancing joys of being so warmly welcomed by such sincere people extending hands of friendship. The men were making sure that everyone had a drink and Mac held the floor briefly while he made an official collective welcome and a toast to the new arrival wishing her a happy new life in Australia. It really was a splendid night; there was no one who did not make an effort to have a personal time with Jess. They talked with Jess about her plans and someone brought her a copy of the local newspaper so that she could advertise for pupils. It was as if everyone had decided that they wished to be home and in bed before ten p.m. People were saying their farewells, wishing happiness for the new arrival and departing leaving Roddy and Jess to thank their hostess and host before stepping out to stroll back to their flats. As they walked, Roddy suggested that Jess may wish to change the furnishing in her flat, sell off anything she did not want, or did not like, and buy pieces of her choice which Roddy would be pleased to pay for.

To set up her 'business' her advertisement had included her doctorate and orchestral experience and she invited students who sought coaching. She was pleasantly surprised with the results of her advertising and soon had enrolled pupils for every weekday and Saturday. A mother wished to enrol her five-year-old daughter and a boy of eight came with his mother to meet Jess. He too was enrolled as was a lady of forty who had just found child-free time and wanted to return to playing. A man of mid-twenties who played for a local quintet enrolled for coaching. She was off to a very good start and eager to be engaged in honest toil, thus paying the scandalously extortionate rent demanded by her villainous moustache-curling landlord which she insisted on paying to preserve her spinsterly honour. Life by the sea was delightful, and when she walked round to her GP who wanted to keep a close eye on her pregnancy, she was proclaimed to be a 'very healthy young animal' and that everything was going famously. Roddy had to go down to Collie to look at a site where a tender was to be let for clearing of the land and site preparation for plant which would produce high-density wood fibre board. On-site he was to meet a member of the engineering company that was going to erect the plant. It looked like a pleasant outing for Jess and she could visit his farming property.

In the process of the site inspection, he saw a little old wooden house raised on stout wooden stumps once, many years ago, home to a tree feller. Between the road edge and the front of the house, a sloping earthen path led up to the steps in front of its door. The house was surrounded by fruit trees and a profusion flowering native shrubs and a blaze of blooms from plants tall and small. There was a big vegetable garden, a greenhouse, and poultry wandered everywhere, goats stared from their pole-fenced yards among deciduous trees, a newer shed where cheese was made and advertised for sale along with the vegetables, fruits and jams, pickles and bread. 'What's going to happen to all of that?' he asked, indicating the house, the gardens, and the outbuildings. It seemed to Roddy that it was with callous indifference that the engineer replied, 'Oh, all of that will go. It will be part of your contract to clear all that away. A couple of women have got it and I think they pay the shire a peppercorn rent.' When they had finished their inspection and the engineer had left for Perth, he told Jess in the very words of the engineer what he had said. 'God, that's horrible! Those poor women will be broken hearted to have to leave what must have been a hard labour of love to put all this together. Even now it must entail never-ending toil, but I imagine that they find the life very rewarding.' She saw that his face had taken on an anxious look: then it fixed firmly. 'I'm going to go and see them,' he blurted out. 'Would you like to come with me?'

'Yes, of course,' she readily agreed.

'My name's Roddy Mckenzie and this is Jessica,' he said to the lady in a white overall coat whom he met as they knocked and entered the dairy shop. 'I'm Enid Brady', she said, 'the cheese maker. How can I help you?'

'Well, I was wondering if we could be of any help to you. I heard just minutes ago that your property is going to be wiped off the face of the earth. How are you feeling about that?'

'Well, Mary and I are broken hearted as you might imagine. We love this place . . . a big part of our hearts is here. All our efforts to have the factory built around us failed miserably. Fortunately we're not too old and we are well and fit. We'll never have this way of life again, but surely we'll find something that we can do together.'

'Look, I own two hundred acres of land on the Hille Headings Road not that far from here where I fatten cattle. I've just had an idea about how we could help. Is your business partner handy?'

'She won't be far away. Would you like to come with me and we'll go and find her?'

They walked down a path through the gardens where a lady with a red bandana over her dark hair was bent over, pulling lettuces from a row in a bed of clay loam soil, with a quick stroke of a sharp knife cutting off the rots and placing them in a shallow wooden tray which she had positioned under a shading umbrella.

'Mary, this is Roddy Mckenzie and Jessica, he says he has an idea about how he can help us.'

'Hello, how are you?' greeted Roddy. 'Let's fill your tray and get it out of the sun first.'

'There's only this one to do . . . a man will be coming to pick it up any time now.'

Roddy bent to the task, picked the lettuce, and passed them to Mary who cut off the roots with the only knife. The tray was filled in a minute and together they went back to an open shed under the trees near the dairy. A man drove up in a Holden ute, paid for the tray of lettuces in cash, and drove off. He would have liked to stop and chat, particularly as he would have liked to know who the two strangers were, but he had to deliver these lettuces to restaurants in Bunbury for this evening's diners.

'It's not much more than an hour ago that I learned that to clear the site for the factory your home, your property and outbuildings are going to be completely swept away. The thought was so sickening I, literally, nearly spewed, and then I became angry and a bit upset. It is my company that is going to do the obliteration. I have signed a contract to do this and I am not able to get out of it now, too many other people would be badly affected, but here's what I want to do. I have the capacity to shift your house and your buildings holus-bolus to a two-hundred-acre property that I use for fattening cattle, just down the Hille Headings Road. That would mean you could have the house that you've been living in with no change, put on a nice spot which we'll pick out. The soil for the gardens will be on pasture land that I have never treated with fertilisers or weed killers and I don't believe anyone did before me. I'll turn that under with a mould board plough. It'll make great gardening land. If the idea appeals to you, we'll have to start planning right away . . . what do you think?'

There was stunned silence as the women stared at each other, speechless. This was indeed a miracle. Each crossed herself—and wept. 'Mr Mckenzie, you have been sent to us by the good Lord,' Mary managed to say.

He had to do what he had now done. How could he be complicit in tearing down what these women had achieved?

The only cost to Mckenzie Earthmoving would be Ray's time in drawing up the plan and organising a crane and the other plant they would need—the rest would be Roddy Mckenzie's personal expense. Jess didn't need to know this. What she did know was that what he had done, what he had undertaken to do, he would do with love and she knew that this was simply his being Roddy Mckenzie.

Jess's pregnancy had reached beyond the halfway mark and all was going well. The neighbourly relationship worked without too much restraint yet privacy was safeguarded; neither paid the other a non-purposeful visit but to drop in for coffee or a cup of tea or a drink at what seemed an appropriate time was usually welcomed and there was always some activity afoot that had to be planned or discussed. If they bumped into each other in their little kitchens, the physical contacts were just like writhing puppies who don't care if another gets in the way. She loved his light-hearted boyish approach to their being together, yet she sometimes wished it were otherwise. 'But wouldn't that be unfair?' she asked herself. She found herself having to summon self-control when she found herself staring at him when she thought he couldn't catch her eye. They each tried not to think of each other in any other way than being good friends, but neither could deny a great, deep, strong affection constantly within them. 'How long can we manage this?' was a question that arose now and again—or more often.

Jess's very first student had departed—the man from the quintet. This was his performance assessment session. He seemed sincere about what he wanted to achieve from his coaching sessions and they had drawn up a programme which their sessions would follow adapting as needs emerged. She knocked on Roddy's open door. 'Any chance that a working girl could get a drink at the cessation of her toil?'

Without looking round, he replied tersely as if turning away an unwanted cadger: 'Yes, there's a pub just down the road.' Then he turned and laughed, saying, 'But if you're my nice-looking Sheila from next door, come on in.' They were sitting on his verandah each with a glass in hand soaking up and sharing the delights of living where they lived when his telephone rang.

—ooo—⟩⊗⟨—ooo—

Jane Dugal had been shattered! She was driving with a friend—well, not a friend by definition but someone who was part of their set whom she had known for a few years and had been thrown together with more frequently since she had married Tobias Pettigrew, and had just passed through a village not far distant from Winchester when she pointed out to her passenger a charming cottage seen through spaces in tall trees and a magnificent bedded roses.

'What a sweet cottage and beautiful garden,' she remarked to her passenger.

'Yes, it really is quite charming. Toby's had it for years, but I suppose you prefer not to go there.'

'Are you saying it belongs to Toby Pettigrew the man I'm married to, and I've never known about it?'

'Good God, then it's surely not possible that you don't know that Toby lives there and commutes to London by train?'

She did just glance in the rear-vision mirror before skidding to a halt by the bank of the road. Two years of a not-very-happy social marriage were wearing to the point of serious thoughts of divorce.

'Does Toby keep a mistress there?'

'Most of the men we know, or are married to, have a mistress just that in Toby's case it's a man, and since homosexuality is a crime, one has to be more than normally discreet. Everyone knows. It's been going on for years.'

'How many years?'

'Oh, at least five that I'm aware of. Does it make any difference—six years, five years, two years?'

'It does to me because it means he was a practising homosexual when he proposed marriage to me! Don't you see, *this* is life. I am just a component of his *other* life.'

Because his elder brother had a son and there was an heir to the estate, Toby was not required to make the conscientious heterosexual endeavour necessary to provide one. Jane immediately began divorce proceedings which were fraught with family rows, 'discussion and counselling' of the church and dealing with lawyers hardened by the trenches of elite family litigation warfare. In oblique advice, it had even been suggested that she keep quiet, enjoy the income, and find someone nice to go to bed with. She was devastated to know that assumed trust had been violated that her body and her husband's had been shared and a travesty made of heterosexual marriage. She had known that marriage within the stud-book system did not require much of showing or of sharing tender emotion. But she had married a cause; the cause of superior-caste maintenance. In that cause, the prime quality required of women was superior skill in sustaining a lifelong charade. It was so ludicrously awful that she looked upon herself with utter contempt.

She had completed her doctor of science postgraduate degree in mathematics with high distinction and prizes and was now happily back at school but keeping an eye open for a mathematics project that suited her. Turning a page in a Maths Journal, she saw, in a blink of electrifying impact, an advertisement for the role of Senior Mistress Mathematics at Presbyterian Girls' College, Cottesloe, Western Australia, written applications were invited and successful applicants would be interviewed at St Andrew's University. Australia! That's it—successful in the application or not! Up! Up and away!—away from this disgusting absurdity. She went to her typewriter immediately, now to get her head mistresses' recommendation, supportive evidence of her brilliance as a teacher, and the published work she had done on the Psychology of Teaching Mathematics and Advanced Mathematics at Secondary School Level. Start packing! She telephoned Miette to ask her where Roddy was in Western Australia. Cottesloe! Was fate taking a hand? 'He's not married yet, Jane darling,' was the first information Miette reported. 'He's too busy building three already very successful big businesses and travelling and he has been here very briefly twice and once we met in France at St Tropez where he and Erik sailed in the classic wooden boats, he still looks very beautiful and is more charming than ever *s'il soit possible* I think that's because he is now so successful.'

'Dear Miette, she could scuba-dive without tanks', thought Jane, and then with a happy, inward, hopeful smile said to herself, 'That's all the information I wanted.' Schools and universities begin their academic years in spring, so Jane would come to complete PGCs second half year.

Roddy lifted the phone. 'Hello, Roddy Mckenzie. Good God, Jane Dugal. Where are you phoning from? From Cottesloe?! Well, I'll be blowed. Jess, it's Jane Dugal from Woodend. She's in Cottesloe.' Panic, concern, fear, loss; felt signals in two hearts and minds; at the sending and receiving points of both telephones a female stomach sank and a heart felt a twinge. 'Where are you now? . . . Heavens, that's about ten minutes away do you have transport?' He told her the straightforward directions to his flat. 'She'll be down in about ten minutes.'

'Would you like me to go?'

'Why would you go? She's Fearnachan but can be a bit snooty. I'm a bit surprised she rang. Miette Verney told me she had married an upper-class real estate agent in London, although they buy and sell property I think they don't like to be called real estate agents. Do you want to save your wine ration until she comes? If she hasn't eaten, perhaps we could go down the road and eat rather than cooking late. Mind you if we'd rather stay here I can go to the Italian kitchen next to the OBH and get some lasagne?'

When she arrived, Roddy met her at the door with a handshake and welcomed her in. 'Jane, I'd like you to meet Dr Jessica Innes of Aberdeen and Edinburgh Universities currently doing some coaching while undertaking another major life promoting project. Jess, this is Jane, daughter of Major Dugal of Woodend—in whose Lodge by grace and favour we have lived and for whom my dad worked as gardener—and if my British intelligence contact is correct, Jane already a considerable mathematician with a master's from Edinburgh is now doctor of science in mathematics of Oxford University. Welcome to Australia, Jane; if you haven't been living here for years without my knowing it.'

'I arrived just three days ago and have been immersed in welcoming hospitality.'

Looking at Roddy, she went on, 'I had this evening free so I thought I should try to contact you having got your address from Miette. Fact is, I'm now a migrant to Australia where I have every intention of staying. I shall never go back to England to live.' She then related to them the whole story of her miserable marriage and how it finally, sordidly, pitifully ended; how she had seen the PGC advertisement, her being appointed and how she had already begun teaching.

'Your story makes me feel very sad,' Roddy said, and his sadness could be heard. 'I know it takes all kinds to make a world, but I can never work out why some people need to be so utterly horrible and so deceitful. However, that's the regrettable past. The future sounds very exciting, I hope you will love Australia the way I do and have all the good luck and friendship that I've enjoyed. Let's have another glass of Prosecco and toast your future.' So they did, and Roddy asked Jane, 'Have you eaten yet?'

'No, but I can later.'

'Neither of us has eaten, so perhaps you'd like to go out somewhere nearby and have a meal, or I could nip down to Enzo's, get some lasagne, and we can eat here?' He looked around for responses and Jane spoke first.

'Why don't you two decide? It's so pleasant here, need we go out?'

Roddy, leaving Jess and Jane together, drove to the Italian pasta house at the side of the OBH.

In his absence, Jess divulged to Jane the entire story of her infatuation for Michel in a trimmed-down version, of how she had become pregnant, the sexual debasement in Basel, her rejection by her parents, Flora Mckenzie's warmth and empathy, Roddy's offered solution, his pledge, and what had happened in her brief period in Cottesloe. Jane was enthralled by every word of the story's unfolding. She was silent for a while. She left her chair and came round the low verandah table. Jess stood up and they embraced. 'Jessica', she said softly, 'you are a wonderful woman. You must love Roddy Mckenzie very much.'

'I do,' she affirmed emotionally, emphatically. 'But I will *not* put him in an awkward situation and cause him to break his word.'

'Jess, please may we meet again after this evening, we must put our heads together on this solvable dilemma?' They had turned to lean on the balcony wall to listen to the sea and to watch the lights flashing seaward signals from Rottnest Island.

Roddy's voice sounded from the doorway, 'I'm sorry I took so long. Enzo had, had a rush of orders and was in the throes of making some more lasagne. Having focused your appetites on lasagne, I decided not to go for pizza or spaghetti Bolognese. Hope you're not dying of hunger.'

'No, I don't think we thought about food, I was unburdening myself of my life's story to Jane which seems to have fitted into Enzo's cooking time. Don't know about Jane, but I'm not going to be able to put up with those lovely smells for too long. Shall I dish up?' asked Jess.

'Brava, Jess, I'll open some red and put on an Italian musical accompaniment.'

Jane watched the pair in the confines of the cramped little kitchen moving around and touching against each other like otters playing in a pool.

They were dining contentedly and listening to Italian tape recordings of popular music as background. Eating lasagne begs for red wine. Jess looked at Roddy with appealing eyes and said, 'Enzo would have put vino da casa in the sauce. Do you think my baby would mind so much if I add half a glass of wine?'

Two loving faces were in mutual regard sharing caring eyes.

'Well, since neither of your doctorates is in medicine, I shall, as a practical bulldozer driver, offer some earthy advice. Since I assume you are not going to make a habit of such tippling, and if you drink a good big glass of water before you go to bed, I surmise your baby will neither suffer harm nor became on alcoholic in later life. There . . . them's my sentiments.' He poured a half glass of wine. Jane observed the care, the predicament, the fun made of the issue, and a seemingly practical solution. Humour and games and care were quite obviously not uncommon between these two.

When Jane left, she had Jess's telephone number. Luckily, having no school duties after classes on that particular evening, she rang Jess early next morning and said she wanted to speak with her urgently. They agreed to meet at the Cottesloe cafe on the corner near the hotel facing the beach.

They met; and the impact of Jane's appearance struck Jess like a blow; just a pink shade on her cheekbones was all that remained of colour on her face. Jess could see that she was wound tightly in some strong emotional binding. She realized that there was something, which Jane thought exceptionally important, that she had to say; something important was so obviously, painfully disturbing her.

As Jane began to speak, Jess could only watch her eyes, the pallid face and the acute tension of her body.

'Jess, I don't know where the start point should be, but I want you to hear a bit about me before I make the statement I must make.' Jess suddenly felt a shiver of fear. 'As I was growing up and into adulthood, I had no idea what love really was. Even what I'd read in romances, novels . . . left me uncertain about whether what the author was describing was what I imagined love to be. I found it difficult to recall or visualize any married couple I had observed who appeared to be in love in the way that I imagined it should be. Most couples or people who were described as lovers showed each other . . . at the most . . . only what I had in mind as fondness.

'Then when I was a woman and met the man Roddy Mckenzie and experienced being in his presence with others, and experiencing the heady happiness of being with him alone . . . doing anything . . . being anywhere, I knew that I had discovered the secret of the riddle. I fell madly in love with a lovely man. With Roddy, I felt . . . complete . . . whole. . . liberated . . . light.' She began to cry as she railed at herself in that memory. 'But I was a stupid. . . arrogant. . . prejudiced. . . idiot and chose the shadow for the substance. When Roddy went away . . . I . . . never . . . ever for a moment experienced that exhilarating, transporting feeling again. With Roddy, I had a sensation of the exquisite . . . something that Roddy had given me that took me beyond just being a woman but a woman in total control of her "self", I felt I belonged with him and that he would never take away those feelings he had given me. Then he went away. He left me to find for myself my flaw . . . the flaw that he knew would make our lives totally unlivable. He gave me all those treasures never elsewhere to be found: and I would find them . . . by social pressure. . . not enough. Good God, when I think of it, I collapse in shame and self-hate . . . pearls before this swine. I know he loved me, and because he did, he did what was painfully right.

'Dear . . . dear Jessica, all these treasures are yours now. God, you must know how much he adores you. You too are a rare person. Ask him to marry you. . . at once, Jessica. . . please. Release him with honour from his stoic compact. Save your love and save him . . . please, Jessica . . . please.' She had seized Jess's hands and now was squeezing them quite painfully, adding beseechingly, 'And save me too.'

Jessica came round, put her head on Jane's shoulder, and gasped, 'Oh, Jane . . . and I thought you had come to take him away from me. It must have been a passage through hell for you to do what you so bravely did this afternoon. You will know, because I know now the beat of your heart, that I can feel how much having to say all those words must have drained you. Come home with me . . . we can prepare a little meal to have together . . . you can borrow a jumper . . . it's beginning to get cooler.'

Whilst this pulsing vein of purification was burning her mind and body, and before she would break down from the torment, it was imperative that Jane see Roddy too—today!

'Jessica, I am sorry, but my organisation skills have been somewhat proscribed by knowledge of local geography. I needed to see Roddy today too, and without knowing what would happen with us . . . it was just as urgent that I should talk with him as with you. I know it's like a scheming intrusion into your lives, but can you see how much pain it might avoid if I can tell him that he must marry you? Can you trust me to do that without hurting him? Jessica, I really can't bear to carry these feelings around much longer . . . and you two really do need to act quickly. The only place we could arrange to meet was at his flat. Will that be too difficult for you?'

She looked at Jane and told her eyes, 'I'll cater for three.'

Roddy had said to Jane that he would 'be waiting at six, at six'.

When she arrived, she saw that Jess's door was closed and Roddy's door was open. Jane knocked and called, 'Are you in, Mr Mckenzie?'

'Aye, come away in. How was your day?' he asked as she stepped into the room.

'Harrowing.'

He drew his head back and said with concern, 'Oh, I'm sorry to hear that. Go you and sit down', he said in gentle command, 'and I'll bring you a dram of your chosen kind.'

'You know', Jane said quite seriously, 'I've just realized what people might mean when they say: "I need a drink." And when you say a "dram", I think of whisky, and when I say whisky, my brain connotes a single aged malt, and I wish I could be as sure as other things of importance about which I'm confoundedly uncertain, I'll wager you've got one.'

'That was a certainty and you would have won. Would a Laphroaig be suitable?'

'Beggars can't be choosers,' she said, matching what she knew well was the McKenzie humour and indicator of friendship.

'I've had a good day, but if I've got someone drinking my best whisky, I'll just have one too so as not to lose all my stock in the displenishment caused through overgenerous hospitality.'

They raised each an Edinburgh crystal glass and the Mckenzie led with 'Slainte math', and she replied, 'Slainte mhor.'

She sipped and put down her glass. He could see that like a horse before a jump she was gathering self-control and strength.

'Roddy, I've only seen you and Jessica together last night when we talked mostly about me; but even that may have had some educational value. I learned something breathtakingly, beautifully heart lifting. I was close to and could observe two people who absolutely adored each other. There was a melody in their words and a study of people in love in every glance, a sublime knowledge of their physical and emotional locations. Roddy . . . Jessica Innes adores you . . . needs you . . . wants you, she is bearing deprivation with grace, but I am sure not without pain . . . as I see her pain, I can imagine yours . . . because you love her just as deeply and feel the pain of disjuncture with equal intensity. Roddy, time is rushing away from you both and away from a newborn child. I am a gross idiot in some regards and certainly have been in particular regards, but as I wagered on the whisky, I would wager with the same outcome that you already love that expected child and think of it as yours. Roddy, please waste no further valuable love, ask Jessica to marry you. She will know you are not breaking your bond, and if she does think so, she will know that you love her more than honour itself.'

The Mckenzie stood up bent over Jane as she sat and kissed her lips. 'Jane Dugal, you are exposed as the angel I always knew you were. Thank you for the leap you took despite your nervousness and taxed temperament.' He paused and, keeping her in his gaze, asked, 'Please, miss, may I leave the room? Here's the bottle. Go for displenishment. It will be my joy that you drink it under my roof and there's more in the cupboard. Should I not return very soon, you will have to check the regimental aid post.' He left and went next door. He was shaking with nervousness and delight. What was he going to say? An enemy with a weapon ten feet away aiming to kill him was less daunting. 'Ease the reins. Let your instinct guide you.'

He knocked on Jess's door and called, 'May I come in?'

'Aye, come away ben. Before you start, may I tell you Jane is coming for supper, and if you'd like to come, I'll put more water in the soup.'

'Yes, Jess, thank you, that would be nice . . . Jess, I love you,' he uttered in wide-eyed relief of having heard his voice making that longed for utterance.

She was trembling, but she sensed a game.

In a failed show of nonchalance, quickly, before he could gather his wits to say more, she said much more softly than she had attempted to sound, 'Yes, I'm aware of that, but before I say another word, I want to ask you a question.'

'Ask, ask, please . . .'

'Roddy Mckenzie, will you marry me?'

That poor unborn child was in danger of having its nest bowled from the bough by the onrush of a strong man overcome by desire to put his arms round the tree. But even in this nigh uncontrollable urge, he squeezed as high up on the bole a he could.

'I will . . . I will . . . oh . . . yes, I will, darling, darling Jess. Thanks for pulling me out of that life of my own prohibition. I couldn't have you feel I wanted to marry for any reason other than love and adoration my treasure. I've loved you every minute since I saw that sad face in Rose Bros. But I wanted you to be sure I didn't love you because you were so sad . . . out of sympathy . . . I loved you when you were throwing snowballs at me in Amsterdam, and when I saw you in Hong Kong and how I was vicariously happy for you when I saw those people who were my friends, good people whom I respect, fall in love with you too. And now I have you near me. You will never believe that I did not contrive this, but now I know you won't and I don't know whether it matters . . . Jess, stop me prattling . . . I've already begun not to make sense.'

She put her finger on his lips and said very quietly, 'I'll take my finger off if you promise to say what you first said, just once more. Promise?'

He nodded; she took her finger away and held his hand. He said quietly but firmly gently and looking at her with his soul in his eyes, 'Jess . . . I love you.'

She gently put her arms around him and put her head on his chest and gasped and cried, 'Oh, Roddy . . . Roddy Mckenzie. . . my dearest man . . . I love you too.'

There were seconds when they did not speak, then Jess said, 'C'mon, Roddy, we must go to poor, wonderful Jane.'

'Jane, I'm sorry we're so selfish and just left you alone,' Jess apologized. She looked at Roddy and back to Jane. 'We'd like to tell you something. We are going to be married.'

Even in the tension and the explosion that was taking place inside her, Jane saw a game as the Mckenzie surely would. 'Pray tell me', she asked, 'to whom and when?'

Roddy said, 'Well I'm going to marry Jess.' Jane turned her eyes to Jess who, on that cue, said, 'And I'm going to marry Roderick Fraser Mckenzie tomorrow if possible.'

Something resembling a rugby scrum ensued with arms seeking holds and heads near heads and dodging, with the added complication of attempts to place congratulatory kisses. Laughter and tears were simultaneous. There was relief of tensions, there was love, and there was great joy.

For the Mckenzie and Jess, the first priority of the next morning was to inform the Sydney people; Doris, and Mauri. Jill would best be telephoned after work. Doris was ecstatic.

'I'm so happy for you, my darling boy, and I won't deny that had kept alive a hope that you and Jill might get together. But your heart has decided; and you are going to marry a delightful, wonderful person. I shall love her as I love you, my Roddy Mckenzie. That little baby is going to be the most fortunate child. Don't you dare neglect me and think that marriage absolves you from caring for me! Is Jess there? I'd love to speak to her.'

First, he replied, 'Thank you so much, Doris. Logic may underlie decisions, but love will always hold the trump card. I could never neglect you. You will always be a star in the galaxy of the ladies I love. Yes, Jess is here, I'll pass the phone. I'll say oo-roo when Jess and you finish.'

'You're going to marry my darling boy, now you will be my darling girl. You're a lovely person, Jess, and you deserve each other. It will be wonderful for your little baby to have Roddy for a dad. Marriage is a busy business and rearing a child complicates things, but please, Jess, try not to forget Mauri and me. We do care about you . . . and love you lots.'

Madge was at work when he phoned. She was overjoyed by the news. Janet McGillivray, Ethel Treloar, and Iris Jones were joyous and congratulatory when both spoke with them.

Yesterday they had run a short rapid and in their river of life and rounded a bend; they sensed a great adventure to come, out in that broad sweep of a future whose horizon would continue to precede them forever and forever until the end of their lives.

There was never any discussion or 'by your leave': the wedding would be held at the McGillivray residence.

Madge, Janet, Jane, and Jess—with long-distance suggestions, guidance, and constant liaison from Doris, who promised to come over a week before the service just to help with last-minute detailing—undertook every detail of the matrimonial ritual including the religious part, even to the point of calling upon the services of a Presbyterian minister renowned for the brevity of his offices, the school chaplain of PGC, to elicit the nuptial vows, and having heard them, complete their registration and bless the union.

Janet McGillivray was in her element; she delighted in the prospect of having Doris resident with her to share the heightening excitement until Mauri would arrive on the day before the wedding when she would move to the hotel. Mind you, all of their efforts were undertaken for no other reason than to relieve Jess, with her parturition now just weeks away, of concern and over-excitement; besides she had her music pupils to consider.

Of the NSW contingent, Bruce Lockwood and Amy wanted to stay in an Australian hotel so they were berthed at the Highway with the McPartlands who were themselves wedding guests. A miracle of personal sacrifice that Bert would come: he had a horse starting at Belmont. The Lockwood's wanted to see the Karajini gorges since they had come thus far. This was arranged by Bert McPartland so that they flew there on a private aircraft and actually stayed on Karajini cattle station. Kate and John Wilson stayed with Rhys and Iris Jones who had wanted to host a couple or more.

Among the wedding guests, now here, now there, always in a talkative group, always very visibly enjoying himself was Reo Ito, always happy to be near Roddy Mckenzie with whom he had worked so ably and enthusiastically on the Ugojim deal. He continued to be a conduit leading back to Asahi Ishikawa through the Japanese trading bureaucracy, sending reports on Ugojim Aust. Pty. Ltd.; and always feeding back to Roddy any whispers of new mining plans or major structural developments in Australia; always on the political network, always benefitting his friend Roddy; and always a sincere friend of Rhys too. He played good tennis and golf, was a welcome hand on sailing crews, a lively companion on fishing trips, and often bumped into in concert foyer crowds. Bruno Brunsden was there too, feeling very pleased to know that the trust he had put in Roddy in taking up the Cocklebiddy work had proved so well founded and was leading to a great future for him and certainly a long-term likelihood of work for Main Roads far into the future.

As she stood in the garrulous gathering at the wedding of Roddy Mckenzie and Jessica Innes, in that lovely house by the Indian Ocean, Jane saw, in a cleansing mental emetic of realization, the contrasting health of this group with the false, insincere, malevolent, carping social gatherings of her past experience. There with innate, attractive aplomb, was the gardener's son from Woodend; and there a brilliant and beautiful concert musician, emanating natural ease and charm daughter of a damned near subsistence tenant farmer, both adored and included into their society by people who had succeeded and were succeeding, in their lives, not only by the measure of making lots of money, but by living in continuing progress, personal growth, loving, sharing, caring. Now she, Jane, had been drawn by them, on sincere invitation, into their society. 'Don't look back, Jane', she was saying to herself, 'Use regret as an impetus to *your* progress, seize this invitation to enlarge your life: absolve yourself. Test your new vision: confirm its reality. Speak to anyone, to the person next to you.' And that would be the end of her regret. She turned to the short man standing within touching distance to her left. He was in a fine-looking double-breasted dark navy suit with thin faint grey stripes about an inch apart, his black shoes were literally sparkling and a university tie was prominent against his crisp white shirt. His face was more ragged than rugged and over and out of the most baggy, crumpled surroundings sparkled two of the liveliest cerulean eyes she had ever seen.

'Isn't this the most beautiful wedding reception . . . such loving guests', she shared what she was thinking with him, 'I'm just so happy for Roddy and Jessica.'

'Yes, I agree with you. I just think Roddy Mckenzie deserves all of this . . . and the respect of the folk here now, and there's many more that would want to be here, all wishing him well. If there's a better bloke than Rod Mckenzie, I've yet to meet him. Do you know him well?'

'We played together as little children, but by circumstances beyond my control, our paths diverged. I came to know him too late. I had to get to know myself first and that was a long hurting experience. I met Jessica only days ago. She's a rather wonderful woman, and she and Roddy are, as we say in Scots language, *sib*, they're of the same spirit. They will from now love each other until the end of infinity.'

Simon, as usual, had listened beyond mere hearing. 'My god', he declared, 'that's pretty powerful language. What's your name if you don't mind my asking?'

'Jane Dugal. And yours?'

'Simon Fraser, I work for Roddy at Mckenzie and Ugojim,' which was all she learned about Simon on that day.

There was a buzz going round about a Flotilla heading for Garden Island on the following day. Lynne came along and introduced herself to Jane.

Lynne: Have you chosen to sail tomorrow, Jane, or go in a stink boat?

Jane: Oh . . . I haven't been asked.

Lynne [to Ann who was with Jane]: I'm crewing for the Mckenzie and Jess.

Ann [immediately suggests]: Plum could probably do with crew for tomorrow. [to Jane] Why don't you and I go with Plum, Jane? Come, I'll introduce you. [Plum with his wife Joyce was with Rhys and Iris Jones.]

Ann: Hello [deferentially to her seniors], have you met Jane Dugal yet?

Plum: No, dear Ann, I haven't . . . but I think I'd like to. [Offers his hand] I'm Harry Plumridge . . . and may I be the agent of introduction to Mr and Mrs Rhys and Iris Jones and Joyce Plumridge?

Jane [having shaken hands]: How d'ye do? Isn't this just the most delightful wedding? And Mr and Mrs McGillivray's house is the perfect setting.

Iris Jones: And Janet and Mac are the perfect hosts which, as a friend of Roddy's you're sure to find out. They think the Mckenzie is the unbeatable champ . . . tell you the truth . . . so do I.

Ann: Plum, do you need crew for tomorrow?

Plum: Yes, if they can stand the sharp edge of my tongue an' maybe the cat, and can keep an endless supply of grog coming up from the 'tween decks.

Ann: I was going to suggest Jane.

Plum [regards Jane with a ferocious scowl]: Have you been before the mast?

Jane: Aye, master . . . an' more'n two year. I was with the admiral when we drummed them up the channel. Ah [scowl as she recalls something horrible], ah, let me tell 'ee captain, when we was slung atween the round shot in Nombre Dios Bay . . . ah, . . . but that's not for young ears.

Plum [to Jane]: Our ship *The Jolly Roger* be green as grass below, her sticks hardly fit for stirring grog, but [Plum turns and smiles at Joyce] she's carried us many a happy mile. We're at Freshwater Bay. Easy for you to get to?

Jane: I'll leave my gig at home and come on my peg and my leg. At what berth shall I find the *Old Superb* lying?

Plum [laughing like a suddenly unchoked drain—turns again to Joyce]: Heavens above, dear mate, what have we got here?

Joyce [immediately]: The ready-made sailing companion [she exclaims, then asks] Jane, are words your business?

Jane: No, Joyce . . . symbols. I'm a mathematician.

But Joyce and Plum knew that here was a literary mind, a store to be drawn upon and enjoyed in the future.

The newlyweds, full of joy that their guests had delighted in the unusually brilliant, exotic food (think Doris), and wines that Mac had invited to his cellar for the short storage of a day; and the even more exotic selection delivered by an agent on the Mckenzie's behalf, having said their thank-you's and farewells left the party as bride and groom, and walked contentedly, hand in hand to their adjacent homes in that little block of flats on Avonmore Terrace.

They sat in Jess's sitting room and cuddled and talked, kissed and talked, about the dizzying wonder of the day, which for them was a scratch upon the slate of time that marked a new, dimension of loving each other that was free from the limitations of a noble pact which now could be happily forgotten. 'Good night, sweet princess, may angels guard thee,' he finally said, and withdrew to the flat next door.

The morning easterly breeze was still in, and when the mast was back up again, having passed under the road and rail bridges which spanned the Swan River upstream of Fremantle harbour. *Satori* set a spinnaker, powered through the heads and trimmed for Garden Island. Plum noted this act of bold enthusiasm and said to his crew, 'That wind won't last for much longer, we don't really want to be repacking a spinnaker after seven minutes; but to use what there is of it we might just pole out the headsail.' Ann and Jane were onto the task and had the big headsail out on a spinnaker pole in seconds, set and pulling well. However, as Plum had predicted the easterly didn't last and *Satori* quickly and faultlessly doused her spinnaker and it disappeared below to be passed through a bottomless bucket and stowed in its bag. *Jolly Roger* slipped its pole aboard, laid it in its deck position, trimmed its headsail in the now non-existent breeze, and awaited the arrival of the sou'-wester when they would finish in Herring Bay on a gentle reach.

When the Flotilla reached the bay, the motor boats had put their anchors down and three had rafted up; Mac in the centre with Rhys to starboard, Peter Gill and Madge to port. Roddy set *Satori's* fluked Danforth anchor on the clear sandy bottom and hailed Plum on his arrival, to raft up if he so wished. So when the fenders had been slung in position and springs and mooring lines made fast, the question was, 'Your place or mine?' But before a decision could be made a sleek royal pinnace which had been sculling around safely clear of the yachts came alongside. 'With Captain Jones's respects, he wishes to invite the skippers and crews of *Jolly Roger* and *Satori* aboard for a pre-Tiffin peg or two,' announced Peter Gill, handling the pinnace, Rhys Jones's tender. Having stepped easily across from *Satori* to *Jolly Roger,* Jess was carefully put aboard over the square transom of Plum's yacht, *Satori* being a double ender would have meant Jess's having to go over the side. The skippers, having to wait for the next pinnace trip, consoled themselves with the icy contents of a bottle of Emu Export.

It was a perfect autumn day; with a comfortable sunny temperature of 75-degree Fahrenheit, the lower cloud comprised scattered bits of cumulus and very high above ribs of stratocumulus giving the shape of a vast vaulted ceiling to the pale blue sky, the wind may have risen to eight or ten knots but the large cruisers, their bows to the breeze provided a lee. Peter Gill, who drops a fishing line whenever he finds himself on a piece of water, already had a dozen garfish aboard before the circling school off his port side, the school moved in its circling action elsewhere. From then on he caught sand whiting and others joined in the fun. There were bubbles galore to drink which somehow the ladies seem skilled at sipping while watching and feeling tensions on a fishing line. The Treloars were talking about football, the finals would be played quite soon but there was talk of food, wine and music with Doris, Jane, Joyce and Plum, Lynne, Ann, and Roddy heavily involved; but people drifted in and out of sub-sets of conversations. Mac and Rhys had taken responsibility for bringing the OBH mob, and Claude was an enthusiastic and erudite participant eager to hear every word that Jess contributed. It was a conversational cornucopia. What a glorious day it was in every conceivable way! Since the inclusion presence and of Jane and Jess was competed for, nay, *demanded* by Claude and Doris, they were taken aboard Mac's big launch for the return trip, getting *Jolly Roger* home to Fresh Water Bay was left to Plum and Ann, while Roddy and Lynne easily managed *Satori*.

There were cars coming from and to yacht clubs up and down the Swan, finding their way to homes and reuniting families, returning crew members as required. For all there was the prospect an early start to the next work week.

Jess had been taken to her door by Mac and Janet; after putting away the fresh fish, some her own catch, she sat down to a gentle background of music from the ABC's classical music, talks and news station, and was sitting looking out at the fast darkening sky going back over the experience of being amongst those very pleasing, bright people. Roddy absolutely swam in their depth, so she felt reassured and supported in the instincts to happiness that she had begun to feel so immediately on introduction,. She now knew the OBH mob and their culturally sophisticated wives who combined their arts and musical orientations with a deeper interest in human life and how practical needs and aspirations shaped their activities and their behaviour. They each, without fanfare, had a chosen a cause in some aspect of community help; the young, the ill, the aged, the especially talented, and the genuinely poor. And except for Doris, who played tennis only if someone was absolutely desperate for a partner, each had one favourite sport but could usually happily partake of another. This applied equally to the men Frank Dalby and his wife played lawn bowls, Claude played golf and tennis, Freddie played any game which involved a ball of any shape. Except for the pulmonary exercise of barracking for the home rugby side, Plum no longer trotted onto the field; but he loved his old *Jolly Roger* and sailing and caring for her wooden hull and rigging kept him exercised and fit; and, he was more than just a 'good cook'.

They continued, when Roddy came home, to sit happily recapturing experiences of the day and Roddy said, at one point, 'I continue to be surprised by some new content from Claude's capacious cranium; it's not that he just remembers a host of random facts by date, or about a historical event, he can always give a small dissertation by way of explanation or context about any of the subjects that have arisen amongst us. I do believe he'd never say anything . . . except . . . . "I don't know", when something he knows only a very little about is put to him.'

It was time for bed. Without any previous discussion, but from sensible tacit agreement, it was decided that until the baby was well and truly born, Jess should enjoy by herself the liberty of spreading herself and wriggling for comfort in her little double bed. Roddy's early bed, early rise regimen, absences to the bush, and his size would make sharing a bed at this point quite uncomfortable at a time when getting what sleep they could was important to their spiritual, mental, and physical health. It also meant that he had better get cracking on the planning and execution of blending the two flats into one larger apartment, which was the reason he had bought the two flats in the first place and which he had delayed when Jess's needs, and his offer, had eventuated. The tactile pleasures of their proximity were not neglected. Spontaneous times arose which allowed them to kiss and caress and to fondle; when he could smoothly touch his hand across Jess's taught belly to let the baby know he was there and in the proximity of him and Jess, let him or her sense the sounds of his voice; he wanted, and Jess wanted the baby to know him.

The natural process of pregnancy was rapidly moving to its climax. Jess's GP had put her in the care of a quite famous obstetrician who had reserved a private room for her confinement in Lucknow Hospital at Claremont. There was a perfectly adequate big sofa in Jess's flat which the Mckenzie could use as a bed for the early days after the baby's arrival and his or her advent.

It was only a few days after this when Roddy had already discussed the plans for his enlarged apartment to be thought of differently now through the much more experienced eyes of a married man with children to consider, that Madge fielded a call from Graham Knight who said that a house had come on the market which Roddy might well be interested in. When he heard where the house was, Roddy was more than just interested.

The flats in which in Jess and Roddy presently lived allowed them to see just the ocean and Rottnest but not the nearer seashore, because the roof of a rather large old stone house immediately in front of them blocked the view. Graham Knight, on the Mckenzie's immediate demand, located the keys and had the family's solicitors' permission to view the property. The house had remained vacant while probate dragged on and the effects of the will decided upon by the benefactors. Two young people had received the house in share. They did not wish to share. It was a large house mounted on high sandstone foundations on large arches of skilled-masonry, two on each side, exposing a vast completely open space, allowing air to pass through and allowing ingress, certainly suitable for garaging. Above that were three floors with big windows onto wide verandahs on the first and second. There were magical views. Roddy was thinking that, what he was prepared to spend on the flats project could now be applied to the interior alterations of this residence. It had been put up for auction and passed in with no further offers made. Not only was the Mckenzie, now a married man with a wife and child, he was going to take on the typical young man's burden of a mortgage. Jess came to join Roddy as the keys were turned in the lock on the big timber door that had stared at the sea for fifty years. She had to trust Roddy not to over-commit but suggested to herself that if she got more students, or took an orchestra or teaching job, their two salaries may be adequate, including, of course, the rental revenue from the soon-to-be-vacant flats.

As with yachts, some will be bought only by certain kinds of people, so with houses, and it looked as if the certain kind of person had arrived to seal the ownership fate of this one. The young beneficiaries of the will had plans for their lives, which they wanted to get on with and in those plans was no place for an old stone house at Cottesloe. Graham, Mac, Jess, and Frank Dalby were called upon in conference and consultation. Their combined wisdom and knowledge of markets, clients, and Roddy's finances, resulted in an offer being made to the young people's solicitors. The Rural and Industries Bank were visibly enthusiastic about offering Mr and Mrs Mckenzie a credit foncier loan for the purchase of their house. 'Ah', thought Roderick gleefully, 'I won't be sleeping on the sofa for long! Put long-term refurbishment plans on hold for a while; just get two of the bedrooms, a bathroom, a laundry (and long clotheslines), a kitchen, and a sitting room quickly ready for immediate use— no painting or redecorating, essentials only—isolate the area from all other services if necessary.' They had vacant possession. Tradesmen were immediately tasked to check and ensure the correct functioning of gas, plumbing, and electricals; cleaners were hired to make it spic and span. The new baby, the new mother, and the new father would, when mother and child were ready to leave hospital, spend their first day and night of occupancy—together.

The house was named *Corriedale* which very much pleased Roddy and Jess; so in honour of the old station owner and the redoubtable Corriedale sheep, bred out of Lincolns and Merinos, simultaneously in Australia and New Zealand; bearers of fat lamb, medium/broad wool and providers of excellent meat, it would happily, with that name, continue to be known

———∘oo-⟨⊗⟩-oo∘———

So far as Western Australian business development was concerned most of his potential Pilbara clients were occupying offices in Perth CBD or inner suburbs, or at this time, worked out of existing offices in Melbourne or Sydney. Roddy was now your city businessman. He never at any time imagined himself in this role, but he had found the challenge of negotiating a deal quite exhilarating.

He was very unhappy about his continuing lack of representation in Victoria, and it was a strain on himself and Billy as they struggled to do Victoria justice, to do the tracking down and door knocking that was essential. Roddy had to go to go to Melbourne again where this time they may have found the man they needed. Roddy called on Billy and Mauri to make up the final selection panel, the preliminary selection process having been carried out by Chris Paton. Billy's back up in NSW was very new appointment. Billy wanted Roddy to come over and do at least three client prospecting calls with him; he wanted the new man to get further knowledge of Roddy and perhaps realize, as Billy had said to Roddy, 'Whatever a bloke knows and whatever his personal skills, there's something about the Mckenzie culture that can only be got from you.'

Queensland was also a burning issue. Ugojim had some big orders from Western Australia and Asahi-san was pleased; but he knew, and he knew Roddy knew, that total penetration was not going fast enough. Yet good men were hard to find and there was not time to breed them up. An objective was written into Roddy's planning and any process of appointing of new, permanent, operators 'was a search for another Billy Grey'.

His life as a newly married man with a new child would require careful, thoughtful planning. He had a belief that a father had a crucial role to play in a child's life, girl or boy. He wanted to ensure that he filled that role. 'Right, let's get Victoria fixed before the baby comes!' Roddy was all the time conscious that he wanted, very much, to be near Jess and the baby; it was important to him and his ideas of love and parenting. Planning and timing were going to be very important.

For Western Australia, there was great capacity in the management team; Freddie Treloar, Rhys Jones, John McGillivray, at the top end; Madge, Simon (more and more), Ray Robinson, Dave Oliver, and old Bill Gray at the second level. Their research and intelligence gathering systems were attracting more and more success. Hiring sub-contractors or 'contract-specific' operators was up to the folk on that second level; 'Get us another Billy Gray', he kept reminding them, 'keep your eyes on the contract-specific blokes' (the men who signed on just for the duration of a project). He saw, many a time, opportunities for Mckenzie 'juicy plums for the picking' everywhere he went, but now was not the time to be expanding Mckenzie Earthmoving. Simon was ready, he had completed his studies, but was he becoming too important in the Ugojim-Mckenzie headquarters to be whisked away to get Queensland set up? Unless—unless—Roddy could re-dedicate himself to Western Australia. With its enormous potential the Pilbara, was a critical market anyway—mm. But 'Fix Victoria first'.

Only a few evenings before he would fly to Melbourne to interview the final applicants for appointment as Ugojim representative for Victoria, they sat eating having their usual 'all topics considered' discussions, that Roddy's work load and the Victorian staff appointment was mentioned by Jess. Without his being specific, there was an unusual note of concern only lightly veiled in the few words he chose as a response. Jess registered this and tucked it away for a little later. After dinner when the dishes were done, they sat together on the settee drifting into pleasurable conversation while listening to music—not for proper listening—just selected to be pleasing to the senses.

With quiet intent, Jess stood up in front of him holding his hand, 'Come to the table, Roddy, I want to be a bit more comfortable and see your face while we're speaking.' It was obvious to him that she wished to say something important.

'Darling Roddy, I am not going to talk to you about how deeply I love you . . . you must know that . . . and anyway, I'd be incapable of describing how deep that love is. I believe you love me just as I love you. I know that you love my unborn baby. I know you believe very much in the important role and contribution of fathering to the life and development of a child as a new human being on its way to becoming a worthy adult. I know that you value human commitment to an ideal. I know that you have committed yourself to that ideal.

'Over the many thousands of years since mankind were hunter-gatherers, humans have had to work often excruciatingly hard amidst the painful effects of hunger, drought, starvation, cold, heat, attack by animals and human competitors, yet breeding pairs survived all of those difficulties . . . pairs. We are a pair, Roddy. We live in a world of greater sophistication and almost all of the elements of living have taken on different forms and are valued in different ways. Or they have been re-evaluated and often discarded entirely. But the essential imperative is still there. We must survive. As we have evolved, we have learned that we must survive spiritually and practically. For a life worth living, to be a deep, enjoyable, fulfilling life, these two must be bound inseparably. Difficulties will be there to be faced . . . one of life's certainties. You are facing great difficulties right now. When you make promises, strike practical business deals, when you choose to make caring for those you employ a matter of personal commitment; you place those deals and bargains in your heart, that abundant Roddy Mckenzie heart. Roddy, my dearest love, never, ever, for a fraction of a second feel that you diminish your love for me by the smallest fraction when you apply yourself to that other aspect of the world, the life we share—the life of work. Just as I adore music and playing music . . . I will want to do it at its highest level for the rest of my life. That love of music will never diminish my love for you . . . nor our baby . . . nor will loving my baby diminish my love for you . . . I . . . we just add some more love . . . not thinned . . . not diluted . . . just more . . . extra. You must get on with fixing the Victoria problem, you must get Queensland going. I know you know that that's an El Dorado waiting to be exploited and Asahi, right now will know that too. You must continue your respectful friendship with Asahi, you must continue your boys' club at the OBH, you must go to the Squadron and sail *Satori*. These are all important elements whose proportions must not be diminished. They are parts of the richness of our lives. I'm going into childbirth with a first-class obstetrician surrounded by the loveliest people on this earth. No woman has ever been so richly befriended. Roddy, go out there and do your duty,' she said vehemently. 'Concentrate! Concentrate! Concentrate! You know the music: just play it! I will be happiest if I know that you are doing that.' She took her hands from his and placed them on his cheeks. He did not move. He had not moved as Jess had been speaking. Hers were the words that had to be heard. Then he said with as much control as he could muster, 'If our baby is a girl, may we call her Helen?'

In Melbourne, Mauri had reserved a room suitable for conducting the three interviews in 'one of his hotels'.

The room was pleasant with a window to the sky, a table behind which Mauri, Roddy, and Billy would conduct the first part of the interview; for the second part, there were comfortable chairs with a small, low table with and an ashtray, beside each. Roddy believed that there was no value in false friendship or making any effort to put an applicant at an ease which the applicant was unable to provide for himself. Human care, civility, and good manners were the ground rules. If the man didn't get in there and fight to get the job, if he couldn't work out the psychology of the interviewers, if he couldn't present the unique selling point that put him far ahead of the other applicants, they would not be appointing the man they needed to further the interests of Ugojim. The morning was spent on three interviews and immediate post-interview discussions with each interviewer giving his own assessment without comment or interruption, then they made their joint assessment and decision. They had sandwiches sent up for lunch. They planned to complete their assessments by five p.m., board their planes, and get back home. Roddy would take their decisions and their notes on his five thirty flight and forward the results to the applicants next morning. One applicant had stood out. He had handled the panel skilfully and proposed by far the best solutions to the 'what-ifs'. He had a prepared plan of what he intended to do for Ugojim from the day of his appointment. Not only was he the best of the three, he actually did appeal to each of the interviewers which had shown up in their personal assessments. Billy would go back to Sydney with Mauri and catch the first ANA flight to Newcastle early in the morning. They knew when they parted that evening that their new Ugojim man, Victor Trumper, would be ready to start in four weeks from the date of resignation from his present employment. Roddy's plan was to get him over to Perth immediately he was available to undergo his Ugojim orientation. He would then go back to Victoria with him and begin a round of planned introductory calls. In the meantime, he would confirm Ugojim's interest in a property which had been an agricultural plant and machinery site just five miles west of Morwell on Prince's highway in the La Trobe Valley. The buildings were quite presentable and with Ugojim's colours and signage would look pretty smart. There being no option to lease it had to be purchased. The Bank of New South Wales, whose valuers had looked at the proposition, were happy that the price was right and that if Ugojim decided to move on, they should not lose money on resale. Next financial demands for premises would be for Queensland and South Australia. The spread of Ugojim Australia's capital and credit would be very thin. The solution to that problem was more sales—quickly! Would it not be perfect to get a Pilbara sale while Victor Trumper was here?

———∘∘∘❍❍❍❍∘∘∘———

The baby was born at dawn after Jess had spent the long night in labour. Roddy was standing by at the hospital. Jess was exhausted but fine when he saw her with the baby in her arms. He looked at the bundle and his eyes lit up as he joyfully gasped, 'Is she a girl?'

'Yes', said Jess, smiling, 'this is your Helen of Troy.'

'Oh, Jess, you little beaut', he cried, 'you've done it!'

Before going to the office, he took time to call Doris, who was delighted to hear the good news, and telling her that Jess had a bedside telephone gave her the number. He also rang Janet and Ethel.

After dashing up at mid-day just to check, he visited the hospital again at the end of the day to find the pair doing well, the mother had had a good sleep. Helen was feeding from an abundance of milk without digestive problems. Jess's beauty had assumed a different dimension, a look of rounder softness which seemed appropriate to a beautiful woman who was now a mother. The downcast woman met in Rose Bros., now seeming to have been so long ago, was someone quite different today. She was now a woman who had about her an aura of fulfilment and serenity. As he drove homeward, he thought it incredible that that meeting with Jess had taken place only nine months ago. It seemed as if a lifetime had been lived since then. He went to *Corriedale* and found that the two bedrooms and the bathroom and toilet had been cleaned to the tiniest detail which was very pleasing; the kitchen and laundry were yet to be done—plenty time for those. There were notes from the plumber and the electrician detailing what they had found and what they had done—good. 'Might just drop in at the OBH, let the boys know, and wet the baby's head.' The visit would also enable passing the news to the wives who no doubt would begin to telephone Jess and pay her visits during her short stay in hospital as Madge had already done after work.

There was a bit of tension being felt by Roddy about cash flow, and just when he had begun to think there may be a drought until the Pilbara opened up, Billy struck oil. A fax from Newcastle arrived in the Fremantle office of Ugojim. It was from Billy Gray. It was an order from Meadowlea Coal Ltd. a green field coal operation in the Hunter Valley. Billy had just sold twenty haulpaks, three top-capacity excavators, three different models of dozers, ten of the biggest road haulage trucks, and a shovel. Roddy was on the phone to Billy immediately. It was answered by the showroom assistant. 'Billy said he was expecting your call and that he would be at the Newcastle Business Club and to give you the number.'

Roddy called at once and a male voice said, 'I'll call Mr Gray to the phone.' Roddy was ecstatic and let Billy know. 'Billy, I'm so pleased for you, old son. What a triumph! You must be feeling highly chuffed. You deserved that order, Billy. I reckon you did a classic piece of work on that from the very first sniff you got. I wish I were there with you now. I'll let you tell your dad yourself, but I want to tell the others if that's okay with you? They'll be damned near as happy for you as I am. Anyway your beer will be getting flat. But before you go, speak to Mauri right away, and get him to have his lawyer draw up a contract to purchase and get Meadowlea to sign it. I'll immediately fax Mauri an exact copy of Meadowlea's order. We can't start shipping from Japan without a guarantee. Okay, the official Ugojim Australia order will go to Hiroshima as soon as I put this phone down. Soon as you've phoned Mauri relax and enjoy your celebration. I just wish I could be there with you, Billy. Well done.'

'Madge,' he called out. 'Come here, come here and hear this.' He told her the news. 'Isn't that great for Billy?' he asked with the excitement of a schoolboy.

'That's excellent: mind you, he deserves it. He worked very, very hard on that sale. And my god, what has it done for Ugojim Australia?'

'You can't imagine, all I know is it's going to speed up our growth . . . fund our expansion. Madge, you've no idea how happy I am for Billy. You're right, he certainly does deserve it. I wish I could be with him right now. C'mon, we'll get that order of Billy's off to Hiroshima.'

To succeed as Billy just had is not achieved by wishing and waiting for the phone to ring. The scraps and fragments of the intelligence picture have to be put together; the plan has to be followed with appropriate responses taken to the inevitable unexpected twists, turns, and new or changing information. Journeys have to be taken and people have to be met and negotiated with; tactics to bring about success in parts of the plan have to be developed and executed.

It had been a long patient track for Billy. He had been onto a company which had formed to operate a new open-cut coal mine on a green field site in the Hunter Valley. He was speaking with them just at the point where their shares had gone on the board. For Billy and Ugojim, it was the classic selling case study.

Since he had come to Newcastle, he had joined Rotary, the local business club, the Chamber of Commerce and had taken up golf for which he showed a notable aptitude. He had really good relationships with the local Fuson dealer and the Treloar Haulage manager, shipping agents, and the Harbourmaster who was a Scotsman and with whom he played golf. He had two vehicles for different uses depending on the level at which he was visiting an organisation and he dressed to match his Fuson pick-up or his classy Fuson sedan. Billy Gray and his work were a perfect match. He had been born and brought up into earthmoving plant, he was convinced on the quality of the Ugojim product, he thought his boss was magic and liked all the people he had worked with in Western Australia. He loved being with people, he loved being out and about and enjoyed and participated in the clubs he had joined. His move to Newcastle had just expanded his life and his way of living it. Mauri had been a great strength to him and a great, true friend. Doris had taken him under her wing and made sure he had a good time in Sydney doing the kinds of things he liked to do. That is the way Roddy Mckenzie wanted people's worlds to be.

At Ugojim Australia intelligence gathering for the Pilbara had already begun before Victor would come on board and accelerated thereafter. Asahi had pursued a report from Roddy which informed him that an American mining company was concentrating its exploration and sampling on one particular area of Pilbara leases on titles held by a local Australian. Asahi had confirmed that discussions were taking place in Tokyo between an American mining group, Sumitomo Metal, and Nippon Steel, about the formation of a consortium to open and operate a mine in the Pilbara.

Roddy must find a way into Sumitomo and Nippon Steel immediately: he must know the moment a deal was struck and a consortium formed. Some time would elapse from that point before the actual people who would make decisions on equipment purchase would be appointed. He would really like to know who those appointed were before they knew themselves. First, he took himself to the Highway on Friday afternoon. The geologists who were almost constantly tracking the Pilbara, and the drillers who were sampling all around, had come across Americans (and indeed were doing work for them) and Japanese geologists and engineers working on behalf of Sumitomo Metal. The 'geos' were talking about *pisolite* a good quality spheroidal crystalline iron ore which was being found on the table tops of huge mesas rising high above vast acres of flats left after the scouring out by rivers draining the ancient seas. He found out who were paying the cheques to the geos and the drillers. He began his first reconnaissances, penetrating peripheries and locating targets. This was a situation where Japanese equipment stood a very good chance against the predilections for brands, and use habits of the Americans in heavy plant and equipment. He had to locate and win over the Americans, as well as the Japanese, because they would finally decide what equipment they were going to buy because they were the miners, theirs would be the responsibility to develop and extract the ore and ship it out, they would manage the mining operations. Roddy, as Ugojim Australia Pty. Ltd., had to confirm precisely where the ore would be mined. He had to overcome any fears the Japanese partners may have that they may be seen as foisting Japanese equipment upon the American operators. He had to convince the Japanese that he was conscious that such feelings may exist and that, as a result, he would work very diplomatically to ensure that, in his duty to sell Ugojim equipment, he would sell it on its merits. He had to be known personally to the Japanese that he was in the field with the purpose of selling Ugojim equipment to the Americans. The Americans must know him too; and they must know that he was a practical heavy equipment man whose only purpose was to provide the people who were going to be doing the hard, dirty work of getting the ore from the top of the mesas to any planned port with the best equipment they could get. He needed to know what relationships Asahi had with Nippon Steel and Sumitomo Metal. He needed to have Asahi's full support in his approaches to these companies and Asahi must be intimate to Roddy's strategy. He would talk with Asahi about his need to have the help of Sato Tanaka in his meetings with the Japanese Pilbara venture partners. They were planning a port and a railway; so much was involved; so many contractors to find out about and to sell to. It looked like a day and night job for him. He knew he was going have to as Simon to go to Queensland. He knew he must not delay Victor's activities in Vitoria. He always gave Jill Lowing concise reports on the progress of Ugojim, his current activities and planning, and he gave her a specific briefing on his strategies on this latest front. She never needed a reminder that she was part of the intelligence network of Ugojim Australia Pty. Ltd. There was action for Mckenzie in all of this. He needed a rep for Mckenzie in WA.

He was impatiently waiting to have Victor come aboard. As well as drawing up a strategic plan for the Victorian operation, he must become totally involved in this new client deal. Roddy and Victor must go to Japan as soon as possible, and Roddy would let him remain there for the remainder of the month to be chaperoned by Sato socially, and given immersion and saturation in the Ugojim products. Roddy would ensure that before he met Asahi Ishikawa, Victor Trumper realized that Asahi was due the greatest respect as a very special kind of man; he must never, ever be let down or his trust betrayed.

Roddy had kept in contact with Piet van Eisen at Big Beauty and he and Bruno and the Collie coal miners would be part of demonstrations to the new client of Ugojim equipment at work and get reports from users about their experience. Now, as a result of Billy's success, they would also be able to see Meadowlea and the big bright orange Ugojim equipment.

The speed at which events in the life of Mckenzie occurred, originated in him a developing talent to store the smallest alterations in the kaleidoscopic scatter of changing elements and images which bombarded his brain. This talent supported a sense of reasonable continuity through an ever altering maze. The salutary, comforting growth and development of his marriage, the growth and development of Helen, Simon, Billy, Madge, Ray, Dave, and Bill, and soon, he hoped, of Victor, of Ugojim, of Mckenzie, of the states one by one, of their network of intelligence, and good relationships all around were all abounding evidence of the goodness of life. He was in that life, a sensing moving part of it: he must neglect nobody and nothing, nor must he miss or become blasé about any fragment of its scattered, wonderful variety.

He had not forgotten that life, as he came to realize it—as it became real for him—had taken its shape from a changing tack. Changing tack; the going-about of a yacht in the Mediterranean; the conviction of Erik Barron all required a change of tack. Erik had seen and understood that the greatest barrier to a good life for Roddy Mckenzie was the schism of caste and saw a way to help him overcome that split. The barrier had been circumvented, it had not been overcome, or ever would it be, but that circumvention was enough, it was a gap in the enemy's wire overcome by throwing his body full tilt upon it, getting to his feet and pressing on. On the way, he picked up a plan of the minefield.

On the home front, planning had to be undertaken too. A new domestic regimen would have to be developed into which the requirements of three inexperienced people might fit with reasonable comfort. Babies had to be nursed by mothers; and in different ways by dads. Babies had to be scrutinized by dads attempting to absorb the wonders of this little living miracle. Little eyes as yet not seeing all, but sensing much; hands to be examined, very small to say the most, but accountably complete; ears and cheeks and noses and toes all there, nothing missing and nothing to spare. She was so quiet and only got noisy and crotchety as even a dad would if wind was trapped in his pipes. There was evidence that more than the milk of human kindness was passing through her tiny crescent corpus. That void inside would need replenishment for which young mothers have been from heaven sent. The eternal child in both of them responded well to the new one in their midst.

————∘○○-⧙◎⧘-○○∘————

That Roddy had continued onward so successfully through the minefield was because Erik had so clearly indicated the gap. Once through the gap, Erik knew that Roddy would be able to scale the encountered obstacles along the path. Roddy made clear in his mind that never would he resort to mimicry. He decided that he had no wish to deceive; that deceit is a complex, mind, and spirit-sapping process fixing ultimately on the most destructively deceived person—himself.

Erik had set Roddy on his development path now he was pursuing his own. Just as Roddy was dealing with venturers who needed to gather capital to fund their plans to form companies Erik had become one of those, seeking money to float *Stags Head Resources* as a copper ore producer with contiguous cobalt, uranium, and titanium, in the now 'province of Katanga' in south central Africa, the onetime Belgian Congo.

The researches carried out by Erik, and the late Bartolemeusz, had established certainty that no overlooked claimants existed. Nevertheless Erik had established an account, a fund into which, before profit, an amount of money and shares would be set aside to provide income for a legitimate claimant should one ever come to light. The investor capital was raised in Britain, with Nora Barron being of great assistance, in Australia where investment in mining ran in the blood, and in Japan whose need for minerals was ever growing. Nora had worked with Jill Lowing who had played an important role.

It had been Erik's objective to staff Stags Head Resources as a totally African operation. On order of priority of birth locations in central Africa, he would select the cream of applicants. However, if an African American, or an Ethiopian, or a Moroccan were a better candidate, he would be chosen before a Katanga. He scoured the British, American universities, and European universities for the best African graduates, threw baits into established mining companies in Latin America and Africa and Australia. Should a European applicant present himself or herself the same exceptional personal qualities would be demanded. He took Eve Arden with him as a mobile office to phone the London office daily, to record every interview and ensure that all documentary evidence was meticulously recorded and filed. His objective was to create the model African enterprise in both technical and human excellence. He and Eve interviewed far and wide from Buenos Aires Lorenzo Marques, Stockholm to Strathclyde, to Manchester, Birmingham, Arkansas, Tasmania, and Johannesburg. He had to create the major executive engineering and operational structure that would raise Stags Head from the ground to a fully operational, profitable organisation, a *toute vitesse*, but without haste; each decision must have been given deepest consideration, the best that Erik could apply, and the best applicant selected.

For operations manager, he needed an engineer, a psychologist, a tradesman, a mental gymnast, someone who could use a marathon runner's energy every day, day after day, who had the courage to make a decision which if wrong would bring the whole mining process to a grinding halt, who could condense a mass of conflicting factors into a whole that was finally interpretable in only one way. They found a man who had decided to turn an age-old underground mining system into an above-ground operation and creating a huge open pit mine of a magnitude never seen in the pursuit of gold anywhere on the surface of the earth. The cost would be enormous just to shift the initial overburden. But after a hundred other factors were astutely weighed and weighted, would combine to simplify the extraction, and strip thousands of pounds of expense from the daily cost of getting tons of ore and ounces of gold. He was the quintessential Australian of lore and legend, lanky, long, and strong with a ready smile twisted almost out of sight by wry humour, with crisp quips delivered in a language only to be heard when Australians are eavesdropped in conversation; adjectives will never attain to the pungency and the imagery of the well-turned phrases that are still whip-crack crisp. One look could turn a challenger to a fight into someone who decided that right now he needed to be somewhere else—mind you, had he decided to stay, the first few seconds of action would convince him he'd made the wrong choice. Tom McGowan knew nothing of Erik Barron: as Erik had to try to discover the essential Tom McGowan so had Tom of Erik. That they felt at ease with each other was because they brought their ease with them. Tom may have looked the taller of the two but side by side Erik was perceptibly the taller. Erik Barron was not a talking cheque book, a man who saw money first and attempted to fit the world around it. Barron played no psychological game of pretending understanding and equality. He made none of those hopeless, pitiful attempts at showing, without disclosing, the superiority

of rank and by inference of personal superiority. Tom felt that
Barron was without fabrication; or using the gulling, matey,
expression 'we'. Implicit in the discussion was 'I' and 'you' left
to be constructed to 'we' by the individuals, the realist adults
in the discussion, the vision must appear in the minds of both
to make it 'ours'.

Two mature men were talking about a task that was
worthwhile undertaking. It would require a big endeavour by
each of them, and together it would be achieved to the great
satisfaction of both.

'Tom, I want you and me to sit down together for a very short
time to talk together about what has to be done. What has to
be done is a huge task. I believe it is possible of achievement. I
know it is not going to be easy. The biggest weight of it will be
on your shoulders and on the shoulders of the chief mining
engineer and a third man will be another for whom it will be
impossible to write a job description. I have chosen you because
I think you are a good man,' Erik said, and he gave those words
a very special meaning that Tom had never detected in their
use before. Without any silly vanity in being so described, Tom
felt the transfer of an honour and an onus. 'And I've chosen
Josef Mosungo because I think he is a good man. Being a good
operations manager or chief mining engineer brings definable
measurable skills. Being a good man is just something identifiable
by some but immeasurable by most; there is no definition for
those men; it is something one just knows. I will tell you that I
searched far and wide for another man to do a very important
job. Henri Mnabeka is a doctor of great academic distinction
an agriculturalist, horticulturalist, botanist; but I wanted him
here with us at Stags Head for much more infinite qualities;
and it's because he has those very qualities that he wants to
come here. Here he has a world to build. In promoting human
well-being and development, he will create an environment
in which education in sciences art and engineering will be of
primary importance, but his burdens will include health and
hygiene, recreation from sports games and athletics to music
art and drama, all generically African; he will help initiate
market gardens and domestic gardens, layout the locations for

each house and design a human environment that works with the natural world. Sewerage and sanitation will have natural conversions from raw sewage via reed beds and trees, willows and melaleucas in flowing water. If, and when, he sleeps, he will dream with the spirits. When, as soon as humanly possible, we are all able to meet together. I want it to be there, in Africa . . . on the site where we shall design our futures. Then we can plan what we want to make Stags Head become.'

Only someone of Erik Barron's character could undertake the attempted transposition of the ephemeral nature of a grand dream into the accountable, dividend producing reality of a continuously functioning ore-producing and processing corporation, in the face of the turmoil of hate and killing, and political mayhem making mockery of reason; with extraordinary difficulties of transportation, the uncertainties of your product ever reaching your clients. He needed around him men of the right spirit—good men.

------∘∘∘⊱◈⊰∘∘∘------

Erik and Roddy had sustained a correspondence; a continuing exchange of ideas, aspirations, challenges; a shared world of determination to succeed in their realization of dreams. For Roddy, the advent of Jess and the baby Helen had added new colour to his dreaming; new directions for his planning; new inclusions, new emphases, new urgencies. It is possible that he would have found it perfectly suitable to live in and live out of his mediocre flat on Avonmore for an indefinite future; it provided all that he desired as a home and as a base, a store for his growing library, art and recorded music, a kitchen where he could indulge his growing pleasure in, and knowledge of, cooking. Its very smallness gave him time for his principal hobby—his work in Ugojim and Mckenzie. That was impossible now: but now there was Corriedale.

His Saturday morning judo tapered to nil, but he could dash down for a swim when he was at home. He could still enjoy *Satori* because Jess enjoyed the club, and the two could come aboard for river cruise picnics. If Jess wanted to crew in a twilight race, there was always a volunteer baby-minder. The farm was not yet playing the role in Helen's experiential development that he foresaw for it. And something had happened there that caused and accelerated a change of thinking about what it should become.

Mary arrived at Corriedale one day bringing some vegetables from the farm her face as long as a mile of bad road, ready to weep at any second. Roddy was at home and met her when she drove up. He went close to her and looking at her eyes and her face said quietly to her, 'You look very unhappy, Mary, something is very wrong. Can you tell me what it is?'

'Enid and I are going to have to separate,' she blurted.

Roddy probably did not hide his dismay. 'Good God, Mary, what's gone wrong?' he cried.

'She says the dairy and cheese making is getting bigger and busier and she wants me give up gardening and give her more help. But I love my garden and gardening. I want to do more gardening and less dairy. Enid won't see it that way. She says we'd barely keep the home together and wouldn't be able to put any money aside if we didn't develop the cheese making and goat breeding.'

'Mary, I don't want to sound heartless, but I see that as a solvable problem. I want to ask you just one question. Do you still care for Enid and would you want to go on living together if you could have your freedom to do all the gardening you want to do?'

'We share some very deep things. I can't imagine a life without Enid, but I couldn't live on that lovely land and just be doing cheese making and looking after goats. To look around me every day of my life and see that lovely land and just potter on it around the house in my free time would be a kind of hell. Enid doesn't see that there's money to be made from the garden. I haven't been able to begin developing it because of bloody cheese and bloody goats.' Her frustration was giving rise to anger now.

'If I could solve the cheese and goat problem and get you out on the land with a solid development plan backed by me, do you think you and Enid could make it up and get back to closeness?'

'Right at this moment it's difficult to say, but if we could live again as we did in the old hut, I know we could be happy again.'

'Mary, I don't like interfering in people's lives, but I care for you two and I'd be very unhappy if you lost each other. Would it be all right with you if I go and see Enid?'

'It can't be any worse, Roddy, if you think you can help, I can trust you, I know. Yes, please speak with her.'

'When do you plan going back down to the farm?'

'Very early tomorrow morning.'

'Okay, that gives me time. I'll go down and see her now. I'll just tell Jess. Cheer up; I'm sure there will be good news. I'll let you know when I get back. Are you going to be with your parents?'

He rushed upstairs to tell Jess what he and Mary had talked about. Jess did not want to come for the trip.

At the farm, Enid was in the cheese making room washing up. She was as dispirited as Mary, and fearful that because Mary saw herself never being able to go back to vegetable and fruit growing, she would hate it so much that she would go away.

'Enid, do you still care for Mary and want to spend your life with her?'

Now Enid, the strong-willed 'tough guy', was showing the power of her care for Mary moving within her. Emotionally she feared a parting.

'Right, Enid, this is what I'm going to suggest.'

He suggested that she immediately employ a full-time worker whose salary Roddy would provide until profits could cover that expense. She was to provide him with a plan for marketing development for her cheeses and stud breeding herd, with costs as accurate as she could quickly ascertain. He said he would be asking Mary to do the same for the gardening investment. He would change the concept of the farm to one where only weaner calves were kept there and the rest of the land devoted to harvesting high-quality meadow hay visually and environmentally rich in diverse herb and flower types; and after he and Mary had discussed it, the growing of fruit trees and aesthetic deciduous varieties. They would grow Shiraz and Grenache grapes from the best clones they could get and make wines with minimum human intervention. He would hasten to get a house built for Jess and Helen and another house, or maybe two, for guests.

'Enid, I won't stay longer now, but please get that employee as fast as you can and the plan to me, within a month from now.' His voice changed now and he spoke more slowly as he looked at her face. 'My fondest wish is that you and Mary should rediscover each other . . . and with the new work arrangements that you'll have a little bit of time to do other kinds of non-farm things which you can enjoy together.'

He returned to Cottesloe and drove directly to Mary's parents' house and there, taking Mary aside, told her what had transpired from his discussion with Enid and gave her directions in the same vein as those he had given Enid. It would have been impossible for Mary to rise quickly from that fearful depth of soul which had trapped her, but somehow she expressed in her face and her voice feelings that moved Roddy's heart, 'Thank you . . . so much for doing what you've done, Roddy . . . I certainly shall never . . . forget this. You are a very unusual person, Roddy . . . what a wonderful day that was when we met you.'

New events and the changes they caused happened so rapidly one on top of the other that the period from Helen's birth to her twelfth birthday was now available to memory only as fragments.

It seemed to have been in a distant past that a blond-haired little girl ran naked with other tiny tots laughing, yelling and screaming on the sandy shore of the river beach in front of the Flying Squadron.

From that same beach, when she was just new at primary school, she pushed out dinghies with other small boys and girls and learned to sail under the tutelage of old Hew Jarman. From the age of 5, she had begun to play the piano, the small grand which had been acquired for their totally sound-proofed music room under the house. It cannot be recalled when it was discovered that she had perfect pitch.

She had discovered her own process of learning by some instinctive process so that she enjoyed learning through inquisitiveness about any subject. Her parents welcomed her incessant questioning by which they too benefitted and never talked down to her. Fairies could be conjured up for delight in a world clearly known and understood as the unreal, the suspension of reality for the duration of the joyful—or scary—fantasy. And her parents asked her lots of questions too; particularly when she had posed one. She began to ask herself, 'Is there another question? Is this the question I should start with?' She learned how to tumble a problem in her brain to view it from different perspectives. She completed junior school with many awards one of which was a special prize for music which delighted her most. She accepted her abilities with aplomb and never had any notion of superiority. She accepted that some were envious of her success and popularity. She saw envy as a vile, corrosive characteristic curable only by its possessor: she found ways to ignore its manifestations. She was in the midst of all the girlish, childlike, and adolescent activities and energetically and enthusiastically revelled in sports, and was never a 'goodie-two-shoes'. It was no surprise when she was appointed head prefect of middle school. From her early hours of living, Helen looked out upon a sunny world across which clouds did pass—even if they hung around for a while. She was very much with her parents; acting, reacting, interacting. She watched her mother 'shmoozelling' up to Dad, she observed their eyes and faces and saw the flow of respect and affection that joined them. Those were the same looks that they shared with her. She saw how they sat and faced each other and how they could be serious when they wanted to make decisions, how they questioned each other, and how they answered. This perspective underlay Helen's consistent sunny, smiling disposition which was reflected back upon her upon her by young and old.

Flora had never seen Jess's little girl. The thought that taking a small child travelling was a joyless experience for a mother; and she could not accept the argument that a child of 8 years old benefitted more from travel than being in school. With Jess's blessing, Roddy hopped on a plane and went to England to fetch Flora for a visit; it was unsurprising that he also had a business objective. He wished to explore the possibilities in a newly developed rough-country vehicle. Before going up to see

Flora, he visited Winchester and said good-bye to the regiment. There being no further obligation under the National Service Act, he left his name on the Reserve of Officers List and 'retired' from the army as Captain Mckenzie, R. F. MID.

He went next to Ranelagh where he had a wonderful, joyous time with the Verneys. He regaled his old companions at the Barley Mowe with stories and descriptions about how much of his good fortune had begun here with them and how much gratitude he would forever owe them. He described his replicate bunch of good men at the OBH and how in similar ways they had helped him in his progress. He invited any and all, husbands and wives, to visit with them in Australia.

He was asked if he wanted to take the Alvis out for a spin, 'It's always ready for you, old boy!' So with the most delightful companionship of Miette, he took the opportunity to drive down to Cowes by winding lanes over fondly remembered ground. Hugh had excused himself from the uncomfortable lunacy of trying to find pleasure in driving an ancient car on a road which he had travelled a thousand times—in comfort. The little Alvis didn't make that much noise, as they purred along the roads through the chalky Hampshire lands covered in green plenty.

Miette was able to hear from Roddy the story about her lovely Jane in Australia. She was delighted to hear about how he had married Jess due Jane's adroit appeals to their senses and sensibilities. Still, there remained for Miette fringes of sadness: had he stayed, he might have saved Jane from the horror of that disgusting marriage. But by Jane's intervention, he married Jess who must be wonderful or her Roddy would not have married her. Oh, how beautiful she looked in all of the photographs, a talented musician. How triste that Roddy had not made her baby. And such a lovely child. Oh, how she wished they were all together here where she could enjoy them.

'Now look here, *ma chere madame* Miette, you and Hugh have got to come and stay with us. Jane lives nearer to us than the Barley Mowe to Ranelagh, we have theatre of course and a grand symphony orchestra; you may be surprised to see the quality of our talent in art, music and dance. *Eh bien*, you could easily recruit two, at least, worthwhile protégées.'

He had programmed enough time in London to go to the Naval and Military, eat a stodgy lunch and chat with some very old and some very new soldiers. He strolled up to the Tate, where there was time to view an Augustus John exhibition. After that, he would follow the worn tracks of exhausted hounds gasping for breath, spirits sagging from physical attrition, scrabbling back to a place that was well-known to them, there to let the tides of pain pass and rise to run again—or just to die. Platform 13, Euston Station. He heard the voice tones again. They stirred his heart, yet he knew that he had forsaken that land. He took the train from Euston, but he was not coming home, his new home was in a new world; a home quickly built from the materials of rich new experiences.

He found Flora was so totally organised and poised to leave, like a woman much travelled in strange lands that she might easily have been Florence Baker ready to journey further in the Sudan. She was full of excitement; her welcome to Roddy was brief, the first mention was of 'the bairn'. Still in her memory, clear in every detail, was of that night when the broken spirited Jess had shared the story of her tragedy. Yes, she had seen and enjoyed the frequently mailed photographs. She wanted to see and hear the wee girl. Jess McDonnell would look after the hens and the garden and come and stop some nights just to keep the house 'lived in'. Flora, though it would not appear so, was almost a rail travel novice. Her first journey under the roaring belching power of steam had caused her no nervous turmoil and getting on an aircraft for the first time was quite inconsequential; a minor though necessary part of simply going with Roddy to Australia to see that lovely wee bairn—and Jess.

At Corriedale, Flora stood on the second floor verandah and gazed out at the expanse of sky and except for the low line of Rottnest Island, the unimpeded view on the horizon, and said, 'Oh my god, it's so big, isn't it, Roddy?'

'Aye, it is mother. You could travel in a straight line from here and touch no land until you reached Africa.'

Soon, her perceptions became more focused on immediate joys; Helen, Jess, and then, in a turmoil of juxtapositions, Jane

Dugal. She found it so difficult to see in her mind the laird's daughter, here with Rod and Jess, all together, talking as if that line that had existed for hundreds of years with the purpose of separating them into their social levels in the shallow seas of human life, had been drawn away. How could you live without these natural separations? How would the world work? How would you know who you were? Flora's Jane, her daughter, had sworn! 'Mam', she asked, 'how can you believe in all that bullshit?' And her Jane knew. Look at her, vice president of an American bank; and putting gas in the Lodge house which the old laird couldn't afford to do. Sandy had marched at his laird's funeral; was it for the laird, for the regiment, or the shared horror of the Somme? It might be wondered whether the laird would have come to Sandy's funeral. Anyway the right folk came. And amongst them, scarcely to be seen in the ranks, marched Brodie of Brodie, the Earl of Leven and Melville and Colonel Baird. And after Sandy was laid in the ground, they came to the Seaforth Club, which the Forty-third Highlanders shared, to raise a glass to the fallen and the dead and to the men whose march to fate they would surely follow. The ranks were thinning. Of the Fearnas survivors of the Forty-third only a handful remained.

Flora spent every possible minute with Helen from her preparation for school in the morning and her arrival home at night. She grudgingly spared Helen to her homework because she championed its importance. The family took her everywhere, to dinners and barbecues, to the farm to the Ugojim showrooms; to meet absolutely everybody; every day demonstrating her amazing stamina. It was time to go and she forbade Roddy to leave work and waste time just sitting in a plane. The girls on the plane would look after, and she had her lovely Australian books to read, and Bob McGregor would meet her at Fearnas station in his taxi. She was adamant. That was that. She was appalled at what must have been the expense of the luxury class fare, but when Roddy told her that there would be copious good champagne being served as she flew, she was somewhat mollified and her brain could almost be felt thinking, 'Ooh, that'll be nice.' They promised to make a family visit before Helen moved to upper school. Roddy was allowed to accompany her to the doorway of the plane where the charming ladies of Qantas smilingly drew her into their care.

The time for a visit to Flora would be upon them and its delightful prospect was almost consciously thrust to the back of their minds each time they opened a new calendar to disclose another year nearer. There was no doubt that the traffic of the Mckenzie family's life would continue its enjoyable yet hectic speed.

Certainly for Roddy, the pace of development whirled about him. Each state had now had a Ugojim manager and three representatives, literally and metaphorically, flying around their states. These men had been selected with meticulous care and brought into the stream moulded, and groomed to fit the strong bloodlines of the Ugojim stable. Their success rate had been phenomenal and each manager was where he wanted to be, each representative was well rewarded, reaping the fruits of applied endeavour. The morale within Ugojim was almost palpably high, nurtured by Roddy's devotion to the well-being of all.

Mckenzie had grown to the size where it was thoughtfully decided that they could profitably halt and consolidate. In every practical sense, it had reached the point of manageability and input-output ratio that Roddy had aimed for even in the early days. A flexible multi-skilled team had been put together allowing Mckenzie to pick and choose the most profitable, future-ensuring, future-extending jobs. Madge was on the Mckenzie board, and although her role had been redefined, she was still intimately close to everyone in Mckenzie, knowing and understanding the people and every detail of company activity. Simon Fraser was group operations manager responsible, with Roddy, for strategy and finance of Ugojim, Mckenzie, and the equipment hire business and business development. Next, Simon had to join the board of the holding company which controlled the units as a group. With Madge and Ray and the unit managers, he was responsible for mine on-site and Leyton workshop service, and with Roddy for corporate development, recruitment, and training. The business was not top heavy and everyone had to work to the peak of every aspect to their capacities. For this, they were rewarded by living in a happy community of successful, committed, contented people, very good salaries and conditions of service. In his corporate role, Roddy was building for the companies and himself, security with growth.

The original Collie farm which was now, of itself, a comfortably profitable operation in which Enid and Mary, happy together, was each following her own favoured path. The property suited the needs of their enterprises and they were very happy to provide dividends for Roddy, Jess and Helen, their favourite people, whose goodness they remembered every day of their lives. In addition to the original farm, the Mckenzie family had bought further property around Collie and were profitably raising cattle for slaughter. They were also enjoying the development of a Highland cattle stud in which Helen took a particular interest. Jess was teaching violin and musicology in the music department of University of Western Australia; and possibly because she had no further aspiration on the academic ladder, enjoyed her students, the congeniality of her work group in the faculty and her work conditions. She still harboured ideas for a quintet and allowed herself to ruminate on how she could have the best of both worlds.

Erik Barron's home was now really at Lubumbashi, although he found it worthwhile to keep an apartment in Kensington for his frequent, necessary, London work visits. With only a little help from an African architect who had trained at Exeter University and University UCLA, he had created an aesthetically pleasing house which functioned perfectly on a flow-through of natural air, balanced and maximized light and shade, private and often needed public spaces, and rooms for guests. It was surrounded by a garden through which waste water and sewage was environmentally dispersed, selected fruits and plants were grown amongst a collection of ornamental species of which a few were being saved from extinction. He treated all needs of, and care for the garden with the greatest enthusiasm. He loved this garden to the extent of feeling, and indeed knowing, that he drew from it spiritual health and inner strength both of which were, in the gruesomely troubled times had been drained almost to the point of drying up. There were still and always would be problems. Was life ever different? But there were great satisfactions and although at times he wrestled with the idea that it smacked of lack of faith and disloyalty, he was building security for himself beyond Stags Head resources. On analysis, he really was at the point where there would be no danger to his personal financial security if he chose to change his life again.

———ooo-⟨◉⟩-ooo———

Inspector Colin Nicol had been working right up until his last official day on the pay strength of Scotland Yard. He was on a case which only one interview with the prisoner remained and Colin's iron core was stiffened for this final step. The arrest had been a fortuitous event engineered around a traffic offence in which the accused had very stupidly taunted hubris in his arrogance when a police officer had stopped him for dangerous driving. The accused had been driving very fast and he had been driving dangerously enough to cause the serious injury to the driver of another car. There was another person in the speeding car, a woman. The police officer had spotted the speeding car earlier and was making a cautious, silent, but fast, pursuit. Then the prang happened. The criminal's colliding car was able to continue and it did—very fast. That's when the policemen, having radioed for an ambulance and police on the scene, turned the noise on and raced to overtake the fleeing car which they very shortly did. The officers drove up and cut it off. They arrested the driver. The driver got out of his car and launched himself at a policeman and actually landed a punch. He was put under arrest. The arrested driver happened, by the bounty of coincidence, to be the villain on whose very last case Detective Inspector Colin Nicol was working. Colin had gone back to go over again some aspects of the file on Carl Caisson.

Nicol had wanted this man for all the death and misery he had caused by drugs, murder, corrupting officials, prostitution, protection rackets, circulating false information, fraud, and what was once called larceny. A charge on any one of these counts could lead to a conviction, but Colin wanted to prove the ultimate. He damned nearly had hanging evidence and this windfall would give him every chance to get it. The woman in the car was a good start point. Now that Caisson had been arrested, and because she just happened to have been in the car at the time, she knew that even if she disclosed nothing her future, to say the least, would be constrained. But she did know quite a lot. Some seemingly innocuous questions led to myriad data of dates, times, persons, items, locations. With what Colin and his team had put together already, it established beyond doubt that they had built a case for murder that was unbeatable. This last meeting with Mr Caisson who was a 'hard man' who could 'take it tough' would leave him little option but to answer and whichever way he tried to frame his responses, he would not be able to avoid putting himself on the gallows. His lawyers would be of little help to him now. The judge and the jury would decide. The conviction of Caisson led to another torrent of convictions of the lower echelons of Caisson's widely spread network of villainy. There were many whose anxiety could take a break, and they had Colin Nicol and his team to thank. There were others who would be duly nicked and do sentences of varying lengths. They, too, had Colin Nicol and his team to thank.

Inspector Nicol left the Yard with a feeling of satisfaction which would be shared by many who had for years lived uncomfortable, fearful lives.

Amongst the incredibly wide variety of horrid, vile human behaviours that many turn their talents and twisted morals to indulge in, Colin Nicol numbered amongst the lowest to be taking another person's life. No matter how poor, pathetic, and painful the lives of many victims had been, the final choice of life or death should have been that person's to make. Policing is policing and soldiering is soldiering and never the twain shall meet. Long ago and still in memory, this principle has made him ashamed and angry that a young man had been killed in Haifa in a corruption of policing.

A section of Scotland Yard, the Unsolved Crime and Open Case Squad had been formed to reopen and investigate unsolved cases. Nicol had decided that without all the trammels of main force policing, he could continue, while still legally retired and pensioned, to devote himself to duty in the service of that part of society, which was reasonable and law abiding, by bringing murderers to justice. It would satisfy, in an almost grotesque way, the intentions of those who, by choosing to take another's life, had chosen to risk their own. For villains who faced the hangman, Nicol believed that they had made their choice. He had a feeling of self-satisfaction in making his choice. It would counterbalance the slothful self-indulgence of the time he proposed to spend paying more attention to his friends, working on lowering his golf handicap and enjoying the world around him. Killers were obnoxious humans. That even one of them could not be brought to justice rankled him to the centre of his gut.

The evening train, the 'Clock', the 'Dinner', the speech by the chief superintendent, the service medal award, the drinks party with the yard detectives organised by them at an old favourite city of London pub, and Colin was on his way to a world that, until only in the last few months, he had never thought about. Even then he hadn't thought about it much.

Walking away from the Yard, he was joining London's throb of clerks and lawyers, jobbers on the stock exchange, civil servants and secretaries of state, and secretaries of Marks & Spencers, shop assistants with fantasies about a future: people who should be able to live their lives free from fear. Those must be good and pleasant lives, and though he did not yet have the slightest notion of it, thought he would be happy to join them.

Erik Barron was at Cowes preparing to take *Fear Naught* to Majorca with a crew of young adventure voyagers and where he planned to keep her moored while he returned to Lubumbashi.

A tall very erect man walked along the finger jetty at Cowes Corinthian Yacht Club, his relaxed pace allowing him to admire the handsome yachts. He stopped at the yacht *Fear*

Naught. There was a tall man on the bow bent over a swivel on a halyard fitting. He was pulling back and releasing the closing pin.

'Having trouble with the halyard fitting, sir?' the tall man called in a friendly tone across to the man on the foredeck.

The big blond man looked up and saw on the jetty a tall slim man clad in a three-piece suit of very lightweight tweed. He was sporting a brown trilby, a fine off-white linen shirt dressed with a Forty-third Royal Highlanders tie, purposely not tied in a Windsor knot.

'Yes. It's sometimes sticky to get open and it should spring closed. Damned nuisance, just at the moment, because when the crew come aboard tomorrow, I want to clear off for the Med. My Corinthians Club doesn't have jetties, so I've got this from a friend who's cruising to make it easy to get stores and gear aboard. I'll just put some "CRC" on it, that'll keep it working until I get the opportunity to put a new one on. The important point is that it stays shut. I'll just have to make sure we don't have to change head sails in a hurry.'

'Wear and tear I guess; and it's had to do some pretty hard work I imagine, if this is the *Fear Naught* of Fastnet fame?'

'Yes, this is the said lady, *Fear Naught,* an S and S 40.'

'She's very beautiful . . . she's a picture of strength and looks . . . we-ell . . . sea-tough. Might I ask if I may come aboard? I'd very much like a close look at a vessel with her record. I'll happily take my shoes off.'

'Hop aboard,' invited the tall man.

Barron could see that the tall man he was addressing was older than himself, but the words 'hop aboard' did not seem inappropriate.

'I should tell you before I do that I'm a policeman—retired from the force—but still active on part-time jobs—and drawing a little pay which is nice—but I'm doing it as a transition to the civvie life. I was Inspector Colin Nicol, now I'm Colin Nicol.'

British people are inordinately conscious of rank. Since they do not treat all people equally, they need to know each person's place in the pecking order to be sure how that person should be pecked. The manner of speaking, questions, idiom, and allusions are changed with great skill—sometimes even subtlety—to ensure that respect is not wasted on people of lower rank or caste.

'Come aboard.'

He slipped off his shoes, squared them on the edge of the jetty, put a hand on a stanchion post and lightly leaped over the fence, landed easily on the narrow deck which ran down the side of the cockpit, and stepped down onto the cockpit floor. 'Good morning, sir, I'm guessing you might be Major Erik Barron?'

'Indeed 'tis I, welcome', and he shook Nicolson's proffered hand. 'I have a tie like that,' observed Erik. 'Are you ex Forty-third Highland?'

'Yes, India, Egypt, Burma.'

'Chindit?'

'No, Imphal.'

'You'd better come below and have a dram.'

His tweed three-piece suit was indeed of lighter tweed than is more often seen and it hung on his lean frame in an intended tailored looseness; the shining moccasin shoes on the jetty were straight from the Via Veneto. He had taken his hat off and was holding it in a competent sun-browned hand. He was a picture of a scene from Scottish Field, or of someone in the crowd at a Lifeguards' race meeting or a polo game at Windsor. You would have to say his face was long and would in a few years be described as 'craggy'. Such a face could be solemn when required but the bright eyes and the shape of the mouth declared the man a 'good companion'.

They were almost exactly the same six feet two inches tall, and as they regarded each other over the binnacle and the helm, their eyes were at the same level.

'Thank you.'

Below, there wasn't the customary austerity of racing yachts and the compromise was a comfortable seamanlike interior. The glass-fibre sides had been covered with a skin of woolly looking material but the thick stainless-steel chain plates, demanding their own inclusion, were on comforting display. In the navigation station to port, there was a working chart on the table, compasses and a parallel ruler, and on the left top corner a fixed ashtray in which a Peterson pipe was held in a clamp. Beside this lay an opened packet of French *Gaulloise* cigarettes.

'I was going to offer you a smoke,' Nicol said, looking at the ashtray while he slipped a flat silver cigarette case from an inside pocket of his jacket. 'Virginia on the left, Turkish on the right,' he said, as he pressed the subtle catch which opened the case, and proffered it to Barron. A powered vessel had just gone by and now the yacht was hit and tossed about in the pen. Nicol had to drop the cigarette case on the table and grab hold of the post at its edge, there for that very purpose. As the yacht was beginning to settle Barron took up the case and selected a Turkish from the side where there were fewer cigarettes.

'How long have those Virginia been in there?' Barron asked, referring to the side which was completely full.

'Mm,' Nicolson murmured thoughtfully. 'I couldn't swear to that, but I've had the case for a long time. Have a look. It's a trophy of the hunt. It wouldn't show up that well on the mantelpiece, so I use it.'

Barron looked at the inscription: *From the OC, Officers, and ORs of B Coy. 2Bn. 43 Royal Highland Regiment to Lt. Colin Nicol, MID on his transfer to Palestine Police Force September 29, 1947.*

'Come and sit down and please call me, Erik,' he was saying as he handed the cigarette case back.

Nicol slid it into the chest pocket of his jacket feeling a very happy man. 'Objective achieved,' said a little voice inside him. While he spoke, Barron was opening an 'odds and sods' cupboard under the galley sink and pulled out an almost spherical container, an ash holder with a spinning opening and closing lid through which he poured some water from the galley tap. He placed it on the table and offered Nicol a chair which he unhooked from its secured position and they both sat down almost facing each other directly across a corner. 'I was in Forty-third Highland too—with a Chindit column in Burma and lastly in Korea.' said Barron.

'I knew you'd been in the army, but the newspaper I saw in Fearnas just said "in a crack highland regiment". I should have known.'

Barron faced squarely, with a conspiratorial look at Nicol's face. 'You're not in a hurry, I hope?'

'If I could stay, Erik, I fear we'd blether here 'til they played *Johnnie Cope*. But I must go and you must bide. I am—though but casually—an employed servant of the realm and I'm sure the beak would not be forgiving if I were found drunk in charge of a motor car. I assure you I won't forget your offer of such hospitality and contrive to find an occasion when I can take it up in earnest. Mind you—and let me hasten to add—only to demonstrate that your present offer of hospitality is not rudely scorned. '

'I'm very sorry too.' Then, with solemn, jocular drama and poetic cadence, he declaimed, 'But I'll make a point of keeping that bottle, even from those who might savour its splendour. And one day, between Last Post and Reveille, we'll blether it to its end.'

'Thank you for letting me come aboard this beautiful—and famous—vessel. It has given me more pleasure than you could possibly imagine. It was grand to meet you.'

Just as easily as he came aboard, he jumped ashore. He slipped on the shoes that were much too elegant for a policeman. Standing erect, and raising his extended right arm long way up to the brim of his brown Trilby, he brought it smartly, shortest way down, to his side. Erik, without a hat, pulled himself erect and his heels together on the cockpit floor. They regarded each other for just a moment, and turning, Nicol walked away up the jetty.

As Nicol walked away, it could be imagined that he felt as if he had drunk at least half that bottle of Islay Malt; and the pipes and drums in his head were playing 'The Black Bear'. Without actually touching it, he felt conscious of the silver cigarette case secure in his chest pocket. Kind fate, providing the little events, was on his side. He was a step on the way.

When the inspector so smartly at a military pace and, with a touch of jaunty parade ground swagger, marched up the jetty, Erik Barron wondered how widely the perimeters of coincidence can be extended.

Colin Nicol's return to the 'Dungeon' at the Met—the name given to the underground space allocated to the "old fellows' club", the people who were applying themselves to the solving of the unsolved—the Unsolved Crime and Open Case Squad—was undertaken at much greater speed and with less attention to the glories of beautiful England than his leisurely, wistful approach to meeting a possible suspect in the south. He now had evidence which might confirm that Major Erik Barron had been one of three men seated in the dead lawyer's office on the day of the murder. That it was a murder, he had no doubt.

Apart from augmenting his information about the suspect, Erik Barron, a highland jaunt to Fearnas whose place of birth it was, would augment his information to enable decisions to be made about his own life after the Met. For this was Colin Nicol's country too.

That Colin Nicol had gone to visit the office of *The Fearnas Courier* was inevitable, the paper had been a part of his acculturation. Or was it part of the rich mould of coincidence which is the seed bed of our lives?

Colin Nicol had not premeditated becoming a soldier, nor had he ever imagined becoming a commissioned officer in HM forces. Nor had he premeditated becoming a policeman in a League of Nations territory mandated to the United Kingdom. Nor had he ever had aspirations to become an inspector in the constabulary of the city of London. When war between Britain and Germany had been declared in 1939, fate had taken the life of Colin Nicol into its thrall. The smells of malting barley, the silent flow of a let from the Cawdor Burn to the distillery at Brackla, would become part of his past.

When, on his retirement, Colin Nicol had visited Fearnas, that visit was indeed driven by a *crie de couer*. Now that the big game was over he could, with a great feeling of contentment, answer that cry. He wanted to go back to visit his old school and to walk on the soil of his birth land. He had an unfading affection for St Ninian's Academy that amounted almost to a passion. His love for the school was bound up with his classmates, with whom he had tried to keep in touch throughout his years of absence. That he had so tried would not have been expected because he had never been a live-wire member of any group and he was neither great conversationalist nor sportsman. He was taller than his classmates, slim and rather stern looking until conversation brought a smile of natural warmth. Within the school curriculum, mathematics and science were his major interests and where he scored highest marks. The limits to his creative imagination meant that he struggled with essay topics in English. However, he knew that there had to be beginnings, middles, and ends, and although his vocabulary was limited, his grammar and punctuation were first class, so he always produced a good plain piece of work which earned him satisfactory marks. His study of history did not inspire in him any high regard for the British Empire, nor a desire to take up arms nor yet to wander the wide world in search of adventure. He would pass well enough in his examinations because he was good at remembering dates, names of people, places, and events; he could pinpoint Plassey or Oudenarde on a blank map with pinpoint accuracy. He had read his share of G. A. Henty, Percy F. Westerman, and Captain Marryat, but he found the wild, clear call of the sea easily deniable.

When it came to considering a career, what imagination he had was not prone to wildness. Certainly he would never have imagined (though that was not really a fault of his imagination) that one day he would answer his nation's call to war and soldier in battlefronts in Egypt, Italy, and Burma. Furthest from his mind would have been the slightest notion that he would spend the bulk of his active years in the London Metropolitan Police and end his career as an inspector.

Another object of powerful affection from his boyhood was the local weekly newspaper the *Fearnas Courier* written in, printed in, and published out of an old stone building in Leopold Street. Its owner and editor a deeply literate, serious historian and was champion for Fearnas in every good cause. Colin read every word that appeared in every issue—he even read the market reports and noted which farms had sold hoggets or steers at what price. He read the reports of council meetings remembering the issues, the names of those in favour or against the question, with no emotional attachment to either side of the argument.

The *Courier* regularly reported the return of errant offspring of Fearnas. In the *Fearnas Courier* office, Colin Nicol had asked permission to see the files of back numbers primarily to see which of the wanderers may be in Fearnas now.

Nicol settled at the tall, sloped reading stand to scan each issue from the current issue, and soon there was gold.

'Ninian Barron Funds Ph.D.s.' The story told of Ninian Barron, a past pupil of St Ninian's who had created from one Fearnas seine netter to an oceangoing trawler, which he owned and skippered, to an organisation spread wide world headquartered in Yarmouth near to his family home in Norwich. The Ph.D. funding was to be open to all students who had completed their entire secondary education at St Ninian's Academy. Candidates for the funding would ideally be in marine-related sciences, but if in any year there were no marine sciences applicants other disciplines would compete.

So the article went on until it reported: *'Mr Ninian Barron's yacht,* Fear Naught, *skippered by his brother Erik, was the subject of a report in this paper when, in mast height breaking seas, in heavy rain squalls, he gave up his lead and making a dangerous gybe, turned back to rescue the crew of a yacht in danger in the Fastnet race. Roddy Mckenzie, also a St Ninian's student, son of Sandy Mckenzie, gardener of Major Ronnie Dugal's Woodlands Estate was in* Fear Naught's *crew at the time. In the Korean War and Kenya, Roddy had served in Major Erik Barron's Company of 43rd Regiment Queen's Own Highlanders. Erik Barron heads up Stag's Head Resources in the Democratic Republic of Congo.'*

My god! Of course! Scarcely credible but here it was. The Fearnas, St Ninian's, Forty-third Highland threads were all in one lay of rope and all connected to the subject of his investigation, Erik Barron. He must follow the lay of the rope in which there would doubtless be bends and hitches. He was following one now leading to Mr Roddy Mckenzie.

The big green bus had dropped him at a stop right beside the ocean beach where today, a moderate surf had attracted some surfers like black seals, bobbing by their boards in the swells, waiting for the wave they wanted. It was hot under the cloudless sky and the sea breeze was very weak that day. Colin

Nicol had stopped to watch them for a few minutes and to scan the coast and across the Cockburn sound to Rottnest Island and south past Carnac to Garden Island. He had come here from the Highway Hotel in Nedlands where he had taken a room for an open-ended stay. The uncertainness of this arrangement seemed not the least to inconvenience his affable host, Bert McPartland who, when they met, made it apparent that they would talk with each other on a first-name basis. Bert was pleased to give Colin information about how to get to Cottesloe where he hoped to call upon a Mr Roddy Mckenzie.

'You know Roddy, do you?' asked Bert.

'No, Bert, but he is on my list of people I was telling you about, some of whom you knew, that I'd like to get in touch with while I'm here. I'm not surprised you know Mr Mckenzie too.'

'Well, you'll find him a good man—you couldn't find a better bloke than Rod Mckenzie, and if you asked anyone else, they'd say the same—except some trade union crooks. Some Mckenzie Earthmoving men drink here and Roddy comes down to get the news on mining and exploration from the geologists and drillers who are regulars and live around here. Say g'day to him from me.'

Colin Nicol turned south from the bus stop and walked on the pathway along the sandstone cliff above the beach as instructed by Bert. A few minutes' walk brought into view the large sandstone house with white verandahs described by Bert. As he came alongside it across the roadway, he saw on an etched flat slab set into the rough sandstone masonry of a low wall the name *Corriedale*. Two heavily beamed wooden gates, painted bright white, were swung wide before the drive which led, sloping upward, to the broad stone steps of the house, between an avenue of flowering shrubs and lower plants and flowers. It was a statement of stolidity and permanence. There was a controlled aesthetic and planning design in the shrub selection. Behind the house there were trees chosen, it seemed, to be of such a height as not to diminish the views of people in the flats and houses on the height behind.

When he had climbed the steps, he had to walk a number of paces across an oiled jarrah-planked deck exaggerating the white bright sheen of the painted timber balustrades and the pale dressed sandstone of the walls. The large door space timbered out in painted white, had three-quarter height, stained glass panels left and right, and a three-piece stained glass fanlight above. The big white door was opened wide screened by a blacksmith's work of delicate iron artistry. Large purple irises their leaves a botanical painting in powdered colours bonded into quite delicate shapes, concealed the utility of an insect screen whose fine mesh added value by an ethereal mistiness softening whatever may have remained in the intrinsic hardness of the iron.

What he was seeing amazed him. Cynicism and the acculturation of life with the criminals in society set his synapses firing demanding to know, 'How did a gardener's son from Fearnas possibly come to own a house like this?' The negative impulses in his brain flashed along the glowing wires conflicting with Bert McPartland's positive words.

Pressing a shiny brass button on the right-hand side set a Glockenspiel sounding through the house. In the moments while he waited, he removed his sunglasses and took his cream-coloured panama hat in his left hand.

'Hail and good afternoon. Please take a pace to the rear and right close or this door of the temple—whether you sing a duet or not—will sweep you from the steps to a doom of broken bones.'

The man who opened the door, and had spoken these words, was dressed in work-worn khaki shorts and shirt, heavy woollen socks which, once white, had been dyed by the dust of red earth. His face, though smudged with dust, was cheerful, open, and confident. He was square but slim and looked lithe and strong.

This was in contrast to the tall slim handsome man who stood before Roddy Mackenzie. Dressed in a well-tailored navy blue jacket, a pale cream shirt, showing the mandatory half inch below the jacket cuffs and regimental tie,: he cut a handsome figure. In the left breast pocket, thrust in with studied carelessness, there was a soft dark-red silk handkerchief. His slacks were light grey and his fine black shoes were highly polished. Blue eyes with no sign of pouches were set under grey eyebrows, which like the dense wavy hair on his head, still sported some remaining black hairs. His skin was clear and healthy looking; on its light tan, there were pink highlights below his cheekbones, there were wrinkles only around his eyes, mouth, and on his forehead that might soon begin to multiply and deepen. He looked as if he took life seriously.

'Do come in', he said, 'and let me see what I can do to help you. I'm Roddy Mackenzie.'

Colin entered a large a square reception area where a highly polished red jarrah floor had upon it a marvellously coloured Oriental rug woven of rich reds and deep blues and dark green and lighter shades of these to create an inexplicable magic. There was a table of a fine, lighter timber possibly Blackbutt on which was a central floral arrangement in a plain-sided glass vase. The non-colour walls gave for visual pleasure a selection of original Australian water colours and oils.

'Thank you, Mr Mackenzie. I'm Colin Nicol, ex-London Metropolitan police, retired, ex 43 Highland and former pupil of St Ninian's Academy. Being retired, time isn't quite the demanding demon it once was, so I thought I'd take a bus down to Cottesloe Beach, while I was in Perth, and see if you were in. I hope you don't mind this unheralded intrusion. May I explain; I'm doing a recce of Australia to assess what it might be like as a place for retirement, and to add interesting dimensions to the exercise, looking up ex St. Ninian's Academy types, police and army chums or men from the same regiment. When I was up in Fearnas before coming here, I was scanning file copies of the *Fearnas Courier* and saw a mention of your name. As a past pupil of St Ninian's Academy and ex 43 Highland, you met two of my search criteria.'

What he said was a simple statement of fact delivered in an even voice of acquired southern English tones, painted by time, over a basic Scottish accent that had a slightly metallic hint. He appeared to be a no-nonsense man.

'I'm pleased to meet you. Come through.' He led Colin through a tall door on the left of the reception hall, but he had no sooner shown him in when he said, almost in alarm, 'Oh . . . I'm not allowed in decent parts of the house wearing these duds. Do you mind if we went somewhere else?' Roddy led away through a door in a set of four stained glass folding doors where a wall, on which there was a large painting, allowed progress left and right. They went through a large kitchen and a space where obviously the family took their 'working' meals through a door and immediately ascended a set of wide stairs with plain varnished wood balustrades leading through a square opening to the next deck. On reaching this level, Roddy said, 'Colin, I've been out in the sun since it came up this morning and I'm as dry as a lime burner's boot! With the record you just described, I imagine you have been known to take a shandy on a hot day? Can I offer you a beer?'

'I can't claim a reward for exertion or early rising but this beautiful heat has dried me out a bit. Yes, please. I'd love a beer.'

Immediately on the left there was a little kitchen with the usual fittings. From the fridge he brought a bottle of Cooper's ale and two glasses. There were some basket-weave chairs around a low table where in an area normally protected from the sea breeze—not necessary on this day—and with a northern view to the ocean.

They had sat down just long enough to toast each other. After a couple of swallows of his icy-cold beer, Roddy asked, 'Look, do you mind if I just have a quick shower and change then I can relax with you and have a blether? Please help yourself to anything from the kitchen. There's a toilet through that door on the left.' He brought some more beer and a dish of nuts. 'Please feel free to wander bout. Upstairs, downstairs—but not in my lady's chamber.'

Roddy returned shortly wearing a bright red polo shirt (which was a polo shirt), crisp white shorts, and tanned leather slippers. The light tan of his exposed skin was accentuated by his outfit.

'Ah, this is much better. Now I can relax with you.'

'In my desk research, I went into the *Fearnas Courier's* office and spent some fascinating hours going through old copies of the paper. That's where I found out about you as an old St Ninian's boy and your service with 43 Highland in Korea. It also mentioned that you sailed with your old company commander in a Fastnet race.'

'Yes, that was a wild and woolly exercise. I've sailed with him in calmer waters since,' Roddy said with a smile, and they both sipped some more beer.

Colin said, 'I notice you don't smoke. Do you mind if I do?'

'Indeed no. I'll get an ashtray and my pipe.' He brought back two ashtrays a heavy stubby briar sometimes described as a shooter's pipe and a soft leather tobacco pouch into which he put his pipe while his hidden fingers filled the bowl. 'This man's been smoking a pipe for a long time,' thought Colin as he observed Roddy's actions. He selected a cigarette from a slim silver cigarette case and taking out his handkerchief gave it a rub and a polish. 'There, that looks better. I shouldn't treat this wee treasure the way I do. It's an item I treasure with a feeling I want to think is beyond sentimentality. Here, I'd like you to have a look. I think you will know what I mean.' With that, he passed the cigarette case to Roddy retrieving his handkerchief. As Roddy read the inscription, Colin spread his handkerchief and, picking it precisely from its centre in thumb and forefinger, shook it into a plume and with practiced insouciance, tucked the gathered end deep into his jacket's breast pocket; a pat and a little final arrangement, and there it was, a decoration and a distinction.

'Yes . . . I can see,' Roddy said, slowly, as if making a pronouncement about the disclosure to him of some profound fact. 'I think I may know what this must mean to you . . . because I know it would mean to me more than even a cherished keepsake.' He went on quite solemnly and quietly, 'It tells of times . . . of you . . . of people you knew and soldiered with . . . and of change. Although these men made this gift, the other blokes . . . other men you had been through hard times with have all been pulled into the symbol of this gift.' He handed it back and went on, 'It was a big life change being marked by this gift, a change of people and a change of system and culture, with many similarities yet an essential difference, the difference between soldiering and policing, then the other very significant change to the Met . . . and now to possibly to the change most demanding of adaptation . . . the change to civilian life. This silver box links all your career experiences from then until now. Yes, there's something much more than sentimentality attached to that cigarette case. It has an almost totemic significance . . . and almost of an amulet . . . it's a reminder that your past ways and habits of thought will confront an ever-changing present and prompt you. . . perhaps . . . to evaluate what of the past is still valuable and what, like a weapon replaced by one that is significantly better, is the one you will use, until something newer and even better comes along.'

Colin listened and found that Roddy was being deeply thoughtful, reverential, as he spoke; his words arising from his perceptions of the significance of this slim silver box and its inscription.

Colin very carefully, almost tenderly took it back, paused to look at it again, then slipped it into the inside chest pocket of his jacket. He could find no words to continue an exploration of the ideas Roddy had exposed. He needed time to think.

'Tell me Roddy; have you any contact with your old company commander anymore?'

'Oh yes. We are religious in our correspondence. Erik has been doing so well in his Congo venture. One of his senior men came here and stayed with us. He was doing a field study of our savannah flora to see what species may be usefully transferrable to Congo and see the work that was being done in using microbes to detoxify mining slurries. He has much admiration for Erik and, if I may say so, a reverence. Mnabeka is himself a charming, erudite man. Helen had him down in the music room and played piano to demonstrate structure in Western music in which he has a growing studious interest. It seems Erik has surrounded himself with first-class top men and women. We were fascinated to hear and see photographs of what has already been achieved of Erik's vision. The community see him almost as a kind of god. Yes, our visitor was Erik's kind of man, generous of strength, intellect, and spirit.'

'My god, Roddy, you have put your Major Barron on a pedestal!'

'Of which I would say he is worthy. Erik Barron made my life. How did he do this? He showed me how I could rise above the English, British caste system. He gave me the key. Whatever I have succeeded in doing—and I hope you may see some of this tomorrow—I'm happily convinced I owe to Ike Barron. Which raises the question, what are you doing for dinner tonight and what have you planned for tomorrow?'

'Tonight I'm having dinner with one Palestine policeman and one from the Met who now live here and they've invited two other migrants from the UK. Tomorrow I would most likely loiter with intent to take in a bit of your city. It looks as if it would be a pleasurable extension of my education. However I should wait to see what the blokes say tonight. It's very kind of you to offer to drive me, and I'd much appreciate your doing that. We're to meet at the Palace at six. One of the blokes is going to pick me up at the Highway Hotel.'

'You've got an RV! What's the time?' He looked at his watch.' We'd better look sharp. Go and visit the loo'— he commanded indicating the door again—'and we're off.'

Nicol jumped up—erect. 'Sah!' he responded and obediently complied.

They went down and out through the front door and turned back under the house where a Fuson pick-up truck with a band of Mckenzie tartan around the doors and the bonnet edges stood next to a large Fuson sedan. From ground level to the floor above stood what appeared like a very large wooden box.

'This', said Roddy, 'is the music room', opening outward a door invisible to all but the knowing. He allowed Colin a quick glance.

The windowless walls had been lined with timber varnished in a light straw colour. On the left was a Bechhstein baby grand piano with open music lying on the closed top. On the floor were some music stands, two of which had open music on them, and some chairs. In the corner was a drum kit. Roddy explained that this was a family music room used principally by Jess who was teaching theory and practice in the Music Department of the University of Western Australia and took private pupils and was developing a chamber music quintet. Helen was very serious about her piano studies—the flute on one of the music stands was his, he added as an aside. Some of Helen's pals, boys and girls, had formed a jazz band, and Jessica and Roddy were delighted to let them use the soundproof room for practice; the drum kit was theirs.

'You are serious about music,' commented Colin, impressed by what he had been told and what he had seen. 'I am, and get great enjoyment through it. Helen is incredibly good, Jess is a maestra and we just accept that and enjoy enjoying her.'

As they drove to the Highway, Roddy told Colin that Jess would be likely to make her evening telephone call from the little red phone box on Rottnest Island any time after six. While she waited her turn, she'd inevitably chat with the other ladies and children waiting their turn to use the only phone. If he timed it right, he would be back in plenty time for her call.

'You should enjoy the Palace, I think. It has a pleasant old-fashioned dining room. It occurs to me, because I can't play host to you in the normal way I would like to tonight, I thought I could offer you this little scheme. Tomorrow I've got to visit Collie Coal in a place called Collie, a couple of hours' drive from here. You could see a bit of Australian countryside and glimpse a bit of how the other half lives. You could also see Ugojim and Mckenzie and hopefully meet some of the people, then we could dine here at the Highway.

'That sounds like a bit of fun and a very attractive offer. I'd like to say yes immediately, but I don't know what the other blokes may have committed to tomorrow.'

Within minutes, they drew up at the hotel. As he let Colin out, they shook hands, and Roddy wished him and his friends a jolly night.

'Just give me a ring when you get back and let me know what you've decided. If you see Bert, tell him Roddy McKenzie was asking after him. Oo-roo!'

As he was going along the hallway to the stairs, Colin did see Bert McPartland. Bert spoke first: 'Did you have a good day out, then?'

'Ah, yes, very pleasant. I went down to Cottesloe to visit Roddy McKenzie. He's a very generous host. He asked me to tell you that he sends his good wishes.'

'That would have been fun, I'm sure. Roddy's a great bloke, one of the best. Are you in for dinner tonight?'

'No, not tonight, Bert, I have an invitation out, but there's a chance Roddy and I will be in tomorrow night depends on what plans my mates may have for tomorrow.'

'Whatever, I'll look forward to seeing you. You'll see most of our clientele are farmers or station owners, they don't bung on side. Neither the men nor, and I'm happy to say, do the women. They understand that many of us have to get a bit grimy to make a living. You might sometimes see a fellow dining in here looking as if he didn't have a zac, yet he's just sold two truckloads of triple-A wool at a pound a pound. We do get professionals in here too, especially on Fridays. You'll see that, like all Australians, they know the score; we live off the sheep's back and we all have to make a quid. Have a good night with your friends. I'll see you tomorrow.'

The first thing that Colin did when he reached his room was to empty his cigarette case without handling its surfaces. He then put it carefully away. The box he put it into was the same gift case in which he had received it on 29 September 1947.

Roddy had not long returned home and was in the kitchen when the phone rang.

'Hi, Dad,' said a girl's happy voice.

'Hello, my little love, what have you been up to today?'

'We took our lunches with us and we all cycled off on a grand tour of the island. The wind wasn't too strong so there wasn't too much hard pedalling west. Mum did pretty well. We all had a swim in the afternoon. We watched some fascinating little birds on the edge of the lake. They were going along, heads down turning the pebbles with their beaks obviously finding wee beasties to eat. We hadn't seen them before, so when we got back, we looked them up in the bird book which I hadn't forgotten to take with us. You're not going to guess what it's called!'

'No idea! What?'

'A Ruddy Turnstone!'

'Are you swearing mildly, or is that its colour?'

'That's its colour. They're such pretty, busy little birds; you'd think ornithologists might have given them a more romantic name.'

'I'm not going to comment now. I'll wait to see how you label things when you're a scientist.'

'Well, after they're fitted into the taxonomy with their Latin names, I'll see if there's a friendlier name people can call them. Don't work too hard. Eat well, Dad. We'll be back soon. Here's Mum.'

'Hello, darling, how are you?'

'I'm well, thank you, love. I'm having an interesting time here. I just came in from work this afternoon, and before I had a shower, a very elegantly attired bloke called at the door. Turned out he was an ex-London police inspector who'd been to Fearnas Academy and served in 43 Highland during the war. We had a couple of beers then I ran him down to Bert McPartland's where a mate was going to pick him up for dinner at the Palace. I've just got back from dropping him off and was commencing the mis en place for tonight's cordon bleu dinner.' He then launched into telling Jess what was planned for the next day if Colin Nicol's cobbers had made no other arrangements.

'God this house is cavernous without my girls. But I haven't been cheating on flute practice. Anything you'd like me to do, or get, before you come home?'

'Not that I can think of now. If there is, I'll tell you tomorrow. There's a fishing expedition on the day after tomorrow, so perhaps you shall have a little fishy on your little dishy when our boat comes in. Maybe some herring or whiting: Jeff McPhie and Jenny are bringing their boat over, so we'll be all at sea.' (Jenny was a maths teacher at the prestigious Perth College. Whatever the crotchety, crinkled, cranky characteristics of the quintessential female maths teacher may be, Jenny, like Jane Dugal, fitted none. Both were brilliant, witty, fun-loving, vivacious women.)

'That should be great fun. I imagine Maggie [their daughter a little older than Helen] will be with them. Give them my good wishes. I'll be on the jetty to get the fish. A few squid would be nice! Helle seems to be enjoying herself. I hope she catches something from 'Davy Jones's Locker'. I bet you're enjoying sleeping on the Geordie Bay beds! [The notoriously uncomfortable beds at Rottnest were the stuff of legend.] I'll be going to Collie and back tomorrow, whatever happens with Nicol's plans. I'll be back here late if Colin comes, because I said I'd take him back to the Highway for dinner. Don't wander out into the darkness to phone tomorrow night. I'll see you at the ferry jetty.'

'Really, the kids are—and this kid is—having a really lovely time. You didn't put in a specific order for the whiting. Did you want Sand or St George? Mind you, there are some pretty voracious appetites over here: you may be lucky to get the left over bait! Will I recognise you on the ferry jetty? It seems so long since I saw you. I love you. I'll look forward to seeing you at the jetty. Sleep tight.'

'You too. Love you, my darling.'

The house felt very quiet and empty, but he sensed their enjoyment. That made him very happy, so he poured a glass of McLaren Vale shiraz and wandered out to sit and gaze at the stars, all of which were lucky, and all of them his.

At about 9.30 p.m., Roddy's telephone rang. It was Colin.

'Roddy? I hope I'm not disturbing you at this hour. I'm under instructions to ring you. Their plans for me were flexible. The boys said not to miss the opportunity for a bit of real Australian life and that I'd see some jarrah forest and a bit of the Stirling Ranges. I'd like to take you up on the offer you made this afternoon if it still stands?'

'Oh, great. I'm pleased. There is an early start though. Could you be ready to be picked up at your hotel at seven o'clock? You won't need to have had breakfast, just have a cup of tea or juice or whatever. I'll organize the rest. How's that?'

'That's fine by me. I'll be on the doorstep at seven.'

'Splendid. You can give me the gory details about your dinner tomorrow.'

The hot wind of the night had begun to blow from about nine o'clock. The air it had brought had spent a searing day sitting atop the sparsely covered rocky hinterland of the north and the wide wheat lands of the east. It came in on the growing wind down off the scarp, out to sea filling the gap left by the hot air rapidly rising from the cooling sea.

The Fuson sedan's air conditioning had been on since Roddy had left Corriedale. He had had a short swim, but the cooling effect vanished before he reached the shower room under the house. It was one of those days of which there were not too many, nor too close together, when the weather seems not to want to move on, refusing to obey the pattern of the area around Perth and Fremantle of the ritual easterly in the morning sou'-wester by noon that characterised the summers. Then, that sea breeze from eighteen knots upwards swept the city's fumes away for a while to be turned back and dumped by the evening breeze out to sea a little bit to hang touching the horizon. But this was one of those other days when the temperatures of concrete stone and iron barely lost a degree of heat. Now the passage of the easterly had slowed, falling to a point where only the fact of its moving at all gave a sensation of coolness to exposed human skin. Humans sweated and dogs panted. Lizards loved it and scurried everywhere hunting to use the energy from their heated blood. There was shade around the Highway Hotel from London plane trees, but the breeze had infiltrated the shade and all that could be said was that fugitives from heat had simply removed themselves from the glaring, grilling heat of direct sunlight.

As they drove south on Stirling Highway, they saw the sea as an uninterrupted, immense sheet of opaque glass The easterly wind, now so gentle and so smoothly hot causing not the smallest ripple, the distant islands like chicken pieces appearing through the surface of blue aspic. Was the sky a reflection of the sea?

He indicated off to the right where from the road, over the railway, between it and the sea lay the headquarters, Ugojim and Mckenzie Earthmoving. They crossed the Swan River by grand swept arches of the new Stirling Bridge. The planned road ahead had not yet been built so, to follow Roddy's choice of route they had do the changes, right and left necessary to get them onto Hampton Road and their main southerly direction.

'Our days of living off the sheep's back have all but gone. Those acres of beautifully built brick woolsheds'—and he indicated off to his right on the edge of the harbour—'which have traded fortunes in millions are mostly empty now and there's some scratching of heads and worries in the souls about what should be their fate. People remember the great part those buildings played in the prosperity of this state. But major changes are happening all the time. Now synthetics clothe the world's peoples.' After the suburban Hampton Road, which had some grand old houses; one or two with tall palm trees bordering the broad paths to their front verandah steps, once had views of the ocean from their higher ground on the eastern side of the road, they joined Cockburn Road. This now would run southward closely along the sound of the same name. On this road, on the seaward side, they passed Robb Jetty where cattle from steamers, laden with cattle herds from the northern stations and which could not use the short jetty, tumbled their wild steers over the side and into the sea, where, driven by men in boats, they were herded ashore to a vast area of paddocks which spread for some miles to the east. But there was a big change. These thousands of head of stock were being slaughtered for Britain and Europe. The advent of the Common Market and the European Union ended that. New markets had to be sought and developed in Asia and the Middle East where animals were preferred to be delivered live so that they might be slaughtered to the rules of local religious customs. Hence the present and increasing trade in shipping live sheep and cattle; and the painful decision to write Finis to the history of Robb Jetty.

'All is change in our world and—and I'm very conscious of this—in us too.' Roddy chuckled as he said, 'I can't remember when I coined this expression; 'One door shuts and another door opens'. Yesterday wool. Today minerals. You'll see as we go on today where enormous deposits of bauxite have been found, mined, and refined. Further on there are riches in mineral sands. This state is bursting at its seams. I arrived too late for the Alcoa development, but it doesn't mean I don't keep contact with the Alcoa people and a watchful eye for opportunities on their intentions and development activities. As with an army, so with business; much success depends on intelligence and a constant state of readiness. We know we can't be everywhere at once and often we have to choose the front on which we should concentrate our forces and launch an assault.'

'I listen to you speak, and on very little evidence, I'd guess that you have been very successful.'

'I'd be disingenuous were I to contradict you. If I am successful, the root of that goes back to Erik Barron. He introduced me to some rather wonderful people; by whom I was supported with indescribable goodwill. Then one good thing led to another. Success is an evolving state. Success is ever a "work in progress". The world isn't totally inhabited by the kind of people I know and love, in whose company I elect to spend my time and who have given me so much, but neither is it totally peopled by crooks. If you go into the water, you will inevitably get wet. Stay out, you will remain dry. If you meet crooks, by-pass them or confront them. Unfortunately in your short stay, you will not be able to meet many of the people to whom I'd like to introduce you. As Erik has done in Arica, I have surrounded myself with good people . . . no, maybe that's wrong . . . maybe they've surrounded me and good people can have all the business virtues of acumen, strategic, and people skills, honesty and desire to succeed without being namby-pamby. I don't know anyone—although such people may exist—who is namby-pamby and successful. I also stick almost rigidly to the principles of warfare and concentration of will. That's about it really.'

Colin was quiet for some moments, he had difficulty in deciding what to say knowing it would be something trite, but he had to respond. When he spoke, it was to say, 'I've never heard a successful man describe his world the way you just have. It seems to me that it is part of a world that I should be learning about. Not too late, I hope.'

'We can all learn new things about ourselves and the world any time. Circumstances can make any of us "too late" for something. Another target will be found. It won't necessarily present itself. I would think having achieved the rank of inspector in the Met a considerable achievement. You must be doing something right and you've been doing it all along and have been too busy to think about it.'

There were not many people abroad in the small township of Collie as they passed through; it looked neither cared for nor cared about. The shops did not attract trade. If you needed something, well, you came and bought it, didn't you? The road narrowed outside the town becoming the main shire council road where a car and a truck could pass each other only if the truck went off the bitumen. After about a mile, they turned east and followed the broader, well-made road to the mine. Collie Coal's administration offices were set amongst its workshops and maintenance buildings on the edges of a regrowth jarrah forest. There was a building with showers and changing space where miners put on their work gear, their helmets, lamps, and air supply emergency apparatus before mounting wagons with bench seats like TCVs to rattle down the black tube bored through the rock and shale to the point on the coal seam where they would work that day. Down there, deep below the surface cables led down from above to bring electric power for machinery and lighting. There were well-lit workshops and 'crib' rooms where miners could have their breaks and eat their 'crib', their lunches, which they had brought down with them.

Roddy's meeting was with David Evans and his team. Dai was the mine manager who controlled every major function of the mine operation above and below ground and reported to the board. Dai and his supervisors and managers wanted to tell Roddy how they intended to extract the coal from the open cut and the tonnage they planned to pull out each shift. Then, with Roddy, they would work out the most suitable models of excavators, haulpaks, front-end loaders, and trucks they would need. Roddy's target was to become—he needed to become— their chosen supplier. Friendship and goodwill would be on his side, but money and the work capacity of the machines would be the final criteria of choice. The management team making the decision had to be able to justify their choice to the board. Today they would get near to working out the units of equipment best suited and needed. Roddy had to know the performance factors of not only his Ugojim equipment, but also the strengths and weaknesses of the competitors. Roddy would have liked to have Simon there with him today so that, were he not available for the continuing negotiations, they could go on seamlessly in his absence. But today Simon was indispensable at HQ.

For the hour's duration planned for Roddy's meeting, Colin had been put into the care of Jim Gates, the mine captain, to be shown over the site. He asked Colin if he would like to make a quick visit underground. Colin had never been near a coalmine in his life and going underground would be quite an experience. He was taken to the change room and fitted out entirely with clean overalls safety boots and the safety gear to descend into the mine. They went down in an inspection vehicle, exactly the same as a crew carrier, along the dark tunnel with the vehicle's headlights reflecting on the dark shale rock, or the cement like coating applied in some stretches only inches away from the four electricians going down with Colin and the captain—it was dangerous to have any part of a body over the edge of the carrier. As the wagon levelled from the long slope of the descent, they could see, far ahead the bright electric light of the work site. Once at the face, Colin was amazed to see an Alpine miner in action. This huge machine accurately steered by a laser beam had a spinning wheel of cutting teeth set vertically, which chewed into the coal seam as it ran from left to right across the face disgorging the cut-out material onto a short conveyor belt which at its end loaded low motor trucks which bore it off to the surface along the tunnel by which Jim and Roddy had descended. Although there were passing bays, the duration of their visit below was controlled by the essential traffic in the tunnel. When their turn came, they made their way back up the long slope away from the fearful sound of cracking coal and rock in the pit's walls which Colin heard very clearly when the cutter had been paused to be shifted forward. Colin felt happy to be out of that gloomy place. The difficult laborious days of lying in narrow tunnels to hack out the coal with pick had passed. The change to clever mechanization had improved the miners' lot. It would change and improve it again with the conversion to open cut.

Jim Gates, and Colin now washed and back in his own clothing, had time for a cup of coffee in his office. He enquired about Colin's friendship with Roddy. Colin again told the story which he had to revitalise; he was becoming tired of its repetition.

Jim had listened intently. He wanted to speak about Roddy and the meeting that was now going on. There was tension in his tone as he said to Colin, 'Jeese, I hope Roddy wins the plant supply deal', he said very earnestly, 'this company owes him a fortune. I'll tell you this: we had a major project on a critical path when suddenly a problem arose. The customer, who'd bought and paid for a shipment of coal, had a sudden cancellation of the designated ship. This mountain of coal . . . hundreds of tons of it . . . was lying exactly on the ground which was the site for the construction of a house for the winding gear and motors for the planned conveyor belt from the new open pit. Construction had to begin in the next five days. The engineers start date could not be changed. There was no time and it would be financial lunacy to bring in a special machine, a reclaimer, to do that kind of job. It was not the kind of equipment which is hired on a short-term lease. Anyway just bringing it here and getting it set up for working would take months. We had five days. All the work upstream and down depended on timing. The only way to do it was to push it with dozers. Roddy and Dave Oliver took on the job. Christ knows when they slept in their on-site caravan they'd brought here, but they were working all the hours of daylight, and during the nights, two on and two off under lights. Roddy had committed Mckenzie to doing it: he was going to live by his commitment. When they dropped the blades and shut off their dozers for the last time, the surveyors had just pulled up and were taking the equipment from their ute to start pegging out the site of the machine house. Collie Coal had been saved from a planning disaster caused by a shipping problem. You wouldn't be able to imagine how much money and trouble that would have cost us. No one here dare say a bad word about Roddy Mckenzie and Dave Oliver.'

Colin was impressed by the captain's sincerity and force in telling his tale. Here was another no-nonsense practical man emphatic in his praise of Roddy Mckenzie. Jim Gates brought Colin round to the office of Dai Evans whose meeting was over and the team was leaving the room. Roddy introduced Dai, with his full title and a bit of description of the magnitude of his role, to Colin Nicol. Colin was quick to say, 'I did appreciate your allowing your mine captain the time to give me that fascinating underground experience. The nearest I'd ever been to a mine was from a train going quickly past the huge slag heaps in Lanarkshire. I think the change from the days of pick and shovel to the Alpine miner must have made a huge change for the better to the life of a miner and to coal production. I know nothing about open-cut mining, but from today's little adventure, I'd say that getting up above ground would have to be like walking into the garden of Eden for a man who's spent all his working days underground.'

'Oh, it won't happen without some degree of culture shock I imagine,' responded Dai. In his tone perhaps an implication might be sensed that he had thought about the social health of that schismatic structure; those below: those above. The men would lose some of their important differentiation and might even now be starting to fear that their special bonded mateship from shared danger may fade, in a way die, to go through a metamorphosis into who knows what new form. 'Change is all around and we have to adopt and adapt,' Dai spoke on and there was a kind of sigh in his sound. Here, too, were one to ask him, he would possibly have had to say it will not be without pain. For some, the society and their social presentation in the larger town and surrounding area hung on the thin thread of their being 'underground' workers. What would there be to give them any status now? Then what about the difference in the ideas of fear? There were a few who had been underground workers since they were old enough to go down the mine. Familiarity had kept the fear of a roof fall and other potential disasters so far at bay as almost to eliminate it. The thought of having to drive one of those towering, broad haulpaks with a fifty-ton load, on narrow, steep winding, and descending pit roads was terrifying, and had already been circumspectly confessed. What would become of them?

Roddy and Colin said their farewells and thanks. The way the meeting members, and finally and significantly Dai, impressed Colin with the evident high regard in which they held Roddy Mckenzie. They left the air-conditioned building and the contrasting heat attacked them in a burning immersion. The car, when they reached it, was untouchably hot. With least and briefest contact, they opened the doors of an oven despite having carefully selected to park in tree shade of spindly jarrah trees. The first effort of the car's air conditioning was used to drive the burning air from the car.

They left the mine road and turned south and the forest continued on the left. On the right of the shire road, the land fell away steeply into a valley where, on the far side of a stream, a small farm had been established. Little paddocks ran off the west and climbed until the steep jarrah-clad hills rose too steeply. The stream and the valley ran south opening and spreading as it went. The forested hill along which they were driving had been eroded away in the distant past so they were descending onto a gentler shoulder of the broadening valley. They may have travelled two miles when a small road beside the shire road led alongside fenced paddocks where low buildings came into view and Roddy slowed the car. This little road continued to pass in front of the buildings before curving back up to rejoin the main traffic road. Their track allowed them to follow a curve into a broad opening, where a wooden gate hung on a stone pillar stood open on each side. A clear painted sign bore the name *Sunny Glen*. Amongst planted wattles and various native broad-leaved trees mixed with deciduous exotics in early years of their growth were the buildings; those by roadside being the frontage of a shop and a well-shaded open air, and undercover a display of fresh vegetables and fruits. The shop was the commercial front of Sunny Glen selling the property's produce particularly a selection of cheeses made from goat's milk, latterly cow's and sheep's milk were added to the range, there was honey and there were jams, marmalades, preserves and pickles of fruit and vegetables These products were elegantly and charmingly displayed in the well-designed space in aesthetically pleasing rustic structures of local timbers inside and out even boasting roofs of wood shingles. Sunny Glen's refrigerated van went daily on a delivery circuit to shops and restaurants form Bunbury and Australind, Busselton, Donnybrook, and places in between. The car was put under the roof of a long open-fronted shed under the shade of the trees.

'Come on, Colin, I'd like you to meet Enid who is the brain and energy behind the cheese-making operation. She'll most likely be in her cheese factory.' They walked out of the heat into a small white-walled cubicle before stepping through an especially thick metal-sandwiched door into the cool gloom of a cheese curing room. They found Enid, clad in white, turning dusty white discs of cheese over on a shelf among many others from floor to ceiling filling this cool windowless artificially lit space.

She turned when she heard the door, 'Roddy!' she exclaimed. 'This is a pleasant surprise. How are you? Are Jess and Helen with you?'

He went forward and kissed her on the cheek. 'No, Enid, they're overseas splashing in the cool waters of the ocean.'

'Overseas?! Jess hasn't said a word about going abroad,' she exclaimed.

'Did she say she was going to Rottnest?'

'Yes, but . . . aw'—she knew she had been taken—'smartie . . . you reckon Rottnest is overseas, do you?'

'Sorry, Enid.' Then, 'Enid, I'd like you to meet an overseas visitor . . . no, he's not from Rottnest. Colin . . . Enid; Enid, Colin.'

'Colin's been down Hille Headings this morning and I thought it be an educational contrast if you could show him your cheese operation. Do you have the time, Enid?'

'No, but for a friend of yours, Rod, I'll make time and it'll be my pleasure. We'll fit him out in whites, no bother.'

'Colin, may I leave you in Enid's care? I need to catch up with Mary. I'll introduce you to Mary later. I'll catch up with you two later,' he said as he waved and departed.

Enid began with the question that Colin was now becoming accustomed to expect: 'Have you known Roddy long?'

'Why that question?' he asked himself.

When she realized that Colin was a very recent acquaintance, she wanted at once to let him know the qualities of this man Roddy Mckenzie.

She launched immediately into passionate detail of the story surrounding her and Mary and their rescue by Roddy when they were going to lose everything. How he had given them land here and a place for their house; their establishment and the growth of their enterprise, the difficulty of their split over the direction their little subsistence farm should take, how he had been like Jesus, solved their problem, and brought their hearts together and how the business had grown and how now the Mckenzie family had become their closest friends and were now their business partners. Whether Colin learned much about the cheese-making process is not clear, but he had learned of Enid's, and through her story, Mary's love and adoration of Roddy Mckenzie. Their tour of the working parts apparently completed, she asked Colin, 'Would you like to come and see the shop now?'

'Yes, I'd like that, Enid, but I don't want to hold you up.'

'No. You must see it.' To see what he did when he entered the shop, at least to a portion of the extent to which it might impress an epicurean, did pleasantly impress Colin. Enid told the short dark lady who looked after the shop, 'This gentleman is a friend of Roddy.' At which point the little lady burst instinctively into ecstatic Calabria dialect. 'Benvenuto Signore. Buongiorno.' She was offspring of one of numerous Italian families who had taken to the woods and hills when Italy joined the side of Germany in the Second World War and the internment of all migrant Italians was announced.

While Colin was with Enid, Roddy had left them and gone out into in the vegetable gardens and potting sheds to look for Mary. 'Ciao, Maria,' he said when he met her and kissed her cheeks. 'Come stai?'

He wanted to talk with her of Helen's enthusiasm about seriously beginning stud breeding based on *Molly,* the farm's pedigreed chestnut Haflinger mare. 'Helen will talk to you herself, Mary, but I thought I ought to sound you out, because even if you have good arguments against the idea and Helen starts on you, you'll just cave in to please her.'

'Well, I'll say now, I'm not against it. It won't require major changes here. We can think seriously about a plan after I hear from Helen. But . . . no, I've no objection.'

'Good, Mary. I didn't want you to get railroaded. I've got a visitor here from UK. If you've got time, can I take him down to meet you and see your operation.'

'Sure. Are you staying down for lunch? Bring him down, then after I've given him a quick tour, you can take him around the rest of the farm and I'll go home and make some pasta. Shall we bring it up, or would you like to come down to us?'

'Mary, it would be perfect to come to you, thank you so much . . . *tu sai tanta gentile cara*, Maria.'

Mary came with him to the shop to find Enid and Colin still there. She and Colin went off on foot to see the farming part of Sunny Glen, while Roddy stayed and had a blether with Enid.

Mary and Colin had gone but a few yards on their way to the propagation sheds when Mary turned to him and asked, 'How long have you known Roddy, Mr Nicol?'

When he explained, it became her opportunity to stand before him and say to him very directly, '*E proprio Santo quest' brav'*, Roddy. He has saved us. He has created happiness and'—she spread her arm and swept with it the entire view—'*quest' paradiso*. We are so near to God here. Jessica and Helen are also saints. I love them. Here I can do what I want to do to the contentment of my heart. *Sono tanto felice.* When you come to know him, you will understand what I say.'

Enid and Mary lived in what looked like (and in fact had been) an old tree feller's house. On its sturdy stumps, it was set into the curving front of a hill facing north-east across the valley to hills and forest on the other side of the stream down before them and the casa famiglia, the Mckenzie family's house. visible; comforting, and memorial of all their good fortune. After the labour of their long days, it was an easy walk for tired bodies. It was beautifully comforting even for visitors used to strange standards.

The walls within were guarding the full happiness of the ladies. There were pictures of the Madonna and Christ on the cross. Prominent, though not all that wonderfully framed, was a photograph of them—Mary, Helen, Enid, Roddy, Jess—taken here at a lunch on some day of joy, where they now were sitting, under the heavy beams and the vines, sharing food together in a happiness that leapt out of the photograph. Colin was uncertain what it was exactly, but something in that scene moved him quite deeply and caused him to pause and look. Roddy noticed the length of his commitment to and absorption of this photograph.

Bread, well of a kind, not focaccia but the simple dough of a pizza pressed down with the hand, thick, just out of the oven; real, first run olive oil and four varieties of cheeses. And vino rosso; pure Grenache from this estate *par la vigneronne* Maria. Colin sipped and, with wide eyes, exclaimed (if one can exclaim sotto voce) in a low gasp, 'This is superb wine! I'm glad that I have seen today the very earth and the vines that these grapes came from.' The salad had cos lettuce which cracked, tomatoes red, flesh-full and round, *melanzane* sliced, fried and stored in oil, *passato* and herbs; asparagus, broccoli, cucumbers, zucchini,

Roddy was deriving very obvious delight in savouring his bread dipped into the fresh green-tinged oil. Colin was being reminded of Palestine on a richer scale.

'E vero contadino quest', Rodrigo!' exclaimed Mary.

When they ate the spaghetti simply with pesto stirred through it, Colin was again surprised. Among all the Italian food he had eaten, he was pleased to enjoy this first-time experience here. Then it was time for desert of lush peaches, creamy yoghurt with mint leaves, and stunning chardonnay from the farm's vines. Mary had described how Roddy had the major influence in the grapes chosen to be grown and how Roddy cooperated amicably in the management of the growing and the making of the wine and how Jess and Helen were enthusiastic and active participants in all of the processes. Roddy drove Colin around the farm on the contoured roads which followed the slopes, shaped to maximize the use of their formed surfaces of packed earth in their water use plan. The trees that grew along these winding roads formed avenues which, as well as being windbreaks and a beauty to behold at all seasons, produced profitable quality pesticide and chemical-free crops sold fresh at a premium, or made into to other marketable products. One field held a herd of young cattle amongst them stud youngsters from the highland cattle herd the others were from stock beef cattle, and two young Guernseys. Ducks and geese wandered freely around and Australorp and Light Sussex were everywhere. There were paddocks of lucerne for hay to sell and to store. The were perpetual meadow grass paddocks rich in variety of herbs and leguminous plants, cut and sold as nutritious hay for race horses; and systematically grazed by growing cattle. Molly was alone in her paddock, but for company, she had cattle next door and daily contact with Mary or the garden workers for whom she pulled a hay rake, or the flat cart on two pneumatic tyres which carted dung, compost, plants, or posts and fencing all around the property. Frames could be dropped in round the edges so that calves or goats or geese could be transported. Whatever her load, Molly cared not a bit. When she wore her collar, she fancied herself to be a mighty work horse stolidly stepping onward, her golden white mane tossing and her head nodding to the rhythm of her march. When she was wearing her breast plate and long traces to the swingle tree of a dung spreading light harrow, she was pulling Boadicea into battle against the Romans. Such information is provided by Helen Innes Mckenzie.

The Mckenzie house at Sunny Glen was a derivative from the classically imagined Australian outback station house, its whole extent on a single-floor level with deep verandahs all round: tall windows and sets of folding doors let in the softened light and circulating air. It stood on a bench sliced from a hillside. The kitchen was a major family space complete with Aga cooker and big sinks for big pots; the shelves held ceramic assiettes and bowls and dishes and plates; not one item that was not used regularly in making healthy, hearty rustic meals for the Mckenzies and gaggles of children and gatherings of adults, friends all, or guests from around the world. This kitchen was where they ate and drank wines. There was another room with an enormous fireplace, shelves of books, paintings where there was space on the walls, sofas to sit in or sleep on; rugs for children to romp on and big enveloping chairs; a couple of table desks for use on the emergency visit of a muse. There were lights and lamps to be moved anywhere and everywhere, to light music stands even. There was a very good upright piano. The room generated, and held a feeling of security, emotional and physical warmth at all times; perhaps most effectively in the freezing nights of winter. Here was the cabin of relaxing contemplative times and arguments galore.

'We spend as much time at the farm as we can and it's never enough. Were there no demands of school or career, Jess and Helle would turn their living schedules around and spend most time here. It's wonderful when it's full of adults and children and especially wonderful when it's just the Mckenzies . . . perhaps with the addition of Enid and Mary who are "of this land" and wonderful companions.'

They went then and said their thanks again and farewelled Enid and Mary. The drove away from Sunny Glen turning right out of the gate, and soon they came to well-fenced pastures where cross-bred Angus Friesian steers grazed on permanent pastures rigidly following a plan of rotation using moveable electric fencing. In a smaller paddock, a hundred and twenty-seven red, shaggy, horned, Highland Cattle grazed on a different composition of pasture type. They looked at home on this hilly rougher rocky ground. This, with the calves at Sunny Glen, was the entire stud herd at this time. They turned off now towards the sea and the Port of Bunbury. He wanted Colin to see Koombana Bay and his mooring for *Satori*. He told how the family could cruise down here on holiday stay on board on arrival night or if the club was having a twilight race or a race next day, otherwise they would go up to the farm. The cruise down and back had to satisfy their sea-time needs.

They left the bay and the little yacht club and turned north from Bunbury towards Mandurah and Fremantle. First the road climbed gently and the sea was out of sight until a place was reached where travellers could pull up at his railed area and take their last view of the ocean panorama before plunging into the forest. Then the narrow road had to climb very steeply to get on top of a long granite ridge, covered in jarrah, running out from the scarp to the sea. Car drivers would become very impatient coming up in low gear behind a truck doing twenty miles an hour at the maximum. Frequently their impatience would overcome them and they would come out from behind the truck seeing the car ahead some distance away but actually speeding towards their car downhill. sufficient power to overtake the truck There were frequent fatal accidents. Roddy told Colin that a plan was in place and contracts would soon be let to widen the road and construct frequent passing lanes. They did not encounter a truck and thanks to the power and flexibility of their Fuson motor they were able to pass on the two occasions they wished to. It was Roddy's view that it would still be dangerous even then.

Through Fremantle and over the river by the older, timber Traffic Bridge, they followed the north berths of the harbour turning north along the shore and in no time turning right into an area of big sheds, oil tanks, and heavy workshops. Then there it was, imposing, bright, and shining amidst its dreary neighbours, the glass-fronted edifice, headquarters of Ugojim Aust. Pty. Ltd. next to it the less-glamorous home of Mckenzie Earthmoving Pty. Ltd. There was a young lady behind a broad desk easily seen by anyone stepping through the automatically operated doors almost invisibly inset into one of the huge glass panes of the front wall. 'G'day, Anya, this is Mr Nicol, my guest today.'

'Good afternoon, Mr Nicol, welcome to Ugojim and Fremantle. I hope you enjoy your stay.'

'You must be just about ready to go,' Roddy said. 'Two seconds later, Mr Mckenzie and you would have had to use dynamite to get in.'

'Phew, Anya, glad we made it. Are you coming out for a drink before you go?'

'No, sorry, I've got basketball tonight, but I think I saw Dave and a new Mckenzie man going round the back.'

'Enjoy your practice or the game whichever, Anya.'

Dave, Madge, Simon, Ray, and a new man who had been going through some tests with Dave for entry to Mckenzie were in the company meeting room where there were facilities for entertainment. These 'meetings' had begun at Mckenzie quite spontaneously as the years went by and it was a chance for most of the people who worked, often very far away from HQ, to speak with other staff who happened to be in town and the people at 'the office'. It was informal, staff initiated, Mckenzie encouraged. Everyone to whom he was introduced gave him a friendly welcome and offered him a drink. He hoped that more than one person would be present when he was asked to answer the inevitable question. But so used were those present to having strangers in their midst that no one asked, instead there were questions about his experiences of Australia.

When Simon heard Roddy say to Colin, 'Let's take just a quick look at Mckenzie and Equipment Hire,' he asked Roddy,

'Would you like me take Mr Nicol to see the other outfits while you catch up with people here?'

'That's a good thought, Simon, thank you. I'd like to meet the new man. Colin, would you like to see the other operations? If you've had enough of underground mines, cheese factories, and market gardens, please have no compunction in saying no.'

'Actually I'd like to, and I'll bet you've got latest business news to catch up on with these folk.'

Simon thought it right to measure this man, so he asked the question. The result was that Colin heard how Roddy Mckenzie had picked him up out of the gutter, had faith in him, and made him into the happy, successful person he now was and how Roddy Mckenzie could never ever be thanked enough for the way he had brought this about.

Roddy spoke with Dave and Frederick Dunbar and was just finishing off by saying, 'Dave will see you right and he'll be the man to talk with if you have any concerns . . . but always put yourself through the exercise of thinking through your problem from every angle first. That's how we grow. I'm sure you can find a way to achieve your goals and do what you want to do in Mckenzie, Ugojim, or any of the other capers we're interested in here. While you're with us, I'm here to help you grow, to achieve, to succeed, and to express your happiness.' Roddy's delivery was inspirational. A new man joining the company was important— he might turn out to be another Billy Gray or a Simon or a Ray Robinson or a Madge Gill.

'Right, I think we should move now, Colin', and turning to Madge, he said, 'We're off to have Colin's farewell night . . . a dinner at Bert McPartland's. Can you imagine it, after lunch with Enid and Mary? I'm going to give Colin a lift out to the airport tomorrow but I'll come in and see you first . . . and I need to see Simon.'

.'Oo-roo, everyone. Mr Nicol and I must leave now. Have a good evening.'

'Every time I'm with these people, I think how fortunate I am,' Roddy said as they got into the car.

There were only diners in the small back bar, which had opened for them when those who had to leave at the six o'clock closing time had been shooed out under legal edict. Bert McPartland was doing the hostly duties and greeted his two guests: 'Well, I suppose you think you've done your bit for national prosperity and deserve a beer?'

'God, it must be wonderful to have a sharp brain like yours!' Roddy said, looking at Bert as if he were making a visual assessment. 'Yeah. I reckon I could force one down. How about you, Colin?' Roddy asked.

'In my case, no force required . . . my round. Are you going to have one with us, Bert?'

Bert agreed to join them and poured a 'glass' into which he added some soda water. Roddy got out his pipe, filled it from a leather pouch and was soon wreathed in comfortable smoke. It was Colin's cue to light a cigarette which he did from a soft, yellow pack of Temple Bar. Roddy could not fail to notice the absence of the cigarette case.

'Cheers', said Bert, 'and how was your day in the Australian bush, Colin?'

'Oh, a memorable day, Bert! I don't think I could have had a better introduction to rural Australia. It was a day of significant firsts for me. From the sights of the busy port of Fremantle through changing countryside and jarrah forest, descent to the depths of a working coal mine, being in a craft cheese making . . . factory seems an inappropriate word . . . shown every detail by a cheese maker passionate about her craft; a biodynamic vegetable nursery and profitable farm, beef cattle, a Highland Cattle stud . . . the Australian headquarters of Ugojim and Mckenzie Earthmoving . . . and each one of the characters I met was fanatically and happily involved in what he or she did . . . and Bert . . . that's not the half of it. No tourists get that kind of experience with an excellent rustic Italian meal and a personal guide to boot. It really was educational and I enjoyed the lot . . . every minute of it . . . except the sound of cracking in the rock walls away down in the mine. I'm just very glad that Roddy offered me the trip.'

'Well, I'm pleased to hear that,' said Bert with sincerity. 'I knew Roddy would give you a good day. Here, have another beer and then I think you should be thinking about going in. There are three not-bad reds on the list tonight to make a pick from; a Hardy's Cabinet-not cabernet-Penfold's Dalwood Hermitage and a Seppelt's Great Western *shiraz*. The choice is yours and you can't make a bad one.'

The dining room, broad and low, had a pleasant hum of conversation from mixed groups of diners. Some husbands and wives, some younger and older mixtures, men locked in discourse, and jollier, noisier groups of men in business suits who had prepared themselves for dining by a session in the bar. The twenties-thirties decor and furnishing engendered a feeling of welcome, of solidity, steadiness, and a sense of the personality of the local history. On the walls, the basically cream-coloured wallpaper, old paintings by local artists, and black-and-white photographs of the early days of the locality, seemed to hang expressively each in its own place. The furniture was heavy and had worn well.

They were shown to two comfortable Queen Anne–style chairs at a table with crisp white napery on which the wineglasses sparkled under small chandeliers in an array of silver laid for four courses. The deep red carpet with its scrolled yellow and dark blue pattern, and the long window curtains of a heavy, similarly red, patterned material, added to the feeling of middle-class establishment, familiarity, and locality.

Colin was looking around taking in what he saw; the men and women, the younger people, the different types each marked by its style of clothing, tweed to serge to cottons and wools; dark greys and white shirts of businessmen's uniforms, tweed jackets and twill or moleskin trousers for the men who conducted possibly even more profitable deals. The women all in dresses; bright, vibrant floral and sometimes frilled around neck and shoulders and young girls with bared, strong brown arms gave delightful feminine lightness to the gathering. Waitresses, mature and younger ladies, with pleasant friendly faces, uniformed in black dresses and white bib aprons, moved with calm confidence and purpose among the tables.

Roddy silently observed Colin as he scanned the diners and their surroundings.

The meal was served with friendly gentleness. It was the customary selection of roasts and fish with the old favourite shepherd's pie. The 'pudding' was treacle pudding, and the 'pie' was apple pie with custard.

'What's your reaction, Colin?'

'I'm getting a feeling of comfort from what I see. It strikes me as being, well, "healthy", as if all is well in the community. I can't even spot the villain.'

'If there's a villain here, you may be certain most people in this room, young and old, know who he is. Suburbs like this one have grown quite slowly and many families are long established. Each has its own institutions; a yacht club, a golf club a respectable, established pub, a church for each denomination, schools private and public, shops run by people who live here. Villains don't find it easy to hide. They are just known about and somehow accommodated. You just don't invite them home to dinner. Should you ever come to Australia, come as soon as you can and pick a setting like this. I see and sense that Australia is changing. I try not to be stupid about it; sadly, social changes will come with increasing rapidity and will not be for the better. Oh, I suppose there are few generations that have not said something like that about the world that awaits the next generation, but were there ever times like these times? How will you see yourself fitting into the new world?'

'I don't have the answer to that question yet Roddy, and from what I have experienced in Britain, I share some of your forebodings. I'm in the process of doing some bridging work to ease the sharp precipice of my own compulsory change and what I have been able to gain from this short visit has been more helpful than you can imagine. I have known what some of my old pals have been through and without exception; each has fitted contentedly into his chosen Australian environment and way of life. Mind, each of them seems to be saying, and some have said so directly, that he came at the right time. I'd like to be part of a community like this before it becomes an anachronism.

'As a retirement occupation, which I'm treating as a transition from demanding days of the yard proper, I've managed to get the Yard to allow me to pursue further investigations of an unsolved murder. I'll be part of the Unsolved Crime and Open Case Squad. Everything about the case seemed so pat. A body, apparently no witnesses, and whatever the motive, it could only be imagined. The major suspect was questioned and the police at that time were satisfied with his response. No murder weapon was found. But something, that was no longer in that room when the police were called in, was used to strike the killing blow.'

Now his face became more serious until it hardened and became steely grim as he spoke directly at Roddy.

'A man is dead and the cause of his death could by no means be described as accidental. I believe, with all my soul that murderers should be brought to justice.' Then there was anger as he said, 'I take it as an insult to the police service that a murderer should possibly think that he could so delude or baffle the police that he could gloat in the triumph of success, or feel safe in the comfort of what he imagined was everlasting security.'

As he spoke, his face had stiffened and his bright eyes fixed Roddy with intensity that conveyed the emotional strength of his feeling. He went on, holding Roddy with his eyes compelling his feelings to be registered firmly with him. It had dramatic focus. That searching, sensing look, and its severe concentration, set a wire of feeling vibrating in Roddy's being. It was as if a volume control had been suddenly turned down: except for Colin's words the room was silent: there was only Colin's voice and his precise, steely enunciation.

Quite suddenly he relaxed and seemed almost to allow every muscle to stand easy. The volume control was quickly being turned up again. The people began to speak. Now the hardness of the tone and the strict enunciation had gone, and Colin Nicol continued to talk.

'While I'm jaunting around having my jollies, I can do a bit of enquiry, enough to keep the aged pensioner-guard, my backup in the office, having their share in the investigation. The approach remains the same and it will lead to the same result—the conviction of a murderer.

'I'm just getting the inkling of a feeling of retirement so far. Resulting from my experiences, and from my first steps into this investigation, I'm thinking, that when it's all successfully over, I might finally hang up my boots.'

'The experience I've had with my old friends here, and most significantly, the experience I have had in meeting you, are big elements in what will be my planning. The learning with you today has been so vivid, really very powerful.

He was speaking now with genuineness, and softness of felt pleasure.

'I have been quite bowled out by what I've seen in and around Sydney, Melbourne, and Adelaide. My old friends from there are delighted with their experiences. They have settled in and are full of praise for what they have found. Your care and kindness has convinced me that I must come back and do a thorough recce and come to a decision. I want a place with sunlight. I have memories of years under clear sunny skies; Malta, Egypt, Italy, Lebanon, and Palestine. None of those places attracts me now, and except for Malta, I see nothing but years of conflict and killing ahead. The south of France or Spain, or Greece though not without their attractions just don't match the style I'm after.

'Here, there's a kind of honest straightforward masculinity in the air. And females seem to be cast in their version of that character. I must say that having shared this little time with you, and while I realize that you don't in the faintest represent the average, you have shown that there is the kind of life and feeling around that I could allow myself to be absorbed into. It's as if the Australian nature, as I've sensed it, is like a ready-made suit that would fit me very comfortably. My outline plan is based on wanting to keep a foot in two camps, one in each hemisphere where ageing bones will feel warmth from the sunshine and I can share life with good friends. I'm imagining spending half the year up around or actually in, Fearnas.'

Now he became almost conspiratorial. 'While I was in Fearnas, I actually looked at a lovely old two-storey house on Loch Loy Road overlooking the Dunbar golf course.' The other half year in Australia is looking more and more attractive and the outline looks like the basis of a workable scheme. At the moment, I'm prejudiced in favour of Perth. But I mustn't jump to conclusions.'

Roddy was still affected by the earlier part of Colin's discourse, but its sharper prickles were softened as the conversation returned to rosier themes. They talked about two local golf courses, a very friendly Naval and Military Club; and "enjoying Mr Bert McPartland's hospitality if it got too hot to be out in the sun". There were one or two spontaneous soft chuckles and non-stop chat.

They had dined well on the roast beef and the magnificent Great Western Shiraz. It was time to go.

'Now we must organize your transport for tomorrow,' said Roddy. 'Your plane doesn't leave for London until late afternoon. Is that right?'

Times were discussed and Roddy said, 'What if I collect you at Bert's at 1530 hours and we toddle out to the airport. That will give you time to go through the admin stuff and we'll be able to have a stirrup cup before you mount Pegasus and fly towards Athens. Mind, if you fall among thieves and need casevac from the Naval and Military, ring Madge and I'll pick you up there'

'You're the RTO. I'm under your command. I'm going to see the lads in the morning and make our au revoirs at the Naval and Military. I didn't want a half platoon of Scotsmen around me, carrying on like Afghans, at the airport. They might make it difficult for me to make a favourable impression on any charming lady I might meet, or more importantly, someone who might have a fishing lease on the Findhorn.'

'Excellent judgement, sir.' 'Roddy responded 'And a wee *deoch an doruis* together afore *ye gang awa* sounds very much the way I'd like it. Have a good sleep and enjoy your farewell with your mates. Bert or his staff will give you any help you need. However, for any change of plan or difficulty arising, just ring Madge at the office. Here's my card.'

Next day, when Roddy arrived and parked at the curved art-deco facade of the Highway Hotel and entered the reception area, he could hear the sound of animated conversation from the public bar. There was no sign of Colin; however, there was a suitcase alongside the receptionist's counter with a tag which read 'Nicol'. A clue perhaps?

Bert McPartland had a good story about Roddy which he was pleased to tell the group. 'A bunch of union toughs came into the bar one evening looking for trouble—and Roddy Mckenzie. They knew he would be here. Roddy had just saved a bloke from bankruptcy by taking over the job he had to abandon because the unions had put a ban on it. Roddy put in the Mckenzie men none of them union members—working for Rod Mckenzie had more benefits than being a union member—and his own and Treloar's trucks and completed the job cutting the unions out. You can imagine they were a bit upset. A great big heavy rough bastard called Roddy a 'cocky little bastard' and said he'd knock the shit out of him. He said to the big bloke, 'Bert McPartland would be upset if my blood and teeth were all over his walls. We'd better go out the back.' Roddy told his blokes to stay where they were 'His union cronies shouted and jeered, 'Fix the little bastard, Ned!' I was in the pantry and saw everything that happened and what I missed I was told.

As they were going out the back door to the yard, the big union bloke walking behind Roddy belted him on the back of his neck between his shoulders, Rod was felled but he rolled off to one side, got himself on his feet. The big bloke was towering in front of him and just going to lunge. Rod raised his left thigh as if he was going to kick and the big bloke leaned forward to grab it and topple Roddy. But Rod's leg was going to come smartly down. For Roddy, the big bloke was now just right. He put his weight on that left foot and I could see the concentration on Roddy's face and body. With the edge of his right hand, he brought down a karate chop to the big bloke's neck where the collar bones join. There was a 'thwack' that they heard in the front bar. 'He's got the little bastard!' someone from the union mob shouted and they all cheered. Then Roddy walked into the bar and said, 'You'd better go and help your mate, I think he's had an accident.'

When Roddy looked into the bar now, a little knot of very sociable chatterers was *en plein vol.* He gave himself a second or two to enjoy listening to and watching these men revelling in being together; talking about experiences and ideas they shared. When there was a two minim rest, he said, in the tones of a senior officer entering a mess, 'Good afternoon, gentlemen.' There was immediate silence and all turned towards the speaker.

'Roddy', said Colin, 'let me introduce you to this fine body of men.'

Introductions were made to the five present, three of whom Roddy acknowledged as having met before, and warm greetings were exchanged as were questions about kith and kin, business and yachts. Keeping Colin very much included, indeed making him feel that this was a meeting at which he might be present as a customary member of the group, the conversation went on and the rhythm continued, the pause sign having been obeyed, people went on to finish the phrase and continue the melody.

In the manner and style of a Wee Free Kirk Minister or a censuring senior rank, Roddy announced, 'You're all *enjoying* yourselves. Now, this sort of thing has got to stop. There's just too much of it going on. I'm RTO for Inspector Nicol's embarkation. If he doesn't board the scheduled aircraft on time, his travel warrant will run out, he will be absent from a place of duty and I think you all understand the consequences.' Then changing tone, he explained that part of his selling pitch for Perth was to show Colin, at the least, the view over the river along the Esplanade and Victoria Avenue, drive him past the Nedlands Golf Club, a bird's-eye view of the Squadron, and take him past University of Western Australia then quickly to the airport. 'They'll be just a few tantalizing images and some that will get his thoughts going, I hope. So, one for the road? Then we'll have to get serious about catching an overseas aircraft.'

Roddy watched from the touch line as these old mates said their good-byes. They'd said them before in their lives, but time was getting shorter now and one never knew which would be the last. Were this day to have been their last, it had been a happy day. It seemed, at least on the visible surface, that this was a hopeful good-bye.

The promised route was followed to the airport. Having said he would not deliver a tour guide monologue but just point out locations and leave Colin to look and think, Roddy had kept to his word.

Perth airport was no grand edifice at this time. It was rather like a collection of very big open sheds with very large windows and it was something of a social hub. At times of departing flights, there were always large groups of family and well-wishers in the open waiting lounge area, crowding into the bar or having a last supper in the dining room. Not everyone in the building had a passenger farewell or welcome mission. Many just came for the bar, the restaurant, and the atmosphere generated by the changing bands of travellers. Of course there were tears too. There were frequent farewells which the parties guessed and feared may be final, or where the departure destination was potentially dangerous or unpleasant.

Colin's booking and luggage-checking took just a few minutes and they repaired to a corner of the bar overlooking the ornamental pond where black swans held little children in exciting thrall.

'I must thank you very much for what you have done for me during my stopover in Perth. Your hospitality was kind, warm, and welcoming,' Colin said with sincerity.

In a flash, his mood changed, and figuratively, he stepped back a pace changing his whole demeanour to the steely, impersonal formality of the evening before. It had hardened yet further. Familiarity was past and he addressed Roddy as Mr Mckenzie.

'I want to return now to my retirement task of unravelling an unsolved murder which took place in London. A lawyer was killed in the private office which he kept in his city residence. Our evidence indicates that Mr Barron was there that night. There was a third man there Mr McKenzie. I don't know for certain who that person was. A man died in that room on that night. The evidence also indicates that someone, who was in the room at that time, may have killed the victim. We know that Mr Barron was there, we also know that there was a third person. I'm almost certain I know who that third person was. But Mr Barron does. That person is not only important to us, he is very important to Mr Barron. You can imagine we have made many enquiries

'Without going into the kind of detail our evidence covers, we know what Mr Barron has achieved in Africa. He would, obviously, ever continue to think that that success is his. It's the sum of all his endeavours, his ultimate dream. We can't imagine how Mr Barron assesses that third person. In a sense that person doesn't know what his danger value is. If it was Barron who caused the victim's death, what he may do, to protect his dream and his present realty, is rid himself of that only source of fear before we ask him to face charges. *Ach weel*, 'Wha sups wi, the deil maun hae a lang speen.' Whoever that third party may be, were I to be speaking with him or her now I'd be saying: 'Come and see me and tell me what you know, or spend many wakeful nights'. Mr Barron is not without determination and he has much to protect.

'He is a soldier. It is doubtful that he could, would, or want to kill someone point-blank who is not a belligerent enemy. Somehow I can't see this man, this third man, or woman, being shot at point-blank by Barron. But years of experience tells me that, even within families, people will protect that which they have striven for, and what they feel to be their own. It's not cowardice that stops that kind of person from shooting a father or a mother or a brother or a sister, it's just that persons of that kind have the ability to fabricate, for their mental comfort, a believable reality of innocence, if another person, at their behest, kills that person who comes between them and their aspirations.

'I'm not sure how Barron will solve his problem. And the lady or the man, who was there that night, is most likely living now, oblivious to the threat. If I knew who she or he was, perhaps I could warn her or him and take her out of harm's way. Should you wish to get in touch with me, this could be helpful.' He handed Roddy his card.

On their way to the airport, their conversation had been about travel, the change of aircraft in Karachi, and his thoughts about what little he had seen of Perth and Western Australia and the other parts of Australia on his brief visit. What troubled Roddy now was the recollection of Colin's conversation in the airport lounge, its meaning and implications. Colin Nicol had found his way to this house. In just a day and some hours pleasantly spent together, he felt that they had rapport. Now he was asking himself whether Colin Nicol's reason, or pretext, for calling on him was a fabrication and his chumminess of those hours together, an extremely well-acted role play. The shocks of the mood change in Colin Nicol, and the shock revival of memory dredged from the past set his brain reeling. How his face may have expressed these mental blows, Roddy Mackenzie could not tell. But it was not the stunning shock which bade him to keep silence. He simply said, 'Good-bye, Colin. I hope you have a safe journey.'

In the minutes or so before boarding, Colin had turned to face Roddy. A dramatic change in Colin's demeanour had flashed into focus. A look of stern seriousness was accompanied by a rigidity of posture. He had begun to speak and now Roddy had been addressed as 'Mr Mackenzie'. Colin Nicol's delivery was in black-white contrast with the discursive pleasantries of their hours together. It had ended on an ominous note.

He thought it good that Jess and Helen were over in Rottnest. It was better that they were not here now. How would he explain to Jessica what was troubling him and the confusion of ideas he was trying to make sense of. It was necessary to analyze, as if from the outside of the action, what had happened during those hours together with Colin Nicol. He needed a clearer view which might help him to plan the action he must take. Now he was asking himself whether Colin Nicol's reason, or pretext for calling on him was a fabrication and his chumminess of those hours together, an extremely well-acted role in a play.

He had gone through in his mind the detail of the hours with Colin Nicol. He was sorting out his mental and emotional reactions; reading the history of his own experience and trying to imagine Colin's views of what he had seen and felt. Considering Colin's behaviour at departure, what would his frame of mind have been from which he might have viewed their hours together? How would he have coloured the people and events? What had he expected to find in Roddy Mckenzie? Could he possibly make a reasonably intelligent guess? Was he, Roddy Mckenzie, the unsuspecting villain that Nicol had come to trap? Why was there no direct question? Perhaps it was McKenzie's next action that Nicol would find important? Had his experience of Mckenzie been so unlike anything in his range of expectations that these had been disarranged by the reality of what he had experienced here at Cottesloe? And had he, by his threat, developed a holding position while he worked out the meaning of the Cottesloe people and events? The shocks of the mood change in Colin Nicol, and the shock revival of memory dredged from the past set Roddy's brain reeling. How his face may have expressed these mental blows, Roddy Mackenzie could not tell. He had simply said, 'Good-bye, Colin. I hope you have a safe journey.'

He knew that he must immediately alert Erik Barron.

It was that season of the year when Erik may be taking a short break on his yacht which he kept at Mallorca when not at Cowes. Roddy checked the time and realized it would be a good hour to ring Erik's London office. Erik shared an office frontline reception with a firm of solicitors, a firm of chartered accountants and a stock broker. The young women who looked after incoming calls were very bright, diplomatic, and efficient; they knew well the subtleties and business ramifications of each of the firms. Rod was extremely lucky; the person who answered his call was Eve Arden to whom he had been introduced when they had all gone out for drinks after a visit he had made to Erik's office.

'Roddy, how are you? How can I help?'

'I'm well, Eve, thank you. I need to speak with Erik absolutely urgently. Can you contact him for me please?'

'He's at Mallorca, Roddy, and could be at sea until late tomorrow. Give me your message and I'll see he gets it *toute de suite*.'

'Mark it "OP IMMEDIATE" or say it's that, he'll understand. Okay? Message reads'—and he paused—'*Op Immediate. Contact me. Will stand by home telephone daily from 1800 hours to 0600 hours GMT, Roddy.*'

'Eve, even if it means you have to send someone to Mallorca by air, I'll pay! I'll get out of your way now. I'll be in touch when the flap is over.'

Eve's telegrammed message from Roddy had been brought to his yacht by the harbour master. Erik checked the time and called from the phone box on the island.

Rod picked up his phone. 'Hello, Rod Mckenzie.'

'Roddy, greetings! What's up?'

'Well done, Erik—swift response,' said Roddy. 'I've just had a visit from a retired police inspector called Colin Nicol. He said he had got himself a retirement job investigating an unsolved murder. That was quietly mentioned, and then he got grimly serious—you should have seen how he looked and heard his voice. He's investigating the death of Bartolemeusz.'

Roddy went on to describe what Nicol had said, 'He's sure, from evidence he claims to have, that you were there and could be responsible. He believes there was a third man present. He intimated that that third man, if he was not in fact the murderer could be bumped off by the murderer so that he couldn't squeal. He was warning me in an oblique way that if I were the third man I'd better look out or come to him and tell him what I knew. I don't know why he didn't ask me outright.'

'Mm. That's interesting,' Erik murmured thoughtfully. 'He called on me when I was just about to leave Cowes on this trip. He mentioned not even a hint to me about any investigation. It was all soldierly affability: no hint of the Bartolemeusz event. I haven't heard from him since. I've got to say, I wondered what the visit was all about. He didn't come because he had a primary interest in *Fear Naught*. Nor did he say anything about wanting to meet me. He let it look like a chance encounter. Just as some confirmation of his 43 Highland credentials I suppose, he showed me a souvenir cigarette case he was carrying. Up to that point he had just said he was a retired police inspector.'

Roddy described the inspector: 'When he came here, I must say he was wearing a very smart rig. There was a regimental hatband round his panama hat, and he was wearing a regimental tie. He only needed a TOS and a stag's head badge to declare he was 43 Highland. Strange you should mention the cigarette case. He proudly gave it to me to have a look at later on.'

'That's it!' exclaimed Erik, 'The cunning bastard! He collected my finger prints from his cigarette case that I'd picked up when it fell on the chart table. Now he's got yours, he'll be having them matched with what we may have touched at Bartolemeusz's office.'

'Well, he'll be upset when he tries to get mine,' chuckled Roddy. 'I'm one of a number of people who, through some physical phenomenon, don't have finger whorls! It was odd though; he made a big display of polishing it before he handed it to me. I assume the police would have a good photographic record of the scene and they'll be trying to work out from where the chairs and glasses were how many people were there.'

'We'll have to work out what appreciation he made and we'll have to make our own of what we think his was,' Erik said thoughtfully. 'So far as we know, he doesn't know that there could have been a fourth man: someone who hadn't accepted a drink. Harry Crossman didn't use his glass. It's highly possible that if he can't get supportive evidence, he may drop you from the suspects and leave you alone.'

Roddy suggested, 'Let's ponder this overnight. I'm wondering whether we shouldn't take the fight to him while he is still trying to reach certainties. He'll be upset to find that his cigarette case doesn't have my prints. Will he think he—or someone on police staff—has accidentally wiped them? Or will he immediately think that I'm one of those printless types? Or will he conclude that I actually wasn't there? That uncertainty gives him three choices: which will he pick? The next thing that he doesn't actually know is how many people were there: another uncertainty. I'm thinking we may have to make that confusion more profound for him to the point where he realizes he has not a case that a court would accept. I think we should, or I should play on the fact that he can't prove that I was or wasn't there. In truth, it really is a coincidence that it I was. Bartolemeusz didn't know I was coming. Did you happen to mention Harry Crossman to him?'

'No, I made the appointment for me. Even I didn't know we three would be turning up.'

Roddy went on, 'Above all things, I think he'd want to avoid having his *derniere acte* to be shown a failure. That could be his weak point. My idea is to strike as soon as possible strike now while Nicol is off balance; with a clear aim, both feeling positive about what must be done, with a concentration of forces in offensive action with the element of unexpectedness in the nature of the attack. Seems to offer a successful outcome. So we'll just go off and give this some hard thought tonight and have a kind of O Group on the phone this time tomorrow night, eh?

'Agreed. I think what you're saying is good strategy. I think we've just got to add the tactical moves so I'll see what strings I can pull. I'll go by road over to Palmas tomorrow. I can probably get a better connection and I've got some friends there who would provide a more suitable place to make the call from. Whatever happens, I'll contact you same time tomorrow.'

'Fine, I'll be standing by. You might remember, Jess and Helen and I have booked a flight to go to UK to see the Grannies before Helen's study demands increase and Jess's work year begins again. We leave this weekend. Being in the Old Dart with the tribe doesn't look like being a problem if I want to confront Nicol.'

'Our plan had better be good and its execution nothing short of brilliant. Failure would be minimal for me—unless there were unforeseen ramifications, roots that may run to affect me . . . and Jess . . . and Helen?' were his first thoughts. Tomorrow would require other important demands for problem-solving skills at Ugojim and Mckenzie. 'Now, Roddy, focus!'

He applied himself to his task.

For Erik, failure in their attack had the potential of crushing, destructive disaster.

He would lose Stags Head, his home at Lubumbashi and all that he had so thoughtfully, skilfully, and lovingly achieved against the many acute problems of operating with any success at all. His fervent hope was to make a positive, measureable contribution to the life of African people that would be same truth at noon as at first light. He had created a mining operation which had become an international benchmark for mining best practice with a workforce whose productivity was away ahead of comparable mining companies. But more than that, he had created an environment where a healthy, happy, thriving community had grown its society to become an exemplar of what was possible despite continuous troubles and taxing problems. The people of Lubumbashi were the complete denial of the gloomy statements of the 'reality' of African social development possibility.

'What about me? Am I an accessory to murder? How will Colin Nicol react to my attempts to save Erik? He had made it very clear how single mindedly he detested anyone, absolutely anyone, who took another's life. How can I measure what danger there is for me; and through me what unhappy consequences may there be for Jess and Helen? What about all the great people who have given me their loyalty and support?' I've got to get this right.

When Roddy had a very clear, argued picture of his plan to put to Erik, he mentally closed it off, locked it in his brain, and when in bed, as he turned his head on his pillow, he was smiling: tomorrow his girls would return from Rottnest.

Of course the story cannot, and must not, end here. We can journey on with our characters, the people we have come to know and follow their fates in the sequel book *Corriedale* which is available now.

Lightning Source UK Ltd.
Milton Keynes UK
UKHW010850260122
397748UK00001B/30

9 781543 407419